Published by POCKET BOOKS

HAROLD ROBBINS

THE Adventurers

POCKET BOOKS

New York   London   Toronto   Sydney   Tokyo   Singapore

POCKET BOOKS, a division of Simon & Schuster Inc.
1230 Avenue of the Americas, New York, NY 10020

Copyright © 1966 by Harold Robbins
Front Cover Illustration by Punz Wolff

All rights reserved, including the right to reproduce
this book or portions thereof in any form whatsoever.
For information address Simon & Schuster Inc.,
1230 Avenue of the Americas, New York, NY 10020

ISBN: 0-671-87482-9

First Pocket Books printing June 1966

66 65 64 63 62 61 60

POCKET and colophon are registered trademarks of
Simon & Schuster Inc.

Printed in the U.S.A.

TO MY WIFE

GRACE

who made so many things possible,
of which this book is the least.

The womb shall forget him;

the worm shall feed sweetly on him;

he shall be no more remembered.

JOB XXIV:20

CONTENTS

CONTENTS

The Adventurers

Epilogue as a Prologue

It was ten years after the violence in which he died. And his time on this earth was over. The lease he held on this last tiny cubicle of refuge had expired. Now the process would be completed. He would return to the ashes and the dust of the earth from which he had come.

The tropical sun threw waves of white-hot humidity against the black-painted crosses on the white clay cemetery walls as the American journalist got out of his taxi at the rusted iron gates. He gave the driver a five-peso note and turned away before the driver had time to say, *"Gracias."*

The little flower stalls were already busy. Black-clad women were buying small bunches of flowers, their heavy dark veils seeming to shield them from the heat and the world from their grief. The beggars were also there, the little children with their large dark eyes set in hollow black circles, their bellies swollen with hunger. As he passed they held out their grubby little hands for the coins he negligently dropped into them.

Once through the gate there was silence. It was as if some master switch had turned off the world outside. There was a uniformed man sitting in an open booth. He went over to him. *"Xenos, por favor?"*

He thought there was a faint expression of surprise on the man's face as he answered, *"Calle seis, apartamiento veinte."*

The American journalist turned away smiling. Even in death they clung to the routines of living. The paths were called streets and the buildings within whose walls they rested were apartments. Then he wondered about the surprise on the man's face.

1

He had been in the lobby of the new hotel, leafing through the local newspapers as he always did whenever he came into a new town, when he found the notice he had been searching for. It was a tiny four lines buried amidst the back pages, almost lost in the welter of other larger notices.

He was walking down a path of elaborate private mausoleums. Idly he observed the names. Ramirez. Santos. Oberon. Lopez. He sensed the chill coming from the white marble despite the heat of the sun. He felt the perspiration damp and cool on his collar.

Now the path had widened. On his left were open fields. There were small graves in them. Small, untended, forgotten. These were the graves of the poor. Thrown into the earth in flimsy wooden caskets, left to disintegrate into nature without care or memory. To his right were the *apartados*. The tenements of the dead.

They were big buildings with red and gray Spanish tiled roofs, twenty feet high, forty feet wide, eighty feet long, of white cement blocks, three by three, and cheating a little on each side so that more tenants could occupy the walls they filled. Each three-foot square bore the name of its tenant, a small cross above the name etched into the cement and the date of death below.

He looked up at the first building. There was a small metal plate attached to the overhanging sheaf. CALLE 3, APARTAMIENTO 1. He had a long way to walk. The heat began to pour into him. He loosened his collar and quickened his pace. It was almost the time and he didn't want to be late.

At first he thought he had come to the wrong place. There was no one there. Not even the workmen. He checked the metal plate on the building, then the time on his wristwatch. They were both correct. He opened the newspaper to see if he had mistaken the date but that was right too. Then he let out a soft sigh of relief and lit a cigarette. This was Latin America. Time wasn't as exact here as it was at home.

He began to walk slowly around the building, reading the names on the squares. At last he found what he was looking for. Hidden in a shaded corner under the overhang on the southwest corner of the building. An instinct made him throw down his cigarette and remove his hat. He stared up at the inscription.

He heard a creaking wagon on the cobblestones behind him. He turned toward the sound. It was an open wagon drawn by a tired burro, its ears flat against its head in protest at being forced to labor in the heat. The wagon was driven by a laborer in faded khaki work clothes. Next to him on the seat was a man dressed in a black suit, black hat, and a starched white collar already yellow from the sweat and dust of the day. Beside the wagon walked another laborer, a pickax over his shoulder.

The wagon creaked to a stop and the black-clad man clambered down from his seat. He took out a sheet of white paper from his inside coat pocket, glanced at it, then began to peer along the walls at the nameplates. It wasn't until he came to a stop before him that the journalist realized that they had come to open the vault.

The man gestured and the laborer with the pickax came over and stared up at the cubicle. He muttered something in soft Spanish under his breath and the other laborer wearily climbed down from the wagon, pulling behind him a small ladder made of pieces of wood nailed together. He placed it against the wall and climbed up. He peered closely at the cement-block vault.

"Dax," he said, his voice unnaturally harsh in the muted cemetery.

The director nodded. "Dax," he repeated in a satisfied voice.

The laborer with the pickax nodded also. There was a sound of pleasure in his voice. "Dax." He spat into the dust at his feet.

The laborer on the ladder held out his hand. "*El pico.*"

The other laborer handed the small pickax up to him. With a tight expert blow the man on the ladder sent the pickax smashing into the dead center of the concrete block. It splintered in radiating lines tearing through the chiseled lettering in all directions just as the sun crossed the corner of the overhang. The laborer cursed at the sudden sun and pulled

3

his hat down over his eyes. He slammed the pickax into the cement again. This time the stone broke through and pieces came flying down, rattling against the cobblestones.

The journalist looked at the director. He was watching the laborers but it was evident he wasn't much interested in what they were doing. He seemed bored with the whole thing. It was just another job. He turned as the journalist came up to him.

"*Dónde están los otros?*" the journalist asked in his hesitant Spanish.

The man shrugged his shoulders. "*No están los otros.*"

"*Pero, en la prensa—*" The journalist stopped. He had almost reached the limit of his Spanish. "*Habla inglés?*"

The director smiled proudly. "*Sí.* Yes," he hissed sibilantly. "At your service."

"I saw the notice in the newspaper," the journalist said with a feeling of relief. "I thought there would be others."

"There are no others," the director said.

"But . . . who placed the notice? Surely there must be someone. He was a very famous man. *Muy famoso.*"

"The office put in the notice. The time has long passed for someone to claim the body. There are others waiting for this space. The city is growing. We are very overcrowded. You can see."

"I can see," the journalist said. He hesitated. "Wasn't there anyone? Family. Or friends. He had many friends."

A veil came across the man's eyes. "The dead are alone."

A muttered cry came from the laborer on the ladder. They turned to look up at him. He had broken through the cement façade and through it could be seen the discolored, termite-ridden wood of the coffin. Now, using the edge of the pickax as a lever, he pried out the remaining pieces of cement from the vault. He lowered the pickax to his assistant and brushed away the final crumbs of cement with his hand. He reached inside the vault and began to pull out the coffin.

The journalist turned back to the director. "What will you do with him now?"

"He will go to the fire," the director answered. "It will be very quick. By now there is nothing left but bones."

"And then?"

The director shrugged. "Since no one has come for him,

4

the ashes will be placed with others in the cart and sent to fill in the land we are reclaiming from the swamp."

The coffin was lying on the narrow strip of cement next to the building. The director walked over and looked down. He brushed his hand over a small metal plate on the cover. He checked the lettering on the plate with the paper in his hand. *"Verificado,"* he said.

He looked up at the journalist. "You want to look in the coffin?"

"No." The journalist shook his head.

"You do not mind then?" the director asked. "When there is no family to pay, the men are allowed to—"

"I understand," the journalist said quickly. He turned away as the men began to lift the coffin lid. He took out a cigarette and lit it. He heard the soft murmur as the men discussed what they found and how it was to be divided. Then there was a muttered curse and the sounds of the lid being nailed back.

The director came back to him. "The men are very disappointed," he said. "There was nothing but a few gold fillings in his teeth and this ring."

The journalist looked down at the ring in the man's hand. It was encrusted with grime.

"I have taken the ring," the director said, "and let them have the fillings. The ring is valuable, no?" He took a grimy handkerchief from his pocket and cleaned it, then held it in the palm of his hand.

The journalist looked down at it. It was gold with a crimson facing stone. He picked it up and read the familiar lettering. It was a Harvard class ring, year of 1939. "Yes," he said, "It's valuable."

"Ten U.S. dollars?" the director asked.

It took a moment before the journalist realized that he was being offered the ring. He nodded. "Ten U.S. dollars." He took the bill out of his pocket.

"Gracias," the director said.

The journalist put the ring in his pocket. They turned toward the laborers. The coffin was already on the wagon.

The director looked at him. *"Vámonos.* We go now to the fire." He climbed up on the wagon and gestured to the space on the seat beside him.

The sun was hotter now than it had been when he first came

into the cemetery and even the faint breeze afforded no relief. The journalist's shirt was wet through to his jacket. They moved through the cemetery in silence. It was almost twenty minutes before they reached the flat dull-gray building that served as the crematorium.

There was a faint smell of smoke in the air as the journalist climbed down from the wagon. He followed the director and the two laborers as they carried the coffin through the wide entranceway.

Once inside he was surprised to see there was no roof; only the sky and the hot sun above. There were six stone open-topped furnaces placed in a circle within the walls of the building. Over each the air shimmered and danced with the heat contained within. A man in a dusty ash-covered gray coat came up to them. "Verificado?"

The director nodded and gave him the slip of white paper. "Verificado."

"Sí," the man answered. He gestured to the laborers. "A las uno."

The laborers walked to the nearest stone furnace and slid the coffin into it. They turned and left the building.

The director took the journalist's arm and they moved over to the furnace. The coffin rested on smoke-blackened steel bars; underneath was what seemed to be a fine wire netting. "For the ashes, no?" the director said.

The journalist nodded.

The man in the gray coat was watching.

The director tugged at the journalist's sleeve. "He expects ten pesos for his work. It is the custom."

The journalist reached into his pocket and held out a bill.

The man's teeth flashed whitely in his swarthy face. "Gracias."

He gestured toward them and, still following the pressure on his arm, the reporter moved back until they were against the far wall. Then the man in the gray coat began to pump the bellows.

There was a faint rumble in the furnace at first, then the rumble turned quickly into a roar. It felt as if thunder were confined in the little box, but still there were no flames visible. The coffin seemed merely to shimmer in the waves of hot air. Then suddenly the man pulled a lever and for a moment it seemed as if all the fires of hell suddenly leaped up.

6

The journalist felt the intense blast of heat against his face, but only for a moment, then the flames were gone and the coffin seemed to disintegrate into gray dust and settle slowly into the furnace.

The director tugged at his sleeve. "We will go outside and smoke a cigarette. Before we are finished, he will bring the ashes."

The hot sun seemed cool compared to the heat he had felt inside. He offered the director a cigarette. The man took it in that delicate manner some Latin Americans have and quickly offered a light to the journalist's cigarette, then to his own. They smoked in silence.

The director was right. They hadn't finished their cigarettes when the man came out with a small gray ceramic urn. He looked at the director.

"The urn is five pesos," the director murmured apologetically.

The journalist found a five-peso coin in his pocket. The man nodded his thanks again and offered the urn to the director.

"Now we go to the wagon," the director said. He led the way around to the back of the building. There a small wagon stood, with a sleepy-eyed burro before it. It was filled with dirt and refuse and flies were buzzing around it. "We empty the ashes here."

The reporter stared at it. Something inside him was suddenly sick. "Is there no other place?"

The director stared at him. He nodded. "There is a farm across the road. For five pesos the farmer will let us scatter the ashes there."

"We will go there."

He followed the director across a field, then over the road. It was a field of potatoes and the farmer who appeared seemingly came from the ground in which they were growing. He vanished as quickly as he received the five-peso coin.

The director held out the urn. "Señor?"

The journalist shook his head.

"You knew him, señor?" the director asked.

"Yes," the reporter said. "I knew him."

The director removed the cover from the urn and with a practiced twist of his wrist scattered the ashes to the wind. Silently they watched the wind scatter them across the field.

"It's all wrong," the journalist said suddenly. "It's all wrong."

"Por qué, señor?"

"This was a strong man," the journalist said. "The earth moved before him when he walked, men loved him and feared him, women trembled at the power in his loins, people sought his favors. And now there is no one here who remembers him." He began to turn away. "You were right. The dead are alone."

The director caught at his sleeve again. The journalist turned to face him. He felt weary and tired. He wanted to be back in the bar at the new hotel with a tall cool drink. He wished he hadn't found the notice, hadn't come out into the terrible sun to this horrible place, to this world without memory.

"No, *señor*," the director said softly. "I was wrong. He was not alone. You were here."

BOOK
1

VIOLENCE
and
POWER

1

I was playing in the hot sun of the front yard when I heard the first thin scream from far down the road toward town. My dog heard it too, for suddenly he stopped frisking around me and the little adobe hut I was trying to build in the hard-baked dirt. He looked up at me, his eyes white and frightened, his yellow tail curving protectively against his testes. He stood very still and began to tremble.

"Quién es?" I asked, my hand reaching to soothe him. I knew he was frightened but I didn't know why. The scream had been eerie and curiously disturbing but I wasn't frightened. Fear is something that has to be learned. I was still too young. I was six years old.

There was the rattle of gunfire in the distance. It quickly died away and then came the sound of another scream, this one louder and more terrified than the first.

The dog broke and raced away to the cane field, ears flat against his head. I ran after him, screaming, *"Perro! Perro! Venga aquí!"*

By the time I reached the edge of the field he was already gone. I stood very still, trying to locate him by sound amidst the heavy stalks.

"Perro!" I shouted.

He did not come back. The sugar cane rustled slightly in the warm breeze. I could smell its pungent sweetness. It had rained last night and the sugar was wet and heavy in the stalks. Suddenly I was aware that I was alone.

The workmen who were there only a few minutes ago were gone. They had vanished like the dog. I stood there thinking that my father would be very angry with them. At ten *centavos* an hour, he expected each of them to give him a full measure of work.

11

"Dax!"

The scream came from the house behind me. I turned around. My older sister and one of the kitchen girls were standing on the *galería* along the front of the house.

"Dax! Dax!" my sister screamed, her arm waving.

"The dog ran into the cane," I shouted back, and turned once more to look into the field.

A moment later I heard her footsteps behind me and before I could turn around she had scooped me up in her arms and was running back toward the house. I could hear her labored breath against my ear and the sobbing husky murmur of her voice. "Ah, *Dios! Dios!*"

My mother was at the doorway even before we reached the *galería*. "Quickly. *A la bodega!*" she hissed. "The wine cellar."

We pushed through the doorway. La Perla, the fat Indian cook, was standing behind my mother. She took me from my sister and began to hurry through the house to the pantry off the kitchen. Behind us I heard the click of the heavy bolt on the front door.

"What is it, La Perla?" I asked. *"Dónde está Papá?"*

She held me tighter to her heavy bosom. "Shh, *niño.*"

The pantry door was open and we clattered down the cellar steps. The other servants were there already, their faces dark and frightened in the shadows cast by the small candle burning on top of a wine barrel.

La Perla set me down on a small bench. "Now sit there and be quiet!"

I looked up at her. This was fun, I thought, more fun than playing in the yard. It was a new kind of game.

La Perla hastened up the stairs again. I could hear her hoarse voice shouting above me. A moment later my sister came down, and there were tears running down her cheeks. She ran over to me and put her arms around my neck and pulled my head down to her chest.

I pulled away angrily. Her chest hurt my face. It was bony. It wasn't comforting and soft and warm like La Perla's.

"Leave me alone," I said.

My mother came down the steps, her face drawn and thin. I heard the sound of the heavy cellar door being slammed and bolted, and then La Perla came too, her face red from the exertion. In her hand she held a huge cleaver, the one she used to chop off the heads of the chickens.

Mother looked down at me. "Are you all right?"

"*Sí, Mamá*," I said. "But Perro ran away. He ran into the cane field. I couldn't find him."

But she wasn't listening. She was trying to hear any sounds from the outside. It was a waste of time. No sound could penetrate this far into the ground.

One of the servant girls suddenly began to cry hysterically.

"Shut up!" La Perla hissed, with a threatening gesture of the cleaver. "Do you want them to hear us? Do you want to get us all killed?"

The girl shut up. I was glad that La Perla had made her because my sister stopped crying too. I didn't like her to cry. Her face gets all ugly and red.

I held my breath and tried to listen. I could hear nothing. "*Mamá—*"

"Quiet, Dax," she whispered sternly.

I had a question to ask. "Where's *Papá?*"

At that my sister began to cry again.

"Shut up!" my mother hissed, then turned to me. "*Papá* will be here in a little while. But we must be very quiet until he comes. *Comprende?*"

I nodded. I turned to look at my sister. She was sobbing under her breath now. I could see that she was frightened but there was no real reason for her to cry. I reached out for her hand. "*No tengas miedo*," I whispered. "I am here."

Somehow a smile pushed its way through her tears. She pulled me close. "My little hero," she whispered. "My protector."

The thud of heavy boots came from the ceiling overhead. Suddenly they seemed to be all over the house.

"*Los bandoleros!*" one of the maids screamed. "They will kill us!"

"Shut up!" This time La Perla did more than speak. Her hand flashed in the dim light. The maid tumbled to the floor whimpering softly. The footsteps seemed to be coming toward the kitchen.

"The candle!" my mother whispered hoarsely. The small light went out abruptly. We sat there in the blackness.

"*Mamá*, I can't see," I said.

I felt a hand press across my mouth. I tried to see in the

13

dark but all I could do was listen to the sounds of the others breathing. The footsteps were over our heads now. They seemed to be in the kitchen.

I heard the crash of a table as it was overturned and dimly the voices of men, the sound of their laughter. There was the creak of a door, and now they were in the pantry. The cellar door rattled. I could now hear their voices more clearly.

"The chickens must be hiding down there," one of them said, and there was a sound of laughter.

"Cock a doodle doo," another crowed. "Your rooster is here."

There was a kick at the door. *"Abre la puerta!"*

I could feel the girls shrinking back against the wall. I felt my sister shiver. "They're only looking for chickens," I whispered. "Tell them they're in the coop back of the house."

No one answered. They didn't seem to mind any more if I spoke. La Perla pushed past me in the darkness and stood at the foot of the steps waiting. A heavy blow against the door reverberated through the cellar.

One of the maids fell to her knees and began to pray hysterically as there was another crash from above. A panel of the door gave way and then it sprang open, as a stream of light came tumbling down the steps to reveal La Perla standing there, resolute as a rock, the cleaver reflecting the light like a silvered mirror.

Some men came down the stairs. There were three that I could see. The others were behind, so all I could see were their legs.

The first one stopped when he saw La Perla. "An old fat hen. Not worth the bother." He knelt slightly and peered under the overhang. "But there are others. Young and juicy ones. The old hen stands guard on her flock."

"Bastardos!" La Perla said through her teeth.

The man straightened up almost negligently and the short-barreled musket in his hand exploded with a blinding flash.

The acrid smell of gunpowder was strong in my nostrils and as my eyes cleared I could see La Perla stagger back against the wall opposite the steps. She seemed to hang there suspended for a moment, then began slowly to slide down the wall. The side of her face and neck was completely gone. There was nothing but a raw red mass of flesh and bone.

"La Perla!"

14

My mother screamed and ran toward her. Almost without effort the man seemed to reverse the musket in his hand and club my mother across the head as she ran past him. She collapsed suddenly, falling across La Perla's body with a curiously crumpled look on her face.

"Mamá!" I started to run toward her but my sister's fingers were like vises and I couldn't move. *"Mamá!"* I screamed again.

The servant girl who had been praying fainted, sprawling grotesquely out on the floor. The man came down off the last step, stepping over La Perla and my mother. He looked down for a moment at the servant, then rolled her casually out of the way with his foot. The others pushed down the steps behind him. There were eleven of them.

He noticed the candle on the barrel. *"La candela,"* he said, gesturing.

One of the men struck a match. Its yellow light danced eerily in the cellar. The leader looked around at us. "Ah, four pullets and a young cock."

My sister's voice came from behind me. It suddenly sounded older and more full bodied than I had ever heard it. "What do you want?" she asked. "Take what you will and go."

The man stared at her for a moment. His eyes were black and they shone like coals. "This one is mine," he said casually. "You are welcome to the others."

The girl who had fainted came to her senses just in time to hear. She screamed and scrambled to her feet. She tried to run past the others toward the stairs but one of them caught her by her long loose black hair. He jerked her back, and she stumbled backward to her knees.

He turned her toward him, holding her head back until her face was almost turned completely up to him, her mouth open, gasping for air. With his free hand he ripped at the front of her dress but the coarse cotton was too strong. It wouldn't tear.

With an angry curse he let her go, then his hand came up with a knife. It slashed quickly down the front of the dress. The coarse shift fell away like the husk from an ear of corn. A thin pencil-like streak, starting at her throat and running down between her breasts and across her brown Indian belly into the heavy matting of pubic hair, suddenly began to well crimson. She screamed and tried to get away, scrambling

15

on her hands and knees, but he laughed aloud and pulled her back by her hair.

She tried to get away again. Quickly he reversed the knife in his hand and hooked the butt end viciously upward between her legs, and this time she screamed in pure agony.

She crumpled to the floor at his feet, writhing in pain. The sharp blade end of the knife reflected the crazy yellow lights from the candle as it stuck upright from between her legs. He put his heavily booted foot on her belly to hold her still and started to pull at the rope belt that held up his *pantalones*.

By now the others were at the other servant girls. Niella, who was my mother's personal maid, was already stripped naked and bent backward across a wine barrel, held on either side by a *bandolero* as a third began to mount her. Sarah, the Indian girl La Perla had brought down from the hills to help in the kitchen, was sprawled on the floor on the other side of the cellar behind a row of wooden crates.

The leader turned. His broad body blocked the rest of the room. "Get rid of the boy," he said quietly, "or I will kill him."

My sister began to push me away.

I turned to look up at her face. It was dull and glazed. Her eyes seemed to have no life in them. "No! No!" I screamed.

"Go behind the boxes in the corner and do not look," she said. It wasn't her voice. It was a stranger's voice, cold and distant. One I had never heard before.

"No!"

The sharp sting of her slap ran down my cheek. "*Vaya!* Do as I say!"

It wasn't the pain. It was the note of authority in her voice. I began to cry.

"Go!"

Rubbing my eyes, I turned away and huddled down behind the boxes. I was still crying. Suddenly I started to wet my pants. How quickly we learn the meaning of fear.

16

screamed again and shuddered. Slowly he disappeared into her as her scream faded away to a low agonized moan.

He moved again on her. Twice more he peered to her into her, and then a peculiar agony of his own seemed to over-ride him, as a curious shuddering animal-like cry escaped him.

But at that moment he looked up and I stared straight into his face. His eyes were red-rimmed and tortured, his mouth open and gasping for air. Then the holster screamed again and I saw the blood bubbling up from her. I felt a terror rising in-side me. I began to tremble. I wanted to kill him.

I heard something sliding to the wooden floor, and I looked

___ ___

2

It was my sister's penetrating scream that stopped my tears. They seemed to dry up inside me as a wave of intense blind-ing hate coursed through me. I sucked in my breath and held it as I raised my head and peered over the boxes.

My sister's back was to me and her naked buttocks were twisting violently as the *bandolero* forced her backward to-ward a crate. Her nails clawed at his face, leaving a red welter of scratches, but he slapped her viciously and she fell backward across the crate.

Her mouth was open and she was screaming but no sound was coming from her lips. Her eyes were wild as they stared up at me without seeing. Her little *tetas* were stretched flat across her chest bones and her belly was almost a concave hollow.

Suddenly I knew what he was going to do. I had seen enough bulls when the cows were led to them. I looked at the *bandolero* as his *pantalones* fell about his legs. His belly was a thick matted rug of hair from which his swollen manhood rose like the white shaft of the broom that was used to sweep the *galería*.

She tried to get up and away but he leaned down on one hairy elbow, resting it in the pit of her stomach, and with his open hand around her throat, he pinned her back against the crate, almost choking her. She screamed again and bucked, sliding away from him, but he cursed and increased the pressure against her throat. She bucked and writhed and angrily he swiped his hand across her face. Her head hit viciously against the side of the crate.

For a fraction of a second he was still, half suspended in the air above her, seemingly balanced on himself. Then she screamed again and shuddered. Slowly he disappeared into her as her screams faded away to a low agonized moan.

He moved again on her. Twice more he seemed to tear into her, and then a peculiar agony of his own seemed to overtake him as a curious shuddering animal-like cry escaped him.

Just at that moment he looked up and I stared straight into his face. His eyes were glazed and tortured, his mouth open and gasping for air. Then my sister screamed again and I saw the blood bubbling up from her. I felt a hatred rising inside me. I began to tremble. I wanted to kill him.

I heard something clatter to the wooden floor, and I looked down. The knife had fallen from his belt. Without thought I scrambled over the crate for it. Slowly, as if with a great effort, he turned toward me.

"Bastardo!" I screamed, plunging it toward his throat with both hands.

He threw up an arm and the knife flew out of my hands, falling between us. I flung myself at him, trying to hit him with my clenched fists, and almost lazily he swung his open fist at me.

I spun back off the wall and crashed into the crates. I could no longer feel any pain. There was only hatred and a wish to kill I never before had known. I am not sure if I realized what could happen. I was only aware that nothing mattered. I had to destroy him.

My sister had twisted her head and was staring at me. Suddenly there was clarity in her eyes. "Dax!" she screamed, grabbing at his hand, the one that now held the knife.

Angrily he tried to wrench his arm free, half pulling her out from under him. "Dax! Run, *por Dios!*" she screamed again. "Run!"

I stood there frozen.

He lunged at me.

"Run, Dax!"

He started to lunge again, and suddenly she seemed to cross her legs, pulling her knees together. He screamed in pain.

"Dax! Run to *Papá!*"

This I understood. This got inside me. I whirled and began to run up the cellar steps. I heard another scream behind me.

18

It stopped almost in the middle, and I heard him shouting hoarsely, *"El niño!"*

I was up the steps and through the house. I burst out into the sunlight. For a moment I was blinded; I could not see. Then I began to run toward the cane fields where Perro had gone. *"Papá! Papá!"*

Some men were coming up the road. I didn't know who they were but I ran toward them. I was out past the fence before the first of the *bandoleros* came out of the house. I streaked down the road screaming hysterically, and then I heard a shout come from up the road, my father's voice.

"Dax! Dax! Gracias a Dios!"

"Papá!" I screamed.

I leaped into his arms crying, *"Papá! Papá! Tengo miedo! Don't let them hurt me!"*

My father's dark face was glistening in the midday heat. He held me closely. "Don't be afraid," he whispered. "No one will hurt you."

"They hurt *Mamá*," I cried hysterically, "and sister. La Perla is dead, and sister is bleeding."

I could see my father's face turn ashen under his dark skin. "This is your army, General?" His voice was savagely sarcastic. "They make war on women and children?"

The slim man standing next to my father stared at him, then those cold gray eyes turned to me. The mouth pressed into a thin line. "If my men have committed any wrongs they will die for them, *señor.*"

He started toward the house, and the *bandoleros* who had started after me stopped when they saw him. *"El jefe!"*

They shrank back against the wall as we pushed past. The general paused in the doorway and looked back at us. "Where are they?"

"En la bodega," I said.

Suddenly my father broke into a run. With me still in his arms he hurtled past the general into the house, through the kitchen, and down the cellar steps.

He stood there for a moment staring at the havoc. Then he put me down slowly. *"Dios mío!"* he cried softly, sinking to his knees and raising my mother's head to his lap. *"Dios mío!"*

My mother's face was white and very still. Her head seemed to be hanging at a curious angle. I looked across the room for my sister. She still lay across the crate, her head dangling backward. I ran over to her. "It's all right now," I cried. *"Papá* is here."

But she didn't hear me. She would never hear me again. The knife was still caught in her larynx where the *bandolero* had plunged it. I stared at her, disbelieving. Then I screamed.

For the first time I realized what had happened. They were dead. They were all dead. *Mamá*. My sister. La Perla. All dead. I screamed and screamed and screamed.

Later, after my father had picked me up and taken me out of that place of blood up into the sunlight, we stood in the courtyard. It was late afternoon, and there were many more men than there had been earlier. There must have been more than a hundred. They were standing around watching silently.

Eleven of them were separated from the others. They were tied together, each with a rope leading to the man on either side of him. They stood silently in the bright sunlight against the wall, staring back at their compatriots.

The general was seated on a chair at the table on the *galería*. He looked out at them and at the other *bandoleros*. He spoke quietly but his thin cold voice carried to the farthest among them.

"Look. And remember. For their punishment will be yours if you, too, forget that you are liberators, not *bandoleros*. You fight for freedom and for your countrymen, not for your own gain or profit. You are soldiers in the service of your homeland, not looters and rapists."

He got to his feet and turned to an aide, who placed a submachine gun in his hands. Slowly he turned to my father. He held the gun out toward him. *"Señor?"*

My father stared at the gun for a moment, then at the general. He took a deep breath, and turned to look at the men standing against the wall. "No, General," he said softly. "I am a man of law, not of war. The hurt is mine but not the vengeance."

The general nodded and walked down the steps from the *galería* onto the hard, sun-baked earth of the courtyard. Holding the machine gun loosely in his hand, he strolled toward the eleven men. He stopped in front of the first in the line, the man who had raped and killed my sister.

20

"You, García," he said quietly, "you I made sergeant. You should have known better."

The man didn't speak. He stared back into the general's eyes without fear. He knew there would be no mercy and he didn't expect any.

A knife flashed in the general's hand as he walked down the line. As he stepped away we could see what he had done. The rope belt holding up each man's *pantalones* had been cut and they fell to the ground exposing their white lower bodies and legs. Slowly the general moved back until he was ten paces away. He started to raise the gun.

I was staring at García. The memory of him poised over my sister exploded back into my mind. I screamed and ran down from the *galería*. "Let me, General! Let me kill him!"

The general turned in surprise.

"Dax! Dax! Come back!" my father called after me.

But I didn't hear. I ran to the general. "Let me!" I cried.

"Dax!" my father shouted.

The general looked back at the *galería*. "It is justice," he said.

"But he's a child!" my father replied. "What could he know of justice?"

"This day he has already learned of death," the general said. "He has learned to hate, he has learned to fear. Let him now learn to kill or it will rankle forever like a cancer in his soul."

My father fell silent. His dark face was somber as he slowly turned away. "It is in his blood," he said sadly. "The cruelty of the *conquistadores*."

I knew what he meant. Even then I knew. The blood that came from my mother, who could trace her family back to the Spaniards who came with Cortez.

The general knelt down. "Come here, boy."

I walked over to him. He rested the gun across his forearm and guided my hand so that my finger was on the trigger. He held the recoil barrel in the crook of his elbow. "Now," he said, "look down the top of the barrel. When you see it is aimed at their *cojones* pull the trigger. I will do the rest."

I squinted along the blue metal barrel. I pointed the gun at García. I could see his white legs and hairy belly just below the end of the short metal barrel. I squeezed the trigger.

21

The noise exploded in my ears and the white body shattered into a thousand tiny bloody fragments. I felt the general sweep the gun down the line. And everywhere it pointed was white flesh dissolving into torn and bleeding flesh. I felt the trigger turn hot under my finger but there was an exultation and excitement in me and I wouldn't have let it go even if it had burned my fingers.

Suddenly the clip ran out and the gun was silent. I looked up at the general in bewilderment.

"It is over, *niño*."

I turned to stare at the eleven men. They were sprawled on the ground, their faces tortured in a last frozen agony, their eyes staring unseeingly up at the white sun.

I began to tremble. "Are they dead?" I asked.

The general nodded. "They are dead."

I shivered now as if the day had turned into ice. Then I began to cry. I turned and ran toward my father. "*Papá! Papá!*" I cried. "They are dead. Now will *Mamá* and sister be alive again?"

---

3

Diogenes Alejandro Xenos. The name was too long for a little boy. At first my mother used to call me Dio. But my father became angry. He thought it was sacrilegious. Somewhere along the line it became Dax. I think it was La Perla who first called me that. The Greek sound of Diogenes was too much for her Indian tongue.

My father was born in the coastal city of Curatu, of a Greek sailor and a Negro woman who ran a small restaurant down near the wharfs where sailors used to eat when they came ashore. I remember once seeing a daguerreotype of my grandparents that my father showed to me.

Even seated, it was apparent that my grandmother was taller than my grandfather, who was standing beside and slightly behind her chair. My grandmother's face seemed very black and she looked into the camera with a kind of poise that indicated an inner strength and purpose. My grandfather had the eyes of a dreamer and a poet, which indeed he had been before he went to sea.

My father had his mother's complexion and his father's gentle eyes. He had loved both his parents very much. Proudly he would tell me that his mother was descended from Bantu princes who had been brought here in slavery and how her father had indentured himself for life after the slaves were liberated, so that she could get whatever small education was available to her.

Jaime Xenos. My father had been named after his maternal grandfather. When my grandmother became too big with child to run the small restaurant, my grandfather took over. But it wasn't for him. Before my father was a month old the small restaurant, and all my grandmother had worked for and accumulated, was sold.

My grandfather, who wrote a beautiful script, then became a clerk to the *alcalde* of the wharf district, and they moved to a small house about two kilometers from the port, where they kept a few chickens and could look out at the blue Caribbean and watch the ships that came in and out of the port.

There wasn't much money but my grandparents were very happy. My father was their only child and they had great plans for him. His father had taught him to read and write by the time he was six, and through the *alcalde* was able to get him into the Jesuit school the children of the officials and *aristócratas* attended.

In return for this honor my father had to begin his day at four-thirty in the morning. His chores were to empty the slops and clean the rooms before classes began. These tasks extended some three hours after classes ended at six o'clock, plus any others the teachers or staff desired.

By the time he had reached sixteen, my father had learned all that the school had to offer. He had inherited the stature of his mother's family, being almost six feet tall, and his father's inquisitive mind. He was by far the brightest student in all the school.

A great *conferencia* was held between the Jesuit brothers who ran the school and my grandfather, at the end of which it was decided that my father should be sent to the University to read for the law. Since his father's salary as a clerk was too meager to pay for this, it was further agreed that he would be sponsored by the Jesuits out of the school's limited scholarship fund. But even this would not have been enough to cover the costs of tuition had not the *alcalde,* for whom my grandfather worked, agreed to make up the difference in return for five years' indenture once my father finished school.

Thus it was that he first began the practice of law without salary in the office of the *alcalde* where his father was a clerk, working in the dank, dark outer room perched high on a stool copying in his flowing hand the early briefs and summations my father prepared for his master. It was there he was working at the age of twenty-three, in the third year of his indenture, when the plague came to Curatu.

It arrived on a ship with clean white sails, a ship that sailed almost jauntily atop the crests of the waves that capped the clear blue waters of the harbor. It was hidden in the secret darkness of the ship's holds, and within three days almost the entire city of three thousand souls was dead or dying.

That first morning when the *alcalde* came in my father was at his desk on the far side of the room in which he worked. The older man was visibly agitated but my father did not ask what had upset him. It was not the thing to do with his excellency. He bent his head over the lawbooks and pretended not to notice.

The *alcalde* came up behind him. He peered down over my father's shoulder to see what he was doing. After a moment he spoke. "Jaime?"

My father looked up. *"Sí, excelencia?"*

"Have you ever been to Bandaya?"

"No, excelencia."

"There is a matter there," the *alcalde* said, "a question of land rights. My good friend Rafael Campos has a dispute with the local authorities."

My father waited patiently.

"I should go myself," the *alcalde* said, "but there are pressing matters here. . . ." His voice trailed off.

24

My father did not answer. He knew what was going on in the office; there were no really important matters. But Bandaya was six hundred kilometers away, high in the mountains, and travel was arduous. Besides, there were rumors of *bandoleros* roaming the hills, waylaying travelers.

"It is a very important matter," the *alcalde* said, "and Señor Campos is an old friend. I would want him to have every assurance." He paused for a moment and looked down at my father. "I think it would be better if you could leave this morning. I have arranged for you to have one of the horses from my stable."

"*Sí, excelencia,*" my father said, getting up from his chair. "I will go home and get a few things together. I will be ready to leave in an hour."

"You know about the matter?"

My father nodded. "*Seguramente, excelencia.* I wrote the petition at your request. It was two months ago."

The *alcalde* sighed in relief. "Of course. I had forgotten." He hadn't forgotten; he knew that every brief and petition that had been issued from his office the past few years had been written by my father. "You will express to Señor Campos my profound regrets at being unable to come personally?"

"*Seguramente, excelencia,*" my father reassured him. He then went into the outer office, where his father sat on a high stool copying a judgment.

"*Qué pasa?*" his father asked.

"*Vengo a Bandaya, Papá.*"

My grandfather smiled. "'*Stá bueno.* It is a great opportunity. Señor Campos is a very important man. I am very proud of you."

"*Gracias, Papá.* I go now. *Adios, Papá.*"

"*Vaya con Dios, Jaime,*" his father said, turning back to his work.

My father took the horse from the *alcalde*'s stable to go home to get his clothes. That way he would not have to walk the two kilometers back to town.

His mother was in the front yard hanging out the washing. She looked up as he tied the horse to the fence. Quickly he explained to her where he was going. Like his father she was thrilled and happy over his great opportunity. Anxiously

25

she helped him select his two best shirts, which she packed carefully with his best suit in an old worn travel case.

They came out into the yard again just as a ship with sparkling white sails came past the breakwater into the harbor. She stopped for a moment and looked at it across the water. "*Mira!*" She pointed.

Jaime smiled. His mother had told him about the ships. About how when she was a little girl her father used to take her up on the hill so they could watch the ships coming into the harbor. And about how he used to say that one day a big ship with white sparkling sails would come and take them home, home to a freedom where a man did not have to bend his knee for his daily bread.

Her father had long since died but she still had the dream. Only her dream was now for her son. It was he who would lead them to freedom. With his strength and with his knowledge.

"Grandpa would have liked that ship," her son said.

She laughed as they walked toward the horse, which was nibbling at the soft grass near the fence. "You are my ship with white sails," she replied.

My father kissed her and mounted the horse. He started up the road behind the house. At the crest of the hill, he wheeled the horse around and looked down. His mother was still standing in the yard, looking after him. He waved to her. She raised her hand. He sensed rather than saw her smile, her bright white teeth. He waved again and turned his horse back toward the road.

As he did he could see the ship heeling toward the quays, the sailors up in the masts running like crazy little ants. The white topgallant was the first to come billowing down, then the foremast, and as he turned to ride away, the ship came easing sideways against the docks, the rest of its sails shuddering down, leaving a tracery of towering masts.

When he returned to Curatu two months later, the ship was still against the dock, a burned black splintering mass of wood that had once proudly sailed the oceans and had finally brought the black death to the city. Of his father and mother he found no trace.

When a servant first brought word that a stranger was riding down from the mountain toward the *hacienda*, Señor

Rafael Campos took his binoculars and went out on the *galería*. Through the glasses he saw a dark man dressed in dusty city clothes astride a dark pony threading its way carefully down the tricky mountainside path. He nodded to himself with satisfaction. The servants were alert. One could not be too careful when at any moment the *bandoleros* might come sweeping down from the mountains.

He peered again through the glasses. The stranger was riding very carefully. Señor Campos put down the glasses and took his gold watch from his pocket. It was ten-thirty in the morning; it would be an hour and a half before the stranger could reach the *hacienda*. It would be almost time for lunch. He clapped his hands sharply.

"Set another place for lunch," he told the servant. Then he went inside to complete his toilet.

It was almost two hours before my father reached the *hacienda*. Don Rafael was seated in the shade on the *galería*. He was dressed in the immaculate white suit of the *aristócrata*, and the ruffles of his white silk shirt and the flowing black tie only served to accentuate the thin delicate structure of his face. His mustache was thin and finely cropped in the latest Spanish fashion and his hair and eyebrows held only the faintest tinge of gray.

Don Rafael rose to his feet as my father dismounted. With satisfaction he noted that my father's suit was clean and brushed, and that his boots were highly polished. My father, aware of the quick appraisal, was glad he had stopped at a stream to make himself presentable.

Señor Campos came to the head of the stairs as my father walked up them. *"Bienvenido, señor,"* he called politely in the custom of the hills.

"Mil gracias, señor," my father answered. "Have I the honor of addressing his excellency Don Rafael Campos?"

The older man nodded.

My father bowed. *"Jaime Xenos, de la oficina del alcalde, a su servicio."*

Don Rafael smiled. "Come in," he said, extending his hand. "You are an honored guest in my house."

"It is my honor, sir."

Don Rafael clapped his hands. A servant came running. "A cool drink for our guest," he said. "See to his horse."

He led my father back into the shade of the *galería* and

27

bade him be seated. As my father sat down near the small table he caught a glimpse of the rifle and two pistols that were placed on the floor next to his host's chair.

The older man caught the glance. "In the mountains one cannot be too careful."

"I understand," my father said.

The servant came with the drinks and the two men toasted each other, then my father made his apologies for the *alcalde*. But Señor Campos would hear no more of the apologies. He was more than satisfied with my father; he was certain that the entire matter would be concluded with satisfaction. Then they went inside to lunch and afterward Don Rafael bade my father go to his room and rest, for there was time enough tomorrow to discuss their business. Today his guest must rest and make himself at home. So it wasn't until dinner that night that my father actually met my mother.

But from the window above the *galería*, María Elisabeth Campos had watched the rider come up to the *pórtico*. The sounds of conversation came clearly up to her through the still quiet of the afternoon.

"He is very tall and handsome, no?" a voice asked from behind her.

María Elisabeth turned. Doña Margaretha, her aunt, who had served as the *dueña* of the household since the death of her sister, stood behind her.

María Elisabeth blushed. "But he is very dark."

"*Tiene sangre negra*," the aunt replied. "But it does not matter. It is said they make wonderful husbands and lovers." She leaned past her niece and looked out the open window. "*Mucho hombre.*"

The sound of Don Rafael's voice, suggesting that his guest rest until dinner, floated up to them.

Doña Margaretha pulled her head back. She looked at her niece. "Now you must go to bed and rest all afternoon," she said. "It would never do to have our guest see you all flushed and tired from the heat of the day."

María Elisabeth protested but did as she was told. She too had been very impressed with the tall dark stranger and wanted to look her best for him.

At last the drapes were drawn and she lay stretched out alone in the cool dimness. She did not sleep. He was an attorney, she had heard him say. That meant he had polish

28

and manners. Not like the sons of the farmers and plantation owners who lived around the *hacienda*. They were all so coarse and common, more interested in their guns and horses than in the polite conversations of society.

Still, she would soon have to make her choice. She was past seventeen and her father was pressing her. Another year and she would be classified as an old maid, condemned to a life like Doña Margaretha's. And even this might be denied her, for she was an only child with no sisters or brothers whose children she could take care of.

It would be nice to be married to an attorney, she thought vaguely as she drifted off into sleep, to live in the city where one met all kinds of interesting and different people.

And my father was very much intrigued by the slim intense young girl who came down to dinner dressed in a flowing white dress that served to accentuate her huge dark eyes and red lips. He sensed rather than saw the wiry body and full breasts beneath her bodice.

María Elisabeth, for her part, was mostly silent through dinner. She listened with half an ear to the familiar voice of her father and delighted in the soft slurring southern overtones of their guest's voice. The speech of the coast was much more gentle than that of the hills.

After dinner the men went into the library for their cigars and cognac and later came into the music room, where María Elisabeth played some simple melodies for them on the piano. After about half an hour she sensed their guest's restlessness and suddenly she began to play Chopin.

My father suddenly began to listen intently. The deep passion of the music stirred him and he stared at the small girl who was almost dwarfed by the huge piano. When she finished playing he applauded.

Don Rafael applauded also. But it was polite and lacked enthusiasm. He thought Chopin too bold and perhaps even immoral. He preferred the more familiar somber music. The wild rhythms of the people he cared for not at all.

María Elisabeth rose from the piano, flushed and pretty. "It is warm in here," she said, opening her small lace fan. "I think I will go into the garden."

My father rose instantly. He bowed to Don Rafael. *"Con su permiso, excelencia?"*

Don Rafael nodded courteously.

My father held out his arm to the girl. She took it graciously, and they walked into the garden. Doña Margaretha followed at a discreet three paces.

"You play well," my father said.

"Not well at all." She laughed. "There isn't much time to practice. And no one to learn from."

"It would seem to me that there isn't much you have to learn."

"In music there is always much to learn," she said, looking up at him. "I have heard it said that it is like the law. One must never stop studying or learning."

"True," my father admitted. "The law is a stern taskmaster. It is constantly in a state of flux. New interpretations, revisions, even new laws almost every day."

María Elisabeth gave a soft sigh of admiration. "I don't see how you can keep it all in your head."

He looked down and saw the deep wonder in her eyes. Right then and there, though he did not know it, he was lost.

It was almost a year later that they were married, after my father had returned from Curatu with the news of the death of his parents. It was my grandfather Don Rafael who first suggested that he stay in Bandaya and practice law. There were two lawyers there already, but one was old and ready to retire. It was a year after that, almost to the day, that my sister was born.

There were two other children between my sister and myself but each was stillborn. By that time my father had become interested in the study of Greek. His father had had quite a library for that time, and everything had been moved to Bandaya from the little house in Curatu.

It was from Doña Margaretha that I first heard the story of my birth and christening. When the midwives and the doctor came down and told my father the joyous news, he sank to one knee and gave thanks. First for the fact that I was a son (all the others had been girls), and second because I was strong and healthy and would live.

Almost immediately the clamor about my name began. Don Rafael, my grandfather, would hear of nothing but that I should be named after his father. My father, of course, wanted me called after his father. Neither would give an inch.

It was my mother who resolved the threatened breach. "Let

him be named for tomorrow rather than the past," she said. "Let him have a name that will embody our hopes for the future and have meaning for all who hear it."

This appealed to the romantic and the scholar in my father and to the dynastic impulses of my grandfather. Thus it was that my father chose these names:

Diogenes Alejandro Xenos.

Diogenes after the fabled seeker of truth; Alejandro after the conqueror of the world. The explanation was simple, my father proclaimed as he held me for the priest's baptismal drops.

"With the truth, he shall conquer the world."

4

I woke as the first glimmer of light came into my room. For a moment I lay there in the bed, then I rolled over and got up and went to the window.

The sun stood on the edge of the horizon, just climbing over the mountains. There was a faint breeze coming from the west and I shivered as the last remaining chill of the night crept into my nightshirt. Suddenly I had to pee.

I went back to the bed and pulled out the small chamber pot from underneath. While I stood there relieving myself I wondered if *Papá* would give me a larger pot now we two men were the only ones left in the house. I felt warmer after I had finished, and I put the pot back and returned to the window.

Across the road in front of the house I could see the faint smoke rising from the small fires around which the *bandoleros*, rolled in their dirty blankets, were sleeping. There was no movement coming from them, no sound. I pulled off my nightshirt and climbed into my *pantalones* and shoes. I put on

31

the warm Indian wool shirt that La Perla had made for my birthday and went downstairs. I was hungry. It was time to eat.

Sarah, who had been La Perla's assistant, was building a fire in the stove. She looked up as I came in, her Indian face flat and impassive.

"I'm hungry," I said. "Are you going to be the cook now?"

She nodded wihtout speaking. Sarah never talked much.

I went to the table and sat down. "I want a *tortilla con jamón.*"

Again she nodded and reached up for a heavy black frying pan. Quickly she threw in two fingers of grease and placed the pan over one of the openings on the stove. A moment later she had diced pieces of ham from the butt hanging nearby and had broken three eggs into the pan.

I watched with approval. She was better than La Perla. La Perla wouldn't have given me a *tortilla.* She would have made me eat porridge instead. I decided to put this new one to the supreme test. "*Café con leche,*" I said. Chocolate was all La Perla or my mother allowed me.

Sarah put the *café* in front of me without a word. I drank it with loud smacking noises after putting three heaping spoonsful of brown sugar into the cup. The sweetness helped kill the awful taste. I never really liked drinking coffee but it made me feel grown up.

She placed the *tortilla* in front of me. It was dark brown and smoking hot and firm like La Perla made them. I waited a few minutes for it to cool, then picked it up in my fingers and began to eat, watching Sarah out of the corner of my eye.

She said never a word about my not using the knife and fork that were lying beside my plate. She merely stood there watching me, a curious expression in her eyes. When I had finished I got up and went over to the pump and ran some water on my hands and wiped my lips, then dried them on the towel that hung there. "That was very good," I said approvingly.

Something in her eyes reminded me of the way she had looked when the *bandoleros* had approached her in the cellar. Her eyes contained that same inscrutable acceptance.

On an impulse I went over and lifted the front of her shift. Her thighs were unmarked and the mat of hair between her legs did not seem in the least disturbed.

32

I lowered the shift and looked into her face. "Did they hurt you, Sarah?" I asked.

Silently she shook her head.

"I'm glad they didn't hurt you."

Then I noticed the faint edging of tears around her dark eyes. I took her hand. "Don't cry, Sarah," I said. "I won't let them do it to you again. I'll kill them if they try."

Suddenly her arms were around me and she was holding me close against her. I could feel her warm breasts against my face and I heard the heavy beating of her heart. She was sobbing convulsively but almost soundlessly.

I was very still within her arms. All I could think of to say was, "Don't cry, Sarah. Please, don't cry."

After a moment she let me go. I slipped down to the floor but already she had turned away and was back at the stove throwing more wood chips into the firebox. There was nothing more to say. I turned and went out.

The house was silent as I walked through the dining room and living room. I went out the front door onto the *galería*.

Across the road there was movement. The *bandoleros* were beginning to wake to the day. The sun was slanting in over the barns and its rays were reaching across the yard toward the house. I heard a faint sound at the far end of the *galería*. I turned toward it.

That part was still in deep shadow but I could see the glowing tip of a cigar and the outline of a man sitting in my father's chair. Instinctively I knew it wasn't my father. He would never smoke a *cigarro* this early in the day.

The face was much clearer when I stepped out of the light into the shadows. The pale-gray eyes were watching me steadily. *"Buenos días, Señor General,"* I said politely.

He answered equally politely. *"Buenos días, soldadito."* He took another puff on his *cigarro*, then laid it carefully on the edge of the table. "How are you this morning?"

"I am fine," I replied. "I got up early."

"I know. I heard you at the window above."

"You were up already?" I asked in surprise. I had heard no one.

His small even white teeth showed in a faint smile. "Generals, like small boys, must be up at sunrise to see what each day has in store for them."

33

I didn't answer. I looked across the road at the soldiers' camp. "They were still asleep," I said.

A slight edge of contempt came into his voice. *"Campesinos.* All they think about is food for the day. And they sleep well knowing that it will be provided for them." He picked up his *cigarro* again. "Have you eaten?"

"Sí. Sarah gave me *desayuno.* She was crying."

The *cigarro* glowed red. "Women always weep," he said casually. "She will get over it."

"I don't cry."

He looked at me for a moment before he answered. "No, you are a man. Men have no time to shed tears for what has already been done."

"Papá cried," I said. "At the cemetery yesterday." I felt a lump in my throat as I remembered. The fading sun throwing long shadows across the little graveyard behind the house. The creaking of the rusted iron gate. The soft squashy sound of the damp black earth as it fell on the coffins, and the unctuous sound of the Latin of the priest echoing hollowly in the morning air. I swallowed the lump. "I also cried."

"That is permissible," the general replied gravely. "Even I wept." He put down his *cigarro* once more and reached for my hand and drew me to him. "But that was yesterday. Today we are men again, and there is no time for tears."

I nodded silently.

"You are a brave boy. You remind me of my own sons." I didn't speak.

"One is a few years older than you, the other a year younger. I have also a little girl. She is four." He smiled and pulled me up onto his lap. "They live in the mountains."

He looked over my head at the distant hills. "They are safe there." His eyes turned back to me. "Perhaps you would like to visit them for a little while? There is much to do in the mountains."

"Could I have a pony?" I asked quickly.

He looked at me thoughtfully. "Not just now. When you are a little older, perhaps. But you could have a surefooted burro."

"Will he be my own, my very own?"

"Of course," the general replied. "No one will be allowed to ride him except you."

34

"That would be very nice," I said gravely. "I think I would like that very much. But . . ." I climbed down from his lap and looked up at him. "But what would *Papá* do? He has no one but me now."

"I think your father would approve," he replied quietly. "He will be very busy this next year. He will have no time to be here. He will be with me."

By now the sun had crept around the corner of the *galería* and the warmth of the day was beginning to make itself felt. A faint scratching came from beneath our feet, then a sudden slithering sound as if someone had been hiding under the wooden floor. Almost before I could move, the general was on his feet, a pistol suddenly in his hand. *"Quién es?"* His voice was harsh.

There was more scratching, then a familiar yelp and whine. I leaped down from the *galería* and stuck my head down into the opening. A cold nose and familiar tongue slobbered all over my face. I reached in and pulled the little dung-colored dog out from under the *galería*, and, holding him wriggling in my arms, got to my feet.

"Perro!" I cried happily. "Perro! He came back!"

5

Manuelo held up his hand to halt us, then drew his fingers quickly across his lips. I sat astride the little pony scarcely daring to breathe. I looked at Roberto; he, too, was very tense.

Roberto was the oldest son of the general, Diablo Rojo. He was almost eleven, two years older than I. I was almost nine but I was taller by a good three inches. He had become very jealous of me, ever since last year when it became apparent that I had grown the faster.

The others sat quietly on their horses. They were listening also. I strained my ears but could hear nothing above the rustling of the leaves in the forest around us.

"They are not far," Manuelo whispered. "We will have to move quietly."

"It would be better if we knew how many there are," Gato Gordo whispered back.

Manuelo nodded. Fat Cat always made sense. He was a thinker. Perhaps it was because he was so heavy; it was difficult for him to move and he thought much.

"I will scout them," Manuelo said, slipping from his horse.

"No," Fat Cat answered quickly. "The leaves are dry, the twigs will give you away. Then they will know we are here."

"How else can we find out?"

Gato Gordo pointed over his head. "Through the trees," he said, "like a monkey. They will never think to look up."

"We are too heavy," Manuelo replied. "A branch might crack under our weight and—poof!—we are dead."

Fat Cat looked at Roberto and me. "But they are not too heavy."

"No!" Manuelo's whisper was almost explosive in the stillness. "The general will kill us if anything happens to his son!"

"Dax can go," Fat Cat replied softly.

Manuelo looked at me. I could see doubt written on his face. "I don't know," he said hesitantly.

Before he could say any more I reached over my head and grabbed a branch. I pulled myself up out of the saddle and into the tree. "I will go," I said, looking down at them.

Roberto's face was sullen and glowering. I knew it was because I was going and he wasn't. But his father made very strict rules, and one always obeyed the leader. Roberto didn't move.

"Be silent," Manuelo cautioned. "Merely find out how many there are and what weapons they have. Then come back and report to us."

I nodded and, turning, climbed higher into the tree. About fifteen feet from the ground, just before the limbs grew too thin to bear my weight, I started to move from tree to tree.

I was very quick, having spent much time in the trees like all boys, yet it took me almost an hour to cover the quarter-mile to their camp. And if it hadn't been for the smoke from their fire reaching my nostrils I would have been there before I knew it. As it was I ended up almost directly over their heads.

I clung silently to a limb, my heart pounding, sure that they could hear it even over their hearty conversation. Slowly I inched my way back until I was completely hidden in the foliage.

From the loudness of their voices I realized that they didn't suspect anyone was within miles. I counted heads carefully. There were fourteen men, their red and blue uniforms faded and dusty. The evening fire had already been started and occasionally one of them would go over and throw wood on it. I wondered why no one among them had started to cook the evening meal but that question was answered almost immediately.

A woman came into the small clearing. One of the men who had been lying closest to the fire sat up and spoke to her. From the markings on his sleeve, I could tell that he was a sergeant. His voice sounded harsh in the quickening dusk.

"Dónde está la comida?"

"It is coming," the woman answered in a low voice.

A moment later two other women appeared, carrying between them a large iron pot. The smell of a meat stew came up to me and I could feel the juices in my mouth begin to bubble.

The women put the pot down near the men and began to dish the stew out onto tin plates. After each man had been served, the women took what was left and retired a few feet off to eat.

I took advantage of their preoccupation with the food to move quietly away. I circled the clearing in the trees until I located where the women had been doing the cooking. There was the remains of another small fire about twenty feet away. There were also a few blankets on the ground nearby, indicating where the women slept. I started to work my way back.

The sun was fast disappearing by the time I arrived. Despite the fact that the others were listening for me, I managed to drop into their midst without a sound. I was very proud of myself when I saw the startled expressions on their faces.

"Fourteen men under the command of a sergeant," I said. "They have already made camp for the night."

"What weapons do they have?" Fat Cat asked.

"I saw rifles and two tommy guns."

"Only two?"

"That's all I saw."

"I wonder what they're doing out here?" Fat Cat said.

"It must be a patrol," Manuelo replied. "They are always sending out patrols to discover where we are." He laughed. "They never have."

"Fourteen men and two machine guns," Fat Cat repeated thoughtfully. "There are only five of us, not counting the two boys. I think we'd better give them the slip."

"Now is the time to do it," I said boldly. "The women have just given them food. They are too busy eating to hear us."

"They have women with them?" Manuelo's voice sounded surprised.

"Yes."

"How many?"

"There are three of them."

"Deserters!" Fat Cat said. "They've run off into the hills with their women."

"Maybe it's true then," one of the others said. "The general has the army on the run. *La guerra* will soon be over."

"The army still controls the ports," Fat Cat replied. "We cannot win until the general captures Curatu. Once we cut them off from the sea the *yanqui* imperialists won't be able to help them. Then it will be over."

"I heard that we're marching toward Curatu," Manuelo said.

"What are we going to do about the *soldados?*" Fat Cat asked, bringing the subject back to the pertinent.

"I don't know," Manuelo answered hesitantly. "They have two machine guns."

"They have also three women," Fat Cat said meaningfully.

"Deserters have no spirit to fight," Diego Gonzalez added. "It has been a long time—"

Fat Cat cut him off with a warning look at Roberto and me. "We could use machine guns. The general would reward us." He looked over at me. "Have they posted a guard?"

"No," I replied, "they are lying around the fire eating. There is no lookout. I could have peed right in their cooking pot and they wouldn't have noticed."

Manuelo came to a decision. "We will take them by surprise. Just before dawn when they are in their deepest sleep."

I rolled over in my blanket, pulling it around me to ward off the night chill. Next to me I heard Roberto move. "Are you awake?" I whispered.

"Sí."

"I cannot sleep," I said.

"Me too."

"Are you scared?"

"No." The answer came quickly in a scornful voice. "Of course not."

"I'm not either."

"I can't wait till morning. I'm going to kill one of those *soldados*. We're going to kill them all."

"The women too?" I asked.

"Of course not," he answered scornfully.

"What are we going to do with them then?"

"I don't know." He thought for a moment. "Rape them, I guess."

"I don't think I would like that," I said. "That's what happened to my sister. It hurts them."

"That's because you're a little boy," he replied scornfully. "You couldn't rape one if you wanted to."

"Why not?"

"You're too small. Your pecker isn't big enough."

"It is so. It's as big as yours!" I replied angrily. "I'm bigger than you."

"But your pecker isn't!"

I was silent. I knew what he said was the truth. I had seen his more than once. He used to play with it in the field back of the house and when it was hard it was twice as big as mine.

"I will rape one anyway," I said defiantly.

He laughed derisively. "You can't; it won't get hard." He rolled over in his blanket and pulled it up over his head. "Now go to sleep. Let me get some rest."

I lay there quietly. I looked up at the stars. Sometimes they seemed to hang so low in the sky I could reach up and touch one. I wondered which was my mother and which was my sister. My father told me that they had gone to heaven and now they were God's stars. Could they see me tonight? Finally I closed my eyes and fell asleep.

I came awake quickly at Manuelo's touch. I was on my feet instantly. "I'm ready," I said. "I'll show you where they are."

"No." Manuelo shook his head. "You stay here with the

horses. Someone has to keep an eye on the horses or they will wander off."

"But—"

Manuelo cut me off. His voice was firm. "You and Roberto will stay with the horses. That's an order."

I looked at Roberto. He didn't meet my eyes. He wasn't so big after all, no matter what he said. If he was, they wouldn't leave him behind too.

"It's getting late!" Fat Cat hissed.

"You stay here until we come back," Manuelo warned. "If we're not back by noon, take the horses and go home. *Comprende?*"

We nodded silently and watched the men disappear into the forest. For a moment we could hear the crackling of leaves and twigs under their feet, then everything was silent.

Roberto looked at me. "We better go see to the horses."

I followed him to where the animals were tethered. They were munching away as quietly as if they were in the pasture at home.

"I don't see why we have to miss all the fun," I said. "The horses won't go far. They're hobbled."

"Manuelo said we have to stay," Roberto replied.

I felt suddenly bold and daring. "You have to. But I don't."

"Manuelo will be angry."

"He will never know," I replied. "I can get there faster through the trees than they can on foot."

I began to shinny up the nearest tree. I paused on the lowest branch. "I'll tell you everything that happened!"

Roberto stared up at me for a moment, then began to run toward the tree. "Wait for me!" he called. "I'm going with you!"

40

6

It didn't take as long to get there as it had last night because I knew exactly where to go. We remained hidden in the trees until I felt Roberto tug at my arm. He pointed and I saw Manuelo and Fat Cat just at the edge of the clearing. Then they disappeared back into the foliage.

From our vantage point I could see our men as they fanned out around the sleeping soldiers. I looked down at the camp. The soldiers didn't stir. They huddled in their blankets around the dying fire. I began to count.

In the dim light I could make out only twelve. I strained my eyes trying to locate the other two but they were not there. Then I understood. They were with the women. I wondered if Manuelo had noticed.

I saw a movement at the edge of the shadows. Fat Cat was signaling to someone across the clearing on the opposite side. I turned my head. Manuelo came out of the foliage. I caught the dull glint of his broad machete as Diego appeared beside him.

Two others were visible next to Fat Cat now. Manuelo gestured with his machete and they ran across the clearing silently. I saw the machetes flash up and down and five of the soldiers were dead before the others had even begun to open their eyes.

The attack was savagely efficient. Two more were dispatched as they tried to roll over. One died as he started to sit up, another just about made it to his knees before Fat Cat, with a broad slash, almost severed his head from his body.

Until now there had been no noise, only the movements of the men as they thrashed in the agonized frenzy of death. Then one of the soldiers broke suddenly and on his hands and

41

knees began to scramble toward the brush in a frantic effort to escape. The loud report of a pistol resounded through the forest, and the birds ceased their shrilling song. The soldier pitched forward face down onto the ground.

The two remaining soldiers threw themselves on the ground, their hands over their heads, screaming for mercy. Their voices sounded thin and reedy in the morning light that was just beginning to filter down through the trees into the clearing. But there was no hesitation in spite of their pleas for mercy.

For a moment there was a silence as our men fought to regain their breath, then Manuelo straightened up. "They are dead?"

"*Sí,*" Fat Cat replied.

"All of them?" Manuelo asked.

Silently they began to check the bodies. Diego raised his head from one he had turned over with his foot. "I think this one still lives."

"Then what are you waiting for?" Manuelo asked.

Diego's machete flashed in the morning sun and a head rolled almost two feet from its body. Diego hadn't even paused to study the result of his blow. He prodded another body with his foot and then walked back over to Manuelo and Fat Cat, taking up a position slightly behind them.

"I count only twelve," Fat Cat said.

"I too," Manuelo confirmed. "The boy said there were fourteen."

"And three women," Diego added.

"He could have been wrong," Fat Cat said. "He's only a child."

"I don't think so," Manuelo answered. "Two must have gone off with the women."

"They can't have gone far. Shall we search for them?"

"No," Manuelo said. "By now they have heard us. We will never find them in this jungle. Gather up the guns and ammunition." He took out a *cigarrillo* and lit it, leaning his back against a tree.

The others had just begun to gather up the guns when I heard a noise almost underneath the tree in which we were hidden. I looked down. It was the enemy sergeant. A tommy gun was crooked in his elbow, and he was just bringing it

42

around to sweep the clearing. Now it was pointing right at Fat Cat.

Without thinking, I shouted, "Gato Gordo, look out!"

Fat Cat's reactions were perfect. He dove sideways into the foliage like the animal after whom he was named. But not Diego. He stood staring up at the tree in which I was hidden, a stupid look of surprise on his face. Then a driving spray of bullets seemed to lift him into the air and tumble him, somersaulting backward.

The sergeant raised his gun toward us.

"Back! Roberto! Back!" I yelled, leaping for another limb.

I heard the chatter of the gun but it ceased almost as quickly as it had begun. I looked down. The sergeant was working the lever as hard as he could. The gun had jammed. I didn't wait to see more.

Roberto screamed behind me. I glanced back over my shoulder. Though he was shorter than I, he weighed much more, and a limb had given way beneath him. He tumbled down through the branches, sprawling to the ground almost at the feet of the sergeant.

The sergeant threw away the gun and flung himself on Roberto. He rolled over and came to his feet holding the boy up in front of him, his knife at Roberto's throat. He stared at our men over Roberto's head. They stared back. Manuelo's gun was now pointed at him, and Fat Cat stood, his machete hanging loosely at his side. The other two moved slowly around behind them.

No one had to tell the sergeant he held the trump. One look was sufficient. "Don't move or the boy dies!"

Manuelo and Fat Cat exchanged embarrassed looks. I didn't have to hear them speak to know what they were thinking. The general wouldn't like this at all; if anything happened to Roberto they might as well not return. Death in the jungle would be a blessing compared to what the general would have planned for them. They didn't move.

It was Fat Cat who spoke first. He pointed the blade of his machete at the ground. "Let the boy go," he said smoothly. "We will be merciful. We will let you go back into the forest in peace."

The sergeant grinned tensely, then spat. "You think I'm a fool? I saw your mercy when the others begged."

"This is different," Fat Cat replied.

43

Manuelo began to inch to one side, and the sergeant's blade flashed. A thin line of blood appeared on Roberto's cheek. "Don't move!" the sergeant shouted.

Manuelo froze.

"Put down your rifle!"

Manuelo looked at Fat Cat hesitantly. Fat Cat nodded almost imperceptibly, and Manuelo's rifle dropped to the ground.

"Now, the others," the sergeant ordered.

Fat Cat dropped his machete, the other two their guns. The sergeant looked down at their weapons for a moment, then decided against trying to retrieve them himself. "Varga! *Aquí, venga aquí!*"

His voice echoed through the forest. There was no answer. He shouted again. "Varga! *Aquí!*"

Still no reply.

"Your *compañero* has fled," Fat Cat said softly. "It will be better if you do as we say."

"No!" The sergeant began to push his way toward the guns, carefully holding Roberto in front of him. "Back!" he warned. "Away from the guns."

Slowly they fell back. Steadily the sergeant inched toward them. He was almost under the tree in which I was hidden when it came to me. It was as if all along I had known what would have to be done. A strange cold rage began to race inside me. It was as if a demon had taken possession of me.

I felt, rather than knew, that I had drawn the knife from my belt. Its hilt lay flat in my clenched fist, the blade outthrust like a sword.

He was directly under me now. A wild scream came up from my throat as I dove from the tree. "*Mato!* I kill!"

I caught a glimpse of the upturned white face as I crashed onto him. A hot searing pain ran up through my arm as the two of us tumbled to the ground. Then two arms seized me and rolled me away. I went over and over and when I scrambled to my feet I saw Fat Cat standing over the sergeant.

There was a look of wonder on his face as he stood there looking down, his machete still hanging loosely. " '*Stá muerto!*" he said. He looked over at me. "He is dead. The little bastard killed him!"

I stared down at the sergeant. His mouth was open, his eyes stared up at the sky sightlessly. Just under his chin, half the hilt of my knife pointed upward.

I looked over at Roberto. He was lying on the ground gasping to catch his breath. When he turned his face toward me I saw the streak of blood down his cheek.

"Are you all right?" I asked.

He nodded without speaking. There was an odd look in his eyes, almost as if he were angry.

I started to walk over toward him when a scream came from behind me. There was a sudden sharp pain at the back of my head and as I spun around I felt nails rake across my cheeks. I fell backward to the ground.

I shook my head to clear my eyes as I looked up. A woman was struggling in Fat Cat's grasp. She spit at me. "You killed him! You're not a child, you're a monster! A black plague from your mother's belly!"

There was a dull thud as the handle of Fat Cat's machete hit her and she slid silently to the ground. There was a faint trace of satisfaction in Fat Cat's voice as he looked around and saw the other two women immobilized by Manuelo's rifle.

"Ah!" he said. "We have found *las putas!*"

7

Santiago, the Indian, pulled some leaves from a bay bush and crushed them by rubbing them together in his hands. Then he bent down and scooped up some mud from the edge of the water hole. "Put this on your face," he said. "It will stop the pain."

Roberto and I did as we were told. The cool mud was soothing. I looked over at him. "Does it hurt?" I asked respectfully.

"Not much."

"I've never been cut," I said.

He drew himself up with a kind of pride, and traced the slight cut with his fingers. "I think it will leave a scar," he

45

added importantly. He looked at me critically. "But I don't think yours will. Scratches aren't as deep as knife wounds."

"Oh," I said, disappointed. I would have nothing to show for it.

I looked over toward Manuelo and Fat Cat. They were huddled under a tree whispering. Occasionally they glanced at the women, who were seated on the ground at the edge of the clearing. The Santiago brothers were guarding them.

"I wonder what they're talking about?" I asked.

"I don't know," Roberto answered. He wasn't looking at Fat Cat and Manuelo. He was staring at the women. "The young one is not so bad."

"Do you think they're angry with us?"

"Who?" Roberto's voice was puzzled. Then he looked over and saw what I meant. He shook his head. "I don't think so. They would have all been dead if we hadn't been here to warn them."

"Sí."

"After all, I did jump the sergeant to try to stop him."

I stared at Roberto. I thought he had fallen. "You're very brave."

"So are you." He glanced back at the women. "I wish they'd stop talking. I'm ready to fuck one right now!"

"You are?"

"Sure."

Manuelo and Fat Cat had finished their conversation, and Fat Cat threaded his way back through the bodies toward us. When he got to Diego he stopped. Santiago walked over to him. "Poor Diego."

Fat Cat's voice was expressionless. "Poor Diego, my ass! He was stupid. I told him many times never to gawk. It served him right."

Santiago shrugged, then turned away as Fat Cat continued over to us. "You boys all right?"

"Sí." Roberto answered for the two of us.

"Bueno," he said. "Do you think the two of you could go back and bring the horses? There is much for us to carry."

Roberto answered before I could speak. "What are you going to do with the women?"

Fat Cat looked at him. "Guard them until your return."

"I will stay and help guard them," Roberto said. "Send one of the others with Dax."

46

Fat Cat stared at him for a moment, then turned and walked back to Manuelo. They whispered again. Once Fat Cat raised his voice but Manuelo shushed him and they began to whisper again. Finally Fat Cat came back.

"If we let you stay, you will say nothing at home?"

Roberto nodded.

I didn't know what he meant but I wanted to stay if Roberto did. "I promise not to say anything either."

Fat Cat looked at me for a moment, then his voice grew softer. "You're going to stay," he said. "We have a much more important job for you than going for the horses. We wish you to serve as lookout. We don't want the soldier who escaped to come back and take us by surprise like the sergeant did. Go back down the path a quarter-mile and keep your eyes alert!"

"I don't know," I said hesitantly. I looked at Roberto but he didn't say anything.

Fat Cat took the pistol from his belt. "Here, take this. If you see him, fire a warning shot into the air."

That convinced me. It was the first time anyone had let me handle a pistol.

"Be careful," Fat Cat said. "Don't shoot yourself."

"I won't," I replied importantly. I looked around to see if the others were watching. "Don't worry. If he's anywhere around I'll warn you."

I was about a hundred yards down the path when I heard the sound of their laughter. I wondered why they were laughing. I was out of sight now but the sound still followed me. Soon I could hear it no more. When I figured I was almost a quarter of a mile away I climbed up into a tree where I could see all around me.

After about fifteen minutes I began to grow restless. If the soldier was anywhere around I hadn't seen him. How long was I supposed to stay? Fat Cat hadn't said anything about that. I waited a few minutes more, then decided to go back and ask him.

I was almost upon them when again I heard the sound of laughter. Instinctively I went up into the trees. Something told me that they would be angry if I came back just then but my curiosity had got the better of me.

They were all gathered at the edge of the clearing. At first I couldn't see what they were doing because they were deep in the shadow of a huge tree. Silently I worked my way around to the other side of the clearing. But all I could see was a tangle of bodies. Suddenly I realized what they were doing.

And yet it wasn't the way I remembered. These women weren't screaming. They weren't afraid. They were laughing, they didn't seem to mind it at all.

Santiago the Older was sitting with his back against a tree, a *cigarrillo* dangling from his lips. There was a curiously satisfied half-smile on his face. I wondered where Roberto was. Suddenly he came out of the bushes, carrying his pants in his hand.

I stared at him. He was right, I thought grudgingly, he was bigger. It stood out in front of him like a small flagpole.

Santiago the younger said something to the others out of the corner of his mouth. Almost instantly there was silence as they all turned to look at Roberto.

Fat Cat sat up. I could see his smooth white belly. He grunted and I heard his voice across the clearing. "It is time," he said. "The general will be grateful. See? He is already a man."

The woman on whom Fat Cat had been lying reached up an arm to pull him back down. Angrily he slapped her hand away. *"Puta!"* He pushed her back to the ground and got to his feet.

Slowly Manuelo and Santiago the younger also got to their feet. Manuelo reached for a canteen and spilled some water over his belly and dried himself off with a bandanna. He turned to Roberto. "It is as we agreed. You have your choice."

Roberto looked at the women. They lay there naked, their bodies still glistening with sweat, staring up at him with noncommittal eyes. "I'll take that one," he said, pointing.

The one he had chosen seemed scarcely more than a girl. I would have picked one of the others, they had bigger *tetas*, but that was the one Roberto had told me he wanted. I could see his legs trembling as he moved toward her. He fell to his knees in front of her. With a laugh she reached up and pulled him down on top of her, raising her legs and locking them around him.

I could see her fat white buttocks and thighs almost encircle him. I looked at the others. They were watching with great interest. After a moment Manuelo turned and fell on the woman nearest him. I heard her grunt as she locked her legs around him. There was another cry and Fat Cat began to couple with the other one.

I looked back at Roberto again. The two of them were moving in a weird almost rhythmless dance. I began to feel an excitement growing in me. I could feel my heart hammering, a peculiar pain beginning to spread in my groin. My mouth was suddenly dry. I couldn't breathe.

Roberto began to scream, thrashing about wildly in a seeming effort to escape the woman's grasp. Startled, I felt myself slipping. I grabbed for the limb but it was too late. I fell from the tree almost at their feet.

Manuelo rolled over and looked at me. *"Perdido!"*

I got to my feet. "You lied to me!" I shouted.

Fat Cat turned his head. "You were supposed to guard the path."

"You lied to me!" I shouted again. I flung myself at the nearest woman, jerking my hips in an imitation of Roberto's spastic dance. "I want to rape a woman too!"

I felt Fat Cat's hands pulling me back. I struggled. "Let me go! Let me go!"

I was still jerking spasmodically when Fat Cat pulled me up off the ground. I wriggled in his arms, hitting out at his face. I began to cry. "If I'm old enough to kill I'm old enough to rape a woman! I'm as good as Roberto!"

But Fat Cat's arms held me close against his sweaty chest. I could smell the man stink of him and suddenly the fight and fever went out of me.

His hand stroked my head gently. "Easy, my little cock," he whispered softly, "easy. Everything will come to you in time. Soon enough you will be a man!"

8

The women were nervous now that the men had dressed. They talked among themselves in whispers, then the oldest, the one who had scratched me, walked across the clearing. "You're not going to leave us here in the jungle?"

Manuelo finished buckling his belt. "We didn't bring you here."

"But we will die," she replied quickly. "There is no one to protect us. To get us food."

Manuelo didn't answer. He took out his pistol and replaced the cartridge that had been fired.

She took his silence for consideration. "Weren't we nice to you?" she asked. "We took on all of you. As many times as you wanted. We did not complain."

Manuelo turned away and looked at us. "Have you got all the guns?"

"*Sí,*" Fat Cat answered.

"Let's go then." Manuelo started down the path.

The woman ran after him. She grabbed for his arm. "*Bandolero!*" Her face was contorted with anger. "You are animals without feelings. Are we just receptacles for your seed? Any one of us might be carrying your child!"

Manuelo pulled his arm free, and the woman fell back a few steps. "Dog!" she screamed at him. "Do you expect us to die here?"

He stared into her face. "Yes," he answered casually, then raised the hand that still held the pistol and shot her.

The bullet knocked her backward against a tree; she fell forward to her knees, slumping finally into a small fetal curl around the trunk of the tree. Her hand clutched at the earth once and then was still.

Manuelo turned and raised the still smoking pistol.

"The other two are gone," Fat Cat said.

I looked across the clearing. Only a ripple in the foliage remained as a sign of their presence.

"Shall we go after them?"

"No." Manuelo returned his gun to the holster. "We have lost enough time with those *putas* already. It is still a full day's journey to the valley for the meat. They will be hungry at home if we do not hurry."

Fat Cat smiled. "It will teach those *putas* a lesson," he said as we began to move down the path again. "They do not own a man simply because once they have put their legs around him."

We did not reach the valley of Bandaya until early the next morning. We came down the side of the mountain in the morning mist. Suddenly the sun broke through the clouds and the valley extended green and beautiful like a thick carpet below us. I straightened in my saddle and peered down trying to locate my home. It had been more than two years since I had last seen it.

I remembered the afternoon it had been decided. My father and the general had been talking quietly on the *galería*. Occasionally my father would look out at me. I was playing in the yard with Perro. I had taught him a new trick. I would hurl a piece of sugar cane as far as I could, and he would run after it, barking wildly. Then he would pick it up and, chewing it ecstatically, bring it back to me.

"Dax?"

I looked back at my father, my arm still holding the piece of sugar cane poised for the next throw. "*Sí, Papá?*"

"Come here."

I threw down the cane and started for the *galería*. Perro picked it up and, chewing it happily, tried to put it between my legs to trip me. When I started up the steps he stood looking up after me with a puzzled expression.

I laughed when I saw the way he stood there. He knew he wasn't allowed on the *galería*. "Wait for me," I called.

Perro lay down in the dirt and began to worry the piece of cane between his paws like a bone. His tail wagged slowly.

I looked at my father as I walked toward him. There were lines on his face I had never noticed before, and his normally

51

dark skin had taken on a weary gray tinge. I stopped in front of him.

"The general tells me he has spoken to you about going to his home in the mountains."

"Sí, Papá."

"Do you think you would like that?"

"He said I could have a burro," I said. "And a pony of my own when I got bigger."

My father didn't say anything.

"He also said you would be going away with him," I said. "Do you have to? I would rather stay here with you."

My father and the general exchanged glances. "I don't like to leave you, my son. But I must."

"Why?"

"It is important," he said. "The general and I have made an alliance."

I still didn't understand. My father continued. "The people are oppressed, there is injustice and hunger in the land. We must do what we can to help them."

"Why don't you bring them here?" I asked. "There is enough for everybody."

Again my father and the general exchanged glances. My father drew me up into his lap. "We cannot do that," he explained gently. "There are too many."

I knew all the *campesinos* in the valley. There weren't that many of them, and I said so.

My father smiled. "There are many more *campesinos* beyond the hills."

"How many?" I asked. "Twice as many?"

He shook his head. "More than that. Thousands upon thousands. If they all came here there would not be enough room for us all to lie down to sleep."

"Oh." I tried to imagine what it would be like if what my father said was true. I couldn't picture it. I had another thought. "Are you going with the general because you are his prisoner?"

"No," my father said, "the general and I are friends. We believe that the people must be helped."

"Then you will become a *bandolero* like him?" I asked.

"The general is not a *bandolero*."

"But his men are," I pointed out.

52

"No longer," my father explained. "He has taken all the *bandoleros* into his army. These men are *guerrilleros.*"

"The army has red and blue uniforms," I said. "They have none. They look like *bandoleros* to me."

"Someday they will have uniforms," the general interrupted.

"Oh." I looked at him. His face was impassive. "That will make it different. Then they will look like an army."

I heard the sound of approaching hoofbeats, and looked out toward the road. It was my grandfather, Don Rafael. "It's Grandfather!" I cried, jumping down off my father's lap. I ran to the railing and waved. "*Hola, Papá Grande! Hola, Abuelo!*"

Usually when I stood at the railing and yelled like that my grandfather would wave and send back an answering shout. This time he was silent. As he dismounted I could see that he was angry from the way his lips were pressed together and from the whiteness of his face.

My father got to his feet as the old man came up the steps. "*Bienvenido, Don Rafael.*"

Grandfather didn't answer but glared at my father with cold stony eyes. "I have come for my grandson."

I started to run toward him but something in the tone of his voice stopped me. I looked at him, then at my father.

My father's face was even grayer as he reached out a hand and drew me back toward him. I could feel his fingers trembling as they pressed into my shoulder. "I do not feel it will be safe for my son to stay in this valley after I am gone."

"You have forfeited your right to him," *Papá Grande* answered in the same cold voice. "By joining with the murderers of his mother, you can no longer be thought of as his father. When one lies down with scum, one becomes scum!"

I could feel the sudden pressure of my father's fingers as they dug into my shoulder. But the evenness of his voice didn't change. "What happened was an accident," he said. "The men who committed the crime have already paid for it."

Papá Grande's voice rose almost to a shout. "Does that bring my daughter, your wife, back? Or your daughter? They are dead, yet the next day you are willing to ride away with their despoilers. You would give your son over into their care?"

My father did not answer.

"You will not be satisfied until you have seen him become as they are! Murderers! Terrorists! Rapists!"

Papá Grande started for me but my father pushed me behind him. "He is my son," he said in that same quiet voice. "I will not let him remain. He will be used as a hostage against me should the army come. It is safer for him in the mountains."

"Sangre negra!" my grandfather spit out at him. "Black blood! The son of the son of slaves! Lowest of the low! I thought you a man or I would not have permitted your marriage to my daughter. Now I see that I was wrong. There is no depth to which you would not sink to abase yourself before your conquerors, just as your parents did to their masters!"

Suddenly the general was out of his chair. "Enough, old man!" he shouted.

Papá Grande looked at him as if he were dirt. *"Bandolero!"* The way my grandfather said it made it sound like the most obscene word I had ever heard.

The general's face went red with anger. *"Basta, viejo!* Is it not enough that we spare you and your property? Or are you so old that you seek death to ease the ache in your bones?"

Papá Grande ignored him. He turned to my father as if the general were not even there. "If you have any love for your son give him to me before it is too late!"

My father shook his head.

"Go!" the general ordered. "Before I lose patience and rescind the favors your son-in-law obtained for you."

Papá Grande glared at him. "I need neither your patience nor his favors. I have seen many of your kind across the years. I will live to see your head impaled on a lance as I have the others!"

He turned and marched down the steps of the *galería* to his horse, his back stiff and proud, his suit white as the snow on top of the mountains. He mounted and wheeled his horse around. "The army will come, and then we shall see how brave you are!"

Then he looked at me and his voice softened. "Good-bye, my grandson," he said sadly. "Already I mourn for you."

He gave the horse its head and galloped away. I looked after him; the horse kicked up small clouds of dust from the hard-packed earth of the road until they were out of sight. I turned to *Papá* whose eyes had a hint of sadness in them, almost like that I had seen in *Papá Grande*'s. Suddenly he lifted me into his arms and held me tight against him. "My son, my son," he whispered. "I pray to God that I do right for you!"

The general clapped his hands sharply, and a man came running across the road. He was a big man, the fattest I had ever seen, yet he ran with a peculiar grace and lightness and swiftness that reminded me of the big wild goats I had seen leaping from crag to crag in the mountains. His hat was already in his hand. *"Sí, excelencia?"*

"Gato Gordo," the general said, "get your gear together and take this boy with you back into the mountains. I charge you with his care. I will hold you alone responsible if anything happens to him."

"Sí, excelencia." The man bowed and turned to look at me. "The boy is ready to travel?" he asked politely.

My father looked at the general. "Must it be now?"

The general nodded. "The danger increases each day."

Slowly my father put me down. "Go inside and have Sarah pack your clothes."

"Yes, Father," I said dutifully. I started for the door.

"Make haste, *niño*," Gato Gordo called after me. "It is best we are in the mountains when night falls."

I was too shy to speak to him then, but later that night when a keening animal woke me from my sleep, I crawled, shivering, to him across the icy mountain ground. *"Tengo miedo*, Gato Gordo," I whispered.

He put his hand over mine. "Hold my hand, child," he said reassuringly, "and I will take you safely through the mountains."

Secure in the warmth of his touch, I closed my eyes and drifted right back into sleep.

But that was more than two years ago and now the sun was clear on the valley and I could see almost across it. I stood up in the stirrups, feeling a kind of excitement rise inside me. It had been a long time since I had been home. *Papá Grande* would be glad that he didn't have to mourn for me after all.

55

9

We had been traveling the road down the mountain for only a few minutes when Manuelo suddenly held up his hand. We stopped as he leaped from his horse and placed his ear against the hard-packed road. He listened intently for a moment, then raised his head. "Gato Gordo," he called, "come listen."

Fat Cat joined him on the ground. Suddenly they were both up and back on their horses. "We must get off the road and hide," Manuelo said. "There is the sound of many horses coming up the road."

Fat Cat looked around. "The mountainside is naked."

"We must go back up then," Manuelo said quickly, turning his horse.

I had played in these hills since I had been a little boy. "Down the road just around the bend there is a small clump of trees. Behind it is a cave. We can hide there."

"Is it big enough for the horses?"

"I heard *Papá* say once that it was big enough for an army."

"Make haste then," Manuelo said. "We follow."

I let loose the rein on my pony, and we galloped on toward the bend in the road. The clump of trees was there just as I had remembered. I turned my pony off the road and up through the trees to the mouth of the cave. *"Estamos aquí,"* I said.

Manuelo was off his horse in a second. "You and Roberto take the horses back into the cave!" he ordered. "The others come with me. We must cover our tracks from the road!"

They slid out of their saddles as Roberto and I gathered up the reins and led the horses into the cave. At first they whin-

56

nied and shied from the darkness but we talked soothingly to them and after a few moments they quieted. Roberto put a loop through their reins and tied them to a boulder, and we ran back to the entrance.

Fat Cat and Santiago the Older were backing toward us through the trees, sweeping the ground with branches. Manuelo and the younger Santiago were setting up one of the tommy guns on its tripod. When it was assembled they picked it up and ran back to the mouth of the cave.

When Fat Cat and the older Santiago were finished, they nodded with satisfaction at the gun. Fat Cat plumped himself down behind it and squinted along the sights with approval.

Manuelo gestured to the younger Santiago. "Up into the trees. Cover us with your rifle if there is trouble."

Santiago was settled among the branches almost before the order was completed. The leaves quivered for a moment as he disappeared from sight.

Manuelo looked at us two boys. "You, back into the cave."

Before we could protest Fat Cat held up his hand. We stood very still, listening. The heavy drum of hoofbeats was clear now. "There are more than twenty," he said, his hand gesturing for us to lie down.

Manuelo went to his hands and knees and crept out toward the road. At the edge of the clump of trees I could see the back of his head as he raised himself to peer down. I tried to look past him to the road but it was hidden by the dipping curve of the mountainside.

The hoofbeats grew louder and Manuelo's head disappeared. The sound rose from the road directly in front of us, then it passed and began to grow fainter.

Manuelo came running back. "Cavalry," he said. "A whole troop! I counted thirty-four."

Fat Cat's lips pursed. "What are they doing here? *El militar* was not reported in Bandaya."

Manuelo shrugged. "They are here."

There was the distant sound of a bugle, then silence. Manuelo listened for a moment more, then sat down behind the machine gun and lit a *cigarrillo*. His eyes were thoughtful.

"*Hola*, Younger!" he called in a low penetrating voice. "What do you see?"

The voice came back muffled by the leaves. "Nothing. The road it is clear."

57

"Not the road, you fool! The valley."

There was a silence, then the voice came again. "There is smoke rising into the air but it is too far to tell what is burning."

"Can you see anything else?"

"No. Shall I come down now?"

"Stay there!"

"My *cojones* are sore from straddling this branch."

Fat Cat laughed. "It isn't the branch that your *cojones* are sore from." He turned to Manuelo. "What do you think?"

"I don't know," Manuelo answered thoughtfully. "It could have been a raiding party passing through the valley."

"What now?" Fat Cat asked. "Do we go home?"

"Guns are a poor substitute for meat."

"But if there are soldiers in the valley—"

Manuelo interrupted. "We do not know that there are. The only ones we saw were riding away."

Fat Cat was silent. Santiago the Older came over and sat down opposite him. They sat there silently staring at one another.

I felt a pressure in my kidneys. "I have to pee." I went over to a tree to relieve myself. A moment later Roberto joined me. We stood there side by side, the two yellow streams arcing golden in the sunlight. I looked at his with satisfaction. Maybe he was older but I could pee farther. He didn't seem to notice. I was just about to call his attention to it when the stream trickled off. I buttoned my fly and returned to the mouth of the cave.

The three men were still sitting silently around the machine gun. Manuelo pinched out his *cigarrillo* and carefully stored the butt in his pocket. "There is only one way to find out. One of us must go down into the valley."

"If there are more *militares* it will be dangerous."

"It will be more dangerous if we return home without meat, or without making sure we could obtain none," Manuelo replied.

"True." Fat Cat nodded. "They would not like that."

"Not at all," Santiago the Older added. "They will be hungry."

Both men stared at him in surprise. It was rare for the Indian to speak.

Manuelo turned back to Fat Cat. "You will go."

"Me?" Fat Cat exclaimed. "Why me?"

"You have been in this valley before. None of the rest of us has. So it is logical that you should go."

"But I was there only one day," Fat Cat protested. He gestured toward me. "Then the general sent me back with him."

Manuelo looked at me. "Do you remember the valley?"

"*Sí.*"

"How far is it from here to your *hacienda?*"

"One and a half hours by horse."

"On foot?" he asked. "A horse would attract too much attention."

"Three, maybe four hours."

Manuelo made up his mind. "You will take the boy with you. He can serve as your guide."

Fat Cat grumbled. "At least we should take the horses. You know how difficult it is for me to walk. Besides, I have a feeling it is too dangerous. We shall be killed."

Manuelo got to his feet. "In that case you will not need the horses," he said with finality. "*Vaya!*"

Fat Cat got to his feet and reached for his rifle.

"Leave it!" Manuelo said sharply. "And hide your pistol under your shirt. Then if you pass anyone on the road you are nothing but a poor *campesino* and his son on your way to Bandaya. If they see you with a rifle they will shoot first and ask questions afterward."

Fat Cat didn't look happy. "How long will you wait for us?"

Manuelo looked at him. I watched him calculating. He glanced up at the sun, then back at Fat Cat. "It is now roughly eight o'clock. If the boy is right you should reach the *hacienda* by noon. We will wait until nightfall. If you are not back by then, we start for home."

Fat Cat stared at him without complaint. Each knew what the other was thinking. Had the situation been reversed Manuelo would have reacted the same way. It was one of the conditions of life.

Fat Cat turned to me. "Come on, boy. Apparently it has also become my duty to return you home."

"My *cojones* are killing me!" The younger Santiago's voice was almost a wail from the tree.

Fat Cat looked up, smiling wickedly. "Too bad," he called.

"Perhaps you would like it better if you could join us for this little walk?"

The sun stood almost at the center of the heavens as we hid in the cane field and stared across the road. The barn and the kitchen had been burned to the ground. I could feel the heat from the charred timbers against my face. There was a sickness clutching in my stomach.

I got to my feet. Fat Cat's hand pulled me down. "Be still! There still may be some of them around!"

I stared at him as if he were someone I had never seen before. "They tried to burn my house."

He didn't answer. His eyes squinted up and down the deserted road. Then he looked at me. "That's why your father sent you to the mountains," he said gruffly.

"If he knew, he should have let me stay," I cried. "I wouldn't have let them burn the *hacienda!*"

"They would have burned it and you too," Fat Cat said matter-of-factly. He got to his feet. "Come. Maybe we learn something."

I followed him across the road. Halfway between the road and the house we came upon a body. It was lying face down in the dirt. Fat Cat turned it over. He looked down and spat. "*Campesino!*" he said contemptuously.

I recognized him. It was old man Sordes, who did the gardening and tended the flowers around the house. I told Fat Cat.

He spat again. "Just as well," he said noncommittally. "He would have been out of a job anyway."

We walked on toward the house. The *galería* was gone too. It seemed to have collapsed into the cellar. I could feel the heat more intensely now.

Fat Cat reached out with his foot and kicked a timber. It fell away from the frame and down into the cellar. Almost instantly a sheet of flame licked up from below.

We walked around the house toward the back.

"Maybe someone is still down in the cellar," I said to Fat Cat.

"If they are, they're well cooked."

It wasn't until we came to the clump of trees that stood between the house and the barn that we saw the two women. They had been lashed to a tree trunk, back to back, and they stared back at us with sightless eyes. One of them I recognized. It was Sarah, the cook. The other I had never seen before.

They had been stripped naked and their bodies were covered with countless tiny cuts in which the blood had dried and caked. Already the ants had climbed up.

"This one is Sarah," I said, "the one who packed my bag."

Fat Cat stared at her. *"La India?"*

I nodded. I closed my eyes and remembered how she had given me breakfast that last morning at home. I opened my eyes. "Why didn't they just rape her and then kill her?" I asked. "Why did they have to torture her?"

"Soldados!" Fat Cat spat again. "They are worse than we."

"Why?" I repeated.

"They thought she had something to tell them." He began to walk back toward the cane field. "Come, there is nothing here. We might as well start back."

We were almost at the road when he suddenly stopped me with his hand. "Your name is Juan," he whispered fiercely. "Do not speak! Let me do the talking!"

I didn't know what he was talking about until the six soldiers suddenly appeared in their red and blue uniforms, their guns pointing at us.

10

Fat Cat took his hat off, a fawning smile on his face. "We are nothing but poor *campesinos* come to Bandaya in search of work, *excelencia.* My son and I."

The young lieutenant stared at him. "What are you doing in this particular place?"

"We saw the smoke," Fat Cat said. "We thought—"

The lieutenant interrupted. "You thought you could steal something."

61

"No, *excelencia*," Fat Cat protested in a hurt voice. "We thought we could be of help. We did not realize it was a military matter."

The lieutenant looked down at me. "How old is the boy?"

"My son Juan is almost twelve, *excelencia*."

"We are looking for an eight-year-old boy," the lieutenant said. "The son of the *bandolero* Xenos."

"We do not know him," Fat Cat said quickly.

The lieutenant looked at me again. He hesitated. "He is supposed to be dark like your son."

"Stand straight, Juan!" Fat Cat turned to the soldier again. "See how tall my Juan is? What eight-year-old has his size?"

The lieutenant was still studying me. "How old are you, boy?" he suddenly asked.

"Tengo once años, señor."

"Why is your skin so dark?"

I looked at Fat Cat. I didn't know what he meant.

"His mother is—"

The lieutenant cut off Fat Cat. "I asked the boy!"

I took a breath. *"Mi mamá es negrita."*

I heard Fat Cat's almost silent sigh of relief. The soldier threw another question at me. *"Dónde vives?"*

I gestured toward the mountains. "Up there, *señor*."

"The boy speaks well for a *campesino*," the lieutenant said to Fat Cat.

"It is the church, *excelencia*," Fat Cat said quickly. "His mother is a great one for the church. He has gone to the school of the Fathers in the mountains."

The lieutenant stared at him for a moment. "Come along."

"Why, *excelencia*?" Fat Cat protested. "Surely there is nothing more you want of us. We wish to return home."

"You can return home later," the lieutenant said. *"El coronel* wishes to interrogate every suspicious person. March!"

The soldiers formed around us quickly. "Where are you taking us?" Fat Cat asked.

The lieutenant spoke briefly. *"A la hacienda de Don Rafael Campos.* Move!"

He started down the road. We followed him. The soldiers followed us. I felt Fat Cat's hand on my shoulder. He whispered, "You will not recognize your grandfather!"

"But what if he recognizes me?" I whispered back.

"We will worry about that when it happens. It has been

62

several years, and you have grown much. It is possible that he may not."

"What are you two whispering about?" the lieutenant asked.

"Nothing, *excelencia*," Fat Cat answered quickly. "Just that we are tired and hungry."

A troop of cavalry came sweeping down the road, and we moved aside to let them pass. The lieutenant called out to one of their officers. "What did you find?"

The cavalryman shook his head. "Nothing." The lieutenant watched as he turned his horse away and galloped down the road to the encampment.

There were men, women, and children standing around the *hacienda* of my grandfather. They looked at us without curiosity, preoccupied with a private misery of their own. Fat Cat drew me to one side. "Do you know any of these people?"

I shook my head. "No one is familiar."

"*Bueno.*" He looked around. "I could use something to eat. My stomach is growling."

The sun was hot, and I was tired and thirsty. "There is a well behind the house."

"Forget it," Fat Cat said quickly. "All they would have to see is that you know where the well is. Then our goose would be cooked." He noticed the expression on my face, and his voice softened. He put out his hand and drew me toward him. "Come, *niño*, we will try to find a place in the shade to lie down and rest."

We found a spot near a wagon in the front yard. Fat Cat slumped down, resting his back against one of the broad-spoked wheels. I stretched out underneath, and in a few moments I was asleep.

I don't know how long I had been sleeping when Fat Cat shook me awake. "Open your eyes, *niño*."

I sat up, rubbing my eyes. The sun was still high in the heavens. I could not have slept for more than half an hour.

The soldiers were pushing everybody toward the *galería* of the house. We got to our feet and moved forward with the others.

A soldier climbed up on the steps and faced us. "Line up by twos."

I looked around. There were perhaps fifty of us in the yard.

There were a few boys about my age but mostly they were adults. I started toward the front of the line but Fat Cat pulled me back behind a fat woman in the center of the crowd.

The front door opened and two soldiers came out of *la casa*. Between them they supported an old man. I sucked in my breath and started forward, but Fat Cat had a grip of steel on my arm.

It was *Papá Grande*, but not the *Papá Grande* I remembered. His once immaculate white shirt and suit were wrinkled and crumpled, and there were traces of blood at the corner of his mouth and down across his beard and on the collar of his shirt. His eyes were almost blank with pain and his chin trembled as he strove to hold himself erect.

They came to a halt at the railing of the *galería* as an officer came out of the doorway behind them. He wore the epaulets of a colonel. He looked at us, then at *Papá Grande*. He had a dark pencil-line mustache, and there was a sneer on his face.

His voice was a thin reedy rasp. "Don Rafael, these people claim to be *campesinos* of this valley. They say you know them and will vouch for them. We want you to look at each and if there is one you do not recognize you will tell us. *Comprende?*"

Papá Grande nodded. "I understand," he said with difficulty. "I have already told you all I know."

The *coronel*'s voice was impatient. "We shall see." He motioned to the soldier on the steps. "Have them file past slowly."

The double line began to shuffle by the *galería* as *Papá Grande* looked down at us, unseeing. Fat Cat and I were almost directly below when the *coronel* spoke. "You, boy! Stand in the front where we can see you."

It was a moment before I realized whom he meant. I stopped, hesitating, then I felt something cold in my back as Fat Cat pushed me into the front line. I stood there looking up at the *galería*, still feeling that cold pressure in the middle of my spine. I wondered what it was.

I looked straight into *Papá Grande*'s eyes. A sudden flicker of recognition burned briefly, then the lids came down over his eyes slowly. When they reopened the eyes contained the same blank look as before.

The *coronel* had been watching us closely. "All right," he said, after a moment, "move on."

The line began to shuffle forward. I felt the release of the cold pressure against my spine as Fat Cat moved away. Then I noticed the lieutenant who had captured us whisper in the *coronel*'s ear.

The *coronel* nodded. "Halt!" he called out.

The line stopped.

"You!" He pointed at me. "Fall out!"

I looked at Fat Cat. His face was blank and impassive, only his eyes glittered. He took my arm as we stepped forward. He bowed obsequiously. *"Sí, excelencia."*

The *coronel* had already turned to my grandfather. "My lieutenant tells me he caught these two near your son-in-law's *hacienda*. They say they are *campesinos* from the hills seeking work. Do you know them?"

Papá Grande looked down at us. There was a curiously distant look in his eyes. "I have seen them before," he replied tonelessly.

Fat Cat moved closer behind me. Once more I felt the coldness against my spine. I started to turn but his free hand kept me facing forward.

"Who are they?" the *coronel* asked.

My grandfather seemed to take a long time in answering. At last he licked his lips and spoke. "I am an old man," he said in a quavering voice. "I do not remember names, but I have seen them often in the valley seeking work."

The *coronel* turned and studied me. "The boy is dark. Your son-in-law is also dark."

"There are many of us with Negro blood," the old man replied quietly. "It has not yet been declared a crime."

Again the *coronel* was silent. He looked thoughtfully at the old man, then drew his pistol and pointed it at me. "Then it does not matter to you whether this one lives or dies?"

There was a sadness in my grandfather's eyes but it was gone when he turned back to the *coronel*. "It does not matter."

Slowly the *coronel* cocked the pistol. *Papá Grande* turned away. The *coronel* didn't look at me; he kept watching my grandfather.

Suddenly I felt Fat Cat push me aside. *"Excelencia!"* he cried. "I beg of you! Have mercy! Do not take my only son! Mercy, *excelencia*, mercy, for God's sake!"

The *coronel* turned his gun from me and pointed it at Fat Cat. His voice was flat and cold. "Would you die in his stead?"

Fat Cat threw himself on his belly. "Mercy, *excelencia!* Mercy *por Dios!*"

My grandfather turned and spat down at Fat Cat. "Kill them both and have done with it!" he said in a contemptuous voice. "Put an end to their miserable craven groveling. It sickens me!"

The *coronel* stared at him, then slowly released the cocked hammer and put the pistol back in its holster.

Fat Cat scrambled to his feet quickly. "*Mil gracias!* A thousand blessings on you!"

The *coronel* waved his hand. "Move on."

Fat Cat pulled me back into the line. Slowly we shuffled away, as the line moved behind us. At last we had passed the *galería.* We stood there silently. I looked at Fat Cat. "He does not know me!" I whispered.

"He knows you!"

"But—"

Fat Cat's hand squeezed my shoulder. The *coronel* was walking down the line toward us. He came to a stop in front of me. "*Cómo se llama?*"

"Juan," I answered.

"Come with me." He turned, and Fat Cat fell into step beside me as we followed him back toward the *galería.*

The *coronel* called up to one of the soldiers. "Bring the old man down, and send the others away."

The soldier locked an arm against the side of my grandfather and began to walk him down the steps. There was a faint sound from the road behind us. I looked back over my shoulder at the people in the road. An angry murmur arose when they saw *Papá Grande* being led down from the *galería.*

"Tell them to leave!" the *coronel* shouted. "Open fire on them if necessary."

"*Vaya! Vaya!*" The lieutenant had his pistol out. "*Vaya!*"

The crowd stared at him. He fired a shot into the air, and slowly they began to move on.

When the road had emptied, the *coronel* turned to me. "The old man does not care whether you live or die," he said in a quiet voice. "Now we shall see if you feel the same about him!"

66

11

By now it was almost three o'clock, and the sun was pouring fire down on the earth. The sweat dried on our bodies and the saliva evaporated in our mouths, leaving the faint sickly taste of salt. Despite the heat I felt a shivering inside me, a trembling I could not control as they brought *Papá Grande* down the steps.

"Take him to the wagon," the *coronel* commanded.

The old man shook himself free. "I can walk," he said proudly.

The soldier looked questioningly at the *coronel*, who nodded his head, and we followed the old man as he walked to the center of the blazing courtyard. When he had reached the wagon, he turned and faced them. There were lines of weariness etched into his cheeks but his eyes were calm and clear. He did not speak.

"Strip him," the *coronel* ordered.

Quickly the soldiers stepped forward. The old man held up a hand as if to stop them but they had already begun ripping the clothing from him. His thin body was almost as white as the clothing he had worn. Without it he seemed small, shrunken, shriveled, his ribs standing out against his flesh. His buttocks and flanks were loose and flabby with the failures of time.

"Lash him to the wheel!"

Roughly two *soldados* spread-eagled him to the wheel, his arms and legs outstretched to the rim. The hub of the wheel protruded into the center of his back, forcing the old man to arch outward in an awkwardly obscene position. His face grimaced with pain as his stiff joints rebelled. He closed his eyes and turned his head to avoid staring into the sun.

The *coronel* gestured. He didn't have to order the soldiers to their duty. One of them snapped the old man's head back against the rim of the wheel and secured a leather strap around his forehead to keep his head from moving.

"Don Rafael." The *coronel's* voice was so low that at first I wasn't aware it was he who had spoken. "Don Rafael."

My grandfather looked into his eyes.

"There is no need for this, Don Rafael," the *coronel* said, almost respectfully.

Papá Grande didn't answer.

"You know where the boy has been hidden."

My grandfather's eyes didn't waver. "I have already told you I do not know. He was taken away by Diablo Rojo."

"That is hard to believe, Don Rafael." The *coronel's* voice was still soft.

"It is the truth."

The *coronel* shook his head in apparent sadness. "Your son-in-law, Jaime Xenos, allied himself with the *bandoleros,* the murderers of your daughter. It is known to us that he has political ambitions. What else can we assume but that you are in sympathy with them?"

"If I were," the old man asked, "would I be so foolish as to remain here in my *hacienda* where you could find me?"

"Perhaps you thought your age would save you."

A dignity came into the old man's voice. "I have never been a traitor."

The *coronel* stared at him silently for a few moments, then turned to me. "Where do you live?"

"In the mountains, *señor.*"

"Why do you come into the valley?"

I looked at *Papá Grande*. His eyes were watching me. "To work, *señor.*"

"Have you no work at home?"

Fat Cat answered quickly. "No, *excelencia.* The drought—"

"I asked the boy!" the *coronel* warned sharply.

"There is nothing to eat," I said. That much at least was the truth.

The *coronel* was thoughtful. He glanced at *Papá Grande*, then at me. "You know this man?"

"*Sí, señor,*" I answered. "He is Don Rafael, the landlord."

"He is Don Rafael, the traitor!" the *coronel* shouted.

I didn't answer.

Suddenly his hand was on my wrist, pulling my arm behind me forcing it upward. I screamed with pain as the fire ran through me.

"He is your grandfather!" the *coronel* hissed harshly. "Do you deny it?"

I screamed again as he applied more pressure. I began to grow dizzy and felt myself beginning to fall. Then there was a blow against the side of my head and I fell to the ground. I lay there too weak to move, sobbing into the dirt.

As if from a distance I heard the voice of my grandfather. It was cold and empty of feeling. "That alone should convince you, *coronel*. Nobody with my blood would give you the satisfaction of hearing him cry. It would be beneath us."

I heard a muttered curse, then a dull thud. I raised my head and looked up. The *coronel* was just moving away from my grandfather, the pistol still in his hand. The blood streamed down the side of the old man's face. His beard was already crimson. But his lips were firmly pressed together.

The *coronel* turned to one of the soldiers. "Wet the leather band around his temples," he said. "Let us see if the sun can persuade the truth to come to his lips."

He strode off toward the *galería*, and I felt Fat Cat's hands lifting me to my feet. My shoulder ached as I moved my arm. I stood there a moment to catch my breath.

Papá Grande stared at me silently. After a moment he closed his eyes and I felt the pain in him. Instinctively I started to reach out my hand. But Fat Cat caught my arm almost as I moved, and forced me to turn away. From the *galería* I could see the *coronel* watching.

A *soldado* walked past carrying a bucket of water. With a snap of his wrist he dashed the water into the face of my grandfather. The old man choked and sputtered as it ran down his face. He shook his head to free the water from his eyes but the leather thong allowed him to move only a fraction of an inch. I could feel the sun on him. Already the white of his body was turning red under its scorching rays. I could imagine the leather band beginning to tighten across his forehead. Almost before my eyes I could see it drying and contracting. His mouth opened and he began to gasp for air.

I heard footsteps behind me. I turned and saw the *coronel* walking toward us. He had a tall glass in his hand. The ice clinked as he walked. He stopped in front of *Papá Grande*.

He raised the glass to his lips and took a sip. "Well, Don Rafael," he said, "would you care to join me in a cool rum punch?"

My grandfather did not answer. Only his eyes were powerless to avoid looking at the glass. His tongue brushed against the surface of his dry lips.

"A word," the *coronel* said. "Just one word. That's all it would take."

With an effort the old man tore his eyes away from the glass. He looked straight into the *coronel's* eyes. There was a contempt in his voice that went far beyond anything I had ever heard. "To think that I might have defended you," he said. "You are worse than the *bandoleros*. They, at least, have ignorance as an excuse. But before God what will be yours?"

The rim of the glass splintered as the *coronel* smashed it against the wagon wheel. He held the jagged edge against my grandfather's naked belly. "You will talk, old man. You will talk!"

My grandfather took a deep breath, and spat directly into the *coronel's* face. Then an involuntary scream caught in his throat and died there as he turned his eyes downward in horror. The *coronel* stepped back, and we saw why the old man had screamed. The glass, with part of his genitals trapped within it, hung embedded in his flesh.

I began to scream, but Fat Cat quickly caught my face to his big belly and smothered it.

"Let the boy watch!"

Slowly Fat Cat released me. But he kept a warning hand on my shoulder. I looked at the *coronel*. His eyes were cold. I turned to look at my grandfather. He sagged weakly against the bindings. The blood dripped slowly from the glass to the ground.

I blinked my eyes to hold back the tears. The *coronel* must not see me crying. Somehow I knew that *Papá Grande* would not want that. A softness came into the old man's eyes, and I knew that he understood. Then he closed his eyes slowly and sagged against the bindings.

"He is dead!" one of the soldiers exclaimed.

Quickly the *coronel* stepped forward and brutally thumbed one of the old man's eyelids up. "Not yet," he said in a satisfied voice. "They don't die that easily. Not when they get to be as old as this one. They wish to live forever." He turned and started back toward the house. "Call me when he revives. I have not yet had my lunch."

We watched him walk up on the *galería* and disappear into the house.

"We are hungry too," Fat Cat called to the *soldados*.

"Be glad you are not with him," one of them answered, gesturing toward my grandfather.

Fat Cat looked at me, then back at the soldier. "He is but a child," he said. "At least be merciful enough to let me move him back into the shade."

The two *soldados* looked at one another, then one of them shrugged. "It is permitted. But try nothing funny."

Fat Cat led me toward the house. He threw himself to the ground in the shade of the *galería*, and I slumped down beside him. We rolled over onto our stomachs so that our heads were toward the house and our backs to the *soldados*.

"Does your shoulder still hurt?" he whispered.

"No," I answered, though it did. But only a little.

He glanced sideways at the sky. "The sun will be gone in a few hours. Manuelo and the others will leave without us."

"What will *el coronel* do to us?"

Fat Cat shrugged. "They will either kill us or let us go." His voice was matter-of-fact. "It all depends on the old one there. If he talks we will die; if not—well, we have a chance."

Suddenly I remembered the cold metal against my back when the *coronel* had called us out of the line. "They wouldn't have killed me," I exclaimed. "You would have!"

"*Sí.*"

"But then they would have killed you!"

He nodded.

I wasn't angry. I just didn't understand.

"To save you," he said. He jerked his thumb over his shoulder. "Or would you prefer that?"

I didn't answer.

"They would force you to betray your father, to tell where we hide out. You could not stop them. And in the end they would kill you anyway."

Now I began to understand. This was the way it had to be. This was the core of our lives, the only thing that mattered. I glanced back over my shoulder. The old man still hung there

71

quietly, the sun burning his flesh. I whispered, "I wish we could kill him."

Fat Cat looked at me. There was a kind of approval in his eyes. "He will die soon," he said quietly. "Let us pray that he dies in silence."

There was a sound behind us. "On your feet! The old one is awake. I go to call *el coronel*."

The *coronel's* voice came from behind me. I turned. He was wiping his face daintily with a napkin. "Don Rafael!"

Papá Grande didn't look at him.

"Don Rafael!" the *coronel* said again. "Do you know me?"

The old man's eyes roved wildly. "Bring me my horse!" he shouted suddenly. "I will ride into the hills to kill the *bastardos* myself!"

The *coronel* turned away in disgust. "Cut him down and kill him. He is of no further use to us."

He started to walk away, then his eyes fell on me. "*Un momento.* You still say the old one is not your grandfather?"

I didn't answer.

He took his pistol from its holster. He spun the cylinder and five cartridges fell into his hand. He closed his fist over them and looked at me. "There is one bullet remaining. You will kill him."

I looked at Fat Cat. His eyes were dark and impassive. I hesitated.

"You will kill him!" the *coronel* shouted, handing me the gun.

I looked down at the pistol in my hand. It was heavy. Much heavier than Fat Cat's. I looked at the *coronel*. His eyes were burning, his face flushed. It would only take one bullet. But then they would kill me, and Fat Cat too. I turned away.

My grandfather remained silent as I moved toward him. The blood was still dripping from his mouth, but his eyes seemed suddenly to clear. "What is it, boy?"

I didn't speak.

"What do you want, boy?" he asked again.

I felt a knot in my stomach as I brought the pistol up. My grandfather saw it. He didn't move. I could swear a faint smile came into his eyes just before I pulled the trigger.

The recoil spun me half around, and the big revolver flew from my hand as I struggled to keep my feet. I looked at the old man. He slumped against the wheel, his eyes staring at us sightlessly.

The *coronel's* voice came from behind me. *"Bueno."* He turned and started back toward the house.

I looked at my grandfather. The tears began to well up in my eyes. I fought them back. Alive or dead, he would not want them. Fat Cat's hand was on my arm as he half led me, half dragged me toward the road. The *soldados* stared at us impassively as we walked past. At last we were out of earshot. The tears came to my eyes now.

"I killed him!" I cried. "I didn't want to, but I killed him!"

Fat Cat didn't slow his rapid pace. "What does it matter?" he asked, without looking at me. "The old one was as good as dead. It matters only that we are alive!"

12

It was three hours after nightfall when we got back to the cave. The others had already gone. I was so tired I could scarcely keep my eyes open. I dropped to the ground. "I'm hungry."

Fat Cat looked at me. "Get used to it," he said tersely. He walked around the cave, his eyes searching the ground in the eerie light.

"I'm thirsty, too."

He didn't answer. After a moment I became curious about what he was searching for. "What are you doing?"

He glanced at me. "I'm trying to figure out how long they have been gone."

"Oh."

He gave an exclamation and went down to one knee. He picked up something and crushed it in his hand, then flung it away. "Get up!" he said abruptly. "They've been gone only an hour. Maybe we can catch up with them."

I dragged myself to my feet. "How do you know? What did you find?"

"A horse turd," he said, already leaving the cave. "It's center was still warm."

I had to trot to keep up with him. I never thought Fat Cat could move so quickly. I could hear his breath coming heavily in his throat as we climbed toward the crest of the mountain. The road was clear as day because of the bright white moon. The night was getting chilly, and I began to feel cold. I ran along, trying to keep my teeth from chattering. "How—how much longer?"

"They will not stop until they are on the other side of the mountain."

I looked up the side of the mountain. It was still a good two miles to where the road crested. I threw myself down at the side of the road. I lay there trying to catch my breath. Fat Cat went a few steps farther, then, not hearing me, stopped and looked back. "What are you doing?"

"I can't walk any more." I said. I began to cry. "I'm cold. I'm hungry."

He stared down at me for a moment. "I thought you were a man," he said harshly.

"I'm not a man," I wailed. "I'm cold and I'm tired."

He sat down beside me. "All right," he said, his voice softening. "We'll rest." He stuck his fingers in his pocket and came out with a stub of a *cigarrillo*. He lit it carefully, cupping his hand against the wind. He wolfed the smoke in deeply.

I looked at him, shivering.

"Here," he said, "take a puff. It will warm you."

I did as he suggested and immediately I began to cough and choke. When I finished, oddly enough I did feel warmer. He slipped out of his blouse and threw it around my shoulders. He drew me close to him.

I snuggled up against the warmth coming from his big body. There was something about the man smell of him that made me feel safe and secure and before I knew it I was asleep.

I awoke with the first rays of sunlight in my eyes. I rolled over, my hand reaching out for him. It hit the earth and I sat up suddenly. He was gone. I looked around wildly. "Fat Cat!"

There was a rustle in the bushes. I turned, and Fat Cat

74

came out into the open. He was carrying a small rabbit impaled on a stick. "So you're awake, are you?"

"I thought—"

"You thought I had left you?" He laughed. "I was only getting us something to eat. Now get us wood for a fire while I skin this little one."

The rabbit was tough and stringy but I never tasted anything so delicious. When we had finished, all that was left was a little pile of bones. I wiped the grease from my face with my fingers, then licked them clean. "That was good."

Fat Cat smiled and got to his feet. "Put the bones in your pocket. Then we'll have something to chew on during the day." He began to kick out the small fire. When he was finished, he turned. "Let's go."

I put the last of the bones in my pocket and followed him out onto the road. "I'm sorry about last night."

"Forget it."

"If it wasn't for me, you would have caught up with the others."

His voice was gentle. "If it hadn't been for you, my bones would be rotting back there in the valley. Besides, we never could have caught up with them."

"What will we do?" I asked. "How will we get home?"

"Walk," he replied brusquely. "Man walked before he learned to ride horses."

I stared at him. Fat Cat hated to walk. It was two and a half days' ride to Bandaya from our refuge in the mountains. On foot it would take more than a week.

Fat Cat's voice cut through my thoughts. "Keep your ears open. If we hear anything, we leave the road. We take no chances. Understand?"

"Sí. Comprendo."

At last we came to the top of the mountain and about a mile down the other side we found a small stream. "We will stop here and rest," Fat Cat said.

I ran to the creek and threw myself down beside it. Thirstily I gulped. After a moment, Fat Cat pulled me back. "That's enough. Rest awhile, then you can drink again."

I lay back against a tree. My feet hurt. I took off my boots and rubbed them, then let them dangle in the running water. I could feel its soothing coolness run up my thighs. By contrast my body felt crawly with the dried-up sweat of the last few days.

"Can I go for a swim?" I asked.

He looked at me as if I were crazy. Mountain people didn't believe in bathing. "All right," he said, "but don't stay in long. You will wash away the protection from your skin."

I dropped my clothes and waded into the stream. The cold sparkling water delighted me and I splashed about happily, kicking up a spray. A thin silver fish streaked past me and I dove after it, hands outstretched. It slipped through my fingers when I raised my head from the water. Then I heard a giggle from the bank. I turned around.

Two young girls were standing on the bank watching me, and Fat Cat wasn't anywhere to be seen. I sat down in the shallow stream quickly.

The smaller girl giggled again. The bigger one turned and called, *"Papá! Diego!* Come quickly. There's a boy in the stream!"

A moment later two men came through the brush, the rifles in their hands pointed at me. "What are you doing in there?"

"I was taking a swim."

"Well, come out!"

I started to get to my feet and then sank back into the water. "Throw me my *pantalones*," I said, pointing.

The older man glanced at the two girls, then back at me. "Turn your backs," he ordered.

The little girl giggled again as they turned. I stood up and waded for the bank.

"Are you alone?" the younger man asked.

"No, *señor*," I answered as I took the *pantalones* from his outstretched hand. "I am with my father."

"Where is he?"

"I do not know, *señor*," I answered truthfully. "He was here a moment ago—"

"And is here again," Fat Cat's voice interrupted. He appeared through the bushes, his plump face shining in a wide-toothed smile. He took off his hat and made a sweeping bow. "José Hernandez, *a su servicio, señores*." He straightened up, still smiling. *"Mi hijo, Juan,"* he added, gesturing toward me. "The crazy one likes the water."

The older man turned the rifle on him. "What are you doing here?" he asked suspiciously.

Fat Cat walked toward him as if he wasn't even aware that the rifle was aimed at him. "My son and I return home from the valley. There is much trouble in Bandaya. *El militar.* It was no place for a peace-loving man and his son to seek employment."

The rifle was almost touching Fat Cat's belly now. "Where do you live?"

"A week's journey from here," Fat Cat replied. "Where are you bound?"

"Estanza."

Estanza was a few days' journey from Bandaya on the way to the coast. The road turned southward two mountain ridges beyond. At that point we would have to leave it and follow the paths through the woods and mountains.

"Perhaps the *señores* would permit us to accompany them." Fat Cat bowed again. "It is said there are *bandoleros.*"

The two men looked at each other. "It is true," the younger one replied. "El Coronel Guiterrez said the road has many bandits." He turned back to Fat Cat. "Where are your horses?"

Fat Cat laughed. "Horses? Who has horses, *señor?* We are but poor *campesinos.* We would be lucky if we could afford one little burro."

The older one looked at Fat Cat for a moment, then lowered the rifle. "All right, we shall go as far as Estanza together."

"But, *excelencia*—" the younger man protested.

"It is all right, Diego," the other said in a slightly annoyed voice. "What harm can one man and a small boy do?"

<hr>

13

I sat on the tailgate of the wagon, my back to the two girls, while Fat Cat rode on the driver's seat with Señor Moncada. Diego rode alongside on a large black stallion, his rifle resting casually across the saddle. Señor Moncada was a farmer who had come to bring his daughters home from a visit to their grandparents.

I stretched wearily and kept a hand on the side of the wagon to keep from falling off in case I dozed. I looked up at the sky. It was almost dark. We would have to stop soon, for the road was too dangerous to travel at night.

"There is a grove around the next bend," I heard Diego call. "We can spend the night there."

The wagon pulled off the road and creaked to a halt on the grass. Fat Cat was down from his seat and pulling at me almost before it rolled to a halt. "Hurry," he said, "gather wood for a fire. Quickly, before the young ladies get a chill!"

I stared at him in surprise. Fat Cat never worried about anyone. Only himself.

"Snap to it!" he shouted.

I began to gather wood. Over my shoulder I could see Fat Cat helping the two girls down from the wagon. By the time I came back with the first armful, the horses had been tethered and watered and were already feeding on the grass. "Where do you want me to put it?" I asked.

Señor Moncada gestured at the ground in front of him.

I started to drop the wood there but Fat Cat stopped me. "I think it is too close to the road, señor," he said apologetically. "It can too easily be seen. It might serve as an attraction for unwanted guests."

Señor Moncada looked hesitantly at Diego. Diego nodded.

Fat Cat walked farther back into the glade. "I think here will be better."

I dumped the wood where Fat Cat pointed. By the time I came back with a second armload a fire was already roaring heartily. I put the wood down and looked at Fat Cat. I was tired.

"More," he ordered. He cut some long branches and trimmed them and formed them into a tripod. The next time I returned there was a heavy iron pot hanging from it, and already the aroma of hot beef stew was beginning to permeate the air.

"Enough?"

Fat Cat looked up at me, his face shining from the flames. "For now," he said. "There is a brook about a hundred yards down the hill. Get another pot and fetch fresh water."

I walked over to the wagon. Vera, the younger girl, looked at me and giggled. I was annoyed. She was always giggling.

"What do you want?" Marta, the older one, asked.

"A pot for water."

Vera giggled again.

I glared at her. "Why are you always giggling?"

She went off into a paroxysm of laughter. The tears began to run down her cheeks.

"What's so funny?" I asked, beginning to get angry. Stupid girls.

She stopped her laughter. "You looked so funny."

I looked down at myself.

"Not now," she said quickly. "This afternoon. When you were in the water. You're so skinny."

I made a face. "It's better than being fat like you."

"Here's your pot," Marta said abruptly. I thought there was a hint of anger in her voice.

I took the pot from her hand. *"Gracias."*

"No hay de qué," she answered, equally polite.

Vera giggled again. "What's the matter with her?" I asked.

Marta shrugged. "She's only a child. She's twelve. She's never seen a boy naked."

"You haven't either!" Vera retorted.

Marta tossed her head. "But I'm fourteen and I don't act like a child about it!"

Diego came up behind me. "Did you get the pot?" he asked suspiciously.

"Sí señor."

"Then what are you waiting for? Fetch water like your father told you to."

Silently I started off. I could still hear his voice as I walked away. "What did he say to you?"

"Nothing," Marta answered.

"Well, stay away from him."

Then I couldn't hear them any more as I went into the woods and down to the stream. Fat Cat was waiting at the bank. "Hurry. The sooner they eat the sooner they will be asleep."

"What are you going to do?" I asked.

"Steal their horses. We can be home in two days. Besides, I like the black stallion."

"It won't be easy," I said. "Diego does not trust us."

79

Fat Cat smiled. "I will kill him."

There was a sound in the underbrush behind us, and Fat Cat got to his feet just as Diego came through the brush. He stood there, a rifle in his hands. Did he never put it down?

Fat Cat wiped his hands on his trousers. "I was just washing my hands."

Some sound in the night awakened me. I rolled over in the blanket Señor Moncada had loaned me and peered over at Fat Cat. He lay there asleep, snoring slightly. I turned my head and looked for Diego. He was not in his blanket.

I turned over and glanced toward the wagon where Señor Moncada and his daughters were sleeping. No sound came from there. I lay quiet for a moment. Perhaps Diego had gone into the bushes to relieve himself.

I heard a horse whinny, and I turned my head. It was then that I saw Diego stealing quietly toward the wagon, his rifle cocked and ready.

"Psst!"

Fat Cat came awake like the animal he was named after. I gestured with my hand and pointed. Fat Cat rolled over on his stomach nearer me. "He's going to kill them!" I whispered.

Fat Cat didn't move. "Let him," he whispered back. "It will save us the trouble!"

Diego crept up on the front of the wagon. I saw him brace his feet and begin to straighten up, the rifle coming to his shoulder, and then a thin scream suddenly rent the night air.

Diego fired wildly as Señor Moncada came down off the wagon. He tried to club him with the rifle, and as they both tumbled sideways against the side of the wagon Fat Cat was on his feet running toward them.

"The rifle!" he called back to me. "Get the rifle!"

He stopped near the struggling men. They rolled over and over, and I saw the flash in the moonlight as Fat Cat lifted his knife. He waited a moment, then suddenly the knife came down. There was a shriek as Diego came up from the ground, his hands reaching for Fat Cat's throat.

Fat Cat stepped back for a moment and waited. Diego moved. The blade stabbed down and Diego doubled like a jackknife. Fat Cat brought up his knee sharply under Diego's chest and he flew backward, head over heels.

Fat Cat turned swiftly, the knife ready in his hand. Señor

Moncada's back was to him as he got to his feet. Fat Cat brought up the knife but at that moment the other turned around, the rifle in his hand.

Fat Cat dropped his hands to his sides. "Are you all right, señor?" he asked, false concern in his voice.

Señor Moncada looked at him, then down at Diego. "The *bandolero!*" he cursed. "He tried to kill me!"

"It was lucky that I awoke, *señor.*"

Señor Moncada smiled. "I am in your debt, *amigo.* You have saved my life."

Fat Cat looked down at the ground. For once he had nothing to say. But after a moment, he found his tongue. "It was nothing, *señor*. It was a small thing to repay your kindness."

He walked to Diego and rolled him over with his foot. "He is dead. Where did you hire such a man?"

"In Bandaya," Señor Moncada replied. "We were told there were *bandoleros* in the mountains and that it would not be safe to travel alone with the little girls. He was recommended by Coronel Guiterrez. He had been acting as a scout for *el militar.*"

"He was nothing but a *bandolero,*" Fat Cat said righteously. "He would have killed you and stolen your horses. He must have wanted your black stallion very badly."

"The black stallion?" Señor Moncada asked in bewilderment. "He wasn't mine. That was his own horse."

Fat Cat's eyebrows shot up. "It was?"

Señor Moncada nodded. "Under the law, he is now yours."

Fat Cat looked over at me. He was smiling. It was the first time any law had worked to his favor. Whatever belonged to a *bandolero* automatically became yours if you took his life.

"Are you all right, *Papá?*" a frightened voice called from the wagon.

I had forgotten about the girls. I turned to the wagon. Marta's face peeked cautiously over the side.

"We are saved!" Señor Moncada exclaimed dramatically. "By the grace of God we have been saved from death! This good man, at the risk of his own life, protected us from that assassin!"

A moment later the two girls scrambled over the side of the wagon. Their arms went around their father and they all began kissing and crying and exclaiming to each other happily. At last Señor Moncada turned to us, his face beaming.

"It was a lucky day for us when we met you this afternoon," he said. "Now I understand why Diego did not wish you to join us!"

"It was a lucky thing for us all, *señor*," Fat Cat answered. He looked over at me and spoke in the voice of a man of property. "Go make sure our horse is properly tethered!"

14

I had finished emptying the last bag of salt into the barrel of beef when suddenly I realized that the two girls were in the barn watching me. I picked up the lid and began to nail it down.

After a moment Marta spoke. "You'll be going home tomorrow?"

It was more statement than question. I nodded. We had been at the *hacienda* almost a week. Señor Moncada had not wanted to make the rest of the journey alone, and the next thing I knew Fat Cat had agreed to accompany him. Especially after he heard that the good *señor* had cattle and was offering to compensate us with four barrels of freshly salted beef and a wagon to haul it.

Of course this meant that Fat Cat would have to leave the black stallion as security, but only until we returned the wagon, so the deal was made and we continued down the road to Estanza.

We had worked day and night to salt the beef and prepare it for the journey. I drove the last nail home and turned around.

"Yes," I finally answered. "We leave tomorrow."

"How old are you?" Vera asked.

"Thirteen," I answered, knowing she was twelve.

"No, you're not," Marta said scornfully. "I heard your father tell mine that you were only ten!"

"My father?" For a moment I had forgotten. Fat Cat, as usual, was out in the cooking hut making up to the cook and probably stuffing his belly.

"Do you have any brothers or sisters?" Vera asked.

I shook my head. Now that I had stopped working it was beginning to feel cool in the shaded barn. I reached for my shirt and slipped into it.

"You're skinny," Vera said. "All your bones stick out." She began to giggle again.

I looked at her in disgust. That's all she ever talked about, how skinny I was.

"Don't pay any attention to her," Marta said. "She's always trying to see what a boy's got."

"You are too! You were the one who followed Diego when he relieved himself!"

"You told me where he went!" Marta retorted. She shuddered delicately. "That terrible man!"

"You didn't think that then. You said his was bigger than Papá's!"

Now I understood.

Marta's voice sank to a conspiratorial whisper. "He saw us watching him. You know what he did?"

I shook my head.

"He came over to where we were hiding. His thing was still in his hand. We were frightened but he laughed and began to massage his thing. In a minute it got three times as big! It was all red on the end like the black stallion's."

"The black stallion?" I asked. I didn't get the connection.

Marta nodded impatiently. "Papá said he will have all six mares knocked up by the black stallion by the time your father brings the wagon back!"

"Oh." Señor Moncada was no fool. One colt alone was worth four barrels of beef.

"He kept playing with it and it got bigger and bigger," Vera continued in a hushed voice.

"Who?" I asked. For a moment I had forgotten what she was talking about.

"Diego," Marta answered in an annoyed voice. "He just stood there with a funny look on his face and kept playing with his thing."

Now I began to be interested. "Then what happened?"

Marta's voice contained a tinge of disappointment. "Nothing," she replied. "We heard *Papá* coming so we ran back to the wagon."

I was also disappointed. I was just as anxious as she to find out what would have happened.

"I didn't like Diego anyway," Vera added quickly. "He would have killed us after he killed *Papá*."

"He would have raped you first," I said with the voice of authority.

My tone impressed them. "How do you know?"

"You always rape girls before you kill them."

"Why?" Marta asked.

I shrugged my shoulders. "How do I know? That's just the way it's done."

Vera stared at me curiously. "You know a lot, don't you?"

"Enough," I answered importantly.

"Can you make yours hard like Diego did?"

"Of course," I answered brashly. "It's easy. Any man can do that."

"I bet you can't," Marta said. "You're too little."

"I am not!" I retorted angrily.

The sisters looked at each other, a strange excitement in their faces. "Prove it," Marta said, in a hushed voice.

"Why should I? Maybe I don't feel like it."

"You're too little," Marta replied. "You're afraid you can't do it!"

"I can so!" I said. "I'll prove it."

I could feel their eyes following my hand as I unbuttoned my fly. I took out my cock and began to fondle it as I had seen Roberto do. After a moment I looked down. Nothing was happening.

"Maybe you're doing it too fast," Marta whispered. "Diego did it much slower."

I looked at her in bewilderment. I wondered if she could know more about it than I did.

She saw my hesitation. "Here," she said, reaching out her hand, "let me show you."

Her hand felt hot and damp. I began to feel its heat and a pressure began to build up in my abdomen. I looked at them both. They didn't raise their eyes; they were too busy watching. I could see Vera move her tongue over her dry lips, and for once she wasn't giggling.

I began to feel a spastic shudder in my loins. I looked down

84

at myself. Pride came surging through me like the heat of the sun in the morning. My pecker was hard. It wasn't as big as I thought it would be, but it was hard.

"I told you I could do it. You better stop or I'll rape you."

"You wouldn't dare!" Marta whispered.

"No? You better let go and get out of here fast!"

They didn't move. I took a step toward them. Their eyes were still on my pecker. I could feel it throbbing. "You better leave!"

"Which one would you rape first?" Marta asked in a low voice.

"I don't care which one," I said. "You just better go, that's all."

The sisters looked at each other. "You're the oldest," Vera said.

I stared at them. I didn't know what to do. I hadn't expected this. "Are you going?" I asked in my most threatening voice.

Marta looked at me. "All right. You can do it to me first."

"You won't like it. You better go."

Marta lifted up her skirt. "Are you going to or not?" she asked impatiently.

I stared at the thin black fuzz between her legs. There was a challengingly expectant look in her eyes.

"All right," I said. "But just remember. You wanted to."

I went at her the way I remembered Roberto had done with the *putas* in the forest. We tumbled backward to the ground. I shoved her legs apart and climbed between them, jerking my hips in a sudden spasmodic motion that seemed to come from deep within me. I could feel myself going everywhere but where I wanted to go. Then I felt her hand on my prick as she guided it to where she wanted it to go. The hair was thin and prickly there, and felt like a thousand tiny needles.

"Stop wriggling," she whispered angrily. "Push!"

But I couldn't. There was a wild exciting pain tearing through my loins that wouldn't let me. No matter how hard I tried I couldn't get past the very edge of her flesh. I heard her grunt with the effort of trying to get me inside her.

"*Qué pasa?*"

I turned around and looked up. Fat Cat was standing in the doorway, a look of incredulity on his face, and Vera was nowhere to be seen. He came over and angrily pulled me to my feet. His hand cuffed me across the side of my face. "Is this the way you return the hospitality of your host?"

I was too out of breath to answer. I looked for Marta. She was already on her feet, running out the doorway. I turned back to Fat Cat.

He was no longer angry; his face was covered with a broad grin. "You'd better button your fly."

I looked down at myself. Embarrassedly I buttoned up quickly.

He rubbed his hand across my head affectionately. "I was wondering how long it would take those two little cunts to get to you," he said, then laughed again. "Come, let us get the wagon ready for an early start."

He started for the barn door. I stared after him. In the doorway, he turned and looked back at me. He saw the wondering expression on my face.

"Do not look so surprised. I told you it would not be long before you became a man!"

15

A shot rang out and before its sound had finished echoing in my ears I had rolled over and was lying flat in the wagon. Another sounded and Fat Cat was on his belly in the ditch at the side of the road. A moment passed and he was on his feet, dripping mud and water, shaking his fist angrily at the mountainside and yelling at the top of his lungs: "Santiago! You blind idiot whelp of a hyena! You jackass braying from your mother's womb! Can't you see it is I, your comrade?"

Ping! A bullet kicked up the dirt not three feet away and Fat Cat was back in the ditch. This time he did not get up. He lay there on his belly in the water, screaming: "Prick! Indian shit! It is me, Fat Cat!"

"Fat Cat?" The older Santiago's voice echoed hollowly down the mountainside.

"Yes, Fat Cat, you sightless, crawling maggot! Fat Cat!"

There was a scrambling through the brush and Santiago suddenly appeared at the edge of the ditch. He looked down into the ditch. "Fat Cat!" he exclaimed. "Why did you not say it was you?"

Fat Cat came up out of the ditch even more bedraggled than before. Water dripped from his hat brim down onto his face, and he sputtered speechlessly.

"Fat Cat, it is really you!" Ecstatically The Older threw down his rifle and embraced his friend. "You are alive!"

"I am alive!" Fat Cat shouted angrily, trying to escape the Indian's grasp. "No thanks to you!"

"We thought you were dead," Santiago said in wonderment. He stepped back and examined Fat Cat. "You are alive and safe. Not a mark on you!"

Fat Cat looked down at himself. The new shirt and *pantalones* that Señor Moncada had given him were filthy with mud. "Not a mark!" he bellowed, lashing out with his fist.

The blow caught Santiago on the side of his face and tumbled him backward into the road. He looked up at Fat Cat with a hurt expression on his usually impassive face. "Fat Cat," he asked in puzzlement, "why are you angry with me? What have I done?"

"What have you done?" Fat Cat roared. "Look at my new shirt. Look at my new trousers. Ruined! That's what you've done."

He aimed a kick at the Indian's head, and Santiago rolled quickly out of the way. Fat Cat's foot went up and suddenly he lost his balance. Backward he tumbled, straight into the ditch. He lay there out of breath, screaming curses into the air.

I heard someone else coming through the brush, and suddenly Manuelo emerged. He glanced at the Indian lying in the road, then walked over to the edge of the ditch and looked down at Fat Cat. After a moment he said in a flat, emotionless voice, "Perhaps when you have done with your childish games, you will tell us what you have in the wagon?"

It had been only twelve days since we had left the mountains for Bandaya, though it seemed as if I had been gone a year. We went on into the camp, where they clustered around us and treated us like heroes. They could hardly wait until the first barrel was opened and the women took the meat away to the cooking pots. For almost all the time we had been away they had been living on small game and roots. Mostly the latter, for the game had fled the mountains because of the drought.

There were eight men, four women, and four children in that small camp in the mountains that Diablo Rojo used as his headquarters and hideout. Three of the women were his, as were three of the children. The other woman and child belonged to Manuelo.

Each of the general's three children had been born of a different mother. Roberto, the oldest and my companion, was dark. He had an Indian cast to his features, as well he might, for his mother was a distant cousin to the Santiagos. Eduardo, the younger son, resembled the general most, though he also bore the mark of his mixed blood in the coarseness of his features. Only Amparo, the daughter, and the youngest, was fair-skinned and blond. Her body was slim and lithe, her eyes bright and alive. They always sparkled with an inner kind of excitement. And there was no doubt that she was the general's favorite, just as her mother was.

The mother was slim and blond, unlike the other two women, who were dark and rather pudgy. They were extremely jealous of her but dared not speak out against her. She had come from somewhere on the coast and it was said that the general had found her in a whorehouse there, though she claimed to be the daughter of an impoverished Castilian gentleman and a German refugee. At any rate she acted the grand lady and the others had to cook and wait on her like servants.

She spent most of her time when the general was away playing with Amparo, dressing and undressing her as if she were a doll. This, plus the favored treatment she received from the general, and every other male in the camp for that matter, was enough to completely spoil the child. For a seven-year-old she was imperious and quick to show petulance when she did not get what she wanted. Most of the time she did, and then everyone basked in the warmth and brightness of her smile.

Amparo stood beside the wagon now, in a pretty white

dress, as I climbed down from the seat. "They told me you were dead," she announced in a rather disappointed voice.

"Well, I'm not."

"I already said a novena for you," she replied, "and Mother promised we could have a Mass said the next time we went to church."

I studied her. We had been children together, and now I felt suddenly as if she had remained a child. "I'm sorry. Had I known, I would have allowed myself to be killed."

A sudden smile brightened her face. "You would, Dax? You would have done that for me?"

"Certainly," I said, humoring her.

She threw her arms around me and kissed my cheek. "Oh, Dax," she cried, "you *are* my very favorite! I'm glad you weren't killed. Really I am!"

I pushed her away gently.

She looked at me, her face glowing. "I've made up my mind."

"To what?" I asked.

"I'm going to marry you when I grow up!" She turned and started to run off. "I'm going to go tell Mother I've decided!"

I watched until she reached the house, a half-smile on my face. Before I had gone away she had thrown a tantrum because she had decided to marry Manuelo and her mother had told her she couldn't because he already had a woman. And just a few weeks before that it had been a young messenger who had come from the general bearing the latest news. I turned back to the wagon and began to unhitch the horses.

On the other side I could hear Fat Cat bragging to the others about the black stallion. Then I became aware of Roberto and Eduardo.

I turned to look at them. "Hello."

Eduardo answered immediately. He was only a few months younger than I but much smaller and thinner. Roberto merely stared at me sullenly. His face was pale, his eyes looked yellowish and sick.

"What's the matter with you?" I asked.

Eduardo answered before his brother could speak. "He's got a dose."

"A dose? What's that?"

Roberto still did not answer, and Eduardo shrugged. "I don't know. The Santiagos and Manuelo caught it too. Manuelo's woman is mad at him."

89

"Eduardo!" his mother called from the house.

"I gotta go."

I finished unhitching the horses in silence. Roberto stood there watching me, so I tossed him one set of reins. "Help me get them into the corral."

He took the bridle and we led the horses off. I opened the gate and we pushed them inside. Immediately they began to graze on the far side, away from the others who warily watched the newcomers out of the corners of their eyes.

"Look at them," I said. "They pretend they don't even see each other. By tomorrow they'll be friends. Horses act like people."

"Horses don't get the clap," Roberto answered sullenly.

"No? How did you get it?"

He spat on the ground. "From the *putas*. We all got it. Manuelo's woman is furious at him."

"Is it bad?" I asked.

He shook his head. "Not so bad. It hurts when you pee."

"What's that got to do with it?"

"You're stupid! That's where you get it, in your pecker. You'll get it too. Manuelo says you're not a man until you've had the clap."

"I had a woman."

"You did?" Roberto said, disbelief in his voice.

I nodded. "Marta, Señor Moncada's daughter. Where we got the meat. I jumped her in the barn."

"Did you get in?"

I wasn't quite sure what he meant. "I think so. Anyway, I wouldn't have noticed. I was too busy. I would still be raping her if Fat Cat hadn't pulled me off."

He stared at me. "How old was she?"

"Fourteen."

He sniffed. "She's just a girl."

"Do you think I'll get a dose?" I asked.

He shook his head. "Nah, she's just a kid. It takes a woman to give you the pox. Does Fat Cat have it?"

"I don't know. He didn't say."

"Maybe he was lucky," he said. "Maybe he didn't catch it."

He began to walk off and I followed him. I didn't understand. If you weren't a man until you got it, how could you be lucky if you didn't catch it?

16

Fat Cat sulked as I followed him up to the lookout post. He turned and looked back at me. "Where do you think you're going?"

"To take a look around," I replied innocently.

"Go ahead and look, but do you have to be behind me every time I turn around? Someday I'm going to trip over you. You'll be squashed like a bug."

I didn't answer as he turned and continued up the path, kicking angrily at the rocks. I followed at a safe distance, not wanting to be squashed like a bug. Fat Cat had been like that all week. Ever since Manuelo refused to let him go back for the black stallion. We were too shorthanded, Manuelo had said.

Ordinarily ten men guarded the hideout. But two of these were already dead. One by the army sergeant, the other before we had gone out for meat. He had got drunk and tried to rape one of the general's women. I think it was Amparo's mother but I wasn't sure. All I had heard was a scream, then two shots. By the time I had got there he was already dead.

The younger Santiago was in the lookout. "It's about time," he grumbled. "I am starving."

"The best thing for a clap," Fat Cat replied maliciously, "is an empty stomach."

The Younger glared at him. "In that case I would advise your getting a dose. If you eat any more no horse will be big enough to carry you."

"Bah!" Fat Cat snorted. "My black stallion could carry me easily were I five times as large."

"I don't believe there ever was a black stallion," The Younger said sarcastically as he started down the path.

91

"You are only jealous," Fat Cat shouted after him. "Dax was with me. Dax saw him. Didn't you, Dax?"

"*Sí*, I saw him."

But Santiago was already out of sight down the path. I turned to Fat Cat. He was looking out over the mountains toward Estanza.

"He is a great stallion, eh, Dax?"

"*Un caballo magnífico!*

Fat Cat sat down, his back against a rock, his rifle across his knees. He still faced south. "Manuelo does not understand what it is to own such a magnificent beast. He never had one, so how could he?"

I didn't answer.

"You'd think I was asking for the borrow of his woman," he continued. "Not that she wouldn't appreciate it, the way he is. But, no. You have to stay here, he says. We're too shorthanded."

He shrugged. "What would they have done if we hadn't come back? I wouldn't be here for Manuelo to refuse such a reasonable request. And they would be starving, eating field mice and rabbit turds and road apples."

I still didn't speak.

But Fat Cat didn't seem to care whether I did or not. "After all I've done for them they have the nerve to doubt I even have such a beautiful beast." He put down his rifle and lit a *cigarrillo*. "I'm telling you it's more than a man can bear."

I watched as he blew out a puff of smoke, then took a last look around. The hillside was peaceful. Dusk was little more than an hour away. "Good night, Gato Gordo," I said, and started down the path.

I looked back for a moment as I rounded the bend. He was still sitting there, letting the smoke curl reflectively from his nostrils. Halfway down the path I heard the cry of a wild turkey. Almost immediately, my mouth watered. It had been a long time since we had such a dish. I was sick of our steady diet of salt beef.

"Gobble—gobble—awk," I called.

It answered, but the sound seemed to come from off to my left. I crept into the brush. I called again. It answered. But it still was moving away from me. It was dusk by the time I caught up to it.

I don't know which of us was more surprised when the turkey's head popped up suddenly out of the bush right in front of me. For a moment we stared at each other incredulously, then the huge bird raised his head to gobble in protest. But he never finished, for quickly I flat-edged my knife like a machete and chopped off his head.

I felt the hot splash of blood against my shirt as the headless body rushed past me, then flopped crazily about on the ground. It was almost ten minutes before he was fully blooded and the body became still. It was almost dark when I picked up the great bird by the legs and hoisted it over my shoulder, the neck hanging down behind me.

Slowly I started down the path. Manuelo was near the corral when I came in. "Where have you been?" he asked angrily. "You know you're supposed to be back by dark."

I swung the turkey around from behind me and dropped it on the ground at his feet. He looked down at it. "Jesus Christ," he said in an awed voice, "where did you get it?"

"I heard him call as I was coming down from the lookout."

Manuelo picked up the big bird and hefted it. "At least fifteen kilos. Estrella, come see what Dax has brought! There'll be a feast tomorrow!"

But there was to be no feast because the soldiers came that night.

It must have been only a few hours before dawn when I heard the first shot. I rolled out of bed and reached for my shoes. I was already dressed, for I had taken to sleeping like the others since our return. I felt for my knife under the pillow.

From somewhere in the house I heard a woman screaming. I didn't go out the door; I turned and dove from the window head first. I hit the overhang and rolled down the back roof to the ground, just as the house burst into flames behind me.

I saw flashes of gunfire and heard men shouting as I scrambled to my hands and knees, then broke for the hillside. I leaped over some low bushes and rolled into a ditch. I caught my breath and then cautiously raised my head.

All I could see by the light of flames was red and blue uniforms everywhere. Manuelo and Santiago the Older came running around the side of the house. I saw the flashes from their rifles. One of the soldiers fell over, another screamed and clutched at his belly. Then one of the soldiers reached behind him and threw something at Manuelo which turned over and over in midair.

"Manuelo!" I screamed. "Watch out!"

But nobody heard me. One moment Manuelo was standing there and the next he seemed to explode into a thousand pieces. Two soldiers were after Santiago now. His rifle was empty and he ran from one to the other, swinging it like a club. Then they lunged toward him and I heard his scream as one bayonet went through his neck, the other drove into his intestines from the rear.

I put my head down and ran along the bottom of the drainage ditch toward the front of the house. When I got to the lookout path, which was hidden by bushes, I peered up over the ditch again. I heard a scream and saw Amparo running past, her white nightdress billowing out behind her. I grabbed for a leg, and she tumbled to the ground. Before she could scream again, I put my hand over her mouth and pulled her down into the ditch.

Her eyes stared up at me, wide, stricken with terror. I put my face close to hers. "Be silent!" I hissed. "It's me, Dax!"

The terror left her eyes and she nodded. I lifted my hand from her mouth. "Lay there and be quiet. I'm going to have another look."

I stuck my head up above ground level. Santiago the Younger lay dead not four feet from me, his sightless eyes staring at me. Others lay dead, nearer the house. The soldiers were still there. A woman, her clothing ablaze, ran screaming from the house. Behind her ran Eduardo, crying, "Mamá! Mamá!"

There was a burst of gunfire, and the woman tumbled to the ground. Eduardo, just behind her, fell over her, and a soldier ran toward them and lunged with his bayonet, again and again.

Another figure came charging out of the house, the fire highlighting the machete he was swinging with both hands. It was Roberto, and the general would have been proud of him. There was no fear on his face, nothing but hatred as he ran screaming toward the soldier.

Taken completely by surprise, the soldier turned and ran. But it was too late. The machete came down and suddenly the soldier's arm seemed to fall away from his shoulder. He yelled in agony and fell sideways, just as a burst of gunfire came from behind him. Roberto seemed to hang in the air for a moment, then crashed backward to the ground, near the bodies of his brother and his brother's mother.

Now there was only the crackling and roaring of the fire. Then I heard the sound of a woman crying. Three women were huddled together to one side of the house. They were surrounded by soldiers. I could see Amparo's mother in the middle. She seemed to be trying to hold up Roberto's mother. Manuelo's woman appeared stony-faced, beyond feeling.

An officer came walking over. I couldn't see his face but it didn't matter. I knew him the moment he opened his mouth. I would never forget that voice, not until the day I died.

"They are all dead?"

"*Sí, Coronel,*" a sergeant answered. "All but these women here."

The *coronel* nodded. "*Bueno.* Do what you will with them. But remember, they must be dead when we leave. I have sworn an oath that not one traitor shall live!"

"*Sí, Coronel.*"

The *coronel* turned his back and walked around the corner of the house, out of sight. The women were already stripped and spread-eagled on the ground, and a line of soldiers was queuing up in front of each. I felt a motion beside me and turned. It was Amparo, her eyes wide. "What are they doing?"

I knew what they were doing. Raping and killing. That was the way it was. But suddenly I knew it would serve no purpose for her to see. She was only a child. How could she be expected to understand what men did in the course of fighting?

I pulled her back down into the ditch. "It doesn't matter," I whispered.

"What are we going to do?" Her voice trembled. She was beginning to get frightened again.

I took her hand and pulled her along after me toward the path to the lookout. But when we got up there, it was deserted. Fat Cat was not there. Suddenly I knew where he had gone.

To Estanza for the black stallion.

I looked down the path on the other side to the south. It lay dark and deserted. If we hurried we might catch up with him. The night was breaking, the day just beginning to appear

95

over my right shoulder. The morning chill lay heavy on the ground.

"I'm cold," Amparo whimpered, shivering in her thin nightdress.

I knew what I had to do. Fat Cat had taught me. I took off my heavy Indian shirt and draped it around Amparo. It came down almost to her calves. Then I took off my shoes and made her put them on her bare feet.

"Now," I said quietly, and with as much reassurance as I could force into my voice, "we'll walk a little while. We'll rest when the sun comes up to warm us."

17

We were no more than a quarter of the way down the mountain when I heard the faint sound of men's voices behind us. I grabbed Amparo's arm and we scrambled through the bushes until I found a spot where the underbrush was thickest. We crawled into the very middle. We weren't a moment too soon.

I heard the heavy tread of boots, and four soldiers appeared almost directly in front of us, their rifles carried at the ready.

"*Hola!*" one said, throwing himself on the ground not more than a dozen feet away. "I've had enough. I can go no farther."

The others stood around looking down at him.

"Sit down," he urged. "You are as tired as I."

"But *el coronel* said to check the path all the way down," one of the others answered doubtfully.

The man on the ground looked up. "Is *el coronel* with us? No, he is down there boozing it up while we exhaust ourselves in these cursed mountains. Fuck *el coronel*."

Another dropped down beside him. "A moment's rest," he said. "Who is to know?"

The others sprawled to the ground. After a moment one of

them propped himself up against a tree trunk. "Which one did you have?"

The first soldier rolled over on his side. "I fucked all of them," he bragged. "As soon as I unloaded in one, I got up and joined another line."

The second soldier shook his head. "No wonder you're so pooped."

"Which one did you screw?"

"The hysterical one. I don't see why she made such a fuss. She had a cunt big enough to accommodate a stallion. I couldn't even feel the sides."

"She wasn't very good," one of the others agreed.

The first soldier grinned broadly. "The blond was the best. You could tell she was getting it regularly. She pressed down the moment you put it in and—pop—you had it. If there hadn't been so many behind me I'd have slipped it to her again. The next time she wouldn't have got off so easy." He reached for his canteen. "I need a drink. All the liquid has been drained out of me."

He held the canteen to his lips, and water trickled out of the corners of his mouth and down his cheeks.

"I'm thirsty, too," Amparo whispered.

"Shh!"

She wriggled and brushed at her face. "There are mosquitoes."

I became aware of them on my back. Before I had been too busy concentrating on the soldiers. Moving very slowly so I would not disturb the underbrush, I pulled her nightdress up from inside my shirt and covered her face. "Lie there and don't move," I whispered. "They can't get at your face now."

But they could get to me; I was bare to the waist. Every few seconds I would feel one sting me, but there was nothing I could do about it. Not while the soldiers were there.

Presently one of them got to his feet. "I guess we'd better get moving."

"What for?" the first soldier asked. "There's nobody down there."

"But *el coronel* ordered us to check the path thoroughly."

The first soldier laughed. "That means we'd wind up at the bottom of the mountain and only have to climb right back up again." He glanced up at the sun. "We can rest here until noon, then report back. Who will ever know?"

"I don't know."

"O.K., go ahead if you insist. We'll rest here until you come back."

The one standing looked at the others, but they made no move to join him. After a moment, he dropped to the ground again. "What you say is true. Who will ever know?"

I turned my head. Amparo's face was hidden by the nightshirt. I could sense her breathing, quietly and evenly. Cautiously I lifted the nightdress. She was fast asleep.

I covered her face again, and turned back to the soldiers. One was already on his back, his arms outstretched and snoring with his mouth open. The others had scrunched themselves down into more comfortable positions and were beginning to close their eyes.

It would be good if I could rest too. But I didn't dare. I fought to keep my eyes open. The sun kept climbing into the sky, the day became warmer. I could feel my back burning with insect stings but I didn't dare brush them away.

I tried to keep my eyes open but every few minutes my head would fall forward. I kept lifting it up but after a while even I must have dozed. But when I heard a noise suddenly I came awake.

The soldiers were all standing now. As I watched they went off to the other side of the road to relieve themselves. A moment later one of them called to the others, "It's late enough now. We can start back."

I watched them move back up the path until they were out of sight beyond the bend. Soon I could no longer hear the sounds of their voices. Amparo was still sleeping. I shook her gently.

She raised her head and pushed the nightdress away from her face. Her eyes were still filled with sleep. "I'm hungry," she said, rubbing them.

"We'll eat soon."

"Let's go home. *Mamá* promised me we would have the turkey you killed yesterday for dinner."

"We can't. The soldiers are still there."

Sleep vanished from her eyes as memory flooded through her. Suddenly she began to cry. "*Mamá! Mamá! Mamá!*"

"Cut that out!" I said roughly.

"I will see *Mamá* later?"

"Sure." How could I tell her that she would never see her mother again? "How did you escape from the house?"

"When the soldiers took *Mamá* I was hiding under the bed. As soon as they left I jumped out of the window and began to run." Tears came to her eyes again. "I ran and ran and ran."

"That was a very clever thing to do."

Her eyes brightened. "It was?"

The one thing that Amparo loved was flattery. She could never get enough of it. "I am clever, aren't I?"

"Very."

She nodded, pleased with herself, and looked out at the path. "Are they gone?"

"They're gone." I got to my feet. "And it's time for us to go, too."

"Where are we going?"

I thought for a moment. We could never catch up to Fat Cat now, but I knew where he was going. "To Estanza."

"Estanza?" she asked. "Where's that?"

"A long way from here. We'll have to walk."

"I like to walk."

"But we'll have to be very careful. We can't let anyone see us. If we hear anybody coming we'll have to hide."

"It might be the soldiers," she said brightly.

"Even if it's not, we'll have to hide. Whoever it was might tell the soldiers they saw us."

"I'll be careful," she promised. "I'm hungry and thirsty."

"There's a brook a little farther on."

"I also have to pee."

That was one thing she didn't have to wait for. "Over there in the bushes."

Amparo went over to the bushes and squatted. Delicately she hiked up her clothes. "I can't pee if you stand there watching me!"

I turned away, smiling to myself. Girls were funny. What difference did it make if I watched her or not?

We reached the brook in about half an hour. I remembered what Fat Cat had told me and cautioned her about drinking too rapidly. I stretched out on the bank and lowered my face into the water. My back began to itch; the hot sun had aggravated the mosquito bites. I reached behind me and scratched. I could feel welts on my skin. I splashed some water over my shoulder.

Amparo stood there watching. "Your back is all bitten. *Mamá* always put bay leaves on my mosquito bites."

"What do they look like?"

"There's a whole clump over there." She pointed to a group of bushes.

I picked off a handful and tried to put them on my back, but they kept falling off. Amparo held out her hand. "You don't know very much, do you?" she asked in an exasperated voice. "Better let me do it."

I stared at her, then silently handed her the leaves. She dipped them in the water for a moment. "Turn around."

I turned my back. I could feel the wet leaves and water running down my back. She was right; after a few minutes the stinging did go away. I sat staring into the brook. Suddenly movement caught my eye, and a small school of fish swam by.

I remembered that the younger Santiago used to spear fish using an arrow. I looked around for a straight branch about as thick. When I found one I quickly stripped it of its leaves with my knife, then made a sharp point and barb at one end. I got to my knees and crouched at the stream's edge.

The fish came by again. I lunged but they were too quick for me; all I succeeded in doing was almost tumbling into the water. I set myself again. After the third try I began to get the feel of it. The fish would break, all going in opposite directions, and the thing was to guess which one would be coming toward you.

I decided it would be the one in the back. I let them swim by the first time because I didn't think the one in the back would come close enough. The second time, however, he was just right. I lunged and felt the spear bite into him.

I turned triumphantly, holding up the stick with the wriggling fish impaled on it. "We eat!"

An expression of distaste crossed Amparo's face. "Raw?" she asked. "How are you going to cook it?"

I could feel my triumph fade. Slowly I sank down on a large flat rock. I yelled as my bottom hit it. The rock was as hot as a griddle from the heat of the sun. I stood there staring down at the rock. If it was hot enough to burn my ass, it was hot enough to fry a fish.

100

18

The fish was good, even if it was a little raw. I caught two more before our hunger was satisfied and each time I had to scrape them from the rock with my knife. It was just as well we ate so much then, because for the next two days all we could find were nuts and berries. The third morning we came across a mango tree and we gorged ourselves so greedily that we both had stomach cramps and had to stay there for the balance of that day.

Amparo began to cry when night came. "I want to go home."

I looked at her silently. There was nothing I could say. I sat there awkwardly, as helpless as any man when confronted by a woman's tears. Her usually pretty face was thin and drawn by the ravages of diarrhea.

"My tuss hurts," she said.

Mine was sore too. I'd know better than to gobble mangoes next time. "Sleep. It will be better in the morning."

She stamped her foot angrily. "I don't want to! I'm tired of sleeping on the ground, half freezing and having bugs crawling over me. I want to go home and sleep in my own bed!"

"Well, you can't."

"I am so going to!" She began to stamp both feet angrily.

I knew what that meant. She was about to throw one of her famous tantrums. I didn't feel like having any of it. I lashed out with my hand, catching her on the cheek, and for a moment she was frozen in surprise. Then the tears really welled up into her eyes. "You hit me!"

"And I'll do it again if you don't shut up!" I said savagely.

"I hate you!"

I didn't answer.

"I really mean it! I'm not going to marry you!"

I lay back in the grass and closed my eyes.

For a moment there was silence. I heard nothing, then I felt her move closer to me. She snuggled against my side. "I'm cold, Dax."

I looked at her. Her lips were pale with chill. I realized that we should not be sleeping out in the open. I'd have to find a place more sheltered from the winds that swept down from the mountains across the prairie.

"Get up," I said, pulling her to her feet.

"But it's dark and I'm tired. I can't walk any more."

"You have to," I said. "We've got to find a warmer place to sleep."

We began to walk. I looked up at the sky. I didn't like the looks of it. The clouds hung low and threatening, obscuring the moon and the stars. A chill damp wind had come up, and I knew that rain could not be far away.

I remembered that earlier that morning I had seen a little forest across the fields. If only we hadn't gorged ourselves on the mangoes we would have been there by now. I tried to see through the darkness but it was no use. All we could do was keep on walking and hope that we would be there soon.

The rain began to come down in great slanting sheets, pelting against our backs from the gusts of wind. In a moment we were soaked through. I pulled Amparo along rapidly, feeling the wet *pantalones* clinging to my legs. The earth turned soft and muddy under my bare feet.

Amparo was crying again. Once she half fell to her knees, and I hauled her up roughly. We began to run again. Suddenly we were there. I pulled her into the forest and stopped under a big tree. It was relatively dry; the rain had not yet penetrated the thick umbrella of leaves. We fought to catch our breaths.

I was suddenly aware that she was shaking from a chill. Her eyes seemed strangely bright and shining. "Dax, I hear voices."

I drew her close to me, trying to warm her with the heat of my body. "No, I hear voices." Her voice sounded strained and thin.

I touched her forehead; she was hot. She must be coming down with a fever. "Shh. Now we can rest."

She pushed me away. "No," she said angrily, "listen."

More to humor her than anything else I did. At first I heard nothing, then I became aware of a low buzz of voices. It seemed to be coming from behind us.

"Wait here," I whispered.

Amparo nodded, and I crept off into the forest. I had gone perhaps fifty yards when I saw them. There were three wagons drawn off from the road under the shelter of the trees, and three men were sitting in one of them. They were hovered around a small lantern playing cards. Three others lay stretched out between the other wagons. They all wore the red and blue uniforms of the army. I could see their rifles stacked along the side of the front wagon.

I wondered if there were more of them. I shinnied up a tree and carefully studied the other wagons. They were empty, but I could see several blankets in one of them. I looked back at the wagon with the card players in it, and wondered if I could get away with one of the blankets.

Then I remembered Amparo's fever and knew I had no choice. She was my responsibility, just as I had been Fat Cat's. There was nothing else I could do. I came down out of the tree and slipped silently up into the back wagon. Moving quickly, I scooped up a blanket and rolled it up tightly. I looked around for anything else we could use. I saw a box of matches and stuck them in my pocket. There was a dried-out piece of fatback lying on the wagon floor, so I took that too.

It took me a few minutes to orient myself when I got back into the woods, then it was easy to work my way back to Amparo. She was lying very quietly as I came out of the underbrush.

"Dax?" she whispered. I could hear her teeth chattering.

"Yes. Quick, get out of your wet clothes!"

I spread out the blanket and rolled her up in it, then took out my knife and cut off a thin strip of fatback. "Here, suck on this."

She nodded and put it into her mouth. I lay down beside her and cut off a little piece for myself. It tasted gritty and salty but the feel of it in my mouth was oddly comforting. I could feel Amparo's shivering slowly subsiding and after a

103

few moments her even breathing told me she was asleep. I remember smiling to myself as I drifted off. For a girl, Amparo wasn't so bad.

A bird singing in a tree over my head awakened me. I opened my eyes and stared upward. Through the branches I could see the clear blue sky. I turned my head to look at Amparo. She was rolled up completely in the blanket.

I looked around for her clothes. They were lying in a damp heap by her feet. I picked them up and hung them on a bush where the sun would dry them. By that time she was sitting up. I held my finger to my lips so that she would not speak.

She nodded.

I cut her another small strip of fatback. "Wait here," I whispered. "I'll be back."

It took me only a few minutes to get to the clearing. The soldiers and wagons were gone. The remains of a small fire was glowing in the center of what had been their camp. I threw a few twigs on to keep it going, and went back for Amparo.

The fire felt good after the cold damp night. I tried to figure out what time it was by the sun. It must have been near nine o'clock. Time to start out again. I rolled up the blanket and threw it over my shoulders, and we moved off toward the road.

Three times that morning we left it to hide in the fields. Once it was several men on foot, another time a man in a wagon, and finally a man and a woman in a wagon. For a moment I was tempted to hail the wagons but I thought better of it. There was no point in taking any chances because from the frequency of the wagons I figured we must be nearing a small town.

When we turned the next curve in the road I could see houses and smoke coming from some of the chimneys, so I pulled Amparo off the road into the field. "We have to go around the town."

She nodded, and we struck out across the fields. It took longer that way and it was nearly night by the time the village was behind us.

"I'm hungry," Amparo complained. "Fatback doesn't fill my stomach."

"We'll have something to eat tonight."

I had spotted a couple of chicken coops and as soon as I found a good place to camp for the night I was going back. I found a place soon enough but Amparo refused to stay by herself.

It was black as pitch as we settled down in a field near the chicken coops. They were out back of a house so we had to wait until I was sure everyone had gone to sleep.

"Wait here. Don't move!" I cautioned Amparo.

I didn't wait for an answer. I sped across the ground on silent feet, taking out my knife as I lifted the latch on the nearest coop.

Almost immediately the chickens set up a racket that could be heard forty miles away. One big red hen ran at me, and I flat-edged her with my knife. I slashed at another but missed, then caught a white pullet as she went by. Quickly I sheathed my knife, grabbed the chickens by their legs, and ran back across the field with their bodies still jerking in my hand. I dove down beside Amparo just as the farmer came out of the house, his nightshirt flapping. He was carrying a rifle and when he saw the open coop he ran to shut it. Then he came running over to the edge of the field near us.

"What is it?" a woman's voice called from inside the house.

"That damn weasel's been at the chickens again! Some night I'm gonna get him!"

He stood there a moment longer, and then went angrily stamping back to the chicken coop. He unlatched the door and went in.

I touched Amparo's arm and gestured for us to leave. The minute he found two hen heads in the coop he'd know that it was no weasel that had raided his flock. We ran all the way back to our hideout, and suddenly we weren't tired any more. Even Amparo was laughing and happy as the chickens dangled over the fire, the lice jumping crazily from their feathers to keep from being incinerated.

19

The days became nights and the nights turned into days and we had lost all track of time when finally we came down the last of the range of hills into the desert. Vaguely I thought it had been about three weeks since we had left the hideout but I could not be sure.

It was about two in the afternoon as we stood there looking across the desert to the next range of hills beyond which lies the green and fertile valley around Estanza. I could see a few wagons on the road, so I knew that we dared not cross by daylight. We would be too easily seen, since there was no place to hide in all that flat hot sand.

I tried to calculate the distance with my eyes. It had taken Fat Cat and me three hours to cross it with the wagon. That would mean about twenty miles. By walking all night we should be able to make it. I turned to Amparo.

Her face was deeply tanned by the sun and her blond hair bleached almost white; her brows and lashes were pale and practically invisible against her dark skin. Her cheeks were thin and drawn and I could see the fine ridges of her bones beneath the flesh and the weariness that pulled down the corners of her mouth. I pulled a chicken bone from my pocket. She put it in her mouth and sucked it gently, letting her saliva soften and moisten it before she chewed. Amparo, too, had learned a lot in these last few weeks.

Several times a day we had had to leave the road and hide. More than once we had nearly bumped into patrols of soldiers but we had developed a sixth sense that warned us when danger was near. I looked out across the desert again. "We'll have to cross it at night. We'll find a place to rest until dark."

Amparo nodded. She knew why without my having to explain. "Have we anything left to eat?" she asked, still sucking on the bone.

"No."

I looked around. This wasn't game country. There were few trees, only scrub brush that seemed to grow only in the desert. That meant there probably wasn't much water either. "But we're not far from Estanza," I said. "There'll be plenty to eat and drink there."

She nodded silently. I watched her look down at the moving wagons along the road. "Do they all hate us? Do they all want to kill us?"

I was surprised by her question. "I don't know."

"Then why do we have to hide all the time?"

"Because we don't know how they feel about us."

She was silent for a moment. "*Mamá* is dead," she said suddenly, "and so are the others. Roberto and Eduardo, too. That's why we can't go back, isn't it?"

I didn't answer.

"You can tell me," she said quietly, "I won't cry."

I nodded.

She stared into my eyes. "Is *Papá* dead too?"

"No."

She turned away and looked out at the desert. For a long time she stood there silently. Then she turned back to me. "If *Papá* is dead," she asked, "will you marry me and take care of me?"

I stared at her. She looked so skinny and helpless standing there. Like Perro used to look when he wasn't quite sure I would give him a bone. I reached for her hand. It felt warm and trusting in mine. "You know I will. We settled that a long time ago."

She smiled. "Do you have another bone?"

I took the last one and gave it to her. She stuck it in her mouth and began to chew on it. "Come on," I said. "Let's find some shade and try to sleep."

The wind came up later that night as we started down the road to cross the desert. We shivered as its chill struck us. I looked at Amparo. "You all right?"

She nodded and pulled the shirt closer around her and lowered her head into the wind.

"Wait," I said, and unrolled the blanket and cut it down

107

the middle with my knife. After tonight we wouldn't need it any more. We would be at Señor Moncada's farm. "Here, use it like a *ruana*."

She wrapped her half around her and I did the same. The wind seemed to be getting stronger. Occasionally it would lift the sand and fling it up in our faces and soon our eyes were stinging. The skin on our faces became raw and chafed, and after we had been walking a few hours even the hard-packed surface of the road was covered with a fine layer of sand.

Several times we stumbled off the road and sank in sand to our ankles. The wind was so fierce now it was hard to see where we were going. I tried to look up at the stars to get my bearings, but even they were obscured. More than once we found ourselves floundering and had to fight our way back to the road.

"I can't see," Amparo cried. "The sand is blowing in my eyes."

"Make a hood." I pulled the blanket up over her head and made a peak with just a narrow opening in the front to see out of it. "Better?"

"Yes."

I did the same and it worked. We moved off again but before we knew it we were off the road again. It seemed like an hour before we stumbled onto it once more.

"I can't walk any more, Dax," Amparo sobbed. "My shoes are filled with sand."

I made her sit down, and I emptied her shoes. Then I pulled her to her feet. "It's only a little way farther."

We struggled on. My throat felt raw and dry. I could feel a rattling in my chest. Suddenly the sky seemed to lighten. One moment it was a faint gray, then the sun popped over the mountains behind us. I stared at it incredulously. It was coming up in the west.

Suddenly I realized what had happened. Sometime in the night we had turned around and begun to backtrack. Now we were caught in the middle of the desert in broad daylight. I turned and looked down the road toward Estanza. There was a wagon coming in the distance.

I took Amparo's hand and we ran off the road. Everything was flat; there was no real cover. I told her to lie down and I stretched out beside her. I pulled our *ruanas* up over our heads. Perhaps they would look enough like the sand to fool anyone passing by.

I heard the creaking rumble of the wheels of the wagon. I raised a tip of the blanket and peeked out. The wagon had gone by. I was already up on one knee when I saw another down the road. Quickly I fell to the ground again.

"What is it?"

"Another one."

The sun was beginning to bake the sand. The heat rose up all around us. "There's nothing we can do," I said. "We'll just have to wait for the night. There are too many people on the road."

"I'm thirsty," Amparo said.

"Lie still; try not to think about it."

I could feel the sweat running down my back and between my legs. I licked my lips. They were dry and salty. I lifted the blanket. The road seemed clear in both directions as far as my eye could see.

"All right," I said, "let's walk for a while. Put your *ruana* up again. It will keep off the sun."

The heat shimmering off the road formed wavy patterns before our eyes. My feet began to burn.

"I'm thirsty, Dax."

"We'll walk a little more," I said, "then we'll stop and rest."

We managed to go on for another half-hour. The sand was so hot now that when we stretched out on it we could scarcely bear it. My tongue felt dry and swollen. I made the saliva run in my mouth for a moment but as quickly it seemed to dry up.

"It hurts, Dax." Amparo began to cry. "My mouth hurts."

She was sobbing quietly. Her shoulders were shaking. I knew she would have to wet her lips somehow. I took out my knife and cut the edge of my finger. The blood suddenly welled up.

"Damn!"

"What did you do?" Amparo asked.

I held up my finger. "I cut myself." I pushed my finger toward her. "Suck it."

She put my finger in her mouth and sucked. After a moment she looked up. "There, is it all right?"

I looked at my finger. I squeezed it, forcing the blood to well up again. "Better do it once more to make sure."

She sucked again. This time when I held up my finger the edge of the cut was white. "It's all right now."

"Good." She lifted the blanket and looked out. "It's starting to get dark."

She was right. The day had almost gone, and night was coming. I could feel the heat beginning to leave the sand. I got up on my knees. I looked down the road that cut through the pass between the mountains. On the other side lay Estanza. "If we walk all night, we could be there by morning."

Amparo looked up at me. "Can't we get a drink of water?"

"There's none between here and Estanza."

She went over to the side of the road and sat down. "I'm tired."

"I know, Amparo." I covered her with my *ruana*. "Try to sleep a little. Tomorrow everything will be all right."

She lay back and closed her eyes. In a moment she was asleep. I tried to, too, but there was a peculiar ache in me that wouldn't let me. No matter how I turned I seemed to hurt. I let Amparo sleep for about two hours.

It was about an hour after sunup when we finally reached Señor Moncada's farm. Several horses were tethered out in front but I saw nobody. I gestured to Amparo to be quiet as we went around to the back.

There was smoke coming from the kitchen chimney. It was so strong in my nostrils that I could feel myself growing dizzy with hunger. We crossed the back yard to the kitchen door. Still holding Amparo's hand, I opened it.

It was dark and I couldn't see until my eyes adjusted, then I heard a woman scream and my vision suddenly cleared. A cook was standing near the stove, and three men were sitting at the kitchen table, two of them facing me. A third had his back to me. The red and blue of their uniforms suddenly registered.

I turned, pushing Amparo toward the door. "Run!"

She took off like a rabbit across the yard. I started after her. I heard a yell behind me and when I looked over my shoulder I tripped over a log and fell. As I scrambled up a soldier ran past me.

"Run, Amparo, run!" I screamed. "Run!"

Another soldier came up to me. I turned to face him, pulling my knife. I began to feel dizzy. Exhaustion and the long night had taken their toll. Then I saw clearly his face, and suddenly nothing remained in me but a burning rage and hatred. I felt the desire to kill rise in my throat. "Fat Cat!" I screamed, and I launched myself at him, my knife outstretched.

He had sold us out. That was why the soldiers had been able to raid our hideout. It was because of him that so many had been killed, and all for a lousy black stallion.

As I slashed upward with the knife I heard Amparo scream. I turned and saw that a soldier had caught her. He was pulling her back toward us, kicking and screaming. I began to feel dizzy again.

I turned back to Fat Cat. He was staring at me, his face white. "Dax!"

I screamed hysterically. "Dax! I'm not dead like the others! I'll kill you! I will cut off your *cojones* and stuff them down your lying throat!"

"No, Dax. No!"

"Traitor!" I took another step toward him but there was something wrong with the ground. It was rolling like the sea at Curatu, where I had once gone with my father. "Traitor!" I screamed again.

"Dax!"

But this was another voice. One I had never forgotten, though I hadn't heard it for more than two years. I looked past Fat Cat toward the kitchen door, where my father was standing. But there was something wrong. I thought I was going out of my mind. My father also was wearing an army uniform.

"*Papá!*" I cried. I took a step toward him, then I remembered Fat Cat and rage once more shook me. I turned and screamed, "I'll kill you! I'll kill you!"

I cocked my arm to throw the knife at his throat, but the sun blinded my eyes. I blinked for a moment, and suddenly everything began to fade. The knife slipped through my fingers. I felt myself falling to the ground, and then a pair of arms caught me.

The darkness started to come again and I remember thinking: how can it be night when it has just become morning?

111

Then out of this darkness came my father's voice. There was love in it. Pain. And sorrow too.

"My son," he said softly. "My son, what have I done to you?"

And then mercifully the night came and covered me.

20

The old man in the black robes leaned back in his chair and placed his fingers together judicially as he waited for my answer. His dark eyes shone behind the lenses of his spectacles.

"I will try to do better, *Monseñor*," I said.

"I hope so, Diogenes." But his voice was as lacking in conviction as mine.

School was just not for me. The routine and monotony of the classroom was too confining. Some things I liked and in those I did well. Languages. English. French. Even German. Latin was a dead language, used only by priests in their mumbo jumbo, and I couldn't have cared less about it. In the two years I had been there I had yet to pass Latin. That was the reason I stood now before *el director de la escuela*.

"Your esteemed father was one of our brightest pupils," *el director* continued pontifically. "He was second to none in his grasp of Latin. If you wish to follow in his footsteps in the practice of law, you, too, must be."

He seemed to expect an answer. "*Sí, Monseñor.*"

"You must also try to improve your grades in the other subjects." He glanced down at the report on his desk. "There are too many in which you have barely managed to receive passing marks. Grammar, literature, *historia, geografía* . . ."

I looked out the window as his voice droned on. I could see Fat Cat lounging outside the gate at the school entrance waiting for me. He made an imposing figure in his bright

112

red and blue uniform, and as usual he was the center of an admiring group of maids and governesses also awaiting their charges. But somehow I had never grown accustomed to seeing him in uniform. Especially that one. Even though the army was now ours and the general was *el Presidente*.

The revolution had been over for almost three weeks by the time Amparo and I had reached Estanza. It had taken us almost five weeks to get there, and in all that time we had not dared talk to another human being.

I remember when the general came into my room at Señor Moncada's *hacienda* several days later. I lay listlessly in the bed, still weak from the fever that had raged through my body. I had heard the sharp click of boots outside my door and turned my head to greet him. He was not a tall man but in the uniform of commander-in-chief of the army he seemed to have taken on added height.

His face was still lean and sharp, his lips thin and cruel under those strangely pale-gray eyes, as unblinking as ever. He came to the side of the bed and looked down at me. His hand was oddly gentle as he placed it on the white bed sheet over mine. "*Soldadito.*"

"*Señor General.*"

"I have come to thank you for returning my daughter to me," he said quietly.

I didn't answer. I couldn't see what he had to thank me for. There was little else I could have done.

"You saw . . ." His voice was oddly hesitant. "You saw what happened to the others?"

I nodded.

"Roberto and Eduardo. Could they still be in the mountains? We never found their bodies. All had been thrown into the fire."

"They are dead, *señor*." I had to turn my face away from the sudden pain in his eyes. "I saw them die."

"Was it . . ." Again the hesitation in his voice. "Was it swift?"

"*Sí, señor*. Like men in battle, *excelencia*, not boys. I myself saw Roberto kill two of them."

Suddenly he exploded. "Damn that Guiterrez!"

I looked at him questioningly. "*El coronel?*"

His pale eyes were glittering. "Guiterrez, the butcher of

113

Bandaya! He knew of the armistice before he went into the mountains."

"Armistice, *excelencia?*"

"A truce, *soldadito*. There was to be no fighting while the surrender was being arranged."

He turned and walked over to the window. His back was toward me as he spoke. "The war was already over when he attacked the hideout."

I closed my eyes. The whole thing then was *por nada*. They had all died for nothing. All of them. My grandfather, he, too. All because of *el coronel*. I felt a black hatred rise in me.

I heard someone in the doorway and I opened my eyes. Fat Cat came in carrying my lunch on a tray. The bandage on his dark-brown forearm where my knife had nicked him showed whitely in the darkened room.

"Well, my little fighting cock, I see you're awake."

The general's voice exploded. "What happened to the lookout? Why weren't we warned in time to flee?" He came back to the bed. "What happened?"

Fat Cat's face went suddenly white and I could see the beads of sweat standing out on his forehead. There was a look in his eyes I had never seen before. Not even when we had faced death together.

I closed my eyes again. I knew what had happened and why. Fat Cat had deserted his post. But I wasn't a child any longer. I knew that one more death could not return life to those already gone. And that even had Fat Cat been there he would only have added another corpse to the others.

I opened my eyes and looked up at the general. "I don't know, *excelencia*. I woke when I heard the first shots. When I became aware that the house was burning I went out the window into the ditch. Then I saw Amparo, and I grabbed her and we fled."

The general stared at me for a moment. "You did well." He covered my hand again, his touch curiously soft and gentle. "My sons are dead but their spirit and courage lives on—in you. I shall always think of you now as my son."

With surprise I noticed the beginning of tears in those pale-gray eyes. The general could not be crying. Men did not weep; he had told me so himself. "Thank you, *excelencia*."

He nodded and, straightening up, started for the door. He

turned at the portal and looked back. "I leave you to your lunch."

Then I remembered. "How is Amparo?"

He smiled. "She is up and about. I am taking her back to Curatu with me. Get well soon and you will join us."

I could hear his boots echoing down the hall as I turned to Fat Cat. His face was still pale but he was smiling. "You have given me back my shirt," he said.

I don't know why but suddenly I was angry. "I have given you back your head!" I pushed the tray back toward him. "Take it away, I'm not hungry."

Silently he left the room, and I turned my head toward the window. But I didn't notice the blue sky and the sunshine, nor did I hear the soft twittering of the birds. All I could see was *el coronel*, and all I could hear was that detestable voice. The black hatred again rose in me, bringing the bitter taste of bile into my mouth. If he was alive, someday I would search him out and kill him!

A few weeks later I was in Curatu. Father had found a house on the side of the hill looking out over the sea not far from where his parents had lived. Soon after that I was registered in the same Jesuit school that he had attended as a boy, and the same *monseñor* who had registered him was now impressing upon me my failures as a student.

Unwillingly I forced my attention back to his droning voice. "You show promise," he was concluding, "but you must work harder to achieve a standing over which your father can take pride."

"I will, *Monseñor*. I shall work very hard."

He smiled. *"Bueno.* Go then in peace, my son."

"Gracias, Monseñor."

I left the small room which served as his office and fled down the corridor. I blinked my eyes at the sudden brightness of the sun as Fat Cat came over from his crowd of admirers. "The car is waiting, *excelencito.*"

Ever since Estanza he no longer called me by name. I had become *"excelencito"*—little excellency. I could go nowhere, do nothing, without his being around. Once he had told me that the general and my father had assigned him to be my bodyguard and I had laughed. I did not need a bodyguard. I could take care of myself. But that hadn't changed things. Fat Cat was always around.

I looked over at the black Hudson limousine with a uniformed chauffeur seated behind the wheel. I gave Fat Cat my books. "I don't want the car. I feel like walking."

I turned and started down the hill toward the city. A moment later I heard the purr of a motor behind me. I glanced back. The car was following, crawling slowly down the hill, the chauffeur and Fat Cat in the front seat. I smiled to myself. In that at least Fat Cat hadn't changed. He would still rather ride than walk.

Later I sat on a piling at the end of the dock and watched a freighter being unloaded. I could hear the sailors cursing, the longshoremen in French and the answering insults in Spanish. My French teacher would truly be surprised at my knowledge of that language if he ever heard me repeat some of their obscenities.

I looked up at the red, white, and blue tricolor flying from the mast. There was a breeze coming in from the sea and it fluttered proudly. I surveyed the port. There were only two other ships being unloaded. One flew the flag of Panama, the other was Greek.

Before the revolution, I had been told, there were never fewer than twenty ships. Mostly *norteamericano* and English. Now both the United States and Great Britain forbade our ports to their ships. My father said it was because they had alliances with the former government and had not yet recognized our new one. I didn't see what that had to do with it. Especially when bananas rotted on the docks, they burned the sugar cane in the fields, and the coffee beans turned brown and maggoty in their bags in the warehouses.

I heard footsteps behind me and turned. Two boys were coming toward me. They wore the torn and ragged clothing that seemed the common garb in this part of the town. They stopped in front of me, and one of them took off his hat and addressed me respectfully. "A few centavos, *excelencia*, for our hunger."

I felt embarrassed. I had no money. I had no need of it. Whatever I wanted Fat Cat got for me. "I haven't any," I said curtly, to cover my embarrassment.

"Just one centavo, *señor*. For the grace of God."

I climbed down from the piling. "I'm sorry, I haven't any money."

I saw them exchange disbelieving looks. I felt strange.

They weren't much older than I and yet their manner had been subservient, almost wheedling. Now they stood directly in front of me on the narrow catwalk leading back to the main dock and there wasn't room to pass.

"Excuse me," I said.

I saw a sullen look come over their faces. They didn't move. "What do you want?" I asked. "I told you I haven't any money."

They didn't answer.

"Let me pass," I repeated, beginning to get angry. Did these fools think if I did have a few centavos I wouldn't give it to them?

"He wants to pass," the larger said mockingly. The smaller smiled nastily, and echoed the other in a mocking sissy voice.

I needed no further invitation. The pent-up rage roared inside me. A moment later the smaller one was flying from the catwalk into the water and the larger one screamed as the toe of my shoe caught him in the *cojones*. He fell to his knees on the catwalk, clutching at his groin, and as I kicked him in the side he too went over into the water.

While I stood looking down at them as they struggled toward a piling I heard footsteps behind me.

"What happened?" Fat Cat asked.

"They would not let me pass."

"*Campesinos!*" Fat Cat spat into the water after them.

I started back to the shore, Fat Cat following me. The big black limousine was waiting at the edge of the dock. I turned to Fat Cat before I got into the car.

"Why do they beg?"

"Who?"

"Them." I pointed to the two boys climbing back onto the dock.

Fat Cat shrugged. "There are always beggars."

"They said they were hungry."

"There are always the hungry."

"But there aren't supposed to be. That's what the whole revolution was about."

Fat Cat looked at me, a strange look in his eyes. "I, myself, have been in three revolutions. Yet I never knew of one that put food in the bellies of the *campesinos*. *Campesinos* are born to starve."

"Then why did we fight?"

Fat Cat smiled. "So that we would not be like them and have to beg for our bread."

I stared at him for a moment, then took my foot off the running board. "Do you have any change?"

He nodded.

I held out my hand.

He put his hand into his pocket and dropped some coins into my open palm. I closed my fist around them and walked back down the dock. The two boys watched me warily, fear clouding their eyes. The bigger one was still holding himself. The smaller spat at my feet.

"*Campesinos!*" I threw the coins down at them and turned and walked away.

21

The *Palacio del Presidente* was in the center of the town. It occupied two city blocks and was surrounded by an eighteen-foot brick-and-concrete wall, which effectively cut off the building from the streets. There were but two entrances, one on the north side facing the mountains at the rear of the city, the other on the south looking toward the sea. It was a fortress within itself. There were always guards at the iron gates and sentries who patrolled the walks atop the high walls.

By a decree of one of the former presidents, who had had a shot fired at him from a nearby building while he was walking from the *residencia* to the offices, all the buildings for two blocks square surrounding the palace had been razed. This kept any windows from overlooking the presidential enclosure. It did not, however, keep that particular president from assassination. After several months of brooding humiliation over his taking a mistress, his own wife had shot him.

The *soldados* at the South Gate snapped to attention as the big black limousine rolled through. I looked out at them carelessly from the back seat. The car turned right and headed for the *residencia*, a white stone building in the southeast corner. When it stopped in the driveway the soldiers there looked at me without curiosity, for my regular weekly visit to Amparo was by then routine.

Amparo's *apartamiento* was in the right wing. The left belonged to her father, and the center of the building contained the public rooms. I was ushered into the large corner room that served as her sitting room. As usual I had to wait. *La princesa,* as she had come to be called, was never on time.

I was standing at the window looking out on the grounds when she came in followed by her *dueña.* She came toward me in a fine white dress, her long blond hair falling to her shoulders and her hand outstretched imperiously.

As was the custom, I kissed her hand. "Amparo," I said gravely.

"Dax." She smiled. "It was good of you to come."

We said the same things each week and now we waited for *la dueña*'s customary words. They came right on schedule. "I shall leave you children to your play."

Amparo nodded. We waited until the old woman closed the door behind her, then turned to each other, grinning. In a moment we were at the window looking down.

Sure enough, *la dueña* came out the side entrance. Fat Cat was waiting there, his uniform cap in his hand, and together they turned and hurried to *la dueña*'s small apartment in the servants' building.

Amparo burst out laughing. "She waits all week for your visit."

"Not mine," I replied dryly.

She laughed again and turned to me. "Shall we watch them?"

I shook my head. I didn't feel like it today. Sometimes we would run into Amparo's bedroom, where from one window we could look down through a skylight just over the bed in *la dueña*'s room. It was dull. They always did the same thing. I couldn't understand why Fat Cat didn't get as bored with it as we did at watching them.

"What do you want to do then?"

"I don't know." I stood at the window looking out.

119

"You're not much fun."

I looked around at her. Amparo at nine was growing into a more beautiful child each time I saw her. And well aware of it. But she was alone too much. She was not allowed outside the walls of the palace. Not even to attend school. Tutors and teachers were brought in.

Every afternoon selected and approved playmates were allowed to visit. Señor Moncada's two daughters, now at a private school in Curatu, came once a week; other children of the local *aristócratas* and *políticos* also had their turn. Once a month there was a party which we all attended.

Beyond that Amparo lived in a world completely peopled by adults. There were times when I felt she was much older than I. She seemed to know so much more about what went on in the world. She was always filled with tiny malicious bits of gossip about people.

She went now to the couch and sat down. "What did the *monseñor* say to you?"

I looked at her in surprise. "How did you know he sent for me?"

She laughed. *"La dueña.* I heard her say that if it weren't for your father you would have been sent down."

"Where did she hear that?"

"From one of *Papá's* aides. *Papá* always asks for your school report."

El Presidente had many more important things on his mind than my marks at school. Why this interest in me?

"Papá thinks of you often. He says that if my brothers had lived they would have been like you." She looked down at her hands, and a wistful note came into her voice. "Sometimes I wish I had been a boy. Then maybe *Papá* wouldn't feel so badly."

"He would rather have you than any of them," I said.

Her face brightened. "Do you really think so?"

"Of course."

"I'm going to be very smart, he'll see. I'll be able to do as much as any boy."

"I'm sure you will," I answered. It was always safe to agree with Amparo. That way we didn't get into any arguments.

"When are you leaving for Paris?"

This time I was really surprised. "Paris?"

"You're going to Paris," she said positively. "I heard my

120

father say so. Your father is going there on a trade mission. *Los Estados Unidos* and Great Britain refuse to send their ships to trade with us. We must find new markets for our products or we will not survive. France seems most logical."

"Perhaps my father is going without me."

She shook her head. "No. He will be gone for several years. Besides, I heard *Papá* say that he will arrange for you to attend a school there."

"It's funny he never said anything to me."

"It was only settled this morning," she said. "I heard them talking at breakfast."

I thought of the French freighter I had seen at the docks. I wondered if we might be sailing on her. I walked to the window and looked out toward the port. I couldn't see her at the pier. She must already have gone.

Amparo came and stood beside me. "Shall we go outside for a walk?"

"If you like."

We went downstairs and out her private entrance, which opened onto a small garden. As we came out of the building two soldiers fell in behind us just out of earshot. We went through the iron gate and strolled down the path toward the *administración* building. Soldiers snapped to attention and saluted as we passed.

A car had pulled up in front of the "little palace," as the guest house was now called. A man got out and hurried into the building. I couldn't see his face. "Who was that?"

Amparo shrugged. "I have seen him several times. I think he is the manager of La Cora."

I knew who La Cora was. She was the latest in a series of residents of the little palace. *El Presidente* liked to have things brought to him.

"I don't think he will be going there much longer," Amparo said suddenly.

"Why?"

"I think *Papá* is already getting bored with La Cora. He has had dinner with me almost every night this week." There was a faintly malicious sound of triumph in her voice.

I knew, of course, about the women who had come to the little palace in a steady procession. They stayed an average of six weeks, then disappeared. A few days later another would appear. Our *Presidente* was a man of diversified

121

tastes. La Cora had lasted longer than most; she had been in residence almost two months. "I wonder what she looks like."

"She's not very pretty," Amparo replied disdainfully.

"I heard she was."

"I don't think so," Amparo answered. "She has big *tetas*. They're out to here." She held her hands out a foot in front of her chest.

"I like big *tetas*."

She looked down at herself. Her own breasts were just beginning to form. "I shall have big *tetas*," she said, "bigger than hers."

"I'm sure you will," I answered soothingly.

"Would you like to see her?"

"Yes."

Amparo turned and walked up to the entrance of the little palace. The soldier on duty saluted, then opened the door. We went into the house, where a majordomo greeted us.

Amparo looked down her nose at him. "I have come to call on La Cora."

The servant stood there hesitantly. I could see that he did not know what to do. Amparo, however, was used to having her own way. "I am not used to waiting!"

The majordomo bowed. "Of course, *Princesa*. If you will follow me?"

He led us to an *apartamiento* in the left wing of the building, and paused outside the door. Through it we could hear the faint murmur of voices. He knocked.

The voices fell silent. A moment later a woman called, "Who is it?"

"*La princesa está aquí*."

"*La princesa?*"

"*Sí, señorita*. She wishes to see you."

There was a quick murmur of voices again, and the door opened. A tall woman with large dark eyes and black hair gathered into a chignon stood in the doorway. She looked at Amparo, then stepped back. "I am honored, *Princesa*."

Amparo swept into the room as if it were her own. "I thought it might be nice if we had tea together."

The woman glanced at the man by the window fleetingly. I saw him nod impersonally. His face was thin and he wore a Vandyke beard. His eyes were very dark and glittered.

"It will be my pleasure, *Princesa*." La Cora clapped her

122

hands, and the majordomo came to the door. "Tea, please, Juan."

Amparo said, "I would like to present my friend, Don Diogenes Alejandro Xenos."

La Cora curtsied, and I bowed. "My pleasure, *señorita.*"

"May I present my manager, Señor Guardas?"

The manager bowed, his heels clicking audibly in the military fashion. *"A su servicio."* He straightened up and looked at La Cora. "I trust you can persuade his excellency to attend. I have arranged a special entertainment for tonight."

"He will attend."

Señor Guardas walked to the door. "I must now excuse myself. I have many pressing engagements."

Amparo nodded, and he bowed again as he went out the door. I watched until it had closed behind him. There was no doubt in my mind that he had once been a soldier. It showed in his carriage, the military cadence of his walk.

La Cora pulled her peignoir closer around her and touched her hair. "Had I known of your visit, *Princesa,* I would have made myself more presentable. If you could grant me a moment perhaps I could change into something more suitable?"

"Of course."

Amparo turned to me as soon as La Cora had left the room. "She does have big *tetas,* doesn't she?" she whispered.

I suddenly heard a voice through the open window. I walked over and looked out. I couldn't see who was speaking, for whoever it was was directly beneath the window and hidden from my view. But the voice was oddly familiar.

"La bomba must be placed on the table exactly at midnight!"

The answering voice was indistinguishable. "It will be done, *excelencia.*"

"See to it. There must be no blunders!"

There was a moment's silence, then two men came into view. One was the majordomo, the other Señor Guardas. The majordomo's hand came up in a half salute as Señor Guardas turned and hurried off. No wonder the voice had seemed familiar; I had heard it only a moment before. I turned to Amparo.

123

She was studying herself in the mirror. "Do you think my *tetas* will get to be as big as La Cora's?"

"I think so," I replied dryly.

She saw my face in the mirror. "What is puzzling you?"

"They must be having a big entertainment tonight," I said. "They're even having firecrackers on the table."

"Where did you hear that?"

"Just now. I heard La Cora's manager giving the instructions to the majordomo. He wanted *la bomba* placed on the table exactly at midnight. I wonder what sort of entertainment they are going to have?"

La Cora's voice came from the doorway. "It is actually only a simple little party for *el Presidente* and a few members of the cabinet. We honor the beginning of his third year as our leader and benefactor."

"Oh, then that must be the reason for *la bomba* at midnight."

La Cora laughed. "The way you say it makes it sound most ominous. Actually, it's to be molded of ice cream."

"That's a very clever idea," I said. "*La bomba de helado.*"

La Cora looked over at Amparo. "You know how your father loves ice cream."

Just then the majordomo came into the room with the tea tray.

"I've changed my mind," Amparo said suddenly. "I've just remembered I have to be back at the *residencia*. Are you coming, Dax?"

I looked at La Cora apologetically, then hurried after Amparo, who was already disappearing down the hallway. I caught up to her just before she reached the front door. "What are you so angry about?" I asked, holding it open for her.

"I hate her!"

The two soldiers fell in behind us as we walked off toward the *residencia*. "Why?" I asked. "What has she ever done to you?"

Amparo looked at me coldly. "You're like all men. You see nothing but a big pair of *tetas*."

"That's not true."

"It is! I saw the way you were drooling. You couldn't look anywhere else."

"What did you expect me to do?" I asked. "There wasn't much else to look at."

Amparo stopped as we started up the walk to her private entrance. "You never looked at me like that."

"I will," I promised, "when you grow up."

"If you were a gentleman you would look at me that way now!"

I looked at her. Then in spite of myself I had to laugh.

"What are you laughing at?"

"There's nothing to look at."

I saw her hand coming and I caught it just before it could slap me. "Why do you want to do that?"

Her eyes flashed angrily. "I hate you!" She pulled her hand away from mine and drew herself up haughtily. "I never want to see you again!"

I shrugged and started down the walk.

"Dax!"

"Yes?"

She held out her hand. "You didn't kiss me good-bye."

22

I felt a rough hand shaking my shoulder. I rolled away from it and burrowed back under the sheets. They were soft and warm. I didn't want to go to school. I might even plead illness.

"Wake up, Dax!" Fat Cat's voice was harsh, urgent.

My subconscious identified the sound. I had heard it before. In the jungle, in the mountains. It meant danger. I sat up in bed, wide awake now. Night was still outside the windows. "What is it?"

Fat Cat's face was tense. "Your father wants to see you right away!"

I glanced out the window, then back at him. "Now?"

"*Inmediatamente!*"

I was out of the bed and dressing. I glanced at the clock; it was two in the morning. I felt a cold dread creep over me. I shivered as I buttoned my shirt. "He has been hurt! He is dying!"

Fat Cat remained grim and silent.

I stared at him as he handed me my jacket. "*La bomba!*"

I saw the surprise come into his face. I spoke again before he could. "*La bomba de helado! Asesinato!*"

He crossed himself quickly. "You knew?"

I grabbed his hand. "Is my father alive? Tell me!"

"He is alive. But we must hurry."

The chauffeur was behind the wheel of the big black Hudson, the motor racing. We got in silently and immediately we roared out the driveway toward the *Palacio del Presidente*. The guards waved us through without the usual identification.

I was out of the car and inside before Fat Cat was off the seat. The foyer was crowded with men. I saw *el Presidente* sitting in a chair in the corner. He was bare to the waist and a doctor was winding a bandage around the upper part of his chest. His face was white and drawn as he looked at me.

"Where is my father?"

He gestured toward La Cora's *apartamiento*. "In the bedroom."

Without another word I ran out the door toward the *apartamiento*. The first room was the living room, where Amparo and I had been earlier that day. Plaster and dust were everywhere. Half the far wall had been blown inward. I ran through what was left of the doorway to the dining room.

It was completely wrecked. The big windows and French doors were blasted open to the night. Tables and chairs everywhere were broken into fragments. The bodies of two men still lay on the floor but I didn't waste even a look at them.

I went through another doorway into a small foyer. There was a closed door at the opposite end which two soldiers were guarding. One of them opened the door when he saw me.

I came to a dead stop in the doorway. Two priests were already there; a portable altar had been set up at the foot of the bed and the flickering light of the candle cast a wavering shadow of a crucifix onto the wall. One was kneeling before the altar; the other, bending over the bed, held a crucifix above my father's face. On the opposite side of the bed was a doctor, a hypodermic needle in his hand.

My legs were suddenly leaden. I stumbled as I came into the room and caught a chair to right myself. *"Papá!"*

Then I was at the side of the bed, tears running down my cheeks. His face was ashen gray and I could feel the cold sweat on his cheek as I bent to kiss him. He didn't move.

I looked at the doctor. "He's dead!"

The doctor shook his head.

"Don't lie to me!" I shouted. "He's dead!"

I put my hands under my father's shoulders to lift him. My father groaned and I lowered my hands as if I had been scorched. There was an empty space on his left side. I stared at the doctor. "Where is his arm?"

The doctor's face was expressionless. "It was blown off by the explosion."

I sensed a flicker of light coming from over my head and, looking up, I saw that the canopy over the bed was mirrored. I could see the weird shapes we made as we stood about the bed. Slowly I looked around the room. It was all red velvet and gilt. On the walls hung paintings of nude men and women. And in each corner were statues of couples in obscene embrace.

My father groaned again. I looked down at him. The beads of sweat stood out on his forehead. The doctor leaned over and wiped them away as I slowly got to my feet. "Take him out of here!"

"No," the doctor said, "it is dangerous to move him."

"I don't care!" I shouted. "Take him out of here! I won't have him die here in this whore's room!"

I felt the priest's hands on my shoulders. "My son—"

I shook myself free. "I want him out of here! A harlot's bed is no place for a man to die!"

The doctor started to speak, then fell silent as a voice came from behind me. It was *el Presidente*'s. He stood in the open doorway, the bandage still around his naked chest. "The child is father to the man," he said. "You will do as the boy commands."

"But—" the doctor protested.

"He will be taken, bed and all, to my own room in the *residencia!*"

El Presidente's voice was final and commanding. He gestured to the soldiers in the hallway behind him. They covered *Papá* with more blankets. It took ten of them to lift the heavy bed and carry it out of the house and down the walk to the *residencia*. Fat Cat and I followed silently, and it wasn't until I had seen my father moved into *el Presidente's* own chamber that I turned to the priest who had come from La Cora's bedroom with us. "Now, *Padre*, I shall pray!"

The faint light of morning was just coming into the room when *el Presidente* opened the door an hour later. He stood looking at me for a moment, then crossed to the bed where my father lay. I watched him as he stood there silently. His face showed no expression.

Then he turned. "Come, *soldadito*. It is time for breakfast."

I shook my head.

"You can leave him. He will live."

I looked into his eyes.

"I would not lie to you," he said quietly. "He will live."

I believed him. He put an arm around my shoulder as we started out of the room. In the doorway I looked back. My father seemed to be sleeping. I could see the rise and fall of the white coverlet over his chest.

We went downstairs. The smell of hot food came to my nostrils, and suddenly I was hungry. I sat down at the table in the dining room and a servant placed a platter of ham and eggs before me. I began to eat ravenously.

El Presidente sat in a chair at the head of the table and another servant brought him a cup of steaming coffee. He wore a loose-fitting shirt, so I could not see whether he was still bandaged, but he moved his arm awkwardly as he lifted the cup.

"Now do you feel better?" he asked as I pushed back my empty plate.

I nodded. A servant put a cup of *café con leche* before me. I raised it to my lips. The coffee was hot and good. I sipped it, then put the cup down. "What happened to La Cora?"

El Presidente's eyes flamed. "*La puta*, she got away!"

"How?"

"She left the room when the ice cream was placed upon the table. She said she wished to freshen up, but instead she left the grounds immediately in a black car. She and another, a man with a beard, were in the back seat. Her majordomo was driving." He picked up his coffee cup again. "But we will find her, and when we do—"

"Didn't the guards stop the car?"

"No, and already they have paid for their carelessness!"

"The bomb was in the ice cream?"

A surprised look came over his face. "How did you know?"

I told him of the conversation I had overheard yesterday under La Cora's window. He sat silently all through my accounting. When I had finished a knock came at the door. He nodded to a servant, who went to the door.

An army officer, a captain, entered and saluted. *El Presidente* negligently returned the salute.

"We have found La Cora and the majordomo, *excelencia*."

"*Bueno*." El Presidente rose to his feet. "I personally shall attend to those two."

"They are already dead, *excelencia*."

"I said I wanted them alive!" *el Presidente* shouted angrily.

"They were already dead when we discovered them, *excelencia*. They were in the black car in which they had made their escape. They had been shot, and their throats were also slit."

"Where was the car found?"

"*La Calle del Paredos, Presidente*."

I knew the road. It led from the mountains to the docks.

"Where on the road?"

"Near the bay."

"And the man with the beard?"

"There was no sign of him. We searched the whole area, even the docks. He had vanished."

El Presidente was silent for a moment, then nodded. "Thank you, *Capitán*."

He turned to me. "Now it is time for you to rest. I have had a guest room prepared for you. You will live here with us until your father has completely recovered."

I slept fitfully, and I was troubled by dreams. And in one of them I was back in the yard of my grandfather's house. The sun was white hot and I could feel it burning into my brain as I kept hearing an oddly familiar voice. "There is one bullet left in the gun. You will kill him!"

I rolled over and sat up erect in the bed, my eyes wide and staring. It was late afternoon, and suddenly I knew where I had heard that voice. La Cora's manager, Señor Guardas, the man with the beard, was Coronel Guiterrez.

I jumped out of bed and began to dress quickly. I didn't know how, but this time I would find him. This time he would not get away. Because I would kill him.

Fat Cat fell in behind me as I came out of the room. I walked down the hall and stuck my head into my father's room. "How is he?"

"He is still asleep," the doctor said.

I turned and continued down the corridor toward the staircase. Amparo was coming up as I started down. Her hand stopped me. For once she wasn't playing the princess. "Is your *papá* all right?"

"Yes. He is sleeping."

"You were asleep, too," Amparo said. "I wanted you to have lunch with me."

"Later," I replied, starting down the steps again. "I have work to do."

I went out the front door and signaled for the car.

"Where are we going?" Fat Cat asked.

"To the docks."

I didn't wait for him to open the door. I jumped in and he climbed quickly into the front seat. He twisted around as the car began to move. "What for?"

"To find the man with the beard, the one who got away."

"How can you do that? The *policía* and *el militar* have searched the whole city. They could not find a trace of him."

I shrugged and directed the car to the pier where I had been yesterday. I walked down the dock to the catwalk. The same two boys were there, fishing around the piling.

"Campesinos!"

They looked up, their faces sullen. They exchanged looks, then concentrated again on their fishing.

"Campesinos!" I called again. "Yesterday you begged for a few centavos. Today I bring you one hundred pesos!"

This time they didn't look away, but stared up at me with disbelief in their eyes.

"Come up, I will not harm you."

They hesitated a moment, then laying down their fishing poles, came up onto the catwalk. The older boy took off his hat. "What is it you wish from us, *excelencia?*"

"To find a man." I gave them a brief description of La Cora's manager, Vandyke and all. "Sometime last night he was in this neighborhood. I wish to discover where he is now."

They looked at each other. "Such a man would be hard to find, *excelencia.*"

"Harder to find than one hundred pesos?" I asked.

"La policia has already been looking for such a man," the bigger one said. "They did not find him."

"They did not offer one hundred pesos for information," I answered, and started back to the car.

"We do not wish trouble with the authorities, *excelencia.*"

I turned. "There will be no trouble."

The two looked at each other. "We will see what we can discover."

"Bueno. I shall be back in two hours. If you bring me information you will be richer by one hundred pesos."

I walked back to the car. Fat Cat looked at me with a curious respect in his eyes. "Do you think they will find out anything?"

"If they are as hungry as you say they are, they will. Now take me home. I must get money."

I went straight to my father's den. I knew where he kept the small iron box—in the bottom drawer of his desk. The key was in a drawer on the opposite side. I opened the box and took out one hundred pesos. Then, because I was suddenly hungry, I went down to the kitchen and asked the cook to give me something to eat.

At four-thirty in the afternoon I got out of the car with Fat Cat and walked out on the dock.

131

"I told you they would find nothing," Fat Cat said smugly. "See, they are not even here."

"They will come."

We went back to the car and waited. It was almost twenty minutes before they did. Then they appeared in the mouth of the alley across the street, where they whistled, gestured, and disappeared. I crossed the street, Fat Cat right behind me, and walked back in the alley where we could not be seen from the street.

"Have you the money?" the older asked.

I took the hundred pesos from my pocket. "Do you have the information?"

"How do we know you will give us the money?"

"How do I know you will tell the truth after you receive the money?"

They looked at each other and shrugged.

"We are forced to trust one another."

The older one nodded. "At three this morning such a man as you describe boarded a ship at Pier Seven. The one flying the flag of Panama."

"If you have lied to me you'll pay for it!"

"We have not lied, *excelencia*."

I gave them the money, then turned and ran out the alley. At Pier Seven I got out of the car and located the ship, then started up the gangplank. But the sailor on duty at the top of the gangplank stopped me.

"We sail in an hour," he said abruptly. "No visitors."

"Come on," I said to Fat Cat, and started back down the gangplank.

I didn't even wait for the car to stop. I ran down the path and past the guards to the office of the president. *El Presidente* looked up from his desk in surprise. There were several men gathered around him, but I didn't give them a chance to speak.

"I know where Coronel Guiterrez is!"

"What has Guiterrez to do with this interruption?"

"He is also Señor Guardas," I said. "The man with the beard, the one who escaped."

El Presidente did not hesitate. He picked up the telephone on his desk. "Tell Capitán Borja to have a squad ready at the entrance to the office building immediately!"

He turned back to me. "Where?"

"On a Panamanian ship at Pier Seven. We must hurry; they sail in less than an hour."

El Presidente started toward the door.

"But we dare not delay the sailing of a ship, *excelencia*," one of the others protested. "It would be a violation of our international agreements!"

El Presidente turned to him angrily. "To hell with international agreements!" Then he smiled. "Besides, who would dare protest a visit from the head of state? It will be an honor." He put a hand on my shoulder and pushed me out the door in front of him.

The ship's captain was obviously upset. "I beg your excellency's indulgence. If we lose this tide we sail a half-day behind schedule."

But *el Presidente* was very suave. "Surely your government would be even more upset if you refused me an inspection of your ship, which I so greatly admire? I have heard much about the wonderful fleet of your great country."

"But, your excellency—"

El Presidente's voice turned suddenly harsh. "*Capitán*, I must insist. Either I inspect your ship or I impound it on charges that you have violated our hospitality by giving refuge to an *asesino*, an enemy of our country!"

"But we carry no passengers, your excellency. Only the crew, who have been with the ship since we sailed from our home port more than four weeks ago."

"Have the crew stand for inspection then!"

The captain hesitated.

"Now!" *el Presidente* ordered.

The captain turned to his first mate. "Pipe all hands to the bow deck."

A moment later the crew began to assemble. There were thirty-two of them and they formed a ragged double line down the center of the deck.

"Attention!"

The lines straightened up. The men stared straight ahead.

"Is this all the crew?" *el Presidente* demanded.

The ship's captain nodded. "*Sí, excelencia.*"

El Presidente turned to Capitán Borja. "Take a detail of two and search the ship. Make certain no one has hidden out below decks."

The captain saluted and marched off with two of his men.

The remaining soldiers stood at the ready as *el Presidente* turned to me. "Now we will look into their faces, eh? The bearded one should not be difficult to recognize."

But it wasn't that easy. None of the men wore a beard. As we started down the line a second time in silence Capitán Borja reappeared. He reported that there were no other men aboard.

"Do you spot him?" *El Presidente's* voice was worried.

I shook my head. But my two informants couldn't have made up a story like that. They weren't smart enough.

The ship's captain came forward. There was a faint note of triumph in his voice. "I trust your highness is now satisfied?"

El Presidente did not answer. He looked at me, and I exclaimed, "No! He is here, he has to be! He obviously has shaved off his beard."

"Then how will you know him?"

I gestured and *el Presidente* bent toward me so I could whisper into his ear. He smiled and nodded. He turned back to the first man in the line. *"Como se llama usted?"*

The sailor remained at attention. "Diego Cárdenas, *excelencia.*"

El Presidente continued to the next man. *"Se llama usted?"*

"Jesu María Luna, *excelencia.*"

Soon we were a third of the way down the line. *El Presidente* paused in front of a slim man dressed in the dirty clothing of an oiler. His face was covered with grease; even his hair was dirty.

"Se llama usted?"

The man glanced at me, hesitated, then spoke in a harsh voice. "Juan Rosario."

El Presidente had already gone on to the next man, but I turned. "Juan Rosario what?"

"Rosario y Guard—" His voice broke suddenly, and he lunged at me, his hands at my throat. *"Bastardo negro!* Twice I should have killed you! This time I shall!"

I clawed at his hands, trying to free them from my neck. I could feel a burning in my lungs and my eyes began to pop. Then Fat Cat moved in behind him, and the grip on my throat was suddenly broken.

I stood there fighting for breath as I glared down at the man on the deck. He shook his head, rolled over, and glared

134

back. His eyes were the same. Cold and cruel and implacable. He might change the color of his hair, shave his beard, even deepen his voice, but he could never alter those eyes. The one glance he had directed at me had given him away.

I loosened my jacket and reached for the knife I had concealed in my belt. I flat-edged the blade and went for his throat as I would for the neck of a chicken, but a pair of hands caught me before I could reach him. I looked up into the face of *el Presidente*. His voice was calm, almost gentle. "There is no need for you to kill him," he said. "You are no longer in the jungle."

Three months later I stood at the rail of another ship as we pulled away from the pier. I looked down and saw Amparo jumping up and down and waving. I waved back. "*Adiós*, Amparo. Good-bye!"

She waved and shouted something back but there was so much noise I couldn't catch it. Slowly the ship moved out into the channel. Now the crowd on the dock had blurred into a single colorful mass. Behind them I could see the city and behind that the mountains, rich and green in the afternoon sun.

I felt my father's arm on my shoulder, and he pressed me to his side. I looked up at him. His face was still thin and he was not yet used to the vacant sleeve on his left side, but his eyes were soft and clear and filled with a look I had never seen before.

"Look well, my son," he said, his good arm holding me tightly against his side. "We are going to another world."

Out of the corner of my eye I could see Fat Cat, and then my father spoke again and I looked back toward land.

"An old world that will be new to both of us," he continued. "So look well, my son, and remember the city and the mountains and the plains of your native land. For when you return you will no longer be a boy. You will be a man!"

BOOK
2

POWER
and
MONEY

1

Efficiently the doctor withdrew the hypodermic needle. He turned to the youth standing at the foot of the bed. "It will make him sleep, Dax, help him conserve his strength for the crisis that may come tonight."

The boy did not answer immediately. Instead he walked around to the other side of the bed and with a touch as tender as a woman's wiped away the moisture from his father's forehead. "But he will die anyway," he said quietly, without looking up.

The doctor hesitated. "One never knows. Your father has fooled us before. It is all in the hands of God." He felt the impact of the boy's dark-brown eyes. They looked deep and seemed to see into him.

"We have a saying in the jungles," Dax said. "For a man to place his fate in the hands of God he must be a tree. Only the trees believe in God."

The boy's voice was soft and the doctor still couldn't get used to the soft, slurring, almost accent-free French. He still remembered the struggle the boy had with the language when he had first met him seven years ago. "And you do not?"

"No, I have seen too many terrible things to have much faith."

Dax walked around the bed to the doctor's side and looked down at his father again. Jaime Xenos' eyes were closed; he seemed to be resting. But there was a gray pallor beneath his warm dark skin and his breath was heavy and labored.

"I was going to summon a priest to administer the last rites," the doctor said. "Do you prefer that I do not?"

Dax shrugged. He looked at the doctor. "It is not what I prefer that is important. What is important is that my father believes."

The doctor snapped his bag shut. "I will come back this evening after dinner."

Dax, with a last look at the bed, followed the doctor out into the hall.

When the front door of the consulate closed behind the doctor, Dax turned and went into his father's office. Fat Cat and Marcel Campion, his father's young French secretary and translator, came forward questioningly. Dax shook his head silently and crossed to the desk. He took a thin brown *cigarrillo* from the box and lit it.

"You'd better send a cable to *el Presidente*," he said to Marcel. His voice was flat, controlled. "Father dying. Please advise."

The secretary nodded and quickly left the room. A moment later the click of a typewriter came faintly through the closed door. Fat Cat cursed angrily. "By the blood of the Virgin! So this is where it ends. In this cold accursed land."

Dax did not answer. Instead he went over to the window and looked out. Dusk was falling and it had begun to rain. The rain softened the dirty gray-black buildings down the street toward Montmartre. Somehow it seemed always to be raining in Paris.

Just as it had been that night they first came here from Corteguay seven years ago. They had looked like a group of country bumpkins, their collars pulled up against their faces as ineffective shields against the sleeting February rain, their luggage piled high on the sidewalk behind them where the cabby had dropped it.

"The damn gate is locked!" Fat Cat had called back to them. "There's nobody in the house."

"Try the bell again. There has to be someone there."

Fat Cat reached up and pulled the bell handle. The clang filled the narrow street and echoed from house to house. But still there was no answer.

"I can open the gate."

"Open it then! What are you waiting for?"

Fat Cat's movements were almost too fast for the eye to follow. The automatic was smoking in his hand and the reverberations were like thunder in the night.

"Fool!" Dax's father had said angrily. "Now the police will come and the whole world will know we couldn't get

140

into our own consulate! How they'll all laugh at us." He looked at the gate. "And for nothing. It's still closed."

"No it's not," Fat Cat replied, touching it with his foot.

It had swung open creakingly on its rusty hinges. Xenos looked at him for a moment, then started through, but Fat Cat's arm blocked his path.

"'I don't like it. There is a stink to it. Better I go first."

"Nonsense, what could be wrong?"

"There is much that is wrong already," Fat Cat pointed out. "Ramírez should be here, yet the house is deserted. It could be a trap. Ramírez may have sold us out."

"Nonsense! Ramírez would never do that. *El Presidente* gave him the post at my own recommendation."

Still, he stood to one side and let Fat Cat lead the way up the path to the house. The grass and weeds had overgrown everything and they felt them tugging damply at their ankles. Unconsciously, Dax's voice fell to a whisper. "Do you think the front door is locked, too?"

"We'll see." Fat Cat waved them to the side of the build-ing, then, flattening himself, he reached out carefully and turned the knob.

The door had swung open silently. They peered into the darkness inside but could distinguish nothing. Fat Cat ges-tured to them, and the automatic appeared suddenly again in his hand. His lips moved in a soft whisper. "I go with God!"

They could hear him stumbling about in the darkness and the sound of muffled curses, then his voice came to them al-most as the lights went on. "There is nobody here."

They stood there blinking. It was as if a tornado had ripped through the rooms. There was litter everywhere, pa-pers scattered over the floor, remnants of broken chairs piled in the middle of the room. A table in the kitchen proved to be the only furniture left in the house.

"Looters have been here," Fat Cat said.

Dax's father looked at him. There was a strange expression of hurt in the older man's eyes. As if he still could not be-lieve what he saw. Finally he spoke. "Not looters," he said sadly. "Traitors."

Silently Fat Cat rolled a cigarette as he watched Dax's fa-ther pick up a piece of paper from the floor and study it. He lit the cigarette. "Maybe we broke into the wrong house," he offered consolingly.

Dax's father shook his head. "No, we're in the right house." He held up the paper so they could both see. It was a sheet of the official stationery of Corteguay.

Dax looked at his father. "I'm tired."

The older man reached his arm out and drew his son close. He glanced around the room for a moment, then back at Dax. "We can't stay here, we'll go to a hotel for the night. I noticed a *pensión* at the foot of the hill as we came up. Come along. I doubt they can feed us but at least we'll get a decent night's rest."

The neatly dressed maid had curtsied as she opened the door. *"Bon soir, messieurs."*

Dax's father wiped his feet carefully on the doormat before entering. He took off his hat. "Do you have three rooms for the night?"

A bewildered look came over the maid's face. She glanced at Fat Cat, standing just behind the consul, his arms filled with luggage. Then she looked down at Dax. "Do you have an appointment?" she asked politely.

Now it was their turn to be confused. *"Rendez-vous?* You mean a reservation?" Dax's father searched his limited French for the right words. *"C'est nécessaire?"*

This had proved too much for the maid. She opened a door off the small foyer. "If you will be kind enough to wait in here, I shall call Madame Blanchette."

"Merci." Dax's father led the way in, and the maid closed the door behind them. From somewhere in the house they heard a faint sound of a woman's laughter. The room was elaborately furnished, with rich deep carpeting and soft upholstered couches and chairs. A fire glowed warmly, and on the sideboard there was a decanter of brandy and glasses.

A happy sound came deep from Fat Cat's throat. "This is more like it," he said, walking over to the sideboard. He looked back at the consul. "Excellency, may I pour you a brandy?"

"I don't know whether we should. After all, we don't know whom the brandy is set out for."

"For the guests." Fat Cat's logic was irrefutable. "Otherwise why would it be here?"

He poured the older man a glass and drank his own in one gulp. "Ahh, that's good." Quickly he poured himself another.

142

Dax sank into a chair in front of the fire. The warmth of the flames reached out and licked his face. He felt his eyes grow heavy with drowsiness.

The door opened and the maid ushered a handsome middle-aged woman into the room. She was faultlessly dressed in a dark velvet gown, a double strand of rose pearls around her throat and a large diamond in a gold setting sparkling on her finger.

Dax's father bowed. "Jaime Xenos."

"Monsieur Xenos." She glanced at Fat Cat, then at Dax. If she objected to Fat Cat's helping himself to the brandy she gave no hint of it. "What can I do for you gentlemen?"

"We need lodging for the night," Dax's father said. "We're from the Corteguayan consulate up the street, but something seems to have gone wrong. There is nobody there."

The woman's voice was extremely polite. "May I see your passports, *monsieur?* It is a regulation."

"Of course." Dax's father handed her the red leather-covered passports.

Madame Blanchette studied them for a moment, then nodded toward Dax. "Your son?"

"Oui. And my *attaché militaire."*

Fat Cat looked pleased at his elevation, and quickly poured himself another brandy.

"You're the new consul?"

"Oui, madame."

Madame Blanchette returned the passports. She hesitated a moment, then spoke. "If your excellency will excuse me for a moment I shall go and see if there are any rooms available. It is late and we are rather heavily booked."

The consul bowed again. *"Merci, madame.* I am grateful for your kindness."

Madame Blanchette closed the door behind her and stood in the foyer for a moment. Then she shrugged her shoulders and went down the hall and opened a door into a room furnished even more richly than the one she had just left.

In the center of it was a gaming table, and at the table five men sat playing cards. Behind them stood several beautiful young women, dressed in the latest fashion. Two other girls sat conversing on a couch near the fire.

"Banco," one of the players called.

"Damn!" answered another, throwing down his cards. He looked up at Madame Blanchette. "Was it anyone interesting?"

"I don't know, Baron," she replied. "It was the new Corteguayan consul."

"What did he want? Information about that rascal Ramírez?"

"No," she replied, "he wanted rooms for the night."

The player who had just bought the bank chuckled. "The poor man probably saw your sign. I told you it would happen sooner or later."

"Why didn't you just send him away?" the baron asked.

"I don't know," Madame Blanchette answered in a puzzled voice. "That was what I intended to do. But when I saw the little boy—"

"He has his son with him?" the baron asked.

"Oui." She hesitated a moment, then turned to the door. "I guess there is nothing I can do."

"Un moment." Baron de Coyne was on his feet. "I would like to see them myself."

"What's the matter, Baron?" the player on his left asked. "Hasn't Ramírez stuck you for enough at this very table? He owed you more than any of us—at least one hundred thousand francs."

"Yes," agreed the banker. "Do you think you can get it back from the new consul? We all know that Corteguay is broke."

Baron de Coyne looked down at his friends. "You are a bunch of cynics," he said. "I'm merely curious to see what kind of a man they have sent us this time."

"What difference does it make? They are all the same. All they really want is our money."

"Do you wish to meet him, your excellency?" Madame Blanchette asked.

The baron shook his head. "No, just to look at them."

He followed her to the adjoining wall, and she drew back a drape. There was a small glass in the wall. "You can see them from here," she said, "but they cannot see us. There is a mirror on their side."

The baron nodded and looked into the room. The first thing that he saw was the boy asleep on the couch, his child's face drawn and tired.

"He's just about my own son's age," he said to Madame Blanchette in surprise. "The child's mother must be dead or he would not be with his father like this. Does anyone know where Ramírez has gone?"

Madame Blanchette shrugged. "There's been some talk that he has a place on the Italian Riviera, though no one knows for sure. One night last week a truck removed everything from the embassy."

The baron's mouth tightened. So that was why they had come looking for a room. If he knew Ramírez, there wouldn't be even a stick of firewood left. As he watched, the tall man walked over to the couch and put a pillow under the boy's head. There was a curiously gentle expression on his dark face.

The baron dropped the drape and turned back to Madame Blanchette. He had seen as much as he wanted. The poor man would have enough troubles once the word got around that a new Corteguayan consul was in Paris. Every one of Ramírez' creditors would be clamoring at his door. "Give them my suite on the third floor. I'm sure Zizi won't mind if I spend the night in her room."

2

It seemed like the middle of the night but it was actually ten o'clock in the morning when Marcel Campion heard the knock at his door. He rolled over and put the pillow over his head. But even through that he could hear the shrill voice of his landlady.

"All right, all right!" he shouted, sitting up. "Come back later. I'll have the rent then, I promise you!"

"There's a telephone call for you, *monsieur*."

"For me?" Marcel's brow knitted as he tried to think who

might be calling him. He got out of the bed. "Tell them to hold on, I'll be right down."

Sleepily he staggered over to the washstand and poured water into the basin and splashed its coldness over his face. His bloodshot eyes stared balefully back at him from the tiny mirror. Vaguely he tried to remember what kind of wine he had been drinking last night. Whatever it was, it must have been awful, but at least it had been very cheap.

He patted his face dry with a rough towel and, slipping into his robe, went down the stairs. The *concierge* was behind her desk as he picked up the telephone. She tried to pretend she was not listening but he knew she was.

"*Allô?*"

"Monsieur Campion?" asked a bright fresh female voice. "*Oui.*"

"Hold on a moment, the Baron de Coyne is calling."

The baron's voice came on before Marcel had an opportunity to be surprised. "Are you the Campion employed at the Corteguayan consulate?"

"Yes, your excellency." Marcel's voice was very respectful. "But I no longer work there. The consulate is closed."

"I know that. But a new consul has just arrived. I think you should return." The baron's voice was clipped.

"But, your excellency, the previous consul still owes me three months' back salary!"

The baron was obviously not used to having his suggestions questioned. "Return to work. I shall guarantee your salary."

He rang off, leaving Marcel staring at the dead telephone. Slowly he put it down. The *concierge* came toward him smiling. "Monsieur is going back to work?"

Marcel stared at her. She knew as well as he; she had heard every word. He started for the staircase, still puzzled. The Baron de Coyne was one of the richest men in all France. Why should he be interested in a tiny country like Corteguay? Most people didn't even know where it was.

The telephone shrilled again and the *concierge* answered. She held the receiver out toward Marcel. "For you."

"*Allô?*"

"Campion," said the now almost familiar clipped voice, "I want you to go there immediately!"

146

Marcel glanced at his watch as he turned into the Rue Pelier and started up the hill. Eleven o'clock. That should be fast enough. Even for the baron.

The grocer sweeping the sidewalk in front of his stall greeted him. "*Bonjour*, Marcel," he called jovially, "what are you doing back in the neighborhood?"

"*Bonjour*. I am going to the consulate."

"Going back to work?" The grocer looked at him shrewdly. "Has that *merde* Ramírez returned? He still owes me more than seven thousand francs."

"Three thousand francs," Marcel repeated automatically. He remembered things like that.

"Three thousand, seven thousand, what's the difference? Ramírez is gone, and so is my money." The grocer leaned on the broom. "What's up?" he asked confidentially. "You can tell me."

"I don't know," Marcel answered honestly. "I just heard that a new consul had arrived. I thought I might get my old job back."

The grocer was thoughtful. "Perhaps my money is not gone after all." He looked at Marcel. "There's fifty percent in it for you if you collect for me. Fifteen hundred francs."

"Thirty-five hundred," Marcel replied automatically.

The grocer stared at him for a moment, then a broad smile cracked his face. Playfully he punched Marcel on the arm. "Ah, Marcel, Marcel. I always said they would have to get up early in the morning to beat you. Thirty-five hundred francs it is!"

Marcel continued on up the hill. He could see the consulate now. On an impulse he crossed the street before he came abreast of it. The first thing he noticed was that the gate hung open, and even from across the street he could see that the lock had been smashed. He nodded to himself. They probably had to break it to get in. He wondered what the landlord would have to say about that.

The second thing he noticed was the boy in the front garden cutting the weeds. Though it was cool he had already stripped to his undershirt, and the fine muscles in his arms rippled as he swung the broad flat blade. There was a look of grim concentration on his face.

Marcel stared at the blade in the boy's hand. He had never seen anything like it before. Then he remembered that he

147

had, in some picture that Ramírez had shown him. It was a machete. Marcel shivered. The savages used them as weapons.

His eyes turned back to the boy's face. He couldn't be French, that much was obvious. Not the expert way he handled the machete. Whoever he was he had come with the new consul. Suddenly the boy looked up and caught him staring.

The eyes were dark and challenging. Slowly the boy straightened up. The machete was still held lightly in his hand but now Marcel felt as if it were aimed right at his throat. The boy's lips tightened savagely, revealing even white teeth.

Involuntarily Marcel shivered again. Then, without even understanding why, he turned and started back down the street. He was willing to swear that he felt the boy's eyes boring into his back until he had turned the corner.

He ducked into the *brasserie*. "Cognac." He drank it quickly, then ordered a coffee. He felt the warmth of the liquor as he sipped at the coffee. If it weren't for the fact that the Baron de Coyne had personally asked him, he would never consider going back to work there. Not among such savages.

From his table Marcel saw the boy entering the grocery store across the street. Impulsively he called for his check, paid it, and crossed over. Through the open doorway he saw the boy select two loaves of bread, a piece of cheese, and a hunk of sausage. Marcel hesitated a moment, then went inside.

The boy did not look around as he came in; he was too intent on watching the grocer wrap his order.

"Three hundred francs," the grocer said.

The boy looked down at the bills in his hand. Marcel could see that he had only two hundred francs. "You'll have to take something back," he said in halting French.

As the grocer reached for the sausage, Marcel said, "Don't be such a crook. Is this the way you plan to get money from the Corteguayan consulate?"

The boy seemed to understand the reference to the consulate, but the rest of it came too fast for him. He looked at Marcel, then recognized him.

"I don't see what it matters to you, Marcel," the grocer

grumbled. But he pushed the sack back across the counter and pocketed the two hundred francs.

"*Merci*," the boy said and started out of the store.

Marcel followed him onto the sidewalk. "You have to watch them all the time," he said in Spanish. "They'll steal your eyeteeth if they think you're a foreigner."

The boy's eyes were dark and unfathomable. In a way they reminded Marcel of the eyes of a tiger he had once seen in the zoo. The same wild tawny lights glinted there. "You're with the new Corteguayan consul?"

The boy's eyes did not waver. "I am his son. Who are you?"

"Marcel Campion. I used to work at the consulate as secretary and translator."

Dax's expression did not change but Marcel sensed rather than saw the slight movement of his hand. The outline of a knife showed briefly beneath his coat. "Why were you watching me?"

"I thought perhaps the new consul could use my services. If not—" He didn't finish. The knowledge of the hidden knife was making him nervous.

"If not—what?"

"There is the matter of the three months' salary the former consul owes me," Marcel replied quickly.

"Ramírez?"

"Ramírez." Marcel nodded. "He kept promising the money would arrive next week. And then one morning I came to work and the consulate was closed."

The boy thought for a moment. "I think you'd better come and talk to my father."

Marcel glanced at the boy's hand nervously out of the corner of his eye. But the hand was empty. Something of the breath that he had withheld escaped. He relaxed. "I shall be honored."

Together they started up the street.

When they arrived at the consulate the new consul was sitting behind a spindly wooden table in the large empty front room, an angry group of men shouting and gesticulating in front of him.

"Gato Gordo!" the boy shouted, plunging through them toward his father.

A moment later Marcel felt himself flung out of the way

as a large fat man hurtled through the doorway. He was spun halfway to the floor before he regained his balance, and when he straightened up he saw that the fat man and the boy faced the crowd together, knives in their hands.

The crowd fell back. A sudden silence came into the room. Marcel saw the pallor of fear enter their faces, and he realized suddenly how afraid he himself was. For a moment they were all in another world. A world of death and violence. Paris had vanished.

And he knew somehow that this was not the first time the fat man and the boy had faced danger together. There had been many moments like this. He knew from the almost unspoken communication that seemed to flow between them. They reacted with almost one mind.

Finally one of the men spoke. "But all we wanted was our money."

In spite of himself Marcel began to smile. This was a method of refusing payment that they had never experienced before. And very effective too. He wished he could do the same with his own creditors.

The consul rose slowly to his feet. Marcel was surprised. The man was taller than he had seemed while seated. But the face was drawn and weary, a weariness more of the spirit than physical. "If you will wait outside," he said in a tired voice, "I will discuss your bills with each of you. One at a time."

The creditors turned and filed silently past Marcel. When the last of them was gone, he heard the boy's voice. "Close the door, Marcel."

This was no longer a boy's voice; it was the voice of a warrior accustomed to having his orders obeyed. Silently Marcel closed the door. When he turned back into the room the knives were gone, and the boy was behind the table, next to his father.

"Are you all right, Father?" he asked in a voice full of love and affection. In some way that Marcel did not wholly understand it was almost as if the boy were the father, the father the son.

3

In the wood-paneled office with the heavy leather furniture, the baron listened attentively from across a massive carved desk. Even with the background of the familiar sounds of the traffic outside coming from the Place Vendôme Marcel could not bring himself to believe in the reality of all that had happened in the week since he had gone back to work. But the baron's voice dragged him back from his moment of unreality. "What is the total of the unpaid bills Ramírez left behind?"

"Almost ten million francs," Marcel answered. "Eighty millions of their pesos."

As was his custom the baron automatically converted the sums into dollars and sterling. One hundred sixty thousand dollars. Forty thousand pounds sterling. He shook his head. "And the consul paid all this himself out of his personal funds?"

Marcel nodded. "He felt it was his duty. Ramírez had been his own recommendation and he felt the government was too poor to have an additional drain placed upon it."

"Where did he get the money?"

"Money changers. He paid a premium of twenty percent."

"It was after this that the consul decided to go to Ventimiglia to see if Ramírez would make some sort of restitution?"

Marcel nodded. "But by then it was too late. The five days of working in that dank, unheated house and sleeping on the cold floor with nothing but a thin blanket had taken their toll. Señor Xenos woke that morning with a bad fever. By afternoon I called the doctor and after one look he insisted that the consul go immediately to the hospital. Señor Xenos protested but in the middle of it he fainted. We carried him out to the doctor's car and off to the hospital he went."

The baron shook his head. "A man's honor is at the same time his most valuable asset and his most expensive luxury."

"I can understand the consul," Marcel said quickly. "He is one of the most honorable and idealistic men I have ever met. It is the boy who puzzles me. He is nothing like the father. Where his father is reflective; he is reflexive; where the man is emotional, the boy is controlled. He is like a young jungle animal, completely physical. In the way he moves, thinks, and acts. He has but one loyalty. To his father."

"And they went to Ventimiglia—the boy and the aide?"

Marcel nodded. He remembered when they had come back to the chilly consulate from the hospital. He had looked at the boy as the door closed behind them. Dax's face was an unreadable mask.

"I think I'd better return for credit the tickets to Ventimiglia issued to your father and myself." Marcel said.

"No." Dax's voice was sharp. He glanced at Fat Cat. Marcel suspected an invisible communication had passed between them because Fat Cat was nodding in agreement almost before Dax spoke again. "Get one more ticket. I think the three of us should pay our friend Ramírez a little visit. It is long past due."

Later they had sat on the side of the hill in the fading Riviera sunlight, looking down into the villa. There were three men seated at a table in the patio, a bottle of wine before them. In the quiet country air the faint sounds of their voices had carried to the hillside.

"Which one is Ramírez?"

"The thin wiry one in the middle," Marcel answered.

"Who are the other two?"

"Bodyguards. He is never without them."

Fat Cat cursed. "I know the big one, Sánchez. He was in *el Presidente*'s personal guard." He spat on the ground. "I always thought him a traitor!"

Some women came out into the patio bringing food. Ramírez laughed and slapped one of them on the behind as she passed.

"Who are they?" Dax asked.

Marcel shrugged. "I do not know. Ramírez always had several mistresses."

152

Dax smiled. Marcel could feel no warmth in it. "At least we know that he does not sleep with his bodyguards." The boy got to his feet. "We must discover which bedroom is his before we go there tonight."

"But how will you get in?" Marcel asked. "The gate will be locked."

Fat Cat chuckled. "That will be no problem; we'll go over the wall."

"But that's burglary," Marcel said, shocked. "We could all be sent to prison."

"And Ramírez stole the money legally?" Dax's voice was dry and filled with contempt.

Marcel did not answer.

Fat Cat leaned his back against a tree and chuckled contentedly. He reached out a hand and affectionately rumpled Dax's hair. "It is like the old days back home, eh, *jefecito?*"

"It is probably the corner room, the one with the balcony," the boy said.

As he spoke the French doors on the balcony opened and Ramírez came out. He stood there leaning against the railing, his cigarette glowing. He seemed to be looking out at the sea beyond the house. Soon a woman came out and joined him. He threw the cigarette over the side of the balcony, and they heard faintly the woman's laugh. Then Ramírez went back into the house with her. The balcony doors remained open.

"Very hospitable of the traitor," Fat Cat said. "Now we won't have to go searching through the house."

Presently the lights went out, and the house became dark. Fat Cat started to move but Dax's hand stopped him. "Give him ten minutes. By then he will be too busy to hear the sound of a thousand horses."

The boy was first on the top of the stone wall; a moment later Fat Cat was beside him. They turned to help Marcel up. Awkwardly he scrambled up beside them. They dropped silently to the ground inside. He took a deep breath and dropped beside them. His knees buckled with the contact and he sprawled, but quickly got to his feet. Dax and Fat Cat were already running toward the house on silent feet. Quickly he followed.

They went around the side of the building and before Marcel had caught up with them they were already on the roof of the veranda. First up the stone balustrade, then hoisting himself on his belly, Marcel gained the roof. Dax had already gone from there to the balcony.

Fat Cat went up alongside him without a sound, then turned and helped Marcel up. His breath sounded like thunder in his ears. It was a miracle that they could not hear him inside the house.

Dax put his mouth next to Marcel's ear. "Wait here until we signal. If you see anyone, warn us."

Marcel nodded. The sick cold feeling of fear spread in the pit of his belly. He swallowed quickly. Dax had already turned away to join Fat Cat. They flattened themselves on either side of the balcony door, their eyes tightly shut, and for a moment Marcel thought they were praying. Then he realized what they were doing; they were accustoming their eyes to the darkness they would find in Ramírez' room. Almost as one their hands moved, and Marcel saw the cold steel of their knives. He closed his eyes. Was he going to be sick? Somehow he fought the nausea down.

When he opened his eyes they were both gone, though he had not heard a sound. He listened intently, his heart beating heavily. There was a faint grunt from inside the room, a squeal from the bed, and a bump as if something had fallen to the floor. After that, nothing.

Marcel felt the sweat breaking out on his forehead. He had an impulse to flee, but his terror over what they might do if he did was greater than his fear of what might happen if he didn't.

Dax's voice was a hoarse whisper from the room. "Marcel!"

He paused in horror in the doorway. Ramírez and the woman, both naked, were lying on the floor. "Are they dead?" he asked in a shocked whisper.

"No," Dax answered contemptuously, "the traitor fainted. We had to knock out the woman. Get me something to tie them up with."

"What?"

"Go through the dresser!" Fat Cat hissed. "The woman will have silk stockings."

Frantically Marcel opened the drawers. In a second he found what he was looking for. He turned. Fat Cat was stuffing one of Ramírez' socks into the traitor's mouth. "Let him taste his own stink," he said with satisfaction.

Marcel held out the stockings wordlessly. Quickly and expertly Fat Cat trussed and gagged them. At last he finished and got to his feet. "That ought to hold them for a while." He turned to Dax. "Now what?"

"We wait until the traitor comes to," Dax said quietly, "then we find out where the money is. It won't be far off."

Dax looked at Marcel. "How much was it my father said he stole?"

"Six million francs over the last two years."

Dax looked down at Ramírez again. "Most of it should still be here. He hasn't had time to spend much of it."

Ramírez was the first to recover. He opened his eyes and saw Dax bending over him, a knife at his throat. His eyes widened in horror. For a moment it looked as if he might faint again, then he steadied and stared up at Dax.

"Traitor, can you hear me?"

Ramírez nodded. A muffled sound came from behind the gag.

"Then listen carefully," Dax continued. "We have come for the money. If we get it no harm will come to you or the woman. If not, you will spend a long time dying."

Another stifled sound came from behind the gag.

Dax raised the knife so that Ramírez could see it. "I'm going to loosen your gag. One move out of you and you will die with the blood pouring from the hole between your legs where your genitals used to be."

Marcel held his breath as Dax loosened the gag. Fortunately Ramírez was no hero.

"Now," Dax whispered, "the money?"

"It's gone!" Ramírez whispered back huskily. "The gaming tables got it all!"

Dax laughed silently. The knife moved swiftly and a thin line of blood traced a path down Ramírez' belly. There was a look of horror on the man's face at the sight of his own blood. His eyes rolled upward into his head and he slumped.

"The coward has fainted again." Fat Cat looked at Dax. "We could be at this all night."

Dax went over to the washstand and picked up the pitcher. He came back to Ramírez and emptied it. Ramírez came up sputtering.

At the same time the woman began to roll around, bump-

155

ing the floor. "Hold her still!" Dax ordered. "She'll have the whole house down on us!"

Fat Cat leaned over the woman and slapped her face. Despite her trussing she tried to kick him. Fat Cat grinned. "At least she has the courage the traitor lacks." He sat down heavily, straddling her hips, and with one large hand spanned her throat, effectively pinning her to the floor.

"Where is the money?" Dax asked again.

Ramírez didn't answer. He was staring at Fat Cat and the woman. His head spun around as Dax swiped at him with the butt of the knife. "It's gone, I tell you!"

Fat Cat looked over at the traitor. "She seems like a nice little piece even though she's a bit small in the *tetas*."

Ramírez remained silent.

Fat Cat looked over at Dax. "It's been a long time. I'm a three-day virgin."

Dax didn't take his eyes from Ramírez' face. "Go ahead," he said quietly. "Fuck her. And when you're finished, let Marcel fuck her too."

The protest rising in Marcel's throat was never uttered. He saw the tawny jungle look in Dax's eyes. The woman began to struggle as Fat Cat forced her legs apart with one knee. He opened his fly. "Be happy, little one," he murmured. "Now you will see what a real man is like. Mine is not a miserable worm like that one's."

The words burst out of Ramírez' throat. "There! The safe in the wall behind the bed!"

"That's better." Dax laughed. "Now, how is it opened?"

"The key is in my pants pocket."

Dax already had the trousers off the chair over which they had been carelessly thrown. He held up a key ring. "Is this the one?"

Ramírez nodded. "Behind the picture on the wall."

Quickly Dax crossed the room. He moved the picture, and inserted the key in the black metal safe. "It does not work!" he said angrily, coming back to Ramírez.

Ramírez tore his eyes away from Fat Cat. "That is the car key. There is another."

Marcel couldn't keep himself from staring. Until now rape had been only a word he had seen in the newspapers. He felt dizzy with a strange excitement. It was nothing like the fornication he had experienced. It was cold and savage and brutal. Fat Cat had already entered the woman. Marcel saw her entire body shuddering under the impact.

"Marcel!"

He tore his eyes away from the two of them and walked over to Dax. The safe was filled with stacks of neatly packaged banknotes. "My God!" he whispered.

"Don't stand there gawking! Get a pillowcase and help me pack this money."

Marcel couldn't keep from glancing back over his shoulder as he held the pillowcase for Dax. He looked at Ramírez. The traitor was staring at Fat Cat and the woman. It wasn't until he ran his tongue over his lips that Marcel realized what he was thinking. The money had been forgotten.

The whole world had gone mad. Nothing in it made sense any more. Dax, after one perfunctory glance at the writhing pair, paid them no further attention. It was as if what was happening was a perfectly ordinary occurrence. Marcel was in the throes of a private sexual excitement all his own; his legs felt weak and they trembled, as they hadn't since the first time he had been with a woman.

"*Bueno!*" Dax's voice was filled with satisfaction. The pillowcase was almost full. Quickly he secured the open end with a silk stocking. He sat on the edge of the bed and looked down at Fat Cat. "Don't take all night," he said casually. "We still have to get out of here."

He looked at the other key on the ring and was about to throw it away. "Do you drive?" he suddenly asked Marcel.

Silently Marcel nodded.

"*Bueno.* There's nothing like a pleasant drive in the cool of the night."

The baron leaned across his desk. "How much did they recover?"

"Almost four and a half million francs," Marcel replied, coming back to the present again.

"I'm glad," the baron said quietly. He stared down thoughtfully at his desk. "That's quite a lad. Has there been any discussion about which school he will attend?"

"I heard the consul mention the public schools. But that was before the money was recovered."

"Unfortunately it won't be of much help," the baron said. "It will hardly cover the personal loans the consul made in order to pay the bills." He tapped the pencil on his desk. "I want you to suggest that the boy attend De Roqueville."

"But that is the most expensive school in Paris!"

"It is also the best. My own son goes there. I will pay the tuition, make all the arrangements. The boy will be offered a scholarship."

The feel of the ten-thousand-franc note in his pocket was very reassuring to Marcel as he left the baron's office. His finances were looking up. The grocer had not been the only one to make a deal with him for the collection of bills.

But there was still one unanswered question plaguing him. He still knew no more about why the Baron de Coyne was interested in the consul and his son than he had the morning of that first telephone call.

4

The buzzer on his father's desk sounded harshly. Dax came back from the window and picked up the intercom. *"Oui,* Marcel?"

"Your friend Robert is here."

"Merci. Ask him to come in." Dax put down the receiver and turned toward the door.

Robert entered and crossed the room, his hand outstretched. "I came as soon as I heard the news."

They shook hands European fashion, just as they always did on meeting or parting, even if they had seen each other earlier that morning on the polo practice field. "Thank you. How did you find out?"

"The steward at the clubhouse," Robert said. "He told me about the phone call."

Dax's lips twisted wryly. Paris was no different from a small town at home. By now the news would be everywhere,

158

and soon the newspapers would have their reporters at the door.

"Is there anything I can do?"

Dax shook his head. "There is nothing anyone can do. All we can do is wait."

"Was he ill this morning when you left the house?"

"No. Had he been, I would not have come to practice."

"Of course."

"Father was not very strong, as you know. Ever since we came to Europe he has been subject to very severe colds. It seemed that no sooner was he over one than he contracted another. It appeared that he had no resistance. Marcel found him slumped over the desk. He and Fat Cat carried him upstairs and called the doctor. The doctor said it was his heart, then they called me."

Robert shook his head. "This is no climate for your father. He should have lived on the Riviera."

"My father never should have come here at all. The strains and tensions were too much for him. He never really got his strength back after the loss of his arm."

"Why didn't he go back then?"

"He had a strong sense of duty. He remained because he was needed. The first credits he worked out with your father's bank saved our country from bankruptcy."

"He could have gone home after that."

"You don't know my father." Dax grimaced. "That was only the beginning. He knocked at every door in Europe to get help for our country. The snubs and rebuffs turned him into an old man. But he kept on trying."

Dax took out a thin brown cigarette and lit it. "You know," he said somberly, "the early years here did him no good either. The previous consul had left a mess and my father cleaned it up. He paid all unpaid bills himself, even though it broke him. To this day he doesn't know that I know that everything went to pay those bills—our home in Curatu, his savings, everything he had. The only thing he did not touch was our *hacienda* in Bandaya, and that was because he wanted me one day to have it." He dragged deeply on the cigarette and let the smoke trickle slowly from his nostrils.

"I never knew that," Robert said.

Dax grinned wryly. "If that scholarship at De Roque had

159

not turned up like a miracle, I'd have attended public schools. As It was, my father deprived himself of things he needed so I would be dressed properly and there would be gasoline enough in the car so Fat Cat could drive me home for the weekends."

Robert de Coyne looked at Dax. Strange that none of them at the school had ever guessed it. There were some poverty-stricken ex-royalty there but everyone knew who they were. They were there because they brought social standing to the school. But Dax was South American and everyone assumed that South Americans were rich. They owned tin mines and oil wells and cattle ranches. They were never poor.

Suddenly, many of the things that had happened during those early school years became clear to him. For example, the incident toward the end of that first week at school. Thursday afternoon, between the last class and dinner. Free time. In back of the gymnasium. They had stood in a small semicircle around one of the new boys.

His dark eyes had looked at them impassively. "Why do I have to fight one of you?"

Sergei Nikovitch looked around with an expression of disgust. "Because," he explained patiently, "next week we have to draw lots to see whose room you will share for the remainder of the school term. If you do not fight, how are we to know whether to accept you or reject you?"

"Do I also have the same right?"

"Only if you win. Then you can choose your roommate."

The new boy had thought for a moment, then nodded. "It seems stupid to me but I will fight."

"Good," Sergei said. "We shall be fair about it. You can decide which one of us to fight, that way you will not have to face someone bigger. But you are not allowed to choose anyone smaller."

"I choose you."

Sergei had a surprised look on his face. "But I am a head taller than you. It would not be fair."

"That is why I chose you."

Sergei shrugged hopelessly. He began to take off his jacket. He looked around at the others as Robert de Coyne had gone up to the new boy.

"Change your mind," he had said earnestly. "Fight me in-

160

stead. I'm your size. Sergei is the biggest and best fighter in the class."

The new boy smiled at him. "Thank you. But I have already chosen. This business is stupid enough as it is. Why make it worse?"

Robert had looked at him in surprise. That was the way he had always felt, but this was the first time he had ever heard anyone dare to say it. Still, it was the custom. He felt an instinctive liking for the new boy. "Whether you win or lose I shall consider myself fortunate if I draw you for a roommate."

The new boy looked at him with sudden shyness. "Thank you."

"Are you ready?" Sergei called.

The boy slipped out of his jacket and nodded.

"You have your choice again," Sergei said. *"La boxe, la savate,* or free-for-all."

"Free-for-all," the other said, only because he wasn't quite sure what the other two meant.

"Bien. It is over when one of us gives up."

Actually it was over before that. It was also the finish of that custom at De Roqueville School. It all happened so quickly that it ended while the boys were still waiting for something to happen.

Sergei had reached out his arms in the conventional wrestler's position and begun to circle the new boy, who turned with him, his arms hanging loosely at his sides. Then Sergei grabbed for him, and the other's movements became a blur of speed. The flat of his hand struck aside Sergei's outstretched arm and as that arm fell limply to his side, the new boy struck again. He seemed to half-spin, which gave his flattened hand additional power as it lashed into Sergei's ribs. There was barely time to see the expression of surprise on Sergei's face as he doubled over, then the other circled behind him and hit him at the base of his skull with the knuckles of his closed fist. Sergei crumpled to the ground.

The new boy stood over him, then turned to them. They stared back unbelieving. This one wasn't even breathing heavily. They watched him go back and pick up his jacket from where he had folded it neatly on the ground. He started to walk away, then turned.

"I choose you for a roommate," he said to Robert. Then

161

he glanced at Sergei, still lying silently on the ground. "You'd better get help for him. His arm is broken and so are two of his ribs. But he'll be all right. I didn't kill him."

The doorman at the Royale Palace was an imposing sight. A tall man, six foot seven in his boots, his high Cossack hat made him seem even taller, and the pink and blue uniform with the golden epaulets and braid across the chest gave him the appearance of a general out of a Franz Lehár operetta.

And he ran his post at the hotel entrance like a general. The luggage racks were neatly folded away in a hidden corner and woe betide any bellhop who neglected to replace them in that exact manner. His stentorian heavily accented voice had been known to summon a taxi from as far away as three blocks.

It was said about him that at one time he had actually been a colonel in the Cossacks, though this was never proved. All that was known was that he had been a count, a distant cousin of the Romanovs, and one wintry day in 1920 he had appeared full blown in the hotel doorway. He had been there ever since. Count Ivan Nikovitch was not a man to invite confidences or even discussions of a personal nature. The sight of the saber scar, half hidden in his cheek by the thick, carefully trimmed black beard, was quite enough to discourage that.

Just now he sat awkwardly in a chair much too small for him and studied his son, propped up in the bed. There was no anger in him, not even sympathy for his son, only annoyance. "You were stupid," he said flatly. "One never fights an opponent who does not know the rules. One can get killed that way. Rules are made for your own protection as well as the enemy's. That's why we lost to the Bolsheviki. They didn't know the rules either."

Sergei was embarrassed. That hurt even more than the pain. The ease and speed with which he had been beaten, and by a boy little more than half his size. "I didn't know that he didn't know the rules."

"All the more reason you should have explained them to him," his father replied. "That alone would have so confused him he would have been easy for you."

Sergei thought for a moment, then shook his head. "I don't think so. I think he would have ignored them."

A sound of voices came through the open window. The boys were coming out of the classrooms. Count Nikovitch rose from his chair and went over to look down at them.

"I would like to see this boy," he said curiously. "Might he be among them?"

Sergei turned his head so that he could see through the window. "There, the dark boy walking alone."

The count watched Dax cross the field to the next building without even a curious glance at the other boys. When he disappeared into the building Count Nikovitch turned back to his son.

He nodded his head. "I think you are right. That one will always make his own rules. He is not afraid to walk alone."

The next year Dax and Robert had moved to the main dormitory, where they would remain, moving only from the top floor down to the first, year by year, until their time at De Roqueville would be over. Now they were "older" boys, as compared with the younger boys, who lived in another building. That was how they had been joined by Sergei. The older boys were lodged three in a room.

It was a policy of the school based on a belief that three was a more productive number than either two or four. Four in a room generally wound up two against two, and two in a room was not economical. Dax and Robert had barely begun to unpack their things when a knock had come at the door. Robert went over and opened it. Sergei stood there, his valise in hand.

It was hard to tell which of them was more surprised. Sergei checked the room slip he still held in his free hand, then the number on the door. "This is the room, all right."

He put his valise down in the center of the room. They stood silently watching him. "I didn't ask for it, you know," he said. "My own roommate dropped out and *le préfet* assigned me here."

They still didn't speak. Since the fight Sergei and Dax had always managed carefully to avoid one another.

Suddenly Sergei smiled. There was warm vitality in that grin. "I'm glad we don't have to fight for this one," he said in mock relief. "I don't know whether my bones could take it."

Robert and Dax glanced at each other; the beginnings of an answering smile came to their lips.

"How are you in literature?" Robert asked.

Sergei shook his head. "Not good at all."

"Math, physics, chemistry?"

A woeful expression crossed Sergei's face as he shook his head to each in turn.

"What are you good at then?" Robert asked. "Those are the subjects we need most help in."

"I don't know," Sergei confessed. "They're my weak ones too."

"History, geography, government?" Dax asked.

"I'm not very good at those either."

Dax glanced at Robert, a secret smile in his eyes. "We need a roommate who can teach us something. You don't seem to be of much use."

"No, I'm not," Sergei answered sadly.

"Isn't there anything you can teach us?"

Sergei thought for a moment, then his face brightened. "I know seventeen different ways to masturbate."

As one, the other two put their hands over their heads and salaamed to him. "Welcome to the club!"

<hr>

5

The black Citroën limousine pulled to a stop at the edge of the polo field and Jaime Xenos got out. He looked across the field at the tangle of riders and horses and squinted his eyes. "Which one is Dax?"

"He's with the ones wearing the red and white caps," Fat Cat said. "See, there he is."

A horse broke from the tangle and came racing down the side of the field. The slender boy swinging the mallet nursed the ball along the ground in tight careful strokes, never allowing it to escape from his control.

An opposing rider came diagonally across the field, and Dax turned his mount swiftly and hit the ball across the field to a teammate. He in turn passed the ball far down the field, where Dax stroked the ball between the goal posts without one member of the opposing team near him. He wheeled his horse and rejoined his team in the center of the field.

"Monsieur Xenos?"

The consul turned. The voice belonged to a thin wizened man who smelled of horses. "*Oui?*"

"I am the polo coach, Fernande Arnouil. I am honored to meet you."

Jaime Xenos nodded. "My pleasure."

"I'm glad you could come, your excellency. You have been watching your son?"

"For just this moment. I must confess I do not know the game."

"It is understandable," the coach replied apologetically. "It is unfortunate but in the past few years the game has lost in popularity." He gestured toward the car. "And I believe the success of that little vehicle to be the major contributor to the decline."

Xenos nodded politely.

"Young gentlemen no longer learn to ride. They are more interested in learning to drive. That is why when such a young gentleman as your son comes along it is important that his talent be developed."

"He is good then?"

Arnouil nodded. "He is like a throwback to the old days. Your son was born to this game. It is as if he came into the world with his feet already in the stirrups."

"I am proud." Dax's father looked across the field. Another play was developing and in the forefront was Dax, guiding his horse with his knees as he fought to retain the ball.

"He realizes he can't keep it," the coach explained. "Observe how he passes the ball to his teammate on the opposite side."

Dax swung low off the saddle and hit the ball back through the legs of his own horse. The teammate picked it up quickly and raced off the field as Dax decoyed part of the opposing team along with him.

"Beautiful!" The coach turned back to Dax's father. "You are wondering why I asked you to come?"

The consul nodded.

"Next year your son will be sixteen. He will be eligible to play in regular interschool competition."

"Bien."

"But in order to be eligible," the coach continued, "he must have his own horses. It is a strict rule."

The consul nodded. "And if he does not?"

Arnouil shrugged in a typical Gallic fashion. "He cannot play, no matter how well qualified."

Jaime Xenos looked across the field. "How many will he need?"

"At least two," the coach replied, "though three or even four are preferable. A fresh horse for each chukker."

The consul still did not look at the coach. "How much is such a horse?"

"Thirty to forty thousand francs."

"I see," Xenos replied thoughtfully.

The coach squinted at him shrewdly. "If it is difficult for you to locate such horses," he said diplomatically, "I could perhaps find a sponsor with several to spare."

Xenos knew what he meant. He forced a smile. "If you think it worthwhile," he said, "my son shall have his own horses."

"I am pleased that you should feel so, your excellency. You will not regret it. Your son will become one of the great players of our time."

They shook hands and the consul watched as the bow-legged little man walked down the field. The consul was aware what Fat Cat was thinking. He got back into the car wearily and waited until Fat Cat slipped behind the wheel. "Well, what do you think?"

Fat Cat shrugged his shoulders. "It is only a game."

Dax's father shook his head. "It is more than that. It is a game only for those who can afford it."

"Then that lets us out."

"We cannot afford to be out."

"We cannot afford to be in," Fat Cat retorted. "There are many more pressing demands."

"In a way Dax could become a symbol of our country. The French can help us."

166

"Then tell *el Presidente* to send the hundred and sixty thousand francs for the horses."

The consul looked at him, then smiled suddenly. "Fat Cat, you're a genius."

Fat Cat didn't know what he was talking about. He studied the consul in the rear-view mirror.

"Not the money, horses," Xenos said. "Those wiry pintos with feet like mountain goats ought to be perfect for this game. I'm sure *el Presidente* would be happy to send some."

The coach caught Dax as he came out of the locker room after the game. "I just spoke to your father," he said. "He assures me you will have your own horses next year."

"He did?"

The coach nodded.

Dax's eyes swept down the field. "Is he here?"

"At the end, near the gate."

But Dax had already seen the car and was running down the field. His father got out of the car and embraced him. "Why didn't you tell me you were coming?" Dax asked.

His father smiled. Dax was growing. He was up to his shoulder now. Another year and he would no longer be able to look down at him. "I wasn't sure that I could."

"I'm glad you did." It was the first time his father had ever come to the school.

"Is there a place we could go for tea?"

"There is a *pâtisserie* in the village."

They got into the car. "The coach told me that you said I would have my own horses next year."

"Yes."

"Where are we going to get the money?" Dax asked. "We can't afford it."

The consul smiled. *"El Presidente* will send us four mountain ponies."

Dax looked at him silently.

"Is there anything wrong?"

There was such a look of concern on his father's face that Dax did not have the heart to tell him that good polo ponies required years of training. Instead he reached over and took his father's hand. "That's wonderful," he said, squeezing it tightly.

"Don't be a fool," Sergei said. "Spend the summer with us at Cannes. Robert's father has a villa there and a boat."

"No. I have to work with the horses if they are going to be any good by fall."

"You're wasting your time," Sergei said positively. "You'll never make polo ponies out of those mountain goats."

"Coach thinks I've got a chance."

"I don't see why your father just doesn't buy regular ponies. Everybody knows you South Americans are lousy with money."

Dax smiled to himself. If Sergei only knew the truth. "It would be a good thing for my country if they turned out well. Perhaps, as my father always says, it would convince Europeans that we can do other things besides grow coffee and bananas."

Sergei got to his feet. "I'm going down to the village. There's a new waitress at the *pâtisserie*. Want to come along?"

Dax shook his head. There were other things he could do with five francs. "No, I think I'll bone up for the exams."

He sat quietly at his desk after Sergei had gone. It was three years now that he had been in France. He felt a restlessness, and got up and went over to the window. He looked down at the rolling lawns and neat gardens.

A wave of sudden homesickness swept over him. He longed for the wild untouched mountains. Everything here was too neat, too orderly. There was no excitement in discovering a new path, a new way to come down from the mountains. Here there were always set roads to follow.

All civilization seemed to be like that. Even his father, who was prepared to observe the rules and respected them, had never thought it would prove this confining. With each new rebuff, each new disappointment, he seemed to shrink more and more within himself. His betrayal by Ramírez had been only the beginning.

There were other incidents, far more subtle and destructive. Promises made to support Corteguay in its quest for independence from British and American political and financial domination. There were lines Dax had never seen before in his father's face. There was a hesitancy, an uncertainness in his manner that marked the beginnings of old age. These last three years of failure had taken their toll.

Dax felt all these things, and at times he wanted to cry out to his father that this life was not for them, that they ought to return home to the fields and the mountains, to a world they understood. But the impulse remained bottled up inside him. He knew his father would not listen, could not. The determination to accomplish his mission, the hope that he might succeed still burned deep within him.

There was a soft knock at the door behind him. He turned. "Come in."

The door opened and the Baron de Coyne entered. They had never met before. "I'm Robert's father. You must be Dax."

"I am, sir."

"Where is Robert?"

"He should be back shortly, sir."

"May I sit down?" Without waiting for an answer, the baron dropped into an easy chair. He glanced briefly around the room. "Things haven't changed much since I was here."

"I suppose not."

The baron glanced over at him suddenly. "I suppose things rarely do change no matter how much we want them to."

"I don't know, sir." Dax wasn't quite sure of the baron's meaning. "I guess it depends on the thing we want changed."

The baron nodded. "Robert mentioned that you might be spending the summer with us."

"I'm afraid not, sir. But I'm very grateful to have been asked."

"Why can't you come?"

Dax felt the lameness of his answer. "I'm training some Corteguayan ponies for polo."

The baron nodded solemnly. "Very commendable. I shall be most interested in what results you achieve. If you are at all successful it could prove of value to your country. It will show France that Corteguay can do other things besides grow coffee and bananas."

Dax stared at him. These were almost the exact words his father had used. He felt his spirits begin to lift. If a man like Robert's father felt this, perhaps things were not so bad after all. Perhaps there was still hope for his father's mission.

6

Sylvie began to pick up the dishes, and Dax got up from the table. A moment later he went outside. Arnouil and Fat Cat leaned back in their chairs. Fat Cat began to roll a cigarette.

Arnouil was silent for a moment, then put the stub of a small cigar in his mouth. He didn't speak until after Fat Cat had lighted his cigarette. "The boy is alone too much. He never smiles."

The smoke drifted across Fat Cat's face. He didn't answer.

"He should not have stayed here and worked all summer," the coach continued. "He should have gone with his friends."

Fat Cat shrugged. "Are not the ponies shaping up?"

"More than shaping up. They were born for this game; they will revolutionize it. But surely his father must see that a boy should have fun."

Fat Cat took the cigarette from his lips and looked at it. It wasn't too bad for French tobacco. A trifle sweet perhaps, but not bad. "Dax is not like other boys," he said carefully. "Someday he will be a leader in our country. Perhaps he will even become *el presidente*."

"Even Napoleon was a boy once," the coach replied. "I'm sure he did not allow his destiny to rob him of his youth."

"Napoleon became a soldier by choice. He had not been a warrior since the age of six."

"And Dax has?"

Fat Cat looked at the coach. He nodded silently. "When Dax was not yet seven *el Presidente* himself held the gun as Dax pulled the trigger that executed the murderers of his mother and sister."

The coach was silent for a moment. "No wonder then the boy never smiles."

The night was quiet and the air cool with the first breeze from the west as Dax walked down to the stable. The horses whinnied when they heard him coming, and he took the sugar he always kept in his pocket and gave them each a lump. Then he went into their stalls and stroked their necks gently. They whinnied again, a soft lonesome sound.

"We're all homesick," he whispered. They didn't like the confinement of the stable. They missed the open corral.

"Dax?" Sylvie's voice came from the stable door.

"I'm in here with the horses."

"What are you doing?" she asked curiously, walking over to him.

He looked out at her over the bars of the stall. "I thought I'd come down and keep them company for a while. They get lonesome so far from home."

She leaned against the bars. "Do you get lonesome too, Dax?"

He stared at her. She was the first person who ever had asked that question. He hesitated. "Sometimes."

"Do you have a girl back home?"

He thought for a moment of Amparo, whom he had not seen in three years. He wondered what she was like now. Then he shook his head. "No, not really. Once when I was nine a girl decided to marry me. But she outgrew it. She was only seven herself and very fickle."

"I have a boyfriend," she said, "but he is in the navy. He has been away for six months, and it will be another six before he returns."

He looked at her. It was the first time he had thought of her as a girl. Until now she was just someone around the stables, riding the horses and fooling around like anyone else. Except for her long hair there had seemed to be nothing feminine about her, no roundness visible in the man's shirt with the rolled-up sleeves or tight dungarees. Suddenly he noticed the female softness of her.

"I'm sorry," he said, without really knowing why he was, except that for the moment she seemed as alone as the horses or himself.

The horses whinnied again. He held out some lumps of sugar to her. "They want you to feed them."

She took the sugar and crawled between the bars. The horses nuzzled against her, each greedy for his ration. She laughed as one of them pushed her with his nose and she stumbled back against Dax. Involuntarily his arms went around her.

For a moment she stared up into his face, her eyes on his, then abruptly he let her go. There was a hard, tight, almost painful knot in his stomach. His voice sounded harsh even to himself. "I guess they've had enough."

"Yes." She seemed to be waiting.

He felt the tightening in his groin, the pounding at his temples. He turned and started through the bars. Her voice brought him back.

"Dax!"

He looked at her, one foot still half through the bars.

"I'm lonely too."

He still did not move. She came toward him and laid her hand lightly on the hardness at his groin. With an almost frenzied moan of pain he pulled her toward him and all the tensions of his youth and loneliness burst into a shattering crescendo of flame.

Later he lay quietly in his room listening to the soft sounds of Fat Cat's breathing in the other bed. The pain inside him was dissolved now. Suddenly Fat Cat's voice came out of the darkness. "Did you fuck her?"

He was so surprised that he did not even try to evade the question. "How did you know?"

"We could tell."

"You mean her father—"

Fat Cat laughed. "Of course. Do you think he is blind?"

Dax thought for a moment. "Was he angry?"

Fat Cat chuckled. "Why should he be? Her fiancé has been away for almost a year. He is aware that a filly in season needs servicing. Besides, she's old enough."

"Old enough? She must be about my age."

"She's twenty-two. Her father told me so himself."

Twenty-two, Dax thought, almost seven years older. No wonder she had made the first move. She must have thought him a stupid boy to wait this long. He felt the tightness begin again at his loins as he remembered how they had lain together. Abruptly he got out of bed.

"Where are you going?"

He turned in the open doorway. Suddenly he laughed. This was a new escape, a new kind of freedom. He should have discovered this long before. "Wasn't it you who told me that once wasn't ever enough?"

172

7

Robert came into the room just in time to hear his father say, "What do you need a swimming pool for? You have the whole Mediterranean."

His sister Caroline pouted. And when she twisted her pretty little face into a pout everyone, including the baron, was affected. "It's so *gauche*." Her lower lip was quivering tremulously. "Everyone goes to the beach."

"What difference does it make?"

"Papa!" Caroline sounded on the verge of tears.

The baron looked at her, then at his son. Robert smiled. He knew better than to take sides. His little sister had a way all her own.

"All right, all right," his father said finally. "You will have your swimming pool."

Caroline burst into a smile, kissed her father, and ran gaily from the room, almost knocking over the butler, who was on his way in. "Monsieur Christopoulos to see you, sir."

"Excuse me, Father. I didn't realize you were busy."

The baron smiled. "No, Robert, don't go. I shan't be long."

Robert settled himself into a chair in a corner across the library from his father's desk. He watched the visitor settle himself. The man's name had sounded vaguely familiar but he wasn't much interested. He picked up a magazine and began leafing through it idly when something his father said caught his attention.

"Have you considered Corteguay?"

Robert looked up.

"Registering your ships there would be of more value than Panamanian registry."

"I can't see how," the visitor answered in a thick Greek accent.

Robert worried his memory until the name came suddenly clear. Christopoulos. Of course; the gambler who along with Zographos and André controlled the syndicate that ran the *tout va* at all the casinos from Monte Carlo to Biarritz. He wondered what a gambler had to do with ships.

"In the event of war," his father said, "Panama would be forced to declare herself on the side of the United States. Corteguay has no such ties. Not to Britain, not to the States, not to anyone. She alone of all the South American countries could maintain neutrality. She would run no danger of the loss of outside aid or financial support. These have already been denied her."

"But in case of war the United States surely would make overtures to Corteguay. How can one be sure that such blandishments would be resisted?"

The baron smiled. "A clearly neutral fleet of ships based in the Americas, with the right to sail the seas free from attack by either side, would be more than worth its tonnage in gold. The beginning should be made now to ensure that neutrality."

The Greek nodded thoughtfully. "It will be most expensive." He looked down at his carefully manicured nails. "It is not easy to support an entire country."

"True," the baron replied quietly, "but that is exactly what must be done." He got to his feet. The meeting was over. "My participation in such a project must be contingent on that."

Christopoulos rose also. "I will inform my associates. Thank you for these moments of your valuable time."

The baron smiled. "Not at all. It was my pleasure to sit across a table from you without a deck of cards between us."

The Greek smiled also. "I have the feeling that without the cards I am rather a child in your hands."

The baron laughed aloud. Christopoulos. The greatest *tailleur* in all the world was seldom given to flattery. "I shall be at the casino tonight to give you a chance to recover your confidence."

"*À bientôt.*" Christopoulos shook hands with the baron and left.

The door closed behind him and the baron looked over at

174

his son. Robert got to his feet. "Do you really think there will be a war?"

The baron's face tightened imperceptibly. "I'm afraid so, though not right away. Five or six years, perhaps. But it must come. Germany is burning for revenge, and Hitler can only survive if he offers it to them."

"But surely it can be stopped. If you see it this far in advance—"

The baron interrupted. "Not everyone agrees with me." He looked at his son. "Why do you think you've been enrolled at Harvard, and your sister at Vassar?"

Robert did not answer.

"How is your polo-playing friend?"

"Dax?"

The baron nodded. "According to the papers his playing has swept the Continent this year."

"Dax is fine." Robert looked at his father. "Did you know he had been invited to play for France in the international matches?"

"Yes, but only as an alternate. He still is rather young, you know."

"He's seventeen. They're just using his age as an excuse. They're afraid of him."

"Perhaps," his father admitted. "They haven't nicknamed him 'Le Sauvage' without reason. Costa is still in the hospital since your friend deliberately drove his horse into his to prevent his scoring."

"Dax plays to win. He says there is no other reason for the game," Robert said defensively.

"There is such a thing as gentlemanly sport."

"Not for Dax. The polo field for him is like the jungles of his homeland. He says to lose there is to die. Did you know his father is the consul from Corteguay?"

"I had heard it. What is he like?"

"Very different from Dax, gentle and much darker. He has only one arm. Dax says the other was blown off by a bomb during an attempt on their president's life."

"Someday we'll have to invite them both down," the baron said casually. "I'd like to learn more about their country."

Madame Blanchette herself opened the door. "Monsieur Christopoulos is expecting you."

175

Marcel nodded. This merely confirmed what he had already guessed, that the syndicate was mixed up in more than gambling houses in France. He followed her through the small foyer into a small salon. The slim dark *tailleur* rose to his feet. "Monsieur Campion, thank you for coming. Please, sit down."

He did not offer to shake hands, nor did Marcel press it. Marcel knew his place. He slipped into an easy chair, curious why the gambler had summoned him. He did not have long to wait.

"We understand that gambling in Florida is about to be abolished. We also have interests in Cuba and Panama but we were thinking, perhaps, of going into Corteguay. Under the right conditions, of course."

Marcel nodded. He didn't speak. On the surface it sounded legitimate but actually it didn't make much sense. Corteguay was too far from the States to attract tourists. Cuba, just ninety miles off the coast of Florida, was all they really needed. But if that was what Christopoulos wished him to believe he would go along with it.

As if sensing this weakness, the other continued. "We realize, of course, that the United States and Corteguay are not on the best of relationships. But we are thinking of the future. Time has a way of altering circumstances. Ten years from now it could be another story."

"True," Marcel admitted.

"We have to take a long-term view in our business. Do you think that perhaps the Corteguayan government might be receptive?"

Marcel hesitated. "It is difficult to say."

"The country is poor. Surely they would welcome the opportunity of sharing in the benefits we could provide?"

Marcel allowed himself a slight smile. "That is the crux of the matter. Corteguay needs assistance now, not promises in the future."

"Perhaps certain officials could be influential," the gambler suggested. "I remember once having a discussion with the former consul, Ramírez. He seemed most interested."

Marcel knew very well that Ramírez had accepted a hundred thousand francs from the syndicate on just such an assumption. Now he was convinced that this was all Christopoulos was interested in. There was no other reason for this meeting.

"Monsieur Xenos is not at all like the former consul."

"Surely he would appreciate financial assistance. I understand he is still paying off certain large debts."

Again Marcel nodded. "True. But Monsieur Xenos is that rarest of beings, an honest man, an idealist. The very thought of self-gain from representing his country would be repugnant to him." He was silent for a moment. "Besides, he would be against any project which siphoned off even a fraction of the income of his impoverished countrymen."

"We might forbid his countrymen entry as we do in some areas."

"Then the benefits from your project would seem extremely dubious," Marcel replied. "The consul would be well aware that there is no other possible source of return for your tables."

The *tailleur* fell silent. After a moment he asked, "What sort of proposition do you think might interest the consul?"

The answers came readily. "Industry. Trade. Investment. Anything that would help Corteguay export its crops. Their economy is geared to their agriculture."

"Might a shipping line prove of interest to them?"

Marcel nodded. "Very much so. Low-rate transportation for their exports would have great appeal."

"I have a nephew in Macao," the gambler continued. "He operates the casinos there. However, he also owns a shipping line, four freighters of Japanese origin. They are too often idle to suit him, and he has been looking for new markets. Perhaps I could interest him in the idea."

"That might prove to be a solution. It would most certainly get your foot in the door. The consul should seriously consider your other proposition once that had been accomplished."

The gambler looked at him. "You realize, of course, that should anything develop from this conversation you would be provided for?"

"Thank you. That is most generous of you."

"You say that Christopoulos is willing to put in a shipping line in exchange for gambling privileges?" the baron asked later in his office.

177

Marcel nodded.

"Have you mentioned the idea to the consul yet?"

Marcel shook his head. "No, your excellency. I thought first I should talk with you."

"*Bien.* You did exactly right. I think perhaps it is time I met the consul."

"*Oui, monsieur.* Shall I speak to him about an appointment?"

"No, he already has an appointment with one of my branch banks. I think it best that our meeting come about under such circumstances."

"As you wish, your excellency."

8

"Caroline is a bitch!" Sylvie rolled out of the bed, her slim boyish figure taut with anger. She pulled a cigarette from the package on the dresser and lit it.

Lazily Dax propped the pillow under his head. "You sound jealous."

"I'm not jealous!" Sylvie shouted. "I don't like the bitch, that's all."

"Why not?"

Sylvie dragged savagely on the cigarette. "She thinks her father's money can buy anything she wants. I saw the way she looked at you after the game last week. Like a cat over a bowl of cream."

"You are jealous," Dax said. "Why? I'm not jealous of Henri."

"He isn't home enough for you to be jealous of him!"

"But when he is. Remember I was in the next room. I heard everything that went on, yet I wasn't jealous."

"No, damn you!" She remembered the night. Deliberately

she had made as much noise as she dared without waking the entire house. And Dax had not given her a sign that it had mattered one way or the other. "You don't care about me at all. I might as well be a stone wall for all I matter to you. And now you're going to spend a week's holiday at their villa in Cannes. I know what will happen."

"You do?" He smiled. "Tell me. I'd like to know."

"She'll drive you out of your mind. I know the type, all promises."

"Don't I have anything to say about that? After all, I don't have to respond."

Sylvie looked at him. "You can't help yourself. Even now. Look at yourself. Just talking about it has got you a hard on. You're an animal."

Dax grinned. "It isn't that. What do you expect when you're standing around naked and smelling like cunt?"

She stared at him for a moment, then squashed her cigarette in a plate and dropped to her knees beside the bed. Tenderly she touched his tumescence. "*Quelle armure magnifique*," she whispered. "So quick, so strong. Already he is too large for both my hands to hold."

She buried her face against him. He felt the warmth of the tiny edges of her tongue tingling his flesh. He crushed her head against him.

Dax felt the throbbing stab of pain race through his groin. Angrily he turned over on his stomach so that his anguish would not be visible to them all. Sylvie was right. The bitch! The cock-teasing little cunt!

He preferred English for cursing. There was something harshly forthright about Anglo-Saxon obscenities. They expressed exactly what you meant. French was too evasive. Spanish was too long-winded; you found yourself short of breath before you had said what you intended. English was a most economical language. It said so many things with so few words.

The sound of Caroline's laughter turned him around again on the chaise. She was standing at the edge of the pool talking to Sergei and her brother Robert. The damp silk of her brief one-piece suit clung to petite breasts and small rounded belly with a kind of insouciance. She laughed again and he caught her glancing at him from the corner of her eye.

He turned his back again angrily. Damn her! She knew exactly what she was doing to him. He looked out over the rolling green lawn to where his father, the baron and his English cousin were seated in the shade of the large wisteria.

Strange how different the baron and his English cousin were. It was hard to believe they shared the same ancestor, the frightened little Polish merchant who had fled from the pogroms of the Warsaw ghetto. He had traveled by night across snow-covered Europe afoot, with a fortune in diamonds sewn into his clothing. And the foresight of the man was equally amazing. More than a hundred years ago he had sent his eldest son across the channel to England, while he and his youngest remained in France where they had set themselves up as moneylenders and pawnbrokers. Quietly they had gone about their business despite the wars that rolled over Europe, and they had prospered until the De Coyne banks in France, and Coyne's Bank Ltd. in London, were among the most powerful in Europe, rivaling even Rothschild's.

Both branches of the family had been accorded honors in their adopted countries. The baron's grandfather had been awarded his baronage by Napoleon, and Sir Robert Coyne, after whom Dax's friend had been named, had been knighted by the King of England for his services during the World War.

The baron had finished speaking, and now Sir Robert was answering. He was tall and blond and his blue eyes were cool as he spoke slowly to his short, dark, brown-eyed cousin. Only his father seemed reflective and thoughtful. Dax wondered how it was going.

Everything seemed to have been marking time until this meeting. The urgent pressures from home were nearly at their peak. Unless new financing could be obtained quickly it appeared extremely doubtful whether *el Presidente* could maintain his control over the country in the face of the rising hungers of the populace.

A splash of cold water hit Dax like an icy shock. He sat up abruptly. Caroline stood laughing down at him. He grabbed for her and she ran, diving into the pool. Forgetting that the water was too cold for his liking, he plunged in after her.

She shrieked in mock terror as she pulled away from him with quick even strokes. She was out of the pool on the far side before he could catch her. He had known he would never be able to catch her. She was a much more polished swimmer. He held onto the side of the pool, glaring up at her.

She stayed just out of reach.

"Coward!" he whispered fiercely. "You're afraid to let me catch you. You know what would happen if I did."

"What would happen?" she whispered back challengingly.

"You know." He could not take his eyes off her breasts, where they pushed up against the tight bathing suit.

She smiled, sure of herself. "Nothing would happen."

"No? You're that sure?"

She nodded.

"You wouldn't like to meet me in the poolhouse after everyone has gone to sleep tonight and find out, would you?"

She stared at him for a moment, then nodded. "All right. Tonight. In the poolhouse."

Abruptly she walked away. He was still treading water watching her when Sergei swam up alongside him. "You're next, friend."

Dax turned. "What do you mean?"

Sergei laughed. "You'll wind up with your prick in your hand like all the rest of us."

Dax didn't answer. His eyes were still following her as she disappeared into the poolhouse.

They both heard the sound at the same time later that night. Footsteps on the concrete walk around the pool. Caroline's voice sounded loud in the darkness of the little poolhouse. "Who could it—"

His hand clapped quickly over her mouth. "Be quiet!"

The footsteps came nearer, hesitated. The two of them held their breaths, then the steps turned away and faded into the night. "That was close," he sighed, then almost yelled out loud as her teeth sank into his hand. "What did you do that for?"

"You were hurting me. I decided to hurt you back."

"You little bitch," Dax said, and reached for her.

But she was already on her feet. In the faint light from

181

the window he could see her straightening her dress. "We'd better go back."

"One little noise and you're scared," he taunted.

"And you're not?"

"No. Besides, I haven't finished yet."

She moved closer to him. He sensed her hand on the rough fabric of his trousers. Quickly he tore at his buttons. He felt the hot moistness of her hand. "Caroline!"

A strange little smile came to her lips. "You're not afraid, are you?"

"What is there to be afraid of?"

This time he screamed aloud with the pain. Her long nails tore into his flesh, then she was at the open door. "Too bad, Dax."

He didn't answer.

Again he sensed the silent sound of her secret laughter. "You didn't think I'd be as easy as a stableman's daughter, did you?"

Then she was gone, and he was alone. He felt the surge of anger rising inside him as he walked over to the washstand and turned on the water. Sergei would collapse with laughter if he ever learned what had happened.

Angrier now than ever, he dried himself quickly and went outside. For a moment he stood looking back at the dark villa, then turned toward the road. Cannes was only a half-mile away. There were bound to be girls there. There always were. To hell with her. Let her practice her black teasing arts on Sergei, or on her brother for that matter. They might be civilized enough to tolerate her petty amusements.

A shadow suddenly materialized from the darkness and fell into step beside him. He did not have to look to know who it was.

"Where are you going?"

"Was it you outside the poolhouse?" he asked angrily.

Fat Cat laughed. "You ought to know better. Do you think I would let you hear me?"

"Who was it then?"

"Your father."

"My father?" Dax's anger evaporated. "Did he know I was inside?"

"Sí. That is why I am here. He wishes to see you at once."

Dax turned and silently followed Fat Cat back to the

house. His father looked up as he came into the room. "What were you doing with that girl in the poolhouse?" he asked in a harsh whisper.

Dax stared at his father. It was one of the few times he had ever seen him so angry. He didn't answer.

"Are you crazy?" His father was distraught. "Do you know what would happen if you were caught with her? Do you think the baron would be willing to make a loan to the despoiler of his daughter?"

Dax still didn't answer.

His father slumped suddenly into a chair. "Everything would be lost. The whole negotiation would collapse. Everything we fought for and bled for would be gone. And all because of your stupidity."

Dax looked at his father and for the first time he noticed the trembling in his hand, the age lines and exhaustion in his face. He walked over to him. "I'm sorry, *Papa*," he said softly, "but there is nothing to be upset about. I didn't touch her."

His father's tension eased. The one real truth of his existence was the honesty that lay between them. He knew his son would not lie to him.

"You are right, I was stupid," Dax said. "It will not happen again."

His father reached out and took his hand. "Dax, Dax. In how many worlds must you learn to live because of me?"

Dax felt the agony and fragility of the man in his touch. Suddenly there was a sadness and an understanding in him that had not been there before. He bent down and pressed his lips to his father's soft dark cheek. "I want to live only in your world, my father. I am your son."

It had been the first time that Dax realized his father was dying.

183

9

There was no pain, although Jaime Xenos knew that he was dying. He looked up into the eyes of the priest. There was so much he wanted to explain. But the words merely flitted across the screen of his mind and never found their way to his tongue.

He was tired. He had never felt so tired. He turned his head on the pillow and closed his eyes. The drone of the priest faded. Perhaps he would find his voice again after he had rested. There was no fear. Only a heavy kind of sadness. There was so much to be done, so much he could still do. But now it was over. Time was coming to a stop.

Dax. The word seemed to burn its way through his mind. Alone. Dax. He was so young. And so alive. There were so many things he had not yet taught him. So many things the boy would need to know. The world was not solved by the sheer physical energy of youth alone. He wanted to tell him that. And much more. But it was too late.

Much too late. He slept.

Dax crossed the room toward the doctor.

"He is sleeping," the doctor said. "It is a good sign."

Dax followed the doctor out of the room, leaving the priest alone with his father. Fat Cat was waiting just outside the door. "How is he?"

"The same." Dax shook his head. He turned to the doctor. "When . . . ?"

"Sometime tonight. Perhaps tomorrow morning. No one can tell."

"There is no chance?"

"There is always a chance," the doctor said, knowing as he spoke that there was none.

Marcel came up the staircase. "A reporter from *Paris Soir* is on the telephone."

"Tell him there is no news."

"That is not why he called."

Dax looked at him. "Why, then?"

Marcel did not look at him. "They want to know if you will continue to play polo."

Dax's face clouded. Angrily he clenched his fist. "Is that all they have to think about? A great man is dying and they worry about their stupid games?"

He remembered when the reporters had first given him the name "The Savage." It was after the game with Italy when he had ridden two of the Italians into the dirt and one of them, seriously hurt, had been taken to the hospital.

They had clustered around him later, asking questions:

"How do you feel about the two men who were injured?"

"Bad luck," he had answered casually. "This is no game for men who can't keep their seats."

"It sounds like you don't care what happens to them."

Dax had looked at the reporter. "Why should I?" he asked. "The same thing could happen to me every time I go out there."

"But it didn't happen to you," another reporter said. "And it always seems to happen to someone on the other team."

Dax's voice turned cold. "What do you mean?"

"It seems strange," the reporter had continued, "that you always become involved in an accident when the other team is about to score. And they are always the ones to be hurt, not you."

"Are you suggesting that I deliberately set about to injure them?"

"No." The reporter hesitated. "But—"

"I play to win," Dax interrupted, "and that means not allowing the other team to score if I can prevent it. I am not responsible for the lack of horsemanship of the other riders."

"There is such a thing as sportsmanship."

"Sportsmanship is a word for losers. I'm only interested in winning."

"Even if you kill someone doing it?" asked the first reporter.

"Even if I kill myself," Dax retorted.

185

"But this is a game," the reporter said in a horrified voice, "not a battlefield."

"How do you know?" Dax asked. "Have you ever been out there with a thousand pounds of horse and man charging down on you? Just try it once. You'd change your opinion."

He remembered that the telephone had rung that night while he was at dinner. It was one of the reporters he had spoken to that afternoon. "Did you know the Italian died in the hospital a little while ago?"

"No."

"Is that all you have to say?" the reporter had asked. "Not even that you're sorry?"

Suddenly Dax had been angry. "What good would it do? Would my words bring him back to life?" He had slammed down the receiver.

How strange that he should recall it all now that his own father was dying. Nothing could change that. Not his hurried return from London after the All-France match with England. Not even the news he brought about the shipping contract, which meant more than anything else. No, it had all come too late.

The only change that the resultant publicity had made was in the crowds. The stands were all sold out for the next game, and there was a murmur from the stands as he came riding out onto the field. He looked up in surprise, then glanced over at Sergei riding next to him.

The Russian smiled. "You're a star. They all came out to see you."

Dax stared at the crowd. They were gawking at him with a curious expectancy. He felt a cold shiver go through him. "They came to see me kill someone."

Sergei looked up at the crowd, then back at Dax. The Russian's mouth settled into grim lines. "Or be killed."

They were almost satisfied. Toward the end of the fourth chukker there was a pileup in the center of the field, and three horses went down, with Dax in the middle. There was no sound as the other two got to their feet and started off the field. But a low soft murmur swelled up as Dax did. Startled for a moment he glanced at them, then turned quickly away to help his pony up.

The horse stood there shaking, its sides heaving, as Dax

slowly rubbed its neck. "We fooled them that time, didn't we, boy?"

Then Fat Cat had come onto the field with another pony. A faint smattering of applause began as he lifted himself into the saddle. Mockingly he tipped his cap, and the crowd began to roar their approval.

Bewildered, he pulled up beside Sergei. "I don't get it."

"Don't try." Sergei laughed. "You're a hero now."

Even the newspapers recognized this, and by the end of that year they were pushing him for the All-France team. He became the youngest eight-goal handicap player ever to ride onto the field. Just a month shy of his eighteenth birthday.

But how empty it all seemed now as he waited for his father to die. Everything. All the plans that had seemed so important then. He remembered one night at school, along toward the end of the term. The three of them had been in the room together.

He had leaned back in the chair and put his feet up on the desk. "How do you think you made out in the exams, Sergei?"

Sergei's handsome face had clouded over. "I don't know. That last examination was rough."

Dax nodded. He looked at Robert, though there was no need to ask him. For almost three years now he had stood at the head of the class. He was beginning to pack away his books. "How do you feel?"

Robert shrugged his shoulders. "Relieved," he said cautiously, "and yet a little sad." He looked around the room. "In a way I hate to leave this place."

"Shit!" Sergei had shouted explosively. "I'll be glad to get out!"

Dax smiled. "What are your plans?"

"What plans? There are no more free schools for me. No more scholarships. I guess they figure the Commies are in power for good, so who needs a White Russian?"

"What are you going to do then?" Robert had asked. "Go to work?"

"At what?" Sergei made a face. "What the hell can I do? Get a job like my father? Be a doorman?"

"You'll have to do something," Robert had said.

"Maybe I'll go to Harvard like you," Sergei replied sarcastically. "Or join Dax at Sandhurst. But who would get me an appointment? My father the general?"

Robert fell silent. Sergei watched him for a moment, then apologized, his voice softening. "I didn't mean to be nasty."

"That's all right," Robert replied in a low voice.

"Actually, I've already decided what I'm going to do," Sergei said, his voice lightening.

"You have?"

"I'm going to marry a rich American. They seem to go for princes."

Dax began to laugh. "But you're not a prince. Your father is a count."

"What the hell's the difference?" Sergei asked. "To them a title is a title. You remember that one at the party the other night? When I took it out she looked at it and said in an awed voice, 'I never saw a royal one before.'

" 'Does it look any different?' " I asked.

" 'Oh, yes. I'd know the difference in a minute. The tip is purple. Royal purple!' "

When the laughter had died down, Robert turned toward Dax. "What about you?"

"I guess Sandhurst," he said. "I got the appointment, and my father wants me to go."

"I think it's a damn shame!" Robert said angrily. "The only reason they gave you an appointment is because they want you to play polo for them!"

"What difference does that make?" Sergei asked. "I only wish they'd asked me."

"I'll bet it was my uncle who arranged it," Robert said. "I saw the way he watched your playing when he came to that game last year."

"My father thinks it may help relations between England and Corteguay. Maybe we'll get that shipping line after all."

"I thought it was all set when my father formed the company. It cost over five million dollars to obtain those shipping rights."

"Only the ships never came. It seems that Greek gambler had leased his ships to the British before he got word that the deal with Corteguay was set."

"Somebody was double-crossed."

"Your father and mine. Yours especially. Actually all your father ever got for that five million was an import-export license guaranteeing him five-percent commission on all freight. It turned out to be worth nothing since there was no shipping."

They fell silent for a moment. Though they were both thinking the same thing, neither of them spoke about it. It was much too obvious.

It was Sergei who broke the silence. "We still have this summer, ten games between now and fall. That means at least forty parties, forty different girls to fuck! Anything can happen."

"I know what will happen."

"What?"

The beginnings of a smile appeared around Dax's mouth. "You'll wind up with a royal purple clap!"

10

The consul came into his office walking slowly, leaning on his cane. "Good morning, Marcel."

Marcel looked up from the newspaper he was folding carefully and placing in the exact center of the consul's desk. "Good morning, your excellency."

Jaime glanced down at the newspaper. "Did they win?"

Marcel smiled. "Of course. And Dax again scored the most points. He is a hero. I understand the whole team is being allowed to stay over for the long weekend."

The consul sat down behind the desk and glanced at the newspaper. It was lavish with praise for his son. He shook his head. "I don't know whether I like this. All this attention. It's not good for a young boy."

"It won't hurt Dax. He has too much sense for that."

"I hope so." The consul changed the subject. "Have we any reply from Macao about the ships?"

189

"Not yet."

"I don't like it. I had heard the British were anxious to release them. They were lying idle in the harbor. And yet, silence."

"These things take time."

"How much time? A month has passed already since Sir Robert promised to expedite things in London. The British may have all the time in the world. We do not."

"The last letter we had from Sir Robert said that he was doing his utmost."

"But is he?" The consul's voice was quizzical.

"It was half his money that the baron put up for the shipping contract."

"And he is also a director of the British lines."

"Two and a half million dollars is a lot of money to lose."

"He could lose much more if the British lost their power to embargo our shipments."

The secretary did not answer.

Dax's father leaned back wearily in his chair. "Sometimes I think I am not the man for this job. It's too much for me. Too devious. There is no one who says what he really means."

"There is no one who could do it better, excellency. It just takes time, that's all."

A wry smile crossed the consul's lips. "True, but I may not have that time."

Marcel knew what he meant. The consul had steadily grown more frail and delicate. The once giant frame of the man had given way to a thin delicacy. Now the cane. And it wasn't all a diplomat's posture, as the consul had so jokingly remarked. Besides, he had contracted another bad cold and actually he ought to be in bed.

"We'd better get another letter off to *el Presidente*," the consul added. "I'll bring him up to date. Perhaps he will have changed his mind about the advisability of allowing Dax to attend the British school."

It was with mixed feelings that Dax rode onto the English playing field. This would be the last time he would be wearing the colors of France. Next year he would be playing for the British and Sandhurst. He glanced down the field toward the stands. Sir Robert and his two daughters were there. The girls saw him and waved. He waved back.

Sergei grinned. "You got it made. Which one are you going to fuck first?"

Dax laughed. "Are you out of your mind? I almost got into enough trouble over Caroline. My father would kill me."

"The blond one looks like she might be worth dying for. I can see her creaming just looking at you."

The sound of the whistle floated across the field. The British team had already come out. "Come on," Sergei said. "Let's go meet your future playmates. And teach them how this game is really played."

The party that night was at Sir Robert's London town house. The British had played well but unimaginatively, and they had lost. But even Dax had to admit they were good sportsmen. Their captain seemed to mean it when he had come over to congratulate them.

Now Dax was standing alone near the huge French doors leading to the garden, watching the dancers. Sergei gave him a knowing wink as he danced by with a tall blond girl. Dax could not help grinning. He knew what that meant. Sergei had already selected his pigeon for the night.

"Enjoying yourself?"

Dax looked around and saw Sir Robert standing next to him. "Very much. Thank you, sir."

Sir Robert smiled. "I think you will like it here. We may not have the style of the French but we try to make it comfortable."

Dax was beginning to appreciate English understatement. Involuntarily he glanced around. He had never seen a more luxurious home. Even the baron's Paris town house could not compare with this. "No one could ask for more, sir. You have thought of everything."

"You must consider this your home while you're at Sandhurst. I have already instructed the servants to set aside a suite for you and we're expecting you for the weekend in the country."

"Thank you, sir. I don't know what to say."

"Then say nothing. Just be at home." He glanced at Dax. "I had a letter from your father this morning."

"You did? Did he say how he was?"

Sir Robert shook his head. "Your father never talks about

191

himself, only about his work." His eyes turned shrewd. "How is his health?"

"Not good." Dax's voice turned somber. "I really don't know whether I should leave him at this time. Perhaps I could somehow ease his burden if I stayed at home rather than coming to Sandhurst this year."

Sir Robert looked at him hesitantly. "If I may speak as your senior?"

"Please do. I would appreciate your thoughts."

"If I were your father you would please me most by going to Sandhurst. The impression you will make here will be far more useful to him and your country than if you had stayed by his side."

Dax was silent. It was exactly what his father would have said. Yet that made neither of them right. There was still the question of his father's health. If only he did not catch another cold. If the damn ships were only freed, then the strain on his father might be lessened. That would make him feel better about leaving. "Thank you, sir," he said aloud. "I suppose that is exactly what I shall do."

Later, after the party, he rolled over and switched on the bed lamp. He glanced at his watch. It was three o'clock and yet he could not sleep. He got out of bed and went to the open window. The traffic had quieted, and he stood there looking out. Idly he wondered when Sergei would come in.

Sergei had borrowed a car to take his pigeon home, so probably he would not return until daylight, if at all. But as he was watching, the headlights of a car spilled into the courtyard. Sergei got out and a moment later was in the room. "What are you doing still up?" His eyes swept the room suspiciously. "You had one of them in here?"

Dax laughed. "Is that all you can think of?"

"Is there anything else?" Sergei took his jacket off angrily. "That one I took home was sure a waste of time!"

Dax laughed again. "You can't win them all."

Sergei flung his jacket onto a chair. "Pretty soft," he said. "She told me that Sir Robert is giving you this suite while you're at Sandhurst."

Dax nodded.

"Did you know the girls' rooms are right across the hall?"

"So what?" Dax knew because both of them had taken special care to tell him.

"You're not going to be able to ignore them," Sergei said, unbuttoning his shirt. "They're both ripe and ready." He slipped out of his trousers. "They're still up, you know. I saw the light under their door."

"Do you have a cigarette?"

Sergei tossed him a pack. "They're probably waiting for you."

"I hope they don't wait too long."

Sergei shook his head in mock sadness. "You're making a big mistake. Somebody else will come along and grab off all that prime pussy." He looked at his friend. "What are you worried about? Their father is over in the other wing. He can't hear you. It must be at least half a mile away."

Dax laughed. "Shut up and go to bed, you horny bastard. It's not my fault you didn't get laid tonight."

But actually Sir Robert was sitting in his study studying the latest report on the Corteguayan situation. Tomorrow he would take it to the country to put with the others. It was safer there where even if the servants should pry it would have little meaning for them. His lips tightened grimly. The pressure was on him now. There were times when he felt an annoyance with his cousin. The baron was too French, too sentimental. What difference did it make that the Corteguayan consul was a man of honor? Besides, he was a sick man. Couldn't his cousin see that if they kept the ships away only a little while longer the government would be bound to fall? He was a fool if he couldn't.

It had to. Already the *bandoleros* were active in the hills. This time with English money and English arms. The peasants were hungry. How long would they continue to starve for *el Presidente*, who was nothing but a *bandolero* himself?

The ships had to be kept away. The loss of the two and a half million dollars was little enough to keep the present government from making an agreement with the Greeks. And when the government did finally fall, he would more than make up that loss once his own ships returned to Corteguay.

11

It was a few minutes past seven the next evening when the station taxi dropped off Dax in the driveway of Sir Robert's country estate. The butler answered the door.

"Welcome, sir," he said, taking Dax's valise. Dax followed him into the house, which seemed strangely quiet, considering the turnout he had been led to expect.

"Where is everyone?"

"You're the first, sir. The young ladies will be coming on the ten o'clock. Sir Robert will be down tomorrow with the other guests."

He opened the door to Dax's room and put down the bag. "Do you wish me to unpack you, sir?"

"No, thanks, I'll manage. There isn't much."

"At what time would you like dinner, sir?"

Suddenly Dax was hungry. He glanced at his watch. "Just give me time to bathe. Eight o'clock will be fine."

Dinner did not take long. He ate quickly and voraciously and by a quarter to nine he had finished. "The wireless is in the master's study," the butler suggested. "And also the newspapers."

Dax nodded. He turned on the radio and sank into a soft leather-covered chair. After a few minutes he was bored, and went over to the desk for the paper. As he picked it up the letter upon which it had rested fell to the floor. Idly he picked it up and was about to replace it when he noticed it was in Spanish. Since it was already open and out of its envelope he casually glanced at it, then the signature caught his eye.

Ramírez.

That alone was enough to make him read the first paragraph.

"I would like again to congratulate you on your foresight in the acquisition of the four Japanese merchant ships, thus preventing them from falling into the hands of our enemies. Information I have received from my compatriots at home indicates that the government is under extreme pressure to secure immediate relief."

Dax felt a cold chill inside him despite the roaring fire in the grate. What kind of man was this who with one hand offered you comfort and friendship and welcomed you into his home, while with the other he was helping your enemies to destroy you? He read on.

"The uprising is slowly gaining momentum. But, as you know, we suffer seriously from a lack of arms and munitions, and since the cost of obtaining these is prohibitive because they must be smuggled across the Andes from neighboring countries, I am reluctantly forced again to request additional funds. I hesitate to place again a burden on your ever so willing generosity but ten thousand pounds is an immediate necessity if our plans are to meet with the success we all hope for. If you cannot spare this, even five thousand would be of great help."

Dax's mouth twisted grimly. He wondered how much of the money Ramírez siphoned off before any of it reached his so-called compatriots.

"I will appreciate hearing from you at your earliest convenience and until then please accept the gratitude of myself and my compatriots for your aid in our mutual struggle to overthrow the despotic bandit who unlawfully seized control of our poor country."

Ramírez. If he weren't so angry he might have laughed. Ramírez the thief, the coward. Ramírez the betrayer. Ramírez was not one to bandy about names. Dax stared down at the letter. His father would have to be made aware of it. And the baron.

Suddenly the thought crossed his mind; could the baron already know? Could he, too, be a part of the scheme? He did not know whom he could trust. He folded the letter and thrust it into his pocket. He would have to caution his father.

He started from the room angrily. He would leave for

195

Paris tonight. Then he stopped. That would be exactly the wrong thing to do. Sir Robert would wonder about his abrupt departure; it might only serve to call attention to the missing letter. He would have to stay for the weekend, perhaps even longer. He forced himself to go back to his chair. When the butler came in to announce the arrival of the young ladies he was quietly reading the newspaper.

They looked enough alike to be twins, though they weren't. Enid, the oldest, was eighteen, her sister, Mavis, a year younger. "See, I told you he'd be down tonight," one of them said to the other.

Dax took her hand. "Hello, Enid."

She laughed. "I'm Mavis."

He smiled. "I'll never be able to tell you apart."

"Did mother and father come down?"

He shook his head. "No. The butler told me they aren't expected until tomorrow."

"Good," Enid said, "then we'll have the house to ourselves tonight."

"We'll have our own private little party," Mavis added. She looked at her sister. "Who might be around that we could ask over?"

"Why bother?" Enid looked at Dax. "I'm sure the three of us can have a perfectly marvie time."

"Parties?" Dax laughed. "Is that all you can think of? I'm so tired the only thing I can think of is another hot bath and a good night's sleep."

"Must you always be so serious? Don't you ever think of having fun?"

"Tomorrow I'll think about having fun."

He leaned back in the big marble tub and closed his eyes. The steam came up to his face and he relaxed, then he heard a faint sound and his eyes opened. He looked back toward the door to his room. There was no one there. The sound came again. A puzzled expression came over his face.

Then abruptly the door opened and the two sisters stood there, along with a cold blast of air from the empty corridor behind them.

"For Christ's sake close the damn door!" he yelled, grabbing for a towel. "You want me to freeze to death?"

But Mavis was quicker. She pulled the towel just out of

196

his reach, laughing, while Enid closed the door. He stared at them, trying to cover himself with his hands. After a moment he gave it up as a bad job. They were still laughing. "What's so funny? Your bathtub out of order?"

Enid sat down on the stool next to the tub. "We thought since you were so tired the least we could do was give you one of our medicinal baths."

"Medicinal baths?"

"Yes, they're very stimulating. All the girls at school take them." She reached over and turned on the cold-water tap.

Dax almost jumped out of the tub when the icy water hit his back. "You're both crazy!" he yelled.

The two girls pushed him back into the water.

"Sit there, don't be such a baby. Here, take a drink of this," Enid said, holding out a bottle.

"What is it?" he asked suspiciously.

"Brandy."

He took the bottle and squinted at it. It was half empty. "Where'd you get this?"

"From Daddy's liquor cabinet."

"Half empty?"

"We were bored," Mavis said. "What did you expect us to do? You didn't want to have a party."

"Then we got the idea of giving you a medicinal bath," Enid added. "Miss Purvis, at school, always claims they're the best remedy for physical tiredness."

That explained it. They were both high. Dax shrugged his shoulders and took a swig of the brandy. At least it warmed him.

Mavis touched the water. "I think it's cold enough now. What do you think?"

Enid put in her fingers. "It's cold enough."

Dax took another swig of the brandy, and lay back in the tub, resigned. "Now what?"

"You'll see," Mavis said. "Get out of the tub."

"All right. Hand me a towel."

"No." She held the towel just out of his reach. "Get out of the tub first."

"I will not."

"Oh, no?" Enid giggled. Quickly she turned on the cold water again.

He was out of the tub almost before the icy spray hit. He

stood there shivering as they began to slap at him with the rough Turkish towels. "Hey, that hurts. Cut it out!"

Instead they flicked the towels harder. He jumped around trying to avoid their attack and at the same time not drop the bottle. Finally he managed to duck past them into his bedroom. He dove into bed, pulling the covers up over him.

They stood at the foot of his bed, owlishly watching him.

"Now that you've had your fun, why don't you go back to bed?"

A curious look passed between them. "All right," Mavis said. "Give us back our bottle."

Dax took another sip. "Why should I?" He began to feel the spread of its warmth. "I think I'm entitled to something after all I went through. I may even come down with pneumonia."

"We won't leave without the brandy."

He was beginning to feel good now. "If you want it you'll have to take it away from me."

They moved toward him threateningly. He pushed the bottle under the pillow and crossed his arms on his chest. Abruptly they snatched the blanket away, leaving him naked on the bed. This time he made no move to cover himself. "Well, what are you going to do about it?"

"Did you ever see anything so immensely beautiful?" Enid whispered in an almost awed voice as she reached up to unbutton the blouse of her pajamas.

Sometime during the night one of the sisters had gone out and fetched another bottle of brandy but Dax was not sure which. They kept changing places so often that he was never quite clear which was which. The one thing he was certain of was that this was not the first time they had played games like this together.

Now Enid—or was it Mavis?—took a drink from the bottle. "I don't know ever when I felt so well screwed." She sighed, and looked down at Dax's face in her lap. "And to think we had you down for a fag."

Mavis—or was it Enid?—raised her face from his lap and saw the puzzled expression on his face. "You know—fagot, queer, homosexual."

He laughed. "What made you think that?"

"So many are, you know," she said seriously. "It's these

damned public schools. They all get buggered so much they begin to like it."

"With girls like you around?" he said, reaching for the bottle.

"That's the only way some of them will do it," Mavis replied. "They say it's better that way." She rolled over and took the bottle from Dax. "Next time we'll try it that way."

"Fongool," Enid said, giggling.

Dax woke at the first morning light. He flung out a hand and touched warm naked flesh. Sitting up in bed, he reached across Enid and picked up his wristwatch from the night table. It was almost five o'clock. He looked down at the sleeping girls. The French were right about English women; they did not have the charm of their own women. But when they were in bed there were none like them; they had all the amatory instincts of alley cats.

He reached over and shook them. Mavis opened her eyes. "It's morning," he whispered, "you'd better be getting back to your own rooms."

"Oh." She sat up and stretched. "Is Enid up?"

But Enid wouldn't open her eyes and in the end the two of them had to carry her back across the hall. Dax dropped her onto her own bed and turned to leave.

Mavis stopped him, her hand on his arm. "Dax."

He looked down at her. "Yes?"

"It was a good party, wasn't it?"

He smiled. "It was great."

She hesitated; her glance fell before his. "Will there be a next time?"

"Of course."

She looked up into his face and smiled. "The house will be too full this weekend. Too bad you can't get down to Brighton during the week. We have our own apartment near school."

"Who says I can't? Will it be all right if I bring a friend?"

"Of course." Then she looked up at him, a worried look in her eyes. "But—"

"He's all right, he knows how to keep his mouth shut. You know him. Sergei. The Russian who plays on the French polo team with me."

"Oh, yes." She began to smile. "That could be real fun. When would you come?"

"Monday night, if that's all right with you."

Later that morning, before anyone arrived, he went down to the village and called Sergei at the hotel in London. As a reward for winning, the whole team was staying over. He wasn't worried about Sergei not coming once he'd explained. Sergei would know just what he was talking about.

12

Sir Robert looked down at the photographs on his desk. His face did not change expression as he looked up. "You could go to jail for this, you know."

Dax remained impassive. He did not answer. He knew that Sir Robert was bluffing. Silence fell into the room; only the faint hum of commerce seeped through the walls from the banking area outside.

Sergei had used almost the same words when Dax had broached the idea to him at the hotel in Brighton but Dax had laughed. "On what grounds? Do you think Sir Robert would want the publicity? Don't forget it's his daughters who will be involved."

"Just make sure my face isn't in the pictures," Sergei had said, acquiescing.

"It isn't your face I need," Dax had answered. He paid the luncheon check and got to his feet. "Let's go. We still have to buy a camera and some film."

"You'd better get developing equipment as well. You can't take pictures like that into the corner store to be developed. But what if the girls won't go along with the idea?"

"When they've had enough to drink they'll do anything," Dax had answered, and he'd been right.

Sir Robert shuffled the photographs and placed them in a

200

small neat pile in front of him. "How much do you want for these?"

"Nothing," Dax replied, "they're yours."

The banker looked at him for a moment. "The negatives then?"

"There are four ships in Macao that were promised to my father two years ago. When they arrive in Corteguay the negatives will be mailed to you."

"That's out of the question," Sir Robert said. "I don't control those ships."

"Ramírez thinks you do."

Sir Robert stared at him. "So that's what happened to the letter."

Dax did not answer.

"Is that your conception of honor?" Sir Robert demanded angrily. "To betray your welcome in the home of your host?"

The beginnings of anger stirred in Dax's voice. "You're not the one to lecture me. When your own value of honor is how much you gain by its betrayal."

It was Sir Robert's turn to be silent. He stared down at the pile of photographs. "I do what I think is best for England."

Dax rose to his feet. "For your sake, Sir Robert, and my own, I would much prefer to believe that than to believe you acted out of greed."

He started for the door. Sir Robert's voice stopped him. "I need time to consider this."

"There's no hurry, Sir Robert. I'm returning to Paris today. If, say, by the end of next week I do not have a favorable reaction to my request, Ramírez' letter will be shown to your cousin the baron, and to my father. Then a thousand duplicates of each of those photographs will be distributed all over Europe."

Sir Robert's lips were tightly pressed together. His eyes stared coldly at Dax. "And if I should, as you put it, react favorably? You surely don't expect me to communicate with you directly?"

"No, Sir Robert. I shall learn of your decision soon enough from my father."

"And Ramírez? Don't you want me to do something about him?"

A yellow light flashed in Dax's dark eyes. The banker felt a chill run through him at the sudden savageness that came into the boy's voice. "No, Sir Robert. I have my own plans for him."

Sir Robert's breakfast coffee slowly turned cold as he read a headline in his newspaper the following morning:

FORMER DIPLOMAT AND AIDE MURDERED ON ITALIAN RIVIERA

He felt his hands begin to tremble as he remembered the look in Dax's eyes. He shuddered, recalling how he had urged the boy to stay with them when he entered Sandhurst. Beneath it all the boy was nothing but a savage; all the education, the polish, was merely a thin veneer covering up the jungle. There was no telling what an animal like that might do. They might all have been murdered in their beds.

It was strange how suddenly near at hand it all seemed. No longer was it merely numbers and notations on a balance sheet at the bank. Now it was people, human beings, himself and his daughters, life and death.

His daughters. He felt a chill as he thought of them coupled with that savage. Whatever had possessed them to behave as they had? They had never given him the slightest trouble before. He hadn't been able to bring himself to talk to them about the pictures. They were such proper young ladies he did not know how to begin to discuss it.

Suddenly he was angry. It all came clear to him. He was a fool for even having doubted them for a moment. Everyone knew that savages in the jungle had access to mysterious potions that even modern science knew nothing about. That had to be it. Somehow the boy had managed to give the girls an aphrodisiac. Perhaps in a harmless cup of tea.

He realized suddenly what he had to do. He had to get them away from here. His wife came into the breakfast room and sat down opposite him. "How are you, my dear?" she asked, spreading marmalade on a slice of toast.

"The girls are going to your cousin in Canada!" he exclaimed angrily.

She stared at him in surprise, her toast forgotten. "But I thought we agreed that they didn't have to. That Chamberlain would never permit a war in Europe."

"He's not prime minister yet! The girls are going, there will be no further discussion about it."

Sir Robert got to his feet abruptly and walked from the room, leaving his wife staring bewilderedly after him. As he walked down the driveway to the car that would take him to his offices in the city he decided that was only part of the answer. The other part was that Corteguay would get her four ships.

Because now it wasn't the threat of scandal or exposure or even for that matter the possible besmirching of his honor if his cousin learned of his betrayal. It was much simpler and more basic than that. For the first time in his life Sir Robert no longer felt protected by his position and his money. They were scarcely the armor that would deflect the thrust of a savage's knife. The ice-cold fear of death danced on his spine.

The sound of the muffled drums echoed hollowly on the dock behind him as Dax followed the flag-covered coffin up the gangplank. The sailors snapped awkwardly to attention in their new and unaccustomed uniforms of the Corteguayan merchant marine. Silently Dax watched as the coffin passed into their hands from the honor guard of French soldiers who had carried it aboard.

Then the soldiers stood at attention as the sailors moved down the deck with the coffin. Slowly he followed them, moving stiffly in his stiff new morning suit and holding his shiny top hat awkwardly. He closed his eyes as the sailors tilted the coffin in order to get it through the narrow doorway of the stateroom.

How ironic, he thought, that his father would never know he was returning in a ship bearing his name. That was the first thing Dax had noticed when the cortege stopped dockside. JAIME XENOS. The white lettering on the black paint was still fresh enough to allow one to discern the former name beneath. Shoshika Maru. It was the first voyage between France and Corteguay for the newly created merchant marine.

It was only a little over a month since the day he had sat in his father's office and Marcel had brought in the cable from England. He still remembered the smile on his father's face when he looked up after reading it.

"Our friend Sir Robert has managed to get the ships for us!"

Dax had smiled at the happiness in his father's eyes.

"Now perhaps when the time comes we shall return home aboard our own ship."

The time had come, Dax thought, but in a way neither of them had foreseen. His father was returning home. But not he. He was to remain. The cable from *el Presidente* had been explicit:

"My condolences over the death of your father, who was a true patriot. You are hereby appointed consul, and will remain at your post until further notice."

He watched while they tightened the straps around the coffin to secure it against the turbulence of the sea. Then, one by one, the sailors left, saluting as they passed, until only he and Fat Cat remained in the cabin.

He turned to his friend. Fat Cat said in a quick whisper, "I will wait outside."

Dax looked down at the coffin, still covered by the green and blue flag with the soaring white eagle of Cortez, from whom the country had taken its name. Then he quietly walked over and rested his hand lightly on the lid of the casket.

"Good-bye, Father," he said softly. "I wonder if you were ever aware how much I loved you?"

13

It was near eleven when Sergei awoke and stumbled blindly from his room into the kitchen. His father was seated at the table. "Why aren't you at work?" Sergei asked in surprise.

The count looked at him. "I am not working there any longer. We are going to Germany."

"What on earth for? Everyone knows that Paris hotels are the best paying in all Europe."

"I am no longer going to do such menial work," his father answered quietly. "I am a soldier. I am returning to my profession."

"In what army?" Sergei asked sarcastically. Ever since he had been a child he had heard about the White Russians forming an army to return in triumph to the motherland. But nothing ever came of it. They all knew it would never happen.

"The German army. They have offered me a commission, and I have accepted."

Sergei laughed as he poured himself a cup of steaming black tea from the samovar on the sideboard. "The German army, eh? A bunch of idiots training with wooden guns and gliders."

"They will not always have wooden guns and gliders. Their factories are not idle."

Sergei looked at his father shrewdly. "Why should you fight for them?"

"I will help lead them into Russia."

"You would lead an army of foreigners against Russians?" Sergei's voice was incredulous.

"The Communists are not Russians!" The count's voice was angry. "They are Georgians, Ukrainians, Tartars, banded together by Jews using them for their own purposes!"

Sergei was silent. He knew better than to argue with his father on this one subject. He sipped at his tea.

"Hitler has the right idea," his father went on. "The world will never be safe until the Jews are exterminated! Besides, Von Sadow tells us that Hitler wishes Russia returned to her rightful rulers."

"There are others going with you?"

"Not at first." His father hesitated. "But they will join us. You had better start packing."

Sergei looked at the count. Long ago he had come to the conclusion that his father wasn't the brightest of men. Somehow he was always in the forefront of every harebrained scheme to restore the monarchy, and somehow he was always the one who lost his money and was made to look the fool. This time would be no different. The others would wait, watching as his father took all the risks, then commiserate with him over his failure. But there would never be any talk of compensating him for his efforts on their behalf.

He sighed. There was no use in trying to talk his father out of it. Once Count Ivan made up his mind, that was the end of it. There was no turning back. The words came to his lips almost before he knew he had spoken them. "I am not going with you."

Now it was his father's turn to be surprised.

Later that week Sergei sat uncomfortably on the edge of the chair across from the desk in the room that used to be the office of Dax's father. In a way it was hard for him to realize that less than a year ago he and Dax had gone to classes together. In the months since his father's death, Dax seemed older, somehow matured.

"So you see," Sergei said, "I've got to find a job."

Dax nodded.

"And there's really nothing I can do. That's why I came to see you. Perhaps you could think of something I could do. I know how busy you are; that's why I hesitated."

"You shouldn't have." Dax did not tell his friend that actually there wasn't that much to do. There still weren't many people interested in Corteguay. The only thing that had really changed was his social life; suddenly he was in great demand for parties. There was something attractive to the French about a young man whose only qualification for the job as consul was an international rating in polo.

"We'll have to find something for you," he said. He smiled at Sergei. "I'd give you a temporary position in the consulate but I'm going home next month. *El Presidente* has decided on the new consul."

"I thought—"

Dax smiled. "It was only temporary. Until *el Presidente* could find the right man."

"What are you going to do?" Sergei was more interested in his friend than in himself.

Dax shrugged his shoulders. "I don't know. *El Presidente* has written that he has plans for me but I don't know what they are. Perhaps go to Sandhurst as he had planned. I'll find out once I get home."

The two young men were silent for a moment. "Perhaps you'd like to come to Corteguay with me?"

Sergei shook his head. "Thank you, no. I would not feel right in a strange land. I wish to stay in Paris."

Dax did not press it. "I understand. I will keep my eyes open. Should I hear of anything I'll get in touch with you right away."

Sergei got to his feet. "Thank you."

Dax looked over at him. "I have some money I can spare if you need it."

Sergei looked down. Five thousand francs. His hand itched to pick it up but he was too embarrassed. "No. Thanks," he said awkwardly, "I have enough to manage."

But he was angry with himself as he left the consulate. The ten francs he had in his pocket would barely last him until tomorrow. And already the landlord was screaming for his rent. Without thinking, he walked all the way to the hotel where his father used to work. Then he suddenly realized, and stared up at the familiar building. Why had he come here? His father no longer guarded the door, he could no longer give him the money he used to ask for.

He walked across the street to a café and sat down in the back row under the awning. He ordered a coffee. He nursed it while he considered which of his friends might be most likely to have something on, a party or even cocktails, where he could unobtrusively get something to eat.

A voice interrupted his reverie. "Sergei Nikovitch?"

He looked up. The man standing by the table was familiar. Then he realized that it was the bell captain from the hotel across the street.

"Hello," he said, unable to remember the other's name.

Without ceremony the man sat down. "What do you hear from your father?"

Sergei considered him coldly. For a moment he was tempted to get up and leave. The fellow was too damned presumptuous. Then curiosity got the better of him. He would not have had the nerve to sit down unless there was something definite on his mind. "Nothing."

The bell captain shook his head. "I do not trust the Germans. I told your father not to go."

Sergei did not answer. He knew very well that the bell captain had done nothing of the sort. He wouldn't have dared. His father would have squashed him like the insect he was.

A waiter came by. "Two cognacs," the bell captain ordered grandiosely, then turned back to Sergei. "And how is it with you?"

"All right."

"Have you found anything yet?"

Damn him, Sergei thought, there are no secrets in this town. "There are several propositions I am considering."

"I was thinking about you only today." The bell captain was silent while the waiter put down their cognacs. "I was wondering if Sergei Nikovitch was doing anything."

Sergei looked at him silently.

"If he isn't, I thought, there is perhaps something that I can arrange. If only while you are making up your mind about the many offers."

Sergei picked up his drink. *"Na zdorovie."* At least the worm had the manners not to say what he must obviously know to be a fact. That Sergei had nothing at all to consider.

"À votre santé."

It was Sergei's turn now to express an interest. If he did not, that would be the end of it. He felt a little better with the warmth of the brandy in his stomach. "What was it you had in mind?"

The other lowered his voice. "As you know there are numerous tourists in the hotel. Among them many rich ladies alone. They are embarrassed to go out at night without escorts."

Sergei's voice interrupted. "You are suggesting I become a gigolo?"

The bell captain held up a protesting hand. "Heaven forbid! These ladies would never entertain a gigolo; they are of impeccable social standing. They would never consider going out with anyone who was not their equal—or better."

"Then what is it you are suggesting?"

"Some of these ladies are interested in meeting the right people. They would be most generous toward anyone who could introduce them into the correct circles."

Sergei stared at him. "Is that all?"

The other shrugged his shoulders expressively. "Anything more would be up to you."

"I don't understand," Sergei said. "Where do you come in?"

"I will arrange the introductions between the lady and yourself. For this I will get fifty percent of what you receive."

Sergei took another sip of his cognac. The bell captain

would certainly get a fee from the ladies for the introduction. "Twenty-five percent."

"Agreed."

Immediately Sergei regretted his generosity. The bell captain probably would have accepted ten.

"There is one in particular," the bell captain continued. "She has been in the hotel almost a week. This morning when I brought her the American papers she spoke to me again about such a possibility. If you are interested, she is in the lobby now."

Sergei hesitated. It was probably the other way around. He was to be brought around for her approval. His lips tightened. For a moment he was tempted to tell this pimp of a peasant to go to hell. Yet the screams of his landlord still echoed in his ears. He got to his feet and unconsciously straightened his tie. "Perhaps. But only if she appeals to me."

"There she is," the bell captain whispered as they entered the lobby, "the red wing chair in the corner."

The woman looked up just as Sergei turned, and a feeling of surprise ran through him. She was not old at all, in her late twenties or early thirties. He had always thought it was only older women who required the attentions of a gigolo. Her eyes were a very dark blue and they looked at him steadily as he felt his face flushing as he turned his eyes away.

"What do you think?"

"Does it matter?" Sergei asked. Then he saw the puzzled look on the man's face. "All right. It might turn out to be amusing."

"*Bon.* She is very nice. You will like her."

"Is she married?"

The bell captain looked at him indignantly. "What kind of a man do you think I am? Would I be fool enough to have you waste your time with a single woman?"

Mrs. Harvey Lakow had two children in boarding school, four million dollars left her by her parents, and a husband who was convinced that if he left the country that summer Roosevelt would find a way to ruin his business.

"I can't go this year," he had said. "Nobody knows what idiotic thing that man in the White House might do next."

"What can he do? And even if he should, we'd still have enough money."

"You don't seem to realize there's a depression," he had replied irritably. "He wants to turn everything over to those damn unions."

"And you're going to stop him?"

He got to his feet angrily. "Yes, by God! At least he's not going to get *my* business!"

She was silent. It wasn't his business. Not really. Her father had founded the company many years ago and had taken Harvey into it when they were married. When her father had died she had inherited the stock and automatically Harvey had become president. But somehow all that had conveniently been forgotten.

"I'm going down to the office."

"And I'm going to Paris. Alone if you won't come with me," she had said, suddenly making up her mind.

"You won't enjoy yourself, you don't know a soul there."

She had waited silently for him to offer to go with her. But he never had and after one week alone in the Paris hotel she thought about what he had said. She was not enjoying herself. She was alone in a city where a single woman was nothing.

She looked at herself in the full-length mirror as she stepped out of her bath. She was thirty-eight years old and though her figure did not have the firmness of her youth she did not look her age. Her breasts were still firm, thank goodness. They had never been overly large so they did not droop from their own weight, and her tummy was almost flat.

But it was her eyes that were her best feature. They were large and a dark blue that shone with a luminosity of its own, an inner fire that time had not wholly dimmed. Suddenly, and without reason, they filled with tears. Angry at herself, she snatched up her robe and, wrapped it around her, walked into the living room just as a knock came at the door.

"*Entrez,*" she called, reaching for a cigarette.

It was the bell captain. "Your papers, madame." And seeing her struggling to light her cigarette, he quickly struck a match.

"*Merci,*" she said, blinking her eyes rapidly.

But he had already seen the tears. "Will madame require the car for this evening?"

She hesitated a moment, then shook her head. There was no place a woman could go alone. It would be another lonely dinner in her suite. She did not even enjoy eating in the large dining room by herself. The bell captain looked at her shrewdly. "Perhaps madame would be interested in an escort for the evening?"

She stared at him, ashamed of her thoughts. "A *gigolo?*"

He caught the faint look of distaste on her face. "Of course not, madame."

She thought of the gigolos she had seen and of the women they accompanied. Somehow you always knew. She could never bear to have people looking at her like that. "I will not have a *gigolo.*"

"I would not dream of such a thing, madame. But there is a young man in the hotel who has seen madame. He is most interested in meeting her."

"A young man?" In spite of herself she felt flattered. "Not a gigolo?"

"Not a gigolo, madame." His voice lowered to a confidential tone. "He is of royal blood."

She hesitated. "I don't know."

The bell captain spoke quickly to take advantage of her indecision. "If madame happened to be in the lobby I could arrange to be talking to the young man. If madame approves, I could then arrange the introduction. If not"—he shrugged

211

his shoulders—"the young man will respect madame's wishes despite his disappointment. He will trouble you no further."

Although she had already made up her mind that she would not go down to the lobby to see the young man, she found herself taking extra special care with her makeup. She looked at herself in the mirror. Her eyes were large and darkly blue and shining with a light that had not been there for a long time. She felt young and excited. I'll be just looking, she told herself as she closed the door behind her; I'll look and then go away. Surely there's no harm in that.

She began to feel the fool sitting there in the lobby. She was certain everyone knew exactly why she was there. She looked at her watch and decided to wait ten more minutes. She was just on the verge of getting up and returning to her suite when the two of them came in.

He is young, was her first startled impression. But then she remembered having read somewhere that Frenchmen preferred women older than themselves. He's very tall, was her second. His six foot three seemed even taller standing beside the short bell captain, and his broad shoulders and dark unruly hair did give him a regal look. She guessed his age at about twenty-four. But it was partly her own age that caused her to overestimate. Sergei was actually not quite twenty.

His dark eyes swept the lobby looking for her. Suddenly their eyes met and she saw him flush. The bell captain wasn't lying, she thought in surprise; only a man who really wanted to meet someone would blush like that.

When he turned his eyes away, without thinking, she nodded to the bell captain. In the same moment, overcome at her audacity, she fled to the elevator.

She had never had an affair during all her marriage and it was because of this that there was an air of unreality surrounding them. Time had been suspended, and if it was not love at least there was romance. Now, three weeks later, she met Sergei at the door with a letter in her hand.

Sergei realized it was over and he felt a regret because he had come to like this quiet, intelligent woman very much. "It is time for you to go?" he asked, accepting a drink.

She nodded. "Tomorrow."

"Tonight then we will have to see all of Paris which you have not yet seen. We will be out all night."

She was silent for a moment. "I have seen enough of Paris."

He put down his drink and held out his arms. She came into them quietly, and he found her cheeks were wet with tears. For a long time they sat silently. The day faded and night came and street by street the lights came on all over the city.

After a while she stirred. "I'd better order something. You must be starved."

"I'm not hungry."

Silence fell again and they looked out at the twinkling lights. "Paris is lovely at night."

He didn't answer.

She stirred in his arms. "I was never young," she said. "I know that now."

"You will always be young."

"Now I will, thanks to you."

"I will take you to the boat," he said suddenly.

"No." She shook her head. "It is better to get used to being alone on the boat train."

"I shall miss you."

Her eyes were dark. "I'll miss you, too."

"But at least you are going home to your family, to those you love."

"And you?" she asked. "What about you?"

"I don't know. My father wishes me to join him in Germany. I don't want to go but—"

"You mustn't go!"

He shrugged. "It is something to do. It is better than hanging around Paris doing nothing."

"No, it's wrong. What the Nazis are doing is dreadful. You must not become a part of it. President Roosevelt says—"

"Your President is Jewish," he said, interrupting. "My father writes that his name is really Rosenfeld, and that he is allied with the Communists."

She began to laugh, and then saw the puzzled look on his face. "You remind me of my husband. He goes around repeating stupid things like that." Then she saw the hurt expression on his face.

"I'm sorry," she said, instantly contrite, "but you know it's not true. I mean about the President being Jewish."

He didn't answer.

"You must find a job."

"Where? Who would hire me? There is nothing I can do."

She sensed the peculiar desperation in him and drew him down to her. The quick male warmth of him reached out and engulfed her. Later, much later, she whispered to him shyly, "It was me you wanted to meet that day in the lobby? Not just anyone?"

He sensed her need. "Yes, it was you. From the moment I first saw you."

It was five o'clock in the morning but the bell captain was waiting as Sergei came out of the hotel. "Well? How much did she give you?"

Sergei stared at him a moment, then negligently, almost carelessly, took the check from his pocket. The other grabbed it and gave a loud whistle. "Do you know how much it is for?"

Sergei shook his head. He hadn't even looked.

"Five thousand dollars!"

Sergei didn't answer. He was still thinking of the woman he had left in the room.

"You must have a cock of steel." The bell captain laughed vulgarly. "You must have screwed her out of her mind."

Sergei looked at him. It wasn't that at all. He knew why the check had been so large. It was so that he could remain in Paris and not have to join his father.

The bell captain drew closer to him. "Was she any good? Some of these Americans are made for it."

Sergei looked at him coldly.

"Well, it doesn't matter, tomorrow she will be gone. There is another woman in the hotel who has seen you in the lobby. When she asked I told her you would be free after today. She would like you to join her for dinner tomorrow night."

Abruptly Sergei walked away. The bell captain looked after him, still holding the check in his hand, and called, "She wants you to wear your dinner jacket because afterward you are to escort her to a *soirée* at a friend's house."

214

15

Dax looked up from the letter. "It seems we are not to go home after all."

"Then we are to stay here?" Fat Cat asked.

Dax shook his head. "No. *El Presidente* has decided that I should follow Father's wishes and go to college. But not to Sandhurst, to Harvard."

Fat Cat's face was puzzled.

"In the United States."

"Los Estados Unidos!" Fat Cat exploded. "Has *el Presidente* gone out of his mind? They hate us! They will kill us!"

"El Presidente knows what he is doing. It is one of the best universities in the world."

Marcel, who was also standing by the desk, said, "Isn't that where your friend Robert is going?"

Dax nodded.

Fat Cat got to his feet. "I don't like it. It is a land filled with gangsters and Indians. We will all be murdered in our sleep. I have seen their films."

Dax laughed. "Can it be that the fat one is afraid?"

Fat Cat drew himself up proudly. "Never!" He started toward the door, then paused. "But I shall never sleep without my knife under my pillow!"

Marcel waited until the door closed behind him, then turned to Dax. "I have been meaning to speak with you for some time," he said hesitantly.

"About what?"

"I am planning to leave the consulate."

"I see."

In a way it did not come as a surprise. Dax had wondered how much longer Marcel would stay for the sort of wages paid by Corteguay. In a way it was lucky for them he had remained as long as he had.

"Naturally I will stay long enough to help the new consul to become acquainted with the routine."

"My country will be most grateful. Have you any plans?"

Marcel shook his head. "I'm almost thirty; it is time I tried something new. Exactly what I do not know. But if I do not go now, I never shall."

Actually, that wasn't exactly the truth. The deal had already been made with the baron and Christopoulos. The gambler's nephew wasn't happy with the shipping lines; he wanted to return to the excitement of the gambling rooms. The *tailleur* had decided to bring him back to France but not until he had spent one more year with the shipping lines. Marcel was going to Macao ostensibly to run the casino, but actually he was going to China to learn the business. He was also supposed to buy as many freighters as he could lay his hands upon.

Marcel had accumulated quite a bit of money of his own that they knew nothing about, and he planned to use this as a down payment. Only after he had secured title would he pass a ship along to the syndicate, and even then it would not be sold to them outright. Only leased on a long term. The rentals would be enough to cover the payments as they came due, and eventually the ships would belong to him. He was certain he would have no trouble convincing the syndicate of the advantages of this. It would reduce their initial investment; they might even be grateful to him for discovering this way of conserving their capital.

Dax's voice brought him out of his momentary reverie. "We will have to find someone to replace you." Suddenly he snapped his fingers. "Perhaps my friend Sergei would be interested. He was talking to me only last month about needing a job."

But Sergei was nowhere to be found. The *concierge* at his apartment said that one day during that week he had packed up all his things and moved out without leaving a forwarding address. The only conclusion that Dax could come to was that his friend had gone to join his father in Germany.

Sergei was bored. Nothing bored him more than gambling. Whether it was cards or roulette, the mere fact that one had to sit and wait was intolerable to him. Already the old woman had forgotten him in her absorption.

This one was not like the American. This was a very wise, very old, very rich Frenchwoman who knew exactly what she wanted. She simply wanted the company of a handsome young man, and Sergei filled the bill. The moment she had seen him in the hotel lobby she had been certain he would.

It was a simple and straightforward arrangement. Sergei was to be her companion. His salary was two thousand francs a day, and she was to pay all his expenses including clothing. Two days later they had left for Monte Carlo.

The casino held two sessions a day and she attended both. Sometimes Sergei would wonder at her grim determination to throw away her money but after a while he no longer thought about it. There seemed to be a never-ending fount. Two weeks had gone by and she hadn't once stopped. Now they were beginning their third at another matinee session.

Idly Sergei drifted away from the table and out onto the terrace. He looked down into the harbor. The white yachts sparkled on the clear blue water, and the palace gleamed pink on the hill beyond. Slowly he walked down the steps into the garden.

The fragrance of the flowers was strong in his nostrils after the thin, aseptic air of the casino. He walked to the edge of the garden and stood, his hands in his pockets, looking glumly out over the water.

"It's very beautiful, isn't it?"

The voice came from behind him. Sergei turned in surprise. It was an almost unwritten rule that one never spoke to strangers on the grounds of the casino. An old man was sitting there on a bench, his hands neatly folded over the gold knob of a walking stick, his white hair and neatly trimmed beard blending almost invisibly into the off white of his silk suit. Sergei did not have to be told who the old man was, though he had never seen him before.

The old man, rumor had it, was the world's largest munitions dealer, and it was also said that he owned the casino in whose gardens he now sat. His yacht was the largest and whitest in the harbor.

Automatically Sergei answered in Russian. "It is very beautiful, Sir Peter."

"You're Sergei Nikovitch?"

"*Da.*"

"What do you hear from your father, Count Ivan?"

217

"Nothing, Sir Peter. I have received only one letter, shortly after he left for Berlin."

The old man's eyes went past him to the harbor. He nodded gently and his eyes seemed to look into the distance. "I don't see why those fools waste their time gambling in there when there is so much beauty out here."

Sergei did not answer.

Sir Peter's eyes came back to him. "Your father, too, is wasting his time," he said, in that same soft voice. "The Mother Russia we loved is lost and gone forever, and we shall never get her back."

Sergei remained silent.

"But then your father is a Cossack," Sir Peter continued, "and what else is a Cossack to do but fight? Even when the battle is already lost he must continue to do so."

The old man's voice suddenly lost its philosophical tone, the blue eyes became sharp and piercing, and the gentle voice hardened. "But at least your father has his reasons for what he is doing. What are yours?"

Sergei was too surprised by this sudden change to answer. He merely gawked.

"You're here with that stupid old biddy who has so much money she does not know what to do with it. So she wastes her days in places like these. And for two thousand francs a day you dance attendance on her like a puppet."

There was nothing the old man did not seem to know. Sergei could only stare at him.

"I am ashamed of you, Sergei Nikovitch!" the old man said indignantly, rising to his feet. "Ashamed!"

Sergei found his voice. "But what else was I to do?"

"You could have gone to work as your father did. He was not ashamed of honest labor."

As the old man turned and started off, two men mysteriously appeared and placed themselves on either side of him. Sergei stared at them in surprise. But Sir Peter was not surprised. His bodyguards were always near him.

"I'll expect you at dinner tonight," he said over his shoulder. "Seven o'clock. Be on time; I'm an old man and I eat early."

The white house with its columns of marble and marbled floors was perched at the very crest of the highest mountain in Monaco. It stood higher even than the pink palace of the

Grimaldis, who were the titular rulers of the little country, for even they accepted the fact that Sir Peter was entitled to look down on them. It was his tax money that paid all the bills.

Sergei looked across the huge mahogany table at the old man, then down the shining expanse at Sir Peter's young French wife. She sat there quietly, her diamonds and pearls glowing in the light of the candles. All through the meal she had scarcely spoken three words.

"My sons are dead," the old man said suddenly, "and I need a young man I can trust. Someone whose legs are stronger than mine and can go where I no longer can. The hours will be long, the work often dreary and exhausting, the pay little. But I offer the opportunity of learning. Would you be interested?"

Sergei turned back to the old man. "Yes. Very much."

"Good," the old man answered, satisfaction in his voice. "Now go back and tell Madame Goyen you will not be returning to Paris with her."

"She has already returned, Sir Peter," Sergei answered, relishing the faint look of surprise that appeared on the old man's face.

There had been a scene that afternoon. It had erupted because madame had felt that she should not be left to dine alone. To appear in the hotel dining room by herself, or even to be served alone in her suite, would be too humiliating. Everyone knew that Sergei was with her. What would they say about her when she appeared alone? But he had been adamant and in a huff she had had her bags packed and left.

Sergei had not actually known of her departure until he came down to leave for Sir Peter's and an obsequious assistant manager had called him quietly to a corner and presented him with a bill. Sergei's mouth had twisted into a wry grin; why, the old bitch had left him with the chits and his room rent. "I'll see to it tomorrow."

The assistant manager was polite but firm. "I'm sorry, sir, we must have the money tonight."

The bill came to almost every franc he had, so now he was about back to where he had started. Tomorrow he would have to leave the hotel and find a cheaper room. He had already made up his mind that he would not return to Paris.

219

"Good," Sir Peter said. "Tomorrow you will bring your things here from the hotel."

"Yes, sir."

Sir Peter got to his feet. "I am tired. I'm going to bed." Sergei rose but Sir Peter waved him back into his chair. "Don't get up," he said sharply. "If you are to stay here you might as well get used to it. I retire immediately after dinner every night." He turned to his wife, his voice softening. "Stay here with our guest, my dear. There is no reason for you to come up early tonight."

There was silence at the table after the old man left. Sergei lifted his *demitasse* and studied her, wondering what kind of a life she could have with such an old man. But she was not thinking about him. She was thinking about Sir Peter. What a kind and wise old man he was.

Sir Peter glanced back down at them from the balustrade at the top of the grand staircase and nodded. He was eighty years old and his wife twenty-eight, and he had lived long enough to know that a young woman required more than jewels and riches and quiet affection. He saw them get up from the table and go out onto the *terrasse*. He went on to his room.

He closed the door behind him. He had done the right thing. Better that she reassure herself with a fine young man like Sergei than with one of those slimy characters who went always around the casino. Besides, with Sergei, he could always keep an eye on things. If at any time it looked as if it might become too serious he could always send the boy away.

16

It did not take Sergei long to discover that he was nothing but a glorified errand boy. Sometimes, during these first few months, he wondered why Sir Peter had even bothered to hire him. And then one day it all became clear.

He had returned that morning from the bank in Monte Carlo with several papers that required the old man's immediate signature. He went directly into the library that served the old man for an office, and found Madame Vorilov there alone. She looked up from the newspaper she was reading.

Sergei hesitated in the doorway. "I did not mean to disturb you, madame," he said respectfully. "I have some papers that require Sir Peter's signature."

"Come in." She smiled. "Sir Peter has gone to Paris."

A puzzled expression came over Sergei's face. Usually he knew when Sir Peter planned to go away. It did not happen often. "Perhaps I'd better go there too. The papers are important."

The smile vanished from her face. "They can wait until tomorrow. He'll be back by then."

Sergei still stood in the doorway. "Very well, madame. I'll run down to the bank and inform them."

"You do take your job seriously, don't you?" A faint smile returned to her face.

"I don't understand."

She pointed to the telephone. "That would inform them much more quickly that the papers can't be signed today."

"But—"

"Don't be silly," she said with a touch of asperity. "Call them, then take the rest of the day off. You haven't had a holiday since you came here."

A smile came to his lips. "That's very kind of you, madame." He came into the room. "But I wouldn't know what to do with myself."

She got to her feet and crossed to the window. She looked down toward the harbor with its white yachts and sails. "Sir Peter doesn't give you much time for fun."

He placed the papers on the desk in a folder. He picked up the telephone. "I didn't think he was supposed to."

She turned to him suddenly. "Do you know why he really hired you?"

He stared at her, the telephone forgotten in his hand. "Sometimes I wonder. It seems as if I'm the last person he needs."

She laughed. "He hired you for me. He thought I needed you."

Slowly he put down the telephone.

"He loves me," she continued, "and he wants me to have everything. So he brought you home."

"Did he tell you this?"

"Of course not; do you think he would be that much a fool? Look, I've brought you home a lover?"

He stared at her, then his eyes fell. "I'm sorry. I did not know."

She turned and looked out the window again. "Of course you didn't, that was what I liked about you. You were too much a gentleman to even think such a thing."

"Tomorrow when Sir Peter returns I'll hand in my notice."

She looked at him. "You *are* a gentleman. Where will you go, what will you do? Do you have any money?"

He thought of the hundred francs a week that Sir Peter paid him and shook his head.

"Then don't be a fool," she said sharply. "You are not to leave here until you have money."

"At one hundred francs a week?"

"That's something Sir Peter taught me," she said. "There is always an opportunity to make money when there is a lot of money around." She came back into the room. "Look for it, you'll find it."

He shook his head. "I'm afraid not. I have no talent for making money."

She looked at him curiously. "You don't like to work, do you?"

He grinned at her. "I guess that's it. Work is boring. There is never any fun. I've had enough of it."

"How do you expect to get money then?"

He shrugged his shoulders. "Perhaps I'll find a rich American girl to marry."

She nodded seriously. "That would be preferable to playing the gigolo to Madame Goyen."

He stared at her. He had not thought she would take him seriously. "But it takes money to make money."

"Perhaps I can help you," she said. "Now go. You have the rest of the afternoon off."

He nodded and left the library, though he did not leave the house. Instead he went to his room and got out of his warm sticky clothing and took a shower. Then he stretched out on the bed and lit a cigarette. Before it was finished the expected knock came at the door.

222

He smiled to himself and, stamping out the cigarette, shrugged into a robe as he opened the door. "Come in."

"I have an idea that may help you."

"Yes?" He saw her eyes fall to the front of his half-open robe. A faint flush began to rise over her face.

She made an effort to look away but in spite of herself her eyes could not leave the fascination of his rapidly increasing tumescence. Her lips parted. "I—"

"I have a better idea," he interrupted, drawing her toward the bed. "I think it's about time I began to earn all of my salary."

"I have to see you," she whispered as he came into the dining room. "Don't go upstairs after dinner."

He nodded to show that he understood and went to his accustomed place at the table. He remained standing until Sir Peter came in, and then the two of them sat down.

After dinner, as usual, Sir Peter retired. Sergei went out onto the *terrasse* and waited. A few minutes later she appeared. They stood at the railing and looked out at the flaming sun going down behind the mountains.

"I'm pregnant," she whispered.

He stared at her in surprise. "With twenty-two bidets in the house you—" He caught himself. "Are you sure?"

She nodded silently. Her face was pale.

He whistled softly. "I wonder if Sir Peter ever considered this one?"

She didn't answer.

"Have you told him?"

She shook her head. "Not yet."

"What are you going to do?"

"Get rid of it. I have asked my doctor to make the arrangements."

"You'll never get away with it. He'll find out."

"I have to take that chance," she said desperately. "What else can I do?"

He pulled a cigarette from his pocket and lit it. He stared at her thoughtfully. "When?"

"Tomorrow. He has to attend the board meeting at the bank all afternoon. You'll have to drive me to the *clinique* and back; I don't dare trust the servants. I'll make up some excuse so I can stay in bed for a few days."

223

Abruptly he flipped his cigarette over the railing. He watched it tumble end over end into the garden below. "What time?"

"I won't come down for lunch. I'll pretend to be sick in the morning."

"What time?"

"After lunch, as soon as he leaves for the bank." She put her hand on his arm. "I'm sorry."

He looked down at her. "I am too."

She started to speak, then changed her mind. She turned and went into the house. He watched her walk up the grand staircase and then turned back toward the harbor. Slowly the sun disappeared behind the mountain and it was night. And still he stood there.

She looked at her watch. It was almost two-thirty. She had heard the big limousine go down the driveway over half an hour ago. Why hadn't Sergei come for her yet? Then there was a soft knock at the door. Quickly she moved toward it.

"What took you so long?" she asked, then the words stopped in her throat.

It wasn't Sergei who stood there.

"May I come in?"

"Of course," she said. She moved back from the door to the center of the room. "Sergei told you?"

He closed the door behind him. "Yes."

He saw the tears in her eyes when he turned. "I suppose there's no use in my telling you that I'm sorry."

His eyes met hers steadily. "There's nothing for you to be sorry about. We will have a beautiful son."

Sergei sat in the train later that afternoon looking out the window at the countryside rolling past. There were times when he could see far out into the Mediterranean from the *corniche* along which the tracks were laid. At other times the mountains hovered over the train like twin guardians.

He looked down at the newspaper on his lap without really seeing it. He had done the right thing. He knew that. And it wasn't only the hundred thousand francs that Sir Peter had given him which made him feel that way. It was the look in the old man's eye when he had told him.

It wasn't that he had been brought to have an affair with

224

her. It was more than that. He had been brought to do what the old man could never do, and now it was done.

A wry grin crossed his lips. Not bad. A hundred thousand francs in stud fees wasn't bad at all. That was the way to do it.

It was better than working for a living.

17

"The first thing we have to do is buy you a few Chinese girls." The language was French, but with a heavily guttural Greek accent.

Christopoulos' nephew was nothing like Marcel had imagined him to be. He was short but slim, and darkly good looking. His suits were immaculately tailored, in many ways superior to anything Marcel had seen in Europe.

"Stay away from the refugees," Eli continued, "the white women will only get you into trouble. If you don't wind up with a clap, you'll end up in a worse mess with the police. They're always involved in one sort of plot or another."

Marcel found his voice. "What do I need any woman for? I can get along without them."

The dark eyes considered him shrewdly. "That's what you think. You haven't met the sort of women we have out here. They keep grabbing for your cock until they get it." He lit a cigarette. "Besides, the Chinese are a strange race. They won't accept you until they see you have accepted them."

"And buying Chinese girls will indicate this?"

Eli nodded. "Yes, and even more. It will show that you intend to stay here. Whether you do or not is immaterial. Once you buy a girl you are always responsible for her; therefore, even if you should go away you will still be here. Understand?"

225

Marcel nodded. It was odd but he understood.

"The next thing is to get you some decent clothes."

"What's the matter with my clothes? I had them all made just before I left Paris."

"They're too European," Eli said. "Only the refugees here wear European clothing. Besides, the French are the worst men's tailors in the world. There are proper tailors in Hong Kong."

"Oh, no!" Marcel groaned. The overnight trip on the ancient rolling ship from Hong Kong had been the worst part of the journey out from Paris. "I won't go back there."

Eli grinned. "You won't have to. My tailor will come here for the fittings."

"But what will I do with all the clothes I already bought?"

"Give them away," the young Greek replied negligently. "Perhaps some Chinese will accept them in trade, possibly for a house girl. But you won't get anything much for them." He got to his feet. "Come. My apartment is in the building behind the casino."

"I'd like to take a look around first if I may."

"Not until you have the proper clothing," Eli replied firmly. "God alone knows how much face you have already lost walking through the casino carrying your own luggage!"

He clapped his hands sharply and a servant came in for Marcel's bags. "We can't even go shopping for girls until after you get your clothing. No respectable Chinese would sell his daughter to a man dressed like you!"

Her name was Jade Lotus. She was fourteen years old and delicately made. Her skin was the color of rose ivory, her eyes large and dark, and her face delicately oval, not round like most Chinese girls. And she walked as gracefully and lightly on her feet as if they had not been bound at all. Marcel could tell with one glance that she was not like the others.

He looked at her father. The old man was sitting quietly, sipping his tea. Marcel turned to Eli. He too was silent. He sipped at the tea.

After a moment he spoke. It was in Cantonese, a language Marcel did not understand. "Your tea has the fragrance of a thousand flowers, Honorable Tao."

"It is but a poor attempt to please the palates of my honorable guests," the old man replied softly.

"I have your permission to speak in French? It is the language of my friend here."

"Of course." Tao Minh bowed graciously. He looked over at Marcel. "French is a language of which I am most fond. It has a music very much like our own."

Marcel could not help his look of surprise but he remembered to be polite. "I thank you for your indulgence of my ignorance."

The old man nodded graciously. He picked up a small mallet from the table and struck a tiny gong. Before its musical tone had faded his tea had been taken away and a long slim pipe placed next to him. He held the thin bowl over a small candle in a glass in the center of the table. After a moment he inverted the bowl so the flame could lick into it. Then he put the stem delicately into his mouth.

Marcel stared at him in fascination. Neither of the men he had bought the first two girls from was like this one. By contrast they seemed common, even vulgar.

"What you need is a girl of high caste," Eli had explained to him. "One of good manners and breeding who will act as your hostess, your number-one wife. It is she who will entertain your friends and run your household. It is she who will maintain your 'face.'"

"Let's get one then." Marcel was tired of the delays—first the clothing, now the girls. He was beginning to feel he would never be allowed into the casino.

"It's not that easy," Eli said. "There are not many such girls around. Usually the wealthy Chinese want them for themselves."

"What am I supposed to do then? Wait forever until we find one?"

"Take it easy, my friend, this is the Orient, not France. Things are not done as quickly here as at home. But do not give up hope. There is one girl I have heard of who might fill the requirements but—"

"But what?" Marcel interrupted impatiently. "Let's get her and have it over with!"

"Not so fast. There must be something wrong with the girl. She is old and not yet chosen. I have asked my agents to investigate."

"Old?" Marcel had asked. "How old?"

"Past fourteen."

Marcel stared at him. "You call that old?"

Eli met his eyes. "It is old in a country where the most eligible are married at eight or ten."

Finally the agents brought back a satisfactory report. Jade Lotus was very beautiful, well educated, and highly trained. She had a lovely singing voice and could play several instruments, including the small lyre of which the Chinese are so fond. It took a great deal of questioning on Eli's part to find out why she had not yet been married, but at last the flaw was revealed.

Jade Lotus walked like a Western woman. It was as if her feet had never been bound. Her father had called in specialist after specialist but there was nothing they could do. He had all but resigned himself to having her forever in his house.

Now the old man nodded benevolently at Marcel. "The fragrance of the poppy is most relaxing after tea."

Marcel wondered at a civilization that allowed one quietly to smoke a pipeful of opium after tea and still persisted in binding a girl child's feet despite all the laws that had been passed against it.

Apparently it was time for the bargaining to commence. "My friend has come here to establish a home."

The old man nodded. "May the gods of fortune attend him."

"He is a man of great standing in the Western world."

"I am honored that he enters my house."

"He seeks a number-one wife," Eli continued, "someone with whom he can share his old age and blessings."

"Many Westerners have so proclaimed," the old man replied, "but in time they all returned to their own land leaving empty homes and broken hearts behind."

Marcel felt his heart sink. This old man was on to him. He looked at Eli.

But Eli was ready with an answer. "My friend is willing to take insurance against such a day, though he knows it will never occur."

Tao drew at his pipe and nodded. "I have come to depend on Jade Lotus," he said. "She is by far the brightest and most beautiful of all my daughters."

228

"She is also the eldest, almost beyond the age of a favorable marriage."

"Only because I have been most careful in the selection of a husband for her. So fair a flower demands a most particular garden."

"Overcaution has placed many a girl in the gardens on the other side of the hill," Eli replied.

They all knew what that meant. Older girls were often sold to brothels on the far side of the port. Tao's expression did not change as he looked at Marcel. "How is one to judge the sincerity of another's affection?"

"My friend offers one thousand dollars Hong Kong as a token of his sincerity."

The Chinese made a casual gesture with his pipe. "A mere nothing compared with the esteem in which I hold Jade Lotus."

Marcel looked up in surprise as Eli got to his feet. "We thank the Honorable Tao for his gracious hospitality and beg a thousand pardons for daring to intrude upon his valuable time."

Tao was upset at this sudden termination of negotiations. In spite of himself words came from his lips. "Just a moment, just a moment. Why are all Westerners always in such a hurry?"

From behind the large screen Jade Lotus watched and smiled to herself as Eli sat down and the bargaining began again. She had noticed that the one who bought her had not got up when his friend did.

The next day a heavyset Portuguese policeman sat in the chair in front of Eli's desk. He took out a handkerchief and mopped his face. "It has been brought to our attention that your friend has been buying wives." He glanced at Marcel. "You are aware that there are laws against such practices?"

Eli grinned. "Is it against the law for a man to hire servants for his house?"

The policeman smiled. "No, of course not." He looked again at Marcel. "But I thought this might be a good opportunity to meet your friend."

Eli introduced them. "Detective Lieutenant Goa keeps an eye out for us in case there should be trouble."

The two men shook hands.

"Once every month he gets an envelope containing ten

thousand Hong Kong dollars. No one has yet been able to figure out where it comes from."

The policeman grinned. "There are always two extra men on duty outside each night."

Marcel looked at Eli. "Has there ever been trouble?"

Eli shook his head. "Not in the years I've been here."

Marcel turned back to the policeman. "Perhaps one policeman outside would be sufficient," he said with a smile. "That way your overhead could be cut in half."

The policeman's hearty laughter boomed through the room. "I think your friend and I will get along. I hear he hired old Tao's Jade Lotus as his housekeeper, the lucky dog. I had an eye on that one myself. But I was waiting until the price came down to where I could afford her."

The fan-tan players at the big table looked up as Marcel and Eli walked through the casino. "The new owner," one of them said.

Another nodded his head. "One can see he is a man of great wealth and stature from his clothing. He is very British."

What he really meant was that Marcel was fair and had brown hair, not like Eli, who was dark.

"Only a man of great wealth could open his house by the purchase of four wives in one week!" a third player said.

"Yes," added the first, "and one of them Tao's daughter Jade Lotus, as number-one wife. You know old Tao. I'll bet he made the Westerner pay plenty even though her feet are not right."

"Begin the game," another said impatiently. "Everyone knows that Westerners are stupid about such things."

18

The smell of the old city was overpowering as Marcel turned into the narrow street. Here there was no chance for it to escape. The buildings kept the street in perpetual shadow and there was barely enough room for a ricksha to squeeze through, much less an automobile.

Marcel turned and looked down the street. At the end were the docks. The faint calls of the fishmongers echoed up the winding street and everywhere was the stench of the unsold catch that lay rotting on the wharfs. The beggars waited hungrily for the fishermen to turn their backs.

A boy pulled at Marcel's arm. The boy was small, he seemed no more than eight, but his eyes were already old. "Poontang, missuh?"

Marcel shook his head.

"Velly clean. Westin style. Oriental. Young, any way you like."

Again Marcel shook his head.

The lad was not easily discouraged. "Eight year old? Five?" He paused. "Boys? You like boys? Velly tlicky."

Marcel didn't bother to answer. He pushed open the door of the house before which he stood, and entered. The heavy odor of incense, intended to hide the aroma of opium, grabbed at his nostrils. He resisted the impulse to sneeze as the young Chinese came toward him.

Behind the closed outer door Marcel heard the boy's voice from the street. "Plick!"

The young Chinese made a face. "I don't know what's happening to the children nowadays. They have no respect for their elders. I apologize a thousand times."

Marcel smiled. "It does not matter, Kuo Minh. The tree is

231

no longer responsible for the fruit once it falls upon the ground."

Kuo Minh bowed. "You are most understanding. My father and my uncles are waiting upstairs."

They climbed the rickety steps to the top floor of the building. Though he had come this way many times now, Marcel always paused in wonder at the change between this floor and the others. Suddenly the halls were intricately inlaid in fruitwood and teak, and the doors were of richly burnished ebony with ivory trim. Kuo Minh opened one and stood back to allow him to enter.

A lovely young girl in classic silks came forward and knelt at his feet to remove his shoes and put on native slippers. When she disappeared Marcel followed the young man into the next room.

There the four men seated at the small table rose and bowed. He returned their greeting and accepted an invitation from Kuo Minh's father to be seated. Almost instantly another young girl brought tea.

The four men waited politely until their guest had refreshed himself. Then as usual it was Kuo Minh's father who did the talking. It wasn't until after they had exchanged polite small talk about Marcel's health and the health of his wives that he got down to business.

"You have word for us about the guns?"

"I have heard," Marcel answered quietly.

The old man glanced at the others, then back at Marcel. "Good. We have a quantity of poppy with which to pay."

Marcel allowed a look of regret to cross his face. "I am most reluctant to report that it is ships my client is interested in, not poppy."

Kuo Minh's father sucked in his breath. "But you have always traded for poppy."

"I am told the market for poppy has fallen off. At any rate it is ships that my client wants."

They began to talk rapidly among themselves. Marcel did not even try to follow the conversation. They were speaking much too rapidly for his limited Chinese. Besides, it did not matter whether he understood. He knew what he wanted.

It was more than a year now since he had arrived in Macao. And in that year he had become rich beyond all his dreams. Almost from the very first deal. It was the guns that had done it. That and the opium. All the warlords wanted guns. The only way they could get them into China was by smuggling them on the little fishing craft that plied the open seas between the mainland and Macao. And the only way they could pay was with poppy.

But the Japanese had proved much shrewder than Marcel had anticipated. As much money as he had to make deals with, it was but a pittance compared to what they wanted for their ships. It was just about this time, when he had been casting about frantically for a way to increase his capital, that he had got onto the traffic in guns.

It had begun when a man's body had been found floating around the docks. Lieutenant Goa was sitting in Marcel's office at the casino when the word was brought to him. He got to his feet, shaking his head. "We'll never solve this one. He was one of Vorilov's agents."

"Sir Peter Vorilov?"

The policeman nodded. "He does a big business here."

Even as he asked the question Marcel knew it was stupid. "I thought selling munitions here was against the law?"

The policeman looked at him peculiarly. "Isn't almost everything?"

Almost before the policeman left the office Marcel was on his way to catch the afternoon steamer for Hong Kong. He did not dare to send a cable from here. He was certain the police got a copy of every one he sent.

The one he sent to Sir Peter Vorilov in Monte Carlo read: YOUR AGENT MACAO DEAD. MY SERVICES OFFERED SUBJECT APPROVAL CHRISTOPOULOS. WAIT YOUR REPLY HONG KONG, PENINSULA HOTEL, KOWLOON, TWENTY FOUR HOURS.

The answer was in his hands less than twelve hours later. SERVICES ACCEPTED. It was signed VORILOV.

Less than two days later Kuo Minh had appeared in his office. Others came and it was always the same. Guns for poppy. In less than a week he found out that the guns Vorilov sold were ancient and had no market anywhere else in the world, and that the price he received abroad for the poppy was more than five times what it cost him. He was actually profiting from both sides of each deal. A year later when the statement came from the bank in Switzerland even he had been surprised. He had over three million dollars in gold to his credit.

It was then that Marcel made up his mind to return to his original purpose. To acquire ships. But if he approached the Japanese they would realize how badly he wanted the ships. The only way was to have the Chinese get them for him.

Now the old man turned and spoke rapidly to his son. After a moment Kuo Minh turned to Marcel. "They say they haven't the money for ships. All they have is poppy. The monkey men won't take poppy."

Marcel pretended to think over what they had said. "Do they know of any ships they *can* get?"

The men spoke rapidly among themselves. This time the old man spoke directly to Marcel. "There are at least ten old ships we can buy but they are expensive. Perhaps they would cost even more."

Marcel kept his face impassive. "How expensive?"

"It doesn't matter," the old man said, "we do not have the money."

Again Marcel pretended to be lost in thought. "Would it help if I found another market for your poppy?"

The old man nodded. "It would be a great help."

"I will make inquiries. But I doubt I can get you as high prices."

"We will be forever in your debt."

"*Bon.*" Marcel got up. "I will be in touch with you soon to let you know what success I have had."

They rose and bowed ceremoniously. After Marcel's footsteps had faded they spoke among themselves. "They are all the same," one said, "sooner or later their greed overcomes them."

"Yes," replied another, "you would think he would be satisfied stealing from both us and the Russian. But no, that is not enough. Now he plans to take even more from us to purchase his accursed ships."

"I think it is time we sent him to join his predecessor in the harbor," said a third.

Kuo Minh came back into the room just as his father held up his hand. "No, good brothers, it is not yet time. We cannot afford to be idle until the Russian finds a replacement for him."

"You are willing to let him rob us even more?"

"He will not rob us," Kuo Minh's father said calmly. "As soon as we find out how much less he will pay us for the poppy, we will double the sum and add it to the cost of the vessels he seeks."

"He has become rich," Christopoulos ranted. "In less than a year he has amassed three millions in Swiss banks. Now we find that he owns the twenty ships he was supposed to buy for us. And he has the nerve to tell us that he can arrange for us to lease them."

Sir Peter looked at him steadily. "What do you want me to do?"

"Surely the money came from somewhere. Since the books of the casino are in order, he has to be stealing from you."

Sir Peter smiled. "Not from me. His accounts are meticulous. He has collected the full amount for me on every transaction."

"Then he must be overcharging your customers."

"That's their tough luck." Sir Peter shrugged. "My prices are high enough to satisfy me. If they wish to pay more I cannot stop them."

"Then there's nothing you can do to stop him?"

"I have no reason to stop him," Sir Peter corrected. "Only you have, only you can."

"How?"

"Don't lease the ships from him. What is he going to do with twenty ships and no cargoes? He will break himself in a month."

"Then the Japanese will repossess them and we'll be just as bad off as before."

"That's your tough luck." Sir Peter looked at his watch. "I must be going now. It is nearly bedtime for my son. I try to be there as often as I can. At my age I can't look forward to being there for too many more."

He walked the *tailleur* to the door. "You know, Christopoulos, you shouldn't be so greedy. A long time ago I learned to stick to my own business. You should do what you do best—dealing cards."

Eli looked up as his uncle got into the car. "What did the old man say?"

Christopoulos cursed.

"He won't do anything?"

"No, he says his books are in order, too." His voice went slightly bitter. "I have the feeling he was laughing at me."

They rode in silence for a few minutes. "What are you going to do?"

"Damn him," the uncle replied, "I told the baron I didn't trust him. If he were here I would kill him with my bare hands."

"Why bother?" Eli asked lightly. "In Macao there is someone who would be glad to do it for you."

The uncle looked over at him.

"If he hasn't been stealing from you and he hasn't been stealing from Sir Peter he must be stealing from someone. So it must be the Chinese with whom he is doing business."

"You know them?"

"Everybody in Macao knows them. All it would take is a letter from me."

"But surely they're not that stupid. They must know what he is doing without your telling them. Why haven't they killed him before this?"

Eli glanced at his uncle. "The Chinese are not like us. In the Orient there is a thing called 'face.' So long as only he and they knew, it did not matter. They still got what they wanted. But should it become common knowledge that he is stealing from them they would lose much face if they did not kill him."

Christopoulos' face twisted in anger. "Give me one month to make the proper arrangements with the Japanese. Then write your friend a letter."

19

Marcel sat behind his desk and studied the American. He was tall and red-faced and his eyes were blue and hard. Marcel glanced down at the business card again.

236

Marcel looked at him again. "And what can I do for you, Mr. Hadley?"

Hadley came right to the point. "I came here looking for ships. You've got them all."

Marcel made a disparaging gesture. "Not all."

"No," Hadley admitted wryly, "only those that are still seaworthy." He leaned forward in his chair. "I am authorized to offer you a handsome profit if you will sell them to us."

Marcel smiled. "That is always good to hear. But I am not yet prepared to sell."

"What are you going to do with them? You haven't yet reached an agreement on your leasing deal. And you're surely not going to eat them."

Marcel was no longer casual. Apparently the American was well informed. "They will lease the ships."

"I have heard they won't. I have heard they made a proposition to the Japanese to buy the ships after they've starved you out."

Marcel stared at him. So that was the reason they were taking so long in answering. "They won't starve me out," he said, more confidently than he felt. "I will find cargoes."

"How?" the American asked. "Here in Macao?"

It was true. It was only small shipping that came here. The big cargoes went elsewhere. There was a saying on the wharfs: If it's too big to be smuggled who needs it? Marcel took a deep breath. "I have agents in Hong Kong."

"You have nobody," Hadley replied positively. "If you don't make a deal with the Greeks you've had it. The Japs will have their ships back in two months."

"In that case why don't you go to them?"

Hadley smiled. "Because we want to make sure we get the ships. I'd rather make a bum deal with you and get them than take a chance on the Japanese."

"You speak frankly."

"It's the only way we do business. My boss has no patience with devious schemes. He goes after what he wants."

Marcel nodded. He knew the reputation of the owner of American Freight Lines. A poor Boston Irishman, he had fought his way up to gain control of many companies and he had amassed tremendous wealth. It was his ruthlessness and determination that gave his shipping line almost a freight monopoly to and from South America.

Marcel tried to remember what else he had heard about James Hadley. In recent years it was said he had turned more and more to politics. He had become important in the political party that had just elected Roosevelt for a second term, and there was talk that the President would offer him an ambassadorship. Already he had represented the country at several important diplomatic negotiations, where he had only succeeded in creating an impression of complete vulgarity. But now he had two sons in his large family at Harvard and there was talk that he was softening. Like all the newly rich he had begun to think of entering the new world to which money alone would not admit him. The world of influence.

Suddenly it dawned on Marcel that the man opposite him bore the same name. He picked up the card again. "You are related?"

The American nodded. "We are first cousins."

"I see."

Hadley waited a moment, then, when Marcel did not continue, said, "Then you are determined not to sell your ships?"

Marcel nodded.

"In that case I have an alternative suggestion. We have fifty ships flying the American flag. We would like to transfer them to foreign registry for tax purposes. I propose that we pool them in a mutual company and register them in a country whose neutrality would be maintained in case of war. That way our ships would be assured of the freedom of the seas."

Marcel shook his head. "That is impossible. They would still be known as your ships."

Hadley looked at him shrewdly. "Not if we sold them to you. Our interest would be vested in a Swiss corporation."

"But what country could we register them in? Swiss registry would never stand up."

"You spent many years as assistant in the Corteguayan consulate in Paris."

Again Marcel stared. The Americans were much shrewder than he had thought. "But Corteguay already has an agreement with the De Coyne interests."

"And what have they to show for it?" Hadley asked

scornfully. "Four lousy ships when twenty would not be enough!"

"Still they do have an agreement."

"How long do you think that agreement would stand up if we pointed out to their president the advantages of doing business with us?" Hadley retorted. "Politicians are the same all over the world."

For the first time in a long while Marcel thought about the dead consul. Jaime Xenos had wanted something like this for his country more than anything else in the world. Still, this would have horrified him. But the American was right. There were not many with the integrity of Dax's father.

"How would you get to *el Presidente?*" Marcel asked. "I was merely a clerk in the consulate. I would have absolutely no influence."

"Leave that to us," Hadley replied with assurance. "All I need from you is an agreement in principle." He got to his feet. "I'm going back to Hong Kong on the afternoon boat. Think it over. I'll be at the Peninsula Hotel for a few days if you should want to get in touch with me."

"I'll think about it."

They shook hands and Marcel stared thoughtfully at the door after Hadley left. He knew why Hadley was remaining in Hong Kong—to talk with the Japanese about the ships. He was taking no chances, whatever Marcel's decision might be.

Suddenly Marcel cursed. Somewhere along the line something had gone wrong. It had to be something he had never suspected. Angrily his fist hit the desk. Damn the Greeks! The old saying that you could never trust one was absolutely true. Already they were trying to stab him in the back. And if it hadn't been for him, they would never have had a chance at the ships at all.

The house was unusually quiet when he came home that night. Even Jade Lotus seemed subdued as she took off his shoes and brought him his slippers. When she brought his evening aperitif he asked, "Are you all right?"

She seemed pale. He looked at her thoughtfully. He knew better than to question her. Suddenly she spoke no French at all, only Chinese, and he would learn absolutely nothing. Besides, he had grown very fond of this quiet lovely girl he had bought.

He remembered the day he had brought her home. His other wives were already there, lined up in the doorway to welcome her. He had thought they might be jealous—of her beauty, of the fact that she came from a better family. But much to his surprise it proved to be exactly the opposite. They exclaimed happily over her beauty and delighted in the profusion of her fine clothing. They clustered around her, squealing in their singsong high-pitched voices, "Welcome, sister. Welcome, sister."

That night when he entered his bedroom there were fresh flowers in the vase near the window, and incense burned fragrantly in front of the smiling Buddha. There were even new silk sheets on his bed. He had just begun to undress when there was a sound behind him and he found himself surrounded by his three other wives.

Laughing and giggling, they undressed him, then pushed him naked between the sheets. Motioning for him to stay there, they left the room and in a moment he heard the sound of a lyre, plucked softly. It came closer and closer. Soon it was outside his door. He turned as the door opened.

Jade Lotus came in first. He could do nothing but stare at her. He had never seen anyone more beautiful. Her hair hung softly around her face, her eyes appeared jet black. The diaphanous silk gown she wore clung to her figure, revealing a body resembling gleaming ivory. She moved slowly toward him on mincing feet.

Behind her came the other wives. One was playing a tiny lyre, another carried a bowl of sweetmeats and candied fruit peels, the third bore a decanter of wine. Jade Lotus stopped in front of the bed, her eyes cast down modestly.

The sweets and the wine were put down quickly on the small table next to the bed, then the two other wives turned to Jade Lotus. Slowly they drew the gown over her head and she stood completely nude. Then they turned to him and pulled back the sheet.

Still she stood there, her eyes cast down modestly. "Come, my sister," one of them said softly. "Sit by your husband."

Without looking, Jade Lotus delicately perched on the edge of the bed. He could see a tiny pulse beating in her throat and the soft puckering of the pink nipples on her

240

breasts. He felt a stirring within him but still Jade Lotus did not look at him.

"Look, my sister," the other wife said happily. "See how you please your husband?"

But Jade Lotus still would not look at him. Impatiently one of the other wives took her hand and placed it upon him. The soft warm touch of her suddenly completed his erection. He reached up to turn her face toward him, and suddenly they were alone.

For a moment her eyes looked into his, then she spoke. "I am afraid to look, my husband," she whispered. "I have heard that Western men are like giants in their parts."

"Is that what the others told you?"

She shook her head. "No, they are your wives, they would never be disloyal. They told me not to be afraid. They said the great size of your part only brought them greater joy and pleasure."

A pleasant sensation came over him. Suddenly he felt strong and powerful. He had never thought of himself as heavily endowed, though he had heard that Orientals were smaller. "Look at me."

She closed her eyes. "I am afraid."

"Look at me!" This time it was a command she dared not disobey. She opened her eyes and slowly turned her face downward. Suddenly her eyes stopped and her breath caught. "I will die," she said, "it will reach into me and stab my heart."

Suddenly he was angry. "Go then if you are still afraid. Send in one of the others."

He saw the pallor spread over her face. He would never know the fear that ran through her at that moment. The disgrace that she would bring to herself and to her family if she allowed him to send her away. "No, my husband. I am no longer afraid."

He laughed and reached up for her, but she stayed his hand. "I do not want you to strain yourself, my husband."

Moving quickly, she suddenly straddled him, one knee on either side of his hips. Then slowly, her hand guiding him, she lowered herself. She was dry and penetration was difficult. Again and again she drew back as the pain became too pressing.

241

He saw her eyes squeeze tight and the tears began to roll down her cheeks. "Stop," he said harshly.

Her eyes flew open and she stared down at him. The fear in her eyes was too much for him. Gently he drew her down beside him. She seemed little more than a child.

"Who told you to do it this way?"

She hid her face in the pillow so that he might not see her shame. "My mother," she whispered. "It is the only way to absorb Westerners, she says, otherwise they will tear you apart."

He stroked her long black hair. "That's not true. Come, I will show you."

He began to kiss and caress her and when he was finally inside even he was surprised at the surge of her passion. And she had come to be his favorite because there was nothing she wouldn't do to bring him pleasure in her frenzy of excitement.

Now she stood before him silent and pale as he sipped at his aperitif. "I will have my dinner and then go back to the casino. I have work to do."

She nodded and left the room silently. A moment later he heard a wail from the kitchen, then the sound of angry words. He had just started for the kitchen when she appeared in the doorway.

Her face was pale and there was a hint of tears in her eyes. "I apologize for the disturbance, my husband."

He stared at her. "What the hell is wrong?"

She didn't answer.

"Well, if you won't tell me I'll find out for myself."

Suddenly all his wives were in the room. They were all crying. Jade Lotus took one look at them and it was more than she could bear. She began to weep too.

Bewildered, he looked from one to the other. "Which one of you will tell what is wrong?"

At this the other wives began to wail even louder. Jade Lotus flung herself at his knees. "Don't go to the casino tonight. Don't leave the house."

"Why not?" he asked angrily. "What the hell has got into all of you?"

"The Tong Minh has already passed the word that you are a dead man."

"What?" He was incredulous. "How do you know?"

242

"This came." Jade Lotus got up and took a box from a closet and opened it. It was filled with white silk.

"What's that?"

"Enough silk to make four mourning dresses. It is the custom of the tongs, so the wife is not caught unprepared for widowhood."

"When did you get this?"

"This afternoon. A messenger came from Kuo Minh and left it at our door."

A cold fear began to run through him. "I'll have to get out of here. I'll go to the police."

"What good will that do?" Jade Lotus asked. "You will be dead before you get there. Already they have men watching the house."

"There was no one outside when I came in."

"They hid themselves. Come, look."

He followed her to a window and peered out through the corner of the shade where she lifted it. A man stood in a doorway across the street, another down the block by the lamppost. He dropped the shade. "I'll telephone the police. They will come and get me."

But the telephone was dead. The wires had been cut. Marcel felt a sinking despair. They had thought of everything. "It must be a mistake. Why didn't they kill me when I came home?"

"Without giving your wives a chance to bid you farewell?" Jade Lotus' voice was shocked. "They are not savages."

For a moment he thought he was going to be sick, then he pulled himself together. "There must be a way to get out of here."

There was no answer. Angrily he turned and went back into the living room. He pulled open a drawer of the desk and took out the revolver he kept there as protection against prowlers. The cold metal was oddly reassuring though he had never even fired a gun before.

His wives came into the room. Jade Lotus whispered something to them in rapid Chinese. One by one they nodded, then she turned to him. "There is one way."

He looked at her, startled. "Why didn't you tell me before?"

"We did not want to see you become a murderer," she

243

said simply. "It is bad enough that the Tong says you are a thief."

He couldn't meet the look in her eyes. "What makes them say such a thing?"

"A letter came from the one who was at the casino before you. It claims you did not give them all the money you got for their poppy."

Now it was clear to him. Why the Greeks were so sure that they would get the ships. They would be returned to the Japanese because of the unpaid balance after his death.

"How can I get away?" he asked almost humbly.

"We have been instructed to leave the house before ten o'clock. One of us will remain here. You will leave wearing her clothes."

"Which one of you?"

"I will remain," Jade Lotus said. "I am the number-one wife, it is my duty. Besides, I am the one nearest to you in size. I even walk like you."

He stared at her. "But won't you be in danger? What will they do when they find you instead of me?"

"I will be in no danger," she said quietly.

But all that night on the little Portuguese smuggler taking him to Hong Kong Marcel would not allow himself to think about her. Or the expression on her pale face as she had watched him go out the door with the three other wives.

It wasn't until late the next night, after the meeting with Hadley at the hotel in Hong Kong, that he woke in his stateroom feeling the throb of the heavy engines. He was on an American freighter bound for its home port in the United States.

"Jade Lotus!" he cried out into the dark. He could see her face and the terrible knowledge in it. That leaving her in his stead had condemned her to death.

Many years later, when he was very rich and there had been many women, he would come to think of her only as the prettiest of the four Chinese girls whom he had bought in Macao.

But that night he cried out her name.

And he wept for the cowardice that had made him flee.

And for her.

20

"I'd like Dax to stay with us here in Boston until he finds a place of his own," Robert said when his sister came down to breakfast.

Caroline hesitated. "But that means his man stays, too. The one who's always with him."

Robert nodded. "Fat Cat."

Caroline shivered. "That's the one. He sends chills through me. He's always watching."

Robert laughed. "That's his job. He's been with Dax ever since he was a kid. Their president made him Dax's bodyguard that time when they were all out in the jungle."

"They're not in the jungle now. Why does he still hang around? It's not as if he were a servant or anything."

"He's part of the family, I guess. And since his father died, he's all the family Dax has."

Caroline picked up her coffee and tasted it. She made a face. "God, this coffee's horrible! Will we ever find a cook who can make proper coffee?"

Robert laughed again. "You say the same thing every morning. You forget that we're in America. Their coffee is different from ours."

"I'm going to write *Papa* and see if he can't send us a cook."

"*Bon.*" There was a sound at the door and Robert looked up. He got to his feet as Caroline's house guest came into the room. "Good morning, Sue Ann."

The pretty blond girl smiled. "Good mornin', Robert," she said in a softly Southern accent. "Good mornin', Caroline deah."

Robert remained standing after Sue Ann sat down. "Then it's all right if Dax stays with us?"

Caroline shrugged. "Why not? The house is certainly big enough."

"He arrives in New York tomorrow. I think I'll fly down to meet him."

Sue Ann looked at Caroline curiously after Robert had left. "That name," she said, "it's oddly familiar. I've heard it somewhere."

"Dax is a friend of my brother's. They went to school in France together."

Sue Ann picked up her coffee cup. "This coffee's delicious," she said absently. "Wait a minute! Isn't he the polo player, the one who became an ambassador when his father died?"

"Yes. But not an ambassador, Sue Ann, only a consul."

"What's the difference? I hear he's fantastic!"

"Fantastic?" Caroline stared at her friend. There were times she didn't understand her friend at all. Why was it every man she was going to meet was "fantastic"? She had heard this phrase at least once a week ever since she had met Sue Ann.

Dax has changed, Caroline thought, as he came into the house with Robert. A feeling of surprise came over her. He was grown now, he wasn't a boy any longer. He was a man. She hadn't realized that less than a year could make that much difference. The last time she had seen him was a few months before his father had died. She had come to America several months earlier than her brother.

Now Dax saw her and smiled. She came forward and turned up her cheek for his kiss, French fashion. "How pleasant it is to see you again, Caroline."

His voice was deeper too, she thought, and alongside him Robert looked like a schoolboy. "I'm so glad to be here to welcome you, Dax. How was your trip?"

"*Bon,*" he said, "until we landed. Then the reporters wouldn't leave me alone."

"You see? We have a real celebrity on our hands!"

Dax smiled deprecatingly at Robert. "Reporters are the same all over. If there isn't any news they will try to make some."

Caroline felt oddly flustered. This wasn't the boy she had teased in the poolhouse. She had the strange feeling that she would never dare do that again. He raised his head, look-

246

ing over her toward the staircase. Without turning she knew that Sue Ann had come down. A faint jealousy stirred inside her. The cocotte had spent all morning in front of her mirror, preening herself.

Caroline turned as Sue Ann came toward them, honey blond and tan. Damn, Caroline cursed silently, why do all American girls have to be so tall? She turned to Dax. "I'd like you to meet my friend, Sue Ann Daley. Sue Ann, this is Dax Xenos."

"*Enchanté*," Dax said, taking her outstretched hand and kissing it.

Sue Ann flushed, then looked up at him. "I'm so pleased to meet you, Mistuh Xenos." Caroline had never heard her Southern drawl so pronounced. "I've already heard so much about you."

Dax turned to Caroline. Instantly he knew what she was thinking. He felt an inward smile. Serves her right, he thought, she has had it too much all her own way. "Why didn't you write and tell me there were such beautiful women in America, Caroline? If I had known that I wouldn't have waited so long."

"Women" was the word he had used, not "girls." Caroline noticed that immediately. He *had* grown up. Suddenly he seemed beyond her and she grew angry.

"I would have," she said, hiding her feelings behind a smile. "But I thought you would be too busy."

Dax looked past her at Sue Ann. "If I had only known," he said, "I never would have been that busy."

Fat Cat came into the room while Dax was dressing for dinner. He stood there for a moment, then sat down heavily. "This country is nothing like I thought."

Dax smiled. "No Indians? No gangsters?"

Fat Cat shook his head. "Not any of those. And the accursed heat. One melts in one's clothing."

"You're always complaining. In France it was the damp and the cold. Don't worry, in the winter there will be snow up to your ears. You will be cool then."

Fat Cat looked at him. "How long are we to stay in this house?"

Dax turned around. "Why?"

Fat Cat shrugged. "The French one, your friend's sister. She doesn't like me."

Dax didn't answer. He knew better than to differ with Fat Cat's instincts. "Until we can find a place to live."

"It had better be soon," Fat Cat said ominously.

Dax turned back to the mirror and finished knotting his tie. "What makes you say that?"

"The blond one looks at you as if already you are between her legs. And the French one looks at you as if she will kill you once you get there."

"You think she's jealous?"

Fat Cat nodded. "More than jealous. She is used to having her own way, that one, and she realizes she can no longer be with you as she was in France. Look out!"

Dax went downstairs and found Robert in the library. "Where are the girls?"

"Where else?" Robert shrugged. "Dressing. I have an aperitif for you."

"*Merci.*" Dax took the drink and tasted it. "*Pastis. Ah. C'est bon.*"

Robert smiled. "I thought you could use it."

Dax settled back into his chair. "Tell me about America."

Robert looked at him. "It's very different," he said cautiously. "I don't mean just different from home. I mean different from what we thought."

"I guessed as much." Dax laughed. "Fat Cat is disappointed. There are no Indians or gangsters."

Robert smiled. "I'll let you in on a secret. So was I when I first got here." When they had stopped laughing, he turned serious again. "What I'm talking about is the American people. Here at Harvard we meet people like ourselves. Aware of the world and of their part in it. But outside the classrooms, in the streets, they are very different. It does not matter to them what happens anywhere else. Their oceans isolate them from world events."

"In a way they are right. They are big oceans, both the Atlantic and the Pacific."

"They won't always be that big!"

"What about school? Is it difficult?"

"The classes? Not very. About the same as any other. It's the other part of school life that is difficult to understand. Their sports. Baseball and football. Basketball. The student who excels in these sports is more valued than the highest scholar."

"It is the same at home. It was like that with soccer. And it was the same for me in polo. By the way, is there a polo team?"

"I do not think so. I have received an invitation from friends to attend the polo games at Meadowbrook."

"Meadowbrook?" Dax's brow wrinkled. "Isn't that the team Hitchcock plays for?"

Robert nodded. "I believe so."

"I would like to go at least once. I have never seen Hitchcock play."

"It's on Long Island. We would have to take the train to New York or fly. It would make a nice weekend; they asked us to stay with them."

"But they don't even know me."

"That's the way Americans are," Robert said. "They think nothing of asking a complete stranger into their homes. Dinner, weekend, even to stay a month. It doesn't seem to matter to them."

"They are a strange people."

"That isn't the only invitation. I must have received twenty calls since you arrived. I'm afraid I didn't realize how much of a celebrity you are."

"I'm sorry," Dax said quickly. "I didn't mean to intrude on you in this fashion. If it inconveniences you, I will be glad to move to a hotel."

"I wouldn't hear of it. This is the first time since I left France I've had someone to talk to." He put down his drink. "It's almost like old times. The only thing that is missing is the big Russian."

"Sergei?" Dax smiled. "I wonder where he is. I tried to call him several times before I left but he had moved out and left no forwarding address. I thought perhaps he had gone to join his father in Germany."

"No, he's in Switzerland. Caroline had a letter from a friend who saw him there. He seems to have come into some money. He's driving a big red Mercedes and seems always to be in the company of rich women."

Dax's eyebrow went up. "I guess our friend was more serious than we thought when he said he would marry a rich American!"

Robert laughed. "He would do better here. You know Caroline's friend?"

"Sue Ann?"

Robert nodded. "She inherited at least fifty million dollars from her grandfather alone. He was the one who started the Penny Saver stores in Atlanta. She'll get even more when her parents die."

"Of course! The Daley Penny Savers. I saw them all over England. But I never made the connection."

"They have even more here." Robert picked up his drink, grinning suddenly. "Can you imagine what Sergei would do with a girl like that?"

Dax laughed. "He would go out of his royal purple mind."

Their sudden shouts of laughter were interrupted by Caroline and Sue Ann coming down for dinner.

21

Her voice was soft and slurry. "Honey, nobody, but nobody, eats me the way you do."

Dax rolled over on his side and looked up at Sue Ann. Her eyes were almost closed and her mouth partly open. Her long blond hair spilled out over the pillow and her full breasts, with their oddly tiny pink nipples rose gently with her deep breathing.

"I can't believe that."

Her eyes opened. They were blue and they looked at him with a fierce intensity. "I mean it, Dax. All the others—well, they act as if they didn't really like eating me, that they were just doing it as a favor."

He grinned, reaching for a cigarette. "Well, they're stupid then."

Her hand stopped his and guided it back. She sighed

softly. Her eyes closed again. "And when you're inside me," she whispered, "man that's so much livin' it's almost like dyin'."

He laughed and rolled her on her side, facing away from him, then, almost jackknifing her, pulled her back against him. He felt her shudder as he went inside her.

"Oh, God!" she cried. "Don't you ever stop?"

"Only when you've had enough."

"I never get enough!" she cried. A frenzied shiver ran through her. "I'm coming again!" She yelled wildly, trying to pull away from him.

His hands gripped her shoulders, holding her tightly. A moment later her frenzy passed but she kept shivering and squirming. "Don't stop! I want to come a thousand times."

"I won't stop."

Her head fell back against his shoulder and her face twisted around to look up at him. Her eyes were almost closed again and her voice was very low. "No wonder they don't want you to fuck niggers!"

He had been long enough in the States to know what she meant. It was all he could do not to hit her. "You dirty cunt!"

Her eyes closed tight and she pressed herself against him. "That's right, honey," she whispered, "eat me, hurt me, talk dirty to me, and fuck me. That's all I want!"

Later she took the cigarette from his mouth and placed it between her lips. Slowly she let the smoke trickle through her nostrils. "I'm glad you got this apartment. Caroline never gave us a minute alone."

He took another cigarette and lit it without answering. "Is Caroline any good?"

He stared at her. "Why don't you try her and find out?"

"You won't tell me?"

"Would you like me to talk about you?"

"Why not?" she retorted. "I talk about you."

He laughed. "You're crazy."

"French girls are supposed to be good."

He nodded.

"As good as me?"

"No one is as good as you."

She smiled. "I love it. That's all I could ever think

251

about. Ever since I was a little girl. I couldn't wait. I used to get excited all the time just thinking about it."

"You haven't changed much."

She put her hand on him. "You're quite a man." A shadow came across her eyes. "I'm going to miss you."

He was surprised. "Miss me? Why?"

"Mother decided I should go to Switzerland to school. And Daddy says there will be a war soon. Mummy said I had to go right away so I'll be home before it starts."

"When are you leaving?"

"Tomorrow."

"So soon?" he asked. "Why didn't you tell me?"

She looked at him. "Would it have made any difference?"

"No. But . . . ."

She glanced at her watch then back at him. "There's just about time for one more." She dropped her cigarette into the ash tray near the bed.

Later she stood watching him in the mirror as she finished putting on her lipstick. She smiled.

"Will you miss me?"

"A little," he said. "There aren't many like you."

She came over to the side of the bed and kissed him. "It's been great, hasn't it?"

He nodded. "Where was it you said you were going? Switzerland?"

"Yes."

"A good friend of mine may still be there, Sergei Nikovitch. Look him up if you can. Count Nikovitch."

Sue Ann's eyes widened. "Is he a real count?"

Dax nodded. "A real count, a White Russian. The Communists drove his family out."

"I just might do that," she said quickly, then hesitated. "Is he good looking?"

"Very handsome. And much bigger than I. He's six foot three. His father was a Cossack officer."

After the door closed behind her, he leaned back in the bed, smiling. Sue Ann was not the type to be alone for long. If anyone was to get anything out of her it might as well be Sergei.

The telephone beside his bed began to ring. After a few moments he heard Fat Cat pick it up in the other room. He was just lighting another cigarette when Fat Cat opened the door. "Every time the blond one is here the French one telephones."

"Caroline?"

"Is there any other French one here? Are you all right? That other one must be screwing your brains out. I am glad she is going away."

"You were listening at the door."

"What else is there to do in this dull place?" Fat Cat retorted. "Will you talk to her?"

"O.K." Dax picked up the telephone. "Caroline?"

"I've called you three times in the last two hours," she said, her voice annoyed, "but that stupid man of yours said you were in bed."

"That's right, I am."

Her voice was shocked. "In the middle of the afternoon?"

"You know South Americans—we like long siestas. Besides, what else is there to do?"

"Robert has classes all day. He asked me to see if you still plan to go down to the Hadleys' with us this weekend?"

"Of course."

"We'll be by at nine tomorrow morning to pick you up."

Dax couldn't resist annoying her. "Is Sue Ann coming with us?"

"No," she answered sharply. Then her voice softened and for the first time he sensed a happy sound to it. "Haven't you heard? She's going away."

"Away?" He pretended surprise. "Where?"

"To Europe." Then Caroline added cattily, "Her parents decided it was about time she got some polish."

Dax was still smiling as he put down the telephone.

"Dax! Dax!" He heard the call and, turning, swam lazily back to shore. A speedboat filled with youngsters started out to sea just as he reached the small dock, its backwash causing him to miss his handhold. A hand reached out and pulled him the rest of the way to his feet. He looked up and saw it was James, Jr., the oldest Hadley brother.

"Thanks." He looked after the speedboat. "Your kid brother seems to be having the time of his life."

"He is," Jim said. "He's busy playing captain. This is the first year Dad has let him take the boat out on his own."

He glanced after the rapidly disappearing speedboat and his eyes softened. "He's only seventeen, you know. Come on up to the beach house. I'll get you a beer."

"Good idea."

They stood in the shade, drinking the beer right out of the bottle. Jim squinted at him in the harsh sun. "How do you like it here?"

"It's great. You were kind to ask me out."

"I don't mean Hyannis Port," Jim said. "I mean generally. The States. Boston. Harvard."

Dax looked at him. The American's face was serious. "I don't know," he answered honestly. "I haven't been here long enough to make up my mind. It's only been six weeks, you know."

"I know." Jim nodded. Then he grinned and there was something warm in the smile that took the sting out of his next words. "And you've been seeing Sue Ann Daley. That wouldn't leave you much time for anything else."

Dax was surprised. He hadn't realized it was common knowledge. "You know Sue Ann?"

Jim nodded. "I know her. I went with her when she first came up here last year. I lasted about a month. She was too much for me."

They both laughed, and the ice was broken. Then Jim's face turned serious again. "We've heard a great deal about you."

"I've also heard about you."

Jim shook his head. "You don't mean me, you mean my father."

Dax didn't answer.

"My father was curious about you. He thought you did a terrific job the way you filled in after your father died."

"I didn't do much. I just hung around until they could get someone else."

"My father says any time a man can hold a job like that for six months without doing anything wrong, he's a wizard."

"Thank your father for me, but it's easy to do no wrong when there's so little to do. And with only four ships between Corteguay and the rest of the world there isn't very much commercial activity."

Jim looked at him shrewdly. "You think my father made a

mistake when he pulled the freight lines out?" he asked bluntly.

"You've been quoting your father," Dax answered quietly, "so let me quote mine. The boycott of Corteguay was not only an act of economic reprisal. It was also an act of cruelty. It condemned a small country to starvation."

Jim Hadley was silent for a moment. "You don't like my father much, do you?"

Dax met his eyes evenly. That was one thing he had already learned. The *norteamericanos* were all alike. They twisted everything around and made it personal. If you approved of their actions, they automatically assumed you liked them; if you didn't, the opposite assumption was equally automatic.

"The answer to that is the same as the answer to your first question. I don't know. I've never met your father."

"Holy cats!" Jim said. "You're brutally honest."

Dax smiled. "If I may quote my father again, never tell a lie when the truth will serve you as well."

Jim stared at him for a moment and then broke into a grin. "I'm beginning to wonder if it's safe to ask you to have another beer?"

"Try me and see."

<hr>

22

Robert was waiting for them as they came out of the classroom. He was carrying a newspaper, and his face was serious. "Have you seen the latest?"

Jim shook his head.

Robert showed them the bold-face headline: MADRID UNDER SIEGE!

"Oh-oh," Jim said, "that didn't take long."

Robert read aloud: "General Mola, in command of the attacking forces, says the end of the war is not far off. In addition to the four attacking columns surrounding the city, he claims there is a fifth column within Madrid itself, helping with the liberation."

"A fifth column," Jim said. "That's a new word for spies and traitors."

"Hey, Jim!" They all turned as Jeremy Hadley came running up.

"What is it, younger brother?"

"Can I use your car tonight? I got a real heavy date."

Jim fished in his pockets for the keys. "Sure. Just don't crack it up. Dad made me work all year for it."

"Thanks."

"Come on up to my place for a beer."

Jeremy looked at Dax. "Me, too?"

Dax grinned. "You, too. We have no personal objections to freshmen."

Jeremy looked at his older brother questioningly. "It's O.K. You're eighteen now. Dad won't object."

They cut across the yard silently. A strange but closely knit family, Dax thought, observing the two brothers as they walked side by side. There was no doubt that their father ruled with an iron hand and yet it was clear that the boys worshipped him. Everything had been spelled out for them.

James, Jr., the eldest, was going into the law school after he graduated, and then into politics. Then came one daughter, followed by Jeremy. He was going the same road, only he would stay in the practice of law. Two more girls and a third brother, Thomas, who was only twelve but destined for the Harvard Business School. It was he the father had decided would carry on with the business interests of the family. One more girl and then the baby of the family, Kevin. Two years old and already they were calling him "Doc." Somehow the girls didn't seem to matter. Dax wondered whether all Irish families were like that.

"What a joint!" Jeremy said enthusiastically as he sank back into a chair with a bottle of beer clutched in his hand. "I go for a place like this." He looked at his brother Jim. "Why don't you talk to Dad? Now that we're both in school, why should we have to go home every night? You can sell him on it; you can wind him around your finger."

"Not me." Jim laughed. "You do your own dirty work."

"I haven't got the nerve," Jeremy admitted. He turned to Dax. "I could never crack a book in a joint like this. How do you do it?"

"It's not easy," Robert said. "You should see some of the girls marching in and out of here. You'd think you were watching a parade."

"It's not as bad as all that," Dax protested.

Jeremy shook his head in wonder. "Now I know where you got your rep with the girls. You got a place to take them." He turned to his brother. "The back seat of your car isn't the greatest place in the world for romance."

"Dad will romance you if you don't get your marks up to where they should be!"

"O.K., O. K., I get the message." Jeremy turned to Robert. "What were you guys looking so grim about when I came up?"

Robert showed him the headline. The younger boy made a face. "Oh, that. So what?"

"It could mean war in Europe," Robert said. "Germany and Italy are openly helping the Falangists. How long do you think we can keep out of it?"

The boy's face turned serious. "That's true. I didn't think of that." He turned to his older brother. "What do you think will happen?"

"I don't know, but Dad thinks there won't be any war—yet."

"But I hear a lot of guys talking about joining up with some kind of international brigade they're forming. And the ROTC boys are yelling to join up now and get all the cushy jobs when the war comes. Personally, I think they can't wait."

"You haven't done anything foolish?" Jim asked sharply.

"No. Why should I?"

"Don't, that's all. Let them shoot off their mouths all they want but don't you do anything. Time enough to get killed in our own wars."

The telephone began to ring, and Dax picked it up. "Oh, hello, honey."

"He's at it again!"

"No, honey," Dax said, "there aren't any girls up here.

257

Just a couple of fellows." He covered the mouthpiece with his hand. "Will you guys shut up?"

"There goes the weekend," Robert said.

"Can't be much. Probably just some Radcliffe girl."

"I don't care what kind of a girl it is," Jeremy said seriously. "I just wish it was me she was calling!"

"Make friends," *el Presidente* had written in one of his letters. "Meet all the people you can. Someday the *gringos* will want to come back to Corteguay and you will have made the contacts that will make it easier for them to do so. This is most important, my boy, more so even than your studies. It is in this way you will help our beloved Corteguay most."

Dax remembered that on his way down to the luncheon meeting with the elder Hadley. He had done as *el Presidente* asked, though it would have been difficult for him to do anything else. Ever since he arrived, the Americans had sought him out. He was for them a new kind of celebrity. His Continental manners and the fact that he had been born in a country of great violences where life was held cheaply seemed to lend a strange attraction to his charm.

Especially for American girls. After a while he almost always knew that each new invitation meant that some girl would be waiting anxiously to find out whether he was actually all that primitive in bed. There were times he wondered about this curious compulsion to sexual challenge. In many ways these encounters—and that was really the way he came to think of them—turned bed into battlefield, rather than a place of romance. The main thing seemed to be to prove the traditional male superiority. And then somehow when this happened there seemed always to be an undercurrent of resentment. Most of the time he never saw the girl again.

Meanwhile with each new conquest his reputation as a Casanova grew. At times he thought of it with a wryness that helped him absorb the jokes and joshing of his friends. He never thought of himself as they did, and he once remarked to Robert that if the Americans thought of him as a Casanova what would they think of Sergei, whose only purpose in life seemed to be to fuck every woman he met.

That this interfered with his studies went without saying. His grades were barely above passing, and had it not been

258

that his being at Harvard had certain diplomatic undertones, he might have been dropped. It wasn't that he was a bad student; there was just never enough time for him to apply himself.

During the summer just past, his second in the States, he had played polo for the Meadowbrook team, and at the end of the season the great Tommy Hitchcock himself had complimented him. But then he had jokingly taken cognizance of Dax's reputation.

As they stood together in the shower after the last game he had said, "You could be one of the greatest polo players in the world if you didn't do all your training in bed."

Dax had merely laughed. He was still too shy in the presence of Hitchcock, despite having played all season with him, to protest.

The snow began to fall as the taxi crossed Boylston Street, and the cabdriver turned. "Here it comes, the first real storm of winter."

Dax grunted in answer. From now until it was gone Fat Cat would leave the house only for the most dire of emergencies. This man who had faced death and survived so many dangers was more frightened of tiny flakes of snow than of anything else. The white blanket of hell, he called them.

Dax pulled his coat tightly around his throat as he paid the cabby. He didn't much care for snow either. He looked up at the building where he and James Hadley were to have lunch. Americans were strange people. They held business meetings at lunchtime when they should be relaxing and enjoying their meals.

"Dad's been wanting to meet you for a long time," Jim, Jr., had said on the phone. "He thought it might be a nice idea if you could meet him at the Club tomorrow for lunch."

Dax didn't have to ask which club. There was only one for the important people of Boston and to lunch anywhere else would have been sacrilegious.

A gray-uniformed flunky met him at the door and took his coat. "Mr. Xenos?"

Dax nodded.

"Mr. Hadley is already at his table. Please follow me." He led Dax past the bar, already crowded with men having a preluncheon drink, into a large dining room.

259

As he walked through the busy room, Dax recognized many of the locally important men. Former governor, now mayor again, Jim Curley sat at a large table in the dead center of the room, where people could always drop over for a word with him. As usual there was a priest at the table. Idly Dax wondered which one this was, nothing less than a bishop or a cardinal, probably. At another table he recognized another politician, James "Honey Fitz" Fitzgerald, together with one of Boston's leading business lights, Joseph Kennedy.

Then they were at the table and Jim, Jr., was getting to his feet. "Dax, I'd like you to meet my father."

"My pleasure," Dax said, his hand reaching out automatically.

But it wasn't at the senior Hadley he was staring. The other man at the table was Marcel Campion.

23

"Well, I have to get back to the office," James Hadley said, getting to his feet. He gestured with his hand. "No, don't get up. There's no reason for you to rush off, Dax. I'm sure you and Mr. Campion have many things to talk about besides the business we discussed."

Young Jim also rose. "I have a class, so I've got to run along too."

A silence fell between them after the others had gone. Dax looked at Marcel. He had changed. No longer did he seem the ordinary little clerk that Dax remembered. There was something about him that was more positive and self-assured. Perhaps it was the carefully British tailored suit, but it seemed more to be in Marcel's eyes. They mirrored the confident look of a man who knew what he wanted and how to get it.

Marcel was the first to speak. "It's been a long time, Dax, almost two years."

"Yes."

"What do you think of him?" Marcel asked, with a gesture indicating he meant their host.

"He's everything I heard he was and more," Dax answered sincerely.

Marcel slipped into French and Dax followed automatically.

"You know what he said?" Marcel leaned forward confidentially. "That their Mayor Curley could have been President of the United States, only he came thirty years too soon. Someday he claims they will have a Catholic as President."

"I can't believe it."

"*En vérité,*" Marcel continued. "I think that is what he plans for his eldest son."

"Jim?"

Marcel nodded. "The man plans ahead many years. Even now he is entrenching himself deeply in the Democratic party. That is why he is so insistent on the boy entering politics."

Dax stared at Marcel thoughtfully. After the other things he had heard at this luncheon he could believe almost anything. "How did you come to him?"

"It was simple. He had ships for sale, and I wanted them."

"But how did you get interested in the ships? I thought you went to Macao to run the casino."

"I did. But it wasn't long before I found out that ships were available."

"How was it that you were able to get them when the De Coynes couldn't?"

"De Coyne is a fool," Marcel said emphatically. "He leaves everything to that English cousin, whose only purpose seems to be to hinder the growth of any line that threatens his own. It is my belief that he joined the deal only to sabotage it."

Marcel leaned toward Dax, his voice lowering. "When I learned this I remembered the need your father expressed for ships. I borrowed money from some Chinese friends and so was able to get twenty. Then I looked about for more, and there was Hadley with fifty to sell. Naturally I went to him.

But that one is no fool either. He guessed my intentions immediately. My impression is that by then he had regretted his hasty decision to join the British in a boycott of your country."

"You mean he regretted the loss of money."

"In the end it is the same thing. Anyway, he was willing to sell me the ships, but only under the condition that his company would remain their worldwide freight agents. Before I could undertake such a thing I realized immediately that I would have to get a firm commitment from Corteguay. Without that I should have no use for the ships."

Dax looked at him. "I don't know how *el Presidente* would feel about doing business with an American."

"Your president is a practical man," Marcel said. "By now he must realize he can expect no more from De Coyne."

"But there is still the five million dollars that was paid for the franchise," Dax pointed out, "and it runs for twenty years."

Marcel took a thin cigar from his pocket and lit it. The clouds of blue smoke rose slowly around him as he stared at Dax. He did not speak until the cigar was glowing evenly. "Don't make the same mistake that your father did," he said quietly. "Your president is not a man of integrity like your father. Do you know what happened to that five million dollars? Do you really think it went into the treasury of your country?"

Dax did not answer.

"I can tell out what happened to it. It is in a bank account in Switzerland in *el Presidente*'s own name."

Dax was shocked. If Marcel knew, then surely his father must also have known. "Did my father . . ."

"Your father knew."

"Then why didn't he—"

Marcel didn't let him finish the question. "What could he have done? Forsake his post? That would not have helped Corteguay. And getting more ships would have. So he kept his mouth shut, though in a way I think it hastened his death."

Dax shook his head. He felt a tightening in his throat. His poor father. If he had only known! But then, what could he have done? Nothing.

Marcel took advantage of his continued silence. "Why else do you think we are willing to pay another five million for a franchise? Because we are sure *el Presidente* will accept it. Dax, it is time for you to grow up and become a realist. If the deal is made, you will be taken care of most handsomely. It is time for you to begin to think about yourself. Unless you also intend to bankrupt yourself paying the bills of thieves."

"I don't know," Dax said hesitantly. "It's hard for me to believe—"

Again Marcel interrupted. "What is hard to believe? Can't you see that is exactly why your president sent you here? Just for something like this, to make it easier for the United States to return to Corteguay? Don't you think he already is aware that he has received all the aid he can get from Europe?"

Dax was silent.

"If I were not so positive would I offer to become a citizen of Corteguay?"

Dax stared at Marcel. "You mean you would live in Corteguay and give up your French nationality?"

Marcel laughed. "Who said anything about living in Corteguay? I merely said I would become a citizen." He glanced around the room, which was almost empty now. "I like the United States, especially New York. That's where the business is and that's where I intend to live."

Later that night, as *el Presidente*'s voice crackled metallically over the long-distance wires, Dax knew that whether Marcel had told him the truth or not did not matter. The only objection to the proposition that *el Presidente* offered was that he thought the amount to be paid, really an indemnity to Corteguay for the misery caused by the boycott, should be ten million dollars instead of five. And when he finally put down the receiver he knew that his job here was done. It was time for him to return home.

Dax looked around the table. Robert and Caroline, Jim and Jeremy Hadley and two of their sisters. It was good of them to give this little dinner for him at the Ritz Carlton on his last night in the States. He felt a wry grin twist his lips. What would people say, he wondered, if they knew that Dax Xenos, the modern Casanova, sat alone, the odd man at a dinner celebrating his leaving them.

The coffee came and Jim cleared his throat, looking around at the others. They nodded and he got to his feet. An expectant silence fell across the table.

"Dax," Jim said in his easy voice, the hint of a Boston accent scarcely noticeable. "We, your friends, though we regret that you must leave us, respect the fact that you feel you can serve your own country best by going home.

"But we did not want you to go without some small remembrance of us, something that would always remind you, no matter how far away you might be, that you are still with us, still one of us. So, bearing in mind that once a Harvard man always a Harvard man, we decided that the small memento we give you will always serve that purpose."

With unexpectedly clumsy fingers Dax opened the small leather box. The gold ring and the crimson stone flashed up at him. Dax recognized it immediately; it was his class ring, class of '39. He looked around at them, aware of the trouble they must have gone to to have it made. Ordinarily such a ring would not be available to any of them until their final year. And that was still more than two years away.

Quickly he slipped the ring on his finger. It was a perfect fit. He looked around at them. "Thank you," he said simply, "I shall always wear it. And I shall always remember."

Then Caroline was at his side and when he rose to kiss her cheek, much to his surprise he saw that she was crying.

He stood at the rail with Fat Cat as the mountains of Corteguay, behind the city of Curatu, appeared through the mists of the morning.

"Home!" Fat Cat said excitedly, his hand suddenly on Dax's shoulders. "Look, Dax, home!"

The mountains loomed larger as they looked, the motion of the ship steady beneath them. Now they could see the green, the beautiful dark green of winter, which was really summer in Corteguay.

Suddenly Dax heard his father's voice in his ear, just as if he were standing beside him. "For when you return you will no longer be a boy. You will be a man."

Dax felt his eyes blur and the tears begin to roll down his cheeks. "Yes, Father," he whispered.

But what neither of them had known was that growing up would prove to be such a painful and lonely process.

264

BOOK
3

MONEY
and
MARRIAGE

Sergei shifted the thin sheaf of paper on the large bare back desk. There was no chair beside Count Nikovitch.

Sergei faced it hesitation contemplatively. Silently he waited for the overlord.

Kastele now joined the surrender. He rose, tall and ad-detours, tall behind ... Take it quite right, your highness, he added in a harmless voice. "We officers are death. Please sit down, Prince Nikovitch, I'm sure we can at last the change of a ... contact if a gentleman."

Adjacently Sergei allowed himself to be led back to his

1

Bankers' offices all over the world smelled the same, Sergei thought, settling himself into a leather chair. Only Swiss banks smelled more so. Older and mustier. Perhaps it was because of their reverence for money. Somehow he got the impression that their money was older and mustier too.

The two bankers behind the great double desk stared at him. Casually Sergei stared back. He was quite content to let them speak first. He didn't have very much to say anyway. He remained silent.

The small bald one spoke first. "I am Monsieur Bernstein," he said in a tight Germanically accented French. "This is my associate, Monsieur Kastele."

Since they made no gesture to shake hands, Sergei remained in his chair. He nodded without speaking.

Bernstein leaped immediately to the attack. "You're not a prince," he said, his eyes accusing behind the gold-rimmed spectacles.

Sergei smiled and shrugged. "So what?" he replied agreeably. "She knows that."

Bernstein's eyes, behind the glasses, went suddenly blank. "She already knows?" he echoed in a puzzled voice.

Kastele quickly joined his partner in the fray. "You're not even a count," he said in a voice thick with disapproval. "Only your father is a count. He's in the German army."

Suddenly Sergei was annoyed. "I wasn't aware we were meeting to discuss my family." He got to his feet. "I don't particularly care whether I marry the girl or not. It's really her idea." As he turned and started for the door, Bernstein, with surprising agility for so small a man, came out from behind the large desk. He reached Sergei before he opened the door. "*Un moment*, Monsieur Nikovitch!"

Sergei noticed the thin beads of perspiration on the little man's bald head. "There was no offense intended, Count Nikovitch."

Sergei gazed at Bernstein contemptuously. Silently he reached for the doorknob.

Kastele now joined the surrender. He rose, tall and cadaverously thin, behind his desk. "That's quite right, your highness," he added in an unctuous voice. "No offense was meant. Please sit down, Prince Nikovitch. I'm sure we can discuss the matter of a marriage contract like gentlemen."

Reluctantly Sergei allowed himself to be led back to his chair. He had the upper hand and he knew it. One word from Sue Ann to her father would immediately cut the bankers off from all future contact with the Daley fortune.

Bernstein walked around the desk and sat down. There was an obvious relief in the look he exchanged with his partner. He imposed a smile over his face as he turned to Sergei. "We have been in touch with Monsieur Daley," he said, "and we are pleased to inform you that he has no objections to your marriage to his daughter."

Sergei nodded silently. This was more like it.

"However, we are instructed to make certain that Miss Daley's interests are protected. You are aware, of course, that she is heiress to a large fortune which is irrevocably bound to the future of the family business. It is up to us to work out an agreement which will act as protection for all parties concerned."

Sergei still remained silent.

"Yourself included," Kastele added hastily.

Now Sergei allowed himself the luxury of a reply. "Of course."

Bernstein's voice was smoother now. "In return for the customary waiver of rights of inheritance and all other claims upon your future wife's estate, Monsieur Daley has authorized us to offer a dowry of twenty-five thousand dollars and an allowance of five hundred dollars per month after the ceremony. Of course all your living expenses, everything, will be borne by Monsieur Daley. You will have to pay for absolutely nothing. He desires for you to be happy, feeling that if you are, his daughter will be."

Sergei stared at the banker thoughtfully for a moment. "I'm afraid I couldn't make his daughter very happy on a miserly arrangement like that. I'm sure Mr. Daley must be aware of that."

Kastele looked at him shrewdly. "What do you think you should have?"

Sergei shrugged. "Who knows? When a man's wife is heiress to fifty million dollars he cannot walk around with only pennies jingling in his pockets. What kind of impression would that make?"

"Would fifty thousand and a thousand a month make a better impression?"

"Slightly." Sergei took out the gold cigarette case that Sue Ann had given him and took a cigarette from it. He lit it from the matching gold lighter. "But still not good enough."

Kastele's eyes remained on the gold case and lighter that Sergei carelessly left on the desk in front of him. "What makes you think you're entitled to make a better impression?"

Sergei drew on the cigarette and let the smoke out slowly. "I'll make it as simple as I can, gentlemen. It's not what I think, it's what Miss Daley thinks."

"We have only your word for what Miss Daley thinks," Bernstein said quickly.

"No, you have Miss Daley's word also." Sergei pressed the catch on the cigarette case and it opened. He pushed it toward the bankers. "Read the inscription."

Bernstein picked up the cigarette case and Kastele leaned over his shoulder. Sergei did not have to see the expression of surrender on their faces to know he had them.

To my Sergei—
An engagement present
to the world's greatest swordsman
from his most grateful scabbard.
Forever yours,
Sue Ann

The terms finally agreed on were a dowry of one hundred thousand dollars and an allowance of twenty-five hundred per month. And there was one additional clause added by mutual agreement. In the event that Sue Ann should ever desire a divorce Sergei would be entitled to a settlement of fifty thousand dollars for each year of their marriage up to five—two hundred and fifty thousand dollars.

269

It had begun a little more than three months ago, toward the end of January, in Saint Moritz. It was one of those gray days when the clouds and the falling snow obscured the crisp mountains and kept everyone at the resort indoors. It was about four in the afternoon and Sergei lay stretched out on the couch in front of a roaring fire in the small chalet he had rented for the season. Suddenly he had heard a knock at the front door.

Who the hell could be out in this stupid weather? he thought as he rolled over and yelled for the maid to answer the door. There was no answer, and he remembered that this was her afternoon off. She would not return until six o'clock.

Sluggishly he got up from the couch and, adjusting his trousers, walked into the foyer as the knocker sounded again.

"I'm coming." He opened the door grumpily. "Oh, it's you," he said, recognizing the snow-covered man standing outside. "I might have known only an idiot would come up the mountain in weather like this."

Kurt Wilhelma, the *skimeister* at the Suvretta, brushed the snow from his clothes and boots and followed him into the house. "Are you alone?"

"Of course I'm alone. Whom did you expect to find here, Greta Garbo?"

"Nothing would surprise me," Kurt replied. "Christ, it's bitter outside. Have you got anything to drink?"

"There's a bottle of vodka on the sideboard." Sergei threw himself down on the couch again. He watched as Kurt poured himself a drink.

"I think I've got a live one for you this time."

"Sure," Sergei replied skeptically, "like the last one. She turned out to be a British showgirl looking for a sure thing herself. We both felt like bloody damn fools after fucking each other half to death and then finding out we were both working the same side of the street."

"Anyone can make a mistake. But this one is legitimate. I checked."

"How?"

"Well, she's up here with two girls as her guests and she has the royal suite, the big one with the three bedrooms. Lastly, her reservation was arranged by the Crédit Suisse and the bill is to be paid by them." Kurt swallowed his drink

270

neatly. "And you know the Crédit Suisse. They won't do anything for anyone who doesn't have a lot of money."

Sergei nodded. He thought for a moment. "Maybe they're a trio of lovers."

"No," Kurt replied quickly, "they weren't in the hotel more than ten minutes before they began making a play for some of my boys. I told them to go ahead with the two others but to leave the blond one alone until I cleared it with you."

"Blond, eh? What does she look like?"

"Pretty good. Long legs. Big knockers. Too much make-up, like most Americans, but not bad. The kind of eyes that always look ready. Crotch gazer. You can almost see her measuring it."

"American, you say?" Sergei looked up at him. "The others?"

"American also."

"What's her name?"

"Sue Ann Daley."

"Sue Ann Daley?" There was a faint trace of recognition in Sergei's voice. "Let me think."

Kurt went back to the sideboard and poured himself another vodka. Sergei's brow was furrowed as he tried to remember. Suddenly he got to his feet and went over to the escritoire and pulled out a drawer. Quickly he went through a bundle of letters and pulled one out. He glanced at it briefly. "I knew I'd heard that name."

"What do you mean?" Kurt asked curiously.

Sergei walked over to the *skimeister*, smiling. "You know, old man, I think this time you really do have a live one."

Kurt smiled. "You know of her?"

Sergei nodded. "A friend of mine wrote me about her about a year ago when she first came to Switzerland. I was too busy to look her up."

Sergei went back to the escritoire and sat down. He pulled a sheet of notepaper toward him. The kind that bore the crest and *Prince Sergei Nikovitch*. He scribbled quickly across the page, then folded it and put it in an envelope. He wrote her name across the front in bold script. He turned to Kurt.

"Here. Send this up to her room with a dozen roses. I'll come by at nine to take her and her two friends to dinner. And tell Émile that I want my special table in the corner, with flowers and candles, a corsage at each place setting, and a magnum of Piper '21."

Kurt looked at him. There was never a question in his mind that the girls might not come to dinner. Only one thing troubled him. "How about the money for the flowers?"

Sergei laughed. "Lay it out. What the hell, you can afford it with a twenty-five-percent cut."

2

Sue Ann stuffed another chocolate into her mouth and rose from the chaise longue. She walked across the room and stopped in front of the long full-length mirror, dropping her negligee. She stared at her naked reflection with dissatisfaction. "Christ! I must have put on at least fifteen pounds since I came to Switzerland."

"It's not that bad," Maggie replied swiftly.

"It's those damn chocolates," Joan said, "they'll do it every time."

Sue Ann turned to look at her friends, sitting on the couch. "How do you two do it? You've been here two years and you're both as thin as you were back home."

"We were the same the first year," Joan said. "But then you taper off."

"It's that damn school," Sue Ann answered. "It's like a prison. There's nothing to do but eat. I couldn't wait for the holidays."

"Well, here we are."

"And I can't get into one of my evening dresses," Sue Ann said. "What the hell can I wear to dinner tonight?"

Maggie grinned. "Why don't you go like you are? It would save a lot of time."

Sue Ann walked back to the box of chocolates and picked

out another. "Don't think I wouldn't like to. I'm so horny I'll probably come when he kisses my hand."

"Is the table to your satisfaction, your highness?" Émile asked respectfully.

Sergei looked it over critically. "It's perfect, Émile. Sometimes I wonder why you aren't at the Ritz in Paris. You should be where your talents would be truly appreciated."

Émile bowed. "You're too kind, your highness. Your usual aperitif?"

Sergei nodded and Émile walked away. Sergei looked around. He had been aware of the curious eyes of the other diners as he came through the room. He knew the picture he made. Evening clothes made him appear even taller and the white of his shirt front contrasted nicely with the deep winter tan on his face. He nodded politely to several people he knew, then picked up the drink that the waiter had unobtrusively put down. He sipped it slowly. His guests should arrive at any moment. He had sent his card up to their suite before he entered the dining room.

He glanced up as the three girls came in. My God, he thought as he got to his feet, she's wearing absolutely nothing under that dress!

Sue Ann was heavy but she was tall enough to get away with it. She walked straight, her flesh and the silk of her dress moving together with a liquid fluidity, her breasts straining against the thin chiffon. She stopped in front of him and held out her hand. "Dax spoke about you quite often."

Sergei smiled. He lifted her hand to his lips. The other girls giggled. That was one consoling thought—at least she didn't giggle. There was some hope for her after all.

"And what shall we call you?" Sue Ann asked after they had all been seated. "It's kind of awkward if we 'your highness' you all night."

"Why don't you just call me Sergei? After all, I'm not really a prince, you know. My father is only a count."

"You enjoy winter sports?" he asked politely a moment later.

"Oh, yes," the other two said almost as one.

"Not me," Sue Ann said bluntly. "I'm from the South. I hate snow and cold."

273

He looked at her with a kind of surprise. "Then why did you come here?"

She stared into his eyes. "For a good time. I like to ball."

"Ball?"

"You know, ball. Have fun. The things you can't do in a girls' school."

"I think I know what you mean." He began to smile. "I must say I approve. Skiing and skating are a waste of time."

The orchestra began to play and he got to his feet. "I trust your dislike for sports does not extend to the dance?"

Sue Ann laughed and shook her head. "Uh-uh. I love to dance."

The music was a tango and he felt the softness and the warmth of her through the thin silk dress as he pressed himself against her. He was a better dancer than she but because he was she never knew it. He led her sinuously into the dance until they seemed to mold into one liquid movement.

He felt the press of her large warm breasts against his chest and looked down into her face. Her eyes were almost closed and her lips were parted. This one is ready, he thought. He let his strength flow into his loins and pressed himself against her.

Her eyes flicked open suddenly and she stared up at him. "Sorry, I couldn't help that."

She smiled. "Don't apologize. I love it." She pressed herself tighter to him as they finished the dance.

He led her back to the table and then dutifully danced with the others. But neither had the demanding, driving sexuality of Sue Ann, though in their own way, they were more attractive to him.

When he sat down again he unobtrusively moved his chair so that their legs could touch. Later he found her hand under the table and placed it on his hardness. And all the while he kept making light conversation as if nothing at all was going on.

After the main course, the orchestra began to play another tango. He looked at her. "Our dance?"

She nodded and started to get up. Suddenly she stopped and sat down again. "Damn!" she said furiously.

"What is it?"

She glanced at the other girls, then at him. "I knew I

should have worn panties. I'm all wet and it's gone through the dress. Everyone will see."

"What will we do?" Maggie asked.

"We could sit here until they close," Joan said.

"Don't be a damn fool, the restaurant doesn't close until two in the morning."

"Don't worry about it." Sergei smiled. "I can handle it. No one will know."

"You can?"

"Sure." He leaned toward her. As if by accident his hand knocked over the glass of champagne, which flowed down into her lap.

"Oh, I'm so terribly sorry!" he exclaimed in a voice loud enough to be heard at the nearby tables. He got to his feet, dabbing at her with his napkin. "A thousand apologies for my clumsiness!"

Sue Ann began to smile as the waiters hurried up solicitously. She got to her feet, the two girls and the waiter surrounding her. "You will come up to the suite for coffee and dessert, won't you?"

"Of course."

He remained standing until they had left the room, then sat down again and called for the check. He signed it with a flourish. As he was crossing the lobby on his way to the elevators, Kurt walked up to him. "Well?"

"Don't worry, this one will pay the rent."

Joan opened the door for him. He entered the room. Sue Ann was seated on the couch in a negligee. "Everything all right now?" he asked, smiling.

She nodded.

"I took the liberty of ordering coffee and sweets. Then a pot of caviar and more champagne."

"Caviar and champagne?"

"It's the best thing for a long happy night."

Maggie got to her feet. "We'll go to our rooms."

Sergei spoke to her but kept looking at Sue Ann. "What for? I thought we were going to have a party."

"But there's only you."

"Why do you think I ordered caviar and champagne?"

Sue Ann began to laugh. This was the kind of language she understood. "You think you're pretty good."

He smiled, looking down at her. "I'm the best there is."

"Enough for all of us?"

"I'm a very simple man. It's the only sport in which I indulge. Everything else is a waste of time."

Sue Ann looked at the other girls. "What do you say, kids? I'm willing."

Maggie and Joan looked at each other hesitantly.

"Come on, what are you waiting for?" Sergei laughed. "I always put on a better show when there's an audience."

"I'm hungry," Sergei said.

"So am I."

"You two go ahead," Maggie said sleepily. "I can't keep my eyes open."

"What about—" Sergei never finished his question, for Joan was fast asleep. He looked at Sue Ann and grinned. "It looks like just the two of us."

"That's the way it would have been," she said with a slight edge of sarcasm, "if you weren't such a showoff."

He laughed again and got out of bed and padded naked into the sitting room. He sat down on the couch and began to spread the thin toast with butter, then liberally covered it with heavy spoonsful of grosgrain caviar.

He looked up as Sue Ann came in and stood beside him. "Help yourself," he said, gesturing, his mouth full.

"You're a pig!"

He didn't answer. He picked up another slice of toast.

"I thought you Continentals were supposed to be such gentlemen."

"If you want to be treated like a lady go put some clothes on," he retorted.

She stared at him for a moment, then turned and went into the bathroom. When she came back she was carrying two white terrycloth robes. She tossed one at him while she shrugged into the other. She sank into the chair opposite him. His robe still lay where it fell, across his lap.

"What are you staring at?"

"Nothing." She hesitated, then asked, "Just between the two of us, what were you trying to prove?"

He stared back at her, suddenly aware that she was brighter than he had thought. "What do you mean?"

276

"O.K., so Dax is your friend. But he wasn't the only man I ever went to bed with."

He didn't answer.

"Were you trying to show me that you were a better man than Dax?"

He grinned. "No, you were right the first time. I'm a pig. I just thought it would be fun to bang all three of you."

She shook her head. "I don't buy that. You're not that stupid."

"O.K.," he said, suddenly angry, "so I was trying to prove I was a better man."

"You don't have to get angry. You are, you know." She smiled. "You've made your point. You're the most man I ever had."

He relaxed suddenly.

"I've never known anything like you. I kept coming all the time. Even while you were with them. Each time they did, I did. After a while I got mad. I wanted you for myself. You knew that, didn't you?"

"Yes."

She stared at him. "What are you going to do about it?"

He got to his feet suddenly. "Come on, get some clothes on."

"Where are we going?"

"To my place, where we can be alone."

She looked at him, hesitating. Then she gestured toward the other bedrooms. "What about them?"

"Fuck them," he said, "let them find their own. You're the only one I want."

3

The March sunshine bounced off the snow, sparklingly blinding. It poured through the open window into the room, where they sat at breakfast.

"I think you're going to have to marry me, boy."

Sergei picked up his glass of orange juice. "What for?"

"The usual reasons. I'm knocked up."

He was silent.

"You never figured on that, did you?"

"I thought about it," he said, "but I figured you'd taken care of things."

She smiled. "Who had the time? Are you angry?"

He shook his head.

"Then what are you thinking?"

"I know a doctor. He's very good."

This time it was Sue Ann who didn't speak. After a moment he could see the tears hovering just behind her eyes. Her voice was flat and dull. "O.K., if that's what you want."

"No," he answered harshly, "that's not what I want. But can't you see what they'll do to you?"

"I don't care. I'm not the first girl that ever went to the altar carrying a package."

"That's not what I mean. Look, it's O.K. for you to be having fun and games with a phony prince. But marrying one is another story. They'll make you a laughingstock!"

"My grandfather left me fifty million dollars, which I get all of when I'm twenty-five or I marry, whichever comes first. With that kind of money we can piss on all of them."

He stared at her. "That's just what I mean. That makes it worse."

Suddenly she was angry. "What the hell kind of a gigolo are you anyway? Isn't my money as good as anybody else's? That old man in Monte Carlo, whatever his name is, or that woman who keeps sending checks from Paris?"

He stared at her. "You know?"

"Of course I know. Don't you think my father's bankers were after me the minute they found out I hadn't gone back to school and was living with you? They gave me the whole dossier."

He fell silent. After a moment he said, "And you still want to marry me?"

"That's the idea."

"Why? I don't get it."

"You're a fool then. You know what I'm like. I used to think there was something the matter with me before I met you. One man was never enough. There were times I used to do it with three men in a day, one right after the other. I was beginning to think there wasn't a man alive who could give me all I wanted. Then I found you."

"And that's reason enough to get married?"

"It's enough for me. What other reason do you need if two people can make it together like we do?"

"There's something called love."

"Now you're beginning to sound like an idiot. Maybe you can tell me exactly what love is?"

He didn't answer. A kind of sorrow came over him, together with a pity for her. Then he looked into her eyes and saw the naked terror revealed there. That he might refuse her. And suddenly he understood. The fear of what she was, had been, and would be if there weren't one man she could cling to.

A kind of smile crossed her lips. "We're very much alike, you and I. We're doers. All the rest are talkers. If what we have isn't love, then it's the nearest thing to it that either of us will ever know."

The pity in him overpowered his reason. He couldn't bring himself to tell her that the very reasons she advanced were the things that would destroy their relationship. He knew deep inside that in time neither of them could keep from seeking satisfaction with others.

"O.K.," he said, wondering which of them would be the first to succumb, "we'll get married."

It was planned as a quiet little wedding in a small church just outside Saint Moritz but it turned out to be something entirely different. The Daley money was just too important to be ignored, and in the end it was held in the cathedral with a hundred guests and throngs of reporters.

"You don't look happy," Robert said as they waited in the vestry.

Sergei came back from the door through which he had been looking into the crowded church. "I've yet to see a happy bridegroom."

Robert laughed. "You'll be all right once we start down the aisle."

Sergei looked at him. "I know, but it's not that I'm worrying about. It's after."

Robert didn't answer. He, too, had his doubts.

279

Sergei turned back to the door. "Dax should have been here. He would have been amused by all this. I wonder if he ever got the invitation. You haven't heard from him, have you?"

"Not one word, not since he left Cambridge a year ago. I wrote him several times but he never answered."

"It's a strange, wild country, I guess. I hope nothing has happened to him."

"He'll be all right. Much more will be happening to us." Sergei shot him a quick look. "You still think there'll be war?"

"I don't see how they can stop it. The war in Spain is almost over. The Germans have finished their warmup. That much you know from your father's letters." Robert laughed. "So now Chamberlain is going to Munich to talk to that madman. It's all a waste of time. Nothing will do any good."

"What does your father say?"

"He's transferring everything he can to America. He even wants Caroline and me to go back there."

"Are you?"

Robert shook his head.

"Why not?"

Robert shrugged. "For two important reasons. I'm Jewish, and I'm French."

"What can you do? You're not even a soldier."

"There will be something," Robert said. "At least I can stay and fight. There are too many of us fleeing before that monster already."

The sound of the organ came into the room. Robert peeked out the door, then turned back. "*Allons, mon enfant.* Now it is your turn to be a man."

The wire-service reporters were standing at the back of the church as the couple knelt before the altar. "Think of it," the AP man said. "In ten minutes he walks out of here gone from broke to fifty million bucks."

"You sound jealous."

"You're damn right I am. At least it should have been an American boy. What's wrong with good old American boys?"

"I don't know," Irma Andersen, who was covering the nuptials for Cosmo-World, whispered cattily from his right, "but from what I heard she tried them all and they were found wanting."

"Now, now."

"I wish I could afford that caviar-and-champagne kick," the INS man said. "It really must do the trick."

"Don't get big ideas. Us poor people better stick to oysters."

The AP man looked at him and smiled. "That's fine, but what are we going to do all summer?"

4

The rustling of fallen leaves brought him from sleep and he reached out, his hand closing over the rifle lying on the blanket beside him. From the corner of his eye he saw Fat Cat, already on his feet, blending silently into the trees. Muffling the sound with his blanket, he pumped a cartridge into the firing chamber of the rifle and waited.

There was silence all about him. He squinted up at the sky. He didn't have to check his watch to know it was around five o'clock in the morning. He put his ear to the ground and listened.

The footsteps had ceased. He took a deep breath. Fat Cat had intercepted whoever it had been. He still did not move. There was a faint hum of voices, and the mere sound reassured him. If it were anything dangerous there would be no conversation. Just the noises of death.

The footsteps began again. Dax raised his head and peered down the trail from the small cave in which he lay. Just as a precaution he raised his rifle and leveled the sight on the corner of the trail.

The bright red and blue uniform of the soldier appeared first. Behind him, Fat Cat, his revolver still in his hand, was almost invisible in his faded and nondescript khaki. Dax waited until they were almost upon him, then got to his feet.

The soldier started nervously, his face still pale from the

encounter with Fat Cat. Then he pulled himself together and saluted. "Corporal Ortiz, *Capitán*," he said formally. "I come with dispatches from *el Presidente*."

"Sit down, corporal." Dax squatted. "We don't stand on ceremony here. Besides, you make too good a target in that uniform of yours."

With a sigh of relief the soldier sank to the ground. "I have been trying to find you for almost a month."

Dax squinted at him. "You did well. One hour more and we would have been gone." He looked at Fat Cat. "How about some coffee?"

Fat Cat nodded and set about making a small fire, where the wind would disperse the smoke before it could rise into the air. He looked down curiously as the soldier opened his knapsack and handed Dax a number of envelopes tied neatly together with a string.

Dax settled his back against the rock and opened the first envelope. He took out an engraved card. He glanced at it for a moment and then began to chuckle. He held it up for Fat Cat to see. *"Mira!* We are invited to a wedding!"

Fat Cat looked at him over the coffeepot. *"Bueno,* there's nothing I like better than a good *fiesta*. Food and music and pretty girls. Who's getting married?"

"Sergei. To Sue Ann Daley."

"The blond one?"

Dax nodded.

"She'll fuck him to death. Maybe there is still time to warn him?"

Dax looked at the soldier. "What is the date?"

"April twelfth."

"Too late; the wedding took place two days ago. In Switzerland."

Fat Cat shook his head sadly. "Too bad." Then he and Dax looked at each other and began to laugh.

Ortiz stared at them in amazement. Was it for this nonsense that he had been sent to find them? To risk his life in these terrible mountains against all manner of unknown terrors merely to bring an invitation to a wedding which they could not even attend? Truly the life of an ordinary soldier was a sorry one.

Quickly Dax opened the remaining envelopes, saving until last the official one bearing *el Presidente*'s seal. One

282

after the other they disappeared into the fire. When he had finished the last he looked up. *"El Presidente* wishes us to come in."

"What for?" Fat Cat poured steaming black coffee into a tin cup and gave it to Dax, then filled others for Ortiz and himself.

"He does not say." Dax looked at Ortiz. "Do you know why?"

"No, *Capitán,*" Ortiz replied quickly. "I am but an ordinary soldier. I know nothing."

Fat Cat swore angrily. "For three months we have lived like animals in these hills and now that we're almost finished with the job we are told, 'Come in.' Why couldn't you wait two more days to find us? Just two more days."

The soldier paled at the anger in Fat Cat's voice. He seemed to shrink inside his uniform. "I—"

"Maybe it's not so bad," Dax said reassuringly. "Days have a way of getting mixed up out here in the mountains. The good corporal really didn't find us until the fourteenth, did you, corporal?"

Ortiz stared from one to the other. He could not make up his mind which of the two was more mad. The young one with his face burned almost black by the sun or the fat one who came upon you as silently as a puma. But there was one thing he did know. If they said he did not find them until the fourteenth, that's when he found them. What difference could two days make out here in the jungle? Especially when it was a matter of life and death. His own.

He cleared his throat. "But of course, *Capitán.* The fourteenth."

Dax smiled. He got to his feet. "Let's get going then. We have still a hard march to where we will meet with *el Condor.*"

El Condor! Ortiz could feel his intestines shrivel. So that was what they were up to! *El Condor,* the *bandolero,* who had been terrorizing the mountains for the last five years and who had sworn to put to death any man who fell into his hands wearing the uniform of the army. "I think I'll be getting back now," he said, starting to his feet.

"I don't think so," Dax said quietly. "You'll be safer with us."

"Yes," Fat Cat replied, "especially in that uniform. It's

283

not good to be wandering around in the hills wearing a monkey suit like that."

"Do you think we can find another set of *pantalones* for him?"

Fat Cat nodded. "I have an extra pair. They'll be a little big but—"

"He'll feel more comfortable."

Ortiz couldn't agree with him more. He couldn't get out of the uniform fast enough.

Dax looked down into the valley. "See?"

Ortiz and Fat Cat followed his finger. A faint wisp of smoke was rising from a corner of the valley.

"They are already there and waiting," Dax said, a note of satisfaction in his voice. "Just as *el Condor* promised."

"What do you think his answer will be?"

Dax shrugged his shoulders. "Only God knows."

"Answer to what?" Ortiz asked.

Fat Cat looked at him. *"El Presidente* sent us with an offer of amnesty. If *el Condor* lays down his arms and comes in to Curatu all is forgiven."

"Amnesty for *el Condor?"* Ortiz shivered and crossed himself. "What makes you think he will believe you?"

"He knew my father," Dax said. "He knows I would not be a party to anything but the truth. It took us all this time to locate him. Last week he told us we would have his answer in seven days. We will spend the night here and go down in the morning."

"Do you really think *el Condor* will come in?" Ortiz whispered to Fat Cat as they spread their blankets on the ground.

"I'll be better able to answer that tomorrow night." Fat Cat then added an afterthought which kept Ortiz in a chill all through the night. "If we're still alive."

Dax stretched out on his blanket on his stomach, his chin resting on his crossed forearms. He looked down into the valley. Gradually the day faded into the purple of evening and night sounds began to come to his ears. The faint wavering smoke from the camp of the *bandoleros* could no longer be seen. Motionlessly he lay there, wrapping the safety of the night around him like a blanket. Everything was different from what he had expected, but that was only because he had thought things had changed.

284

It wasn't until he got home that he realized that nothing ever really changes. Someone had once said that the more things change, the more they are the same. It seemed to him that none of the things that his father had hoped would be achieved had yet been realized. There were still not enough schools, and those there were had quickly been pre-empted by the officials and minor officials for their own children. That was in Curatu. In the small villages and the countryside there were no schools at all.

And though around the capital there was a network of paved asphalt roads they went nowhere, ending abruptly in swamps or jungles only a few miles beyond the outskirts. In the mountains and valleys of the back country the *bandoleros* still struck terror into the hearts of the *campesinos*.

There had been a sadness in him those first few weeks he had been home. He was glad that his father was not there to see what he saw. It was not for this his father had spent his days.

He had gone down to the port and watched the ships come and go and the fishermen return with their catch. In the early hours of the morning he had wandered through the marketplace listening to the cries of the vendors. And everywhere he went he saw the small concrete statues of *el Presidente*—on the street corners, on each new building, at every pier in the port and entrance to the marketplace. And there was always the red and blue uniform of the soldiers.

It wasn't until a week had passed that he became aware that soldiers were following him. It wasn't until a few days later that he realized that the people looked at him as if he were a stranger, that the sound of his voice had a different accent from their own, that the cut of his clothes was of another society.

A sense of loneliness and isolation began to possess him. Suddenly the atmosphere of the city began to choke in his throat. It was not until then that he realized he was no longer the same person who had left here years ago. He was something else, someone else. What he was he did not know. Instinctively, hopefully, he left the city for the *hacienda* in the mountains where he had been born.

There, where the sky and the earth seemed to stretch forever before him and the mountains thrust their purple, craggy

285

fingers at the sun and stars, he hoped to find again the sense of freedom he had lost. The reason for his being.

5

On an afternoon several weeks later he was sitting in the patio looking out toward the mountains when Fat Cat came out of the house and sat down next to him. "It is not the same?"

Dax picked up a thin cigar and lit it before he answered. "No," he said, his voice flat and empty.

"Things are never the same." Fat Cat looked at Dax shrewdly. "But you must have known that."

Dax let out a cloud of blue smoke. "I knew."

A tinge of anger came into Fat Cat's voice. "I thought surely that *el Presidente*—"

"Would what?" Dax prompted.

The anger was strong in Fat Cat's voice. "Find something for you to do."

Dax smiled. "Such as?"

Fat Cat did not answer.

"*El Presidente* has many things on his mind besides me."

Fat Cat turned toward the mountains. After a moment he said, "There are men coming on horseback." He listened again. "Soldiers."

Dax got out of his chair and walked to the railing. There was nothing he could see or hear. "How do you know?"

"Only soldiers' horses move in step." He looked at Dax. "Are you expecting anyone?"

Dax shook his head. There, now he could hear a faint muffled beat of hooves. He turned. Fat Cat was checking his revolver. "I thought you said they were soldiers."

Fat Cat shoved the revolver into his belt. "They are soldiers. Still, one stays alive by not taking chances."

They stood there until the first red and blue uniform came

286

into sight, then Fat Cat turned. "They will be hot and thirsty. I will see to their refreshment."

Dax watched the soldiers approaching. There seemed to be a full squad, about fourteen men, all mounted on the wiry brown mustangs that the army preferred. From his uniform Dax knew that the leader was a captain. But there was another, a slim young officer, though Dax could not distinguish his rank because his uniform bore no insignia. The captain held up a hand and the squad wheeled to a halt just beyond the gate.

The two officers started up the walk to the house. It wasn't until then that Dax recognized the younger officer. Despite the slimness of the body, the tightly fitting uniform seemed only to accentuate the young feminine curves. She turned and suddenly her face broke into a familiar grin and she began to run toward him.

He hurried down the steps to meet her, then suddenly she stopped and stared up at him. It was almost as if she were a little girl again and was suddenly surprised to see how tall her older brother had grown.

"Dax?" Her voice was husky, almost breathless.

"Amparo."

Still she stood, her eyes searching his face. She seemed to want to speak but no words came. It was he who finally broke the silence. "Take off your hat."

"What for?"

His face broke into a teasing smile. "So I can make up my mind whether to kiss or salute you."

Her blue eyes crinkled in an answering grin and with a gesture she flung her hat across the yard. Her blond hair tumbled down almost to her shoulders. "Dax, Dax, I could not believe my eyes. You're so—so big!" And then she ran into his arms.

He held her close, feeling the warm femaleness of her. "You've grown a little, too, *Princesa*."

She looked up into his face. "How could you leave Curatu without seeing me?"

"You were in Panama," he said. "No one seemed to know when you might return."

"Daddy knew."

Dax's face clouded. "I only saw *el Presidente* once. And then only for a few minutes. He was busy."

"Daddy's always very busy."

Dax heard the captain clearing his throat behind them. Awkwardly Amparo turned. *"Capitán de Ortega, Señor Xenos."*

The soldier saluted, then stepped forward to take Dax's outstretched hand. "Your excellency."

"Capitán de Ortega. Welcome to my house."

There were footsteps on the veranda and Amparo whirled around. "Fat Cat," she cried, "you haven't changed at all!"

Amparo appeared in a white gown at dinner. A diamond-and-emerald necklace was at her throat and matching ear clips accented the blondness of her hair. The candlelight seemed to add a warm ivory tint to her tanned skin.

Dax smiled at her over coffee. "You're the first guest I've had since my return. You'll have to stay for a few days. We have much to catch up on."

"I'd love to," she replied, then hesitated and looked at Captain de Ortega.

"I promised your father we would return tomorrow."

Dax glanced at de Ortega. The captain's face was expressionless as his eyes turned to Amparo.

"I'm afraid the captain is right," she said reluctantly.

Dax didn't press it. "Come, we shall have a liqueur on the *galería.*"

The soldier got up. "I must see to my men, your excellency. And then, if you will permit, I shall turn in. We must be on the road early."

Dax nodded. "Of course, Captain."

When the soldier left the room, Dax turned to Amparo. They sat in silence for a few minutes, then Dax took out one of his thin black cigars.

"May I have a cigarette?"

"Excuse me." Dax pushed the box toward her, then held a light.

Amparo took a deep drag and leaned back. "Well?"

He thought for a moment, then took the cigar from his mouth and studied it. "Many things have changed," he replied reflectively. "It has been a long time."

"Ten years is not so long." Her eyes were large and dark blue. "I haven't changed, have you?"

He shook his head. "You have changed, and so have I. Everything has changed."

"Some things never change."

They sat looking out into the night. The stars twinkled brightly in the velvet blue sky and the fires of the soldiers were like fireflies in the field across the road.

"Do you always travel with an escort of soldiers?"

"Yes."

He looked at her. "Why?"

"Father insists. There is always danger. Thieves. *Bandoleros.*"

He grinned wryly. "Still?"

She nodded seriously. "There are a few who still oppose my father. They refuse to see the good." She looked at him suddenly, aware of how he must feel. "You're disappointed, aren't you? You expected everything to be changed."

"In a way I did."

"It's not that easy," she replied quickly. "I know how you feel. I felt the same after I returned from five years at the university in Mexico. But after I had been home for a while I began to understand."

"You did?"

"Yes. You have been away even longer than I, Dax; you've forgotten the way it is. Most of our people don't want change. They want to be given things, not to work for them. Even sending their children to school is too much of an effort."

"Maybe it's because there is no room for them in the schools, and only the children of officials can get in."

"It wasn't like that at first. But after a while they just stopped going."

Dax didn't answer.

"Father's biggest concern is to prepare for the war."

He looked at her questioningly.

"You've been abroad. You know a war is coming."

"What have we to do with that?" he asked. "Corteguay is not involved."

"Not directly, no. But *el Presidente* says it will be a great opportunity for our country to become self-sustaining. Someone will have to supply them with food."

"Wars aren't fought on bananas and coffee."

"He knows that. More than three years ago he approached

289

the big cattle ranchers in Argentina. He granted them special concessions to set up operations here. By next year we will have close to a million pounds of beef available for export."

Dax knew what concessions *el Presidente* had probably made. He wondered how much had ended up in his pocket. "And how much meat is available to the *campesinos?*"

"You *have* been away a long time," Amparo said. "Have you forgotten that *campesinos* don't eat beef? They prefer their own foods. Vegetables. Chicken. Pork."

"Maybe that's because beef has always been too expensive."

She was suddenly angry. "My father was right—you're exactly like your father!"

Dax looked at her. *"El Presidente* said that?"

She nodded.

He smiled suddenly. "That's one of the nicest things he ever said."

She placed a hand on his arm. "Dax. Dax. I didn't come here to quarrel with you."

"We won't, I promise."

"What are you going to do? You can't stay here in the hills doing nothing."

He took the cigar from his mouth and looked at it for a moment, then threw it over the railing. It burst into a scatter of sparks. "I've thought about that," he said slowly. "But I don't see that there's anything for me to do. I hung around Curatu for almost three weeks. No one offered me anything so I came home."

"El Presidente is very hurt that you did not come to talk with him before you left."

"How could I? Every time I sent in a request to see him he was too busy."

"How could he have known you were planning to leave?"

"Would it have made any difference? What was I supposed to do? Hang around forever like a dog hoping for a bone?"

"Come back to Curatu with me and see him."

He looked at her. "Is that your idea or his?"

She hesitated a moment. "Mine. He would never admit he is hurt and longs to see you."

Dax looked at her for a moment, then shook his head.

"No, I think I'll stay here. When your father wants me he'll send for me."

That had been almost a year ago, and Dax had remained at the *hacienda* for almost nine months before *el Presidente* had summoned him. When he was ushered into the office *el Presidente* threw his arms around him and greeted him as if it had been only yesterday when last they had seen each other.

"Your father's greatest ambition," he said to Dax, "was to see the country united under one government representing all the people equally. It is also mine. This has been almost accomplished. But in Asiento *el Condor*, the old *bandolero*, still resists. *El Condor* knew your father and respected him. He would listen were you to approach him with an offer of amnesty. His participation in the government would be without prejudice."

6

"I am not a *político*," the old *bandolero* said. "I am only a simple murderer so there is much of which you speak that I do not understand. But this I do know. I would like my son to go to school. To learn to read and write and speak with the smoothness of your tongue. I would not wish for him to spend his life in these hills engaged merely in a struggle for his existence."

Dax looked across the fire at *el Condor*. The old man was seated on the ground, his legs crossed in front of him Indian fashion, the thin cheroot gripped between his lips, his hawk-like face tight over the bones. He glanced around at the others. The *bandolero*'s lieutenants stared back at him expressionlessly. The morning sun glinted on their knives and guns. Behind the old one stood the son of whom he spoke.

291

Slim and straight, he stared at Dax, his fourteen-year-old eyes filled with an animal wariness. Like his elders, he had a knife and revolver in his belt.

Dax turned back to *el Condor*. "Then you will accept *el Presidente*'s offer?"

"I am an old man," the *bandolero* replied. "It does not matter much if I die. But I would not wish my son to die with me."

"No one will be harmed. That is the personal guarantee of *el Presidente*."

"I do not desire to become governor of Asiento," *el Condor* went on as if he had not heard. "What do I know of government? I just do not want that my son should die." He took the cheroot from his mouth and looked at it, then raked out an ember from the fire and relit it. "I had eight sons and three daughters. They are all dead but this one."

"No one will die," Dax repeated. *"El Presidente* himself guarantees that."

The old man kicked the ember back into the fire. "Diablo Rojo is a fool. Guiterrez will kill us all."

Dax stared at the *bandolero*. The old one's face was impassive; only the faint glitter in his coal-black eyes betrayed his Indian heritage. He wondered how to explain to a man for whom time did not exist that Guiterrez had long since gone. That this was a new government, even though the soldiers wore the same uniform. That it had been many years since Presidente de Cordoba had been Diablo Rojo, a *bandolero* in the hills, and that he himself had seen Guiterrez captured and taken away to die. Before an answer had taken shape in his mind the old man spoke again.

"If you will guarantee the life of my son. You personally, swearing on the soul of your sainted father whom we all loved and respected. Then I am prepared to accept Diablo Rojo's offer."

"I swear it."

El Condor sighed softly. *"Bueno."* He got stiffly to his feet. "Go then to Diablo Rojo and tell him I will meet him in the village of Asiento on the last day of this month. There will be no more war between us."

El Presidente waited until the door had closed behind his

secretary before he spoke. "You have done well in the mountains."

Dax did not answer, for no answer was expected. He looked across the desk at *el Presidente*. The man seemed never to change. Save for the slight graying of his hair he looked exactly as he had the first time Dax saw him. He was dressed in the uniform of a general but without medals, insignia, or braid. This, he believed, showed him to be a man of the people.

"There will be peace now. *El Condor* was the last of the important ones. The others, they are nothing. We can pick them off like flies."

"Perhaps the same arrangement could be made with them? They would be willing once they saw how *el Condor* was received."

El Presidente dismissed this with a gesture. "They are not worth the bother. We shall take care of them." He clasped his hands on the desk and leaned forward. "At any rate you will not have to concern yourself with such problems. I am appointing you consul at large. You are going back to Europe."

Dax stared at him. "To Europe? What for?"

El Presidente opened his hands. "The war in Spain is drawing to a close. It is time we established relations with the new government of Francisco Franco."

"But what of General Mola?" Dax asked. "I thought he was to be president."

El Presidente shook his head. "Mola talks too much. I realized that as soon as I heard his statement about the fifth column before the siege of Madrid. With those words he lost his power, because Madrid did not fall immediately. The first thing a leader must learn is to keep his mouth shut. He must never let anyone, friend or enemy, know what he is thinking or planning."

Dax was silent for a moment. He wondered how many men besides his own father had been deceived by *el Presidente*'s calculated silence. He pushed the thought from his mind. "What do you expect me to do in Spain?"

"Spain will need food. We have food to sell. Spain will also need supplies with which to rebuild. All kinds. The stupidity of the *gringos* will keep them from doing business with Franco. We can obtain whatever is required from them and transship it to Spain."

Dax looked at the older man with a growing respect.

Suddenly he understood what had set him apart from the countless other *bandoleros* who had come down from the hills. Now he knew what had attracted his father. Right or wrong, selfishly or unselfishly, *el Presidente* always planned ahead. And no matter how much disappeared into his own pocket, Corteguay benefited.

"You will go to Franco," *el Presidente* continued, "and you will make a deal with him. We will be the agents for Spain in the markets of the world."

"What if Franco is not interested?"

El Presidente smiled. "Franco will be interested, I know the man. He is like me, a realist. He knows that he can no longer count on his allies Germany and Italy once his war is over. They will soon be involved in a war of their own. Have no fears, Franco will make a deal."

"When do you want me to leave?"

"On the third of next month a ship sails for France. You will be aboard." He got out of his chair and walked around the desk to Dax. "And now there is just one more thing."

Dax smiled. "Yes?"

El Presidente did not answer immediately. He pulled a chair close to Dax and sat down. Subtly his voice changed. "You know for a long time now I have thought of you as my own son. I remember when my two boys died, when you came down from the hills with Amparo. I think often of you two."

Suddenly Dax knew what was coming. He raised his hand to try and stop the older man. "We were only children then."

But *el Presidente* was not to be stopped. "I remember even thinking how well you looked together. She so fair and blond, you so dark and fiercely protective. I recall turning to your father and saying, 'Someday.' "

Dax got to his feet. "No, excellency, no. It is much too soon to speak of such things."

El Presidente looked at him. "Too soon? Is it too soon for me to want a son to take my place? I am getting no younger. Someday I would like to lay down the burden of this office and retire to the peace of a small farm knowing that the country would be in the hands of my son."

El Presidente's face was sincere, his eyes warm. For a moment Dax was almost convinced that he meant it. But the very next words dispelled the illusion.

"The marriage of the two of you will truly unite the country. The respected name of your father joined to mine will convince the people of the mountains that we are sincere in our efforts."

Dax did not answer, and *el Presidente* took advantage of his silence to continue. "Amparo is wonderful. But she is only a girl. And there is only so much a girl can do. What I need is a son. You. To be my right arm."

Dax sank back into the chair. "Have you spoken to Amparo?"

A look of surprise came across *el Presidente*'s face. "What for?"

"She might not want to marry me."

"Amparo will do what I wish. She will do whatever is best for Corteguay."

"I still think she should have the right to choose her own husband."

"Of course. Then you will ask her?"

Dax nodded. He would ask her, perhaps next year when he returned from Europe. By then many things might change. Even *el Presidente*'s mind.

"Excellent." *El Presidente* went back behind his desk. The meeting was over.

Dax got to his feet. "Is there anything else, sir?"

"Yes." *El Presidente* looked up at him, a faint smile around his eyes. "I would appreciate it if you spoke to Amparo as soon as you leave here."

"Must we be in that much of a hurry?" A faint suspicion that he had been outmaneuvered entered Dax's mind.

"Oh, yes. We must," *el Presidente* replied, smiling. "You see I have already given out the story of your engagement. It will be in all our papers tomorrow morning."

7

Dax thought he noticed traces of tears around Amparo's eyes. "You've been crying?"

She shook her head. "You just saw my father?"

He nodded. "Congratulations, we're engaged."

She looked at him a moment, then turned and walked across the room to the window. When she spoke her voice was so low that at first he could scarcely hear her. "I told him not to do it."

He didn't answer.

She turned and looked at him. "You believe that, don't you?"

"Yes."

"*El Presidente* has his own way of doing things. I told him that you should be allowed to make up your own mind."

"What about you? I'm not the only one involved."

She didn't answer for a moment, then her eyes met his steadily. "I made up my mind a long time ago." A hint of a smile came to her lips. "Have you forgotten?"

He laughed. "I haven't forgotten. I thought you would outgrow it."

"I thought so, too. But when I came to see you in the mountains I knew I hadn't."

"Why didn't you say something then?"

"Why didn't you?" she retorted. "Girls aren't supposed to suggest such things. Were you so blind you could not see?"

"I'm sorry. It never entered my mind."

Suddenly there was a flash of her childish temper. "Oh, get out! You're as stupid as all men!"

He reached out for her. "Amparo."

She shook off his hand angrily. "You don't have to marry me! Nobody has to marry me! I don't have to beg any man!"

She ran out of the room. Dax stood for a moment, listening to her angry footsteps on the stairway. Just as he started out *el Presidente* came in.

There was a smile on the older man's face. "What's wrong?" he asked slyly. "A lovers' quarrel?"

Amparo had just finished repairing her makeup when she heard a knock at the door. "Who is it?"

"Me."

She walked to the door and opened it. *El Presidente* followed her into the room, closing the door behind him. He peered at her from under his bushy eyebrows.

"I hope you didn't make a fool of yourself."

296

She shook her head.

"You didn't tell him?"

Again she shook her head.

"Good," he said, satisfaction in his voice. "De Ortega is gone. He won't cause us any trouble."

"You didn't hurt him?" she asked, sudden concern in her voice.

"No," he replied, lying. A bullet through the brain never really *hurt* anyone. "I sent him to a station in the south."

"It wasn't his fault."

He felt the anger rise in him. "Whose fault was it then? I placed you in his charge. He was supposed to protect you, not rape you."

"He didn't rape me."

"That makes it worse," he said wearily. He stared at her for a moment. "I don't understand you. I sent you to the university in Mexico for five years. To become a lady. To be educated. Was it only to have you tumble into bed with the first good-looking *caballero* that came along, like any common *puta* off the streets?"

She didn't answer.

"Well, thank God, it's over." He sighed. "Dax will make you a good husband. You will have children and there will be no more nonsense."

She looked directly into her father's eyes. "I am not going to marry him."

"Why not?"

"I am already with child."

His mouth hung open. "Are you sure?"

She nodded. "I am entering my third month." She turned to pick up a cigarette from the dressing table. "I won't marry him. He would know in a minute."

El Presidente seemed paralyzed for a moment. Then he exploded. Viciously he slapped her across the face, tumbling her backward onto the bed.

"*Puta!* Whore!" he shouted. "Isn't it enough that I must defend myself against my enemies? Must I also bear the cross of betrayal by my own?"

A photographer came over to them. "One more picture, your excellency, please."

"Of course, of course." *El Presidente* was very much the

297

proud father. He moved closer to Amparo and stood on his toes. At least this way he appeared to be taller than she. Not as tall as Dax on the other side of her, but tall enough not to seem ridiculous.

The flashbulb popped. They blinked their eyes. "Thank you, your excellency." The photographer bowed and moved away.

Dax looked at Amparo. She seemed pale and drawn. "Are you all right?"

"I'm just tired."

"It's too much, too quickly," he said. "Just yesterday we were engaged. Today this—"

He gestured at the room. The large reception hall in the presidential palace was filled. For the first time he realized that a whole new society had sprung up since he had been away. There were so many people whose names he did not even know. New people who had become important. Many of the old families were still there, but they were the window dressing. It was the new people who really held the power.

"What you need is a vacation, Amparo."

"I'll be all right, Dax."

"You've become a political adjunct to your father. The Women's League. The Worker's Association. The Children's Society. It is too much."

"Someone has to do it."

"You can't do it all yourself. It is unfair of your father to think you can."

"I go where my father cannot. How else do you think he can retain the support of the people? I have to do it. Governing has a responsibility all its own."

"The responsibility is your father's."

"It is mine also," Amparo replied. "They look to me for the little things they dare not bring to him."

Dax looked out over the hall. *El Presidente* was talking to a group of men. Every few moments he would glance toward them as if to reassure himself that Amparo was still there. He wondered what the old man would do after they were married. Amparo would be his wife, not *el Presidente*'s political assistant.

He turned back to Amparo but she was already deep in a conversation with a small group of women. He caught fragmentary snatches about a campaign for the improvement of certain health conditions. There was no doubt that Amparo dominated the small group. When she spoke the others listened with respect.

The women were all strangers to him, members of the new class that had evolved while he had been away. He took out one of his thin *cigarros* and lit it. So many things had changed. Nothing seemed the same any more.

The graciousness of the old society of his grandfather's time, and even of his father's, was gone. The new society just evolving from the middle and lower classes still carried traces of these backgrounds. But their speech, though carrying the stamp of education, still had overtones of the common people; and their manners were a curious overlay of form and style upon the rough directness of the *campesino*.

And their dress. He half smiled to himself thinking of the women of Europe and the United States whom he had known. Corteguayan ideas of fashion ran the spectrum of colors, and featured elaborate laces, frills and furbelows that reminded him of old photographs. But there was an energy and vitality about them that awakened his sympathy and pride. His father would have been proud of these people.

He looked again toward the men surrounding *el Presidente*. The men had not changed as much. They were still much the same. The fawning sycophants with the same inbred respect for power and carelessness about the privileges of others. They groveled to those above them, spat on those beneath them.

Suddenly he was glad to be returning to Europe. In a way he was more at home there than here. As a matter of fact he was more at home almost anywhere than here. He was Corteguayan. But he felt himself almost an outsider among a primitive people.

Amparo came toward him. "You have a strange expression on your face."

"I was thinking."

"About what?"

"How nice it would be if you and I, just the two of us, could go up into the mountains to my *hacienda*. Alone."

She stared at him. "Father would not like it. He wants me near him."

Dax shrugged. "Your father has had his way with us. Sooner or later he will have to get used to the idea. When we are married you will no longer be at his beck and call."

Amparo knew her father. That was not the way he thought at all. Things would not change with their marriage. They would only become more so. Dax, too, would join the circle which continually orbited around *el Presidente.*

"Tonight," he said suddenly, mistaking her silence for consent, "after everyone has gone. We will leave quietly. No one will miss us."

Suddenly she felt sorry for him. In many ways he was much more sophisticated than they and in others far more naïve. He did not yet understand the demands of power. He did not appreciate how much her father dominated the people around him, how completely he controlled their lives. But he would find out. In time. For now, let him retain the illusion.

"It's a wonderful idea. We can leave after the banquet tonight."

<hr>

8

<hr>

Dax was sitting on the *galería,* the usual thin cigar in his mouth. He looked up as Amparo came out from the house. "How did you sleep?"

Her eyes moved out across the fields toward the hills. "Very well. It's so quiet here. The mountains whisper you to sleep."

He looked at her approvingly. In just the two days and nights they had been here the blue shadows under her eyes had disappeared. The color had come back into her cheeks and no longer was she so tense and strained. "I told you it would be good."

She turned and looked at him. "If only it could remain like this."

He didn't answer.

She sat down opposite him as Fat Cat came out with a tray of coffee. He placed it on the table between them. She filled her cup. "Would you like more?"

He shook his head. "No, thanks. I've already had mine."

Amparo took a sip. The coffee was strong and hot and she was grateful for its warmth. "It is time we talked."

"Yes?"

"It must seem strange to you after having been away so long to come home and suddenly find yourself betrothed." She hesitated, waiting for him to answer, but when he said nothing she continued. "It was not so for me. Somehow I always knew, when I did marry, that it would be at my father's own time, not mine."

"And you do not resent it?"

"No. You see, duty has always been drilled into me. Ever since I was a little girl. I wish only that you had been given more time. Perhaps we might have found our way to each other without his help. As we did when we were children."

He took the cigar from his mouth and looked at it. "Perhaps that would have been better. Still . . . ."

She felt surprise grow in her. "You feel as I do?"

"I don't know," he confessed. "But I wasn't really as shocked when your father spoke to me as I thought I would be." He began to smile. "I'm afraid I'm not being very romantic."

She returned his smile. "Neither of us is." Suddenly she felt shy. "But I am glad it was you."

For the first time he reached out and touched her. She stared at him for a moment, then leaned forward, and he kissed her. She felt the light touch of his lips and there was something very young about it despite the faint aroma of the tobacco that clung to him. Suddenly a deep sadness welled up inside her and the tears came to her eyes.

"What is it?"

She shook her head violently. She could not stop her tears. She got up and ran back into the house.

A few minutes later she came out again. "I'm sorry, Dax."

"Don't apologize."

"I think you'd better take me home."

He looked up at her questioningly.

"I shouldn't have come here, people will talk."

"That's not the reason."

"Whatever the reason," she said with a flash of temper, "I want to go home. Will you take me or must I go alone?"

He got to his feet. "I'll take you."

301

Only once on the way back did he speak to her. "Sooner or later you will have to tell me what's troubling you," he said. "I have a feeling that the sooner you do the better it will be for us both."

She glanced at him out of the corner of her eyes, wondering just how much he knew or had guessed. But his face betrayed nothing. And she couldn't bring herself to tell him, not yet.

The small village of Asiento wore a festive air. The streets were decorated with the green and blue flag of Corteguay and bunting draped the doors and windows of the small stores along the dusty main street. In every other window there was a photograph of *el Presidente*.

Dax stood on the *galería* of the one small hotel and looked over the crowds lining the streets awaiting the arrival of *el Presidente*. Everywhere there was an air of excitement, peddlers hawking sweets, small boys running in and out of the crowds with tiny flags clutched in their grubby fingers. A roar came up from the crowd further down the street as the head of the presidential cavalcade turned the corner.

First came a company of mounted cavalrymen on dark chestnut horses. In perfect cadence, four abreast, they came down the narrow street, their red and blue uniforms bright and gay in the sunlight. Behind came the first automobile. Two soldiers were in the front seat, one of them driving. There were two officers in the rear seat. Between them sat *el Presidente*, dressed in a simple khaki uniform, its very simplicity making him stand out from the others. The crowd began to shout:

"Viva el Presidente! Viva!"

El Presidente raised his head, his white teeth flashing in a smile. With a gesture he removed his hat to the crowds. Again they roared their approval. A second car turned in behind them. Again soldiers were in the front seat. This time between the two officers in the rear, her blond hair uncovered and shimmering in the sunlight, sat Amparo. Her face was alive, animated, as she smiled at the crowds. This time there was true affection in their cheers.

"Viva la princesa! Viva la rubia!"

Dax turned to Fat Cat. "Quite a reception."

302

Fat Cat's eyes were narrowed against the sun. "I don't like it," he said. "Too many soldiers."

"You didn't expect *el Presidente* to come alone."

"No, but he didn't have to bring the whole fucking army."

The automobiles had stopped in the square. The *alcalde* came down the steps of the city hall to greet *el Presidente*. At a command from their officers, the cavalrymen wheeled into formation and came to attention. Slowly *el Presidente* got out of his car and walked over to assist Amparo. Then they turned and walked over to where the officials were standing.

The *alcalde's* voice was loud enough to be heard all over the square. "It is with deep feelings of humility and honor that the proud city of Asiento welcomes *el Presidente* and his lovely daughter."

Dax turned to Fat Cat. "Come on, let's go inside for a drink."

They sat in the dark, almost cool bar, sipping cold glasses of beer. "I don't think he will come," Fat Cat said unexpectedly.

Dax looked at him.

"*El Condor* is no fool. By now he must know how many soldiers *el Presidente* has brought with him."

"The old *bandolero* is a man of his word. He will come."

Fat Cat was silent. He sipped at his beer.

"It seems almost as if you wish he wouldn't."

Fat Cat looked across the table at Dax. He shook his head gloomily. "If he is smart he will not come." He picked up his glass and looked into it. "Mark my words, there will be bloodshed if he does."

There were footsteps from behind them and they turned. It was Ortiz, the little soldier who had found them in the hills. He saluted smartly. "Señor Xenos?"

Dax nodded. "Yes, Ortiz."

"His excellency wishes you to join him and *la princesa* in the garden of the *alcalde*."

Dax finished his glass of beer and got to his feet. He looked down at Fat Cat. "Coming?"

Fat Cat shook his head. "*Con su permiso,* I shall remain here. The beer is cooler."

Dax glanced at his watch, then at Amparo, seated next to

303

him at the long table in the *alcalde*'s garden. "It is almost time."

Amparo stared at him. "Four o'clock?"

He nodded, looking up. Already the table was being cleared. *El Presidente* got to his feet and the others also rose. They followed the *alcalde* through the garden to the *galería* of the building, which faced out onto the square.

El Presidente gestured to Amparo. She joined him beside the railing. "You too, my son," he said to Dax.

Dax took his place on the other side of Amparo. He looked across the square. The soldiers had drawn up in front of the building in two files, forming a lane between them leading up to the *galería*. Behind the soldiers the crowd was suddenly quiet. Across the square Dax saw Fat Cat come out of the hotel.

There was a flutter of excitement as a small boy's voice shrilled, "They're coming! They're coming."

Expectantly the crowd looked across the square. Dax caught a glimpse of *el Presidente*'s face. It was grim and expressionless. Then he joined the others in looking toward the street from which the *bandolero* would appear.

El Condor was riding the first horse, a large bay stallion. He rode silently, glancing neither to right nor to left, his wide-brimmed hat pulled down over his face to shade his eyes. Behind him Dax could see the others. One was *el Condor*'s son. The boy rode defiantly, glaring back at every curious eye.

There was still no sound from the crowd as the *bandolero* rode past and up the lane of soldiers. The old man reined in his horse and held up his hand. The others stopped.

He took off his hat and the thick black hair seemed to tumble almost to his shoulders. He looked up at *el Presidente*. "I have come, your excellency," he said, in a loud clear voice, "in response to your request. I accept your offer of amnesty. Let there be peace between us."

El Presidente looked at him for a moment, then quickly came down the steps. Stiffly, the old *bandolero* dismounted, and behind him the soldiers snapped to attention.

"In the name of our beloved country," *el Presidente* said, "I bid thee welcome. Too long has our house been divided." He stepped forward and enfolded the old man in an embrace.

A roar welled up from the crowd. It came from the

heart. For this meant the end of terror, of sleepless nights. Of the fear that at any moment the *bandoleros* or the *soldados* might turn their beloved city into a battlefield. At last it was over.

Dax looked out over the heads of the crowd and the horses of the dismounting *bandoleros*. Fat Cat was nowhere to be seen. He had probably gone back into the bar, disappointed that his predictions had proved false.

El Presidente was leading the old man up the steps. The reporters hurried forward and the two of them turned for their photographs. Dax glanced at Amparo. "Your father should be proud. It is a wonderful thing he is doing."

A strange look crossed her face, but before he had a chance to ask her what it meant he felt a hand on his sleeve. He turned. It was *el Condor*.

"I have kept my word," the old man said. "I have brought my son and hereby hand him over into your care. You will see that he attends the school as you promised?"

"I shall keep my word."

The old man gestured, and the boy came closer. "You will go with Señor Xenos, and you will obey him as you would me."

The boy nodded silently.

"You will be a good boy and someday will return to the mountains with the knowledge and the words that will keep you forever free." He reached out a hand and lightly touched the boy's cheek. "You will do nothing that will make me ashamed of you."

Almost roughly the old man pushed the boy toward Dax. "His name is José. You may beat him if he does not do what you say."

El Presidente stood at the old man's side now. "Come into the house for a cooling glass of wine," he said. "There is much we have to talk about."

The *bandolero* laughed. "Wine and talk. The years haven't changed you at all!"

9

"It will take all night to reach Curatu," Dax said. "We could be at my place in a few hours. Why not spend the night there, then we will go on in the morning."

Amparo looked questioningly at her father.

He nodded. "It is a good suggestion. You will certainly be more comfortable there. I will see you in Curatu tomorrow."

"Bueno. I will go and find Fat Cat."

But Fat Cat was nowhere to be found. The barman at the hotel remembered him leaving with a soldier shortly after *el Condor* had arrived. The soldier had come back but Fat Cat had not. The soldier was at the table in the corner.

It was Ortiz and he was sleeping, his arms on the table. Dax shook him awake and he looked up, his eyes drowsy with wine. No, he did not remember where he had left Fat Cat. There had been a *cantina,* and there had been some women there. Also singing and dancing, but after a while they had left. Then Fat Cat and he had become separated.

Dax shrugged. Fat Cat had probably found a woman and would come dragging home the next morning. He laughed to himself. Some things never changed.

Amparo was waiting in one of the cars. Two soldiers were already stationed in the front seat.

"The car will never make it over the mountains," Dax said. "There aren't any roads, only narrow old wagon trails. If we take it we'll have to drive halfway to Curatu before we can cut back."

Amparo seemed to hesitate.

Dax smiled. "You have changed. I remember when you couldn't wait to get on a horse."

306

She got out of the car. "Go get a horse for me," she said, with a trace of temper. "I'll be ready to leave as soon as I get into some other clothes."

Dax went around the hotel to the stable and picked up Fat Cat's horse and his own. He grinned to himself. Fat Cat would be angry, but it was his own fault.

He led the horses around to the front. It was just turning dark. As he came out from behind the building he saw the boy standing there, holding his own horse. He had almost forgotten about him.

"Are we ready to leave, *señor?*" the boy asked softly, falling into step.

"*Sí.*"

They stopped in front of the *alcalde*'s house. Dax looked down at the boy. "Do you wish to say good-bye to your father?"

José's dark eyes were expressionless. "I have already said good-bye to my father."

The night was bright and clear and the moonlight made the path as easy to follow as in daylight. They rode single file, Dax leading, followed by Amparo, and the boy bringing up the rear. At the crest of the mountain Dax stopped and looked back down at the village. The houses were bright with lights and in the still night air occasional distant sounds of music floated up.

Dax laughed. "There won't be much sleep in Asiento tonight."

"I guess not."

A group of fires to the north of the village caught his eyes. "What are those fires, I wonder?"

Amparo did not answer.

"They are the campfires of the *soldados,*" José said.

Dax looked at him. "How do you know?"

"We saw them as we came in. It was then my father sent most of his men back into the mountains."

Dax looked at the boy for a moment, then turned to Amparo. "What for?"

She shrugged her shoulders evasively. "Father never goes anywhere without his personal escort."

"I thought they entered the town with him."

"My father said they were Guiterrez' *guerrilleros.*"

Dax turned in his saddle.

"I'm tired," Amparo said suddenly. "Are we going to sit here all night talking?" She turned her horse around and started down the path.

Dax glanced back at Asiento for a moment, then turned to the boy. José was watching him impassively. "Let's go."

José pulled in behind him silently. They went down the mountain through the night after Amparo, then across the valley and the fields to Dax's *hacienda*. It was almost midnight when they arrived. They hadn't exchanged more than a dozen words all the way.

Dax escorted Amparo to her room. Her face was drawn and pale, and suddenly he felt sorry for her. Being the daughter of *el Presidente* must not be the easiest job in the world.

He put José in the room he had occupied when he was a boy and came back downstairs. He lit a thin *cigarro* and slowly puffed on it. There were questions bothering him, things he felt Amparo should answer. But there would be time enough for them in the morning. This day was over, he thought. But he was wrong.

He had been asleep for only a few hours when the thud of horses' hooves awakened him. At first he merely stirred sluggishly in the bed, thinking that Fat Cat was making a lot of unnecessary noise. Then he leaped from the bed, and went to the window. There were two horses coming through the front gate. He recognized the heavy figure of Fat Cat on one but he couldn't make out who was on the second. Whoever it was was slumped over the saddle, clinging to the pommel and barely managing to retain his seat.

Quickly Dax slipped on his trousers and ran down to meet them. Fat Cat was getting down off his horse and the other turned his face when Dax ran down the *galería* steps. It was pale and drawn and caked with dried blood. Dax stared at *el Condor*, his surprise immobilizing him.

"Help me get him into the house," Fat Cat said gruffly. "The soldiers cannot be far behind."

Automatically Dax reached out an arm toward the old man. It was amazing how light and fragile the old *bandolero* had become. "What happened?"

"I told you there were too many soldiers," Fat Cat replied. "There were many more outside Asiento."

The old *bandolero* coughed and a new spot of blood bubbled up through his mouth as they put him down on the bench beside the staircase. The *hacienda* was beginning to come awake. One of the women came in from the rooms behind the kitchen.

"Get water and towels!" Dax ordered. He looked at Fat Cat. "Send one of my men for the doctor."

Fat Cat turned and ran out of the house.

El Condor coughed and grimaced with pain as he tried to speak. Dax took a damp towel from one of the women and wiped the old man's face. "Don't try to talk. We've sent for the doctor."

El Condor grimaced. "For what?" he asked in a rasping whisper. "I am already a dead man."

"You will not die."

"I warned you that Guiterrez would kill us all."

"It wasn't Guiterrez."

"It *was* Guiterrez." Fat Cat's voice came from the doorway. "We were stupid, the old one was right. He's now the head of *el Presidente*'s secret police."

Dax stared at him. There were footsteps on the stairs in the hall and he turned to see Amparo descending. Her face was white and drawn. She moved silently down the steps. For a moment Dax caught a glimpse of José's face behind her, then it disappeared.

"They set up an ambush as the *bandoleros* were coming out of the town on their way back to the mountains."

Dax's eyes turned from Fat Cat to Amparo. "You knew about this!"

Amparo didn't answer. She moved around Dax and looked down at the old man. There was no expression in her eyes. "Is he dead?"

Dax looked down. The old man's jaw hung open; his eyes stared up sightlessly. "He's dead."

A scream came from the staircase and Dax whirled as the boy launched himself at Amparo, the flat edge of his knife extended. Automatically Dax shoved her to one side; she tumbled over a chair as he intercepted the boy. Dax went down to one knee under the impact but the knife clattered to the floor. He kicked it out of reach and got to his feet.

The boy was still on his hands and knees. He stared up at Dax, his eyes streaked with tears. "You lied! You knew all the time!"

"I did not," Dax said, moving forward to help the boy to his feet. "Believe me, I did not!"

"Don't touch me!" José sobbed, and shook him off. "Liar! Traitor!" He turned and ran to the door. "Someday I will kill you for this!" He disappeared into the night and a moment later there was the sound of a horse racing off in the darkness.

Fat Cat started after him. "He'll go back to the mountains!"

"Let him go!" Dax said, then turned back to Amparo, still sprawled out on the floor. He bent over her. "Let me help you up."

"Don't move me!" she said, suddenly savage. "Can't you see I'm bleeding?"

He looked down at her, his eyes widening. The lower half of her nightgown and robe was already stained.

"What is it?"

She glared at him, a curious mixture of anger and sorrow in her eyes. "You poor damn fool! Can't you see? I'm losing my baby!"

He straightened up, a sick feeling inside him. What a fool he must have seemed to them all. With all his knowledge, with all his experience, with all he had learned about the world outside, he must have seemed a child in their hands. There was not one of them who hadn't lied to him, who hadn't used him. Even Amparo.

There was the clatter of many horses outside, then heavy boots on the *galería*. He turned as the soldiers thronged through the doorway. They filled the hallway with their red and blue uniforms.

A moment later, Guiterrez pushed his way through them, the silver braid shining on his uniform. His beady dark eyes swept past Dax, taking in the body of *el Condor* and the sight of Amparo watching them from the floor. He didn't have to be told the *bandolero* was dead. His lips moved tightly as he looked at Dax. "Where is the boy?"

"He's gone."

Guiterrez stared at him. "I don't believe you." Then his eyes fell on Fat Cat. "Arrest that man!"

Dax's voice held the soldiers motionless. "No!"

A light began to dance in Guiterrez' eyes. *"El Presidente*

310

will not be pleased, *señor*. That man tried to help the *bandolero* escape."

"I don't give a damn what *el Presidente* likes!"

A faint cold smile came to Guiterrez' lips. "Your own words betray your treason." He pulled his revolver from its holster and pointed it at Dax. "Arrest them both!"

The soldiers pushed forward to get to Dax but before they could reach him, he scooped up the knife that the boy had dropped on the floor.

Guiterrez leaped backward against the wall. He glared into Dax's eyes. "I've waited a long time for this," he said softly, a tight smile coming to his lips as he raised the revolver.

"So have I!"

Dax's arm moved with the blur of light, and the smile on Guiterrez' face changed to an expression of surprise as the hilt of the knife appeared suddenly in the center of his throat. The revolver fell from his fingers as he raised his hands frantically to grab at the knife. But they never made it; he began falling almost before they were halfway there.

Dax felt the soldiers seize him and roughly pull him back. He twisted, trying to pull himself free, but they held him tightly.

"Let him go!" *El Presidente*'s voice rang out sharply from the doorway.

He strode past them without a second glance at the men lying on the floor. He knelt down to his daughter. A whisper passed between them too quickly for Dax to hear. Then *el Presidente* slowly got to his feet, turning back to him.

"You have done well, my son," he said, his pale-gray eyes expressionless. "I, myself, was coming to kill Guiterrez for violating the amnesty!"

10

The New York offices of the Hadley Shipping Company were located on the edge of the financial district overlooking

Battery Park. They were in an old building, on the nineteenth floor, the penthouse of which had been converted into the personal offices of Mr. Hadley. It was a large five-room suite consisting of an office facing west, surrounded by glass, which gave a clear view in all directions. To the south lay the Statue of Liberty and harbor, to the north and east the towering spires of the Empire State Building, the Rockefeller Center complex, and the needle of the newly completed Chrysler Building. The other rooms were a board room, which also served as a private dining room, a completely equipped kitchen, a large bedroom and a bath.

Marcel turned from the window as Hadley came into the office.

"I'm sorry to have kept you waiting," the older man apologized. "The directors' meeting took rather longer than I had expected."

"That's all right, Mr. Hadley. It gave me a chance to admire the view."

"It is nice," Hadley replied without feeling, as he went behind the desk and sat down.

The way he said it made Marcel wonder if the old man had ever really looked out of the windows. He went over to a chair opposite the desk and sat down.

Hadley didn't waste a minute. "My information from Europe is that war is a matter of months, possibly even weeks, away."

Marcel nodded. There was nothing, as yet, for him to say.

"American representation in Europe will become difficult," Hadley continued. "Especially since the President is avowedly prejudiced toward Britain and France. He has promised them every assistance short of war. It will make it equally difficult in America for certain European interests."

Marcel nodded again. He had a feeling he knew what was coming.

"How many ships have we still committed to the sugar trade?" Hadley asked abruptly.

Marcel thought for a moment. There were nine of them at sea but four were carrying cargoes destined for his own personal warehouses in Brooklyn. "Five. And they will all be in New York by the end of the month."

"Good. As soon as they're unloaded, every ship we have must be sent to Corteguay. If war breaks out, any shipping from here bound for Europe will become fair game for German submarines." He picked up a paper from his desk and looked at it. "Have you had any recent word about Dax?"

"*El Presidente* informs me that he is still in Spain. The agreements with Franco are almost complete."

"We must get word to him that the agreements are to be concluded as soon as possible. I've decided that he should be our representative in Europe when war comes."

Marcel looked at him. "How do you know Dax will do it? After all, he is not working for us."

A look of annoyance crossed Hadley's face. "I know that; that's what makes it practical. Dax represents a completely neutral country. He will have the freedom of Europe no matter how the war goes."

Marcel was silent. He was beginning to understand Americans. Now he knew how the great fortunes were built. War or no, the business of making money brooked no interference. "Have you spoken to *el Presidente* about it?"

"Not yet. I'm leaving that to you. After all, he's your partner, not mine."

It was still early when Marcel left Hadley's office. He checked his watch. There was still time to go out to Brooklyn before his luncheon appointment at one o'clock. He stood on the sidewalk and flagged a taxi. "Bush Terminal in Brooklyn."

Idly he looked out the window as the taxi made its way toward the Brooklyn Bridge. How different the Americans were than the Europeans. They were complacent, safe behind their oceans. If war came it could not touch them.

It would merely be something to read about in the newspapers, to listen to on their radio between "Amos 'n' Andy" and the "Fleischmann Variety Hour," or to watch in a newsreel before the latest Clark Gable movie came on. The threats, rantings and ravings of Hitler could never really reach them. Europe was on the other side of the world.

The humid heat of early August poured in through the cab windows. Even the breeze brought no relief from the pounding heat of the pavements. Slowly the taxi fought its way through the traffic in downtown Brooklyn after coming off the bridge. Up Flatbush Avenue, past Fulton Street with its crowds of shoppers and elevated trains, and then turning into Fourth Avenue toward Bay Ridge. It didn't cool off until they were near the bay.

Marcel told the cabdriver to wait. The cabby mumbled something about losing money while waiting, but Marcel ignored him. A man was seated inside behind an old desk reading a newspaper. He looked up as Marcel came in, and put down the paper. "Good morning, Mr. Campion."

"Good morning, Frank. Everything all right?"

"Right as rain, Mr. Campion," the watchman replied, getting to his feet. He was used to these visits by now. Marcel had a habit of appearing at odd times. There was no telling when, sometimes even in the middle of the night. As usual he followed Marcel through the door into the warehouse proper.

Marcel stood just outside the doorway and looked across the warehouse. The building covered a complete city block and row after row of burlap bags filled with sugar reached almost to the fire-sprinkler line under the high-girdered roof.

Marcel felt satisfaction surge through him. More than a year had passed since he first thought of the idea. By the third of September, when the four ships he expected tied up at the dock outside the warehouses, it would all be over. The last warehouse would be filled and then all he would have to do was wait. The coming war in Europe would take care of everything.

He remembered when he had been a small boy during the last war. There were two things his family could never get enough of—sugar and soap. He remembered once hearing his father complain that he had had to pay twenty francs for a few hundred grams of coarse brown sugar. They had hoarded it and used it carefully for more than a week. That was where the idea originated.

Sugar. Everything in America was sweet. Soda pop, chocolates, buns and cakes, even their bread. Everyone consumed sugar in copious quantities, everyone took sugar for granted. There had always been enough of it. War or no war, they would still expect it. And they would willingly pay for it.

Now there were four buildings like this one, all filled with sugar. He was perhaps the only man who could have done it. He controlled the ships. It was he who could supply falsified bills of lading that diverted the attention of the customs officials who screened every ship that entered the harbor.

But it took money. A great deal of money. More than Marcel had. It was almost as if the sugar producers were aware of what he was up to. He had to pay a bonus of twenty cents on every hundred-pound bag to ensure that they would sell only to him. Additional money went to key officers on his ships who were aware of the real nature of the cargoes. Even the leasing of the warehouses through a blind cost him thousands of dollars over the market.

Quickly the figures flashed through Marcel's mind. There was almost eight million dollars tied up in this project, most of it borrowed. He had never had that much money, and if it hadn't been for Amos Abidijan he never would have had.

Marcel was under no illusions as to why Abidijan had lent him the money. It wasn't because he had been willing to put up his share of the ships as collateral; Abidijan had more ships than he needed. It wasn't even that Abidijan was participating in the profits that might accrue from the project. Abidijan couldn't care less; he hadn't even asked what Marcel wanted the money for. Amos was interested in only one thing. Marrying off his eldest daughter.

In all there were five of them, and until the eldest was married none of the others could marry. It was beginning to seem as if they would never marry, because no one appeared anxious for Anna's hand, despite the dowry that was certain to come with it. It was genuinely unfortunate that of all the daughters Anna most favored her father. She was short and dark, with the slightest hint of a mustache over her upper lip, which no amount of electrolysis had been able to eliminate satisfactorily. And no couturier, no matter how expensive, could hide the square peasant lines of her body.

It seemed as if she had collected all the bad points in the family; the other girls were slim and taller, almost average American in complexion and appearance. Only poor Anna looked and acted like her father. Deciding that men were not for her, she became interested in her father's business and began to work in his office. It was there that Marcel had met her.

He had come in to see her father by appointment but had had to wait. The receptionist had ushered him into Abidijan's outer office, which had been empty. He had just sat down when Anna came in.

"I'm sorry, Mr. Campion," she said, in her husky, almost manlike voice, "my father will be a little late."

By the time the English "my father" had reached Marcel's brain and had been translated into *mon père*, she had already gone behind her desk. Marcel got to his feet. This was a time for true Gallic courtesy.

But to poor inexperienced Anna, who was not used to any attention from the opposite sex, mere Gallic courtesy seemed like romance and before Marcel knew it he was involved. Lunch, then dinners, finally evenings at Amos' home. And ending with weekends at their country place. It was almost two years now, and it had become more or less accepted that they were going together, though Marcel had never said a word to her.

That was the way it had been when Marcel had gone to her father for the loan a little over a year ago. He had thought about asking Hadley for the money, then decided against it. James Hadley had a curious kind of morality. There was practically nothing in business he would not do but this was something else. The ugly words "hoarding" and "black marketing" were anathema to him. Whatever he did had to be justified somehow by overall civic benefit. If he should happen to profit by it, so much the better. And he usually did.

"I need four million dollars," Marcel said to Amos. "I can raise perhaps two on my own—"

"Say no more," Amos had replied, holding up a hand and reaching for his checkbook.

Marcel stared at him in amazement. "But don't you want to know what the money is for?"

Amos shook his head, smiling. "I don't have to. After all, it's all in the family, isn't it?"

Marcel's mouth hung open. Then he caught himself. "But I may need more in a short time."

Amos tore the check out with a flourish and held it out toward Marcel. "When you need more just come in and ask."

Twice more Marcel had asked. Each time the check was tendered and there were never any questions. But it was almost over now.

A little while longer and Marcel would be able to repay the loans. Just as soon as he had he would then make his position clear to all of them. It was only a question of time.

316

11

Dinner at Abidijan's was long and dull and as boring as usual. After dinner they went into the library for coffee and cognac. Silently Marcel took the cigar proffered by the butler and, carefully clipping the end, lit it with a sigh of satisfaction. One thing Amos did do right. He smoked good cigars. The Havanas were always in perfect condition. Not too moist, not too dry, and with a flavor that seemed to caress the palate.

Amos slipped into his favorite leather chair and looked over at Marcel. "You are acquainted with the Baron de Coyne?" he asked in his peculiar-sounding English.

Marcel nodded. "I worked with him," he said, twisting the truth a necessary fraction. His curiosity was piqued but he knew better than to ask questions.

Amos thought for a moment before continuing. "Perhaps you can help me. There are certain companies in which he and I are mutually interested. We have both submitted offers and now they are playing us off one against the other, forcing up the price."

Marcel shook his head. "Always there are greedy ones." He had heard that De Coyne was transferring most of his assets to the States but he hadn't realized that the baron planned also to become active in American business. "What can I do to help? It will be my privilege."

"Perhaps De Coyne and I could make a mutual agreement. Before the price gets so high it will not be profitable for either of us."

"That sounds reasonable. I'm sure the baron would not be averse to that."

317

"That was my thought also. But there seems to be no way I can contact him. The lawyers representing him here refuse to talk."

"Let me think about it," Marcel said. "I'll see if I can come up with something."

"Good." Amos got out of his chair and went to the window of the apartment and looked out at the East River. He stared for a moment, then looked at his watch. "She's late."

Marcel was puzzled. "Who's late?"

"The *Shooting Star*. She was due to pass here at nine-twenty."

Marcel stared at him in surprise. Abidijan owned or controlled one of the largest fleets in the world and yet he knew when an individual tanker was due. Marcel looked at his watch. "Give her a few minutes. It's just nine-thirty now."

Amos came back from the window and sank back into the chair. "Sometimes I think of retiring," he said, "and then I think of all the people depending on me and wonder how I can. I am not growing any younger."

"You're a long way from being old. I only wish I had your energy."

"No, no," Amos replied quickly, "you are a young man. That's why you can say such things. But me—I know better." He puffed at his cigar and sighed. "If only I had sons, even one son, I wouldn't worry." He peered at Marcel shrewdly. "Not that there is anything wrong with the girls. But girls—well, they are girls. If I had a son I could turn the business over to him, then I could take it easy."

Marcel smiled. "With five girls you will have many grandsons."

"Now if I had a son like you," Amos said, ignoring what Marcel had said, "I could leave the business in his hands."

Marcel refused to bite. He knew better. Amos would give away nothing. He would always remain in control. Until he was dead. And even after, if Marcel knew him at all. He was saved the bother of answering by Anna.

"Father," she called excitedly from the living room, "the *Shooting Star* is coming up the river!"

Marcel looked at her standing in the doorway and something inside him shivered. For a moment she had sounded exactly like the old man.

Abidijan got up and went to the window. "It's the *Shooting*

Star," he said, looking at his watch, "and fifteen minutes late, too." He looked at Anna. "Remind me to send a note to her captain in the morning. The reason we publish schedules is because they are to be kept!"

Marcel left a little after ten o'clock, pleading a headache. Anna saw him to the door. "Get some rest," she said, a worried expression on her face. "You look very tired."

He resisted the impulse to tell her that he wasn't tired. He was merely bored. Instead he replied, "A good night's sleep will set me right."

She nodded. "Go right to bed."

"I will. Good night."

The door of the Sutton Place town house closed behind him. He stood in the night and breathed deeply. After the heat of the day the breeze coming from the river seemed almost cool and fresh, though as soon as he started across town the heat returned. After walking a block he could feel the perspiration start trickling down his chest.

He stood on the corner of First Avenue looking for a taxi. As usual when one wanted a cab there were never any around. He looked down the street. Only the lights of some cheap saloons beckoned. He looked at his watch. There were only two places to go at this hour. El Morocco or the Stork. He decided on the first; it was nearer. Only a short walk.

The maître d' bowed. "Monsieur Campion, good evening. Alone?"

Marcel nodded, his eyes flicking around the room to see who was there. "A small table in a corner if you have one."

"Of course, Monsieur Campion." The maître d' led Marcel to a table in the corner of the small outer room. It was a good table and he slipped the bill Marcel gave him discreetly into his pocket.

Marcel ordered a small bottle of champagne. He sat there sipping the wine slowly, feeling the air-cooled room erase the torture of the humidity outside. Several people he knew came by, and he nodded politely. Little by little the restaurant began to fill up. Still he sat there, dreading the thought of returning to the heat.

A young woman's voice came from behind him. "Marcel?"

Automatically he rose before turning around. "Mademoiselle de Coyne!"

She held out her hand and he kissed it. "I was hoping I would run into you."

"I'm so glad you did." It was a moment before he realized they were speaking French. "Won't you sit down?"

"Only for a moment," she replied. "I'm with some people."

He pulled out a chair and a waiter hurried over with another glass. "*À votre santé.* And how is your father?"

"He is well. But things do not go well at home."

"I know."

She glanced around the restaurant. "But here it does not seem to matter."

"They are fortunate; they don't realize how lucky they are." Marcel put down his glass. "I have heard that your father is planning to come here."

"I don't know," Caroline replied. "At the moment everything is so upset. I am returning on the *Normandie* tomorrow."

"Give your father my regards. And please inform him that if there is anything I can do for him here he has only to command me."

"Thank you." Suddenly she was looking directly into his eyes. "I have inquired everywhere but without success. Would you know where Dax is?"

He might have known that she hadn't stopped merely to see him. There had to be another reason. To her he would always be merely a clerk. His impassive face hid his disappointment. "Of course. Dax is in Europe. Didn't you know?"

She shook her head. "No, I didn't."

"He's been there almost a year."

Her disappointment was almost visible. "We never heard from him. He never called."

Suddenly he felt sorry for her. "He's been in Spain on a mission for his government."

"Oh?" A look of concern crossed her face. "Is he safe? He might have been hurt."

"No," he replied reassuringly, "I'm sure he's quite safe. As a matter of fact I have heard that he will soon be in France. Perhaps he will look you up then."

"Can you get word to him? It's very important. My father would like very much to talk to him."

"I will try." Now things were beginning to make sense. That was why Hadley had wanted Dax to go to France. Not

320

just for the vague reason he gave. He had probably heard directly from De Coyne. Another piece fell into place.

It was Hadley he should speak to about Abidijan's problem. The lawyers were just a blind. He made up his mind to check them out in the morning.

"Please try to reach him." Caroline got up from the table and held out her hand. "I will be extremely grateful."

He kissed her hand. "It will be my greatest pleasure to be of help to you."

He stood watching her make her way back to her table. He saw her speak to the man on her right and averted his eyes just in time to avoid theirs. Still, he managed to catch a glimpse of the smiles on the faces of the other two at her table, and he felt a tightness inside him.

It was the old story. He had almost forgotten. Europe was still Europe. For a moment a curious kind of hatred boiled up within him. The mere fact that she hadn't offered to introduce them was sign enough that he was not their equal. It would serve the Old World right if they destroyed themselves in their own holocaust.

Now the wine was bitter in his mouth, and he called for his check. He paid it and went out into the night.

12

When Robert de Coyne came down to breakfast his father was already at table. An opened cablegram lay beside his plate. Silently his father picked it up and handed it to him.

ABIDIJAN BIDDING TWELVE MILLION UP MASTER PRODUCTS STOP HOW HIGH SHALL I GO STOP HADLEY

Robert threw the cable down on the table, a look of disgust on his face. "I don't like it. They're holding us up."

"What can we do about it?" The baron shrugged. "That company is the key to our American operation."

"I thought Hadley was a better trader than that. How did Abidijan hear about it?"

"It doesn't matter now," the baron replied. "We'll have to go to fifteen million."

"That's three times its worth!"

The baron smiled. "Beggars can't be choosers. And in the American market that's just what we are."

Robert picked up his coffee cup just as the butler came into the room. "There's a Monsieur Campion to see your excellency."

"Marcel Campion?" Robert's voice reflected his surprise.

"I believe that was the name, sir."

Robert looked at his father. "I thought Marcel was still in New York."

The baron looked up at the butler. "Have him wait in the library. I shall be in as soon as I finish breakfast."

Marcel was dozing in a chair when they entered the room a half hour later. He got to his feet apologizing. "I beg your pardon, but I just arrived from Lisbon, after flying over from New York."

"Quite all right," the baron answered, but he didn't offer to shake hands. He walked around behind his desk and sat down. "You know my son, Robert?"

Marcel bowed. "Monsieur Robert."

Robert nodded casually. "Marcel."

Marcel waited for them to ask him to sit. Instead the baron asked casually, in an almost patronizing voice, "What is the occasion for this extraordinary visit?"

Marcel felt the weariness of the long trip seeping through him. Suddenly he seemed to have lost his voice. He stood there gawking.

An annoyed look crossed the baron's face. "Come, speak up. What's on your mind? I have a very busy day before me."

A surge of resentment flooded through Marcel. Nothing had changed, nothing ever would. These people had too long been used to having people crawl to them. It wasn't that way in America. There it was what you were that counted, not who your family had been.

What was he doing here? He no longer needed the

baron. Or his money. Or even the association. In America they were beginning to accept him for himself. To hell with the old man. Let him find his own way in America. The whole elaborate scheme he had developed went out the window. Why should he let the De Coynes ride in on his back?

But quickly he found his voice. "My good friend Amos Abidijan suggested I see you in connection with certain companies you both are interested in."

The baron flashed a look at Robert. "Yes?"

"Perhaps there could be a merger of your interests," Marcel continued. "It could possibly result in substantial savings to you both."

The baron looked up at him shrewdly. "And how do you figure in this?"

Suddenly Marcel began to laugh. For the first time he found himself thinking and speaking in English. "Not one fucking bit. I just came for the ride!"

He never regretted that outburst. Never. Not even when he stood in Amos' office two days after Hitler had marched his troops into Poland, and asked for four million dollars to keep from going bankrupt.

It was the sugar that did it. The scheme that was going to make him rich beyond all his wildest dreams. The day after war had been declared in Europe, Roosevelt had put a ceiling on the price of sugar. Four dollars and sixty-five cents per hundred pounds. Marcel had paid $4.85. That was twenty cents per hundred pounds he was out. Four million dollars. And the processors were in no mood to wait for their money. They had him where it hurt and they knew it.

Silently the Armenian wrote the check and handed it to him. He closed the checkbook and looked up.

"Thank you," Marcel said humbly.

"Speculation is a dangerous business. I got very badly hurt during the last war."

Marcel looked at Amos in surprise. So he had known about the sugar. "It's still a good idea," he said defensively.

"Yes, if you get the sugar out before the government requisitions the warehouses."

"Do you think they'll do that?"

Abidijan nodded. "They'll have to. Roosevelt promised to supply the allies. Every warehouse along the waterfront will be requisitioned."

"Where will I ever find a place big enough for all that sugar?"

Amos laughed. "You're a bright young man. But you still have a lot to learn. You don't want it all in one place; that would make it too noticeable. What you must do is scatter it around. Hide it. In obscure places where they will never look. A little at a time like the bootleggers used to do with whiskey."

"I'll never find enough places in time."

"I know how you can," Amos said. "I have a friend. He used to be a bootlegger and he still has many of his old hiding places. I have already spoken to him. He'll take care of you."

Marcel stared at him. "You've saved my life."

Amos laughed. "I do no more than you did for me."

"Did for you?"

"I have had a letter almost two weeks. From Baron de Coyne. He told me you went there to see him about my proposition."

"Oh, that. It was nothing."

"Nothing?" Amos cried. "You fly to Europe in one of those crazy machines just because I ask you a favor and you say it is nothing? I wouldn't go up in one of them for my own father." He got to his feet and walked around the desk. "The baron and I just bought the Master Products Company for three million dollars less than my own offer."

Marcel stared at him. So the baron wasn't that proud after all. Money was the great equalizer.

Amos put his hand on Marcel's shoulder. "Now, that's enough talk about business. Let's talk about more important things. I think October is a very good month for a wedding, don't you?"

13

Sue Ann put down the telephone. "Father wants us to come home."

Sergei raised his head from the newspaper. "You know the baby can't be moved from the *clinique*."

Sue Ann got to her feet angrily. When she moved quickly she appeared even heavier. After the baby she had made no attempt to get back her figure. Instead it seemed as if she had welcomed the excuse to stop caring about her appearance. Now she could eat all the cakes and chocolates she wanted, drink and stuff herself with all the delicacies she had formerly denied herself. The only thing that hadn't changed was her insatiable appetite for sex.

"I know that. But if we go home it won't matter to her. We're not doing anything for her by being here. The only people she really knows are the sisters at the *clinique*."

"She's still our baby. We can't just go off and leave her."

Sue Ann looked at him, her full face settling into grim lines. "You won't give up, will you? You won't admit she's beyond hope, that she'll always be like she is?"

"The doctors say there's a chance."

"The doctors?" She snorted contemptuously. "They'll say anything. They like the money they're getting."

Sergei didn't answer. Instead he got to his feet and started for the door.

"Where are you going?"

He looked back at her. "To the *clinique*. Want to come along?"

"What for? Just to stand there and look at her?"

He shrugged.

She crossed the room to the liquor cabinet and took out

325

a bottle of Scotch. "I'm booking passage to the States for next week."

"If you do," he said quietly, "you'll go alone."

Sue Ann put some ice in her glass and poured whiskey over it. For a moment she sloshed it around in the tumbler, then turned to face him. "There's someone else. That nurse at the hospital. The English one."

"Don't be a fool."

"My friends saw her in your car."

"I was only dropping her off on my way home."

"Yeah?" Sue Ann said skeptically. "My friends say different."

"What do your friends say?"

"They saw you drive by from their balcony. They could look right down into your car. Your fly was open and she had your cock out."

"In broad daylight?" he asked derisively. "You believe that?"

"I know you," she said, finishing the whiskey in her glass and adding some more. "You can't drive a car without having someone to shift your gears. Someday you'll kill yourself doing that."

Sergei laughed harshly. "It's as good a way to die as any. At least I won't expire from stuffing myself like a pig."

Her face clouded. "Don't try to change the subject. I'm not the same girl I was when we got married. I'm wise to you."

"You're very wise," he replied sarcastically, "and do you want to know something? You were much more attractive when you were stupid!"

The door slammed behind him. For a moment Sue Ann stood there, then angrily flung the glass at the closed door. It shattered, the pieces scattered over the rug. "Screw you!"

Suddenly she ran to the window and flung it open. She looked down into the courtyard. He was just getting into the car. "Fuck you! Fuck you! Fuck you!" she screamed out the open window like a fishwife. She was still screaming as the car roared out of the courtyard into the street.

Sergei's hands gripped the wheel tensely. He could feel the throb of the big engine under the hood of the Mercedes responding. It had been a mistake, just as he had known it

326

would be. But that was no consolation to him now. Having been right didn't make him feel any better. Only worse.

It was just as he had said. They were too much alike. And much too different. Now it was over, only in one way it would never be over. Not for him. There was the baby. There would always be the baby. No matter how old she would become, Anastasia would always be a baby.

"Elle est retardé." He could still hear the voice of the specialist. Flat, trying to be unemotionally professional, but still filled with a world of sympathy for the pain of the parents.

He had looked across the room at Sue Ann. There was no expression on her face. At first he had thought she did not understand because the doctor had been speaking in French. "He says she is retarded."

Her eyes looked at him coldly. "I heard him," she answered in an emotionless voice. "I thought something was wrong when she was born. She never cried."

He had looked down into the crib. Anastasia was lying there quietly. Her dark eyes were open but there was no curiosity in them. She was three months old, long past the time for her to show signs of awareness. He felt a constriction in his chest, and fought back the tears. "Is there nothing that can be done? An operation?"

The doctor looked at him, then at the baby. "Not now, perhaps later when she is older. One never knows about such things. Sometimes it just clears up by itself."

"What can we do now?" he asked desperately. "She's such a tiny thing. So helpless."

Sue Ann had turned away from the crib and gone over to the window. It was as if she had divorced herself from whatever was going on in the room behind her.

"Keep her here," the doctor urged gently, "she needs special care. She's too delicate in many ways to be moved. That's all we can do for the present."

"Kill her!" Sue Ann's voice was suddenly savage as she turned from the window. "That's what you can do! Her blood is bad. Papa warned me about old European families. She'll never be any good. She'll be an idiot!"

The doctor couldn't hide his shock. "No, madame, she will never be an idiot. She is merely retarded. A little slow perhaps, but she will be a lovely child nonetheless."

Sue Ann stared at them both for a moment, then turned and walked out of the room, slamming the door behind her. After a moment the baby started to cry. The doctor bent over the crib. "See, she responds. A little slowly, as I said. But she responds. What she needs is care and love."

Sergei looked at him silently. The doctor knew what he was thinking with the intuitive knowledge of experience. He straightened up and came over to Sergei. "Your wife is upset. It is not your fault, these things sometimes happen in intrauterine pregnancies. The baby almost strangled in its umbilical cord. There was some damage to the brain before we could get oxygen into her. But it was very slight. Very often these things repair themselves with time."

Sergei still did not speak.

"You must not blame yourself, my friend," the doctor said gently.

But in a way, he did.

Sergei parked the car in the driveway of the *clinique* and went directly to the baby's room. The sister who was changing the bed linen smiled at him. "The baby's in the garden with the nurse."

Sergei walked through the tall French doors into the garden. He looked across the green lawn. The nurse was sitting on a small bench, the baby carriage in front of her. She looked up as she heard him approaching.

He walked around the carriage and looked into it. The baby was awake. She looked at him with lackadaisical eyes. "How is she this morning?"

"Fine. It was so lovely and warm I decided to give her a little air."

"Good." He took out a cigarette and lit it. His voice lowered. "Where were you last night? I waited at the inn until nine o'clock."

"I couldn't get off; the matron kept me in her office until late. By then I couldn't get a bus so I slept here."

He looked at her. There were tired lines in her face. "Is there anything wrong?"

"I didn't sleep very well, I guess. The matron gave me my notice."

"Your notice?" The surprise showed in his voice.

"Whatever for? There've been no complaints about your work."

She still didn't look at him, and a slight bitterness crept into her voice. "Oh, yes, there have. The matron told me."

Suddenly he was suspicious. "Did she say who?"

The nurse looked at him with her clear gray eyes. "Oh, no, the matron would never do that. But from the nature of the complaint I could guess."

He stared at her. "My wife?"

She nodded.

"She wouldn't! She knows how important you are to Anastasia."

"She did though," the nurse said. "She's the only one who could have. The complaint wasn't about my work, it was about my behavior."

Sergei got to his feet angrily. "I'll see the matron."

"No," she said firmly, "let it go. It would only make it worse."

"What are you going to do? Have you made any plans?"

She shook her head. "I'll have to find something here. There's no way of getting to England now that the Germans have occupied France." She squinted up at the sky. "It's getting a little cloudy."

Sergei followed her back into the room and stood there while she changed the baby and put her back into the crib. Anastasia lay there uncomplaining. He watched them silently. There was something profoundly touching about the gentle way the nurse handled the child. If only Sue Ann had taken the time to see how much the baby needed her perhaps things would have been different.

"She's really a very good baby," the nurse said.

Sergei walked over to the crib and bent over it. "Good morning, Anastasia."

The baby stared up at him for a moment, then her face lit up and her eyes and lips crinkled into a smile.

"She's smiling at me!" Sergei said, looking over at the nurse. "See, she's beginning to recognize me."

The nurse smiled back sympathetically. "I told you she was improving. In another few months you won't know her."

Sergei turned back to the crib. "It's your daddy, Anastasia," he said happily. "It's your daddy, who loves you."

329

But the smile was gone now and once more the baby looked up at him with lackadaisical eyes.

14

Suddenly Sue Ann began to feel sorry, as sorry for Sergei as for herself. It was over between them. In a way it had been over a long time. If only she hadn't become pregnant. Or if she hadn't been afraid to have an abortion. Why hadn't she paid more attention to the calendar and not let it get so far. If—But there were so many ifs and none of them was of any help now.

But most of all she felt sorry for the baby.

She had wanted to love the baby. She had wanted to care for her and cuddle her and play with her but somehow once she saw her, her empty expression, she couldn't. She had tried at first. But when she had looked at her still discolored face, at the screwed-up, almost strangled expression, she had gone sick inside. Silently she had pushed the baby away, and the nurse had taken her back to the incubator.

Sue Ann leaned her head back against the couch and closed her eyes. It went a long way back. A long, long way to when she was a little girl.

Her father was never home. Perhaps at Christmas and on other holidays, but at other times he always seemed to be away on business. It was always the stores. She could see the yellow and blue signs against her closed eyelids. DALEY PENNY SAVERS. The stores were Daddy's life, just as they had been his father's before him.

Her mother had been one of the beauties of Atlanta. Many times Sue Ann had heard her expressions of disappointment because her daughter took after her father, who was big and

330

heavy, and had none of the beauty that all the girls in her mother's family had possessed.

By the time she was fourteen Sue Ann was taller than most of the boys in her class at high school. She was already fighting a weight problem unsuccessfully, because the more nervous she became about her weight the greater was her compulsion to eat. And with the onset of the menses she developed a chronic adolescent acne.

She remembered the tears of frustration she had shed in front of the mirror, and how she had not wanted to appear in public or go to school. But her mother had forced her and she remembered how most of the boys had laughed when they saw her pimpled face, usually covered with the remains of the latest healing ointment. After a while she began to hate boys because of this cruelty, yet in spite of this she always felt an inner excitement whenever they spoke to her or even noticed her. Her sexual responses even then were so great that no matter how hard she tried to control them she would soon be soaking wet. And she was always desperately afraid that they would notice.

She didn't remember exactly when or how she came to masturbation but she could remember the relief she got from it, and the quiet and lassitude that would steal over her afterward. It was only then that she no longer felt the tensions or the desire to stuff herself. She remembered how pleasant it was just to lie in bed in the morning after she had done it, to close her eyes and dream of how beautiful she had become. And then her mother had come into the room and caught her.

She could still see the startled, angry expression on her mother's face as she stood in the doorway staring at her lying naked on the bed, her legs drawn up, her fingers busy. Almost before she could stop, her mother had slammed the door and snatched a leather belt from the dresser and begun to beat her.

The first lash across her naked flesh burned into her with an almost exquisite pain. She screamed, then rolled over on her stomach trying to escape the furious slashes. She could feel the burning welts rising on the flesh of her back and buttocks and legs. A fiery heat ran through her and suddenly she was screaming and writhing in the throes of the first real orgasm she ever experienced.

But in spite of it she could still hear the angry shouting of

331

her mother as she belabored her with the leather belt. "You dirty child! Do you want your children to be idiots? Do you want your children to be idiots?" Again and again, over and over, until it melded with her pain and tears. Idiots idiots idiots . . .

About the only thing she learned from that experience was always to lock her bedroom door. Nothing more interfered with her preoccupation with her own physique. It kept on like that until her first real sexual experience, which happened when she was sixteen. Actually it would have happened sooner had the choice been hers. But at first she could not attract boys. And then when she finally managed to they were afraid; her family's reputation was too awesome, or perhaps the local boys still had some vestiges of southern gentlemen.

It finally happened in the back seat of a convertible parked in the dark of a local lovers' lane after a high-school dance. Almost before the boy realized it things had gone so far that it was impossible for him to back out. Yet at the final moment he hesitated.

"What are you stoppin' for?" she demanded angrily.

"I don't know, Sue Ann. Do you really think we should?"

She exploded in a burst of pragmatic practicality. "Are you never goin' to get tired of me jackin' you off?"

And in the end it was almost as if she had to do it herself. She guided him inside her. But when he came up against the obstruction of her hymen he stopped again. "Ah cain go no fuhther," he whispered.

By then she was half out of her mind. The thought that she was this close and it might come to nothing was too much for her. She dug her nails into his buttocks. "Push harder, goddam it!"

The boy gave one last convulsive shove, and the deed was done. A moment later he had his orgasm and started to withdraw.

"Where you think you're goin'?" she asked.

"You're bleedin'," he said. "I doan want to hurt you."

"You're not hurtin' me."

"You sure?" he asked doubtfully.

"Of course I'm sure. Come on, do it to me again. Hurry, I want it. Do it to me, goddam it. Hurry!"

Almost overnight her acne went away and no more did she

332

have to lock her bedroom door. There were lots of boys and lots of automobiles and when she went away to school for the first time a brand-new wonderful world opened up for her. And the beating her mother had given her and the things her mother had said were forgotten. Or so she thought. Until the night the baby was born.

She seemed to be fighting her way up out of a fog. She opened her eyes. The bright light was still shining into her eyes. She was lying on the table in the delivery room. She blinked her eyes to clear them. Her vision was still fuzzy.

The doctor and two nurses were bending over a table in the corner. Vaguely she wondered what they were doing. After a moment it came to her. "My baby!" she cried, trying to get up, but the straps held her down.

The doctor looked back over his shoulder and said something to one of the nurses. The nurse came over to her. "Lie back and rest."

"What's the matter with my baby?"

"Nothing. Just rest. Everything will be all right."

"Doctor," she screamed, "what's the matter with my baby?" When she tried to get up this time the nurse held her down. A moment later the doctor came over. "My baby's dead!"

"No, the baby's all right. We just had a little trouble."

"What kind of trouble?"

"The umbilical cord was wrapped around the baby's head."

The nurse in front of the table moved and she could see the baby's face covered with an oxygen mask. "What are they doing?"

"Giving the baby oxygen. Now try to rest."

She pushed away his hand. "Why?"

"In case the baby was damaged. Oxygen helps in cases like that. We don't want to take any chances, do we?"

Suddenly she knew. "She was deformed, wasn't she? Or the brain. That's the first thing that's damaged, isn't it?"

The doctor looked at her. "One never knows in cases like these," he answered reluctantly.

She stared up at him. Maybe they weren't sure but she was. From deep within came the memory of her mother's words. "Do you want your children to be idiots?"

333

She closed her eyes in sudden pain. Mother was right, she thought. Her mother was always right. "Doctor?"

"Yes?"

"Doctor, can you fix it so I won't have any more babies?"

He looked down at her. "I can. But don't you think you ought to talk to your husband first?"

"No!"

"This was an accident," he said, "it probably would never happen again. It's one chance in a thousand. But once your tubes are tied it can't ever be undone. What if you want another baby?"

"I'll adopt one. That's the one way I can be sure of what I'm getting!"

The doctor studied her for a moment, then gestured to the nurse. The cone came down over her face and she gulped deeply. She felt the tears come into her eyes as she closed them, then the room began to recede. There was a curious pain and she felt that all her insides were crying, and that if she were awake she would be crying too.

Why? Why did her mother always have to be right?

15

Sue Ann turned to him suddenly while they were taking the first of her valises and trunks out to the limousine. "I don't want a divorce."

Sergei didn't answer.

"The bank will send your regular check every month, and of course they'll pay for the baby's care."

"You don't have to," Sergei said tightly. "I can take care of her."

"I want to."

Again he didn't answer.

"I'll come back," she said. "I just want to go home for a while. Until I feel better."

"Sure." But they both knew she would never come back. That was the way it had to be.

"Everything's so different here. The language, the people. I never really felt right."

"I know. That's normal enough, I guess. Everyone feels better at home."

The last of her bags were on the way out. She looked up into his face. "Well," she said awkwardly, "good-bye."

"Good-bye, Sue Ann." Sergei bent and kissed her, French style, on both cheeks.

She looked up at him for a moment. Suddenly the tears came into her eyes. "I'm sorry," she whispered, then turned and ran out, leaving the door open behind her.

Slowly Sergei closed it and went into the living room. He poured himself a small whiskey and drank it neat. He felt weariness course through him and sank into a chair. There had been other good-byes with other women but this one was different. None of them had been Sue Ann. None of them had been his wife.

Still he could not say that he had not expected it. Ever since she had come out of the hospital and told him what she had done.

"You must have been crazy," he'd shouted. "Only an idiot would do a thing like that!"

Her face had gone pale and stubborn. "No more children. One like her is enough."

"The others did not have to be like her!"

"Would not have to be." She corrected his English. "But I'm not taking any chances; I've heard about you old European families."

He stared at her. "There's never been anything like that in my family. It was merely an accident."

"Not in my family either," she replied with finality. "Anyway, I don't want any more children."

An awkward silence came down over them. He stood in front of the fire looking down at it. She came over and stood at his side. "We really fucked it up didn't we?"

He didn't answer.

After a moment she spoke again. "I think I'll go up to bed."

He still did not say anything.

She walked over to the foot of the stairs and turned. "Coming up?"

"In a little while."

She went silently up the steps. He stood there until the logs burned down. When he came into the bedroom she was in his bed waiting for him. But it wasn't the same. It would never be the same between them. Too many walls had suddenly sprung up.

She had realized it almost as quickly as he. Suddenly all her desire to get back to normal vanished. She went off her diet and gave up her exercises. She grew careless about her appearance and weight seemed to cling to her. Once he suggested that it wouldn't hurt if she had her hair done and bought a few new dresses.

"What for?" she asked. "We don't ever go anywhere."

That was true enough; the war had limited their movements. Travel in Europe was a thing of the past. No longer could they run down to the Riviera for the swimming or dash up to Paris for amusement. It was like being locked on an island.

Bit by bit, one by one, people seemed to be disappearing. They became caught up in the vortex of the conflict and returned to their own country. Soon there was nobody left but the Swiss. And they were very dull. All they seemed to be really interested in was money, and the principal topic of conversation seemed always to be which of the current crop of leaders was salting away the most money in Switzerland.

From the proprietary manner in which they spoke about it one gathered that the Swiss had no intention of ever having to return it. When the war was over most of the deposits would remain there because a great percentage of the depositors would not have survived, and they would have died without making adequate provision for the transfer of their funds. Thus they would properly become Swiss property. When the Germans outflanked the Maginot Line and overran France it looked as if the Swiss were right. It was as if a curtain had suddenly been drawn across western Europe.

It had been less than a month after that that Sergei happened to be in the bankers' offices. Bernstein had looked at him and said, "Your father is a colonel in the German army?"

Sergei was curious. They knew it as well as he. "Why?"

"We should get in touch with certain of our clients," the banker had answered, "and now there is no way we can do this."

"Why don't you just go to them?" Sergei suggested. "You're both Swiss. You should have no trouble."

"We couldn't do that," Kastele replied quickly. "The Swiss government would not permit it. It might be viewed as a hostile act by the Germans."

Sergei stared at them, then suddenly he realized the answers. Their clients were Jews. He didn't speak.

"If your father got you a permit," Kastele said, "I'm sure we could arrange for a Swiss passport."

Sergei was intrigued. "You mean I would become a Swiss citizen?"

The bankers exchanged glances. "That, too, could be arranged."

Sergei was thoughtful. As it stood he was neither French nor Russian. He was merely one of the many people who drifted around Europe after the last war. Stateless persons they were called. But it had been recognized that they were entitled to settle down somewhere, and most of the White Russians had done so in France. A Swiss citizenship might be very useful to him one day.

"What would you want me to do?"

"Merely try to locate our clients and obtain instructions about their holdings."

"And if they can't be found?"

"Try to determine if they are still alive. We will need that information to settle their accounts."

Sergei wondered if what he had heard was true, that the unclaimed balances were divided equally between the banks and the Swiss government. If it was true, then he could see why the bankers had a big stake in what happened. "And what would I get out of it?"

"I'm sure we could work out an equitable arrangement," Bernstein said. "We haven't been such bad fellows to get along with, have we?"

By the time Sergei left their office he had agreed to write his father and find out what could be arranged. That had been several months ago. The reply from his father had finally arrived that morning. The day Sue Ann left.

His father was in Paris, quartered in a suite at the same hotel at which he had been employed as doorman. Something could be done. His father would be very glad to see him once again.

Sergei put down the empty whiskey glass. He had made up his mind to accept the offer of the bankers. Later that afternoon he would go to their offices and inform them of his decision. But first there was something else he had to attend to. He picked up the telephone and gave the operator a number.

A woman's voice answered.

"Peggy," he said quickly, "this is Sergei."

"Yes," the brisk English voice replied.

"Sue Ann is gone. How long will it take you to get the baby ready?"

A faint note of happiness came into the voice. "The baby's been ready all morning. I've been awaiting your call."

"I'll be there in ten minutes."

16

The only sound on the Avenue George V was the sound of his own footsteps on the sidewalk. Dax looked up the street toward the Champs Élysées. It was a feeling he could never quite get used to. Paris at midnight, deserted.

The streets were empty. All the French at home in their flats behind locked doors. Fouquet's on the corner closed, and the cafés with their deserted tables and chairs still outside. The shops, their windows usually filled with bright-colored goodies to attract the ladies, were shuttered. Paris in the summer of 1940, with no lovers strolling arm in arm pausing to kiss beneath the heavy-leafed chestnut trees.

He pulled a thin cigar from his pocket and lit it. As he struck the match he heard footsteps and turned. A girl came out from the shadow of a doorway. In the glow of the match he could see her face. Sharp, thin, hungry.

"Wohin gehen Sie, mein Herr?" she whispered. The sound of her German was alien to the night and clumsy on her tongue.

He shook his head gently and spoke to her in French, then watched as she scurried back into the shadows from which she had come. He turned and began to walk again. Even the whores seemed defeated.

It hadn't been that way at the party he had just left. There the lights had been bright behind the heavy drawn drapes. There was music, laughter, champagne, attractive women. There were the Germans and the Frenchmen who accepted them. But after a while the party had palled. The French were too eager, the Germans too condescending, the laughter too forced. He decided to leave and had looked around for Giselle.

He found her in the center of a group of Germans, her birdlike little French manager hovering on the fringe, and watching her with careful tiny glances. Her pert, bright face was alive and sparkling as she looked around at the men surrounding her. Giselle was an actress. She loved an audience.

He smiled to himself. There was no point in asking her to leave. She was having too good a time. Quietly he slipped away. In the morning she would call him. Early, her voice still fuzzy with sleep, so that he would know she had left instructions with her maid to wake her. "Why did you leave without me?" she would ask reproachfully.

"You were having too good a time."

"I wasn't. I couldn't stand them. German men are all so pompous. But I had to. Georges said so. It was business."

Georges always said so. Georges did not like Dax. Dax could not get him film for his cameras, or permission to make movies. Dax could only distract Giselle. And Giselle was Georges's principal product. Without her he was just another producer.

"Will you come over for lunch?" she would ask.

"I'll try."

"Until later then," she would say in her sleepy, husky voice, and Dax would turn back to his desk knowing that she would go right back to sleep.

It was more than a year now that he had known her. He

saw her first at the railroad station in Barcelona. A mob was milling around the entrance.

"What's happening?" he asked a friend, a member of the Spanish purchasing commission.

"It's the movie star Giselle d'Arcy. She's just come back from Hollywood and is on her way to Paris."

The name did not mean anything to him but when he saw her in the center of the crowd passing by he knew her instantly. He could not help but know her. Her photograph had been on billboards and newspapers all over the world.

The photographs did not do her justice. Her breasts were not as large as they seemed to be in the pictures, nor were the hips so round or the legs so long. And what the photographs did not catch was the sheer aliveness of her, the joyous vivacity of her walk.

Dax stared and a real physical pain shot through him. It had been a long time since he had wanted a woman. Suddenly he was afire. This one. Only this one. He had to have her. It was as simple as that.

She looked out over the crowd and caught him staring at her. Automatically she started to look away, then inexorably, as if drawn by a magnet, her eyes came back to his. He did not avert his. He saw her face pale slightly and then something in the crowd turned her away and she disappeared through the gate to the train. He followed.

But he waited until the train was a half hour out of the station before he went looking for her. He found her alone in her compartment, Georges having gone to the lavatory. She looked up from her magazine and saw him through the glass door. She watched silently as he opened the door. He closed it behind him and stood leaning against it. His breath constricted his chest. After a moment he said, "I've got to have you."

"Yes," she answered, "yes, I know." All she could feel was the sheer animal power, almost as if there were a powder keg contained within him.

He reached down and took her hand. It was trembling slightly. "I know you," she said, almost in a whisper, "though we've never met."

"No, not before this day. But now we have. Now, this time, this place, this day."

By the time Georges made his way back to the compartment the shades were drawn and the door was locked. Nervously he knocked on the door. "Giselle, Giselle," he called, "are you all right?"

"Go away." Her voice was throaty.

He stood very still for a moment. He knew that sound; he had heard it before. He made his way to the bar and ordered a drink, then sat back in the seat and philosophically watched the countryside go by. He wondered who it was that she was with. Usually he was able to spot them in advance. He shrugged and ordered another *pastis*. You couldn't win them all and, anyway, tomorrow they would be back in Paris where everything would be all right. He could control her in Paris.

That had been more than a year ago. Many things had happened in that year. The Germans overran the Continent. France was trampled under the marching boot of the Nazis. There was a new government in Vichy. Desperately Georges tried to cling to the illusion of autonomy.

But it wasn't quite that easy. The Germans had the last say on everything. Now there were signs that they might allow some of the studios to go back into production, and Georges wanted to be among the first. Carefully he cultivated all the right people. The Germans and their French collaborationists. They, like everyone else, were impressed with Giselle.

The only thing that bothered him was her attachment to Dax. It had lasted a great deal longer than he had expected. He didn't understand it. Dax could do nothing for her, offered her nothing. Yet still she saw him. Dax never mentioned marriage, yet she showered him with gifts. Studs and cuff links of gold and diamonds.

Georges would never understand it. It was all backward. Usually it was Giselle who received the gifts, not gave them. That was the long-time prerogative of an actress.

Once he had gone to her with a proposition from an important German officer. Giselle had merely laughed and told him to go away.

"But he can help us."

"Help you," she said with her peculiar direct acumen. I'm happy the way I am."

"Don't you want to go back to work?"

She shook her head. "I do but I have a feeling it wouldn't

341

be right. There's beginning to be a lot of talk about the collaborationists."

"They're fools!" Georges snorted. "The war is over, we are beaten."

"There are still Frenchmen fighting overseas."

"It's 1870 all over again. This time it's the Germans' turn, the next it will be ours."

She looked at him, her large blue eyes sad. She knew how badly he wanted to return to work, how much he needed it. Without it he was nothing. "If we don't win this time," she said softly, "we may never have another chance."

But she did go to the parties and other functions he suggested. But always with Dax, never with him alone or another Frenchman, or even a German. She was determined that there be no talk about her having been a collaborationist.

Once there she behaved normally; there were no outward signs that she was not going to cooperate. But she refused every offer with one excuse or another, and she avoided every affair that had any political significance. The proof that she had been discreet was that the average person on the street, when they saw her, still smiled and nodded. They did not avoid her or give her the contemptuously silent treatment they gave to so many of the others. As far as they were concerned she was still a star, whether she currently was making movies or not.

Once when she and Dax were having lunch in her apartment, which overlooked the Bois de Boulogne, they had heard the sound of marching. She went over to the window and looked down at the goose-stepping Germans. After a moment she turned to Dax. "Do you think they will ever leave?"

"Not until they're forced out."

"Will it ever happen?"

He left the window and went back to the table. He didn't answer.

She was suddenly angry. "You don't care, do you? You're not French, you're a foreigner. Besides, you're doing business with them. You'd do business with anyone!"

He took the cigar from his mouth and placed it carefully in an ash tray. "I care," he answered quietly. "I have friends who are both French and Jews. I don't like what is happening to them but I dare not interfere. I am a representative of my government."

342

She stared at him. It was the first time she had ever heard him express himself about the war. And she sensed the anger under the pleasantness of his voice. Contritely she walked over to him. She bent and pressed her cheek against his. "I'm sorry, darling. I should have known. It's not easy for you either."

He looked up into her face. "It's easier for me than it is for you French."

17

Fat Cat was waiting for him as he entered the consulate building. "There are some Germans waiting for you in the office."

"Oh? Who are they?"

"I don't know; two officers."

"I'll see them."

Fat Cat stopped in front of the door. "I'll wait out here in case there's any trouble."

Dax smiled. "Why should there be?" he asked, a faint sarcasm in his voice. "They're our friends."

"They're nobody's friends!"

Dax opened the office door and went in. The two officers leaped to their feet. Automatically their hands shot out. "Heil Hitler!"

"Gentlemen." Dax walked around behind his desk and sat down. "I don't believe we've met."

The older of the two straightened up. "Permit me, your excellency." He clicked his heels in a military bow. "Lieutenant Colonel Reiss. My assistant, Lieutenant Kron."

Dax nodded and took a thin cigar from the box on his desk. He lit it without offering them one. "It's late and I'm tired. Please state the purpose of this visit."

The Germans exchanged glances. He could see that they were not used to being so received. Noting the SS emblem on

343

their uniforms he could understand why. They were used to evoking fear when they appeared. He smiled inwardly. To hell with them. They needed him more than he needed them.

No agreement had been reached with the Germans over Corteguayan beef, though discussions were still going on. As a matter of fact he was to attend another tomorrow. He was aware that Spain was sending them a good share of the supplies they received from Corteguay. It was one of the prices that Franco had to pay for their past assistance.

The colonel took out a paper from his tunic and glanced at it. He spoke a heavily accented French. "You are acquainted with one Robert de Coyne?"

Dax nodded. "Yes, we went to school together. He is a friend of mine."

"You are aware of course that he is a Jew?" The colonel's voice was thick with contempt.

Dax's was equally full of contempt. "I also have some friends who are German."

The colonel ignored the sarcasm. "Have you seen him recently?"

"No."

"Where were you tonight?" the younger officer asked suddenly.

Dax stared at him. "None of your business!"

"I remind you, sir," the colonel said stiffly, "that we are here on the business of the Third Reich!"

"And may I remind you," Dax replied angrily, "that you are in the embassy of Corteguay." He got to his feet. "You may now leave!"

As if by magic the door behind them opened. The officers stood there awkwardly.

"You may leave, gentlemen!"

"General Foelder won't like this!" the younger officer said.

Dax's voice was cold. "You may inform your superior that after this when he wishes to approach me he may do so through regular diplomatic channels. This may be arranged through your own foreign ministry."

He turned his back as they left the room. A moment later Fat Cat was back. "What did they want?"

Dax smiled. "You already know, why ask? Unless you've lost your skill at keyholes. Or have you grown so fat you can't bend down?"

344

"Have you heard from Robert?"

"No." A worried look crossed Dax's face. "Nor have I heard from his sister in the past few weeks." He was angry with himself for not having thought of it sooner. He and Caroline spoke on the telephone at least once a week.

He had seen her only a few times and then at her house. Caroline did not go out much any more. He still thought she should have gone to America with her father when the Germans had begun their invasion of France. But she hadn't. In a way she was very much like her brother. She didn't believe in running either.

"I'd better call her," Dax said, reaching for the telephone. He dialed the number. There was no answer. He let it ring for several minutes.

When he put the telephone down there was genuine concern in his eyes. Someone should have answered. Even if Caroline was not in, there was always a servant or two around.

"There's no answer?"

Dax shook his head silently.

"What do you think?"

Dax took a deep breath. "I'm afraid that our friends may be in trouble."

Caroline sat on the edge of the chair staring at the ringing telephone. A German sat opposite her, leaning back comfortably in his ordinary gray business suit. "Why don't you answer it?" he asked. "It might be your brother. He may be hurt and in serious trouble."

Caroline tore her eyes away from the telephone. It was almost a relief not to look at it. "I haven't heard from my brother in months. Why should he call now?"

"I told you," the German said patiently, "there was an attempt at sabotage in the freight yards. It failed, of course. We killed all of them except one, who got away. He was wounded. We believe it was your brother."

"What proof have you?" Caroline retorted. The telephone finally stopped ringing. She drew a breath of relief. "The last I heard he was in a prison camp after you captured him on the Maginot Line."

"He escaped. I told you he escaped." For the first time the German's voice contained a note of impatience. "Besides, one of the saboteurs confessed that it was your brother before he died."

Contempt crept into Caroline's voice. "I've heard about such confessions."

The voice hardened. "Nevertheless, it was your brother. And he is hurt and somewhere in Paris. Possibly not far from here, perhaps bleeding and dying. If we can find him there is a chance his life may be saved."

"By whom?" Caroline asked sarcastically. "And for what? To be tortured and stood up against a wall and shot?"

"We're not as bad as all that. You must not believe all the propaganda that our enemies are spreading."

Caroline did not answer. She took a cigarette from a box on the table in front of her. Quickly the German leaned over and held a light for her.

"Why can't you be reasonable? Surely you must understand; you were German once. At least your family came from there."

Caroline took a deep drag on the cigarette and stared at him. "That was almost a hundred years ago, and we left because we were Jews. Things haven't changed so much we'd forget."

The SS man sank back into his chair. "Despite what you have heard, the Third Reich is not unreasonable. Once a German, always a German. It could even be forgotten that you were once Jews."

Caroline looked into his eyes. "Perhaps by you. But could we?"

The German's lips tightened. He reached over and snatched the cigarette from her mouth. All politeness disappeared from his voice. "Jew bitch! Next time the telephone rings you will answer it!"

"And if I don't?"

He moved quickly, the back of his hand swiping across her face. She fell sideways from the chair to the floor and lay staring up at him. He got out of his chair and stood over her, his eyes cold with hate. "If you don't," he said slowly, "you'll wish you had!"

Robert huddled in the doorway across the street, his hand clutching the shoulder where he had been shot. He felt

346

the warm sticky blood seeping through his fingers. He looked over at the house.

It was almost morning and there was still a dim light escaping around the edges of the heavy drawn drapes in the library. The German staff car with the two soldiers in it was parked in the street in front of the house.

Suddenly the front door opened, and the two soldiers sprang out of the car and stood stiffly at attention. Caroline and a man came out. The man was dressed in an ordinary business suit. One of the soldiers opened the door of the car and Caroline got in as the man spoke to him for a few moments.

In the crisp morning air Robert could hear his brisk "Jawohl." Then the man got into the car beside Caroline and closed the door. The driver got back into the car and started the motor. The remaining soldier stood for a moment watching the car drive off, then turned and entered the house.

Robert waited until the door had closed behind him before he came out of his hiding place. He stood indecisively in the street. For the moment the fact that they had Caroline was more important than his wound. He did not have to be told what Germans did to their prisoners. A cold dread began to run through him. Something would have to be done to get her away from them.

Briefly he thought of giving himself up, but then reason took over. It would do no good; the Nazis would simply have both of them. He felt a sharp pain in his shoulder. The quick movement had started the bleeding again, and he felt weak and on the verge of tears as despair coursed through him. Then the sound of heavy boots rang out from down the street.

He didn't wait to see whose they were. He knew the cadence of the goose-step too well. He went down an alley into a dark doorway and huddled, shivering. He didn't even stick out his head until the sound completely faded away.

After that he moved through the early-morning streets almost aimlessly. There was no place for him to go. All the others were dead, and when he had gone back to the hideaway there had been Nazis all around it. He began to feel weak, almost lightheaded from the loss of blood. If he did not find help soon he would no longer have to hide from the Germans. They would find him lying in the streets.

18

The woman's voice over the telephone was hushed and guarded. "Monsieur Xenos, this is Madame Blanchette. Do you remember?"

"But of course." From the first night Dax had spent in Paris, he had passed her house almost every day. "How are you, Madame Blanchette?"

"I am fine. But I am so disappointed. You have not come to visit us since your return."

For a moment Dax was puzzled. He had never been a client of her establishment. Then he remembered. The baron had. "I am sorry, madame. I have been too busy."

"A man must never allow himself to be so busy he cannot relax once in a while," Madame Blanchette said reproachfully. "It is only by the leisure time spent away from his work that a man can maintain his peak."

Dax laughed. "I apologize again, madame."

"I took the liberty of calling in the hopes that you could visit us this evening. I am giving a very special *soirée*. It might be quite amusing. I think you will find it most novel."

Dax looked down at his desk calendar. "I have another appointment——"

"We should be most disappointed if you did not come, Monsieur Xenos," she interrupted. "In a way the entire *soirée* is planned around you."

There seemed to be a strange insistence in her voice. "All right, I'll come. But it will have to be late."

"How late?"

"One in the morning?"

He sensed the note of relief in her voice. "That will be quite satisfactory. Nothing much will happen before then."

As Dax put down the telephone Fat Cat came into the room. "Well, what did you find out?"

"She's gone all right. None of the servants will talk. There are two Germans hanging around the house."

"Did you check the neighborhood?"

Fat Cat nodded. "The same everywhere. Nobody knows. Or dares talk."

Dax thought for a moment. "I just had a curious phone call from Madame Blanchette down the street. She was a friend of the baron's. Could Caroline be hiding there?" He reached for one of his thin cigars. "Madame Blanchette seemed very set on my coming there tonight."

The telephone began to ring again, and when Dax picked it up a familiar voice greeted him. "Good morning, darling." Giselle's voice was still fuzzy with sleep. "Why did you go off and leave me at that horrible party last night?"

Dax glanced at his watch. It was nearly noon. "You were enjoying yourself."

"But, darling, that was because I was with you."

"And six other men. I couldn't even get close to you."

"But I'm alone now. You could come over for lunch?"

Dax could almost see her sprawled across the huge bed, her breasts pushing up against the décolletage of her night-dress as she lay on her stomach talking into the telephone.

"I'd like to, but I can't."

"Oh, darling, I'm so disappointed!"

He laughed at the patent fakery in her voice. She was a good enough actress to make her voice do exactly what she wanted it to do. "No, you're not. You're going right back to sleep again, which is what you planned to do all along."

She laughed and the sound was warm in his ear. "Then dinner tonight?"

"Yes, but I shall have to leave by midnight. I have another appointment."

"At midnight?"

"Yes."

A jealous note crept into her voice, and now she was no longer acting. "There's another woman."

"No. How could there be? You have never given me enough time to find one."

"You won't have strength for another woman when you leave me tonight!"

"Is that a threat or a promise?"

"Don't joke with me," she said. "I am a very jealous woman."

"Good. That is the best kind."

Sergei stood in front of the Hotel Royale Palace. There was a curiously faded air about it since the Germans had taken it over. He went through the doors into the lobby. He noticed that the paint was peeling from the walls behind the front desk as he stepped up to it.

The German corporal looked at Sergei's expensive clothing respectfully. "*Ja, mein Herr?*"

"Colonel Count Nikovitch."

"Do you have an appointment? The colonel is extremely busy."

"He'll see me. Just tell him his son is here."

The soldier picked up the telephone, and a moment later Sergei was escorted to an office on the second floor. He paused for a moment at the door bearing his father's name, and then opened it. He stopped momentarily, as he always did when he saw his father, realizing once again the tremendous stature of the man. Then he was caught in a powerful bear hug as his father came around the desk and almost crushed him against his breast.

"Sergei, Sergei," he said over and over, and tears flowed freely from his eyes. "Sergei!"

Sergei looked up into his father's face. There were lines there that were new, and the once jet-black hair was now shot through with gray. "How are you, Papa?"

"I'm fine now," the count replied in his gruff hearty voice. He went back behind his desk and lit a long Russian cigarette. "You look well. How is your wife?"

"She's gone back to America."

The old man looked at him shrewdly. "She's taken Anastasia with her?"

Sergei shook his head. "No, Anastasia is with me."

Count Nikovitch slipped down into his chair. "How is the child?"

"She's improving. But it will take time."

"Is your wife coming back?" the count asked bluntly.

"I don't think so."

A momentary uncomfortable silence fell between them. Sergei looked around. "It's a nice office."

350

"I don't belong here," his father replied tersely, "but the General Staff considers me an expert on Paris, so here I am."

Sergei laughed. "And you left Paris because you thought the Germans would send you into Russia!"

His father didn't smile. "All armies are the same. But we shall invade Russia yet."

"But they have a nonaggression pact with Stalin."

The count's voice lowered. *"Der Führer* has made many pacts. He hasn't kept one of them. He's too smart to open up another front and fight a war on two fronts. After we get through with the English, then you'll see."

"You really believe that, don't you?"

His father looked at him steadily. "A man has to believe in something." He ground his cigarette out in an ash tray. "After I left Russia there was nothing to believe in. Our whole world vanished overnight, ground into the dirt by the stinking feet of the Bolsheviki."

"What makes you think Hitler will permit that world to rise again? Why should he want any other world than his own?" Sergei walked over to the window and looked down into the street. "I don't think he will, Papa. He already has more power than any czar. Why should he let any of it go?"

His father didn't answer. After a moment he got up and came over to the window beside Sergei. They stood there looking out silently.

"When I was just a boy, once a year your grandfather used to bring me to Paris. It was essential for every young nobleman, he used to say. Paris was where one learned to live. I remember how we used to stand together in a window of this very hotel and look down at the streets and the pretty cocottes and the beautiful horses and carriages. And at nights, the grand parties!" He fell silent for a moment, then began again.

"Then when I came here after the Revolution the owner, who had liked my father, was kind enough to give me a job as doorman. He would stop by every once in a while and we would talk about the good old days. Sometimes I would look up at the windows and wonder if I would ever be on the inside again, instead of outside in the cold and snow and rain. Now everything has turned around again and once more I am."

"But the whole thing's different."

"What do you mean?"

"Where are the people? The pretty cocottes, and the laughter and the gaiety? It's not Paris any more." Sergei turned back into the room. "Even up here it's not the same. This used to be a fine suite, now look at it. And the owner? What happened to him—was he a Jew?"

His father didn't answer. He went back to the desk and sat down heavily. "I don't know. I am a soldier, not a politician. I do not involve myself with things which do not concern me."

"But the man was kind enough to help you when you needed help. You said so yourself."

His father looked at him. "Since when have you become so concerned about Jews?"

"I'm not. I'm only concerned about Paris. Somehow, somewhere, all the laughter has gone. Perhaps the Jews took it with them."

His father stared at him. "Why did you come here?"

"On business. I represent the Crédit Suisse. I'm trying to contact certain of their clients."

"Jews?"

"Some of them, yes."

The count was silent for a moment. When he spoke, his voice was heavy. "I might have guessed. The first time in your life you have a decent job, and you get yourself involved with the wrong kinds of people."

Caroline was cold. She had never been so cold in her life. She went over to the door of the little cell and banged on the bars. The matron sitting across the hall looked up.

"When will they return my clothes? I'm freezing."

The matron stared at her blankly, and Caroline realized that she must not understand French. Haltingly she repeated her question in German.

"Ich weiss nicht."

The sound of footsteps echoed down the corridor, and the matron suddenly snapped to attention. A man's voice spoke but the man himself was just out of the range of Caroline's vision.

"Das Fräulein Caroline de Coyne?"

"Dreiundzwanzig."

"Öffnen Sie die Tür."

The matron came toward the cell, turning the ring of keys. Finally she found the right one, and opened the steel door. Caroline shrank back into the corner of the tiny cubicle as the matron stepped back to allow a man to enter.

He had to duck his head to get through the small door. Slowly he straightened up, kicking the door shut with his foot. A faint smile crossed his lips as he saw Caroline trying to cover herself with her hands. "Don't be embarrassed," he said in French. "Think of me as you would your doctor."

"Who are you?"

He smiled again, seemingly enjoying the hint of fear in Caroline's voice. "Or perhaps it would be better if you thought of me as your priest," he continued softly. "You see, in a way I am your confessor. It is to me you will confide all your secrets, all those little things you never tell anyone else."

She felt herself begin to shiver. But this time it wasn't the cold. It was the fear running through her. "I haven't any secrets," she whispered. "I told only the truth. I know nothing about my brother."

He shook his head slowly, disbelieving.

"Please, please. You must believe me." She looked down at herself and suddenly the humiliation of her nakedness got through to her and she began to cry. She sank to the floor, covering her face with her hands. "Oh, God! What must I do to make you believe me?"

Through her fingers she saw the shining brown shoes come nearer. The voice came from directly above her now. "Tell me the truth."

"But I am telling the—" The words stuck in her throat as she looked up. His fly was open and the erect phallus and testicles hung obscenely over her. She froze for a moment, then his hand brutally gripped her by the hair and pulled her face against him.

"Kiss it," he said, in a cold, quiet, almost disinterested voice, "kiss it and swear you are not lying to me. Go ahead, bitch Jew. Kiss it. It will not choke you. It is not pork."

19

"You're being most mysterious," Giselle said as Dax got up from the table. "Where are you going?"

He turned from the mirror, where he had been straightening his tie, and a smile crossed his lips. "You won't believe it, but I'm going to meet an old friend."

"An old friend?" she repeated skeptically. "At this hour of the night? Where? The only places that are open are the brothels."

"You guessed it."

"In a *bordello*?" She was beginning to get angry. "And you expect me to believe that?"

"I told you you wouldn't."

"And you're going to meet an old friend and just talk to him? That's all?"

"It's not a him, it's a her."

"If I thought you were telling me the truth," she said, glaring at him, "I'd kill you!"

He went back to the table and kissed her upturned cheek. He tried to capture her lips but she turned away. He laughed. "You know, jealousy becomes you. It makes you even more beautiful."

"Go!" she said angrily. "Go to your whorehouse. I hope you get a clap."

He went to the door and opened it. Her voice stopped him. "After your business is finished, will you come back?"

"It may be late; I might even be all night."

"I don't care. Whatever the time, don't go home, come here."

He looked at her for a moment, then nodded.

"And, Dax, you will be careful, won't you?"

He smiled. "I will."

He went downstairs, and the sleepy night *concierge* let him out. Fat Cat was waiting in the street. "What are you doing here?"

Fat Cat grinned. "You don't think I'm going to let you go to Madame Blanchette's alone? She always had the most beautiful girls in Paris, and usually I can't afford them!"

Madame Blanchette herself greeted them after the maid had opened the outer door and taken their hats and coats. "Monsieur Xenos, how good of you to come. It has been a long time."

"It has been a long time."

"Come with me into the *grande salle*," she said, taking his arm. "We have a very special entertainment tonight. You will see what you have been missing by not paying us a visit." She dropped her voice to a whisper. "After the entertainment you will go with the Eurasian girl. No other." Then her voice returned to its normal level. "You look very well."

Dax smiled. "And you, madame, are even more beautiful than I remember from my first night in Paris."

"*La,*" Madame Blanchette replied, "you have grown into a *galant* as well."

They entered the *grande salle*, where a small trio was playing in the corner. Ringed around the room were small conversational groupings of couches, tables and chairs. Each formed a small nucleus of its own, giving an impression of intimacy.

The conversation stopped for a moment, and Dax felt many eyes turn to him. He glanced around the room. Of the twenty-odd men in the room Dax guessed that fifteen were German, despite the fact that not one of them was in uniform. The hum began again as Madame Blanchette led him to a small sofa near the center of the room. As they sat down a waiter hurried to fill their glasses with champagne. Dax raised his to her. "*À votre santé, madame.*"

"*Merci, monsieur. À la votre.*"

They drank. "There are many Germans here," Dax said in a low voice, "but no uniforms."

"I do not permit uniforms. *C'est une maison du plaisir.* The war must remain outside."

The conversation faded as the girls began to drift in. There was much heel-clicking and bowing and hand-kissing as the Germans endeavored to be polite and Continental, but they were too stiff, too military. They were much too preoccupied with their roles as conquerors to successfully play the *galant.*

Dax got to his feet as a girl approached the table. She was small with startling tawny green eyes in a faintly Javanese face. Long black hair framed the golden ivory of her face. "Mademoiselle Denisonde, Monsieur Xenos."

The girl held out her hand. *"Enchanté, m'sieur."*

Dax kissed her hand. "Mademoiselle Denisonde."

The girl sat down next to him on the couch. Madame Blanchette clapped her hands sharply and the lights suddenly dimmed, then went completely out. For a moment everything was in darkness but in a moment the great chandelier in the center of the room began to glow.

Revealed in the center of the parquet dance floor were two men and three girls—nude and frozen in a tableau of bizarre intertwining arms and legs. For a moment Dax was conscious only of the beauty of the slim lithe bodies, then suddenly he became aware that all were coupled together in sexual embrace. None of them was without a partner. From the corner came the slow persistent beat of a drum, then gradually the throb of a plucked bass amplified the pulsing sound as slowly the tableau began to come to life.

Despite himself Dax stared in fascination. Whether the passion displayed was real or simulated did not matter. The pure sexuality of the act was one of the most exciting things he had ever witnessed. He felt the pain rise unbearably in his loins. The girl's hand searched him out but he was almost unaware of her touch; his only involvement was with the actors playing out their little tableau in the center of the floor.

Almost when the agony had become exquisitely unbearable, the room plunged once again into darkness. There was a moment of complete silence. Abruptly the girl withdrew her hand as the lights came back on. Dax blinked his eyes.

All over the room, men were doing the same thing. They were returning from a secret world of their own. They avoided each other's glances until they were once more in control of themselves.

356

Madame Blanchette rose to her feet. "Gentlemen," she said with a faint smile, "I trust you have enjoyed our little performance." She waited, still smiling, until the applause died down. "Now I leave you to your own pleasures."

Regally, like a queen taking leave of her subjects, she left the room. The door closed behind her and the hum of conversation began again.

Dax looked at the girl. "Now?"

She nodded.

He got to his feet. The girl took his arm and as they started to leave the room a voice stopped him. "Herr Xenos?"

Dax turned. "General Foelder."

The general smiled. "I did not realize you knew this place."

Dax returned his smile. "How could I not know it? It has been just down the street from the embassy for years."

"Join us for a drink."

"No. Thank you, another time."

"Ah," the general said, "you hot-blooded South Americans. You can't wait."

Dax did not answer.

The officer's voice lowered. "Not that I blame you. These decadent French know how to appeal to our sensuality, don't they?"

Dax nodded.

"By the way," General Foelder continued, "please accept my apologies for any discomfort my men may have caused you the other day. Overzealous youngsters, you know. I reprimanded them thoroughly."

"I felt certain you would, General. That's why I did not bother to call you. I am aware how busy you are."

"The matter is taken care of." The general looked at the Eurasian girl. "I say, that's an interesting bit you have there. She must be new." He turned to the aide sitting next to him. "You must arrange a rendezvous for me." He spoke as if the girl did not exist. "You know how much I admire the exotic."

He looked at the girl again, then at Dax. "I envy you, my boy. I shan't keep you any longer."

Dax bowed. *"Auf Wiedersehen, General."*

The girl nodded and they walked out of the room. Madame Blanchette turned from her peephole in the wall, and for the first time Dax saw her angry.

"That pig of a Nazi! The decadent French, indeed! Until

the Germans came there was never the need for such circuses in my place!"

Dax looked at her quizzically. "You do not have to keep open, you know. I'm sure you don't need the money."

Madame Blanchette shrugged. "Once a place like this closes, it never opens its doors again. The Germans will not be here forever. When they are gone we will once again go back to being our quiet little selves."

Dax followed the girl up to the second floor. She stopped in front of a door and took out a key. Then with a quick glance to see that no one else was in the corridor, she opened it quickly and pushed Dax inside. Not until she had locked the door behind her did she turn on the light.

Dax looked around the room. It was elaborately furnished with a four-poster bed on a raised platform. The curtains around it were drawn. Quickly he crossed over and pulled back the curtain. The bed was empty. He looked at the girl. She shook her head. "No, follow me."

She took him into a small closet. In the confined space he could smell the muskiness of her perfume and was aware of the warmth of her body. He saw her fingers searching along the wall. Suddenly the back part of the closet slid open and he found himself in a small windowless room. In a moment the wall closed behind them and she turned on a small lamp.

It took a moment for Dax's eyes to adjust, then he became aware of a man lying on a narrow cot against the unpainted wall. "Denisonde?"

Quickly Dax was at the side of the bed. He knelt beside his friend. "Robert?"

Robert moved again and groaned. Dax noticed the wound in his shoulder. He heard the girl behind him, and he looked up. "What happened? How did he get here?"

The girl's face was impassive. "We were lovers once, now we are friends. There was no place else for him to go."

At the sound of her voice Robert opened his eyes. "Denisonde," he whispered, "get Dax. We must help Caroline!"

"Robert, I'm here."

Robert looked around, and Dax saw the raging fever in his eyes. "It's me, Dax."

It was as if Robert could not see or hear. He moaned again. "Denisonde, I saw them take Caroline away. Get Dax."

358

20

"We shall take care of him," Madame Blanchette said. "It's mademoiselle you must worry about."

"But Robert needs a doctor."

"The doctor sees him every morning when he comes to examine the girls. He will be all right. As soon as he is well enough we will get him to England."

Dax looked past her at Fat Cat, then at the girl kneeling by the side of the cot. With all of them in the tiny room there was scarcely room to turn around. "I think it would be better if we went outside."

Madame Blanchette nodded, and Fat Cat and Dax followed her through the closet into the other room. He turned as she closed the door. "Madame, I owe you an apology."

Madame Blanchette smiled.

"Now, about Caroline—Mademoiselle de Coyne. Is there any way that you might help me?"

The woman shrugged. "We know a few things. Whether they will help or not, I do not know. She was arrested by General Foelder's staff, so we can assume she is at his headquarters."

"But the general's headquarters are in the Royale Palace Hotel."

"In the second basement they have installed a security prison. Chances are you will find her there but if she is, there is no way to get to her except through the hotel itself."

"Is there any other place she might be?"

"She might be at the prison of the secret police, though I doubt it. There is no love lost between Himmler and Foelder, but in Paris everything comes under Foelder's command." She sat down on a small chair. "Perhaps we may know more tomorrow. The general is spending the night here."

Dax thought for a moment. "I don't think we have to wait that long. I spoke to the general as I was leaving the *grande salle*. He told me the matter was closed. Since we know he doesn't have Robert it must be Caroline he is holding."

"It sounds logical, *monsieur*."

"There must be some way we can make certain."

Fat Cat suddenly said, "I forgot to tell you that earlier this evening your friend Sergei called, from his father's office. He said he would call you again in the morning."

Dax stared at him. Sergei's father had an office in the Royale Palace Hotel. He would surely know about Caroline, and though he might not be willing to talk to Dax, he would certainly tell Sergei. But would Sergei be willing to help?

Sergei looked at Dax. "You have changed."

"So have you," Dax retorted. "Only the dead never change." He reached for one of his thin long cigars. Before he lit it, he offered one to Sergei, who shook his head.

"I was sorry to hear about Sue Ann."

Sergei's eyebrows went up in surprise. "You knew?"

Dax nodded. "A friend of mine ran into her in Lisbon. She was on her way home."

"That's right."

"Are you upset?"

Sergei thought for a moment. "No, not really. It had been coming for a long time, ever since the baby was born."

"I gather the child is with you. My friend made no mention of a baby."

Sergei smiled humorlessly. "The baby is retarded," he said bluntly. "Sue Ann feels the fault is mine. So . . ." He held out his hands expressively. "The baby will be all right in time."

Dax was silent for a few moments. "Perhaps it's just as well. At least you won't have to face one another and torture yourselves every day."

"What about you?" Sergei asked. "There was talk about your marrying *el Presidente*'s daughter when you were in Corteguay. Now there are rumors about you and Giselle d'Arcy."

"Talk." Dax smiled. "People must always have something to talk about."

"I know. But you didn't ask me over just to make small talk, did you?"

"No." Dax carefully put his cigar down in the ash tray. "I'll make it simple. The day before yesterday the Germans

360

seem to have taken Caroline de Coyne into custody. I suspect she is being held prisoner in the basement of the Royale Palace Hotel, which General Foelder has converted into a private jail. I intend to get her out."

Sergei let out a long whistle. "You don't ask for much, do you? How do you expect me to help?"

Dax relaxed. He picked up the cigar again. The mere fact that his friend hadn't said no reassured him. "Your father's headquarters are in the same hotel. I must know where she is. Exactly. Then what I must do to get her out."

"And what if my father doesn't know, or won't tell me?"

Dax shrugged. "Then we'll have to find another way."

Sergei thought for a moment. "All right. I'll see what I can do."

"Thanks."

Sergei smiled as he got to his feet. "Don't thank me. The De Coynes are my friends too."

Two hours later he was back in Dax's office. "Why didn't you tell me she was being held under suspicion of being involved in a sabotage ring with Robert?"

Dax looked at him. "I didn't know."

Sergei stared back. "That's a damn serious matter."

"Have they proved anything?"

"No. They're still questioning her."

"That's the end of it then. A week of their kind of questioning and she'll be ready to confess to setting the Reichstag fire." Dax slumped down in his chair. "Then I gather your father didn't tell you where she was?"

"My father told me exactly where she was. He also informed me who was in charge of her case, and the one way we could possibly get her out."

Dax stared at him. "I don't understand. Why would he do that?"

"Don't you know who owned the Royale Palace Hotel?"

Dax shook his head.

"Baron de Coyne. He was the only man in all Paris who would give my father a job when we came here from Russia."

Dax was silent for a moment. He put down the cigar carefully. "So, how do we get her out?"

"It's really quite simple, old man. You're the key to getting her out."

Dax was puzzled. "Me?"

361

Sergei nodded. "The Germans are very anxious to make that beef deal with you. Everyone of them has been ordered to put himself out for you."

"I still don't understand."

Sergei took an envelope from his pocket and placed it on the desk. "In that envelope are four passes to visit Caroline. All you have to do is to walk in there with a priest and two others to act as witnesses. You marry her, then go upstairs to my father's office and demand that he release your wife. He'll sign a release."

"But what about General Foelder? Won't he have to approve it too?"

"Foelder left for Berlin this morning. Something's come up with Himmler and he's gone there to straighten it out. Until his return my father is commanding officer."

"I'll need two witnesses," Dax said thoughtfully. "Fat Cat can be one of them but—the other?"

Sergei got to his feet quickly. "Don't look at me. You ought to know better."

Dax nodded thoughtfully. Sergei was out because of his father. It would be too direct a link. "I'm not thinking of you."

"I'm sure you'll find someone," Sergei said, "you know how the French love weddings." A faint smile came to his lips. "And may I be the first to offer my congratulations?"

"You can go to hell!" Giselle shouted.

Dax stood there quietly as she crossed the room. "What kind of a man are you anyway?" she demanded. "You ask me to be a witness to your marriage? Don't you think I have any feelings?"

"If I thought that, I wouldn't have asked. But you were the only one I dared even suggest it to."

"Great," she said sarcastically. "How would you like it if I asked you to be a witness at my wedding?"

He stared at her for a moment. "I wouldn't like it. But that's not what I'm really asking you to do. I'm asking you to help save a girl's life."

"Why should I care about her?" Giselle retorted. "What does she mean to me? I don't even know her."

"She's French. And the Germans have her. Isn't that reason enough?"

362

Giselle didn't answer.

"Or has Georges finally got you over on their side?"

She looked up at him. "I love you, Dax. Did you know that?"

He nodded silently.

"Don't you think I wanted to marry you?" she asked. "Why didn't you ever ask me, Dax?"

He held her gaze steadily. "I don't know," he answered slowly. "There always seemed to be so much time. I wish I had."

He saw the tears come into the corners of her eyes. "You mean that, don't you?"

He nodded. "I've never lied to you. I wouldn't start now."

She buried her face against his chest. "Dax, Dax," she cried. "What will happen to us now?"

He stroked her hair gently. "Nothing. Soon this will be over, then things will be as they were before."

"No," she whispered. "Nothing is ever the same when you come back to it."

They got to their feet as the matron opened the door and led Caroline into the small room. "You have fifteen minutes," she said curtly in German, then closed the door behind her.

Caroline stood there trembling, blinking her eyes at the light. "I don't know anything," she whispered. "I'm not lying. Please, don't hurt me any more!"

Dax glanced at the others. Fat Cat and the priest were staring at Caroline, but Giselle was looking at him. He turned and walked over to Caroline. He reached out his hand but she shrank away. "Caroline, it's me, Dax. I won't hurt you."

She shook her head violently. She blinked her eyes, trying to focus. "I don't believe you. It's a trick."

She began to cry and gently Dax took her by the shoulders and turned her toward him. "It's no trick, Caroline."

He felt shocked at her appearance. He could see puffy black and blue marks on her face, and her clothing hung on her loosely. When he looked down he saw the vivid red welts across the upper part of her breasts. For a moment he couldn't speak, then he pulled her to him. She hid her face in his shoulder, still sobbing. He tried to raise her face but she wouldn't let him.

363

"Don't look at me," she cried harshly. "They did such terrible things. I can still feel the dirt on my face!"

"Caroline," he said, speaking very slowly. "I've come to marry you. It's the only way I can get you out of here. Do you understand?"

She shook her head against his shoulder. "I can't marry you," she said, her voice muffled against his jacket. "Not after what they've done, not after what they made me do."

"That doesn't matter. Nothing matters. You must listen to me."

"No!" She tore herself from his arms. She ran to the door and huddled against it, her face averted. "You wouldn't want me if you knew what they did. Nobody would." She sounded hysterical. "You wouldn't want me if you knew what I did just to stop them from hurting me! They made me—"

"Stop it!" Giselle's voice was loud in the tiny room.

Caroline's voice caught in her throat. For the first time she raised her face. Quickly Giselle crossed the room. Her voice was harsh and flat. "Stop feeling sorry for yourself! You're alive, that's all that matters." She caught Caroline by the shoulder and pushed her roughly back toward Dax. "Now shut up and do as he says before you get us all killed!"

Giselle's eyes met Dax's over Caroline's head. She turned to the priest. "Begin the ceremony."

The priest opened the small black book and motioned for them to stand in front of him. Fat Cat and Giselle took their places immediately behind him. The priest's voice was gentle as he began to read:

"We are gathered here in this simple ceremony, before the eyes of God and of man, to unite this man and this woman in the bonds of holy matrimony. . . ."

It was over in a moment. Caroline's face was still buried in his shoulder as Giselle came toward them. Dax looked at her. "Thank you."

The tears came suddenly to her eyes. She leaned forward and kissed him, first on one cheek, then the other. Then she put her arm around Caroline and tenderly drew her nearer. "Come, child," she said, "I have some lipstick. This is no way for a bride to look on her wedding day."

Dax stared at them.

Giselle suddenly became aware of his eyes. "Don't mind me," she said, "I always cry at weddings."

364

BOOK
4

MARRIAGE
and
FASHION

1

The smoke hung heavily in the air of the dimly lit cellar. In the far corner the small combo made up in noise what it lacked in quality. Robert looked up as Denisonde made her way through the crowded tables. He did not get up as she came to a stop beside him. He ignored her, looking down at his *pastis*.

"Bobby?"

He still didn't look up.

"Come on, it's time to go home."

"You all through for the night?"

"Yes."

He looked at his watch. "It's only two o'clock."

"There's no business."

For the first time he looked up at her. He gestured toward the crowded tables. "They have plenty of business here."

"Outside the streets are empty."

He reached across the table and took the small evening bag from her. Opening it, he emptied its contents onto the table. A lipstick, small compact and mirror, a few crumpled bills spread out before him. He picked up the bills and counted them. "Only six thousand francs?"

"I told you there was no business."

He threw the bills back on the table angrily. "I spent more than that sitting here waiting for you."

"I'm sorry."

He picked up the bills again and stuffed them into his pocket, pushing the rest of the articles back at her. "I'm not ready to go yet."

Denisonde stared at him for a moment, then put the

things into her bag. "May I sit down?" she asked, almost humbly. "I'm tired."

He didn't look at her. "No, go sit somewhere else. I don't want you."

She hesitated a moment, then turned and made her way back through the tables to the bar. The bartender put a *pastis* in front of her as she climbed onto a stool. "He's in one of his moods again?"

She nodded.

"He's been sitting here all night like that. He won't talk to anybody."

She didn't answer.

"I don't see why you bother with him," the bartender said, leaning forward confidentially, "a girl like you. You should have a man who appreciates you. One who goes out and helps you in the business. He should get customers for you, not just sit there and expect you to do all the work."

"He's a gentleman."

"A gentleman!" The bartender snorted. "If that's what a gentleman's like give me an old-fashioned mac any time." He went down the bar to fill an order. When he had finished, he came back. He leaned across the bar.

"You're wasting yourself. Get rid of him, and I'll put you onto something good. Really good; no more pounding hard pavements in freezing weather."

She laughed. "I don't want to go into a house. I like working for myself."

"No house. I just got the O.K. from the boss. Get a few good girls, he told me, and right away I thought of you. Denisonde, I thought, that's the right sort of girl for a place like this. Real class."

Before she could answer he left and went down the bar to fill another order. Just then the combo stopped playing, and the trio came down from the stand to the bar. The thin Negro who had been playing the drums stopped alongside her. He pulled a cigarette from a beat-up package, and stuck it in his mouth. "Hello, Denisonde."

"Jean-Claude."

He leaned his back against the bar so he could look at her and out over the room at the same time. "Bobby hasn't said a word all night."

"There wasn't any trouble?" she asked anxiously.

Jean-Claude shook his head. "No, we're kind of used to Bobby by now. Everybody's walking wide around him."

"Good." She glanced back over her shoulder. Robert was still staring down into his drink. "I wish he'd come home. He's in pain."

"How do you know?"

"I can always tell. I knew it the minute we came out tonight. I couldn't work for worrying about him. That's why I came in early."

"You're really gone on him, aren't you?"

She looked at Jean-Claude. "He's alone, he needs somebody."

"From what I hear he doesn't have to be alone."

"What do you hear?"

"That man was around again last night. You know, the one who was asking about Bobby?"

"Did Robert talk to him?"

"No. Same as usual, he told him to go away. After that Bobby went out and didn't come back until just before you did. From what the man said, Bobby's papa wants him to come home."

Denisonde didn't answer.

"That boy's a pure fool," Jean-Claude said. "He don't have to spend his life sitting in joints like this."

"The war did some funny things to people."

"I was in the war, and I'm the same as I always was."

Denisonde looked at him out of the corners of her slightly slanted eyes. "You were lucky."

The bartender came over to them. "I got a live one for you, Denisonde," he whispered. "Down there at the end of the bar."

Denisonde turned slowly. A small man, almost insignificant in his gray suit, stared back at her. She looked at the bartender and shook her head. "No, thanks. Bobby doesn't like me to pick up anybody in here."

"Don't be a fool. He'll meet you outside, and Bobby will never know. Five thousand francs."

"No, thanks."

Jean-Claude's voice came from behind her. "That's the man I was telling you about, the one Bobby wouldn't talk to. He must have just come in."

Denisonde looked down the bar again. Suddenly she made

369

up her mind. *"D'accord,"* she said to the bartender. Quickly she scooped up her bag from the bar and glanced back over her shoulder at Robert. He was still staring into his drink. She got off the stool and went out the door.

She shivered a little at the cold night air and pulled her coat around her. She walked down to the corner and stepped into a doorway. A moment later the man came out and walked down toward the corner.

"Over here," she hissed from the doorway.

The man turned and came toward her. "M'am'selle," he said politely.

"The bartender said five thousand francs."

Without a word he reached into his pocket and came out with a few bills. She took them and put them into her evening bag. "Your place or mine?"

"Your place."

"Follow me. It's just around the corner."

Denisonde walked briskly past him and turned the corner. About halfway down the street she turned into an apartment house. They stood silently in the hallway as she opened the door of her apartment.

"The bedroom's over here," she said, leading the way. She threw her coat onto a chair, and closed the door. She began to slip out of her dress, when she noticed that he was still standing there. He hadn't made a move. She let her dress settle back around her.

"What's the hurry?" he asked. "I've paid you five times the rate. Let's talk first."

She shrugged and sat down on the edge of the bed. "O.K., if that's what you want."

He took off his coat and sat down on the edge of the chair facing her. He took out a package of cigarettes. "May I smoke?"

She shrugged.

He lit a cigarette, and after a moment he said, "His father wants him to come home."

"Why talk to me?" she said. "Talk to Robert."

"He won't listen."

She held out her hands expressively. "I'm not keeping him prisoner here. Robert can leave any time he wants to."

"His father will give you one million francs if you can get him to come home."

"His father doesn't have to give me anything. If Robert wants to he can go."

"You're not being very smart. A million francs is a lot of money. You wouldn't have to live like this. You could do anything you wanted."

"I can do anything I want now. Robert isn't holding me any tighter than I'm holding him." She got to her feet. "You tell his father that if he really wants him back the only way is by coming here and talking to Robert himself."

"His father is a proud man. He wouldn't do that."

"That's the baron's affair, it's his son. There's nothing I can do."

He sat there silently for a moment smoking his cigarette. "The baron is a dangerous man to have for an enemy."

"The baron is also a sensible man. He knows that Robert is safe with me, that I am looking out for him."

The man didn't answer.

"Is there anything else?" she asked in a tone of finality.

"Yes," he said, getting to his feet. He began to take off his shirt. "Five thousand francs is a lot of money for just conversation."

Robert was still at his table when she came back into the cellar club. She stopped beside the table and silently dropped the banknotes on the table. Without glancing at her, he picked up the money and stuffed it into his pocket. He got to his feet. "Come on. Let's go home."

Silently she followed him back through the club and out into the street. They walked round the corner and up the stairs to their apartment. Denisonde closed the door and bolted it as he went into the bedroom. In a few moments he returned and his hand lashed out suddenly, catching her across the face. She fell backward into the chair in stunned surprise.

His face was contorted with anger. "How many times have I told you to change the sheets after you're through work for the night?"

2

The sharp knifelike pain raced through him and Robert moaned softly in his sleep. Vaguely he felt her hand soothing his cheek. "Denisonde," he whispered, then fell back into the uneasy blackness. He still heard the screams echoing down damp stone corridors, the heavy clump of the soldier's boots on the cement floor outside his cell.

He moaned again in his sleep, then suddenly sat up. He reached out his hand; he was alone in the bed. "Denisonde!" he screamed, fear mounting uncontrollably. "Denisonde!"

The bedroom door opened. "I'm here, Robert." She held out a glass. "Drink this."

Gratefully he took the glass and sipped the warm liquid. It was sweet and soothing. "I thought you had gone out," he said huskily.

"You know I wouldn't do that." She took the empty glass. "Now try to go back to sleep."

He stretched out again, his hand still clutching her fingers. Already the opiate was clouding his eyes. "I don't know what I'd do without you."

She watched and when he was asleep she went out into the other room. The coffee was hot on the stove and she took a cup to the table and sat down. Idly she glanced at the clock. It was almost noon. She reached for the telephone and dialed a number. A girl's voice answered.

"Yvette?"

"*Oui.*"

"Are you dressed?"

"*Oui.*"

"I have a date I can't keep."

"How much?"

372

"Twenty-five hundred francs."

"It's not worth it," Yvette said quickly. "I give you half, there's nothing in it for me."

"You don't have to give me half. I'll take five hundred francs."

"*D'accord.* Where do I meet him and how will I know him?"

When Denisonde put down the phone she stared at it for a moment. There were too many like this. She had lost too many customers lately, but there was nothing she could do about it. She could not leave Robert when he was so sick.

She sipped at the coffee and lit a cigarette. Men were such fools. Even with whores they liked to feel they were something special, and when she didn't show up for a date that was generally the end of a client. And in the two years she had been with Robert she had lost far too many. Most of her steadies were gone and everyone knew that the foundation of any girl's business was the repeaters.

For the last few months, in order to earn enough for them to live on, she had taken to the streets again like a rank beginner. Twice already she had been picked up by the flics, but luckily she had been able to talk her way out of it. She stared thoughtfully at the bedroom door.

Something would have to be done soon. What it would be she did not know. Only the man asleep behind that door knew. Only he could supply the answers. Even now she didn't know the whole story of what had happened that day he appeared at her door two years ago.

The war had been over for almost a year, and for a while they had lost touch. His father had come back from America and Robert had gone to work in the bank. The one time he had come to see her, oddly enough, he had taken her out to tea. Nothing more.

She had looked at his thin drawn face across the table. "You still have pain?"

"A little. But the doctors assure me it will pass in time."

"Your sister, she is all right? I hear she married that South American."

"Dax? Yes, she is with him in the United States."

A memory of the dark intense face came to her. "I hope she is happy."

He looked at her sharply. "What makes you say that?"

"I don't know."

"The war changed many things for my sister and me. I don't know if either of us can ever really be happy again."

"You will be happy again. In time the war will recede. Look around you; already people are beginning to forget. You will, too."

Robert had glanced around the crowded tearoom. Suddenly his lips tightened and he got to his feet. He threw a banknote on the table. "Come on, let's get out of here."

She had followed him into the street. He turned and looked at her. "I'll walk you back to your place."

"I don't want to take you out of your way. You must be very busy."

His lips twisted wryly. "I am; my father has acquired the world's busiest errand boy. Me."

"I'm sure he has other plans for you."

"If he has he's keeping them a secret." He put a hand under her arm. "Let's go."

"You sound angry. Is it my fault?"

"No, it's not your fault. Really."

When they had reached her building she had said, "Would you like to come up?"

He had shaken his head.

She was silent for a moment, then held out her hand.

"Thank you for the tea," she had said, almost primly. "It was very nice."

"Denisonde?" He held onto her hand.

She looked up into his eyes. They were darkly somber. "Yes, Robert?"

"Is there anything you want? Anything I can do for you?"

She laughed, shaking her head. "There is nothing, thank you. I have everything I need. I manage very well."

"You do."

"Robert, what is wrong? What is it?"

"Nothing." Then his voice had turned bitter, and he had dropped her hand. "There must be something wrong with me. I don't manage very well at all."

She had watched him turn the corner before she had gone up to her apartment. Right then she had sensed that he would be back. How, when or why, she was not sure. But he would come back. And she was strangely sad because she knew that when he did it would not be good for either of them.

Later that same afternoon Robert sat at his desk studying the papers in front of him. The heading across the top of the first sheet fascinated him:

DER KUPPEN FARBEN GESELLSCHAFT

Beneath it were fifty other pages, each containing the details and balance sheets of the many different companies which had made up the largest industrial complex in Germany. During the war these companies had been the primary targets for all Allied bombers. Now they were merely pieces of paper on his desk.

They had been brought in to him by his father's personal secretary several days ago. Attached was a short note in his father's hand. "Study these, then see me Friday morning."

As he opened the folder he wondered why his father was interested in the Kuppen companies. He had read in the papers the week before that the Allies had formed a commission to study the overall company and formulate plans to dissolve the complex. They felt that like Krupp, Kuppen had too great a war-making potential.

A thought entered his mind. It might be that his father was being asked to represent France on the commission. A smile came to his lips; in that case it would be a pleasure to work on such a project. It seemed almost as if he had grown up with a hatred for the name because it was somehow tied up with every engine of destruction that had come out of Germany. Aircraft, submarines, the Kuppen V4 bombs that helped rain destruction on England, even the Kuppen rifle, which had been standard equipment in the Nazi army. It would be a joy to tear such a company apart.

The telephone on his desk rang. He picked it up. It was his father's secretary. "The baron is ready to see you now."

"I'll be right in."

His father looked up as Robert came into the office. He gestured to a chair. "You read the reports?"

"Yes, Father."

"You also are aware that last month the Baron Von

375

Kuppen was sentenced to five years in prison for his part in the war crimes?"

Robert nodded.

"And that also last week a commission was formed to break up the various companies?"

"And about time!" Robert burst out. "It should have been done after the first war. Perhaps then the Nazis might never have got started."

The baron looked at him placidly. "Is that why you think I gave you those reports to study?"

"What other reason could there be? Obviously the commission has requested your expert advice."

His father was silent for a moment. "Either you're a complete idiot or a naïve fool, and I don't know which is worse."

Robert was confused. "I don't understand."

"You've read an analysis of the stockholdings, I presume?"

Robert nodded.

"You noticed perhaps that the largest stockholder exclusive of the Von Kuppen family is Credit Zurich International of Switzerland?"

"Yes, they own thirty percent." Suddenly a rocket exploded inside his head. "C.Z.I.!"

"That's right," his father said dryly. "C.Z.I. Credit Zurich International. Our bank in Switzerland."

"It doesn't make sense. That means we own thirty percent of the Kuppen Farben?"

"Exactly," his father answered quietly. "And that's why we can't let them break it up."

"Then we've been making war against ourselves? And receiving a profit out of it at the same time?"

"I told you not to be an idiot. We made no profit out of the war. Our equity was confiscated by Hitler."

"Then what makes you think we have it back now?"

"Baron Von Kuppen is a gentleman. I have an assignment from him to the effect that he did not recognize the edict of the Nazis. He will honor his obligation."

"Sure," Robert said, his voice turned sarcastic. "What has he got to lose? His seventy percent of what we may save for him will be worth a hell of a lot more than the hundred percent of nothing he will have if the commission breaks the company up."

"You're talking like a child."

"Am I?" Robert got to his feet. "Perhaps you've forgotten. These are the people who set out to wipe us off the face of the earth. These are the ones who dragged your daughter into a prison and raped and beat her. These are the same men who tortured me to get me to betray my countrymen. Have you forgotten all this, Father?"

His father's eyes were steady. "I haven't forgotten. But what has that got to do with it? The war is over."

"Is it, Father?" Angrily Robert took his jacket off and rolled his shirt sleeve up over his forearm. He leaned over his father's desk. "Is the war over, Father? Look at my arm and tell me if you still think so!"

The baron looked down at Robert's arm. "I don't understand."

"Then let me explain. See those tiny punctures? They're needle marks, and you can thank your Nazi friends for them. They couldn't get information out of me any other way, so they turned me into a drug addict. Day after day they shot me full of heroin. Then one morning they stopped. Do you have any idea what that is like, Father? You still say the war is over for me?"

"Robert." The baron's voice trembled. "I didn't know. We'll get doctors. You can be cured."

Robert's voice suddenly broke. "I tried, *Papa*. It's no use. I live with enough pain as it is, I can't take any more."

"You must go away and rest. We'll find a way to help you. I'll figure out another way to handle Kuppen Farben."

"Let it go, *Papa*, we don't need it! Let them break it up!"

His father looked at him. "I can't. There are others, our cousins in England and America. I'm responsible to all of them."

"Tell them how we feel then. I'm certain they'll agree with us."

His father was silent.

Slowly Robert rolled down his sleeve and picked up his jacket. He walked toward the door. "I'm sorry, Father."

The baron looked at him. "Where are you going?"

"I'm going away," Robert said. "That's what you said I should do, didn't you?"

3

Denisonde got up from the table in answer to the knock on the door. *"Monsieur le baron!"*

Baron de Coyne looked at her hesitantly. "Is my son here?"

She nodded. "But he's asleep, *m'sieur.*"

"Oh." The baron stood outside the door awkwardly.

"Excuse me, I seem to have forgotten my manners. Won't you come in?"

"Thank you." The baron followed her into the apartment.

She closed the door and studied him. The baron had grown old. His face was lean and lined, his hair thinned, gray. "You don't remember me, *m'sieur?*"

The baron shook his head.

"We met once, before the war. At Madame Blanchette's."

"Oh, yes." But looking at him, she realized that he did not. "You must have been just a child then."

She smiled. "Let me get you a coffee. Then I will go and see if Robert is awake."

As she placed the cup before him he said, "If he is asleep, don't disturb him. I can wait."

"Oui, m'sieur."

Robert was awake, sitting on the edge of the bed. "Who's out there?" he asked suspiciously. "I told you not to make any dates until I had gone for the day."

"It's your father."

He was silent for a moment, staring at her. "Tell him to go away, I don't want to see him."

She stood there without moving.

"You heard me!" he shouted, suddenly angry.

She still did not move.

He glared at her angrily but at last it was he who had to

give in. "Oh, all right." He swung a leg off the bed. "I'll see him. Help me to dress."

Left alone, the baron took a cigarette from the long thin gold case and lit it. Delicately he sipped at the coffee and glanced around the meagerly furnished apartment. Nothing was right any more. Not since the war. All the old standards seemed to have vanished.

When he was a young man, new to his father's office, he had been content to spend the long years necessary to gain the experience which would earn the confidence of his elders. The young people of today were in too much of a hurry. He could sense it in almost every department of the bank. He could feel it as he walked through the offices. It was apparent in the almost diffident manner in which the juniors regarded their superiors. It was as if they knew the answers before the questions were even asked.

More than once he had become aware of the skeptical, challenging look on their faces at his own orders. What makes you think you're right? they seemed to be asking. What makes you think you know so much? He should have recognized it long ago. He had seen it on the faces of his own children when war broke out and he had wanted them to come to America. They chose to remain, like the run-of-the-mill man in the street who had no choice. They had no conception of their position in society, or that it raised them above the vulgarity of the conflict.

It was a *malaise de société. Liberté, égalité, fraternité.* Even revolutionists recognized the differences within their own society and that such slogans must apply differently to each level.

The sound of voices came through the thin wall from the bedroom and he twisted his cigarette nervously. It scattered shreds of tobacco in his hand and he looked around for an ash tray. Almost furtively he stubbed the cigarette out in the saucer under the coffee cup. He got up from his chair and went to the window. The narrow street off the Pigalle seemed even more squalid than by night. The electric signs over the nightclubs, which seemed so bright and colorful in darkness, appeared drab and dingy now. The gutters were filled with the litter of the night before.

As he watched, a woman and a man came out of a doorway opposite. The woman smiled and opened her purse. Handing him a few bills, she kissed him on the cheek and left him, walking down the street toward the Pigalle with an unmistakable walk.

A sudden feeling of shame ran through the baron. That man might be his own son. Robert was no better. What personal demons had driven him to such depths? If it had been pride that had sent him away, how could one reconcile that with the squalid way in which he now lived? He remembered how he had learned about it.

A phone call had come from Madame Blanchette. "Your son, *m'sieur*, has taken up with one of my girls."

The baron had laughed. "Ah, the hot-blooded young! Don't worry about it, *madame*. I shall reimburse you for the time she is away."

"No, *m'sieur*, you don't understand. She has left with him. They have taken an apartment off the Pigalle. She is going into business on her own."

He still hadn't understood. "But what will Robert do?"

Madame Blanchette did not answer.

Suddenly the baron was angry. "The fool! Doesn't the girl understand? She won't see a sou from me!"

"She knows that, *m'sieur*."

"Then why did she go with him?" he had asked, bewildered.

"I think she's in love with him."

"Whores don't fall in love," he had replied brutally.

Madame Blanchette's voice changed subtly. "She's also a woman, *m'sieur*, and women do."

The telephone had gone dead in his hand and he had replaced it in its cradle angrily. There was much to do and he erased the conversation from his mind. The boy would come back, he thought. Wait until he found out there would be no money.

But the weeks had gone by and still no word had come from Robert. Then one day his secretary came in with a curious expression on her face. "A gentleman from the police wishes to see you. An Inspector Leboq."

"What does he want?"

"He says the matter is personal."

The baron had hesitated a moment. "Show him in."

The detective was a short man in a gray suit, with a manner that was almost fawning.

"You wished to see me?" the baron asked brusquely. He knew how to deal with presumptuous public servants.

"*Oui, monsieur.*" Inspector Leboq's voice was almost apologetic. "In a raid last night we picked up a few girls and their macs. One of them identified himself as your son, this one." He handed a photograph to the baron.

The baron looked down at the uncompromising police mug shot. Robert stared back at him with harsh defiant eyes. His face is thin and drawn, was the baron's first thought, he can't be eating enough. Then he turned back to the policeman.

"Is that your son?"

"Yes." The baron glanced down at the picture again. "What is the charge against him?"

The policeman sounded embarrassed. "Living off the proceeds of prostitution."

The baron was silent for a moment. Suddenly he felt very old. "What will happen to him?"

"He will go to jail, that is, unless he pays the fine. He says he has no money."

"He sent you to me?"

The detective shook his head. "No, *monsieur*. He did not mention you at all. I merely came to verify his identity." He got to his feet and picked up the photograph from the baron's desk. "Thank you for your assistance, *monsieur*."

The baron looked up at him. "How much is the fine? I will pay it."

The policeman shook his head. "I am not permitted to interfere in these matters, *monsieur*." He studied the baron. "But my brother is a private detective, also an *avocat*, and very discreet. I am certain that he could handle the matter for you, and there would be no publicity."

"If you will be kind enough to have him call on me, I shall be most grateful."

"It will be necessary also to pay the fine of the girl. They are charged jointly."

"I understand."

That very same afternoon the policeman's brother came to the baron's office, almost a carbon copy of the inspector. By the time he had left everything had been arranged. There would be no further trouble for Robert or the girl. After all, his brother was in charge of the vice squad in that *arrondisse-ment*.

That had been almost two years ago. And ever since then the little private detective came to the baron's office each week with a report about Robert, then left with a pocketful of banknotes. Three weeks ago the baron learned that Robert had been taken ill and sent to the *clinique public*. But before he could act, Robert had left the hospital of his own volition. When the medical report came to the baron's desk it seemed clear that Robert was slowly but surely destroying himself. It was then that he had decided to act.

And now the door from the bedroom was opening. The baron felt the nervousness in his stomach but forced himself to look up. Robert stood in the doorway, silently.

The baron felt a sadness almost choke him. It was Robert, and yet it was not. The unfamiliar gauntness, the thinness of the pale flesh stretched tightly across his cheekbones, the dark eyes in deep sunken hollows—could this be his son? "Robert!"

Robert didn't move from the doorway. His voice was strange, harsh, not the voice his father remembered. "Didn't you get the message? I told them I didn't want to see you."

"But I wanted to see you."

"Why?" Robert asked bitterly. "Are there other Nazis you wish me to save?"

"Robert, I want you to come home."

Robert smiled. At least it was supposed to be a smile, though it was nearer a grimace. "I am home."

"I mean—" The baron felt helpless. "You're ill, Robert, you need care. You'll die if you keep on going the way you are."

"It's my life," Robert replied almost carelessly. "It doesn't matter, I should have died during the war."

The baron became angry. "But you didn't! And to kill yourself this way is a sheer waste. It's a child's notion. Is this how you hope to punish me? With a childlike fantasy of my weeping at your grave?"

Robert started to speak but the baron wouldn't let him. "I will weep, but not for you. For my son. For what he could have been. With so much to do in this world, with so much that you profess to believe in, with so many things you still could do if you really cared, you wish to throw your life

382

away? No, you're a spoiled little child who's on a hunger strike because his daddy won't play the way he wants."

He met Robert's eye. "You may not agree with what I do but at least I do what I believe in. I work. I don't run away and hide when things don't work out the way I want them to."

He walked to the door and opened it. "I was worried about my son," he said coldly. "I'm not any more; I have no son. No son of mine could be a coward!"

He started to close the door. *"Papa!"*

He turned back into the room.

"Close the door," Robert said. "There is something I would like to do."

The baron leaned against the doorjamb, a curiously weak feeling in his legs. He looked at Robert silently.

"I would like to go to Israel, *Papa*. There, I feel, I could find a purpose. I could feel useful again."

The baron nodded without speaking.

"But first there is something I would do." Robert turned to the girl. "Denisonde, will you marry me?"

The girl looked at him steadily. After a moment her answer came in a clear, steady voice. "No."

It was then that the baron smiled; his son had come home. "Nonsense," he said, feeling the strength come back into him. "She will marry you, my son."

4

Dax came out of the surf and walked up the beach toward the cabaña. The sand was already warm to his naked feet and the hot Florida sun sparkled in the drops of water still clinging to his body. He glanced down the beach, then up beyond the pool to the big white winter home of the Hadleys.

Nothing stirred this early in the morning. He picked up his watch from the table near the cabaña. Nine o'clock. He sighed with a curious pleasure. He could look forward to almost two hours of solitude. No one at the Hadley's ever came outdoors before eleven. He went into the cabaña for a towel.

He stood in the doorway for a moment to let his eyes get used to the dim light, then he noticed her lying on the couch. At first all he could see was the pale-blond hair, but then she suddenly sat up and he saw that she was completely nude.

"I thought you'd never come out of the water, Dax."

He pulled a towel down from the rack and threw it at her. "Sue Ann, you're an idiot!"

She made no move for the towel. It slid to the floor beside the couch. "Everyone's still asleep."

He pulled another towel from the rack and turned and went outside. He spread the towel on the sand and dropped on it, rolling over on his stomach so he could rest his face on his arms. A moment later he felt the sand move near him and he opened his eyes. Slowly he turned his head to look up at her.

She had put on a white bathing suit that did very little to conceal her lush body. "What's the matter with you?" she asked in an annoyed voice. "And don't give me that shit about Caroline. I know better. All New York was talking about you and Mady Schneider."

He didn't answer. Instead he reached out a hand, grabbing her by the ankle and tumbling her into the sand.

"What's the idea?" she asked angrily. Then she saw the white teeth against his dark face. "Oh, Dax!"

He rolled away slightly, still smiling. "Without making a thing of it, look up at the house. The big windows near the corner on the second floor."

She rolled over on her stomach and lay there for a moment, her face against the sand. Then she raised her head casually. There was a flash of light just behind the window. She continued raising her head until she was looking at Dax. "That's James Hadley's room. He's watching us."

Dax smiled. "And with a pair of binoculars too." He rolled over on his back and stared up at the sky. "So you see we're not the only ones awake."

"The old goat!" She giggled. "So that's how he gets his kicks."

"He's got more than that going for him. He just likes to know what's going on."

"No wonder all those boys are so horny. They get it from the old man."

Dax laughed, getting to his feet. "It's getting too hot. I'm going back into the water and cool off."

He came up out of the light surf just in time to catch a glimpse of Sue Ann flying through the air at him. She crashed into him and he went over backward into the waves. He came up sputtering but by this time she was swimming away with clean long strokes. He set out after her.

"You want to play rough!" he yelled, grabbing her with one hand.

Without a word she grabbed a mouthful of air and let herself sink into the water. He felt her slipping from his grip and turned after her, but already she was back at him under the water. He felt her hands grabbing for his trunks, pulling at them, and then one hand was inside holding him.

Her head came out of the water in front of him. "Surrender?"

He felt the heat rushing into his loins. He looked back over his shoulder. The flash of light glinted at the window. Hadley was still watching them. Well, to hell with him, he thought, they hadn't yet invented binoculars that could see into water. He turned to Sue Ann. "A Corteguayan never surrenders!"

"No?" She tightened her grip.

He laughed, tensing himself against her fingers. Then he put his hands under the water behind her and found the seam in the crotch of the silk bathing suit. With a quick motion he ripped the light fabric then, reversing the grip, thrust two fingers inside her.

He laughed at the sudden surprise on her face. She squirmed, trying to push him away, but he held her easily. Then his feet found the bottom and she couldn't move at all. "Best you get is a draw."

"Let go," she said, pushing at him. "The old man is watching!"

"Let him. He can't see what's happening under the water."

Suddenly she was soft against him. "Oh, God. Oh, God!" Frantically she climbed on him. "Put it in me," she cried wildly, "get it in there!"

He braced his legs and pushed himself into her. He felt the heat of her body close him off from the water. "Put your arms out straight and keep your upper body away from me," he said harshly. "That way it won't even look as if our bodies are touching."

She leaned back in the water, her arms straight out, her legs around his hips, almost as if she were floating. "Oh, God," she moaned, already in a paroxysm of delight. Suddenly her blue eyes were on his face. "I can't hold it, Dax! I can't!"

"You'll hold it," he replied grimly, his fingers tightening unmercifully into the flesh of her buttocks. She started to scream. Violently he thrust her head under the water. She came up sputtering and coughing, then went limp in his arms as she climaxed.

A moment later, she looked up at him smiling. "I needed that," she gasped, "it's been so long." She glanced over his shoulder at the house. "You better let me go, he's still watching."

Dax shook his head, not letting go of her buttocks.

She looked at him in surprise. "You're still hard," she exclaimed, a note of wonder coming into her voice. She threw her head back in a half scream as he thrust himself into her again. "Oh, God!" she cried. "Oh, God! God!"

Hadley wasn't the only person watching. Caroline turned away from the window as they came up on the beach out of the water. Something had happened between them. She was sure of it even if she hadn't been able to see what or how. She knew Sue Ann well enough to tell just by the way she walked.

She walked back into the dimness of the room and got into bed. Despite the heat she shivered and pulled the sheets up over her. What's the matter with me, she thought. I'm not even jealous.

She heard the soft slap of footsteps outside, then the sound of the door opening. She closed her eyes and pretended she was asleep. When she heard Dax come over to the side of the bed she opened her eyes as if she had just awakened.

He looked down at her. "Good morning."

She forced a sleepy smile. "What time is it?"

"A few minutes after ten." He looked at her carefully. "Are you all right?"

"I'm fine, I just felt tired." She sat up in bed. "How is it out?"

"Beautiful. I was in the water. It's nice and warm." He

turned and walked over to the dresser and slipped out of his bathing trunks. "Oh," he added, as if it were an afterthought, "Sue Ann was down on the beach."

She looked at the band of white around his hips and buttocks. She never could get over how dark he became; she knew of no one who took to the sun the way he did. He took off his wristwatch, and came back to the side of the bed.

"I think we'll go out to Hollywood. I have an invitation from Speidel. He wants me to play polo."

A powerful male odor emanated from him. She closed her eyes so she would not see him standing over her. Something had happened with Sue Ann, now she was sure of it. "Will Giselle be there?"

He shrugged. "I suppose so. She's starting a picture."

Joe Speidel was the head of one of the big studios. He was also a producer, and in his own estimation a great polo player. He had organized a team that pandered to his vanity and he loved attracting important players. Dax was his prize catch, even more important than the Oscars that lined his studio mantelpiece.

She opened her eyes and looked up at him. His face was impassive. A faint annoyance came into her voice. "Go put something on. You know I can't stand your standing over me like that."

"I'm going to take a shower." He walked toward the bathroom, then in the doorway he turned. "What do you say?" he asked politely. "Shall we go?"

"Does it really make any difference?" Then when he didn't answer her she said, "Oh, all right. I suppose we might as well."

The bathroom door closed and a moment later she heard the sound of the shower. She rolled over and got out of bed. She crossed to the dresser and picked up his swimming trunks. Then angrily she flung them back on the dresser.

She went back to the window. Sue Ann was lying on the beach, stretched out like a cat basking in the sun. She turned back into the room and threw herself across the bed. An animal, she thought, that's all he is. He'd couple with anything.

A goddamn animal.

5

Caroline had not felt like that in the beginning. Then she had
felt only gratitude and shelter in his presence. Even in Paris
during the long weeks they were waiting for the Germans to
approve her exit visa she had felt safe living in the consulate.
Eventually the approval came through. They had to let her
go. They did not dare disturb their relationship with Corteguay
so long as there was a chance that they might get Corteguayan
beef.

They went down to Lisbon by a rickety uncomfortable old
train and waited there for a Corteguayan ship that would take
them across the Atlantic. Even then she felt relatively secure;
she had gained a little weight and the nightmares that tortured
her sleep were beginning to stop. Until she saw the man in
the restaurant while they were at dinner.

Dax paused, his fork halfway to his mouth. Her face had
suddenly gone white. "What's the matter?"

"That man!" she whispered hoarsely. "He's come to take
me back!"

"Nonsense," Dax said sharply. "No one can take you back."

"He can," she insisted, sick fear knotting her stomach. "He's
come after me. He knows he can make me do anything he
wants!"

Dax turned to look. The man was wearing an ordinary
gray suit, not even glancing in their direction, His tightly
cropped blond head was bent over his plate as he shoveled
spoonsful of soup into his fleshy mouth.

"Take me upstairs!" Her voice turned him back to her.
"Please, Dax!"

He got instantly to his feet, sensing her near hysteria.
"Come," he said, taking her arm.

388

He felt her trembling against him as they walked past the German. They crossed the lobby and went up to their room. Once the door was closed, she dissolved in a paroxysm of tears.

He held her to him closely. "Don't be afraid," he whispered, "I won't let him harm you."

"He made me do such terrible things," she sobbed. "And all the while he laughed at me because he knew I would do them."

"Don't think about it any more," he said, his voice hardening. "I promise you he'll never bother you again."

But it took more than his promise to calm her. It had taken three of the pills the doctor had prescribed for her insomnia. At last she was asleep and he had stood there looking down at her. Her face was flushed and glistening with self-induced fever. Gently he drew the sheets up around her, and then went out silently, locking the door behind him.

She awoke in the morning with a heavy drugged feeling. She got out of bed and, putting on her robe, went into the other room. Dax had been sitting at the table having coffee, smoking one of his thin black cigars. He looked up at her. "Have some coffee."

She sat down, glancing at the newspaper beside her plate. The photograph of the German leaped out at her from the front page, with bold black type over it.

O ALEMÃO ASSASSINADO!

She looked up at Dax. "He's dead!"

"Yes," he answered, his eyes hidden in a veil of smoke. "I promised that he would never bother you again."

She should have felt reassured but there was something in the matter-of-fact way in which he had spoken that suddenly gave her a new picture of him. And this, oddly enough, frightened her even more. The savage sleeping just below the polished civilized exterior needed but a word to revert to violence.

The nightmares came back, and it wasn't until they had almost reached New York many weeks later that they began to disappear. Then another feeling for him began to take over. There was a warmth between them then. A kind of love. Not the sort she had imagined she would one day feel before

389

the Germans had taken her off to prison. But more like what she had for her brother, Robert. A feeling that he would protect her and care for her. Or what she felt for her father, that nothing would harm her so long as he watched over her.

The baron had been at the dock to meet them. So had the Corteguayan consul, along with the reporters. There had been a great deal of noise and confusion and at the end of it she had found herself alone with her father in his limousine as they sped up Park Avenue. Dax was in another car with the consul. Something had come up and he had to go directly to the consulate. But he would join them later for dinner.

The baron leaned back in his seat and studied her. There was a strangely contemplative look in his eyes.

"What do you see, Daddy?"

Unexpectedly, tears came to his eyes. "My little girl. My baby."

Then for some unknown reason she, too, had started to cry. Perhaps it had been the way he said it, or the realization that she would never again be his little girl.

"Robert. We haven't heard a word from Robert." The baron took out his handkerchief. "I'm afraid they've captured him."

"No, Robert is safe."

He looked at her. "You know? How? Where is he?"

She shook her head. "I don't know, Daddy. But Dax says he's safe."

A strange look had flashed over his face. For a moment she thought it was an expression of resentment. Then it was gone, and his voice was flat and unemotional. "How does he know?"

There was an almost childlike faith in her answer. "If Dax says so, it is so."

For a moment the baron recalled the first time he had seen Dax—the boy, half asleep in his father's arms, in Madame Blanchette's parlor. It seemed almost as if he had known then how inextricably entwined their lives were to become. "Your husband," he said, "do you love him?"

Caroline looked at him in surprise. As if it were the first time she had even thought about it. "Of course."

The baron was silent for a moment, then he said quietly, "He is a very strong man. And you—"

"He is also a very kind man, *Papa*. And very understanding."

"But you're so frail. I mean—"

"It's all right, *Papa*, Dax understands. And I won't always be like this. Now that I am back with you I shall get my strength back. You will see. Perhaps soon there will be grandchildren for you to play with—"

"No!" The baron's voice contained almost a note of anguish. "There must be no children!"

"*Papa!*"

"Don't you understand?" he asked savagely. "They might be black! There must be no children."

She had just awakened from her nap when Dax came into the room. "There must be a mistake," he said. "My room is across the hall."

She couldn't meet his eyes. "*Papa* thought it might be better this way for a while. Just until I'm myself again."

"Is that what you want?"

"I don't know—"

He had not waited for her to complete her sentence. "For this one night it won't matter," he said angrily. "But when I come back it will. By then I hope you will know what you want." He started for the door.

"Dax!" she cried after him in sudden fear. "Where are you going?"

He stopped and turned. "I received word at the consulate that I'm to leave for home tomorrow. From there I'm going back to Europe."

"But we just got here. You can't go!"

"No?" There was an ironic smile on his face. "Does your father also say that?"

The door closed behind him and she stared at it. Slowly the tears came to her eyes. It wasn't right. Nothing was right any more. If only she could feel the way she had before the war.

He was in his robe, seated at the small desk, when she came into his room later that night. There were sheets of paper spread out on the desk before him. He looked up at her, then at his watch. "It's almost one o'clock. You should be sleeping."

391

"I couldn't sleep." She hesitated in the doorway. "May I come in?"

He nodded. She walked over to the bed. "What are you doing?"

"Reading reports. I am far behind in much of my work."

For a moment she was surprised. Somehow she had never associated him with work, at least not the dull, routine kind. Then she felt foolish. She should have known better. "I didn't realize," she said half apologetically. "I must have been a great interference."

He reached for a cigarette. "It doesn't matter. I was due for a change."

She looked at him. "Must you go back to Europe?"

He smiled. "I go where my president sends me. That is my life."

"But the war—the danger."

"My country is neutral. I am neutral."

"For how long? Sooner or later the United States will get into it. Then all of South America, your country included."

"If that happens, I will come back here."

"If the Nazis let you, you mean," she said somberly.

"There is an international law governing such matters."

"Don't talk to me as if I were a child! I know what the Nazis think of international law."

"It is my work. I have no choice."

"You could resign."

He laughed. "What would I do then?"

"My father would be delighted to have you in the bank."

"No, thanks. I'm afraid I wouldn't do at all well as a banker. I'm not the type."

"There must be something else you can do."

"Sure." He smiled again. "But professional polo players don't make much money."

"You're treating me like a child again," she said petulantly. "I'm not a baby any more."

"I know."

She felt her face flush under his eyes. She looked down at the floor. "I haven't been much of a wife to you, have I?"

"You have been through a great deal. It takes time to recover."

She still did not look at him. "I want to be a good wife to you. I am very grateful for what you have done."

He put out his cigarette and got to his feet. "Don't be grateful. I married you because I wanted to."

"But you weren't in love with me." It was more a statement than a question. "There was that girl Giselle."

"I am a man," he said simply. "There always have been girls."

"She was not just a girl," Caroline persisted, "you were in love. Even I could see that."

"What if we were? You are the one I married."

"Why did you marry me? Was it because there was no other way to free me from the Nazis?"

He didn't answer.

"Would you like a divorce?"

He looked at her, and shook his head. "No. Would you?"

"No. May I have a cigarette?"

Silently he held open his case and lit it when she took one. "I wanted to marry you," she said. "Before the war I had already made up my mind. But—"

"But what?"

"In prison." She felt the tears coming to her eyes, and tried to hold them back. "You don't know how I felt. I wasn't clean. What they did. Sometimes I wonder if I'll ever feel clean again."

She was crying now and couldn't stop. He reached out and brought her head into his lap. "Stop," he said softly, "you must stop blaming yourself. I know what fear can make one do. Once, when I was a boy, I put a bullet into my grandfather's heart so I myself would not be killed."

She looked into his face. There were lines in it she had never noticed before, lines of pain and sorrow. Sympathy suddenly flowed through her. She caught his hand and kissed it. "I'm sorry," she whispered. "I've been a fool thinking only of myself."

His eyes were soft and gentle. "Come, it is time you returned to your bed."

She stayed his hand. "I want to spend the night with you."

His eyes were questioning.

"I can't keep you from going away, but it's time I became your wife instead of just the girl you married."

And she tried. She really tried. But when the moment came and he entered her, she felt only panic. All she could think

393

of was the prison and the long probing instruments they had used to torture her.

She screamed and raved and tore and fought him away from her. Then she turned her face into the pillow and cried. After a while she fell asleep. In the morning when she awoke Dax was already gone.

6

Somehow the phrase stuck in Caroline's mind. "I am a man. There have always been girls." With the war and afterward, many things had changed. Not that. The stories would come back to her. In many ways, from many places. There were always girls wherever he was.

Once toward the end of the war, after an especially messy scandal had been headlined in the papers, her father came angrily into her room waving the newspaper. "What are you going to do about this?"

Caroline took the paper from his hand and glanced at the headline blazoned across the front page of the New York tabloid:

INTERNATIONAL PLAYBOY-DIPLOMAT
NAMED AS CORRESPONDENT

In Rome, where Dax lived under special diplomatic immunities, he had been charged with conducting an affair with the wife of an Italian count. She handed the paper back to her father. "Dax will be pleased," she observed dryly. "At least they got in the word 'diplomat.' "

Her father stared at her. "Is that all you have to say?"

"What more is there to say?"

"He is making a fool of you. Of me. Of our family. The whole world is laughing at us."

"He is a man. When a man is away from home only a fool would expect him not to get involved with women."

"He's not a man," her father retorted angrily, "he's an animal!"

"Papa, why are you so upset when I am not? He is my husband."

"Do you like this kind of notoriety?"

"No, but I have no control over the headlines. What would you have me do?"

"Divorce him."

"No."

He stared at her for a moment. "I don't understand you."

"That's right, Papa, you don't understand me. Nor do you understand Dax."

"I suppose you do?"

"In a way," Caroline answered thoughtfully. "If any woman can really ever understand the man to whom she is married.

"Perhaps Dax is an animal as you say. Press the right buttons and he reacts. I've seen it. To hatred and danger with violence; to pity with gentleness and understanding; to a woman . . ." She paused, hesitating a moment, then added almost apologetically, "I can guess though I've never really been a woman for him. To a woman he reacts like a man."

Her father was silent for a moment. "Then you're going to do nothing?"

"That's right. Because, you see, Dax knew all this and married me in spite of it. It was the only way he could help me, and for that reason alone I would never ask him for a divorce. If he wants one, I will not object. But until he does, the least I can do is keep my end of the bargain."

But that became more and more difficult as time went by. Dax's return hadn't made it easier for her. It was one thing to hear about something happening three thousand miles away, another to find yourself living with it. The day-by-day infidelities. Caroline would have had to be superhuman not to feel resentment.

The recent affair in New York, for example, with Mady Schneider. The silly little fool had gone so far as to leave her husband and take an apartment in a hotel, telling all her friends that she and Dax were to be married. Somehow the papers had got on to it and one of the reporters had come to their apartment. He had caught Dax and Caroline in the hall, surrounded by their luggage, just as they were leaving for Palm Beach.

The reporter was obviously embarrassed. He cleared his throat finally and asked his questions. Dax had smiled easily and turned to look at Caroline before he answered. "I'm afraid you've been misinformed. Mrs. Schneider and I are good friends, that's all. Obviously nothing more than that." He gestured at their luggage. "Because, as you can see, my wife and I are leaving for Palm Beach to visit friends."

The reporter left, and they had hurried down to the car. On the way to the airport Dax had said, "I'm sorry you had to be annoyed like that."

"Don't apologize. I'm quite used to it by now."

He hadn't answered. Just lit a cigarette and looked at her thoughtfully. They were almost at the airport before he remembered the letter in his pocket. "This came for you this morning. I'm sorry, I forgot to give it to you."

She accepted the letter wordlessly. It was from her father, and reading it she learned for the first time about her brother's marriage.

"Robert's married!"

"I know."

She looked at Dax in surprise. "How? Why didn't you tell me?"

"It was on the diplomatic teletype from Paris. I thought you would prefer to hear about it from Robert or your father."

"Who is the girl? I can't seem to place the name."

"Denisonde. She will be very good for Robert."

"You know her?"

Dax nodded. "She was in the underground with him. She was the one who saved his life."

"Oh, then she's the same one he's been living with?"

He studied her for a moment. Obviously she knew the truth. "Yes, the same one."

Suddenly her eyes filled with tears and she turned her face away. Poor *Papa*, she thought, there is so little he is getting from either of his children.

James Hadley was the only one at the table on the terrace when Caroline came down. He got to his feet and held her chair for her. "Good morning, my dear."

"*Bonjour*, Monsieur Hadley." She smiled. "Am I too late?"

"No, my dear. Everyone else was too early." He raised a hand and a servant appeared.

"Just coffee, please."

Hadley looked at her. "What kind of a breakfast is that for a young girl? You should eat more than that."

She shook her head. "No, thank you. That is all I can eat in the morning. We French do not eat the big breakfasts you Americans do."

"At least some buttered toast?"

She laughed. "You remind me of my father. He was always trying to get me to eat more."

"That's because we both care."

She glanced at him. Was there more than mere politeness in his voice? He met her eyes steadily and suddenly she found herself flushing. "Just coffee, please."

Hadley nodded and the servant disappeared. They didn't speak until he had returned with the coffee. Caroline sipped from her cup and looked down at the beach. "Where is everyone?"

"They've gone sailing." Hadley chuckled and again there was that curious inflection in his voice. "They're like children, always looking for something to do. They can't sit still."

"Oh." She was silent for a moment. "It's a lovely day for sailing."

"It is, but I think I will take advantage of their absence and lie on the beach. The rarest thing down here is a day to yourself."

Caroline smiled. "I was thinking of going in to Palm Beach to do a little shopping."

Almost casually his hand covered hers on the table, patting it gently. "You can do your shopping any day. Why don't you take advantage of a quiet day on the beach, too?"

She looked down. His hand was tanned and strong and curiously youthful. She felt the heat come into her face again as she looked up at him. But she made no move to take her hand away. "If you're sure I won't disturb you?"

She felt his approving eyes as she came out of the cabaña. "You're quite lovely."

Again she found herself blushing. "Not really, not like your American girls. They're really lovely. Tall, long legs. I'm too small."

"I like small women," he said. "A man always feels taller when he's with a small woman."

She took out a tube of sun lotion and began to apply it. "I burn very easily."

"My skin's like leather. I never get tanned, I merely turn red."

"I'd feel better if there were a little shade."

"There's an umbrella in the cabaña," he said, "I'll get it."

Caroline watched him as he got to his feet and went into the cabaña. She knew that he was somewhere in his late fifties but it didn't show in the way he moved. Though he was almost her father's age he seemed much younger.

A moment later he was back, sinking the shaft of the umbrella into the sand beside her. After he had opened it he dropped down next to her. "That better?"

"Much better." She smiled, and held out the sun lotion. "Another favor? My back. I can't reach."

His fingers were gentle and Caroline closed her eyes for a moment. The question, when it came, did not altogether surprise her. "Do you love him?"

Caroline's eyes flew open. For a moment she did not know what to say. "Who?" she asked almost stupidly.

"Dax," he replied gruffly, "your husband."

After a moment she said accusingly, "You wanted to get me alone, that's why you didn't go sailing with the others."

"Of course," he answered without hesitation, "but you still haven't answered my question."

"It's a question I do not have to answer."

Hadley again put his hand over hers. "That's answer enough." He looked steadily into her eyes. "How long do you intend letting it go on like this?"

Caroline looked down at her hand. "Until it's over," she whispered.

"It's been over a long time. It's just that neither of you is grown up enough to admit it."

"It's not his fault," Caroline said quickly, "it's mine. There's something wrong with me."

"There's nothing wrong with you."

"Yes, there is. During the war the Nazis did something to me, inside. I'm not a woman any more."

Hadley put his hand under her chin. "Look at me."

Slowly she raised her head. His face was set, almost im-

398

passive. "What you mean is that you're not a woman for him. That doesn't mean you couldn't be a woman for the right man."

She began to cry. The tears rolled silently down her cheeks. "I tried to be a woman for him. Really, I tried. But I couldn't." She turned her face away. "I'm afraid I never could for any man."

Once again Hadley turned her face back to his. "How do you know? Have you ever tried?"

Caroline looked at him steadily. Her tears had stopped. Somehow she felt like a very young girl, as if he could see into her mind and into her heart and that she had no secrets from him.

"Do you have to make that stupid trip to Hollywood with him?" he asked, almost harshly.

She felt as if she were being turned inside out. "I—I promised."

"Do you have to?" he repeated.

"What are you asking me?"

"Tomorrow I'm going back north. I want you to meet me there."

Caroline took a deep breath. "If you want to have an affair with me I'm afraid you will find me a disappointment."

He didn't speak.

"And if you're asking me to become your mistress," she added, "it wouldn't work. I was never any good at intrigue."

"Before I could ask you that I should first have to prove to you that you are a woman."

Then he drew her face to his and she felt the softness of his lips. There was a warmth inside her that she hadn't been aware of for a long time. When Hadley let her go there was a troubled look in her eyes. "I don't know."

But she did know. That evening she told Dax that she was returning to New York, and that he would have to go to the Coast alone.

399

7

"I have enough ships," Abidijan said emphatically. "If you think they're such a good thing, you buy them. And you pay the storage too; there ain't all that much business."

Marcel studied his father-in-law. The old man glared back belligerently. "I might just do that."

"You do that, but tell me one thing. What are you going to use for money?"

Marcel didn't answer.

"Well, don't come to me for it. I had one good sample of your half-assed schemes. It was me had to bail you out of that sugar deal."

Marcel got to his feet. There was a burning sensation in his chest. "You didn't lose by it," he said tightly. It was true, neither of them lost. In fact they had ended up making a lot of money.

"But it took how long?" the old man asked. "I got better things to do with money than tie it up in worthless ships I might someday find a use for."

"O.K., but remember I came to you first!"

"I'll remember," Abidijan said. A sudden smile came over his face. "If you don't mind a little advice, why not ask your partner, Hadley? He can afford to finance you out of the profits you made him on that Corteguayan franchise. I wouldn't feel too bad if you lost him a little money."

In spite of himself Marcel found himself smiling. The bad blood existing between Hadley and the old man was well known. Hadley was Amos' greatest competitor. He had been able to reach a rating agreement with the Greeks but Hadley couldn't have cared less. He underbid them time after time.

Abidijan saw Marcel's smile and immediately his mood

changed. He got to his feet and came around the desk. "I'm talking to you like a father. What do you need more money for? You got enough money. You got a wife, three beautiful children. And someday when I'm gone, all this." He made an expansive gesture around the office.

Sure, Marcel thought ironically, all mine. But it would belong to Anna and her sisters. Even to my children. But not to me. He forced a warmth into his voice that he did not feel. "I know, Father. But you were young once. You know how I feel."

"I understand." His father-in-law placed a friendly hand on his shoulder. "But you're young yet. Don't be in such a hurry. There's plenty of time."

Marcel left his father-in-law, and walked down the corridor to his own office. His secretary looked up as he came in. "Mr. Rainey called while you were out. I have the operator's number in Dallas."

"Call him back." Marcel continued on into his office. He sank into the chair behind the desk and stared thoughtfully down at the papers. Presently he picked up one and studied it. "Government Surplus" was the heading, a mimeographed form on poor-quality paper listing items the government was putting up for sale. Halfway down the sheet there was a blue circle around one of them: 20 liberty-ship class-two oil tankers.

He put down that sheet and picked up another. Much the same, even the heading. Only the district where the sale was to be held was different. This time the blue circle was around an item consisting of five tankers. Quickly he riffled the papers and made a neat stack of them. One hundred and thirty tankers in all were up for sale.

Already this was the third offer. An asterisk next to each of the items stated that. If the tankers were not sold this time around they would be junked. The government already had enough such ships in mothballs.

Marcel placed his hand angrily on the stack of reports. His father-in-law was a fool. So were the Greeks. All they were interested in was freighters. They had enough tankers. Now that the war was over there would not be the same demand for oil, and if there ever was they could always add to their fleets. For now there were much more profitable cargoes to carry.

401

The telephone rang and Marcel picked it up. "Campion here."

"Cal Rainey." There was an undercurrent of excitement in the flat Texas drawl. "You were right. I managed to get ahold of the geological surveys. There's an oil shelf off Venezuela, and it looks as if it might run down the whole continent."

"Corteguay too?"

"The best chance of all."

"What about the other thing?"

"They're interested," Rainey said, "but they won't talk until they are positive you can guarantee transportation. Abidjan and the Greeks tell them the costs will run too high."

"I see." Marcel took a deep breath. Once again he stood in the pit at the gambling house in Macao watching the cards turn over. One at a time, with a fortune riding on each one, and never knowing whether the next one would be the one that broke you. But the fascination was there, the dangers that drew him like an irresistible magnet.

Perhaps his father-in-law was right. Maybe he didn't need the money. But he could no more help himself than he could stop breathing. "Go back and tell them I will guarantee the transportation."

"But they will want to know how you can guarantee that."

"I'll bring them a list of available ships when I come down there the day after tomorrow." He put down the telephone.

Marcel waited a moment, then pressed the buzzer for his secretary. When she came in he held the stack of papers out to her. "Get me the war-surplus agent in each of those areas on the phone."

"Yes, Mr. Campion."

"Wait a minute. Before you do that get me the Corteguayan consulate. I want to speak to Mr. Xenos."

His secretary went out and a moment later the telephone on his desk buzzed. "Mr. Xenos is not in New York. They don't know where he is."

Marcel thought for a moment. Dax must be around somewhere. He had seen Caroline only last night, at El Morocco with a group of people including James Hadley. He had meant to go over and speak to her but something had interfered. "Start on that list. I'll try to locate him on the other phone."

He changed telephones and dialed Dax's apartment in the De Coyne town house. After a moment a servant answered.

"Is Mr. Xenos there?"

"No, sir."

"Madame Xenos then?"

"Madame Xenos left for Boston last night, sir."

"Is Mr. Xenos with her?"

"No, sir, he's in Hollywood. Mrs. Xenos can be reached in Boston at the Ritz."

The light on the telephone indicated that his secretary was still putting through the first call, so he phoned the Ritz in Boston himself. "Mrs. Xenos, please."

A man's voice answered.

"Mrs. Xenos, please."

"Who's calling?"

"Mr. Campion."

Marcel heard the phone being put down. In the distance he could hear the faint sound of two voices, a man's and a woman's.

"*Allô*, Marcel?" Caroline's voice sounded strained.

Marcel slipped into French. "I'm sorry to trouble you, but it is necessary that I contact Dax. Could you tell me where he is?"

"He's at Monsieur Speidel's home in Beverly Hills, Marcel. Is anything wrong?" Her voice still sounded strained.

"It is only business. But I do have to talk to him."

They exchanged a few more polite words and then he hung up. It wasn't until almost ten minutes later, in the midst of his first telephone conversation with the Philadelphia war-surplus office, that it came to him. For a moment he was so startled he lost the thread of his own conversation. The man's voice. There was no mistake about it. There was no one else with that particular Irish-sounding Bostonian brogue. It had to be James Hadley.

When the conversation was completed he had made a deal for the first five ships. He told his secretary to hold the next call for a few minutes while he placed a call to a private detective who had done some very personal work for him in the past. By six o'clock that evening he had the whole story.

They had to be fools. They had made almost no attempt to cover their tracks. Hadley had even installed her in the company suite his office maintained in the hotel.

But that wasn't all he had. Marcel now owned one hundred and thirty liberty-ship class-two oil tankers. At an average price of one hundred thousand dollars, this meant that he would have to come up with a minimum fifty percent of the purchase price, six and a half million dollars, by tomorrow evening.

Marcel was waiting in James Hadley's office in Boston the next morning when Hadley came in. Hadley didn't act surprised. "I half expected you."

There was something about the man that Marcel admired. Suddenly he knew what it was. Hadley was as much a gambler as himself. "You did? Why?"

"Mrs. Xenos went back to New York last night."

"This morning, you mean," Marcel said, calling the bluff. He was nothing if not a Frenchman. He knew the ways of an affair, and that nothing could ever interfere with an evening.

Hadley sat down behind his desk. A curious paleness showed under the sunburn on his face. "She is still in the hotel."

"That is your business," Marcel said quietly. "I have come here to discuss mine."

8

Cal Rainey was waiting at the airport when Marcel came through the gate. The thin Texan walked toward him with an outstretched hand. "Welcome to Dallas, Mr. Campion."

Marcel smiled as he took his hand. "It is good to see you again, Mr. Rainey. I apologize for arriving so late but unfortunately I was detained on other business in Boston."

"That's O.K., Mr. Campion. All the arrangements have been made. As soon as you get your luggage we'll leave for

404

the ranch. Mr. Horgan has placed his private plane at our disposal."

Marcel looked at him in surprise. "I thought we were to meet here in Dallas. I have asked a friend to fly down from Los Angeles to meet me."

"No problem, Mr. Campion. Mr. Horgan has said that any friend of yours is welcome at the ranch. We'll just send the plane back for him. When is he expected?"

"About midnight." Marcel looked at his watch. "That's only about two hours; perhaps we could wait for him?"

"As you wish, Mr. Campion. In that case let's head for the bar."

The headwaiter bowed. "Good evening, Mr. Rainey." He led them to a small table. "The usual?"

"Right," Rainey said, then looked at Marcel.

"*Pastis,*" Marcel answered automatically. Then he noticed the confused look on their faces. "Pernod and water."

He looked at the Texan after the waiter had brought the drinks. "Now, tell me exactly what arrangements have been made."

Rainey took an appreciative sip at his bourbon. "Mr. Horgan thought that the meetings had better be held at his ranch over the weekend. He's already invited the other interested parties. Dallas is still very much a small town, and word gets around."

Marcel smiled. One of the first things he had learned was that there were no secrets that could be kept if someone was really interested enough in discovering them. Still, the precaution was a good one. The less people knew about it the better. He sipped at his *pastis* and leaned back. It was good to be able to stretch after the long hours on the plane. He glanced around the room. "Is there a telephone here? I'd like to call home."

"There's a row of booths just outside the door."

Anna was upset when he got through to her. "What are you doing in Dallas? I thought you were in Boston."

"Something special came up. I didn't have time to call before I caught the plane." He could not tell Anna what he planned to do. She would immediately report it to Amos.

"How are the children?"

"The twins are fine, but I think young Amos is coming down with a cold."

"Did you call the doctor?"

"What for? It's only a cold."

Marcel shook his head. Despite their wealth her father had done his work well; Anna was as penurious in personal matters as Amos. "If he has a fever call the doctor."

"He has no fever," Anna said sullenly, "and I'm keeping him away from the girls."

"Good." Marcel couldn't think of anything more he had to say to her. "How's the weather?"

"Raining. When are you coming home?"

"About the middle of the week."

"Where can you be reached if Daddy has to talk to you?"

Marcel was silent for a moment. "I'll be moving around. Tell Amos I'll call him." He hesitated. "And you, too."

Marcel walked thoughtfully back into the cocktail lounge. There was no doubt in his mind that Anna would be on the telephone to Amos the moment after he hung up. It was a good thing he was not staying in Dallas. It would take the old man that much longer to find out what he was doing. And by that time it would be too late for Amos to do anything about it.

"That's the ranch off there to the left," the pilot said. "The landing field is about a mile and a half beyond."

Marcel looked out the window. It was a dark night and he couldn't see much. But there were a few lights and he could make out the faint outlines of the house. He straightened up and checked his safety belt. It was tight.

He glanced toward Fat Cat on the seat next to him. Fat Cat was sleeping, his head leaning back against the seat. In front of him were Dax and Giselle d'Arcy. Rainey occupied the seat next to the pilot in the six-place Bonanza.

He should have been more specific over the telephone. Then Dax wouldn't have brought the actress. But he hadn't dared. There was no telling how many extensions there were in Speidel's house. But perhaps it was just as well. With Giselle around few people would guess the real purpose of the visit. It would seem more like a social weekend.

The pilot pressed a button on the panel in front of him. Immediately the lights flashed on at the field below. "Radio signal," the pilot said laconically. "Puts on the landing lights. Saves keeping a man on duty all night." He reached up and began to crank down the flaps. "Y'all's belts good and tight?"

Marcel felt the slight tremor as the wheels hit the ground, and a moment later they were taxiing smoothly toward the hangar. The pilot took the plane right inside before he cut the engine. In the sudden stillness his voice seemed very loud. "A car will be here in a minute to take y'all up to the ranch. I hope you folks enjoyed your flight."

By the time they got off the plane the station wagon was waiting. The driver got out, a slim man dressed in cowboy garb. "Welcome to the Horgan Ranch, folks," he called pleasantly. "Y'all just get into the wagon and have yourself a drink while I get your luggage."

Marcel followed the others to the car. Just behind the driver's seat there was a completely equipped little bar. Rainey was already pouring them drinks by the time he got there.

"I've never seen a car like this even in Hollywood," Giselle said.

"I reckon you won't see one like this anywhere else, ma'am." Rainey smiled. "It was built especially for Mr. Horgan by the Cadillac people."

Giselle looked at Marcel and smiled. "These Americans," she said in French. "They will never cease to amaze me."

Marcel returned her smile with an expressive shrug of his shoulders. He felt much the same way.

Marcel heard a soft knock at his door just as he came out of the bathroom. "Who is it?"

"Dax."

He opened the door and Dax came into the bedroom. "I thought we'd better talk. What is this mysterious thing that's so important I had to come down here?"

Marcel pulled out a package of cigarettes. He held it toward Dax, who shook his head and took out a thin cigar. Marcel held the light for him, then himself. After a moment he went to the door and opened it. He looked out. The corridor was empty.

His voice dropped to a whisper. "Offshore oil."

Dax looked puzzled. "What?"

"In the water," Marcel explained, "the Gulf of Mexico. Off the shores of Texas and Louisiana. They found oil in the ocean bed."

"What's that got to do with us?"

"Horgan had the idea, but the others froze him out. He was angry, so he sent a team of geologists off to Venezuela. And now they have come up with what they think may be an even greater strike."

"I haven't seen anything in the papers. How come you know about it?"

"From the captain of one of my tramps. He was down there trying to pick up a cargo and they offered him a charter. The money was good so he grabbed it. They played it real cute but he's no fool. It didn't take him long to figure out what they were up to. As soon as he told me I put Cal Rainey on it. It took him only two days to confirm it. That's why we're here."

"Why me?"

Marcel looked at him. "Don't you understand? The oil shelf probably runs down the whole coast. The only country in South America that hasn't got a mineral-rights development deal with the oil companies is Corteguay."

Dax looked at his cigar. "So that's it. You want the mineral-rights concession?"

"What would I want that for?" Marcel asked. "I'm not in the oil business. That's for Horgan and his associates. What I want is the transportation of all that oil, not only from that one field but from their wells all over the world. I figure it's worth it to them for the Corteguayan development rights."

"*El Presidente* is no fool. He will know what those rights are worth."

"He'll get the same deal from Horgan that he would from anyone else. Besides, there is one extra if he'll play it my way. A shipping line that is truly Corteguayan-owned. No outside partners. No Hadley, no Abidijan, no De Coynes, no Greeks. Just the three of us."

Dax had long since passed the age of illusion. His world was very different from the one in which his father had believed. And even with all the stealing, more managed to finally find its way down to the people than ever before. There was only one flaw in the whole idea. "Where will the ships come from?"

Marcel smiled. "Yesterday I closed a deal with the American War Surplus for one hundred and thirty surplus tankers."

Dax took the cigar out of his mouth and let his breath out

slowly. He could make a guess at the cost. "And what do you do with them if you cannot make this deal?"

Marcel took out another cigarette and lit it before he answered. Then he waved the match out and looked at Dax somberly. "I'll kill myself," he said quietly. "Because if I don't make this deal I have no other way to pay for them."

9

It was after seven o'clock in the morning when Dax came down dressed in an old shirt and a faded pair of Levi's. He went through the empty dining room to the kitchen. None of the other guests were down yet.

Fat Cat looked up as he appeared in the doorway. "Come in," he said, his mouth full of food. "This one, she knows how to cook."

The Mexican woman simpered and smiled.

"Later," Dax said. "I thought we'd try some of their famous horses before breakfast."

Quickly Fat Cat shoved in a last mouthful of food. He got to his feet, sticking a toothpick in his mouth. He smiled at the cook. *"Está muy bien. Mil gracias."*

She flashed a shy smile at him. *"De nada."*

He walked over to Dax. "What time is lunch?" he asked from the doorway. "With cooking as good as this I don't want to be late."

"Twelve o'clock."

"Bueno." Fat Cat let out a satisfied burp. "I shall be here."

They went out into the bright morning sunshine through the kitchen door. Fat Cat squinted up at the clear blue sky. "It will be hot today."

Dax didn't answer. He led the way toward the stables just behind the kitchen. Three hands were in the corral putting a

409

saddle on a skittish young mare. The two of them went over to the fence, and leaned over it. Each time one of the hands approached the animal she would turn, her ears flat back against her head, her teeth bared.

"The mare she is a very nervous one, no?" Fat Cat called pleasantly.

The men glanced at them, then at each other. They did not speak. One of them moved toward the mare, but she spun away from him.

"Why do not you cover her eyes?"

Again the hands glanced at them, pointedly silent.

"I thought we might take some horses out," Dax called.

This time they all paused in what they were doing, and looked at Dax. They studied the old shirt and the faded Levi's before one of them answered, a faint tone of contempt coming into his voice. "Mistuh Horgan doan allow no greaser servants to ride his horseflesh."

Fat Cat glanced quickly at Dax. Dax's face gave no hint of his feelings; only his eyes were suddenly dark and angry. "Not even that one?"

The three men looked at each other, then a grin came to their faces. The one who had answered turned toward Dax. "If'n you can git the saddle on her you're free to ride her."

"Thank you," Dax said politely. He placed two hands on the top railing and vaulted over.

Fat Cat bent down to crawl through but it was no use. He was too big. When he straightened up he saw the grins on their faces. Angrily he put his foot on the bottom rail to climb over. The rail broke under his weight.

He stood there looking down at the broken rail while their shouts of laughter echoed in his ears. When he looked up a pleasant smile was back on his lips. "I think I better use the gate, no?"

He opened the gate and came into the corral. "Your fences are not made for the weight of men. They must be made for boys, no?"

"Not men like you, Mex," the youngest of them said.

"I am not Mexican, señor," Fat Cat said in a dignified voice. "I am Corteguayan."

"Same thing," the hand holding the saddle said, "all them greaser countries."

Fat Cat turned toward him, his eyes beginning to glint dangerously deep in their layers of fat. Dax's voice kept him from answering. "Take the saddle, Fat Cat."

Silently Fat Cat took the saddle, while Dax walked around to the head of the mare. The man who had given it to him picked up a lariat and began to twirl it idly. Dax picked up the mare's lead rope. "You men go back to the fence," he said pleasantly, "you are making her nervous."

Silently the men drew back against the fence. Dax began to whisper softly to the animal in Spanish. "You are the most beautiful of mares." Horses and women. They were all the same. They loved flattery. He kept on talking to her softly, singing her praises, until at last she allowed him to take her head against his chest, his arm shielding her eyes. He nodded to Fat Cat.

In a moment the saddle was in place and cinched tightly. Before the mare even had a chance to react, Dax was on her, his legs and knees gripping tightly against her sides. The mare stood there for a full second before she realized that he was on her. Then she went straight up in the air and came down stiff legged.

Dax took up the shock with his legs, all the while still speaking softly to her. She took off on a tangent down the corral, bucking and twisting as she went, but there was nothing she could do to dislodge the man on her back. At the far end she turned and began sunfishing her way back. Halfway she ran out of strength and stopped in her tracks, her sides heaving.

Dax still kept stroking her neck and whispering. After a few moments he reined her in and started back up the corral with her. In front of the hands at the fence he turned her around until her rump was toward them, then he agilely slipped from the saddle. "You don't have to be afraid of her now."

They stared at him. He was still stroking the mare's neck. "Are you callin' us cowards?" The man's voice was harsh, the lariat still twisting in his hands.

Dax glanced at him contemptuously for a moment, then turned back to the horse without answering. A moment later the lariat dropped around his shoulders, pulling him roughly away from the horse. He half stumbled backward, almost fell, then caught his balance and turned.

The man holding the other end of the lariat was smiling. "Were you callin' me an' my friends cowards, greaser?"

From the corner of his eyes Dax caught a glimpse of Fat Cat moving toward them. With a quick gesture he stopped him. The hand took the gesture for a sign of fear and pulled at the rope. Dax stumbled, went to his knees and pitched face forward onto the ground just as Marcel and Horgan and several other men came into view around the house.

Marcel reacted swiftly when he saw what was happening. He still remembered the savagery at Ventimiglia. "You better stop your men, Mr. Horgan. They will get hurt!"

Horgan chuckled in a pleased voice. He was a big man. And this was his kind of Texas humor. "My boys kin take care of themselves. They're just funnin'. They love to josh tenderfeet."

Marcel looked at his host, who was surveying the corral with a pleased smile. He shrugged with typical Gallic resignation.

Fat Cat was leaning against the fence, and the hands had moved forward until they were standing over Dax. The man with the lariat looked down. He jerked sharply at the rope. The grin on his face froze into a look of surprise as it suddenly came away in his hands, then turned into a scream of pain as Dax broke his knee with the flat of his hand. He hadn't quite hit the ground when Dax, coming up, caught the second man with a straight arm in the rib cage.

Horgan and the others were standing more than twenty feet away but they could hear the sharp snap of the man's ribs cracking as he collapsed. Dax began to straighten up as the third man came up behind him. But that was about as far as he got, for by then Fat Cat had him garroted with part of the rope that had fallen to the ground, and was shaking him like a terrier with a rat.

"Fat Cat!" Dax's voice was sharp.

Fat Cat's eyes turned toward him.

"Basta!"

Fat Cat nodded. Abruptly he let go of the man. The hand sank to his knees, gasping for breath, his face still congested and almost purple, his fingers rubbing his throat. The other two stared up in pain and horror.

412

"In my country, *señores*," Fat Cat said in a voice thick with contempt, "even the children can take better care of themselves. You would not last one day in the jungle."

Dax turned back to the mare, who was still standing there, her sides heaving, her legs trembling. Soothingly he stroked her neck. "Get some water for the mare, Fat Cat," Dax said quietly. "She must be very thirsty."

Fat Cat turned. His round smooth face didn't change expression as he saw Horgan and the others hurrying into the corral. "*Buenos días, señores,*" he said politely.

Marcel came into the room. He was carrying a sheaf of papers under his arm. "I hope I haven't kept you waiting, gentlemen?"

"No, Mr. Campion," Horgan said. He closed the door behind Marcel. "If you're ready, we can start now."

Marcel nodded. He looked around the room. There were five men there besides himself. Dax, Cal Rainey, Horgan and his two associates, Davis and Landing, both well-known oilmen. Their faces were expressionless; they were sure of their own position, and waiting for Marcel to prove his. Marcel took a deep breath.

"I shall speak frankly, gentlemen. I know you are curious how I learned of your survey, and that you possibly suspect a leak in your organization. Let me put that fear to rest. It really was quite simple. The ship you chartered in South America happened to be mine."

Horgan looked at his associates. "I'll be damned. Didn't anyone think to check that?"

Marcel smiled. "If you had you would have found out nothing; the ship is registered in the name of its captain. The day after I learned of the existence of your survey I got in touch with Mr. Rainey. At the same time I had my attorneys in Washington institute a search to determine which South American countries had already granted mineral agreements for offshore development. Within a few days I learned they were pretty well taken up by the major companies. And those that weren't were already controlled by men like Hunt, Richardson, Getty and Murchison. I also found out that such individuals were pursuing an independent course. They were not a part of your syndicate."

Marcel paused for a moment to light a cigarette. "My attorneys inform me that the only country which thus far had not made any offshore-development deal is Corteguay. Mr. Rainey confirms that your survey indicates a high possibility of oil in that sector. My traffic department has completed a study of your worldwide shipping needs. At that point I asked Mr. Rainey to contact you directly with my proposition." A faint smile crossed Marcel's lips. "Now, gentlemen, you know. There are no more secrets."

Horgan was silent for a moment. "Thanks, Mr. Campion." He glanced at his associates. "If I may, I'll speak as frankly. I don't exactly see where you come in. What's to keep us from negotiating an agreement with Corteguay without your assistance?"

Marcel glanced at Dax, then back to Horgan. "Nothing. Anyone can negotiate. But it is one thing to negotiate on the basis I suggest and quite another to compete in an open market."

"Are you suggesting that it will cost us less by negotiating with you?"

Dax looked at Marcel. "I think I should answer that." Marcel nodded.

Dax turned to Horgan. "You will pay just as much, perhaps even a little more. But you will get it."

Horgan smiled at him. "Then I can't see the advantage. What you and Mr. Campion seem to have forgotten is the simple fact that there may be no oil there. In that case we are not only out our investment but we'll also have gone to the expense of rearranging our shipping contracts in favor of Mr. Campion."

"You have to have ships anyway, Mr. Horgan," Marcel said. "And I'll be shipping your oil for four percent less than any of your current contracts."

"Maybe so," Horgan said, "but if we can't make a deal for less, I feel we're better off on the open market. We'll take our chances."

Dax glanced across the table at Marcel. Marcel's face was expressionless but Dax knew him well enough to recognize his faint pallor. Dax got to his feet abruptly. He was tired of playing games with these rich, self-centered men. "You're not taking any chances, Mr. Horgan."

The Texan looked up at him. "What do you mean, Mr. Xenos?"

414

"You'll never get the contract on the open market."

Horgan got to his feet and faced Dax. "Am I to understand, sir, that you'll stand in our way?"

"I won't have to." Dax smiled but there was no humor in his face. His voice was very cold. "Because once we are home I have no way of keeping my friend from talking. And you don't really believe that my country would make an agreement with you after Fat Cat tells the story of how you stood there and watched while your men called us greasers and attacked us?"

"But they were only funnin'," Horgan protested.

Dax looked at him. "Were they?"

Horgan sat down again. He looked at his associates and then back at Dax. After a moment he turned to Marcel. "O.K., Mr. Campion, you got your deal."

Marcel looked at Dax. There was a faint smile behind Dax's eyes. Suddenly Marcel realized that it had all been a bluff. Marcel looked down at the table. He didn't want the others to see the relief in his own eyes. "Thank you, gentlemen."

That was the beginning of the Campion Lines, which in less than ten years would be the largest privately owned fleet of ships in the world.

10

"It is over with the two of you then?"

Giselle looked at Sergei. *"Oui."* Her eyes grew thoughtful. "It is strange after so many years to realize that the thing you loved is no longer a part of the man you fell in love with." Her hands moved restlessly toward the cigarettes. "Dax has changed."

Sergei leaned across the table and lit her cigarette. He glanced around the restaurant and caught the waiter's eye to bring them two more drinks. "Everybody changes. Nothing, no one ever remains the same."

"I left him in Texas," Giselle said as if she had not heard him. "Suddenly I couldn't stand it any longer. I had to come home, to Paris. I am through with America. I shall never go back there again."

"Not even to Hollywood?"

"Even that. Here I am an actress, there I am nothing but a symbol. A French sex symbol. Like the post cards the Americans take home from Pigalle."

"What did Dax say when you left?"

"Nothing. What was there for him to say?" Her expressive dark eyes studied him. *"C'est la fin.* But I had the feeling it no longer mattered to him. Perhaps that was the hardest of all, that it just didn't matter."

Giselle sipped at her drink. "There he was with all those horrible men. All they talked about was money and oil and ships. I might as well not have been there at all. And then one evening I came into the room, and Dax didn't even look up. He kept on talking to those men. I looked at him and it was as if I were seeing Dax for the first time. And I saw all the children we could have had and hadn't, and the life we might have had and wouldn't. Suddenly I wanted those children and that life we'd never had."

Sergei saw the tears start to come to her eyes. She didn't look at him, and her voice was very low. "Once, when I first met Dax, I felt that after the war, after all the mess was over, we'd make it. And I thought that deep inside he felt as I did. But that night I realized I'd been wrong. That all he had ever wanted from me he had taken, and all he had ever wanted to give had been given."

Giselle was silent for a moment. "It's not too late for me, is it, Sergei? I'm still young enough to love, to have children, and a man?"

Sergei saw her into a taxi and looked down the street. The taxi stand was empty. He hesitated a moment, then decided to walk back to his apartment. It was only a fifteen-minute walk.

The blistering heat of August came up at him from the pavement. For Paris the streets were almost deserted. Any Frenchman worth his salt, from the highest executive to the lowliest clerk, was on vacation. They had gone either to the mountains or to the shore, or simply stayed at home, shutters drawn against the oppressive heat. The small signs on the doors or in the windows of most shops bore eloquent testimony to that. *Fermeture Annuelle.*

Idly Sergei wondered what he was doing here. But he knew the answer. It was always the same, he was short of money.

Bernstein, the Swiss banker, had put it even more succinctly. "You have no head for business, young man," he'd said. "It wouldn't matter if you had an income of fifty thousand pounds a year instead of fifty thousand dollars. You'd find a way to make it insufficient."

That had been only a few weeks ago. He had already borrowed against his payments from Sue Ann over the next two years.

"What shall I do then?"

The banker's voice was very acid. "The first thing I'd do is get rid of some of your stupid investments. That *couturier* for example. Ever since you invested in his business you have been furnishing him with an additional twenty thousand dollars a year just to keep him from bankruptcy!"

"I couldn't do that!" Sergei's voice was shocked.

"Why not? Are you in love with the little faggot?"

"Of course not. But he is very talented. Someday he'll break through, you'll see. The trouble is he's far ahead of his time."

"And by that time you'll be bankrupt!"

"What he needs is a sponsor."

"That's what you said a year ago, so you persuaded Giselle d'Arcy to have him do her wardrobe. It didn't help."

"I mean an American. It is the Americans who really set the styles. What they accept goes, what they reject doesn't."

"Why don't you speak to your ex-wife?" the banker asked.

Sergei looked at him. He had never suspected the banker had a sense of humor. But Bernstein appeared to be quite serious. "Sue Ann a style leader? No, it has to be someone else. Someone the Americans already accept as the height of fashion."

"Get rid of the business," the banker urged with finality, "there is no such person. And if there were, she would already be involved with Dior, Balmain, Balenciaga, Chanel, or Maggy Rouff. Anyway, no one like that would come to an

417

unknown like your friend. There is no prestige in buying clothes from a nobody."

Sergei got to his feet excitedly. "Prince Nikovitch! That should do it."

"Should do what?" the banker had asked.

"The Americans love titles. Perhaps not all of them can marry one but they could be dressed by one."

"Ridiculous," Bernstein said.

"Not really. All we have to do is show that we are accepted by prominent Frenchwomen. Then the Americans will come."

"But how will you attract an important Frenchwoman?"

"Caroline de Coyne—Madame Xenos," Sergei said. "Caroline would do it for me."

"But she is in America."

"She can be persuaded to return."

"But how?" the banker asked. "It is already July. All the showings have been held. No one will come."

"If Caroline comes from America everyone will come, if only to see what brought her. We will have our showing on the first of September. And we will advertise it as the only true fall showing."

"It might just work," Bernstein said. "But what will you use for money?"

Sergei smiled. "You will give it to me."

"Are you out of your mind? I have already told you, you are on the verge of bankruptcy!"

"Madame Bernstein would be most unhappy if she were to discover that she missed an invitation to the *première* of a Paris collection because of your niggardliness."

Bernstein looked at him. A faint hint of a smile began to show in his frosty eyes. "You are a completely unscrupulous scoundrel!"

Sergei laughed. "That is quite beside the point."

"All right, I will lend you the money. On two conditions."

"What are they?"

Bernstein leaned back in his chair. "One, that you show me an acceptance from Madame Xenos. Two, that you remain in Paris at the *maison de couture* until the showing is completed."

"I accept," Sergei said, and reached for the telephone.

"What are you doing?" the banker asked nervously.

"What quicker way to reach Madame Xenos than by telephone? You don't think I'm going to give you time to change your mind, do you?"

Halfway to his apartment Sergei changed his mind. Instead he went directly to the *maison de couture*. He paused in front of the small building and studied the brass plates bearing his crest on either side of the entrance. The doorman hastened to open the door. "Your highness," he murmured respectfully.

Sergei glared at him. "The brass is too shiny," he said, pointing to the *plaques*. "Rub dirt over them, they look too new."

Sergei entered and hurried up the grand staircase that led to the main salon. The painters and decorators had been hard at work. Already his crest appeared everywhere in the building. He walked on through the grand salon into the workroom beyond.

Here was a bedlam of activity. The little *midinettes* were running back and forth carrying bolts of cloth, and models stood about petulantly, some with gowns already pinned around them, others half nude, their tiny breasts casually displayed. Over all this he could hear Jean-Jacques's voice screaming in the office. Jean-Jacques sounded almost hysterical.

Sergei walked through the workroom and pushed open the door. A model was standing on a small stand. Around her stood two of the assistants and a cutter. Jean-Jacques was behind his desk, the tears streaming down his cheeks. When he saw Sergei he came forward wringing his hands.

"What am I to do?" he shrieked. "They all are so untalented and stupid! They cannot do even the simple things I ask of them." He clutched his hands dramatically to his forehead. "I'm on the verge of a breakdown. I tell you! A breakdown. I shall go completely out of my mind!"

He pulled at Sergei's arm and dragged him over to the model. "*Regardez!* Look what they do to my design! Ruined!"

"Calm yourself, Jean-Jacques," Sergei said soothingly, "explain to me what you are trying to accomplish. Then perhaps I can help them to give you what you want."

Jean-Jacques stood in front of the model. "*Regardez*. A completely new idea for the cocktail hour. I see a series of triangles suspended from milady's shoulders like mobiles, thus providing a freeness at every important point. The bust, the hip, the knee."

Sergei looked at the model. The dress was exactly as Jean-Jacques had described it, exactly like the design he held in his hand. But he could understand the designer's frustration. The dress itself did not do what Jean-Jacques intended it to do. He looked at the design, then back again at the model.

A silence came over the office as everyone waited on his word. Sergei nodded after a moment, and turned to the designer. "Jean-Jacques, you're a genius! I understand your problem completely. And I think I know what is bothering you."

"You do?" Jean-Jacques's voice was a mixture of pride and confusion.

"I do," Sergei said with assurance. "It is this!" Dramatically he pointed to the model's hips. "Here, where the triangle should be wide, as you intended, it is apexed and tight."

Jean-Jacques was utterly confused. "It is?"

Again Sergei nodded positively. "It was your word 'freeness' that gave me the answer. The dress must swing wide at the bottom so that milady can feel the breeze on her cunt as she moves, thereby always reminding herself of her femininity."

Jean-Jacques was silent as he studied the model. Sergei did not give him a chance to answer. "I must hurry to my office, I have an appointment. Thank you for giving me this opportunity to bask in your genius."

Sergei paused in the doorway. He looked at the assistants, then at the designer. "I am sure now that they will be able to give you exactly what you want."

When he was gone from the doorway, Jean-Jacques muttered something almost inaudibly under his breath about having something further to take up with his highness, and ran from the room. The two assistants looked at each other. "Did you understand what his highness said?"

The other shook her head. "No." She turned to the model. "Did you understand?"

"Who the hell understands anyone in this business?" the model said with a bored expression as she stepped down from the stand. "They are all crazy. If I got any more breeze on my cunt than I do now, I would probably come down with pneumonia."

420

11

Irma Andersen was a thickset woman in her middle fifties, with a pudgy, rather square face under her heavy, black-rimmed glasses. She held out her hand toward Sergei. "Your highness, so good of you to come!"

Sergei kissed her hand. "Who could resist a summons from so renowned a hostess?"

Irma laughed. Her voice was surprisingly deep but still quite feminine. "Sergei, you phony bastard." She chuckled. "At least you were honest enough not to call me beautiful." She placed a cigarette in a long thin holder and waited until he held a light for her. "It's been a long time," she said, letting the smoke come out through her nose like a man.

"Since my wedding."

"You remembered?"

He nodded. "You were doing a column for Cosmo-World."

"I didn't think you'd remember." Irma placed the cigarette holder on the edge of her desk and picked up a sheet of paper. "I suppose you're wondering why I called?"

"I was a little curious."

"I got a cablegram from my New York newspaper. They heard that Caroline Xenos was coming over with a group of friends especially to attend the opening of your new salon. They asked me to look into it."

"Oh?"

"Are you trying especially hard to keep it a secret?" she asked. "Why didn't you get in touch with me right away?"

It had to be like this, he thought, the push had to come from the States. If he had called as she suggested, she would have killed the showing. "I didn't dare," he replied with just the proper amount of modesty. "You're much too important for me to approach without a major reason."

421

"Anything that has to do with fashion and society is important to me, Sergei."

"But this is just another *couturier*."

"Sergei, you must be an idiot! It isn't every day that a prince opens a *maison de couture*."

He dared a grin. "You know I'm no prince."

"You are honest!" Irma laughed aloud. "I know it, and you know it. But so far as the folks back home go, you're a prince. Anyone who was once married to Sue Ann Daley would have to be."

"That's because they don't know Sue Ann!"

"Sue Ann has a new one, a good-looking young Mexican boy. She found him in Acapulco diving from the mountain into the ocean. He must be all of seventeen."

Sergei smiled. "Good for her; at least he's young enough."

Irma Andersen stuck the cigarette holder back in her mouth. "You'll invite me to the collection, of course?"

Sergei allowed himself a moment's hesitation. "We weren't planning to ask the press."

"I don't care what you're doing about the others, I'm coming."

He was silent.

"I can be a great help to you," she said, "you know that."

He nodded.

"I was on the telephone only this morning to Lady Corrigan in London. I just happened to mention to her that I knew you. She expressed a great interest in joining me at the showing."

Sergei could almost feel a glow of triumph inside himself. Lady Corrigan was one of the richest heiresses in Great Britain. She had also been on every ten-best-dressed list for the past two years.

"There are several others I could interest in visiting your salon," Irma added quickly, "names that will help you gain a quick acceptance. That is if you have anything worthwhile to show." She looked at him shrewdly. "You're not afraid of such a critical audience, are you?"

"No," he replied hesitantly.

"Well, then?"

He looked at her and suddenly he held open his hands in a gesture of defeat. "All right, you're invited. But you realize this means I shall have to invite the rest of the press?"

"I don't care whom you invite. Just make certain I sit in the front row with the customers and not back with the help!"

"Of course," Sergei replied. "You didn't have to ask."

"I have another idea."

"Yes?"

"Why don't you let me give a dinner for you after the collection? We'll keep it small. No more than fifty or sixty of the right people."

"It's a lovely idea, and I am deeply touched. But there is just one difficulty, if I may be frank."

"You can be very frank with me always."

"Money," he said. "I put all I have into this collection."

"What are you trying to tell me? I ran a check on you. Bernstein's bank in Switzerland is behind the showing."

"I'm three years into Sue Ann's settlement already. They won't go beyond that."

"They're fools!" Irma said vehemently, suddenly on Sergei's side. "I think we should have the party anyway."

"But where will I get the money?"

"Leave that to me. It will be my investment in you. I suddenly have the feeling that you're going to make a lot of money."

"I hope you're right. Tomorrow morning I shall have delivered to you, say, five percent of my stock."

"Ten."

"Ten percent," he agreed.

This time Irma held her hand out across the desk like a man. Solemnly he shook it.

"Now," she said, ejecting the cigarette from her holder into the ash tray. "As soon as I can reload this damn thing, I want to hear about your collection. I want to get a story into my next Sunday feature."

Sergei lit the cigarette for her and waited until she fed a sheet of paper into her typewriter. "What is it you would like to know?"

"First, how did you get interested in women's clothes?"

He laughed. "That's easy. As you know, I've always been interested in women."

Irma laughed. "I know that, but isn't it a switch for you to get them clothes rather than out of them?" Abruptly she stopped laughing and grew serious. "That's fun but not what

423

I need for a family newspaper. I need something else. Something fairly controversial but not too far out to start with."

Sergei thought for a moment. "How about the new look? Everyone seems afraid to criticize it."

"That's a point." She nodded thoughtfully. "What have you got to say about it?"

"The new look was designed to cover up ugly people, with the result that it turns all women into the same image. The covered-up, ugly image. My collection is not like that at all. It is designed primarily for the beautiful people. The—"

"Wait a minute," Irma interrupted, "that's it!" Abruptly her fingers began to fly over the typewriter keyboard.

Sergei lit a cigarette and waited until she stopped and turned back to him. "That's what?"

" 'The beautiful people.' I've been looking for a phrase like that for the last year, ever since I started my daily column. Listen to this. 'The heading you see at the top of the column this Sunday, "The Beautiful People," was suggested to me by the most exciting new personality in the world of fashion today, Prince Sergei Nikovitch, a member of the former ruling family of Russia. Prince Sergei's name for the people for whom he has designed his collection is the most exact description of the people we are all most interested in. The people in the forefront of everything—society, politics, the theater, art, diplomacy, you name it. "The Beautiful People" are the leaders. And by the secret intelligence that passes invisibly amongst them the word is out. From all over the world they are flocking to Paris on the first of September to view Prince Nikovitch's collection. From the United States, Caroline Xenos, the former Caroline de Coyne, with a group of her friends; from London, the Lady Margaret (Peggy) Corrigan, one of the world's best-dressed women: from South America, from Europe, from all over the world, "The Beautiful People" are coming.' "

Irma looked up. "How's that for a starter?"

Sergei smiled. "I only hope my collection is as good!"

The tension was like an immense knot in the pit of his stomach. Sergei peered through the curtain into the grand salon. The chairs were placed in a horseshoe, to allow the models a full parade around the room. They went back row after row until they almost reached the wall, and every one of them was occupied. And behind them people were standing. The overflow crowd spilled out into the open corridor.

Irma Andersen had been as good as her word. The front row, in which she sat, looked like a royalty list gleaned from the pages of *L'Officiel* or *Vogue*. Caroline sat at Irma's left, and James Hadley, former American ambassador to Italy, was next to her. At Irma's right was Lady Corrigan and her husband. The front row looked like the *tout va* table at Monte Carlo during the season.

The sound of the string quartet came to Sergei's ears as he stepped away from the curtain and walked back into the workroom. The noise and pandemonium was greater here than any he had ever experienced before. If what had previously existed had been confusion, this was chaos. It seemed as if suddenly everyone had gone out of his or her mind.

Jean-Jacques came running in from the salon behind him. "Get ready, girls!"

The silence that suddenly fell across the room bothered Sergei's ears even more than the noise. He heard the orchestra lead into the first presentation. A thin model whose face was pale under her makeup came forward. She paused before the two of them and pirouetted slowly.

"Beautiful, beautiful!" Jean-Jacques enthused. He kissed the model on both cheeks. She looked up at Sergei questioningly. He, too, bent and kissed her. "Be brave, *ma petite.*"

She smiled suddenly, shyly, and walked out of the workroom. Behind him Sergei could hear the swell of applause that greeted her entrance.

"Where is Charles?" Jean-Jacques asked hysterically, "where is he? He promised to be here. He knows I can't go through an opening without him."

Suddenly Sergei was furious. He had had six weeks of this. It was too much. "He's upstairs in your office fucking a girl!"

Jean-Jacques glared at him. Suddenly his face went white, and he flung the back of his hand to his forehead. "I feel faint, I am fainting!"

He staggered back into the arms of his two assistants. A moment later a young man hurried up with a glass of water. "Drink this, darling."

Jean-Jacques sipped the water. The color came back into his face. He stood up and faced Sergei. "Don't *ever* say such a thing, you naughty boy," he said reproachfully. "It gave

425

me such a turn! You know that Charles and I are faithful to each other."

Behind them the music began to lead into the second introduction, and the next model started forward. "You can handle this," Sergei said suddenly to Jean-Jacques. "I'm going up to my office for a drink."

Sergei closed the door behind him. Silently he took a bottle of vodka from the closet and poured a large slug into a glass. He sat down, the vodka still in his hand, and stared at the picture of the little girl on the desk.

Anastasia had been about seven when the picture was taken, and the blue dress with the white piping made a lovely frame for her light-blond hair and blue eyes. Her slightly uncertain but sweet smile heartened him. He held the drink up. "I pray to God this works, baby," he said. "Daddy's getting awfully tired of running."

Sergei swallowed the last of the drink just as the door opened. He looked up in surprise.

"I thought I would find you here," Giselle said. "No one should ever have to spend an opening night alone."

12

Irma Andersen was having a ball. The real reason she gave parties was because she loved them. Irma loved everything about them. The sights, the sounds, the smells, the excitement. Beautifully dressed people living exotically in a way that even her childhood dreams had never anticipated. It had never been like this in the back room of the tiny delicatessen in Akron, Ohio, where she had been brought up. There it was never anything but a nickel's worth of liverwurst and potato salad and rye bread.

Irma had hated liverwurst and potato salad ever since, and these were the only two items she had never allowed on her menu. So instead of liverwurst there was *pâté de foie gras,*

426

and instead of potato salad there were avocados, sliced and cut and prepared with a deliciously different mayonnaise.

She looked around with a feeling of satisfaction. This was a good party. All you needed was the right mixture of people. Talkers and listeners. About sixty-five percent of the former. It was always better to have more talkers than listeners. There was something livelier about noise. A quiet party was a dead party. A failure.

Irma used to have nightmares about giving a party at which no one spoke. Just the thought had been enough to keep her awake nights. But that had been a long time ago. It could never happen now. Now there was another reason she enjoyed giving parties. They were the greatest source of information in the world. In the first few minutes of that evening she had picked up some very choice tidbits of gossip.

The thing between Caroline Xenos and James Hadley. It was odd, but delicious. The difference in their ages, for one thing. Hadley was old enough to be her father. Besides that, Caroline's husband had the reputation of being one of the world's great lovers and playboys. What was it that Sue Ann Daley had once been quoted as saying?

"With Dax it's like having a machine gun inside you. It never stops shooting and neither does he."

But that was the marvelous thing about people. You could never know what they really wanted. Apparently Caroline desired something else. And she didn't seem to care who knew it, not from the way she kept looking at Hadley.

Irma made a note to ask Sergei what he knew about it. After all, he had been a close friend of Dax's. He would know. And it wasn't to use in her column. Chances were she would never include an item like that in her newspaper. These people were her friends. She would never do anything to hurt them.

In a strange way Irma loved them all. With all their pettiness and amoral attitudes of selfishness, she looked up to them. They had never known what it was to eat liverwurst and potato salad. They really were the beautiful people. And just being with them made her feel beautiful, too.

It was almost midnight when they left the party, and as they stood waiting while the doorman went in search of their chauffeur Caroline said, "I'm glad for Sergei."

"Do you think he's made it?" James Hadley asked shrewdly, "or is it the illusion of the opening?"

"He's made it. Some of his things are very good, a few extraordinary. Tomorrow he will need police to control the crowds."

"He's that good, eh?"

Caroline nodded. "If I did not know him personally, I still would never complete my wardrobe without considering Sergei."

The car pulled up and the doorman stood holding the door. Hadley pressed a five-franc note into his hand and they got in. The car rolled away from the curb.

"Ask the chauffeur to drop me at my father's house."

Hadley was surprised. He took down the speaker and gave the chauffeur the instruction before he answered her. "Wouldn't it be better to wait until morning?"

Caroline shook her head. "I told *Papa* I would be over after the dinner."

"You spoke to him?"

"This afternoon."

"How is he? I have a great respect for your father."

Caroline gave him a penetrating look. "I never know about *Papa*. He's as much a mystery to me as you must be to your children."

"Did he say why he wanted to see you?"

Again that curious look. "He's my father. I've been here almost a week without calling him. So *Papa* called me."

"But he must have said something."

"He didn't have to, I know what he wants."

Hadley regretted the question almost as soon as he asked it. "You do?"

Her eyes were steady on his. "The same thing you would want to know if your daughter were having an affair with him. What does she intend doing about it?"

Hadley was silent. He looked out the window for a few moments but he couldn't keep his thoughts to himself. "Do you know what you're going to say to him?"

Caroline nodded. "I know exactly what I'm going to say."

Hadley felt that if he asked her she would tell him. But he didn't. Something inside kept him from it. Perhaps it was because he already sensed that he knew what she had decided and didn't want to hear it.

428

Instead he got out of the car when it stopped in front of the baron's town house. "Shall I send the car back for you?"

"No," she said, "I'll see you at lunch tomorrow." She turned up her cheek for a good-night kiss. *"Bon soir, mon cher."*

Hadley realized it was over when she kissed his cheek. He felt he should say something gallant, something understanding, but the words did not come readily to his lips. There was just a large empty feeling as he watched her run up the steps to the front door.

The baron was waiting in the library. He got up as she came into the room. His face seemed tired and his hair was grayer than she had remembered. A small warm smile came to his lips as he saw her.

"Papa!" she exclaimed, her eyes suddenly filling with tears. She ran into his arms. *"Papa!"*

"Caroline, *ma petite, ma bébé."* The baron's arms were around her, his fingers brushing the tears from her cheeks. "Don't cry. All will be well."

"I have been a fool," she whispered against his chest, "I have done so many things wrong."

"You've been neither wrong nor foolish," her father said softly. "The only thing you're guilty of is being young and a woman. Both contain a large margin for error."

She looked up into his face. "What do I do now?"

He met her eyes. "You already know that. You tell me. This thing with Hadley, it is over?"

Silently she nodded.

"That is not the problem then. The problem is Dax?"

"Yes."

The baron walked over to the sideboard and poured a small glass of sherry for her. "Here, drink this. It will make you feel better."

The wine warmed her and he waited until she had finished before he spoke. "What do you plan to do about Dax?"

"Divorce him. I have been unfair to Dax all these years. I know that now. I made him wait, pretending that I was trying to be what I could never be. Now I must tell him, and I don't know what to say."

Her father's eyes were steady. "Just tell him the truth. Exactly as you just told me. I think he will understand."

429

"How could he?" she asked. "How could anyone? I've even been lying to myself."

"I think Dax already understands."

Something in his voice made Caroline look up. "Why do you say that?"

"Dax has been in Paris all this week."

"In Paris?" Caroline was surprised. "But there's been no word of him. He hasn't been to any of the regular places. He hasn't even called."

Her father nodded. "That's what leads me to the conclusion that Dax does understand. He's remained in the consulate all week without even putting his head out. And there is only one reason why he would do that. To keep from embarrassing you." The baron came toward her and took her hand. "Indirectly, that's why I called you."

Caroline looked puzzled.

"Dax is planning to leave early tomorrow morning for Corteguay. I thought you two should see each other before he went away. He's waiting in the drawing room."

Dax was already on his feet when Caroline entered. She came directly across the room. His smile of greeting was warm and genuine. "Dax, I've been a child. I've never been a wife to you."

He took her hand. "Sit down."

She sank into a chair. "I don't know what to say. I'm sorry."

"Don't apologize. I haven't been that good a husband that you should feel you owe me apologies."

Caroline looked up at him. "Then what does one say at a time like this?"

Dax took a handkerchief from his pocket and handed it to her. He waited until she brushed the tears away. "Let us say this. Because of circumstances there were two friends who found themselves married to one another, and they were true friends because when their marriage was over they found that it had not destroyed their friendship."

"Is such a thing possible?"

"It is, if it is the truth."

A weight seemed to lift from Caroline's heart. She smiled for the first time. "You are a strange man, Dax. So many people think they know you and yet they don't. They see only what they want to see. Even I was that way. Now I realize that I was just as stupid as the others. I, too, saw only what I wanted to see."

Dax looked at her. "And what do you see now?"

Caroline leaned forward and took his hand. "I see a very kind and gentle man, and a very, very true friend."

13

The wheels of the huge airplane touched the ground, and Dax turned to Fat Cat in the seat next to him. "Well, we're home."

Fat Cat looked past him through the window. The plane was taxiing toward the new airport building. "I do not like it. I prefer to come by sea."

"Why?"

"By sea you are approaching a large country; from the air one sees how truly small we are."

Dax laughed. "We are not a large country."

"*Sí*, I know. But I do not feel this. I like to think we are big, important."

The plane came to a stop, and Dax began to unfasten his seat belt. "We are. But only to ourselves."

The hot Corteguayan sun pained their eyes as they came off the plane. At the foot of the landing stairs an officer moved forward in a smart salute. "Señor Xenos?"

"*Sí.*"

"*Capitán Maroz, a su servicio. El Presidente* has asked that I bring you to him immediately."

"*Gracias, Capitán.*"

"I have a limousine waiting." Captain Maroz said, leading them through the airport doors. "Arrangements have already been made for your luggage."

With a wave of his hand Maroz passed them through customs, and they emerged into a large waiting area. He noticed Dax's eyes taking in the elaborate decorations, the large mosaic murals. "It is beautiful, no?"

Dax nodded. "Very impressive."

The captain smiled. *"El Presidente* says it is important for the *turistas*. They must first be impressed by the airport."

Dax looked down the long waiting area. There weren't many people in evidence, and most of them were in uniform. "How many planes land here in a day?"

Captain Maroz looked embarrassed. "There are but two international flights a week, one from the United States, another from Mexico. They pause here on their way south. But soon there will be more. And *el Presidente* plans to have our own airline operating by next year. Our people are most enthusiastic."

Dax imagined they would be, since it provided work for them. By now they had reached the limousine. Captain Maroz opened the door. Dax got into the car, and the captain climbed in beside him. Fat Cat got into the front with the driver.

The automobile swung around and came out onto a huge six-lane highway. Over their heads was a mammoth sign— BOULEVARD DEL PRESIDENTE. Dax glanced at his companion.

"It is also new," Captain Maroz said. "Of what use is an airport if there is no access to it?"

"Where does it go?"

"To the city, and then on to *el Presidente*'s new winter palace in the mountains." Captain Maroz looked out the window of the car. "It is very impressive. *El Presidente* imported a group of *gringo* engineers to build it."

The horn blasted and the big car swerved to pass a mule-drawn cart loaded with manure. Dax turned in his seat to glance back. The *campesino* dozing in his seat had not even looked up as they passed. Dax could see all the way back to the airport. There was not another car in sight.

The captain's voice came over his shoulder. "Actually the *campesinos* are forbidden to use this road, but it is impossible to keep the stupid fools off."

Dax leaned back in the seat silently. In the fields they passed, some of the *campesinos* looked up as the car sped by but most simply ignored it. Abruptly the car began to slow down. Dax looked up. They were approaching the city.

"I know exactly what those Texans think," *el Presidente* said. "They think we are stupid, that we are children to be

432

led around by our noses." He got up from behind the desk. "In time they shall learn differently."

Dax looked across the huge desk, *el Presidente* seemed hardly to have changed. If anything his hair seemed darker. A vague suspicion flashed through Dax's mind; there used to be a hint of gray in *el Presidente*'s hair. Could it be that the old man was dyeing it?

"They are fools," *el Presidente* continued, "they think there is oil there. Well, let them think so. It will be five to seven years before they discover otherwise."

Dax looked at him in surprise. "But what about the surveys?"

El Presidente grinned. "Geologists, too, can be bought."

"But—"

El Presidente smiled. "Oh, they are right, the shelf does continue all along our coast. But it is more than three hundred miles out and almost two miles down. I doubt that even their Yankee ingenuity will find a way to make it practical for them to drill at that depth." He looked at Dax. "But in those five years they will spend many dollars here. It will be a big boost to our economy. It will also help make the American *turistas* aware of us."

He crossed to a window and looked out. Then he turned and beckoned to Dax. "Over there on the Hill of the Lovers— it will be a good place to build a hotel, no?"

"But there are no tourists yet."

El Presidente smiled. "There will be. Already Pan American Airlines has approached me about the location. They think the view will be *magnífico*."

"And they will supply the financing?"

El Presidente nodded. "Of course."

"And who will supply the land?"

El Presidente shrugged, and went back to his desk. "First the land must be acquired, then we will lease it to them."

"Who owns the land?"

El Presidente looked at Dax and smiled. "Amparo."

Dax returned to his chair and sat down. "Your excellency has thought of everything. I can't see why you sent for me."

"You are very important to our plans. You are the only one of us known outside this country. You are hereby appointed head of the Tourist Planning Commission."

433

Dax was silent.

El Presidente looked at him. "I know what you are thinking —that I am a dishonest, unscrupulous old man. And perhaps you are right. But everything I have done brings us more money, and helps raise the standard of living in Corteguay."

Dax got to his feet. He smiled to himself at the thought of all the clever men this old *bandolero* had hoodwinked. The rich greedy Texans. Marcel. Yet in the end what difference would it make?

For the Texans it would merely be another field that didn't come in; they would continue to make it from their other wells. And Marcel would have his fleet of ships. They would fly the flag of Corteguay and bring in taxes. So Corteguay and *el Presidente* would benefit no matter what happened.

"Your excellency, you never cease to amaze me."

El Presidente smiled. "Now we must think of a way to attract the American *turista*, something that will establish in his mind that Corteguay is an attractive and romantic place."

"There are companies in the United States that specialize in such matters. They are called public-relations firms. I shall get in touch with several of them and we'll see what they come up with."

"An excellent idea." *El Presidente* pressed a buzzer on his desk. The meeting was over. "I shall expect you for dinner tonight. We can talk more then."

Captain Maroz was waiting in the antechamber. "I have another invitation for you, excellency," he said respectfully.

"Yes?"

"It is from her excellency, the daughter of *el Presidente*. She wishes you to join her for tea at five in her apartment."

Dax looked at his watch. It was a little after three. More than time for a siesta and to shower and change his clothes. "Tell her excellency I look forward with pleasure to seeing her again."

14

Jeremy Hadley pushed the accelerator down to the floor, and with a surge of power the big car abruptly crested the hill. For a moment it seemed suspended breathlessly, with the entire Riviera spread out below, from Monte Carlo to Antibes, then it hurtled down toward the blue waters of the Mediterranean.

The girl moved closer and suddenly he felt her hand at the inside of his thigh. He glanced at her out of the corner of his eye. Her lips were partly open, almost as if she were in the throes of sexual excitement. "You Americans and your automobiles!" she shouted over the roar of the wind and the motor.

He grinned. It worked every time. No matter how sophisticated they were, no matter how snide about things American. All you had to do was get them beside you on that front seat. Whatever it was—the speed, the sense of power, the masculine smell of new leather—it never missed.

He looked at her again. There was a place just off the road around the next turn, and there was no doubt about her being ready. She fell on him almost before he had time to cut the motor, her fingers frantically tearing at the nonexistent buttons. He pulled down his zipper, and she gasped as his youth and life sprang free. Then her hot moist mouth covered him.

The sun was beginning to fall beyond Antibes when the big car nosed its way out onto the road once more. She had pulled the visor down and was repairing her makeup in the mirror clipped to its underside. She caught his eyes as she finished with her lipstick. She snapped the visor up and leaned back in the seat. "I don't expect you to believe me but that was the first time I have ever been unfaithful to my husband."

Jeremy didn't answer. There was no need for a reply. If it

435

was the first time, he was certain from the way she had acted that it would not be the last.

"You do not believe me?"

He smiled. "I believe you."

She pulled the cigarette from his mouth and dragged on it. Then she gave it back to him and let the smoke out slowly. "I don't understand myself. I don't know what got into me."

He laughed aloud. "I do. Me."

In spite of herself she laughed. "Don't joke, this is serious."

"I'm not joking."

She glanced at the clock on the dashboard. "How long will it take us to get there?"

"I don't know." He shrugged. "It depends on how long we're held up at customs. Perhaps two hours."

"Two hours?" There was a note of dismay in her voice.

"What difference does it make? Nobody's going to question it."

"My husband will. He didn't like the idea of my driving alone with you."

"I asked him to come. He preferred going on the yacht with the others."

"That doesn't matter," she said, "he'll still want to know what took us so long."

"Tell him we ran out of gas."

He turned on the car radio, and music from an Italian station swelled up. That should stop the conversation, he thought. He glanced at her out of the corner of his eye.

She was leaning back against the seat, her eyes half closed. He wondered what she was thinking. German girls were very strange. And Marlene Von Kuppen was stranger than most.

But perhaps the oddest thing about her was her husband. Fritz Von Kuppen was the second son of the old baron. Tall and blond, an officer in the German Air Corps during the war, he had been shot down early and discharged almost before the war had really begun. When they had first met, Jeremy had been almost certain that Von Kuppen was a homosexual. There was something about the way the man moved on a tennis court. It was almost too classic. He had beaten Jeremy easily, and afterward had invited him back to the clubhouse for a drink.

It was there that he had met Marlene. She had been seated at a table on the terrace talking to another woman.

436

"My wife, Mr. Hadley," Von Kuppen said. "Mr. Hadley plays a very hard game of tennis, Marlene."

Jeremy had smiled and taken her outstretched hand. "But not hard enough. Your husband took me quite easily."

Marlene smiled. "Tennis is the only thing in the world that Fritz is really serious about."

He had cocked his ear. He wondered whether there was something hidden in that statement. But she had quickly introduced her companion, and a moment later the waiter had come with drinks. In the course of their conversation he had learned that the Von Kuppens had stopped off in Italy on their way to the French Riviera, and planned to go on sometime within the next few days.

In a moment his younger brother Thomas came up. Jeremy introduced him and ordered him a drink. "What about the boat?"

"The captain says he'll have everything ready. We can take her up to Antibes in the morning."

"Dad will be pleased. You go on up with the yacht, I'll drive."

"Is that the new yacht I saw in the basin?" Von Kuppen asked.

Jeremy nodded.

"I admired it from a distance. She's a beauty."

"You're going up to the Riviera anyway; why don't you both join my brother for the trip? It will really give you a chance to look her over."

"I'd love to, but—" Von Kuppen looked hesitantly at Marlene.

"I'm afraid I'm a big disappointment to my husband. Boats are his second love, and I always get seasick."

"I could drive you up if you'd like," he'd suggested. "We'd be there by evening."

She shook her head. "No, thank you, Mr. Hadley. It would be too much of an imposition."

But unexpectedly Von Kuppen had spoken up. "I think it's an excellent suggestion, *liebchen*. I'd love a day on the water." He turned to Jeremy. "Thank you very much, Mr. Hadley. We'd be delighted to accept your offer."

When they had gone Tommy had grinned. "You got somethin' going with that girl?"

Jeremy had laughed. "I only met her ten minutes before you got here."

Tommy shook his head. "Some guys have all the luck."

Jeremy rumpled his brother's hair affectionately. "Stop bitching, Tommy. You didn't do so bad those last few weeks in Switzerland."

"I didn't come up with anything like that," Tommy complained. "How come you always wind up with the cream?"

"Make the most of it, younger brother," Jeremy said, suddenly serious. "I have a feeling playtime will soon be over."

"What do you mean?"

"Jim and Dad should be back by the weekend. And you know why they flew back to Boston."

"Do you think they'll let Jim go for Congress? Really, I mean?"

"If they don't, it won't matter. Dad will convince them. He usually does."

"Well, what the hell, that shouldn't bug us too much. There's still more than a year until election."

"You're kidding yourself and you know it. If Dad's made up his mind, the campaign has already begun. And we're all going to be in it. The way Dad looks at it it isn't only Jim who will be running, it will be the whole family."

The yacht was tied up at the private dock and Tommy and Von Kuppen were out on the porch when they pulled up in front of the villa.

"Have a nice drive up?" Von Kuppen called as they got out of the car.

"It was lovely," Marlene said, "but we ran out of gas."

"Bloody damned careless of me," Jeremy added. "I should have filled up before we left."

"Those things happen," Von Kuppen answered casually. He got to his feet. "You must be exhausted, darling. Come, I'll show you to our room."

"That would be lovely." Marlene turned to Jeremy. "Thank you for the ride up."

"You're welcome."

After they had gone into the house, Tommy came down the steps and got into the car beside his brother. He let out a sigh of relief as Jeremy drove the car around in the back to park it. "Man, I'm glad you showed when you did. Things were getting a little bit sticky."

Jeremy looked at him. "What do you mean?"

"Von Kuppen didn't like it at all. And yet I had the feeling it was just what he expected. Maybe even what he wanted. Very sick."

"Yeah," Jeremy said thoughtfully. Probably he had been right in his appraisal. The marriage could be a cover. It was not uncommon. He pulled the car into the parking lot and turned off the motor.

"The hell with him. It's his problem." He was suddenly annoyed at himself for being caught in the middle of something he hadn't anticipated. "Let's go get a drink."

Marlene did not come down for dinner, and the three of them ate in a curiously polite silence. It would be another day before any of the others arrived. His sisters and mother from Paris, where they had been shopping; his sister-in-law, Jim's wife, and their two children from New York; and Jim and their father from Boston. At the end of dinner, Tommy looked across the table at him. "Are you using the car tonight?"

Jeremy shook his head.

"I'd like to run over to Juan-les-Pins and see what's goin' on."

"Go ahead, I'm turning in early."

Von Kuppen turned to Tommy. "If you wouldn't mind, I'd like to come along."

"I'd be glad to have you."

"Thank you." Von Kuppen got to his feet, "I'll be back in a moment. I'll just tell Marlene so she won't wait up for me."

The two of them looked at each other when he left the dining room. "What do you make of that?" Tommy asked. "I was willing to bet he wouldn't leave the two of you alone again."

"We're not exactly alone." Jeremy nodded at a maid and the butler, who were busy clearing the table.

"You know what I mean."

"I'm not going to worry about it, I'm just going up to bed."

Jeremy came out of his bathroom rubbing himself vigorously with a huge bath sheet. He tied the towel around his

439

waist, and took a cigarette from the dresser and lit it. He looked at himself in the mirror with a feeling of satisfaction.

He was in pretty good condition considering his age. His belly was still flat and hard, his weight the same as it had been when he went into the army in 1941. That was eight years ago. Sometimes it seemed almost like yesterday. He had been twenty then.

"Go in now," his father had urged. "We'll be in it before the year is over. I want you boys to be ready for it."

Jim had gone into the air force, he into the infantry. By March of 1942 they were both overseas. Later that same month he had looked up into the sky from where he clung precariously to a sheltering rock and seen the insignia of his brother's squadron on the underwings of the planes that were flying over him. Suddenly, somehow the stupidity of the token raid on Dieppe no longer mattered, the danger from the murderous crossfire in which the Germans had entrapped them was no longer so frightening. His brother was up there watching over him.

Jeremy came back from that raid a first lieutenant, earned his captaincy on the beach at Anzio, and attained his majority in the fields of Normandy, together with the silver star and the purple heart.

That had been the real end of the war for him. After he came out of the hospital he'd been transferred to General Staff and he hadn't complained. He'd had enough. But Jim kept on flying the big bombers right up until VE Day, and came out a full chicken colonel.

Two days later, by a prearranged agreement between them, they had met here at the villa on the Cap d'Antibes, which had belonged to their father for so many years and where they had spent many fun-filled summers.

Old François, the caretaker, and his wife had come out to greet them. "Look, *messieurs*," the old man said proudly, "we kept the pig *Boche* out."

They had nodded, smiling, and murmured their approval despite the knowledge that the Germans for one reason or another hadn't been interested in that area. Still, there was something very sad about seeing the condition of the grounds, the shutters nailed to the windows, the covered furniture.

When they were alone, the two brothers had looked at each other. Jim was older by only four years but already there was gray in his hair and deep lines in his face. The strain of the more than a thousand hours in war-torn skies had left their mark. By contrast Jeremy seemed almost unchanged, untouched. Perhaps it was due more to the prolonged rest in the hospital than to the comparative ease of headquarters duty.

"How is it?" Jim asked about the wound.

"Just a scratch. Nothing. How is it with you?"

Jim held up his hands in a mock punchy fighter's pose. "Look, Maw, they never touched me." But there was no humor in his voice.

"They touched you all right. I was lucky. You didn't get off that easy."

"You *were* lucky," Jim said, a sudden bitterness in his voice. "At least all you fought were soldiers. They were trying to kill you, and you were trying to kill them. That made you even. But when I dumped one of those big ones I never knew whom they might kill. You should have seen Cologne after we got through with it. And Berlin. Each time we came back it was easier. You didn't need eyes, you just followed the aroma of burning houses reaching three miles up in the sky."

"Wait a minute, Jim. You're not feeling sorry for the Germans?"

His brother stared at him. "You're damn right I am. They weren't all soldiers, all Nazis. How many women and children do you think I killed? The soldiers were safe at the front."

"We didn't make the rules for this war," he said harshly, "they did. In Holland, Poland, France, England. They didn't care where their bombs fell or whom they killed. They didn't give a shit because whoever was left they planned to take care of at Dachau and Auschwitz."

"Did that make it right for us?"

"No, nothing makes war right. But when war comes you have no choice. You either fight back or you get killed. And in our time the rules of warfare are made by the aggressor." He pulled out a cigarette. "Any time you doubt that take a walk around Coventry."

Jim looked at his younger brother, a sudden respect growing in his eyes. "Maybe you're right. I'm just tired. I guess I've had it."

"We've all had it, but it's over now. At least for us."

"I hope so," Jim said wearily.

Just then old François had stuck his head into the room and

announced dinner. He was dressed in his old butler's uniform, which had been pressed carefully. Silently they followed him into the dining room.

From somewhere François had got fresh flowers for a centerpiece, and candles were burning at either end of the table. The silver was sparkling, the linen soft and creamy white. And François's wife was standing in the doorway to the pantry, her blue eyes shining behind her glasses. "Welcome home, *messieurs*."

Jeremy had laughed, and run around the table to kiss her on both cheeks. *"Merci."*

She retired to the kitchen in confusion, and they sat down. François had barely finished pouring the wine for their first course when they heard the sound of an automobile on the gravel driveway outside. For a moment they stared at each other, for no one was expected. Then as one they got up and went to the front door.

They were just in time to see their father get out of the old Citroën taxi that had brought him from the station. When he turned and waved to them, they could scarcely believe their eyes.

"I knew exactly where to find you guys," their father called happily.

Then they were all crying at once, and there were a thousand questions. All through dinner they kept looking at each other and at the snapshots of the rest of the family that their father had brought. After a little while it was almost as if the war had never happened.

That year had been the first since the war that the villa was in full use. Not much time had been necessary to restore it, but other concerns kept some of them away. Jim had been married one month after his return home in June of 1945, and now there were two children, both boys. The senior Hadley took Jim into the office and bit by bit let him take over the general operations of his complex businesses.

Jim had almost completed his takeover by the time Jeremy picked up his diploma from Harvard. He had gone back for the one year he had missed, but once he was out he was still uncertain of his future. As usual his father had known exactly what was necessary.

When he accepted an appointment to the reparations commission he had taken Jeremy along as his assistant, and for two years Jeremy had walked in and out of government offices in every major country of Europe. His tall good looks and easygoing manner made him a favorite everywhere he went. The fact that he was American and very rich hadn't hurt either.

He enjoyed both his position and his social life to the hilt. European women were far more sophisticated than their American counterparts. If he had a slight tendency to become overinvolved with any particular one, his job took care of that. He rarely stayed in one place long enough to develop problems.

At the end of the job he came back to the States and spent a year in Washington working on a report dealing with the work of the commission. In April that job was finished, and he returned to Boston with an offer from the State Department.

Again his father was quite definite. "Don't take it, take a year off. Go back to Europe and enjoy yourself."

"I have to decide where I'm going with my life, Dad."

"There's no hurry, you'll know when the time comes. Besides, it's time Tommy spent a little time there too. He'll need someone to show him the ropes. He's never had the chances you had."

Jeremy smiled at the way his father put it. Tommy had just graduated from Harvard, and since he was only twenty-two he had missed the war. But if what he had heard from Jim was correct, Tommy had missed very little else. Half the mothers in Boston locked up their daughters whenever he came around.

In a way he had enjoyed showing his young brother the Europe he had come to know. It was like seeing himself as he used to be before the war. And yet there was a sophistication about his younger brother that he and Jim had never had. It was almost as if the six years between them made Tommy of another generation. It was purely and simply the war; the naïveté and innocence had gone never to return. There was a bomb and it had made death a constant companion to everyone who walked the earth.

Thoughtfully Jeremy came away from the mirror and, taking his pajamas from his suitcase, slipped into them. Thinking of his brother going down to Juan with Von Kuppen to catch the action, he smiled. They were all in too much of a hurry.

443

For the first time he thought he understood what his father meant when he had said there was no hurry. He was still young. He was only twenty-eight.

He stretched out on the bed and turned out the light. Lying on his side, he watched the shadows move across the curtained window. His eyes were just beginning to close when he suddenly became aware that one shadow was all wrong. It didn't move with all the others.

He watched for a moment, then suddenly it disappeared. He leaped to his feet and flung open the French doors to the terrace. No one was there. It wasn't until the next morning that he discovered his imagination hadn't been playing him tricks. For at breakfast he discovered the Von Kuppens were gone.

15

There was a note from the German on the breakfast table thanking him for his hospitality and apologizing for having to leave so early. He looked up as François brought his coffee. "Have they already left?"

"Oui. I called a taxi for them at seven. They have gone to the Negresco in Nice."

Jeremy picked up his cup thoughtfully. It was strange. Another hour and he could have driven them over himself.

"Ham and eggs, *monsieur?"*

Jeremy nodded.

"Me too," Tommy said, coming into the dining room. He sank into a chair and reached for the coffee. "Oh, my head!"

Jeremy smiled. "You must have had yourself a time last night. I don't see how Von Kuppen got off so early."

"Oh, he wasn't with me," Tommy said. "Have they left already?"

Jeremy handed him the note. "Didn't he leave with you?"

"He did, only by the time we got to the gate he had changed his mind. I offered to drive him back to the house but he said

444

not to bother because he liked a little walk after dinner. So I let him out and went on."

"I didn't hear him come back." Then Jeremy remembered. Or had he? The shadow on the terrace, could it have been Von Kuppen?

"You look odd. Anything wrong?"

He shook his head. He wondered whether Marlene had suspected that her husband might be laying a trap for them. Then François came in with their breakfast, and he pushed the thought out of his mind. The Von Kuppens were gone now, there was no point in thinking about them. He had been lucky.

By that afternoon he had completely forgotten about them. As usual his mother and sisters brought guests down from Paris. Sergei Nikovitch, who was doing their wardrobes that year, and Giselle d'Arcy, the actress. There was some talk that they were planning to get married; they had been going together for several years. Jim's wife, Angela, and the children arrived in the afternoon.

The house began to fill with people and in a few short hours Jeremy was certain the decibel rise on the Cap d'Antibes had alerted everyone that the Hadleys had returned.

Dinner that evening was the usual family madness. In the middle of it François bent over him. "There is a telephone call for you, *monsieur*."

He went into the study and picked up the extension phone. "Hello."

"Jeremy?"

Even though the voice was a mere whisper he recognized it instantly. "Yes, Marlene?"

"I must see you." There was a strained urgency in the whisper. "He is going to kill me!"

"Don't be ridiculous."

"He is," she interrupted harshly, "you don't know him. You don't know what he is capable of, he is crazy. The reason I did not come down to dinner last night was because he had beaten me black and blue. That's why we left so early this morning."

He was silent for a moment. "I don't understand. He had no reason, unless you told him."

"I told him nothing. But he says he will keep beating me until I tell him the truth."

445

"Why don't you leave him?"

"I can't. When he leaves me alone he handcuffs me to the bed."

"Handcuffs?" His voice was incredulous.

"Yes." She began to cry. "It's been like this ever since we got married. Whenever he goes out."

"Then how will you be able to see me?"

"He is going to the casino about eleven. I heard him reserve a seat at the *tout va* table. Come at midnight. I'll have the porter let you in."

"But—"

"Come!" she said suddenly, fiercely. "I hear him coming now. I have to hang up."

The receiver went dead in his hands. He looked down at it a moment, then replaced it on the cradle. He didn't like what was happening but her terror seemed very real.

He pulled up in front of the Hotel Negresco a few minutes after midnight. He got out of the car and stood for a few minutes hesitating, then walked a few blocks down the Promenades des Anglais to the Casino de la Méditerranée. He bought an admission card and went into the casino.

It was early in the season but already the roulette tables were jammed. He walked past the *trente-quarante* and *chemin de fer* tables. Behind the railing at the end of the large room was the *tout va* table, no-limit baccarat.

The usual crowd around the outside railing was watching the big-money players with fascination. Keeping well to the back, he peered over their heads. At least she had been telling the truth. Von Kuppen sat just to the dealer's left, staring down at the table with fierce concentration. He didn't even look up when the dealer threw two cards in front of him.

He turned and went back to the hotel and picked up a house phone and called her.

She answered in a whisper. "Room 406."

"I'll be right up."

He replaced the phone, and went to the elevator. When he got off on the fourth floor, he walked to the hall porter's desk. The hall porter silently got to his feet and led him down the corridor. In front of 406 he took out a key and opened the door.

"*Merci.*" Jeremy pressed a coin into his hand.

446

"Merci, monsieur," the porter answered expressionlessly.

He closed the door behind him and stood in the entrance to a living room. He crossed to another door on the far side and knocked.

"Jeremy?" Her voice was muffled by the door.

"Yes." He tried the door. It didn't open.

"He took the key and locked it from the outside. You'll have to get the porter back."

"That would be stupid." He was beginning to get angry. Von Kuppen must really be out of his mind. "There must be another key around somewhere."

There was, in the door to a hall closet. And with typical French frugality all the doors were fitted with the same locks. In a moment he stood in the doorway staring at her. Marlene had not been lying. A handcuff around her ankle linked her securely to the bedpost.

She lay there staring back at him, the sheet up tightly under her chin. "I look terrible," she said unexpectedly, and began to cry.

"Don't," he said harshly, crossing to the bed. "I'll get you out of here."

He tested the handcuff. It was locked, all right. "I'll have to find something to open the lock."

He went back into the other room. Behind the small bar he found an ice pick. "Slide down toward the foot of the bed, I'll need as much play in the chain as I can get."

It took him almost an hour, but finally he managed to snap the tumblers on the lock. Suddenly it sprang open. He stared down at her ankle. It was raw and bleeding. He looked at her with a new respect. She hadn't made a sound.

"Can you stand up?"

"I'll try." Marlene swung her legs off the bed and, still clutching the sheet, reached for his hand. She got to her feet, swaying slightly.

"You O.K.?"

"I'll make it." She gestured toward a closet. "My clothes are in there."

He came back with a dress and a coat. Marlene was leaning against the bedpost. "My brassiere and slip are in the top drawer."

When he brought them to her she looked at him with a wry smile. "You'll have to help me."

447

"Better sit down. It'll be easier."

Marlene sank onto the bed with a sigh of relief. She let the sheet drop, and held out her hand for the brassiere. He stared at her, shocked. Her full breasts were covered with dark bruises, and there were ugly red welts down her belly and across her back. She saw his expression. "You didn't believe me. Nobody would."

She rolled over on her stomach. He stared down at her naked buttocks. Traced across each cheek was an evenly spaced row of raw blistered circles. "He did that with a cigar."

"Last night?" he asked incredulously.

"Last night."

"But how? We heard nothing."

"He put a gag in my mouth."

"Get up," he said harshly. "I'm getting you out of here." Suddenly all his wartime hatred of the Germans came back. He felt almost sick.

It was not until they were in the car and he had automatically turned back toward the villa that she spoke.

"Where are we going?"

"I'm taking you home."

A sudden fear came into her voice. "No, you mustn't. That's the first place he'd look."

"Where else can I take you? You're going to need medical attention."

"Anywhere, just not there."

"I can't take you to another hotel; he has your passport." He glanced at the dashboard clock. It was almost two-thirty. "How late does he stay at the casino?"

"Generally until the game closes down."

"The most we have is two hours then. That doesn't give us much time to make up our minds."

He drove along silently for a few moments, then he had a sudden idea. He didn't know how it came to him or where he had seen it—maybe in the morning *Nice-Matin* that François always left beside his plate. But somewhere he had read that Dax had taken a villa at Saint-Tropez for the summer.

He sped past the Antibes turnoff and headed on up the coast road. Fervently he hoped that Dax would be there. He hadn't seen him since that time in Palm Beach more than a year ago, just before Dax and Caroline had been divorced.

"Where are we going?" she asked anxiously.
"Just around to the side." He smiled at her. "Don't worry,
everything's all right now." And for the first time that night

16

He managed to get the location of Dax's villa from the *gendarmerie*. It was out toward the end of the peninsula near Tahiti Beach, on an old narrow road over which he drove carefully and slowly. He glanced at Marlene. She seemed to be sleeping, her eyes closed. The villa was almost at the water's edge. With a sense of relief he saw lights blazing from the windows. At least he wouldn't have to wake anybody up.

A faint hum of conversation came to him from the open windows as he went up to the front door. He pulled the old-fashioned bellpull. Its loud clanging echoed in the night.

Her voice called from the car. "Where are we?"

He looked back at her. "At a friend's house."

The door opened and Fat Cat looked out. *"Quién es?"*

"It's me, Fat Cat." He moved so the light shone onto his face. "Is Mr. Xenos here?"

Fat Cat recognized him. "Señor Hadley. Come in."

A burst of laughter issued from inside the house. Jeremy hesitated, then turned so Fat Cat could see the girl in the car. "Could you ask Mr. Xenos to come out here, please?"

Fat Cat glanced at the car, then back at Jeremy. He nodded knowingly. *"De seguro, señor."*

He disappeared into the house and came back in a moment with Dax. A warm smile came over Dax's face when he saw him. "Jeremy." He held out his hand. "Why don't you come in?"

Jeremy took his hand. "I have a problem."

Then Dax, too, saw the girl in the car. He raised a quizzical eyebrow but didn't hesitate. "Drive the car around on the other side of the house. Fat Cat and I will meet you there."

With a sense of relief, Jeremy went back to the car. He got in and started the motor.

"Where are we going?" she asked anxiously.

"Just around to the side." He smiled at her. "Don't worry, everything's all right now." And for the first time that night he believed it.

It was near five that morning when Jeremy turned the little red MG into the villa on the Cap d'Antibes. He nodded to himself with satisfaction. Dax knew what he was doing. "Take my car," he'd said. "I'll return yours about noon. The police may be on the lookout for it tonight."

The house was dark and silent. He wondered how long it would be before Von Kuppen would come with the *gendarmes*. Maybe he would have time to get a little sleep. He was exhausted. He went upstairs to his room and was asleep almost before he got out of his clothes.

The sun was streaming through the windows when Tommy shook him. "Wake up."

He rolled over and sat up, rubbing his eyes. "What time is it?"

"Almost noon," his brother answered. "You been playing Sir Galahad?"

"What do you mean?" Jeremy was wide awake now.

"Von Kuppen's downstairs with a couple of *gendarmes*. He claims you kidnapped his wife last night. And Dad's blowing his cork!"

"Father's here already?"

"Half an hour ago. They both arrived almost at the same time."

He staggered out of bed and went into the bathroom. He got under the shower and turned on the cold water. The icy stream hit him, and he swung his arms about wildly until he felt the blood pumping through him, then turned off the water. "Hand me a towel, will you?"

Tommy threw him one. "You're taking this pretty calmly."

"What do you expect me to do?" he asked, rubbing himself briskly.

"I don't know. But I'd be worried if I put the snatch on some guy's wife."

"Maybe it wasn't me."

Tommy looked at him. "I'm glad you said maybe. It kind of keeps the faith."

450

Von Kuppen was at him almost before he entered the room. "What did you do with my wife?"

He stared at him coldly. "I don't know what you're talking about."

His father was watching. "Mr. Von Kuppen claims you took his wife from his hotel last night."

He looked at his father. "Did he see me with her?"

Von Kuppen turned angrily to the *gendarmes*. "I didn't have to see him. The night doorman saw her get into a Cadillac convertible. It was his car all right—they're not that common around here."

"Did he see me get into the car?"

"What does that matter? He recognized my wife. That's enough."

Jeremy smiled. "Not quite. You see, I wasn't driving the Cadillac last night."

They stared at him. Jeremy looked at the policemen. "Come outside, I can prove it."

His father fell into step beside him. "I hope you know what you're doing," he whispered.

Jeremy glanced at him. There was nothing if not complete honesty within the family. "I hope so, too."

His father didn't answer but Jeremy saw his lips tighten. The old man wouldn't be exactly happy if a scandal exploded in the family right now. Especially with Jim going into politics.

He stopped in front of the little red MG. "That's the car I was driving last night."

Von Kuppen stared at him. "It's a trick." He looked around the parking lot. The Citroën was the only other car there. "Where's the Cadillac?"

Jeremy stared at him coldly without answering.

The senior policeman spoke up. "Where is the Cadillac, *monsieur?*"

Jeremy shrugged. "I don't know."

"You don't know, *monsieur?*" The *gendarme's* voice was skeptical.

"That's right. When I went out last night I met a friend in front of the Casino de la Méditerranée. He said he'd like to try out my Cadillac for the evening so we swapped cars."

"Swapped?" The policeman's voice was puzzled.

"Exchanged. The last I saw he was driving it down the Boulevard des Anglais."

"What time was this, *monsieur?*"

He shrugged. "I don't remember exactly. Ten-thirty, eleven o'clock."

"You must know this man very well to exchange your big car for this one."

"Well, you don't swap cars with strangers."

"He's lying!" Von Kuppen shouted angrily. "Can't you see he's just playing for time?"

Jeremy's voice filled with contempt. "You're sick, you know. Has anyone ever suggested you see a psychiatrist?"

Von Kuppen flushed and took a threatening step forward. Unobtrusively the *gendarme* stepped between them. "Do you mind giving us the name of this gentleman to whom you gave your car?"

Over the policeman's shoulder Jeremy saw the Cadillac turn into the driveway. "Not at all," he said casually. "As a matter of fact, here he comes now. Monsieur Xenos. You may have heard of him?"

"We know the gentleman," the *gendarme* replied dryly. He turned as the Cadillac pulled to a stop.

Jeremy walked over. "How do you like it, Dax?"

"It's a beauty. But a little too big for the roads here, I'm afraid."

Von Kuppen was raging. "It's a plot," he shouted. "Can't you see they're in this together?"

Dax turned to stare at him. "Who is this man?"

"His name's Von Kuppen," Jeremy answered. "He thinks that—"

"Von Kuppen?" Dax interrupted. "That saves me a great deal of trouble. I was going to look him up after I returned your car."

He got out of the Cadillac and walked around to the other side. "I have a message for you from your wife."

"You see?" Von Kuppen was almost hysterical. "I told you there was a plot!"

"Plot?" Dax looked amused. "What plot?"

"Von Kuppen claims I kidnapped his wife from their hotel last night."

Dax laughed. "I'm sorry," he apologized, "I did not mean to involve you in my—er—affairs." He turned to the *gendarmes* and spoke rapidly in French. "Mrs. Von Kuppen was not kidnapped. She came with me quite willingly. She said that

452

she was through with her husband, that she had had enough of him and wanted to get away. I stopped by for her after she telephoned me."

"He's lying!" Von Kuppen shouted.

Dax took an envelope from his pocket. "Before you make any accusations you may have to answer for in a court of libel, I suggest you read this note from your wife."

Von Kuppen tore open the envelope. From where they were standing, Jeremy thought the contents looked like photographs along with a piece of note paper.

Von Kuppen's face was white. "I don't understand. I demand to see her. I must speak with her."

"She doesn't wish to see you," Dax replied. "She asks that you return her passport at once."

"But I must see her," Von Kuppen said, "she's my wife. You can't stop me from seeing her."

Dax's voice was cold. "I can and will. She's at my villa, and for your information I am Ambassador at Large of the Republic of Corteguay on a diplomatic mission to France. This automatically places my residence under diplomatic immunity." He turned to the senior *gendarme*. "Is that correct *monsieur?*"

The policeman nodded. "If it is a matter of diplomacy," he said with typical French relief at getting out of a difficult situation, "of course it is out of my jurisdiction."

Dax turned back to Von Kuppen. "In addition to the message I gave you, of which I have copies, I have also a statement from your wife sworn before a *notaire*. I also have one from her doctor, regarding her physical condition. I trust it will not be necessary to take these to court to force the return of her passport. Shall I instigate an injunction barring you from contacting her physically?"

Von Kuppen stared at him silently, then turned to Jeremy. "What did you do to her?" he asked bitterly. "We never had any trouble before you came along."

"You've got to be sick if you believe that." Jeremy turned his back and spoke to his father. "Let's go back in, Dad. I need a good breakfast."

Silently they walked back to the house, leaving Von Kuppen and the policemen in the yard. A few minutes later they heard an automobile pull out of the driveway. When the sound of the car faded, Hadley looked at Jeremy. "You did take her from the hotel, didn't you?"

"Yes."

"Why did you ever do such a damn-fool thing?"

Jeremy looked at Dax. "They were photographs, weren't they?"

Dax nodded and took another set from his pocket. Silently Jeremy handed them to his father without even looking at them. The old man opened the envelope and stared at the pictures. "My God!"

"That wasn't all, Dad. When I got to the hotel he had her handcuffed by her ankle to the bed. I said the son of a bitch was sick and I meant it."

His father looked at the two of them. "We were lucky Dax was around to bail us out of this one. I hate to think what a mess this could have turned into if he hadn't."

"Don't you think I thought of that?" Jeremy asked. "Do you honestly believe I liked the idea of prejudicing Jim's chance of going to Congress?"

"Jim's chance?" His father glared at him. "I thought you understood by now."

"Understood what?"

"Why I told you not to take other jobs offered you. It's not Jim who's going to run for Congress. It's you!"

17

Robert was reading the newspaper when Denisonde came into the small apartment, the almost empty shopping bag hanging from her hand. She stopped in the doorway. "You're home early."

He didn't take his eyes from the paper. His lips still moved as he painfully translated the Hebrew into French.

454

At last he completed the sentence and looked up. "There was nothing to do in the office. They gave me the afternoon off."

Denisonde closed the door behind her and walked into the kitchen. In the doorway she turned. "A new *France-Soir* came in the mail. I put it on the table near your bed."

"Thanks." He got to his feet, then, not wanting to appear too eager about the newspaper, asked, "How did it go with you today?"

She shrugged. "The same as usual. I'm sure the butcher understands French but he pretended not to. He made me speak Hebrew, and when all of them had had their laugh at my expense he told me he didn't have any meat anyway."

"But the new ration stamps are effective today."

"That's what I told the butcher. He said that I knew it and he knew it but somebody forgot to tell the steer."

"What did you get?"

"Potatoes and a piece of fat lamb."

"You went to the black market again?"

"Did you feel like plain boiled potatoes again?"

Robert didn't answer for a moment and when he did his voice was bitter. "Perhaps the Arabs don't want us here but they're getting rich off us."

"The Arabs aren't the only ones who don't want us here."

"It will be different now that the British have gone."

"So I've been hearing for months." Denisonde wearily pushed her hair away from her face. "Besides, it wasn't the British I was talking about."

He stared at her without answering, then turned and went into the bedroom. In a moment he came back with the newspaper in his hand. "Did you see the picture and story about Dax on the front page?"

"No." She came over and stood beside him. "What does it say?"

He read for a moment, then his face broke into a smile. "Dax never changes. It seems he kidnapped some rich German's wife from their hotel in Nice. And when the German came to get her back Dax claimed he couldn't because his villa was covered by diplomatic immunity."

"Does it give her name?"

Robert shook his head.

She turned back to the sink and ran water into a pot.

Then she took a small brush and began to scrub the potatoes.

"Why don't you peel them?"

"There are good minerals in the skins. Besides, there are only five small ones. That's all I could get."

"Oh." He sat down and buried himself in the newspaper.

They were silent while she busied herself. She cut the potatoes in quarters, the lamb into small pieces, then put it all into the pot with some greens she had been hoarding. She took one small onion from the closet, and dropped that in the pot. She stood looking at it for moment, and then opened the closet door again. The remaining onion went in with the first one. She added salt and pepper and put a cover over the pot. It wasn't exactly gourmet cooking but it was better than nothing.

"They have two whole pages on the new *couture*," Robert said without looking up. "Would you like to see them?"

"Thank you." She walked over and took the part of the paper he held out. She sat down in a chair opposite him and looked at the first page. One headline ran across the top:

LA PREMIÈRE PRÉSENTATION DE LA SAISON
Chanel, Balmain, Dior, Prince Sergei Nikovitch

The page was covered with pictures of the new clothes. She studied hungrily the poses of the models staring haughtily back at her. She closed her eyes. Paris. The time of the showings.

It was electric. No matter who you were, princess or butcher's wife, all the talk would be about the new fashions. Copies of *L'Officiel* would pass from hand to hand with oohs and aahs over each new trend, and everyone had her opinion as to whether the style would go or not. It didn't matter whether you had bought a new dress in ten years, you still had a right to an opinion. And your neighbors listened as if your name had appeared at the top of the ten-best-dressed list.

Paris was thrilling at that time of the year. The buyers would be there from all over the world. North and South America, Germany, England, Italy, even the Far East. The restaurants and theaters and clubs would be jammed.

456

How long had it been since she had been in a gay laughing group of people? The Israelis had no sense of humor. They were a grim people. Not that she blamed them. It was a grim world and making a nation was not easy. There wasn't very much to laugh about. Not for them. And when they did laugh their laughter seemed strange and empty, as if it had been torn from them reluctantly.

Denisonde turned the page and a familiar face looked up at her from the center of the sheet. She knew the girl, they had been at Madame Blanchette's together. She had always said that she would be a model. She had finally made it.

Once Denisonde had had such ambitions. It was when she had first come to Paris. But the *haute couture* houses couldn't use her. Her bust was too large; the suits didn't fall right. She had dieted madly, until there were hollows in her cheeks and large black circles under her eyes, but it didn't help. She was still too busty for *haute couture*. But finally she did manage to get a job at a lingerie house. The salary was small, and there were two showings a day, plus one in the evening.

Denisonde had been very naïve then. The buyers were all men, and she thought nothing of parading around the room clad only in a brassiere and panties. She kept her eyes impersonally on the ceiling as she opened the brassiere and took it off, then put it back on, to demonstrate its construction. And if occasionally a buyer's hand, as often happened, would linger caressingly on her breasts she merely considered it a normal hazard of the business.

And then one day after she had been there almost a week the boss had come back to the dressing room. She looked up at him from where she sat on the chair in front of the mirror. Her brassiere, the last for the evening, which she had just removed, lay on the table. She made no move to cover herself. After all, he was the boss, and he had already seen her and all the other girls more times than she could count.

"Tomorrow you get your first pay."

She nodded with satisfaction. "A week already?"

"Yes, one week."

But there was something in his voice that bothered her. "Are you satisfied with my work?"

"So far. But it's time you paid attention to the other part of your job."

"Other part of the job?" she asked, puzzled.

"Yes. There's a very important buyer here tonight. He wants you to go out with him."

Denisonde was beginning to feel like a parrot. "Go out with him?"

"You know what I mean," he said, his voice suddenly harsh. Then abruptly it softened. "It's not for nothing, you know. You get a hundred francs extra and a five-percent commission on his order."

Denisonde stared at him. It wasn't that she was shocked. Or even offended. After all, she was French and a realist. Sex was nothing new to her, but until now it had always been at her option. It was just that she was surprised because nothing had been said to her when she took the job.

"And if I don't want to go out with him?"

"There wouldn't be much point in your coming to work tomorrow. I can't afford any girl who won't do her fair share of the work."

Denisonde sat very still for a moment, then picked up her own brassiere from the chair next to her. "No, thanks. If that's the way it is I'd rather be a cocotte. I would make more money."

"You would also have to carry a police card, and you know what that means. No one would ever give you a decent job again. That's the first reference they always check out."

Denisonde didn't answer, merely picked up her skirt from the chair and stepped into it.

"You're being very foolish."

She smiled at him and reached for her blouse. "You mean I've been very foolish."

After that there had never been any question in Denisonde's mind as to her occupation. She had a shrewd mind and an agile body. It hadn't taken her long to secure a good connection with Madame Blanchette. Actually she had been recommended by an inspector of police who told her to come and see him after she got out of the jail where he'd sent her.

"You look like a nice young girl," he'd said in a kindly manner. "I'll find you a nice house to work in. It's dangerous for a young girl to be on the streets so late at night. You never know whom you might meet."

The smell of burning meat brought her out of her reverie.

She looked up, startled for a moment. Robert was asleep in the chair opposite her, the paper hanging loosely from his hand. Then she saw the pot, and she was out of her chair and to the stove. Quickly she snatched off the pot, burning her fingers, and dropped in into the sink. It turned over and the burned meat and potatoes rolled out.

She stared down in horror at the mess. Suddenly it was all too much for her. *"Merde!"* Suddenly, hopelessly, she began to cry.

"What happened?" Robert was at her shoulder. He stared into the sink. "You burned the dinner," he said accusingly.

She looked at him for a moment, the tears rolling down her cheeks, then angrily ran into the bedroom. "Yes," she shouted back over her shoulder. "I burned the fucking dinner!"

She kicked the door shut behind her and threw herself across the bed in a paroxysm of sobbing. The door opened behind her and Robert came across the room and sat down on the bed beside her. He reached over and put his hand on her shoulder.

She came up into his arms, her face buried against his chest. "Oh, Robert, I want to go home."

He sat silently, his arms tightening around her.

"Can't you see? This land is not my land, these people are not like me. I'm French, I don't belong here."

Robert still didn't speak.

She pushed herself away from him. "And you don't belong here either! You're no refugee, you didn't have to come. You're French, too. They didn't ask us to come, they don't even want us. We do nothing but take up space others need far more than we do. We even eat their food."

"You're tired," Robert said gently, "you'll feel better after you rest a little."

"I won't! What I said was the truth, and you know it. If they really needed you they would give you something more important to do than a clerk's job in a translating office. You know what they need far more than either of us? Money. Money to build with, money to buy food with, clothing. You could do more for Israel in your father's bank than here."

He stared at her. "I can't go back."

"Why not?" she demanded.

459

He didn't answer.

"Because your father is a realist and knows you have to do things you don't like to stay alive in this world?"

"It's not that."

She stared at him. "Because of me? Because I wouldn't fit into your world?"

He didn't answer.

She looked into his eyes. "You needn't worry about that. Just go home where you belong. We'll get a divorce. You won't have to be ashamed of me." The tears came back into her eyes. "Please, Robert, I can't take it any more. I want to go home."

She began to cry again. She hid her face against his chest, and after a moment she heard his voice rumbling softly in his chest.

"I love you, Denisonde. Don't cry any more, we're going home."

18

It was less than six months later and Denisonde was standing in front of the full-length three-way mirror in her room in the De Coyne town house in Paris. She looked at herself critically. Strange what a difference which side of the counter you stood on made. As a model they had told her that her bust was too large. As a client they even more effusively maintained that it was perfect for their designs. She half-smiled to herself.

The designer at Prince Nikovitch's had almost gone out of his mind. He had clapped his hand to his forehead dramatically and closed his eyes. "I see it now, a simple dark-green sheath, tight, clinging to the figure just so. The neck high, coming to a point at the base of the throat, then a bold daring *décolletage* cut out in the shape of a crescent to highlight those magnificent breasts. And a tapered skirt slit from the floor almost to the knee, *à la Chinois. Formidable!*"

He had opened his eyes and stared at her. "What do you think?"

"I don't know, I never wore green."

The dress had been everything that the designer had hoped it would be, though the final touch had come from Robert: the world-famous De Coyne emerald, a fifty-five-carat stone cut into a brilliantly faceted heart set in a framework of tiny baguetted diamonds, and suspended from a simple thin platinum chain. The emerald glowed now against the golden tones of her skin in the exact center of the *décolletage* between her breasts. Even her tawny eyes seemed to reflect its rich green.

Suddenly Denisonde was nervous. She turned from the mirror and glanced at her sister-in-law, seated on the small love seat behind her. The sounds from the party already in progress downstairs came faintly to her ears. "I don't know what's the matter with me. Suddenly I'm afraid to go down."

Caroline smiled. "You don't have to be afraid. They won't devour you."

Denisonde met Caroline's eyes evenly. "You don't understand. Some of those men have had me. What do I say when I meet them now? Or their wives?"

"To hell with them!" Caroline said. "I could tell you things that would make you seem like an innocent."

"Perhaps, but they did not do them for money."

Caroline came toward her. "Look in the mirror. Do you know what that emerald means?"

Silently Denisonde shook her head.

"My mother wore that emerald," Caroline said, "and my grandmother and her mother before her. No one ever wore it unless she was or was about to become the Baroness de Coyne. When my father gave it to Robert to give to you, that was the end of your past so far as we were concerned. And there is no one down there who doesn't know it."

Denisonde felt the tears behind her eyes. "Robert never told me that."

"Robert wouldn't. He would just take it for granted, and so will everyone else. You'll see."

"I'm going to cry."

"Don't." Caroline smiled and reached for her sister-in-law's

461

hand. "Come downstairs before you do—you'd ruin your makeup."

The baron made his way through the guests toward Denisonde. "May I have this dance, *ma fille?*"

Denisonde nodded and made her excuses. He took her hand and led her to the edge of the small dance floor. The orchestra broke into a slow waltz as they moved out on the floor.

The baron smiled as she came into his arms. "You see? I have them well trained. They show respect for my age."

She laughed. "In that case they should play the American lindy hop."

"No, not any more." He looked into her eyes. "Are you enjoying the party?"

"Very much, it's like a dream. I never knew the world could be like this." She kissed his cheek. "Thank you, *mon père.*"

"Don't thank me, it was you who made it possible. You returned my son to me." He hesitated. "Is Robert all right?"

She met his eyes. "You mean the drugs?"

He nodded.

"Yes," she said, "it is over. It was not easy for Robert. He was very sick for a long time but now it is over."

"I am glad. That is yet another thing I have you to thank for."

"Not me, the Israelis. They are very strict about such things. They made him get well."

They were near the entrance to the library, and the baron led her from the floor. "Come in, I have something to give you."

Curiously Denisonde followed him through the door. There was a fire burning in the fireplace. He opened a drawer in the desk and took out some papers and handed them to her. "These are yours."

Denisonde looked down. They were all there—the police cards, the medical certificates, the record of her arrests. She looked up, bewildered. "How did you get these?"

"I bought them," he said. "Now, so far as the records are concerned, your name has never appeared anywhere."

"But why?" she asked. "They must have been very expensive."

Without answering he took the papers from her hand and

462

walked over to the fireplace. He dropped them into the flames, and they began to burn brightly.

"I wanted you to see that," he said, turning to her. "That Denisonde is gone forever."

She looked into the fireplace, then back at him. "Is she?" she asked. "Then who is left? Who am I?"

"My daughter-in-law," he answered quietly. "Robert's wife, of whom I am very proud."

Robert came down the corridor and walked into his father's office. "It's not worth it."

His father looked up. "What makes you say that?"

"I was there," Robert replied heatedly. "Have you forgotten I lived in that country? As important as the project is, Israel will never be able to pay for an irrigation pipeline across the desert. Not in a hundred years. We'll never see our money out of it."

A strange expression crossed his father's face. "But you do agree that such a project is possible?"

"Oui."

"And necessary?"

"Of course, I do not dispute that. What I am questioning is the economics."

"Sometimes it is good banking to invest in things that do not show an immediate profit," the baron said. "That is one of the responsibilities of wealth. To make certain that some benefits for all result from it."

Robert stared at his father curiously. "Doesn't that reflect a rather broad change in your attitude?"

His father smiled. "As much probably as your objections reflect one in yours."

"But this responsibility you have to the rest of the family," Robert persisted. "Was that not the reason you gave for saving the Von Kuppen works?"

The baron got to his feet. "It is part of the same thing. If we had not done what we did someone else would have reaped the benefit. It is the money we made from saving Von Kuppen that makes this possible."

Robert was silent for a moment. "Does it mean then that you are not interested in making money on this project?"

"I didn't say that," his father answered quickly. "As a

banker I must always be interested in profit. But profit alone is not the major motive here."

"But you would accept a profit if I could show you how one could be realized?"

"Of course." The baron sat down again. "Exactly what do you have in mind?"

"The Campion-Israeli Steamship Company. We are about to turn down their request for underwriting because Marcel is greedy and wants to keep all the profits."

"That's right," the baron said. "Our good friend Marcel wants to gobble up everything in sight. In a little more than a year he has got his hands on almost as many ships as his father-in-law owns, more certainly than any of the Greek interests. But his ships are so heavily cross-collateralized that I am afraid any new acquisition might be the one to bring the lot tumbling down."

"But if the profits from the Israeli line were not funneled back into his other companies, might not that be enough to carry the operating deficit on the pipeline?"

His father looked thoughtful. "It might, though the margin would be a very narrow one."

"If we tied the two projects into one and loaned Israel the money at, say, one-half of one percent, instead of the usual five, six or even seven, would that carry them both?"

"That would do it."

Robert smiled.

His father looked up at him. "But what if Marcel won't go for it? Chances are there wouldn't be any profit if he were forced to carry more than his share."

"We can ask him," Robert said. "If he wants the ships as badly as you think he does, he'll go for it. Will anyone else be more eager to underwrite him than we are?"

The baron looked at his son with a new respect. It was basically a sound idea, and if it worked there would be much benefit in it for Israel. "Marcel is in New York," he said, "perhaps you could go there and talk with him."

"Good. I think Denisonde would like that. She's never been there."

The baron watched the door close behind his son. Idly he picked up a sheet of paper and studied it, but his mind refused to concentrate. He was getting old. When he was younger, even a matter of a few years ago, he would never have overlooked such a possibility. Perhaps it was time for him to think about retirement.

It wasn't so much that he was tired. It was just that he had carried the burden long enough. Or possibly it was just that he hadn't been ready to step aside until he was certain someone was capable of carrying on for him. As he had for his father.

19

The crowd began to cheer almost before the long black limousine rolled to a stop beside the flag-draped platform. Quickly a man in uniform, a captain, leaped forward to open the door. There was a glimpse of a silk-clad knee, then the sun glinted brilliantly in the soft gold of her hair as Amparo got out.

The crowd went wild. *"La princesa! La princesa!"*

Amparo stood there for a moment, almost shyly, then smiled at them. A little girl ran up to her and thrust a bouquet into her hand. Quickly she bent and kissed the child, her lips barely moving in a whispered *"Mil gracias."* Then she was surrounded by officials and escorted up to the platform, where she took up her position in front of the battery of microphones. She waited patiently until the photographers had stopped taking pictures and the shouts from the crowd began to die down. When she finally spoke, her voice was low and soft and warm, so that it seemed as if she whispered to each of them alone.

"My children. *Campesinos.*"

Again they began to scream with delight. For was she not one of them? Had not her father come down from the hills to assume his exalted position? And did she not concern herself continually with the peasants and workers, the ordinary people? It was she who saw to it that there were schools for their children, hospitals for their sick, food for those no longer able to work, and care and respect for the aged.

Even now she stood in front of the magnificent building, white and gleaming, which had given so many of them employment during its construction and would provide a means of livelihood for many more during its operation. But even more, the land on which this magnificent new hotel stood, which belonged to her and for which she could collect rent for a thousand years, she had also given to them. It was little enough honor for the one who had done all this, who had given them so much, to have the new hotel named after her. La Princesa.

Amparo held up her hand, and the cheering died away again. She looked down at them, her eyes not even blinking in the harsh hot sunlight. The microphone amplified her low husky voice into a roaring intimate whisper.

"This is a day of which all of us can be proud. A day of which all Corteguay can be proud. It is a day that marks a new beginning of prosperity for our beloved land."

They began to cheer again but her hand stopped them.

"I am here before you only as a symbol. A symbol of the true humility and great modesty of my beloved father, whose work and concern for his people does not permit him to leave his labors for their behalf."

This time she let them roar.

"El Presidente! El Presidente! El Presidente!"

When the sound had faded she began again.

"Tomorrow this hotel will be open. Tomorrow three great airplanes from the United States will land at our airport, and a great ship will drop its anchor in our harbor. Each will be filled with visitors from the countries to the north. They are coming to enjoy the wonders and beauties of our country. It is for us to say to them, *'Bienvenido,'* welcome.

"It is these same *turistas* who have brought wealth to our neighbors, Cuba and Panama. Now they are bringing their wealth to us, so we must share our wealth with them. The happiness of each is a sacred duty. We want them to carry home the message of the beauty and kindness of our beloved land and its peoples.

"We must demonstrate that our beloved country, Corteguay, is a glorious land. A country ready to take its membership in the community of the world."

466

The crowd began to cheer again. Its roar of approval reached up to her. She smiled again and held up her hand. "That is tomorrow—tomorrow it will be open to them. But today it is for us. Today all of us, all of you, can enter and see the marvels you have made possible because of the faith and trust my father has in his people."

Her voice faded and she turned to the bright sparkling ribbon across the entrance behind her. Someone handed her a scissors. It shone briefly in the sunlight as she held it aloft. Then suddenly she lowered it and the ribbon fell fluttering to the ground. With a roar the crowd surged forward through the entrance of the hotel. It jammed up the opening until the two lines of soldiers pushed it into an orderly procession.

Dax stood on the platform watching until the dignitaries and officials had made their polite thanks, then he went over to Amparo. She was alone, except for the soldiers, her bodyguards, who were always nearby. She looked thoughtfully down into the pushing crowd.

"You were very good," he said quietly at her elbow. "Very good."

A quick polite smile came to her lips as she turned, then she recognized him and the smile changed. It became warm and personal. "Dax! I didn't know you were here."

He bowed over her hand, kissing it. "I got in last night." He straightened up. "You were very good."

"I should be, I've had enough practice."

He glanced toward the hotel. "Are you going inside?"

"With that mob?" she asked. "I'm not that crazy. I can't stand them. It's a good thing we have soldiers stationed there or they would tear the place apart. They have no appreciation for anything."

"You haven't changed," he said, looking at her. "At least you're honest."

"Why should I change? Do you change?"

"I like to think so. I grow older. Wiser."

"No one ever changes," she said positively, "they only think they do. We're still the same people we were when we scratched our way down from the hills."

"You sound bitter."

"I'm not bitter, I'm just realistic. Women are more hard-headed than men. New airports, new roads, and new buildings don't impress us."

467

"What does impress you?"

"You."

"Me?" His surprise was reflected in his voice.

"Yes. You escaped. You got out. To you the whole world is not just Corteguay." She frowned suddenly. "I need a drink. I have a headache from squinting into that damned sun."

"The bar is open inside the hotel."

"No, come back to the palace with me. It will be more comfortable there." She hesitated. "Unless you have something better to do."

"No, *Princesa*." He smiled. "I have nothing better to do."

It was hot in the car, and he leaned forward to roll down the window. Her hand stopped him. "No, not until we're out of the crowds. There are still wolves around us."

Dax leaned back thoughtfully. Perhaps she was right. People did not change.

The face of the slim young man leaning against the speakers' platform offered no clue to his thoughts as he watched the big black limousine turn and make its way slowly through the crowds.

I could have killed them, he was thinking, just now as they walked in front of me and the soldiers were looking the other way. I could have killed them the way they killed my father. Without mercy. From ambush.

He straightened up and put his hand inside his jacket, and feeling the gun in his belt gave him comfort. Quickly he took his hand away and put it in his pocket lest it betray him. Still lost in his thoughts, he joined the crowds pushing their way into the hotel.

But what good would killing them have done me? None at all, he thought. The soldiers would have killed me, and all I came back to do would remain undone. *El Presidente* would go on forever. It was not for this I went away to school across the sea.

He paused in the doorway and looked back over his shoulder at the hills. Tomorrow I will begin my journey home. To the land of my father, to my father's people. They will listen to my message. They will discover that they are not alone, that we are not alone, and they will believe. When the guns come will be time enough for the murderers of my father to die. And they will know it is the son of *el Condor* who is their executioner.

He was too busy with his own thoughts to notice the two men fall into step behind him. When he did notice, it was already too late. They had him.

"The *comunistas!*" El Presidente spat on the marble floor. "It is they who are behind this new trouble in the hills. They are sending in guns, money, and *guerrilleros*. There is not a night that passes that another of them does not slip across our borders."

"If we had solved the problems of the *bandoleros* earlier we would not have had to worry now."

"Dax, you are being stupid! Do you think that alone is the answer? I wish it were. But not any more; the disease has spread throughout the world. It is not our country alone. It is Brazil, Argentina, Cuba. In Asia it is Vietnam, Korea—"

"A truce has been in effect in Korea for almost a year now," Dax said. "Both the United States and Russia have withdrawn their troops."

"I have not the advantage of your worldwide knowledge," *el Presidente* answered sarcastically. "But I know enough about the uses of power to understand that the Korean truce will not survive the summer. How long do you think the North Koreans will continue to sit and allow their southern brothers to grow rich and fat in the valleys below the thirty-eighth parallel while they starve in the mountains?"

Dax did not answer.

"Just this afternoon my police picked up a young man who has returned to this country after attending a school in Russia. He was less than three feet away from Amparo while she was making her speech. They found a gun in his belt. He had been sent there to assassinate her."

"Yet he did not fire," Dax replied. "Why?"

"Who knows? Perhaps he got buck fever, possibly he was afraid he would be killed first. There could be a thousand reasons."

"What will happen to the young man?"

"He will be tried," *el Presidente* said. "If he cooperates and gives us information he will live. If not . . ."

He turned and went back to his desk. "In three weeks our application for membership in the United Nations comes up again. This time it will be approved. The Western powers can no longer hold it against us that we remained neutral throughout the war. All of us now face a common enemy."

"It will not be that easy. Russia still has a veto."

"When war comes in Korea," *el Presidente* continued, "Russia will not dare exercise that veto in the face of world opinion. It is then we must be ready. You must let the United Nations know we are ready to pledge three battalions to their service." He picked up a sheet of paper and handed it to Dax. "Meanwhile, here is your commission as a *coronel* in the army."

Dax stared at the paper. "Just what is this for?"

El Presidente smiled. "I am sending Amparo on a visit to the United States. A—what do you call it?—a good-will mission? You are to be in charge of it."

"I still see no reason for the commission."

A wise grin spread over the old man's face. "There is nothing like a uniform to make a woman appear more feminine and fragile."

20

"La princesa called twice while you were out," Fat Cat said, "she wishes to see you right away."

"Did she say what she had on her mind?"

Fat Cat shrugged. "No. The usual thing, I imagine."

Dax frowned as he shrugged out of his military tunic. It had been like this the entire trip. Amparo demanded constant attention. He started to remove his tie. "Was the correspondent from the London *Times* here?"

"He left almost an hour ago. Amparo began phoning almost the instant he left."

"Call her back and tell her I'll see her as soon as I shower." Dax pulled off his shirt. He walked into the bedroom and stripped down the rest of the way.

He let the hot water play over his body. Slowly he felt the tensions ease. The Southern congressman who was so influential on the Foreign Affairs Committee had not been the easiest person in the world to get along with. If it were not for the help of Jeremy Hadley it might have proved impossible.

But Jeremy had a way with him, an open kind of ingenuousness that belied the shrewd political turn of his mind. Gently, ever so gently, he had managed to get across that the privileges currently enjoyed in Corteguay by the Texas oil syndicate could as easily be revoked. He was certain that this would not happen, of course, but no one could really tell. Corteguay was the only country in South America that hadn't made demands on the United States foreign-aid program. Whatever they had accomplished had been wholly on their own, and that made them very independent.

The Southerner had been no fool. He got the message. Besides, he liked the idea that Corteguay had no demands to make on the United States. It was very refreshing, he said, to find a country that chose to stand on its own feet in the great tradition of the Americas. Dax was sure that in the back of the congressman's mind was the tremendous campaign contributions he had already received or been promised by friends in the Texas oil syndicate. At any rate, the meeting had concluded most satisfactorily. The congressman would recommend most strongly to the State Department that the United States favor Corteguay's application.

Dax was so absorbed in his thoughts that he failed to hear the bathroom door open. He was not aware that Amparo had come into the room until he heard her voice.

"What are you doing in there?" she demanded angrily.

"Taking a shower," he called sarcastically through the opaque glass shower doors. "What the hell did you think I was doing?"

"In the middle of the afternoon?"

"What's wrong with that?"

"You've been with a woman," she said accusingly, "that German girl."

"Don't be ridiculous."

471

"I saw the way she was looking at you at lunch."

Angrily he turned off the water. There was no point in explaining to Amparo that Marlene had actually been with Jeremy Hadley. "Stop behaving like a jealous *campesino*. There are reasons other than fornication for bathing in the afternoon. This is the United States; water is plentiful here."

He pushed open the glass door and stuck his hand out, groping for a towel. He found one on the rack and wrapped it around him, then stepped out of the shower.

Amparo was standing in the doorway watching him. Silently he took another towel and began to dry himself. Glancing in the mirror, he could see the anger fading from her eyes.

"Did the interview go well?"

"I guess so, but you should have been with me. I never feel right with reporters when I'm alone. They seem so ... superior."

"All newspapermen seem that way. I think it's an act. To make you think they know more than they do."

"What were you doing?"

"I had that meeting with the American congressman. You knew about it."

"It went well?"

"It went well."

She was silent for a moment. "I would like a drink."

He met her eyes in the mirror. "Ask Fat Cat, he'll make you whatever you want."

"What was it we had before lunch?" she asked. "That cocktail. I liked it."

"A dry martini."

"It was good. These *gringos* know how to make good drinks. They do not merely swill straight raw rum."

"Watch out for them, they are very potent. They sneak up on you and cloud your mind and loosen your tongue."

"I had three at lunch," she said. "They didn't bother me. I just felt good."

Amparo turned and walked away. Silently Dax finished drying himself, then, pulling on a robe, went through the bedroom into the living room of his suite. Amparo was standing by the window, a martini in her hand, looking down at Park Avenue.

She turned. "There are so many of them."

472

He nodded. "This city alone has three times the population of all Corteguay."

"They live and work together. There is no war here, no *bandoleros* in the mountains."

"Not in our sense, but they have their problems. Their criminals are social, not political."

Amparo turned back to the window. "Everyone here has automobiles, even the poorest." She finished her drink. "Not even Mexico, which I thought very wealthy, was like this. It is a very rich country. Now I am beginning to understand what my father means when he says we have a long way to go."

Dax didn't answer.

She turned. "May I have another of these martinis?"

"I am your escort," he said, "not your *dueña.*"

He waited until Fat Cat had brought her another and then said, "Don't drink too much, we have an important dinner tonight. It would not create a good impression if you were to fall asleep in the middle of it."

"I won't fall asleep," she replied angrily. Her face was slightly flushed.

"I am going to take a little *siesta.* I suggest you do the same. It will be a long, late night."

"I'm not sleepy."

"Suit yourself. If your highness will excuse me?"

"You don't have to be sarcastic," she said, following him through the bedroom door.

He sat down on the edge of the bed. "I'm not being sarcastic. I'm just tired."

She watched as he stretched out on the bed. She took another sip of her drink. "You were with that German woman this afternoon!"

He smiled up at her. "See? I warned you about the drink. Already it is making your tongue foolish."

"I am not foolish!" She stood over the bed looking down at him. Her face was quite flushed now. "I know about you. If you had not already been with a woman you would not allow me to stand here like this!"

He put his arms behind his head. "What do you know about me?"

"You forget I see all the foreign newspapers. They are not like the papers in Corteguay, which are not allowed

473

to print anything bad about you. You have been involved with many women."

"So?"

Unexpectedly Amparo felt the tears come to her eyes, and she became even angrier. "Am I not a woman?" she demanded. "Is there something the matter with me?"

He laughed aloud. "You are very much a woman. There is nothing the matter with you. But—"

"But what?"

"Your father has entrusted you to my care. It is a question of honor. How do you think he would feel if he were to learn that I betrayed that trust?"

"You are not smiling when you say that? You are serious?"

"Yes."

Suddenly she began to laugh. "My father is right, you are the best diplomat Corteguay ever had."

"What do you mean?"

She looked down at him. "You know damn well what I mean! Why do you think my father threw us together on this trip if not in the hope that we would become involved?"

Dax didn't answer. For the first time he thought about it. It was exactly what the devious old *bandolero* might do. The direct approach would always be too simple for him.

"It is over between us," Dax said, "he knows that."

She stared at him. "That is really the reason, isn't it? You have never forgiven me for what happened."

"There was nothing to forgive."

"It was not my idea to deceive you; my father insisted. I wanted to tell you."

"It doesn't matter."

"It does matter," she insisted, "now. Then it didn't." Abruptly she finished her drink. "It always was you. But I was young then, and you were never there. So I fell in love with a man who reminded me of you, and my father had him murdered. After you left there was nothing, no one. When I learned of your marriage I cried all night."

"You don't have to tell me all this."

"I have to tell you," she replied, almost harshly. "How long must I be punished? How long must I bear the pain of your thinking that I tried to deceive you?"

He didn't answer.

She sank to her knees beside the bed. Putting the empty

474

cocktail glass on the floor, she pulled his robe away. He felt her tiny hot kisses on the soft flesh of his underbelly, and the power flooded into his genitals. She captured his surging phallus; her sharp teeth scraped him, and her tongue laved him.

Abruptly he sank his hands into her hair and twisted her face up to him. "Amparo"—his voice was harsh, his eyes searching—"it is not the *gringo* liquor in you?"

She looked at him almost shyly. "It is not the liquor," she answered in a low voice, "nor is it my father. This is for me. He will never know."

He still held her in his firm grip, his eyes demanding the truth.

"A few minutes ago you said it was over between us," she whispered, "but you were wrong. It never began." She pulled his hand from her cheek and buried her lips in its palm. He scarcely felt the movement of her lips. "Now it begins."

21

Marcel picked up the telephone on his desk, and the secretary in his office downtown answered immediately. "Anything special this morning?" he asked.

"No, Mr. Campion. I kept the morning free as you suggested."

"Good. I should be at the office before lunch."

"If anything comes up can I reach you at Mr. Schacter's office?"

"No, I don't want to be disturbed there."

Marcel put down the telephone and went out through the private side entrance where his car and chauffeur were waiting. He paused for a moment and looked back at the gray stone building. A glow of pride came over him. It was one of the last decent town houses on Park Avenue. And a corner, too.

Fortunately it was not large enough to house an embassy or the price would have been prohibitive. Still, it was more than large enough for him. Thirteen rooms. The agent had laughed embarrassedly. "Some people think it's an unlucky number."

Marcel had laughed, remembering all the gamblers who had fetishes about the number. One number had been the same as any other for him. The house did just as well on the lucky numbers as it did on the unlucky ones. "I don't mind. I'm not superstitious."

The deal had been made, and he had moved in even before the workmen had finished the renovation. He couldn't wait to get out of the hotel to which he had moved after his separation from his wife. He had the feeling that too much about his private affairs filtered back to her and her father. Hotel employees were very susceptible to bribes.

Another thing he liked was the private entrance. Through it he could go directly up to his quarters, if he so desired, without passing through the rest of the house. This was most useful when he didn't particularly care to have his servants know his comings and goings, or the identity of certain of his guests.

Marcel had no illusions about himself. He had not suddenly become more attractive merely because his name was constantly in the newspapers. It was the money, purely and simply. It was amazing how attractive that made him.

Anna, her father, and their lawyers were already waiting for him when he arrived at his attorney's office. "Good morning," he said pleasantly.

Anna didn't answer, she merely stared, a sullen look on her face that accentuated the shadow on her upper lip, which persisted despite the elaborate and expensive electrolysis. Amos Abidijan grunted some indistinguishable answer. Their two attorneys shook hands and Marcel sat down.

He glanced at his attorney questioningly. Schacter cleared his throat. "I thought it best to wait until you came."

Marcel nodded. "Thank you."

"We'll begin then." Schacter turned to the others and cleared his throat. This was old routine to him. Rich people and their divorces. Money was always the great complication. No matter how much there was, there was never enough for two. One or the other always felt he or she had to have the lion's share.

"Ordinarily I would try to effect a reconciliation," he said smoothly, "but we all are agreed that matters have progressed

476

beyond a point where any such attempt would be practical."

He waited for a moment, then continued. "What we are faced with then is the best way to reach an agreement between both parties to a divorce which will have the least possible bad effects on the children involved. To that end my client, because of his love for the children, is willing to agree to any reasonable determination we can work out. He has no desire to see the children involved in a long disputed court action."

"There is nothing your client could do that would involve the children," one of the other attorneys said quickly. "There is no question that Mrs. Campion has been an exemplary wife and mother."

Schacter smiled agreeably. "We do not dispute that here. However, in a court we should be forced to act in quite another manner, regardless of our personal feelings. You understand that."

Amos Abidijan couldn't remain silent. "What about the money he owes me?"

"What money? So far as I know my client owes you no money."

"It was my money he used to found his business. We were working together on the deal, and he stole it."

"That's not true," Marcel replied quickly, "you know very well that you turned me down on the proposal. It was you who suggested I look elsewhere for financing. You didn't want any part of it."

"Gentlemen." Schacter held up his hands. "Please, one thing at a time. This is not the subject under discussion at the moment."

"You can't separate them," Abidijan replied angrily. "He used my daughter. He used me. Now he thinks he can throw her over because he has what he wanted. We'll agree to nothing until that question is settled."

"In other words, Mr. Abidijan," Schacter said smoothly, "a divorce between your daughter and Mr. Campion is contingent entirely upon a financial agreement with you?"

"I didn't say that! I'm only interested in seeing that my daughter and grandchildren are amply protected. I don't want anything for myself."

"Then you would have no objections if a settlement was worked out for their benefit exclusively?"

"I would have no objections," Abidijan replied stiffly.

"Neither would we," Schacter said quickly. "Now, since we are agreed in principle we can proceed to actualities. Do you have any suggestion as to what you would consider an equitable settlement?"

"It's very simple," Abidijan said before his attorneys could answer. "An outright settlement of five million dollars to cover past indebtednesses, and a division of all properties after that fifty-fifty."

Marcel got to his feet. He was not surprised at the demand. But it was stupid and Amos should have known it was. He did not have that kind of money and even if he had he would never agree to it. He looked down at his father-in-law. "Amos," he said quietly, "you've gone completely senile." He turned to Anna. "I suggest before we meet again that you have a guardian appointed for your father."

Anna stared back at him. There was a thin white line of tension around her mouth. "It isn't my father who has gone mad but you with your desire for money and power. What do you think all those women who are hanging around you want? You're not that handsome. What are you trying to prove?"

Marcel turned to his attorney. "I told you a meeting would be useless. I will file suit in Corteguay as originally planned."

"It would not be recognized here," one of her attorneys said quickly.

"I think it will," Schacter replied quietly. "You see, my client is a citizen of Corteguay, and under their laws so are his wife and children. Our laws are quite specific on that point. Any divorce, if valid in the country of the participants, is valid here."

"Mrs. Campion is an American citizen."

"Not according to the laws of Corteguay," Schacter replied smoothly, "and I'm willing to dispute that in court with you after my client has obtained the divorce."

Abidijan looked at his attorneys. This was something he hadn't expected. And he was familiar enough with laws of other countries through his shipping business to know that anything was possible. "I would like to speak privately with you."

Schacter got to his feet. "Don't move," he said. "My client and I will go into another office."

478

Marcel looked at Schacter as the door closed behind them. "What do you think?"

Schacter nodded confidently. "We got them. I just hope the information you gave me about Corteguayan law is correct."

Marcel smiled. "If it's not, he said, "I'm sure I can arrange the necessary legislation. And that would be much less expensive than Amos' demands."

22

"I'll go to Paris for my wedding gown," Amparo said, "and from there Dax and I will go on a grand tour of Europe."

"You are not going anywhere," *el Presidente* replied quietly, "you are staying here. Your gown will be made locally as your mother's was."

Amparo walked over to the front of his desk and stared down at him. "What gown of my mother's?" she asked sarcastically. "You were never married."

"That has nothing to do with it; your mother never went to Paris for a gown."

"How could she?" Amparo retorted. "You were even afraid to let her out of the house for fear she might leave you."

El Presidente got to his feet. "You will call in a dressmaker; you will remain here. There is much for you to do—"

"I have done enough already! Now I want to see what the rest of the world is like. I don't have to stay here and wallow in the filth along with the *campesinos*."

"Don't forget that you owe your exalted position to the *campesinos!*" the old man roared. "Who gave you the name *la princesa?* They did. Who set you up as an example to Corteguayan women? The *campesinos*."

"So I must spend the rest of my life being eternally grateful to them?"

"Exactly. You do not belong to yourself, you belong to the people."

479

"I might as well be in prison." Suddenly a new thought struck her. "You mean I am to remain here while my husband goes gallivanting all over the world?"

El Presidente nodded. "He has his job to do just as you have yours."

Amparo began to laugh. "You must be out of your mind. You know what kind of man he is; women won't leave him alone. At a party in New York, out of the twelve women there he had been to bed with eleven of them."

El Presidente was suddenly curious. "He told you that?"

"Of course not, but I am no fool. I can tell from the way a woman acts whether she has been to bed with a particular man."

El Presidente was thoughtful for a moment. "The twelfth woman—what was she like?"

Amparo stared at him. "Too old, much too old."

"You're a fool," he said, "the marriage will be good for you. You know how the people feel about Dax. They worship him. Just as they do you."

"It will be no good," she said darkly. "Not for him nor for me. We're too much alike. We're physical people."

"Don't talk like that!" he shouted, angry again. "Remember, you're a lady."

She glared at him. "How can I be with your blood in me? Look at you. At your age most men would be glad to sit down in the evening with a cigar and a brandy. But no, you must have a new woman every week."

He glared back. "Men are different."

"You think so?" she taunted. "What makes you think I am not my mother all over again? And you know how she was."

He was suddenly silent. After a moment, he said, "I would have married her if she had lived."

"I don't believe you. If she had lived she would have fared no better than all the others. You would have tired of her and thrown her out."

He thought for a moment. "I have changed my mind. You will be married within the week, and Dax will not go to Paris. Instead I shall send him to Korea with the battalions I have promised the United Nations."

Amparo jumped to her feet angrily. "He will be killed. He is no soldier."

"He will be perfectly safe," *el Presidente* replied. "Colonels never get killed, they remain safely behind the lines at their headquarters. At least then you won't have to worry about him. There are no attractive women there."

"If there are, he will find them," Amparo said sullenly. Then she noticed the look on his face. "You would like to see him killed, wouldn't you? He has become too popular."

El Presidente met her eyes steadily. "How can you say that? Dax is like my own son."

"You are some father," she said sarcastically. "It is not enough to marry him off to me; no, that might make him even more popular. So you send him off to get killed."

El Presidente ignored her accusations as if he hadn't heard them. He glanced at his watch. "Come, it is time for us to get dressed. The ceremonies are due to begin at three o'clock."

"We are a big-shot country now. The people must see how important we are to the *Naciones Unidos*."

"We are important. The Secretary General does not visit each new nation when it is admitted."

"It is not the Secretary General who is coming, it is only his assistant."

"What difference does that make?" he retorted. "The *campesinos* will not know the difference."

Amparo got to her feet. "I need a drink, my mouth feels dirty."

"It is too early in the day for you to drink. It is not yet noon."

"Then I will not drink rum," she answered lightly. "I will drink a *norteamericano* drink called a martini. It is one o'clock in New York."

El Presidente watched as she walked to the door. He spoke just before she opened it. "Amparo?"

She looked back at him. "Yes, Father."

He was silent for a moment, staring into her eyes. "Trust me."

Amparo's head rose as if she were thinking about what he had said. Then she answered but there was a kind of hopelessness in her voice. "How can I, when I dare not even trust myself?"

A man shuffled along the crowded streets, his worn dark suit hanging loosely on his emaciated frame. He kept his face

481

averted, his eyes looking downward toward the ground, for they were not yet accustomed to the bright sun of day after the many months in the tiny dark cell. He moved awkwardly in a kind of old man's shuffle because the broken leg had not set evenly, and he kept his right hand in his pocket to hide the ugly, twisted, broken fingers that were too repulsive for even his own eyes.

A passerby bumped into him and he apologized, revealing a mouth empty of teeth. The guards had knocked them out savagely with their rifle butts. He saw the expression on the passerby's face and quickly he averted his face again. Moving aimlessly he allowed himself to be caught up in the flow of the crowd and carried along.

He was free, though he didn't quite believe it yet. It had all come too suddenly, too unexpectedly. Just that morning the heavy steel door to his cell had opened. He had been lying on the small heap of rags that constituted his bed, and instinctively he had tried to make himself smaller as he peered up at the guard. Dully he had wondered what they were going to do with him now.

A small bundle had thumped to the floor beside him. "There are your clothes. Put them on."

He didn't move, wondering what trickery they were up to now. Brutally the guard kicked him. "You heard me, get dressed!"

Slowly, on his hands and knees, he crawled over to the bundle. He couldn't undo the knots in the string because of his maimed right hand. The guard swore and bent over. A knife flashed and the cord fell apart.

Trembling, he picked up the pants and studied them. They were not his; his suit had been new when they brought him in. These were old and faded and dirty and torn. He looked up at the guard.

"Hurry up! I haven't got all day."

As quickly as he could he got into the clothes. At last he was dressed. The guard grabbed him by the shoulder and pushed him toward the door. "Outside!"

He half stumbled through into the corridor, and stood there waiting until the guard had locked the cell door. He had difficulty keeping up as they marched down the cell block.

Purposely he kept his mind blank until they had passed the

stairway that led to the subterranean interrogation rooms. Only then did he allow himself to speculate about where they were going. At least there was to be no torture this time. Somehow the possibility that they might be taking him to his execution did not disturb him. Death seemed preferable to the room downstairs.

They passed through the steel door at the end of the cell block and turned down the corridor. Silently he followed the guard into the office of the warden.

A burly sergeant major looked up as they came in. "Is he the last?"

"*Sí.*"

"*Bueno.*" The sergeant looked at him, his face cold and impassive, then down at the sheet of paper on the desk. "You are prisoner 10,614, otherwise known as José Montez?"

"*Sí, excelencia,*" he mumbled.

The sergeant major pushed the paper toward him. "Sign this."

He tried to pick up the pen. But the fingers of his right hand were of no use to him. He looked at the sergeant major questioningly.

"Use your left hand, make a mark. You probably can't write anyway."

Silently José picked up the pen and made a cross at the bottom. The sergeant major picked up the sheet of paper and studied it. He nodded and cleared his throat. The short speech sounded as if it had been learned by rote.

"In accordance with the wishes and the kindly beneficence of *el Presidente,* you hereby are granted amnesty for your political crimes in honor of the occasion of our acceptance this day into the United Nations. You are hereby released on your honor upon signing a written pledge of loyalty to the government. You hereby solemnly swear that you will no longer indulge in acts against the government under the penalty of the forfeit of your life."

The sergeant major looked at the guard. "Escort him to the front gate."

He stood there dully, uncomprehending, until one of the other guards shoved him. Then he began to understand. He was being freed.

"*Gracias, excelencia.*" Unexpectedly the tears began to come to his eyes and he tried to blink them away. "*Gracias.*"

The guard shoved him again, and he followed him down the corridor and out into the huge courtyard. The harsh sun burned into his eyes. Not until then did he remember the hat he still had in his hand and he jammed it down on his head so the brim would shield his eyes.

They crossed the courtyard and stopped in front of the huge steel gate. "This is the last," the guard yelled up to the man in the tower.

"It is about time. It is not easy opening and closing this fucking gate."

Slowly and with much creaking it rose up into the tower. José stood there watching but even when the gate was completely open he did not move.

The guard pushed him again. *"Vaya!"*

He turned to look at the guard.

The guard laughed. "He doesn't want to leave us. He likes us," he called up to the tower.

The man in the tower laughed. The guard gave José another shove and spun him halfway through the gate. *"Vaya! I have not got all day."*

He stood there on the outer side of the opening, staring as the huge gate lowered. Finally it settled into the ground with a loud clang, but still he stood there.

"Vaya!" the guard shouted. *"Vaya!"* He made a threatening gesture with his carbine.

José turned suddenly and broke into an awkward run. He moved desperately, clumsily, the sudden fear of a bullet in his back almost choking him. The burst of laughter from the guards followed along behind him.

He ran until he could no longer hear their laughter, until the breath was rasping in his throat and he was spent. Then he sank into the shade at the base of a building, slumped against the cool stone. There was nothing but the frightened beating of his heart sounding in his ears. He closed his eyes and rested. After a while he got to his feet and began to walk.

There was an air of gay fiesta about the city. Everywhere flags were flying. Corteguayan flags and the banners of the United Nations, side by side. And in every other window was a picture of *el Presidente,* smiling and resplendent in his bemedaled uniform. But José felt no part of it. He merely drifted with the flow of the crowd. Soon they were in the

484

great square in the center of the city in front of the *Palacio del Presidente*.

The people were screaming as he came to an abrupt stop. There was no longer room for him to move. He looked up and a sudden cold chill came into him. He could taste the bitter bile of hatred rising up into his throat. The two of them were there on the balcony in front of him.

El Presidente, his medals glistening in the sun, and his whore-bitch daughter, her blond hair giving the lie to her birth. Next to her stood a man he did not know, a Negro but a *gringo* by the cut of his clothes. Beside him stood Amparo's smiling, deceitful fiancé, awkward in the new uniform tunic of a colonel.

I should have killed them when I had the chance, he thought bitterly. Now, if I had the gun . . . but even now what good would it do me? The hand that cannot grasp even a pen could not hold a gun, much less aim it and pull the trigger.

He turned and began to push his way through the crowd. Someday he would kill them, though. He would learn to use his left hand. To write. And to shoot a pistol. But first he must get home to the mountains. There he could find shelter and rest and regain his strength. There he would find friends and sympathizers.

Then a cold realization ran through his mind. By now they must know of his betrayal, that he had screamed their names when his fingers were crushed in the press. He had tried to still his tongue but the pain had opened his mouth.

He stopped and leaned against a building, trembling, but after a moment he regained control over himself. They would not know of his betrayal. By now they must all be dead. If any of them were still alive he would not have been let out of prison.

Slowly he began to walk again. A sense of relief flooded through him. Better they were all dead. This way no one would know. He would have another chance. And this time he would not fail.

great square in the center of the city in front of the Palacio del Presidente.

The people were screaming as he came to an abrupt stop. There was no longer room for him to move. He looked up and a sudden cold chill came into him. He could taste the bitter bile of hatred rising up into his throat. The two of them were there on the balcony in front of him.

El Presidente, his medals glistening in the sun, and his whore-bitch daughter, her blond hair giving the lie to her birth. Next to her stood a man he did not know, a Negro but a wyszo by the cut of his clothes. Beside him stood Apt-caro's smiling deceitful fiancé, awkward in the new uniform tunic of a colonel.

I should have killed them when I had the chance, he thought bitterly. Now, if I had the gun . . . but even now what good would it do me? The hand that cannot grasp even a pen could not hold a gun, much less aim it and pull the trigger.

He turned and began to push his way through the crowd. Someday he would kill them, though. He would learn to use his left hand. And to write. And to shoot a pistol. But first he must get home to the mountains. There he could find shelter and rest and regain his strength. There he would find friends and sympathizers.

Then a cold realization ran through his mind. By now they must know of his betrayal, that he had screamed their names when his fingers were crushed in the press. He had tried to still his tongue but the pain had opened his mouth.

He stopped and leaned against a building, trembling, but after a moment he regained control over himself. They would not know of his betrayal. By now they must all be dead, if any of them were still alive he would not have been let out of prison.

Slowly he began to walk again. A sense of relief flooded through him. Better they were all dead. This way no one would know. He would have another chance. And this time he would not fail.

BOOK
5

FASHION
and
POLITICS

1

When Dax came out of the doors of American Supreme Headquarters in Tokyo the two soldiers saluted him smartly. Negligently he returned their salute and walked down the steps. A boy passed him carrying a bundle of the latest edition of *Stars and Stripes.* The headline shouted of another major battle in Korea. Dax was standing there on the sidewalk, looking across the busy street at the Emperor's palace, when Fat Cat came up.

"We go home?" Fat Cat asked.

Dax nodded absently, still looking at the palace. "We go home. They do not need us any more."

"They never needed us, they didn't want us to begin with."

"*El Presidente* promised them a battalion. Perhaps if he had kept his promise—"

"*El Presidente* makes many promises. Now the war in Korea is almost over. The new American President will make the peace and we still will not have fought."

Dax turned to look at him. "Have there not been enough wars for you already?"

Fat Cat shrugged. "What else is there for a man to do? He fucks or he fights. Each makes him better for the other."

Dax turned and looked back at the palace. "I wonder what he thinks about in there. It must seem more a prison than a palace to him."

"He is lucky, they let him live. But I am sure if he does think he has only one regret. That he did not win." Fat Cat took a package out of his pocket and began to roll a cigarette. "Now he is a god only to his flowers and butterflies."

"Come on, let's go back to the hotel. I want to get out of this uniform. I am tired of playing soldier in an army that does not exist."

The army existed. Dax had realized that on the day of his marriage to Amparo. But not for export.

The soldiers had lined the streets in front of his house that morning—the streets leading to the cathedral in which the ceremony took place; the streets through which they drove in the big black armor-plated car of *el Presidente* to his palace, where the reception was held, and then along the new highway out to the airport. They even stood along the airstrip where the specially chartered American plane was waiting to take Dax and Amparo on their honeymoon.

What had been the first-class section was completely redecorated as a living room. There were several comfortable armchairs spread about and two banquettes that could serve as beds curved around the dividing wall that separated them from the other passengers. There was a card table, small coffee tables next to the chairs, and a bar set up in the forward section just aft of the galley. And on the opposite side was a small curtained dressing room, complete with vanity table and chair and a private door into the lavatory.

When they reached fifteen thousand feet, the seat-belt sign went off and the hostess in her neat blue uniform came into their compartment. "We will be in Mexico City in approximately four hours. If there is anything you want please ring for me."

"Would you have my maid come up forward?"

"Of course."

Amparo looked at Dax. "I've got to get out of these clothes. I'm dying. The heat has stuck them to me like glue."

Dax nodded. He got to his feet. "I will present my compliments to the captain while you're changing."

When he returned about a half hour later the compartment was dark, the curtains drawn. In the dim light he saw Amparo lying on the banquette wrapped in a silk robe. Her eyes were closed, and a half-empty bottle of champagne stood in a nearby ice bucket.

Dax stood for a moment looking down at her. The silk clung to her body; obviously there was nothing under it. Quietly he took off his jacket and threw it into a chair, then pulled at his tie and began to open his shirt. Then he noticed that her eyes had opened and she was looking up at him.

"I was beginning to wonder if you would ever come back. I thought I might have to fly to Mexico City alone."

It was then that he noticed her hand, moving slowly under the robe between her legs. "What are you doing?"

Amparo smiled, moving sensuously. "I am making myself ready for you."

Angrily he pushed her hand away with his own and sank two strong fingers within her. "Have you not yet learned that when I want you I will make you ready?"

A choked cry of pain rose in her throat and she thrust her self forward violently, seeming to climb. With his other hand he held her away until her eyes opened again and looked up into his own.

"With me you are not *la princesa*," he said harshly, "you are my wife."

"Yes, yes," Amparo said quickly, her arms reaching up for him. "You are my husband and I am your slave. Without you I am nothing, not even a woman."

He stood very still, his eyes searching her face. "Remember that."

"I will," she cried wildly, "I will! Now give me your cock before I die of the distance between us!"

Mexico City. Miami. New York. Rome. London. Paris. Lisbon. Then home. For three months it was the most public honeymoon of the year. Everywhere they went the reporters and photographers besieged them. There was scarcely a newspaper or magazine in the world which did not feature their pictures.

From Rome came the famous picture of Amparo, kneeling to kiss the Pope's ring, her blond hair falling forward from beneath the black lace veil, her eyes turned up as he smiled gently down at her.

Afterward, in their suite at the Hassler, Dax teased her. "I didn't know you were such a religious."

"I'm not."

He tossed the evening paper before her. The picture was on the front page. "You look as if you were in a rapture."

She laughed suddenly. "I was."

"What?"

"He was so pure it was the most exciting thing I ever experienced."

Dax stared at her, shaking his head. "I'll never understand women."

Amparo came over and threw her arms around him. She kissed his cheek. "Don't try, it's better that way."

Dax turned her face up to his and looked into her eyes. "You haven't changed much from the little girl I once knew."

Amparo kissed him lightly on the lips. "It's so wonderful. I wish we never had to go home."

But it was Paris where Amparo really came into her own. All the other cities were exciting, but they were cities masculine in concept and merely tolerant of women. Paris was a woman's city. The very air seemed to contain the perfume of woman, which even the stench of the automobiles could not erase. The grace, the beauty, the style, the very tempo was feminine.

Amparo discovered Paris and Paris discovered her. She was the kind of woman who belonged there—haughty, autocratic, imperious, with the wide excited eyes of a *jeune fille* and the demanding sensuous mouth of a *femme du monde*. She was the center of attraction wherever she went. At dinner. At the theater. Even at the oldest and haughtiest of *couturiers* they fell all over themselves trying to please her.

For once Dax was content to stand quietly to one side while Amparo basked in the limelight. It was at one of the receptions that a familiar voice came from behind him. "She is very beautiful."

He turned, smiling. It was Giselle, holding out her hands to him. He took them in his and kissed her once on each cheek, French fashion. "Thank you. You are looking quite lovely yourself."

Giselle shook her head slightly. "Not like her; already there are lines around my mouth, my eyes."

"Nonsense, you are as beautiful as ever."

"Don't lie to me, Dax." She smiled. "I am a professional. My face is my business."

"Then only you can see such lines. The rest of the world must be blind."

Giselle turned away from him and looked toward Amparo again. "Are you happy with her, Dax? Is it she you always wanted?"

"I am happy."

"You did not answer all of my question."

He stared at her silently.

492

"All right," she said after a moment. "I had no right to ask."

A waiter came by with a tray full of glasses filled with champagne. Dax lifted off two and held out one to her. He raised his. "To those who care."

She emptied her glass quickly and put it down. "I must go."

"But you just arrived."

"I forgot," she said, "I have another appointment." She turned to leave, then abruptly turned back to him. There was a trace of tears in her eyes. "Before you leave Paris I would like to see you once more."

Dax started to answer but she stopped him with her hand. "Not like this; at my apartment. I know you can't get away in the evenings but I am still in the same place. You used to know how to find your way there in the mornings."

Then she was gone, and he was left staring after her.

Later Amparo broke away from her group and came over. "Who was that woman you were talking to?"

"Giselle d'Arcy, the movie star."

"I know that," she said impatiently. "What was she to you?"

Dax stared at her. After a moment he answered, "She was my mistress during the war."

"You're not thinking of seeing her again, are you?"

He smiled. "Not seriously. But now that you mention it, it's not such a bad idea."

"If you do, I'll kill you," she whispered fiercely. "She's still in love with you."

He laughed aloud. But when they left Paris he still had not gone to see Giselle.

Three days after they returned to Corteguay the North Koreans crossed the 38th parallel.

493

2

Amparo came storming into her father's office, brushing aside the two soldiers at the door as if they did not exist. Slamming the door behind her, she crossed the room to *el Presidente*'s desk. "You're sending him to New York!" she said angrily.

El Presidente shrugged. "He must go there before Korea. I explained that to you."

"Alone?"

He nodded.

"I told you I wouldn't let him go alone!"

"He has his work to do."

"You know what will happen." She began to shout. "I warned you about what kind of man he is!"

"So?" Her father's voice was without interest. "That is your problem, not mine."

"I am going with him!"

For the first time since Amparo had come into the room *el Presidente* reacted. He got to his feet and walked around the desk toward her. "You will stay here and do your own job!"

"I will not! You are trying to ruin my marriage just as you have ruined everything in my life! If he goes tomorrow, I go with him!"

He moved quickly, unexpectedly. One hand caught her by the arm, spinning her around, the other came up swiftly against the side of her face, knocking her to the floor. She started to get up, but he placed a heavy boot on her chest, the toe against her neck.

His voice was very cold. "Listen, *puta*, you will do exactly as you are told. I have not come this far to let some stupid girl with a hot cunt interfere with my plans. It would not

494

bother me one bit if you were to spend the rest of your life languishing in prison."

"You wouldn't dare," she whispered, but there was a trace of fear in her voice. "I am your daughter."

El Presidente's teeth flashed in a smile. "Are you? By whose word? Mine and mine alone. Everybody knows that your mother was nothing but a *puta*. All I need say is that a mistake was made, that I had been misled all these years."

Amparo stared up at him silently. After a moment he lifted his foot slowly and went back to the desk. She got to her feet, still glaring at him. Then she turned and started for the door. His voice stopped her. "Not like that," he said quietly. "First wash your face. There are people out there."

Without answering Amparo went into the bathroom. A few minutes later she came out. *El Presidente* looked at her and nodded. Amparo stared back at him, her face pale. "I need a drink."

"That's more like it." He turned in his chair and opened a small cabinet behind him. He took out a bottle of rum and a glass. He splashed a good-size shot into it, and replaced the bottle in the cabinet. He handed her the glass.

She downed the drink and placed the glass on his desk. A little color had come back into her cheeks.

"Now go," he said, "and see to it that you give your husband a hero's farewell. He may be gone for a long time." He watched her walk to the door, and just as she opened it he spoke again. "See if you can get yourself pregnant. It will keep you busy while he is away."

For the first time a faint smile came to Amparo's lips. "That is the one thing I cannot do on your orders."

"Is there something the matter with your husband?"

Amparo shook her head slowly. "Not with him, with me. The baby I lost, the child of De Ortega, whom you had murdered. Well, De Ortega had his revenge; I am barren, sterile. You will never have grandchildren to play at your knee."

Dax sat across the desk from the military aide to the Secretary of the United Nations. Behind them, through the huge window, the evening lights of New York were beginning to show. "I don't know, Colonel Xenos," the aide said slowly, the faintly musical lilt of his Norwegian permeating his somewhat stilted English. "It is very difficult to give an immediate answer. The Americans are very reluctant to entrust new weapons to anyone further."

"You mean MacArthur does not trust his allies?"

"I did not say that."

"Of course not," Dax answered smoothly, "but that is the way it is beginning to seem. As if this is his exclusive, personal war. Someday soon even the American President will begin to see that."

The general was silent.

"Perhaps if I could be assigned to headquarters in Tokyo I could persuade him otherwise?"

"Perhaps," the aide said, then fell silent again.

"I have eight hundred men available," Dax continued, "trained jungle fighters. In a short time there will be two thousand. But they are of no use until they have been taught the use of the new weapons. *El Presidente* wishes to help the cause of the United Nations but he does not wish to send men who are ill-equipped."

The aide turned and looked out the window. Night had come swiftly. He sighed. "Halfway across the globe from here men are fighting a small war so that there will not be a bigger one. I wonder how many small wars we shall have to fight before there is peace?"

Dax did not answer.

The aide swung his chair back around. "Eight hundred men, you said?"

Dax nodded.

The aide thought for a moment. "Perhaps something can be done." His voice was definite now that he had come to a decision. Even a small force from a South American country might have an important psychological effect. "I will assign you to my staff and send you to Tokyo as you suggest. Meanwhile I shall see what I can do to obtain the new weapons for your men."

"Thank you, sir."

"I suggest that if you have any influential friends in the United States government you try to enlist their aid."

"I understand." Dax knew the general was fully aware who his friends were. "I shall certainly ask their assistance."

The aide got to his feet. The meeting was over. "Of course,

you realize that if you are unable to convince MacArthur there is nothing further I can do?"

Dax, too, got to his feet. "I understand that also."

"Good." The aide nodded and held out his hand. "I shall have your orders drawn. You should have them before the week is out."

Dax smiled. "Things go well then?"

Marcel's expression darkened. "Things are not always as they seem. I have enemies."

Dax looked at his father's former clerk. Power and wealth had not seemingly added to Marcel's sense of security. If anything, he seemed more nervous and secretive than ever. "A man like you must expect to make a few enemies."

Marcel stared back at him. "Those I know about I can deal with. But there are those whose identity remains hidden. There is much resentment and jealousy because of my success. I am convinced that many are plotting against me."

"Nonsense."

"It's true." Marcel's voice lowered and he glanced around the crowded dining room at El Morocco, then leaned forward confidentially. "You have heard about my troubles with the draft board? They wish to take me into the army. Me, a key figure in their defense program. The father of three children."

"How can they?" Dax asked. "You're not even a citizen."

"I am a resident alien, and therefore subject to their draft, or so they maintain. Of course, I have lawyers and influential people working on it, but they are stupid, they claim nothing can be done. Powerful people are out to get me."

"Do you have any idea who they might be?"

"I can't be sure. I can only guess." Marcel was whispering now. "It could be Horgan and his group; they never really forgave me for the Corteguayan oil venture. Especially after they discovered there was no oil there."

"But you are still in business together. Surely they would not disturb that relationship."

"They need my ships," Marcel replied, "not me, and they have a contract."

"Could it be your former father-in-law? He probably hasn't any great enthusiasm for you."

A look of contempt crossed Marcel's face. "Not Abidijan,

497

he's too greedy. My children are heirs to my estate, and they're his grandchildren. No, Amos would do nothing." His voice dropped even lower. "I don't know who they are. But I will find out, I have ways. And when I do they will regret ever having tried to make trouble for me."

Dax stared at Marcel. There was a sickness in his voice he had never been aware of before, an expression on his face that seemed almost psychotic. Dax forced an easiness into his voice he did not feel. "It will pass, Marcel. Everything will turn out all right, you'll see."

"It had better," Marcel replied. "I do not intend to go down alone. There are many who will go down with me." He looked up and suddenly the grim expression on Marcel's face changed to a smile. He started to his feet.

Dax rose also. A tall, darkly dramatic young woman was being escorted to their table by the headwaiter. A kind of hush fell across the tables she passed.

Marcel bowed over her extended hand, his lips caressing it. "You know Dax, of course?"

"Of course."

She turned her dark eyes on Dax and smiled, extending her hand. Dax also kissed it. Her fingers were cold as ice. "Madame Farkas."

"And how did the performance go?"

Dania looked at Marcel as they sat down, and made a weary gesture. "As usual, I was magnificent. But that tenor! I told Bing as I came offstage, never again. Either he goes or I do."

In the center of the big room the orchestra blared. The dance floor was jammed and a faint haze of smoke that even the air-conditioning could not wholly eliminate hung over the dimly lit room. Dax sat at the table alone, drawing on a cigarette, watching Dania Farkas and Marcel.

The tall blond girl moving toward a table behind her escort stopped suddenly. "Dax?"

Dax looked up. He smiled suddenly and got to his feet. "Sue Ann."

"It is you, Dax. What in the world are you doing in that uniform?"

He smiled again. "I've been drafted."

"Are you alone?"

498

He shook his head. "No, I'm with Marcel Campion and Dania Farkas."

Sue Ann's eyes followed his gesture and picked them out on the dance floor. "You're alone," she said definitely, "I'll join you."

"But your escort?"

"A nothing, a real bore. He's one of Daddy's trust lawyers. I had nothing better to do."

At her gesture, her escort walked back to her. "Yes, Miss Daley?"

"I ran into an old friend," she said imperiously, "I hope you won't mind if I join him?"

"I won't in the least mind," he replied quickly, almost too quickly. "I'll say good night then."

Dax made room for Sue Ann on the banquette, and as she sat a waiter put down a champagne glass, which the wine steward quickly filled. Sue Ann looked at Dax approvingly. "You look marvelous in that uniform. What a perfect piece of casting. I wonder why no one thought of it before."

Dax laughed. "*El Presidente* decided that in time of war a uniform looks more impressive."

"I'm impressed. What are you—a general or something?"

"No, merely a lowly colonel. There is only one general in our army, *el Presidente* himself."

"Your wife? Is she with you?"

"No, there is too much for her to do at home. *El Presidente,* her father, thought it best she remain. And your new husband?"

Sue Ann shrugged. "A stupid boy; we were divorced over a month ago. I don't seem to have much luck with husbands. How come you never wanted to marry me?"

He laughed. "You never asked me."

"Is that the only reason?"

"Yes. You see, I have a secret. I'm shy."

"And I'm stupid. I really asked for that one. But I shan't make the same mistake twice. Next time I'll ask."

"How do you know there'll be a next time?"

"I know you, and I know women. I've almost come twice just sitting here rubbing my leg against yours. If your wife is the kind of woman who can let you go away alone, even on her father's orders, there'll be a next time."

"You're all wrong," he said, still smiling.

"No, I'm not. I can wait. You're going to be my next husband." Suddenly a mischievous grin came to her lips. "Now that everything's all settled and we're formally engaged, let's get the hell out of here and go someplace and fuck!"

Over Marcel's head Dania had seen Sue Ann come to the table and sit down next to Dax. An almost instant resentment ran through her which had nothing to do with Dax. In a way she did not like him either; he was the kind of man she had always resented. Positive, sexual, and sure of himself with women. But her real resentment was directed at Sue Ann.

The blond hair, the blue eyes, the fair skin. The casual sensuality and the awareness of her importance. There had always been girls like that in the schools that she had gone to, in the world to which she aspired. Girls who had to do absolutely nothing to get what she had had to struggle so desperately for.

Dania had always been the dark one, the Greek girl, the one with the accent, the tall, skinny, unattractive child with the strange complexion. And they were the goddesses—the blond leaders, the ones the boys always ran after. And then one day when she was about twelve something had happened.

She had begun to bleed, and the strange-sounding voice had suddenly taken on a richness. It burst forth from her throat and soared beautifully and majestically above the others in the class. Abruptly the teacher had silenced the singing and peered down from the platform through her steel-rimmed glasses. "Who was that?"

Dania remained silent, afraid that she had done something wrong.

"Who was that?" the teacher repeated.

Several of the others turned and looked at Dania. She could no longer hide. She stepped forward. "It was me."

The teacher stared at her unbelievingly, wondering what sort of miracle had touched this strange plain girl and transformed her. "You will come back after school with your mother."

There it began. The years of struggle. The study and self-denial. By the time she was seventeen Dania realized that she

500

would never be beautiful. But her breasts filled out with the exercises, and she took on some of the dramatic depths of the music she was studying. Bit by bit this began to reflect itself in her makeup and her dress. She learned to accentuate her best feature, her eyes, which were large and dark. And she trained her hair down over her brow to disguise her height, and shaded her cheekbones because they were too high and prominent. A pale lipstick made her mouth appear less wide.

At first there were many men, for Dania was aware that her mother could never furnish the money necessary to complete her musical training. But they did not reach her. It was almost as if from a distance she watched them writhe and spend themselves upon her, then took from them the little they had to offer. Then there was one, and that he was thirty years older did not matter. He was fifty-five, but rich enough to afford all that remained to be done. More important, he was well enough connected to make it possible. She was twenty when they married.

In her own way Dania had been honest enough with him. There was to be nothing between them but music, nothing that might interfere or distract her from her career. Blinded by her talent, he humbly forswore the few remaining years of his manhood and not once in the ten years of their marriage had they ever gone to bed together.

There were other men, and he knew it. Like the tenor who had got her the role of Carmen at La Scala, or the famous composer-conductor who brought her to the Metropolitan in New York. Now Dania was thirty and needed no one, not even him, and even this he accepted. He was content that she bore his name and he could bask in the bright sun of her talent.

But now Dania was no longer content. She thought she could detect the first faint traces of a weakening in her voice and suddenly she was filled with the fear that when it did go she would have nothing, that she would be condemned to spending the rest of her life in genteel splendor with an old man.

It was then that she had met Marcel. In him already rich, already powerful, Dania saw traces of herself. The same selfish greeds and desires. That he was married and had children did not matter; she as an artist was above such things. What did matter was that he like all the others was subservient to her talent, and that he mistook her passion and fire upon a stage as also a sexual capacity.

She waited confidently. Marcel obtained his divorce as she had thought he would. But then something went wrong. He did not ask her to divorce her husband and marry him. He seemed quite content to drift along as they had. Dania realized there were many problems besetting him, and after a while she settled into a routine of watchful waiting. That he would marry her in time she had no doubt. Meanwhile there would be nothing lost since she still had her husband in reserve.

Over Marcel's head she saw Dax and Sue Ann talking and laughing. Suddenly Dania was bored with his mechanical dancing. She tapped Marcel on the shoulder. "Come, let us sit down. I am tired."

"I'm sorry," Dax apologized, "but I must go. I have an early plane to catch for Boston in the morning."

"But it's scarcely three o'clock," Marcel protested.

"I know, but I have a lunch appointment with James Hadley."

"I'm tired too," Dania said suddenly. "It's been a long day, Marcel, let's go."

Suddenly Marcel became stubborn. "No, I wish to stay."

Dania stared at him. She knew instantly that he was trying to assert himself. Well, this was as much her game as his. "Stay then," she said, rising. "The world does not have to stay up all night merely because you can't sleep."

"I'll have to go, too," Sue Ann said.

Marcel looked up at them, from one to the other. Suddenly his eyes were hooded and veiled. "All right," he replied, his voice unexpectedly soft, "take my limousine. But tell the chauffeur to come back for me after he drops you off."

Dax settled into the back seat of the big car between the two of them. The chauffeur turned and looked back questioningly. "You can drop me off first," Dax said. "The consulate is nearest."

The chauffeur nodded, and the window between him and the back seat rolled up. "You don't mind?" Dax asked.

The two women shook their heads.

He was reaching for a cigarette when he felt their hands. Dania on his right, Sue Ann on his left. He smiled to himself in the darkness and slipped his own hands up under their dresses. Sue Ann was already wet but Dania was hot and dry, her pubic hair crinkly under his fingers. At almost the same moment, their hands found his manhood. And each other.

They stared across him in surprise. He could feel his own juices begin to rise as they leaned forward to look down at him, then at each other.

Dax laughed aloud. He raised his hands and placed one on each of their heads pontifically. "Bless you, my children."

3

James Hadley leaned back in the chair. "You have already spoken to Jeremy about this?"

Dax nodded. "He said he would give me all the help he could. But he suggested that you might be able to do even more. That's why I came to see you."

Hadley glanced out the window at the rain, then back at Dax. "Perhaps I can." He leaned forward unexpectedly. "Did Jeremy tell you that he is leaving politics?"

"No." Dax was surprised. "He said nothing about it to me."

"Well, he is; at least, elective politics. He is more interested in going into the State Department. The rough and tumble of the other does not appeal to him."

"Surely that is not the only reason?"

Hadley grinned ruefully. "No, Jeremy has made up his mind to marry that German girl. And he knows that the voters would never vote for a congressman with a foreign wife, especially a divorcée, in Catholic Boston."

Dax did not answer. There was a moment's silence, then Hadley continued. "Jeremy has pledged his support to Jack Kennedy. Kennedy will go for the Senate in fifty-two, the vice presidency in fifty-six, the presidency in sixty. Jeremy promised him he would go down the line."

Dax felt a wave of pity for the old man. It had to be a bitter pill for him to swallow. Those were his exact plans for his own son. Now it was someone else who had taken them over.

"So that is what Jeremy meant when he said you might be able to help me," he said softly. "Do you know the Kennedys?"

Hadley nodded. "They have a place not far from us at Palm Beach. They're a big family."

Dax smiled at the description, for Hadley's wasn't exactly a small one. "Do you think they might be interested in helping?"

"They might," Hadley said. "I don't doubt that Jeremy will talk to Jack, and I'll see what I can do with his father. They're very much interested, I understand, in bringing the South American countries more actively into the UN."

Suddenly he changed the subject. "Did you see Marcel while you were in New York?"

"I had dinner with him last night." Dax took out a cigarette. "He seems overly upset about his draft call."

"Marcel is a fool. What does he expect when he flaunts himself in everyone's face? People are bound to resent him. I told him to lay low, to keep out of the nightclubs and the newspapers. But he wouldn't listen."

"What should he do?"

"I advised him to go in quietly. At his age he'll wind up at a desk job anyway. Then after he's in, a discharge could be arranged for him. But Marcel won't. He won't listen."

"What will happen then?"

Hadley looked across the desk. "If Marcel keeps on like this he'll destroy himself. The one thing you can't beat in this country is public opinion. He's already identified in the public's mind as a draft dodger."

Dax got to his feet. "You must be very busy. I won't presume on any more of your time."

Hadley watched him to the door. "Dax?"

Dax turned. "Yes?"

"You're a strange man, Dax. We've spoken much about business, but never once did you mention Caroline."

Dax shrugged. "What was there to say?"

Hadley met his gaze steadily. "In my own way, you know, I loved her."

"So did I," Dax answered quietly. "Also in my own way."

"She was not for you, and evidently not for me either."

504

Dax did not speak.

"Have you seen her or heard from her?"

Dax shook his head. "No; from what I hear she is still living with her father in Paris."

"I have not seen her either," Hadley said, a curious note of sadness in his voice. "Is it too late for me to apologize for what I have done?"

Dax looked at him silently for a moment before he answered. "There's no reason for you to apologize. Perhaps it's both of us who should apologize to Caroline."

James Hadley stared at the closed door for a moment, then picked up the telephone on his desk. Perspective, he thought, everything was a matter of perspective. Jeremy's decision to abandon politics, Marcel's to fight the draft board. Even Dax's viewpoint about Caroline.

His secretary's voice in his ear interrupted his train of thought. "Yes, Mr. Hadley?"

What had he picked up the telephone for? "Oh, yes," he said aloud, remembering. "Get Joe Kennedy for me."

Sue Ann and Dania were in Dax's apartment at the consulate when he got in from the airport. He raised his eyebrows in surprise. "What are you two doing here?"

"We came to take you out to dinner," Sue Ann said.

"Not me." Dax crossed the living room to his bedroom door. "I'm staying in tonight and going to bed early. I'm leaving for Japan in the morning."

Sue Ann grinned. "Then we'll stay and have dinner with you. You don't think we'd let you spend your last night before going off to war alone, do you?"

"I have a lot to do. Papers to sign and that sort of thing."

"You go right ahead," Sue Ann said quickly. "We'll just make ourselves comfortable, and I'll call a caterer to send up a divine dinner."

Dax stared at her. "Exactly what do you have on your obscene little mind?"

"Obscenities, what else?" Sue Ann's expression changed swiftly to a look of mock horror. "Do you know what I found out last night?"

"No."

"Dania is twenty-seven years old. She's been to bed with

505

more than a dozen men and she's never once had an orgasm. Isn't that terrible?"

"It all depends." Dax looked at Dania. "How does she feel about it?"

Dania met his gaze evenly, her face impassive.

"Well, I think it's horrible. When I heard about it I knew just what I had to do. Once, just once, she has to have a real man."

Still looking at Dania, Dax said, "Maybe she's queer?"

"Not a chance, I've been with enough dikes to know."

Dax turned back to Sue Ann. "And where do you expect to be while all this is going on?"

"Right here, honey." She grinned. "I wouldn't miss it for the world. And I'm not selfish, there's more than enough for the both of us."

"She's passed out," Dax said, rolling over on his side and looking up at Sue Ann.

"So would I if I'd waited twenty-seven years for my first orgasm." She made a face. "I don't know what took her so long, though. You were banging her for more than an hour. I came three times just watching. I was beginning to think you'd never get her over the hump."

She reached her hand down. Her expression changed swiftly and a hunger came into her face. "You're still hard!"

Suddenly Dax's private telephone began to ring.

"Now who the hell is that?" Sue Ann asked in an annoyed voice.

Dax reached for the phone. "We'll see."

"Who is it?" Sue Ann whispered.

Dax covered the receiver with his hand. "Marcel." He moved his hand. "Yes?"

"Is Dania there with you?"

"No."

"She is with you!" Marcel shouted accusingly. "I checked everywhere. She has to be with you. I just heard her whispering."

A withering look crossed Sue Ann's face. She took the telephone from Dax's hand. "Marcel, this is Sue Ann. Don't be an idiot, and please stop bothering us! We're in bed."

Calmly she dropped the telephone back on its cradle. "That ought to hold him," she said in a satisfied voice. She looked down at the sleeping Dania. "I don't know what she sees in that greedy little bastard." She reached for him again. "You're amazing. Nothing distracts you, does it?"

He shook his head.

She settled back against the pillows. "You know, in a way I'm glad we're kind of alone. I thought it would be kicky, you know, the three of us together. But after a while I found myself getting jealous."

"It was your idea," he said, moving over her.

"Not yet," she said, her hands on his shoulders, pushing him down. "Eat me a little. You know how I love it when you eat me."

4

There were perhaps a thousand ways Dax could have died in Korea but not one of them was in battle. The closest he was ever allowed to the front lines was at the officers' club in Seoul, where once a week they gathered to look at the newsreels about the progress of the war flown in from Tokyo. For fifteen months he sat at a special desk in GHQ, in charge of liaison with the Latin American forces. But there was very little for him to do. There weren't any Latin American forces.

At first he would report promptly at eight o'clock and spend a full day at his desk doodling on a yellow pad of paper. At five o'clock he would return the yellow pad neatly to the empty drawer of his desk and lock it. Then he would walk over to the officers' club to have a drink and listen to the latest gossip. At seven he would go to dinner, and by ten he was usually in bed.

Once a week he would present himself to the assistant to the Chief of Staff and inquire whether there was any news about the availability of his troops, and each week the answer would be the same. After a while he stopped coming to his desk every day. Once a week was enough. And if he missed a week now and then, no one seemed to care.

He moved from the officers' quarters and took a small house out near the officers' country club. Each morning and afternoon now found him on the golf course. In three months he had brought his game down into the low seventies.

One afternoon after almost six months in the new house, he came home unexpectedly. The sound of voices came to him from behind the house and, curious, he strolled around to the back of the house.

Fat Cat was standing in the center of a group of women, a bored expression on his face. The women were all jabbering at once.

"What's going on here?"

At the sound of Dax's voice Fat Cat jumped, and the women immediately fell silent, hiding behind him.

Dax looked at them, then at Fat Cat. "What do they want? What are they doing here?"

Fat Cat's voice took on the ingratiating tone he always used when he had got himself into something he didn't want Dax to know about. His round face had the innocent look of a cherub. "Don't you recognize them, excellency?"

"No, I don't, who are they?"

"They are our servants."

"Our servants?" Dax turned to look at them. They giggled and tried to hide, one behind the other. He turned back to Fat Cat. "All of them?"

"Yes, excellency."

Dax looked at them again and counted. "But there are eight of them!" It was only a four-room house—his bedroom and Fat Cat's, a combination living and dining room and a kitchen. "Eight," he repeated, turning back to Fat Cat. "Where do they all sleep?"

"Here, excellency." Fat Cat led him around another corner of the house, the women trailing along behind them.

Against a wall of the house there was a kind of lean-to. The roof was thatched, and on the open side there were curtains made of old burlap bags. Dax parted the curtains and peered inside. On the ground were seven neatly made straw pallets. He let the burlap curtain fall and straightened up. "But there are only seven pallets."

Fat Cat began to look unhappy. "That is all they need."

Dax stared at him. He knew the answer almost before he had asked the question. "Where does the eighth one sleep?"

Fat Cat didn't answer. His face turned slightly red with embarrassment.

"Well?" Dax asked, staring at Fat Cat. He had no idea of letting him get off that easily.

"You see, excellency, that was what we were talking about."

"No, I don't see."

"Well"—Fat Cat took a deep breath—"they were arguing about whose turn it was to sleep in the house."

"With you?" Dax asked coldly.

"Yes, excellency." Fat Cat hung his head for a moment. "You see, three of them are already pregnant. The others feel I am not being fair if I do not let them have their turn."

"I think I need a drink," Dax said. He walked around to the front of the house and went inside. He took off his cap and sank into a chair.

A moment later Fat Cat was at his side. "A nice tall cool gin and tonic, excellency," he said in a soothing voice. He put the glass on the table next to Dax's chair and started back quickly toward the kitchen.

Dax's voice stopped him. "Get rid of them!"

Fat Cat's voice was injured. "All of them, excellency?"

"All of them."

"Couldn't I just send away the pregnant ones?"

"All of them!"

"Couldn't I even keep the two best ones?" Fat Cat wheedled. "It's not healthy for a man to live alone in this climate."

"No," Dax said flatly. "In case you don't know it, we're attached to a foreign military force. We could both be courtmartialed and shot for what you've done. There isn't anyone who would believe that you could run a harem right under my nose without my knowing about it!"

He picked up his drink and sipped at it. "I can't even believe it myself."

It was not until seven months later, after MacArthur had been summoned home, in 1952, that Dax was summoned to the office of the new Chief of Staff. The weather had been freezing along the Inchon Valley and the casualties heavy in the face of the new drive by the North Koreans and the Red Chinese.

The assistant to the new Chief of Staff smiled at him. "At ease, Colonel, I think I have some good news for you for a change."

"Yes, sir."

"The Commander-in-Chief wishes you to confirm to him that your force, which has been held in reserve, has now received its training in the use and care of the new weapons."

"I can confirm that, sir. I received a dispatch from my president just last week. Over two thousand of our soldiers have been trained in the new weapons and are ready to be called."

"Good. I will inform the Commander-in-Chief of your confirmation. He will forward a request to have your troops shipped out at once."

"With your permission, sir, I would like to send a diplomatic dispatch to my president direct. I wish to alert him of the request."

"Good, you have it. I was hoping you'd do that, it should speed things up. Your men should be ready to embark the minute the orders arrive."

But two days later Dax was back with a cablegram from *el Presidente*. White-faced and silent, he handed it to the aide.

PLEASE INFORM COMMANDER-IN-CHIEF MY DEEP RE-GRETS. DUE TO EXPIRATION OF ENLISTMENTS LESS THAN FIFTY OFFICERS AND MEN NOW TRAINED IN USE OF NEW STANDARDIZED WEAPONS. IMMEDIATE STEPS BEING TAKEN TO TRAIN NEW ENLISTERS. YOU WILL BE NOTIFIED WHEN QUOTA IS FILLED.

EL PRESIDENTE

The aide looked at Dax. "It looks like someone's been playing politics with you, Colonel."

Dax did not answer.

"Do I have your permission to show this to the Commander-in-Chief?"

"Yes, sir. And may I request a favor of the Commander-in-Chief, sir?"

"What is it?"

"I feel my usefulness here is at an end," Dax said through

tight lips. "I request permission to be relieved of my duties."

The old aide stared at him for a moment. "I suppose that would be best," he said thoughtfully. "You'll have your permission in the morning." He held out his hand. "I'm sorry, Colonel."

Dax took his hand. "I am too, sir."

It was a war without secrets, and the news was all over Seoul in a matter of hours. Even the North Korean radio announced that the Corteguayan president had refused to send troops to fight in an imperialistic war of aggression.

Dax sat at a table in the officers' club alone with a half-empty drink. He lit another cigarette and stared moodily down at the table. Occasionally a friend would come over with a word of sympathy, but since they didn't know what to say, mostly they left him alone.

Then an American Marine major came in. He was only back a few hours from the battle line. His clothes were still dirty with the mud of the field as he walked up to the bar and ordered a drink in a voice still used to making itself heard over the rumble of war. The other soldiers gravitated around him, eager to hear the latest.

"Man, it was a bitch!" He drank his drink hurriedly and ordered another. "I lost almost half the men in my command. Those damn slant-eyes just kept on comin' an' comin'. I never saw so many of the yellow gook bastards in my life."

The major turned, his elbows on the bar, and looked around. Then he noticed Dax. He stared at him for a moment and, without lowering his voice, asked of no one in particular, "Is that the colonel who comes from a whole country of chickens?"

A silence suddenly fell over the room. Dax looked up and met the Marine's eyes steadily. He had been around long enough to understand the play on words. Slowly he got to his feet. He counted out the money for his drink and placed it carefully on the table, then walked up to the major at the bar.

"I envy you the battle from which you come. Perhaps it gives you the right to say such things, Major," he said quietly, "but I don't envy you the ignorance out of which you speak."

After a moment the major's eyes lowered, and Dax turned and walked out of the club. The next day he was in Tokyo.

511

Less than a month later he was on his way back to New York. It was almost two years from the day that *el Presidente* had sent him out as head of an army that never existed.

5

Sergei sat behind his desk, his eyes thoughtful, his hand toying with the gold letter opener. He looked at Irma Andersen, then at the man sitting in the chair beside her. "I don't know," he said after a moment's silence, "we're doing well enough here. I wouldn't like to upset the apple cart, as you Americans say."

Irma snorted derisively. She spoke rapidly in French, too rapidly for the American sitting next to her to follow. "You're an idiot, Sergei! You gross two hundred thousand a year, maybe net seventeen thousand for yourself. You call that enough? Lakow is offering you millions!"

"But here we know what we can do," Sergei replied. "America, that's another story. It's a different kind of business entirely. Wiser and smarter men than I have lost their shirts in the mass market. Besides, how do I know what it might do to our business here? We could lose it all if our customers decided we had become too common, too ordinary."

"But copies of your dresses are sold all over America now, and it hasn't made the slightest difference."

"Copies, that's something else. Our prices are maintained. Not everyone can afford an original, and the royalties are not bad. But we would surely lose all that if we went into a straight twenty-to-fifty-dollar line."

"It's not just the dresses," Harvey Lakow said, "it's everything. A complete new way of life for the American woman. The Prince Nikovitch name will be on everything. A complete line of cosmetics and perfumes. Lingerie. Sport wear, from bikinis to ski clothes. Even husbands won't be forgotten. We'll have men's toiletries as well as ties and sport shirts. I don't think you quite realize what this could mean. We'll have an investment of over five million before we see a single sale."

Sergei still hesitated. "If the idea is so good, why haven't any of the other houses gone for it?"

Harvey Lakow smiled. "Because we haven't asked them. We asked you."

There was no doubt in Sergei's mind that Lakow was telling the truth. Amalgamated-Federal was the largest association of department stores and women's-wear shops in the world. There were over a thousand outlets in the United States alone, ranging from the largest of department stores in the big cities down to medium-size quality shops in a variety of smaller towns.

"If you could have anyone you wanted, why me?"

"If I may speak bluntly?"

"Go ahead," Irma said, "the truth won't kill him."

Lakow turned back to Sergei. "Once we had decided on what we are temporarily calling 'Paris in Your Home,' we began to look around for the one house we thought would best suit our needs. The older, better-established houses were immediately rejected because we were convinced they were too set in their ways. Then we considered for a while taking one of their designers and building him up. But that seemed hardly practical. It was Dior's name that was known, not the designer's. We were looking for a name that any American woman would immediately associate with Parisian *couture*. That's why we decided on you. Oddly enough, it was my wife who brought up your name. I've learned to trust her judgment, she has very good instincts. She pointed out that although you were a comparatively new house you had survived for over five years, and thanks to Miss Andersen's column and others, you are in some ways more widely known than most of the older houses. Besides, my wife said she met you once and that you seemed a bright, capable young man."

"Your wife?" Sergei's brow wrinkled.

Harvey Lakow smiled. "She said you probably wouldn't remember her. It was before the war, when she came to Paris on a holiday. She was alone; I couldn't get away because of business problems. You were a student then and very helpful to her. You acted as her part-time guide."

"I'm sorry," Sergei said, "I don't seem to remember her."

"It's not really important. The important thing is that you have a good house, and a moderately successful one. But in Paris you will never really achieve the status of a top house. Yet to American women the others are just names, while you are a personality, a man whose pictures they have seen in newspapers and magazines. They know of you through your marriage to Sue Ann Daley, and through the extensive reportage of Miss Andersen. You represent to them glamour, excitement, the high life. There is no doubt in our minds that if you come in with us and go to America we could practically dominate the fashion world there in a very short time."

Harvey Lakow got to his feet. "Look, I know this is all very sudden. I imagine you want time to think about it. I'm going to Rome tomorrow but I'll be back on Saturday. Could you call me at my hotel then and give me your answer?"

There was a silence after Lakow had left the room. "What do you think?" Sergei finally asked Irma.

"He's right," she said, quietly for once, "you will never make it here as a top house. You know that because you wanted to hire other top designers and they wouldn't come."

Sergei nodded. He had long felt the need of another designer; his own little fairy was beginning to lose his sparkle. "It's still dangerous. I could lose everything."

"All you need is a few good years, and then it wouldn't matter. The fifteen percent they are offering you is worth twenty times what this place is. And they are quite willing for you to keep this for yourself alone."

Sergei stared at her. "America, I've heard so much about it. I've always wanted to go there. And yet . . . I'm afraid."

Irma smiled. "You have nothing to worry about. American women are no different from any other kind. You should know that by now. They are all in love with what a man has in his britches."

Sergei reached for a cigarette. "I can always rely on your honesty to make me face myself for what I really am, Irma."

"That's why your name is better known than that fairy designer you've got downstairs. Don't knock it, boy."

Sergei put the cigarette in the holder and lit it.

"Tell me something," Irma said suddenly.

"Yes?"

"Was it true that you really didn't remember Lakow's wife?"

"No." Sergei looked across the desk at her, his eyes gentle and in a way sad. "I remembered her very well."

"I thought so," Irma said with satisfaction. "I didn't think you were the kind of man who ever forgot *any* woman."

"I should be excited about it," Sergei said after the waiter had filled their demitasse cups and gone away, "but I'm not."

Giselle said nothing, just sat there looking at Sergei with her huge blue eyes.

"I'm thirty-five, and for the first time in my life I've found a place for myself. I don't want to chance losing it. I guess it's because I find it too comfortable. Or am I getting old?"

Giselle smiled. "You're still a young man."

Sergei looked at her somberly. "I feel old. Sometimes when I think of my daughter—she's almost thirteen now—I'm reminded of how much time has gone by."

"How is Anastasia? Is she doing well?"

"As well as can be expected. That's another thing; I'd hate to leave her and yet I'm afraid to take her to a strange new place. Things are difficult enough for her as it is. New faces, a new language—it would be too much."

"There are better schools for her in America than there are here."

He sipped his coffee. "You sound as if you think I should go. I thought you didn't like America."

"Professionally America was no good for me. But for you it could be a whole new world."

"You say that, but would you go back?"

"As an *artiste*, no. But if I were you, still young and in search of a world to conquer, I would not hesitate."

Sergei thought for a moment. "No, it's impossible. I cannot leave Anastasia alone."

"Go," Giselle urged, "try it for a year. If you do not like it you can return. I will look after your daughter while you're away."

The telephone began to ring while they were having breakfast in front of the bay window of the suite overlooking the Champs Élysée. Harvey Lakow got up and crossed the room. "Hello."

"Mr. Lakow? This is Prince Nikovitch."

"Yes?"

"I have thought about your kind offer, and I have decided to accept."

Lakow's voice filled with satisfaction. "Good, I'm very pleased. You won't regret it."

"I feel that way, too."

"If you are free Monday morning I'd like to come by your office. Perhaps we can begin to set the wheels in motion."

"I am at your complete disposal."

Lakow put down the telephone and walked back to the table. "Well," he said in a pleased voice, "he's coming in."

"I'm glad," his wife said, looking up at him with a smile.

"Wait until the Allied Stores hear about this," Harvey said triumphantly. "It will knock them for a loop."

"I'm sure it will, Harvey."

"It was a lucky thing that you thought about Nikovitch. All the others just looked down at us when we talked to them. As if our money wasn't good enough for them."

"Don't you worry, Harvey. They'll regret it."

"You're damn right they will! Especially when they see what we plan for Nikovitch." He sat down and sipped his coffee again, then made a face and put it back on the table. "You'd think the French would learn to make a decent cup of coffee!"

She laughed.

"Strange, you remembered him but he didn't remember you. I wonder why?"

"It's not strange at all, Harvey," she said gently, her eyes going past him to the window. "I was probably just one of the many Americans for whom he acted as guide. And he was such a young boy at the time, and frightened too."

"If it were me, I'd never forget you."

Her eyes came back to him and for a moment there was all the beauty of her life in them. She bent across the table and pressed her lips to his cheek. "That's because you're you," she whispered, "and because I love you."

6

The heavy roar of the engines forward in the nose of the chartered DC-7 muted suddenly as they reached cruising altitude and the pilot modified the propeller pitch. Wearily Sergei loosened the catch and his seat belt fell to one side. He pressed a button and adjusted the back of the seat, then lit a cigarette and glanced out the window. Below the lights of New Orleans flickered and then fell away behind them as they circled out over the Gulf of Mexico toward the Florida peninsula.

"Mr. Nikovitch?" Norman Berry, the thin, white-faced PR man slid into the seat beside him, the usual sheaf of papers in his hand and the same worried expression on his face. "I thought we might take a moment to go over the plans for tomorrow."

"Later, Norman. I want to see if I can catch a little rest." Sergei saw the expression on Berry's face worsen. "Leave the papers. I'll look them over and call you when I'm ready."

"Yes, sir." Berry got up and, leaving the papers on the seat, walked out of the forward cabin. The voices of the models chattering excitedly came through the door as it opened and closed behind him.

Idly Sergei glanced down. The blue and red print of the multigraph was headed: "PRINCE NIKOVITCH PROMOTION. September 19th, 1951, Miami, Fla., Airport Reception, 9 A.M., Airport Reception Committee: The Mayor; Members of City Council; Greater Miami Chamber of Commerce; Bartlett's (A-F Miami) Dept. Store; Reporters; Photographers; Newsreel and TV Personnel."

Everything was there, logged and detailed, minute by minute like a train schedule. Nothing was forgotten. And so on through the entire day right up to midnight, when the plane would take off again on its final flight back to New York. Sergei turned the sheet of paper over and glanced across the aisle.

Irma Andersen was already asleep, her mouth slightly open. Sergei shook his head in mild wonder. He was younger than she, much younger, and yet he was exhausted. Where did she find the drive and energy for each day? There had been ten days of this, starting in New York. Then San Francisco, Chicago, Los Angeles, Dallas, New Orleans. Flying by night. A different major city every day.

And it wasn't only this trip. The whole of the past year had been hectic. Now, only now, was he beginning to understand the power and drive of business in the States. No wonder American businessmen conquered the world, then died young. They never stopped. Not for a moment, not for anything.

It had all begun less than two months after he met Lakow in Paris. It started innocently enough, like a pebble dropped into the water, its ripples reaching out wider and wider. Only a line of black type. But suddenly it appeared in thousands and thousands of advertisements, placed by the various A-F stores all over the country.

Dress—or hat, or shoes, or whatever—from the Prince Nikovitch Collection.

Makeup by Prince Nikovitch, the Royal Look of Beauty.

And most of it long before a single item had been put into actual production. So that it always seemed to Sergei like a deadly race against time. Everything was happening at the same time in the penthouse offices on the seventieth floor of the A-F building in New York. There was a continuous pandemonium that made the most hectic day he had ever known in Paris seem like a vacation.

There were three conference rooms adjoining his office, and there were times when even three were not enough. He would race from one to the other. Everything was departmentalized and specialized and yet, somehow, coordinated in a way that only Americans seemed able to accomplish. And between all the office meetings was the press, the publicity which never let up.

He was the symbol, the name, the entire campaign. His pictures were taken at every important Broadway opening, at the opera, at every charity ball, at each important social event. Irma Andersen saw to that, just as she arranged for his name to appear in all the important columns at least twice a week. Not a day passed but somewhere in the United States at least one interview appeared. Not a week passed when his voice was not heard on radio or he was not seen on television in one of the many programs with a special appeal for women.

A few months ago Norman Berry had come into his office excitedly waving a copy of *Advertising Age*. "We made it! We made it!"

Sergei had looked up from the drawings on his desk. "Made what?"

"*Advertising Age* says that you're now the best-known male in American advertising. Better known even than Commander what's-his-name!"

"Commander what's-his-name?" Sergei asked, puzzled.

"You know," Norman said, "Commander Whitehead. The 'Schweppervescence' man."

"Oh, him." Sergei's eyebrows lifted ironically. He looked at Berry quizzically. "Do you think we've been missing a bet? Perhaps we should add a vodka to our line. Prince Nikovitch Vodka."

"That's a hell of an idea! A natural!" Norman seemed enthusiastic, then he stopped suddenly and stared at Sergei. "You're kidding!"

Sergei allowed himself a smile.

"I'm all wound up, nothing like this ever happened to me before."

"Nor to me," Sergei answered quietly.

The target date was September 10 in New York. The collection would be presented exactly as it had been in Paris. Even the models would be flown over by Air France for the showing. Then the entire cast would board a chartered plane and fly to another major city to present the collection again. Ten cities. Ten days.

Lakow had been right. Sergei bent down and picked up the copy of *Women's Wear Daily* that lay beside him on the seat. The big black headline stared up at him:

NIKOVITCH! TWENTY MILLION THE FIRST YEAR?

Harvey Lakow himself was at the airport when the big plane touched down in New York the next morning. He was on the plane before any of them had a chance to get off. "I had to see you before the reporters got to you."

"The reporters?" Sergei asked. "What do they want? The tour was over yesterday."

"You don't understand." Lakow smiled. "They want to talk to you. You're news. The biggest thing to hit the American fashion world in the past hundred years."

"My God!" Sergei sank back into his seat. "All I want to do is get into bed and sleep for three days."

"There'll be very little sleep for you, my boy. We have to keep on the ball. It's time to start planning things for the spring!"

Sergei stared at him wordlessly.

"And by the way" Lakow added, "the directors and officers of A-F are throwing a little dinner for you tonight at '21' in appreciation of the terrific job you've done. Besides, all our wives are dying to meet you."

As it turned out, the day wasn't long enough. Sergei barely had time to get into his dinner jacket and get to the restaurant. When the flurry of introductions had died down he found himself alone for a moment with Myra Lakow.

Very little about her had changed, her eyes least of all. They were still the same dark blue. "Thank you for remembering me," Sergei said in a low voice.

Her smile was exactly the same. "Thank you for *not* remembering me." The smile vanished. "Then I wanted to feel young. And free."

He looked at her for a moment. "And now?"

"And now?" She looked across the room to where her husband stood talking. A warm gentle look came into her eyes. "Now I'm content. And quite happy to act my age."

7

The model stood with the bored expression usual to her trade. The flowered chiffon blouse wrinkled awkwardly as she turned.

"Let's see the unlined one," Sergei said.

Her expression unchanged, she unfastened the blouse and slipped out of it. Her small, hard breasts were pushed up by the padding in her brassiere. Casually, without thinking, she settled them back into the cups and finished buttoning up the other blouse.

Sergei studied her. Now the blouse fitted properly, falling smoothly and outlining her waist without awkward wrinkles. But through the sheer chiffon could clearly be seen the brassiere, which was the crux of the problem.

In France it would not have mattered. French women expected their brassieres to be visible through their sheer blouses. That was why they wore such interesting ones—lace, frills, gay colors. But American women were different. They felt it was gauche if their brassieres showed. So over them they would wear slips, and as a result chiffon blouses, no matter how well made, never draped properly.

Sergei looked at the designer and shook his head. "I'm afraid we still haven't got it."

The designer dismissed the model and turned back to Sergei. "What do we do? These blouses are an integral part of our suits for the spring line."

"Don't blame yourself," Sergei said sympathetically, "blame the American woman. Despite the fact that everyone knows she wears a brassiere, she refuses to destroy the illusion they create. Otherwise why would she go to such extremes to hide them?"

"I'll go back and try again."

"Do that," Sergei replied, "but don't expect too much. Unless——"

"Unless what?"

"Would it be possible to make a brassiere of the same chiffon as the blouse?"

"Not really. The material hasn't enough support to it."

"Then how about a covering of chiffon over the brassiere?"

"That might be possible." The designer's face began to brighten. "The print on the material would have to be selected very carefully though. If the flowers were too large it might not work."

"Try it. If it works we might have a *sensass* for the spring line." He smiled suddenly. "As a matter of fact, if it works we might even call it 'Sensass.' "

" 'Sensass'?"

"That's French slang for 'sensational.' "

The designer laughed. "Good night."

"Good night." Sergei picked up the phone. "Would you ask Mr. Berry to come in?"

He got up from his desk and stretched. The clock on the cover of his engagement book read six o'clock. He walked over to the window and looked out. It was almost dark and the lights of New York had begun to come on.

He turned as Norman came in. "I just wanted to check. What are my plans for tonight?"

"Tonight?"

"Yes, tonight."

"I thought they had already told you—you have no plans tonight."

Sergei went back to his desk and sat down. "You mean I have nothing to do?"

Norman held out his hands.

"You mean I'm off, I have an evening to myself?" Sergei asked sarcastically. "I can even get laid if I want?"

The sarcasm was wasted on Norman. "My God! I never thought of that."

"Thought of what?"

"Broads," Norman answered. "Somehow I was under the impression you were getting all you wanted."

Sergei laughed. "How could I? When did you allow me even a minute to myself?"

"I'll remedy that right now." Norman went over to the telephone.

"Don't bother, I'm too tired anyway. All I want is to go home, take a hot bath, and have dinner. I'll be in bed by ten o'clock."

"Sure?"

Sergei nodded. "Positive."

Later when he came out of the office building the chauffeur jumped out of the black-and-gold Rolls-Royce the company had placed at his disposal.

"Home, Johnny," Sergei said, smiling pleasantly. "You can have the rest of the night off."

"Good, boss. I sure could use it."

Sergei looked out at the street. Traffic seemed unusually heavy and the sidewalks were jammed. "There seem to be a lot of people out tonight. What's up, Johnny?"

"Be that way every night for the next three weeks, boss. Christmas. That's why I'm glad to get the night off. Gives me a chance to get some things for the kids and the old lady."

Sergei leaned back in the seat thoughtfully. Three weeks until Christmas. It was almost fifteen months since he had left Paris.

It was nine forty-five. Sergei had had dinner sent up and he was sitting over the remains watching television when the door chimes sounded. "Come in," he called, thinking it was the waiter.

A moment later the chimes sounded again, and he got up and went to the door. When he opened it a tall beautiful girl was standing in the hall.

"Prince Nikovitch?"

Sergei nodded.

"May I come in?" Without waiting for an answer, she crossed in front of him into the living room. "I'm Jackie Crowell. Norman Berry sent me, he said to give you this."

Sergei took the small envelope and opened it. It was a calling card. One word was scrawled across it. "Enjoy."

In some strange way he was embarrassed. He felt a blush creep into his face for the first time since he had been a boy. "I'm afraid there's been a mistake. You see, I've just

523

finished dinner." He gestured toward the table. "I didn't expect to go out."

"That's all right." The girl smiled. "Neither did I." She took off her mink coat and dropped it casually across a chair. Apparently she knew her way around the hotel because she went directly to the bedroom.

By the time Sergei got to the door she had already slipped out of her dress and was standing there smiling, clad in nothing but a brassiere and a pair of panties. She reached behind her back to unfasten her brassiere.

"Please," he said, "don't."

She hesitated a moment, a puzzled look in her eyes. "You're not queer, are you? I usually can tell right away."

"No, I'm not queer, I'm just tired. Very tired."

"Oh." The smile started coming back as she finished unhooking her brassiere. "That's all right. Norman told me you'd been working hard. Don't worry, you won't have to do a thing. Just lie back and enjoy it."

Sergei stared at her breasts. It was not until that moment that he realized how Americanized he had become. They were firm, full, strong-nippled, sex-symbol kind of breasts, and he felt the heat suddenly rise inside him. Almost as if mesmerized, he stepped into the bedroom and kicked the door shut behind him.

The girl looked into his face and grinned. "It's amazing how quickly most men forget how tired they are once they get a good look at my titties."

In the morning Sergei lay in bed watching as she finished putting on her lipstick. Then she went into the other room and came back with her mink coat hanging around her shoulders. She stood at the foot of the bed looking at him. "You feeling all right?"

Lazily Sergei propped his hands behind his head on the pillow. "I feel fine."

"You'd feel even better if it weren't for one thing."

"What thing?"

"If you weren't in love."

"In love?" Sergei started to laugh, then suddenly stopped. "What makes you think that?"

"I'm a pro, I can tell whether a guy takes it from the top or goes all the way. And you don't go all the way."

"Am I supposed to?" he retorted, suddenly angry. "Any more than you?"

She stared at him silently, her face expressionless. "I guess not." She went to the door. "Well, in case I don't see you before, Merry Christmas!"

"Merry Christmas," Sergei replied but she was already gone. He heard the front door close. More angry with himself than with her, he punched the pillow up behind him. That was all he needed on top of everything else. Merry Christmas from a whore.

His eyes fell on the telephone. Sergei stared at it for a moment, then impulsively picked it up. "Get me Harvey Lakow in Palm Beach, Florida."

Less than a minute later he had Lakow on the phone. "Harvey, I need a vacation."

Lakow's voice was shocked. "My God, man, you can't go now. They're just beginning to cut the suits!"

"It's fifteen months since I've been home," Sergei shouted angrily. "I haven't seen my daughter in all that time, and I'm not going to let Christmas pass without seeing her!"

"That's no problem." Harvey's voice relaxed suddenly. "Isn't it about time you realized that your home is in New York now? Fly her over here."

The reporters pushed at Sergei and several flashbulbs popped. "Prince Nikovitch, look this way a moment."

He turned and another flashbulb went off in his face.

"Does your daughter look anything like her mother?" one of the reporters asked.

Sergei smiled. "I hope so," he answered easily, "Sue Ann is a very beautiful woman."

"Is there some special reason why Miss d'Arcy is coming here with your daughter? Is there something on between you two?"

"No, Giselle is just a very old and close friend. We decided the child should not have to travel alone."

Overhead the speakers announced the landing of the flight.

"Will Miss Daley see her daughter while she's in New York?" another reporter asked.

"I expect her to," Sergei answered, then held up his hands. "Please, gentlemen, enough for now. The flight is down. I very much want to see my daughter."

For once Sergei was grateful that Norman had thought to get him a special customs pass. The reporters parted and he went through the gate, holding up the card. He walked down the long barnlike room and through the doors into Immigration.

It seemed like an hour, though it was only a few minutes before they came through the door. Sergei shifted the big fluffy panda and the flowers to one hand and waved. Giselle saw him first and pointed him out to Anastasia. The child looked up, smiled, and began to run toward him. An immigration officer saw her and started to hold out his hand to stop her, then noticed Sergei. He smiled and let Anastasia run through.

Suddenly shy, she stopped just before she reached him. A tentative smile came to her lips. He dropped to one knee and held the panda out to her. The golden-blond hair and blue eyes were Sue Ann's, all right. But there was a gentleness in the child she had never got from her mother. *"Bonjour, Anastasia. Joyeux Noël. Bienvenue à New York."*

"Hello, *Papa*," Anastasia said slowly, with just the faintest accent. "Merry Christmas!"

Then she took the panda and was in his arms and his eyes were wet as he kissed and hugged her. "You speak English! How did you learn, who taught you?"

Anastasia spoke slowly and very carefully. *"Tante*—uh —Aunt Giselle taught me." She looked at him, then up at Giselle, and smiled proudly.

Sergei turned just in time to see Giselle's warm answering smile. Suddenly he realized many things. That the whore had been right, and that he had been wrong. Slowly he got to his feet.

Silently he held out the flowers. As silently Giselle took them, and came into his arms. Her lips were trembling as he kissed her.

"It's like a miracle," he whispered, "how can I ever thank you?"

Giselle's hand went down and she drew the child into their embrace. "It's no miracle. All Anastasia ever really needed was a mother."

They were married Christmas morning at Harvey Lakow's home in Palm Beach.

526

8

"Marcel's a damned fool," Jeremy said. "He began to think he was more important than the government. The worst thing he could have done was let it go into court. He had to lose there."

The baron looked across his desk. "They sentenced him to eighteen months?" He picked up a thin cigar in his delicate fingers. "Of course he had the right to appeal?"

"The appeal had already been denied. And Marcel made such a stink about it that even though the judge was inclined to suspend sentence he had no choice but to let it stand."

The baron studied the cigar carefully. "That is the trouble when you tell too many lies. Sooner or later they catch up to you. He will get time off for good behavior?"

"Yes. In six months he'll be eligible for parole. That is, if he keeps his mouth shut and behaves himself."

The baron lit the cigar slowly. "How do you think it will affect him?"

"In his business?" Jeremy shrugged. "In what he already has, not very much, I imagine. But if Marcel has any plans for the future he'll have to move carefully. He'll be subject to a great deal of public scrutiny."

"I see," the baron replied thoughtfully. Already he had mentally decided against renewing Marcel's note on the Campion-Israeli lines. True, it would force Marcel to dispose of his equity, but the shipping company was well enough established now for the Israelis to take it over themselves. With the bank's support, of course. He drew gently on the cigar. "Your President did a very brave thing in recalling Mac-Arthur."

"It was the only thing he could do. If he'd let MacArthur

527

have his own way we might have found ourselves in the middle of another war."

"What is there about the military mind?" the baron mused. "Your MacArthur and our De Gaulle. They are very much alike, you know. Each thinks he is God. Though of course MacArthur is only the Protestant version."

Jeremy laughed. "You French seem to have sidetracked De Gaulle. His party doesn't seem to have much power."

"The R.P.F. is a joke. In a few more years it will disappear. But not De Gaulle. He will not fade away like your old soldier."

"What can he do, then?"

"He can wait," the baron replied. "You see, he is aware that we French are not as wedded to the democratic process as are you Americans. In France there are too many political parties—some say one for each Frenchman—and power is always maintained by coalition. And since there are new coalitions every day, so will there be new governments. De Gaulle knows this, just as he realizes that a lack of continuity in government must inevitably lead to disaster. So he will wait and when the time is right he will come back. And that will be the end of the Fourth *République*."

"Surely the people won't stand for it?"

The baron smiled slowly. "That is a common mistake you Americans make. You are so steeped in self-governing that you forget what we French are really like. The average Frenchman, like the average European, will still prostrate himself before a man of power. We may have had our revolution before you had yours, but we still blindly follow the leader whenever one comes along. Napoleon returned. So may De Gaulle."

Jeremy laughed. "Certainly you don't think he has ambitions to become king?"

"Who knows?" The baron shrugged. "Only De Gaulle, and he talks to no one, only to himself. One thing is certain though—when he returns he will return to rule, not to govern." His voice turned reflective. "And who knows but what he may be right. Quite possibly the only way for France to regain her pride and power is to be driven to it."

After Jeremy left the baron leaned back wearily in his chair and closed his eyes. One more year, he thought, then Robert will be ready and I can let go. To say the things they wanted to hear and still say the things that had to be said, that was the strain. Perhaps he was mistaken but it seemed to him that not too many years ago things had been much simpler.

He thought of the young man who had just left him and smiled. He liked Jeremy—his quick mind, his openness, even the strange American brand of idealism he professed. Now, that was the kind of young man that Caroline should have married. Strange that she should have fallen in love with his father. And yet perhaps not so strange; in many ways the father was very much like the son.

Idly he wondered whether Jeremy was still seeing that German girl. There had been talk a while back that they were to be married, but more than a year had passed and nothing had happened. Probably it never would now.

An idea suddenly came to him and the baron sat upright in his chair. His hand hesitated a moment over the telephone, then he picked up the receiver. After all, why not? It was not such a wild scheme after all. It would not be the first time that a son had married a woman who at one time had been the mistress of his father.

Denisonde answered the telephone. Quietly the baron told her to give a dinner party that Saturday night and to be sure to invite Jeremy Hadley.

Marlene was angry; Jeremy knew all the signs. As they rode silently back to the hotel he once or twice looked at her but she steadfastly kept her face turned away. But it wasn't until they reached their suite that she exploded. "Damn them!" she said, throwing her evening bag angrily across the room. "I never want to see them again, any of them!"

"What's the matter? I thought it was a very nice dinner party."

"Then you're even stupider than I thought! Couldn't you see what the baron was doing?"

Jeremy stared at her. "No," he answered stubbornly. "You tell me."

"He was throwing her at you. All night it was 'Caroline this, Caroline that.' Couldn't you see?"

"I didn't observe any such thing. Your imagination is running wild."

"It is not! And couldn't you see how they treated me? As

529

if I did not exist. You sat at the head of the table opposite Caroline, next to the baron. I was put down at the foot next to two nobodies!"

"Cut it out, Marlene," he said wearily. "I'm too tired for an argument. Besides, the whole thing is ridiculous. Caroline and I have been friends for years."

"What's so ridiculous about it? If Caroline was good enough for your father, why shouldn't the baron think her good enough for you? Everybody knows she was your father's mistress!"

Jeremy's face whitened suddenly. "You'd better stop," he said grimly. "You've said too much already!"

But she was too wound up. "Don't go putting on that Holy Hadley act with me. I've been around you too long. I know all about your family. I'm aware of the second family your big brother Jim keeps in that sedate little house in Brookline. And the silent-movie star your father is still supporting. I also know all about your younger brother Kevin, swinging with the pretty boys down in New York, and how your sisters think nothing of switching husbands for the weekend—"

Marlene's voice choked off in her throat as he grabbed her by the shoulders and began to shake her violently. "Stop it! Stop it! Stop it!"

She reeled dizzily when he let her go, and almost lost her balance. She stumbled as she sank into a chair, glaring at him, her breast rising and falling. "Now I suppose you're going to beat me like Fritz did," she said sarcastically.

Jeremy stared at her for a moment, then shook his head slowly. "That's what you'd like, isn't it? It would satisfy your German sense of guilt."

Her mouth twisted into an ugly line. "At least I'm not her, offering herself first to the father, then to the son. I know all about French girls like her. Soldiers told me how they came running after them in the streets, lifting their skirts."

An icy calm seemed to settle over Jeremy. "Haven't you got the story a little mixed up? The first time I heard it they were German girls with the Russians, and later the Americans."

"Is that what you really think? That I ran after you?"

"Is there any other way to look at it?" He smiled coldly. "Remember, it was you who called me."

"I'll" The President thought.

9

The President's secretary got up from behind his desk and held out his hand as Jeremy was ushered into his office. He smiled. "It's always a pleasure to see you again, Congressman."

The handclasp was firm but brief. Jeremy made no reference to being called congressman. The secretary knew as well as he that he no longer was a member of that august body.

"Have a chair," the secretary said graciously. He sat down again behind his desk and pushed a box of cigars toward Jeremy.

"No, thanks." Jeremy took out a cigarette. "I'll stick to these."

The secretary came straight to the point. "The President read your letters with a great deal of interest. He thought many of the points well taken, and wished me to express his gratitude."

Jeremy nodded. He didn't speak, for he wasn't expected to.

"We had a long discussion about the question of your appointment. And the President came to the conclusion that this was just not the time for it."

"Oh? The Senator gave me the impression that the matter was settled."

The secretary smiled bleakly. "I'm afraid the Senator was laboring under a misapprehension. The Senator is rather young, you know, and sometimes his enthusiasms run away with him."

"Yes?" Jeremy's voice was expressionless. The man was a fool. Young the Senator might be, but not in politics. That was a subject he had been nurtured in since the cradle. He never misunderstood anything.

531

"This is an election year," the secretary continued smoothly, "and the new President would expect your resignation as a matter of course. So rather than risk upsetting the apple cart with an interim appointment, we thought it would be best not to make any appointment at this time."

"The President thought so, too?"

The secretary's eyebrow shot up. He didn't like being questioned. "Of course," he replied icily.

The Senator was expecting him and Jeremy was ushered right into the office. "Well, Congressman?"

Jeremy looked back at him. "Well, Senator?"

"Jeremy, we've been screwed."

"You know already?"

"This morning," the Senator said, "right from the White House. The old man called me himself."

"Then why didn't you stop me? Why did you let me go over there?"

The Senator smiled and then his expression changed as he said, seriously, "I wanted you to see for yourself that I hadn't gone back on my word."

"You know I wouldn't think that."

"Thank you."

"I wonder what fucked it up?"

"I don't have to," the Senator replied. "I know. It wasn't the old man and it wasn't State. That leaves only one possibility."

"You mean our friend the secretary?"

The Senator nodded.

"But why? I've always gotten along with him pretty well."

"I guess he just doesn't like Harvard men." The Senator smiled. "The prick went to Yale, you know." The smile left his face. "I'm sorry, Jeremy."

Jeremy shrugged. "That's all right. It was a nice try."

"What are your plans now?"

"I don't know. I haven't given it that much thought."

"Coming out to the convention?"

"Of course. I wouldn't miss that."

"We're getting behind Stevenson."

"Do you think they'll be able to talk Eisenhower into it?"

"I don't think they'll have to try very hard," the Senator

replied. "They'd really rather go with Taft but more than anything they want to win. They'll go with Eisenhower."

"Ike will take it in a walk."

"I think so too," the Senator replied thoughtfully. "In a way it's too bad, because I know Stevenson would make a hell of a President." He glanced at Jeremy suddenly. "We'll need all the help in Congress we can get. It's not too late for you to get on the ticket, you know."

Jeremy shook his head. "Thank you, no. That's not my game. I'm strictly an amateur. I'd rather leave it to you pros."

"If the Republicans get in," the Senator said, "I may not be able to do anything for you for a long time."

"That's all right. I understand."

The Senator got to his feet. "Well, when you decide on something, let me know. Maybe I can be more help then than I have been in this."

Jeremy also rose. "Sure, I'll let you know. I'll have to think of something soon or my old man will be on my back."

"I know what you mean." The Senator grinned. "I have a father too."

Actually it was his father who was responsible for the newspaper offer, as the publisher explained to Jeremy over lunch at "21." "I was having dinner at your father's the other night. A question about French politics came up, and to make his point he brought out a folder of your recent letters. I read one. I was intrigued. I read another, then another. Finally I asked your father if I might take them away with me. That night I stayed awake until three in the morning reading them. At first I thought what a marvelous collection they'd make for a book. You can write, you know. Then I thought, no, the great thing about them was that they were written while the events were still fresh in your mind. With a facility like that the only logical step would be a newspaper column. Would you be interested?"

"I don't know. Every day? I'm really not a writer, you know."

"Who is?" the publisher asked. "At one time the major requisite for becoming a novelist seemed to be a GI background. Earlier, truck drivers were very popular. The way I see it, the only requirement for being a daily columnist is that you write interestingly and have something to say. Well, you say it simply and clearly."

Jeremy laughed. "If you want it simple you came to the right guy."

"Then you'll consider it?"

"I might, if I knew what the hell to write about."

"The conventions are coming up. Just for the hell of it why don't you go to them both and send me a few columns on what goes on. Not for publication, you understand, just to try it out and see if maybe we can come up with the right formula."

Jeremy was intrigued. "I'll give it a spin, but the chances are we'll merely find out how wrong I am for something like this."

But his very first column proved how wrong he had been. After a frantic call from the publisher for permission to run it, which Jeremy gave with reluctant misgivings, the column appeared throughout the country the day the convention opened.

It was headed: "A Foreign Country."

"Foreign countries all over the world are pretty much the same," the first paragraph read. "The average man seems happy to see Americans and likes them very much. Only the politicians, hotel clerks, and taxicab drivers seem to hate us. Chicago is like any other foreign country."

Within a year the column was appearing three times a week in over two hundred newspapers.

In Paris, the baron finished reading that first column in the European edition of *The New York Times* and pushed it across the breakfast table to Caroline. "Did you see this?"

Caroline looked down at the paper and nodded. "Yes. I think it's very clever."

"He's an extremely bright young man."

"Yes," she agreed, "extremely."

"Very strange," the baron said, his brow wrinkling, "we never heard from him after the dinner party."

"Denisonde received a lovely bouquet of roses and a thank-you note the next morning."

"I mean, he never called you or anything like that?"

"No." Then Caroline smiled her secret smile. Poor *Papa*,

he was always at his most obvious when he thought he was being devious. She couldn't resist teasing him.

"Why, should he have?" she asked innocently.

10

The hand gently shook Amparo's shoulder. *"Perdón, Princesa.* Your father is downstairs and wishes to see you."

Amparo felt the band around her temples tighten as she sat up in bed. There was a heavy taste still in her mouth. She looked sleepily at the anxious face of her maid. "My father?"

"Sí, Princesa." The maid cast a sideways glance at the naked young man on the bed beside her. "His excellency is very much in a hurry!"

Amparo shook her head. Something had to be very wrong if her father came here this early in the morning. He had never done so before. "Tell him I'll be right down."

"Sí, Princesa," the maid replied and hurried out of the room.

Amparo turned to the young man. "Stay here. I'll let you know when he's gone."

He nodded silently as she reached for the negligee lying across a nearby chair. Before her hand could reach it, however, the door opened again and *el Presidente* stomped in.

"Excellency!" the young man cried out in terror, and leaped from the bed, to stand stiffly at attention.

El Presidente brushed past him as if he did not exist. He stood at the side of the bed glaring down at Amparo. "I must talk to you immediately!"

She held the negligee over her breasts as she looked first at her father, then at the young man. "Jorge, don't be such a fool! There is nothing more ridiculous than a naked soldier trying to stand at attention. Get out!"

Frantically the young man gathered up his clothes and fled.

When the door had closed behind him Amparo looked up at her father. "What is it?"

"I know that you're not much interested in what your husband is doing," *el Presidente* answered in a sarcastic voice, "but you might have let me know he was arriving today."

"Today?" Her voice was incredulous.

"Yes, today."

Her lips parted in a humorless smile. "I didn't know. This must be the one time your censors sent you the photocopy before I had seen the original."

El Presidente walked over to the window and looked out. "If I'd only known yesterday I might have stopped him."

"What good would that have done?" Amparo asked, getting up off the bed. "Sooner or later he would have found out what you were doing."

"But today of all days." Her father took a folded newspaper from under his arm and handed it to her. "*El Diario* is running a front-page editorial demanding a court-martial over the cowardly resignation of his commission in Korea. They say it reflects disgrace on all Corteguay."

Amparo didn't even open the paper. "I suppose you didn't know about this either?" she asked sarcastically.

"Of course I knew about it," he replied angrily, "but I didn't know he would be here today. If I had I would have had them print it later."

"Blame your stupid spies, don't blame me." Amparo pulled the bell cord behind the bed. "I want some coffee. Would you like some?"

He nodded.

"I'll go to the airport and meet him. I'll explain to him—"

"You will explain nothing. You are not even to see him!"

"Not even to see him? But I'm his wife. What will people think if I'm not there when he gets off the plane?"

"I don't give a damn what they think!" he shouted angrily. "You are also *el Presidente*'s daughter. You will have nothing to do with an accused traitor!"

"So that's the way it's going to be?"

El Presidente didn't answer.

"You've finally figured out a way to get rid of him," she continued in a low voice. "I could see it coming. Ever since our honeymoon, when the papers began to speculate openly about his being your successor."

536

El Presidente stared at her. "And you were loyal to him? As soon as he was gone you leaped into bed with the first man who came near you."

Amparo smiled. "You'll never convince me that I'm not your daughter. We're a fine pair, you and I, exactly alike."

El Presidente suddenly relaxed. The maid came in with coffee and then hurriedly left the room. He walked over to the table and filled his coffee cup. He sipped the coffee with satisfaction. "I'm glad to see you're beginning to make some sense at last."

Amparo came to the table and filled her own cup. She sank into a chair. "You're not going to kill him as you did the others," she said quietly. "I won't allow it."

"You won't allow it?" he asked skeptically. "What can you do?"

Amparo smiled again. "A few days after Dax left I wrote a long report. In it I recorded everything I knew about you— what you've done, whom you've betrayed, where you hid the money you stole, everything. That report is in a bank vault somewhere in the United States, with instructions that it be opened and published if anything should ever happen to Dax or myself."

"I don't believe you. Nothing of yours gets out of the country without my knowing about it."

Amparo smiled and sipped at her coffee. "No? You know so much about me I'm sure you are aware that I went to bed with a man a few days after Dax left. Do you by any chance happen to remember who it was?"

There was a curious expression on her father's face but he didn't answer.

"An attaché to the Mexican Embassy on his way to the United States. And from time to time there have been further additions to that report. Others have been only too happy to do a small favor for *la princesa* in exchange for her own."

El Presidente was still silent. After a moment he sighed. "What do you expect me to do with him then?"

Amparo looked down at her coffee cup. It was empty. She leaned forward to refill it, careless of the way her negligee fell away. "You will send him away," she said. "There are still many ways he could serve you abroad. As soon as he is out of the country I shall divorce him. That will show the people he is out of favor."

"And you will bring your report back into the country?"

Amparo shook her head. "No. The report will remain where it is, an insurance policy against my life and his."

Her father stared at her silently for a moment, then his hand shot across the table. He seized an exposed breast and squeezed it savagely, digging his fingers into her flesh.

Her face went white but the expression in her eyes did not change, even though beads of perspiration broke out across her forehead.

Abruptly he let her go. There was a curious look of respect on his face as he spoke. "You are just like your mother," he said. "Blond hair, black pussy."

The three soldiers snapped to attention as Dax and Fat Cat approached. The lieutenant in the center saluted. "Colonel Xenos?"

Dax nodded. *"Sí."*

"El Presidente has asked that I bring you to him immediately. This way, please." Instead of going through the gate and past the customs desk, he turned toward a small side door. Dax and Fat Cat started after him, but two soldiers stepped in front of Fat Cat.

"You will remain here," the taller of the two said sharply.

Dax saw Fat Cat's hand sneaking toward the gun in his shoulder holster. With a gesture of his hand he stopped him.

"I don't like this," Fat Cat whispered.

Dax smiled bleakly. "What is there to be afraid of?" he asked in English, then reverted to Spanish. "We are home now. Do as the lieutenant asks. Wait here for me."

Dax turned and walked after the lieutenant. Politely he opened the door and stood aside as Dax walked through. Dax blinked his eyes at the hot bright sunlight and waited until the lieutenant caught up with him.

"This way," the lieutenant said, leading him around the building.

There, hidden from ordinary view, stood *el Presidente's* bulletproof limousine. The lieutenant opened the rear door.

"Come in, Dax," *el Presidente* called from inside.

Dax got in and the door immediately slammed behind him. He blinked his eyes, for the curtains were drawn across the windows. The interior of the limousine felt cool, and it was a moment before he realized that both the motor and the air-conditioner were running. He looked at *el Presidente*.

Despite the air-conditioning the old man's face was shiny with perspiration. "Why didn't you let me know you were coming, my boy?" he asked almost unctuously. "Fortunately I learned of your impending arrival from Amparo."

Dax looked directly at him. "I didn't think it would matter. Where's Amparo?"

El Presidente avoided his eyes. "She is dedicating a new clinic at the free hospital."

Through the glass partition both the lieutenant and the chauffeur were watching them, and each held an automatic pistol at the ready.

"Don't pay any attention to them," *el Presidente* said, "they can't hear us."

Dax smiled. "I wasn't concerned about that."

El Presidente smiled back. "The other is just routine. They are very zealous about protecting me. My boy, you have chosen a very inopportune time to come home. You should never have resigned your post."

"There was nothing else I could do when you did not send the troops you had promised."

"There were valid reasons, problems you know nothing about."

"But you gave your word," Dax replied, "and I gave mine. I used my friends, my influence. I pleaded and cajoled them into sending you the new weapons. Surely you don't think they believed your lie about the term of enlistment having expired."

"What difference does it make what they believed?" *el Presidente* answered in an annoyed voice. "There was trouble again in the mountains. The soldiers were more important to me here than in Korea."

"It was a lie from the very beginning," Dax accused. "You never intended sending them. It was merely a way to get the new weapons."

El Presidente's face went white with anger, and with difficulty he controlled his voice. "I have had men shot for saying less!"

Dax leaned back against the seat and smiled tightly. "Go ahead. At least then my friends would realize I had nothing to do with their betrayal."

El Presidente was silent for a moment. When he spoke he

539

had regained control over his voice. "I choose to forget your insult because it was made in the heat of anger. But remember this one thing. My first and only concern is Corteguay. Everything else in the world is important only by its relationship to that. Do you understand?"

Dax's lips twisted bitterly. "I understand very well."

"You may not appreciate it but I have saved your life by coming here to meet you."

Dax was silent.

"The newspapers are screaming for your head. They would like to see you court-martialed for resigning your post under fire."

Dax looked at him. "You wouldn't be interested in telling them the truth, would you?"

"If they would listen I might," *el Presidente* replied, "but it is too late. They wouldn't listen."

"Why didn't you stop them at the beginning?"

"It developed too quickly," *el Presidente* answered smoothly. "Before I could do anything, they had already inflamed the people."

Suddenly Dax began to laugh. "No wonder you were able to persuade my father to believe in you. You control everything printed in the newspapers, yet you calmly sit there and expect me to believe that?"

El Presidente sat stiffly, silently.

"All right. You wish me to go back on the plane that brought me here?"

"Yes, there is still much you can do for us abroad."

"No," Dax replied with finality. "You've used me enough, just as you used my father. Find yourself another boy."

"You say that because you are bitter. But you are Corteguayan. The day will come when you will change your mind."

"I shall always be Corteguayan, but I will never change my mind."

El Presidente was silent.

Dax looked at him. "I would like to see Amparo before I leave."

"Amparo does not wish to see you," *el Presidente* replied coldly. "She has asked me to inform you that she is filing for divorce. She feels it improper, as my daughter, to continue the relationship with you."

Dax pulled back the curtain and looked out the window of the car. The mountains in the distance shimmered in the heat. After a moment he turned back to *el Presidente*. "Very well," he said quietly. He reached for the door. "I am ready to leave now."

"Just a moment." *El Presidente* gestured to the chauffeur in front. "The door locks are controlled by the driver."

The lieutenant got out of the car and came around to open the door. Dax started to walk away but he was stopped by *el Presidente's* voice.

"Vaya con Dios, mi hijo."

Dax turned. *El Presidente* was leaning forward at the open door of the car. There was a curiously sad expression on his face. For a long moment the two men looked at one another, the tired old man whose face seemed held together by a thousand wrinkled lines, and the weary young man whose face had lost its illusions.

"Gracias, excellency," Dax said gravely. *"Vaya con Dios."*

El Presidente ordered the door shut and disappeared behind the curtains as the big car took off, leaving a cloud of dust behind as it cut across the airfield toward the road. Dax watched until it had disappeared from sight, then started back to the terminal.

The big plane banked slowly over the sea, then moved back inland. As the no-smoking sign went out, Dax reached for a cigarette. The stewardess came down the aisle and stopped by his seat. "Señor Xenos? The messenger who brought this asked me to be sure you got it the moment we were airborne."

"Thank you."

The stewardess walked away as Dax opened the envelope and stared down at the note.

> Dax,
> I am sorry. Please forgive me.
> Amparo

Slowly he tore the note into tiny pieces and stuffed them into the ash tray. He lit a cigarette and looked out the window. They were approaching the mountains now. He felt the vague pressure holding him against the seat as the plane continued to lift. He looked down.

The blue, jagged, snow-topped mountains of Corteguay. Suddenly his eyes blurred with tears. He closed them and leaned his head back wearily against the seat.

He would never see them again.

11

"Over there," Sue Ann said, pointing to where Dax lay outstretched, face down on the sand.

"Oui, madame," the beach boy replied, grinning. Sue Ann followed him silently past the early sunbathers. Expertly the boy rolled out the *matelas* and draped a towel over it. Sue Ann took a *franc* from her beach bag and handed it to him. He touched his finger to his forehead and went away, still grinning his toothy grin.

Silently she dropped onto the mattress and stretched out on her back. The sun felt good, warm on her skin. She stirred lazily and turned slightly on her side.

Dax had one eye open and was looking at her. "Hello."

"Hello," Sue Ann replied. She took out a bottle of sun lotion and began to apply the cream to her face. When she had finished she held out the bottle. "Would you do my back, please?"

"Of course." Dax sat up and she turned her back. His fingers were strong as they touched her.

Sue Ann looked out over the blue water. The sailboats were out early that morning and just beyond the bathing ropes a speedboat roared by towing a pair of water-skiers. "You're a hard man to catch up to."

"I don't think so," Dax replied. "I've been on the beach all morning."

"I read about your divorce in the papers. I went to New York to find you, but you'd already gone." She still was not looking at him. "They told me you had gone to Paris, so I went there, but you'd already left for Rome. In Rome I found you'd gone to Cannes. I was surprised to find you here. I really expected you'd go back to New York."

Her back was completely anointed. "Enough?"

"Enough." Sue Ann turned over on her stomach and looked at him. "What are you running away from?"

He smiled, meeting her eyes. "I'm not running from anything. I just have nothing better to do."

"Your actress friend," Sue Ann asked, glancing around the beach, "where is she?"

Dax laughed, his teeth white against his dark face. "Dee Dee? Too early for her; she never gets up until one."

"What do you see in her anyway?" Sue Ann asked. "She's such a bad actress."

"She's fun."

"I find it hard to believe. She looks so soft and mushy. A good stiff prick would let all the air out."

Dax laughed. "Don't let appearances fool you. She's a better actress than you think. She's quite strong, really."

"Could be. But not strong enough for a man like you. Not like me."

Dax studied her for a moment. "There's no one quite like you."

"Good or bad?"

"Both."

She seemed satisfied with his answer. "Her husband has filed suit for divorce in New York, naming you as corespondent. Are you planning to marry her?"

He shook his head. "No. We both agree that I am not wealthy enough to afford her."

She smiled. "They say he found you both in bed. It must have been rather embarrassing."

"It wasn't really." He smiled slightly at the memory. "It was really quite civilized."

He remembered the night when the lights had come on suddenly in her bedroom and her husband had been standing there in the doorway. He was blinking both at the light and at the sight of them sitting up naked in the bed. "Oh, I beg your pardon."

"Hugh!" she had cried. "What are you doing here? I didn't expect you until tomorrow."

543

Her husband looked down at his watch. "It is tomorrow. I came in on the midnight plane from the coast."

"Those damn schedules! I never could understand them." Dee Dee had looked at Dax, then back at her husband. "By the way, you two haven't met. Hugh, this is Dax."

Her husband had made a sort of stiff bow from the doorway. "How do you do?" he mumbled politely.

Dax nodded gravely. He didn't speak.

"Well, I think I'd better be going."

A look of concern crossed Dee Dee's face. "But where will you find a place to stay, Hugh, at this hour of the night?"

"I'll go to my club."

Dee Dee nodded. She seemed relieved. "But make sure they give you an air-conditioned room. It's so damn hot here in New York."

For the first time her husband seemed horrified. "You know how I detest air-conditioning!" He turned in the doorway. "Well, good night."

"Hugh!" she cried out suddenly.

"What is it?"

"I'm such a featherhead, I almost forgot." Dee Dee turned to Dax. "Give me that pillow."

Dax had taken the pillow from behind him and held it out to her. "This one?"

"No, silly," Dee Dee had replied in an annoyed voice, "not that one. That's your pillow. The one next to it, Hugh's."

Wonderingly, he had watched as she put her hand inside the pillowcase. She seemed to be searching for something, and at last she found it, a small gift-wrapped package. She jumped out of bed oblivious of her nakedness and ran to her husband. "Your birthday present!"

Her husband took the package and looked down at it. "Thank you."

"I hope you like it." Dee Dee smiled, then kissed him on the cheek. "Happy birthday, Hugh!"

"Er, yes." He had stood there for a moment more, looking at her, and when he finally spoke, his voice was unusually mild. "Better get back into bed, dear. You'll catch your death with that damn air-conditioner blasting on you like that!"

"What have you been doing with yourself since your return from Korea?" Sue Ann asked, bringing him rudely back to the present.

544

"Nothing very much," he said casually. "Actually, I've been taking flying lessons. I just got my license."

"Planning to get a plane?"

Dax shook his head. "No. The one I'd like is a twin-engine Cessna but they're too rich for my blood. The others haven't the range or the speed."

"I'll buy it for you," Sue Ann said suddenly.

Dax looked at her. "Whatever for?"

"Just like this." Sue Ann snapped her fingers. "I can afford it."

"No, but thanks. An airplane like that is like a yacht. The upkeep is higher than the cost."

Sue Ann was silent for a moment. "Have you made any plans?"

"Not really. I'm still getting used to the idea of having nothing special to do. Next month I've been invited on a safari in Kenya."

"Going?"

"I haven't decided yet."

"What about your friend?"

"Dee Dee's going to Paris to work on some picture, so I probably will go on that safari. The idea of spending the hot summer in Paris doesn't appeal to me all that much."

Sue Ann felt a glow of satisfaction spread over her. If Dax felt like that there was no need to be concerned. There was a mild commotion on the beach behind them, and they turned to look. Dee Dee was coming down the steps to the Carlton *plage*, and the photographers were falling all over themselves trying to get her picture. She was dressed in a flowing pastel summer chiffon print. A large picture hat and a parasol of the same material as her dress shielded her face from the sun. The photographers parted finally and she came down the beach toward them, her high heels sinking into the soft sand.

Dax got to his feet. "Dee Dee, this is Sue Ann Daley. Sue Ann, Dee Dee Lester."

"Miss Daley," the actress said with a faint hint of malice. "I've heard so much about you all these years. I'm glad to meet you."

Sue Ann smiled, getting to her feet. "And I've just heard all about you." She looked at Dax. "Well, I've really got to be going."

"Oh, don't let me interrupt anything," Dee Dee said quickly, "I can't stay but a moment. I can't take the sun. My skin is so delicate, you know. I just came out to see how Dax was doing."

Sue Ann smiled. "Dax is doing fine," she said sweetly. "You weren't interrupting anything important." She picked up her beach bag. "So nice meeting you, Miss Lester."

Dee Dee smiled back. "Nice meeting you."

"Just be good to him," Sue Ann continued, "after all, we are going to get married."

Sue Ann turned her back on them and walked away.

12

The hostess was still a very attractive woman, Jeremy thought, in her mid-forties but still possessing traces of the exciting beauty she must have had in her youth. "Come along to the cocktail party," Dax had urged, "there are always some interesting people at Madame Fontaine's," and since he had had nothing better to do until his dinner appointment, Jeremy had come along.

Dax had been right, there were some interesting people there. Just the proper blend of politicians, diplomats, writers, artists, show people, and the ordinarily wealthy. It was a bright salon and from the pleasantly casual manner in which everything was carried out Jeremy suspected the hostess had been giving such little affairs for a long time.

"It is fascinating," the man on his left said, "the way you Americans can elect a new President and until he takes office the old one remains completely in charge. He still makes many decisions and even appoints people who will survive his own administration."

Jeremy smiled. "Perhaps it is because the new President is aware that in a few months he will have the same oppor-

546

tunity." From the corner of his eye he noticed the hostess, summoned by a maid, pick up the telephone.

"But Eisenhower is going to Korea to end the war. Is he not usurping some of the duties of office?"

"Not really," Jeremy explained. "You see, he's still acting wholly as a private citizen. He cannot initiate any of his plans until he assumes office."

"It is too much for me to understand," the other said in a puzzled voice. "In my country if a man is elected he becomes President that very day. Thus there are never two Presidents."

In your country if a man is elected to office, it is a miracle, Jeremy thought, though he wasn't much interested in what was being said. He was far more curious about the telephone conversation between the hostess and whoever she was speaking with. Whatever it was affected her visibly. Almost before his eyes she seemed to be growing older.

Finally she drew a deep breath. *"A demain,"* she said into the telephone, and put it down. She stood there silently for a long moment as if she were trying to pull herself together. Bit by bit some of the mask of her vitality fell back into place. She took a glass of champagne from a passing tray and walked over to the big bay window overlooking her garden and stood there, staring out silently.

Jeremy was curious about what was holding her interest for so long. By stretching his neck slightly he could see into the garden where, as usual at these affairs, there was a variety of small dogs, yapping and scampering about, left there by their mistresses. And as usual there was one little poodle, hornier than the others, jumping around crazily, trying to mount first one dog, then another. As Jeremy watched, he discovered one bitch who did not throw him off, and with an almost visible expression of satisfaction, he settled down to his task.

The hostess, too, seemed fascinated. Silently she stood there, alone in the window, the room behind her obviously forgotten. When she finally spoke it was as if her thoughts, meant only for her own ears, came from her lips without her being aware of them.

"Look at the little bitch, how happy she is with that cock dancing inside her. She looks around at all the other bitches so proudly. She alone has the cock and she wants them to envy her. And the dog, the damn fool. He thinks he is doing

547

it all, that the triumph is his alone. In his stupidity he thinks he has conquered her but in the end it is she who will triumph."

Jeremy turned to Dax, who had come up beside him. "Do you hear what she is saying?"

Dax nodded.

"I'm sure that everyone else can, too." Jeremy looked around the room. They could hear, all right. Bit by bit the other conversations were fading as they all began to listen, secretly at first, not looking in each other's faces, then more overtly.

"Why doesn't someone stop her?" Jeremy asked in a horrified whisper.

"Let her talk, it is good for her. For years she has been the mistress of Monsieur Basse, the *ministre*. It is in this very same salon that she courted favors for him and helped promote his career. Now there is talk that he has found a younger woman and no longer has time for her." But despite what Dax said, he crossed the quiet salon to stand beside her in the bay window silently.

"What does that little bitch know about what to do with that jabbing cock or with the male to which it is attached? I know what I would do. I would caress him, kiss him, lick him, praise him until he was really swollen with his own strength and power and then I would make room for him inside me and drain his every drop."

Jeremy saw Dax gently take her arm. She turned toward him, a startled expression on her face as if she had just been awakened from a deep sleep. Then slowly she turned and looked around the quiet salon. Her face was faintly pale beneath her makeup. "He is not coming!" she said, in a suddenly loud clear voice.

Almost immediately the conversations began again where they had been dropped. But the party was over and, one by one, the people began to drift away. Jeremy looked at his watch. It was almost time to change for dinner. He caught Dax's eye. "I've got to run. I'll see you in the morning for breakfast."

"Ten o'clock, at my place."

Politely Jeremy sought the hostess but she was nowhere to be found so he left without saying good-bye.

548

Jeremy followed Fat Cat to the dining room. Dax was waiting, still in his dressing gown, his face drawn and tired. He was holding a big glass of tomato juice in his hand.

He grinned at Jeremy. "Probably America's greatest discovery, that tomato juice, lemon, and Worcestershire cure the common hangover."

"My God! You look like the wrath of God. Where did you go last night?"

"Nowhere," Dax answered, taking a sip of tomato juice and making a face. "Now if they could only find a way to make this stuff taste good!"

"I thought you were going to the theater."

"I changed my mind," Dax answered. "I remained at Madame Fontaine's after all the others had gone."

Jeremy stared at him. Suddenly it came to him. "You mean you fucked her?" he asked incredulously.

"It was the decent thing to do," Dax replied noncommittally. He shrugged. "Someone had to give the poor woman back her pride."

Jeremy stared at him speechlessly.

Dax smiled. "And you know, she wasn't bad. She knew what to do, it was exactly as she said it would be. That Basse must be an idiot." He took another sip of his tomato juice. "You know, I think that every once in a while we should oblige an older woman. They are so appreciative, it is great for your ego."

"Oh, brother!" Jeremy said, taking a swallow of the tomato juice Fat Cat had placed before him.

"You do not agree?"

"I do not anything," Jeremy said. "Mostly I do not understand."

Dax laughed. "You Americans are strange, you think a hard is only for making love. But it can also be used to say so many other things."

"I don't get it. I would find it very difficult to—"

"What is so difficult to understand?" Dax interrupted. "Your cock is a part of you, like your hands or feet. You would not let them do or take you where they wanted. What is so different about the penis that it should be considered beyond your control?"

"I quit," Jeremy said, holding up his hands in mock

549

surrender. "You're either too civilized or too primitive for me!"

Dax finished his tomato juice in a gulp. "To carry along that line of thought, a French breakfast of brioche and coffee is too civilized for me this morning. How about primitive American ham and eggs?"

Jeremy laughed. "That I understand."

Later, after they had finished eating and were lolling over their coffee, Jeremy looked at his friend. "You seem restless, changed, not the same somehow."

Dax glanced at him sharply as he lit a thin *cigarro*. "It is not such an easy life being a playboy, whatever your American newspapers seem to think."

"I can believe that," Jeremy said with mock solemnity. "You even have to fuck some broads that you don't like."

Dax laughed. "Even that."

"Seriously, what are you going to do? You're not the sort of man who can sit around doing nothing."

"One never knows until one tries."

"Marcel would give his eyeteeth if you would come in with him. It would take the public's eye off him and let him operate more freely. I'm not sure that it wouldn't be good for both of you."

"Marcel told you that?" Dax glanced at him shrewdly.

"No," Jeremy confessed, "I haven't seen him since he got out of prison. Very few people have. He stays locked up in that house on Park Avenue and makes everyone come to him, even his girls."

"What made you think of Marcel?"

"My father. He seemed to think it might be a good idea. He's ready to talk to Marcel if you wish. You interested?"

Dax shook his head. "Not really. I can't quite see myself as a businessman."

"The money would be good."

Dax glanced at Jeremy and smiled. "I have enough money. I don't have any ambitions to own everything in the world."

"You still should not remain idle. It's a waste. You're too young."

Dax's eyes seemed veiled. "Perhaps it's that I'm too old," he said quietly, "and I can't find any more ways in which to fool myself."

For a few moments there was a silence between them, then

Jeremy broke it abruptly. "Sue Ann's telling everyone she's going to marry you."

Dax did not answer.

"Are you going to marry her?"

Slowly Dax let some smoke drift from his mouth. He held the *cigarro* in front of him and looked at it critically. "I don't know. Possibly, someday, if I'm bored enough."

Then he looked at Jeremy and Jeremy thought he had never seen such sadness in a man's eyes before. "In many ways Sue Ann and I are very much alike, you know. Neither of us has any illusions left."

13

Marcel looked through the gate and saw the reporters and photographers. He turned to the guard who was waiting to let him out. "Is there no other way out of here?"

"There is," the guard answered with grisly humor, "but I doubt that you'd like it."

Marcel gave him a withering look. They were all very funny with their uniforms and petty little bureaucratic ways. It probably gave them a great sense of power to order a man like him around. The guard opened the gate and he walked out.

The reporters were on him instantly. Flashbulbs exploded in his face as he pushed his way through, trying to reach the curb and the waiting limousine. But it was almost impossible to move.

"How does it feel to be out, Mr. Campion?"

"You look like you'd lost some weight, Mr. Campion. How much?"

"Did the prison food agree with you?"

"What are your future plans?"

"Did you know that the immigration authorities have begun deportation proceedings against you?"

"Do you plan to leave the country?"

To all of them Marcel kept muttering the same answer as he pushed his way to the car. "No comment, no comment."

The car sped away from the curb and he leaned back and closed his eyes wearily. It was then that he first became aware of the faintly musky scent of perfume. He turned his head slowly and opened his eyes.

Dania sat there looking at him, her large eyes luminous and dark. "You've grown thin, Marcel," she said softly.

For a moment he did not answer. "Why did you come?" he finally asked, almost harshly. "I wrote that I wanted no one to meet me."

"I thought—" Her eyes suddenly filled with tears and she turned away.

"What did you think?" he asked. "That I would be so hard up from being in prison I would fall into your arms?"

Dania didn't answer.

"I don't need you, I don't need anyone. They'll see. I'll fix all of them who sent me to prison. My turn will come."

"No one sent you to prison, Marcel," Dania replied in a low voice. "You did it all yourself. You listened to nobody."

"It's not true!" he shouted. "It was a plot. They were all out to get me!"

Dania's eyes were dry now and a subtle change had come over her face, a hardness that had not been there before. "They? Who?"

"Abidijan. Horgan. The others." A crafty look came into Marcel's eyes. "They didn't think I could do anything while I was in jail but they were wrong." He began to laugh. "Wait until they discover that it was I who has been buying up their stock on the open market. Wait until they find out that I have acquired the controlling interest in Abidijan Shipping and the Caribtex Oil Company. They won't think then they're so smart. They'll come crawling on their hands and knees. And you know what I'll do?"

She looked into his face and shook her head.

"I'll shit in their faces." He laughed. "That's what I'll do! Shit in their faces!"

For the first time Dania realized how sick Marcel really was. She waited until he had stopped laughing before she spoke. "You're tired, Marcel," she said gently, "run down.

Take a vacation before you do anything. Perhaps a cruise. A long rest while you get your strength back."

"They already know! They sent you to distract me!"

"Marcel!" Her voice was shocked. "I knew nothing about it. Not until this moment."

"I don't believe you. You're in it with all of them. You're all against me!"

Dania stared at him, shocked.

"Now I understand why you cling to that decrepit husband of yours. All the time you were only spying on me. For them!"

"Marcel, that's not true," Dania said, almost desperately. "I couldn't be spying on you. I don't even know them."

"You're lying, you're lying!" he shouted. He signaled to the driver through the glass.

Startled, the chauffeur slammed on the brakes and veered to the curb and Dania almost pitched forward onto the floor. By the time she straightened up Marcel had pushed open the door. "Get out!"

She stared at him for a moment, then smiled. Her voice was thick with contempt. "You sick little man. Get out? Get out of what—my own car?"

Marcel glared back at her, his face paling. Then silently he moved around her and through the open car door. In his haste his heel caught and he pitched forward, tumbling into the gutter.

Dania didn't waste a glance, just pulled the door shut. "Drive on."

It was that photograph, a shot of Marcel sprawled out on his hands and knees in the gutter of an Atlanta suburb staring after the departing limousine, that pushed the Korean War from the front pages of most newspapers the next day. It was taken by a persistent news photographer who had been following Dania's car.

There was a crew of electricians working elsewhere in the house when Schacter was finally shown into the study that Marcel was temporarily using as his office. "What are all these men doing?"

"I'm having the house wired," Marcel answered. "They're installing a burglar-alarm system."

"What on earth for?" the lawyer asked. "You're right on

553

Park Avenue, one of the best-policed areas in the city. Who's likely to break in?"

A peculiar look crossed Marcel's face. "Twice already they've tried since I've been home."

"Did you tell the police?"

"Yes. I even asked for extra protection but they only laughed at me. They said to call them if anyone else broke in. I suspect there's been a payoff."

"The police?" Schacter laughed. "Don't be silly." He sat down and lit a cigarette. "They couldn't care less about your problems."

"You forget I've been to prison," Marcel answered stiffly. "That sets them against me automatically."

Schacter didn't answer. There were some subjects one just couldn't talk reasonably about with Marcel. "Well, so long as you feel better about it."

"Much better." For the first time Marcel smiled. "When I'm finished no one will be able to get into this house without my knowing. Unless they get through the walls by osmosis."

Schacter opened his briefcase. "I brought some papers for you to sign."

"What papers?"

Schacter laid the first group on the desk. "That's the agreement with General Mutual Trust to purchase their holdings in Caribtex at eleven and a half."

"I told you eleven," Marcel said suspiciously.

"You said I could go as high as twelve." That was one thing Schacter did not like about Marcel. After he agreed to something he always carped about it.

"How much does that give us?"

"Another 421,000 shares. About nine percent."

"That's more than Horgan and his group own?"

Schacter nodded. "About 42,000 shares more. You now own 26.1 percent, and they have only 25.3 percent."

"Good." Marcel smiled, and swiftly signed the agreements. He pushed the papers back at the lawyer. "What else?"

"I spoke to De Coyne in Paris this morning. They say they can't renew the note. The money market over there has gone very tight."

Marcel's face flushed with sudden anger. He slammed the desk with his fist. "They've turned against me, too." He stared

554

at the lawyer. "I have half a mind to go over there. I'd make them change their minds!"

"You can't and you know it," the lawyer answered, "so long as Immigration has a deportation case pending against you."

"They might as well have kept me in jail."

Schacter was silent. He thought about the steel bars that had gone up on all the windows in Marcel's house last week. And now the burglar alarm.

"Did you talk to the Boston banks about taking over the note?"

"Yes. They're not interested."

Marcel glared at him. "I started the Israeli lines. I was the only one who was willing to take the risk. The De Coynes were so anxious for me to do so they all but fell over themselves to lend me the money. Now that those Jews see a way to make more money I'm being pushed out."

Schacter returned his gaze steadily. "I don't think being Jewish has anything to do with it," he said steadily. "The De Coynes are bankers. They know how far you're stretching yourself on your other deals. You can't have everything, you know."

"Why not?" Marcel asked. "Who has a better right?"

It was late and the party was beginning to break up. Suddenly Dax looked around. Only he and Marcel and a few girls were left. He caught Marcel's eye. Marcel left the blond girl he had been talking with and came over to him. "Everything all right?"

"Everything's fine," Dax answered, "but it's getting late. I promised to go out early tomorrow morning on Jacobsen's yacht. I'd better be leaving."

"What for?" Marcel asked. "It's early; the best part of the evening is coming up."

"The best part? But everyone has gone."

Marcel smiled secretively. "The girls are still here."

Dax looked at him, then around the room. There were still five girls left, and every now and then he had noticed one of them glancing at him speculatively.

"They're all on my payroll."

"They work in your office?" Dax's voice was incredulous. They didn't look like the type.

"Of course not." There was a faint note of triumph in Marcel's voice. "But they do work for me. The tax laws are getting so strict about expenses it's cheaper to put them on a salary. That way they're deductible."

"Oh."

"A man has to keep on his toes every minute," Marcel said. "They're always out to get you."

Dax didn't answer.

"Now that the others are gone," Marcel continued, "we can go upstairs to my suite. I can promise you won't be bored." He turned to the girls. *"Allons, mes enfants."*

Silently Dax followed them up the staircase to the second floor, where Marcel stopped in front of a door. He took a key out of his pocket and inserted it into a slot. In a moment there was a soft whir from above.

"The only way to my suite is by elevator," he said. "I had the stairways taken out." He opened the door. "We'll go up first with two of the girls. Then I'll send the elevator down for the others."

"But the servants? How do they get to their quarters?"

"There's a stairway in the back, but I've had the entrance to my floor closed off with brick." They got out of the elevator, and Marcel turned and pressed a button on the wall. "I have a button in each of my rooms up here. No one can get up unless I release the elevator."

A moment later the other three girls got off the elevator and Marcel led them all into a large sitting room. There was a table already laid with hors d'oeuvres, caviar, and a pâté. Several bottles of champagne were cooling in buckets, and in the corner was a completely equipped bar.

The girls seemed to know what was expected of them and disappeared through a door on the far side of the room. "That's the guest room," Marcel said. "My room is on the other side. How about a drink?"

"I've about had enough."

"You must," Marcel urged with a peculiar smile, and took Dax by the arm. "Come."

Marcel pressed something under the bar. A panel slid open, revealing a television set, and a moment later it came on. What appeared on the screen was the guest room. The girls were milling about, and in a moment the sound of their voices came through the speaker.

One of them was taking off her dress. "What a drag," she said, in a disgusted voice.

Marcel smiled. "The newest thing—closed-circuit television. They don't even realize we're watching. I'm thinking of putting one in every room of the house. That way I'll know exactly what's going on."

Marcel seemed completely absorbed. Most of the girls were undressed by now. One of them walked over to a closet and pushed back the sliding door. "Well, kids, what'll it be tonight?"

"I don't know," another replied. "What did we wear last time?"

"The white virgin bride outfits."

"Then how about the slinky black bit? It's been a long time since we did that one."

One of the others had moved over to the closet. She had unfastened her brassiere and her rather large breasts pushed free.

"That one does a fantastic trick." Marcel was speaking in a half whisper as though they might hear. "She holds your balls between her tits while she nuzzles you and massages your prostate with her finger. She's a terrible liar, though. She doesn't realize that I know all about the boyfriend who comes to her apartment. Sometimes I feel like throwing her out but they're all alike. You can't trust any of them."

"How do you know she has a boyfriend?"

Marcel smiled his secretive smile. "I know everything. Their telephones are tapped; I even have bugs planted in the springs under their beds." He laughed, turning back to the screen. "You should hear some of the tapes!"

Dax looked back at the screen. The girls were mostly dressed by now. They were all wearing the same costume. Black lace see-through brassieres and garter belts to which were attached long black mesh opera hose. One of the girls turned toward the camera and suddenly the screen went dark. Automatically the panel began to close.

"There's a switch under the rug just in front of the door. It turns the set off automatically the moment anyone starts to leave the room."

Dax looked at Marcel. "I think I'll have that drink now."

It was almost four o'clock in the morning when Dax finally got around to leaving. Marcel watched owlishly from the couch between two of the girls as Dax said his good nights. He was more than a little drunk. Like most Frenchmen he had no tolerance for hard liquors, and had consistently drunk Scotch all night. He struggled to his feet. "I will go downstairs with you. I have something I want to talk about."

Dax followed him into the elevator. Marcel smiled. "What do you think of my little employees, eh?"

Dax laughed. "I must say they're very experienced. But kind of expensive, I imagine."

"You pay for experience. But it doesn't matter, I can afford it."

When they left the elevator and walked downstairs, Marcel said, "Come into my office a moment."

Dax followed him into the library. Marcel closed the door behind them and sat down behind his desk. "I suppose you wonder why I wanted to see you?"

Dax didn't answer.

"I think *el Presidente* was very foolish to treat you as he did. Someday he'll regret it."

Dax shrugged noncommittally.

Marcel stared at him. "But that is not what concerns me. You must be very bored."

"Not really. How can I be bored when I have friends like you?"

Marcel smiled. He was pleased. Then his face went serious. "But how many girls can you fuck? Sooner or later you must wish you had something else to think about."

"I don't know," Dax replied, "it seems to me that I've spent most of my life thinking about other things. What good has it done me?"

"But there must be many things you want to do," Marcel persisted.

"I haven't thought of any yet."

"Have you ever considered going into business? Indirectly you've made a lot of money for others. Isn't it about time you made some for yourself?"

"I haven't felt the need of it."

"You are very much like your father," Marcel said. "He never thought about himself either, he put other things first. I remember when I first came to work for him I was amazed. I had never encountered a man like him before."

"You will never meet another."

"But that was why he died a poor man."

"Perhaps, but to the dead riches do not matter."

"It's all very well to talk like that, Dax, but the world doesn't look at things that way. The only important things are money and power."

"I'm very lucky then." Dax smiled. "I've found a way to get along without either."

Marcel looked at him for a moment. "That's a pity, because I was hoping I could interest you in coming in with me. Together we would do very well. I'm not well liked, you know. I have enemies who go out of their way to do me harm. With you in the picture I could gradually merge into the background, and in time they would forget about me. It would be very worth your while."

Dax looked at him without answering.

"You're the only person to whom I'd make such an offer," Marcel added sincerely. "There's no one else in this world I trust that much."

Dax took a deep breath. In some odd way he knew that Marcel was telling the truth. There was no one else. The closed-circuit television, the tapped telephones, the microphones under the beds. How long would it be before Marcel used the same things to be sure of him? Because there was no doubt in his mind that eventually he would. Marcel was already too far gone to ever retain his faith in anyone. Dax shook his head slowly.

"Thank you, Marcel, but no. If I thought I could be of any real help to you I might have considered it. But I know better. I'm no businessman; in time I'd become a liability, believe me. But I am flattered at your offer."

Marcel looked down at his desk. He did not meet Dax's eyes. "Everyone has turned against me."

"I haven't. If I had, it would make it easier to accept such an offer. I could do more harm inside your organization than outside."

Marcel looked at him. He seemed to be weighing what Dax had said. "That's true." He smiled, suddenly cheerful again. "I know you, you old faker. You have an easier way to make money up your sleeve."

"I have?"

"I've heard the talk about you and Sue Ann," Marcel said knowingly. "In a way I don't blame you. It's easier to marry it than work for it."

Dax smiled. He wasn't annoyed at Marcel's assumption. If that was what Marcel chose to believe, let him. He got to his feet.

"I'll let you out."

Dax waited until Marcel cut off the alarm system and opened the front door. As usual there were no cabs on the street at that hour of the morning. "Let me call my chauffeur to drive you home."

Dax looked up at the sky. It was already turning gray over to the east of Park Avenue. "It's a short walk and I think I could use the fresh air."

From Fifth Avenue, a few blocks away, a large black car was coming toward them. Marcel glanced at it nervously. "I think I'd better be getting back in. I'm beginning to feel a slight chill."

"Good night, Marcel."

"Good night, my friend," Marcel said through the already closing door, "call me whenever you're in town. I'll be here."

Dax stared at the closed door for a moment. He heard the click of an electric switch and knew that Marcel had turned on the burglar alarm again. He turned and walked down to the street.

If this was the price one had to pay for money and power, he wanted no part of it.

15

Marcel was sitting behind his desk when Schacter came in. "Well?"

Schacter shook his head. "Abidijan says you can go to hell. He wouldn't even listen to anything I had to say."

Marcel's face went pale. "Is that all?"

"Not really. He said a few things."

"Like what?"

"They weren't relevant."

"Tell me." Marcel's voice was flat and hard. "I want to know what Amos said."

The attorney felt uncomfortable. "He said you were sick and that you didn't know what you were doing. He claimed he would like nothing better than for you to start a proxy fight. The publicity you've had before this would be nothing compared to what he's prepared to give you. After he got through he said there wouldn't be one stockholder who would go along with you. He also told me that if you tried to vote your children's stock as trustee he was prepared to go into court and have you certified as incompetent."

Marcel's face was almost completely white now. He could scarcely contain his rage. "But he doesn't expect us to go into court with a stockholder's action in which he would be the defendant, does he?"

The lawyer shook his head. "No. He hardly anticipates that."

Marcel smiled thinly. "That's what we do, then. We have enough on him to force the court to appoint a receiver for the company, maybe even put him in the jail where he put me."

"But what good would that do? The court would never turn the company over to you."

"That's unimportant," Marcel said. "The main thing would be that Amos won't have it."

"But have you thought of your children?" the lawyer asked. "What it might do to their inheritance? The trust fund is made up almost wholly of Abidijan stock. It might be worth nothing under a receiver. For that matter the stock you have probably won't be worth the paper it's printed on."

"I don't care!" Marcel shouted. "I can take care of my children! Go into court!"

The lawyer looked at him steadily. After a moment he shook his head. "No, Marcel, I won't do it. I went along with you on most things but not this. It serves no purpose at all. You're simply being destructive."

"You won't do it? You say you won't do it?"

Marcel rose and leaned across his desk. For a moment Schacter thought he was going to strike him. Then words came spilling from Marcel's mouth. "You've sold me out! You sold out to them!"

A look of contempt crossed Schacter's face. "I won't even bother answering that one."

"This is your last chance!" Marcel screamed. "Either go into court or I'll get another lawyer!"

Schacter got to his feet quietly. "That's your privilege."

Marcel came running around the desk still screaming. "I'll have you disbarred! You can't walk out on me! You can't change sides merely because they offered you more money!"

"No one offered me any money," Schacter said, turning at the door, "they didn't have to. Besides, how could anyone believe even you would be crazy enough to pull everything down on your own head just to get even with one man?"

Marcel glared at him wildly. "You Jews are all alike! On sale to the highest bidder!"

For the first time since he had been a young man Schacter lost his temper. He had fought too many times, both publicly and privately, over such slurs. He was a big man, over six feet tall, and his hands shot out and grabbed Marcel by the lapels. For a moment it seemed as if he would pick him up bodily and hurl him across the room. Then he regained his self-control and abruptly let Marcel go.

For a moment they stared at each other. Schacter reached around behind him and opened the door.

"Why are you glaring at me like that?"

"I must have been blind," the attorney said slowly. "Now I believe your father-in-law. You are crazy!"

The next morning Marcel was on the telephone as if nothing had happened. "I've been thinking over what you said, and I've decided you are right. There's no point in going into court. Abidijan's an old man, he won't live forever. When he's gone I'll be able to take it over. I'm still the second largest stockholder."

"You mean you're not going into court?"

"Of course not."

"But yesterday you said—"

"That was yesterday," Marcel answered quickly, interrupting. "Surely you're not holding against me what I said in anger? You're too big a man for that, Schacter. You know the terrible strain I've been under."

At the end of the conversation Schacter found himself once again Marcel's attorney. But somehow he could never bring himself to feel that things could ever be the same. Something had gone out of the relationship.

Schacter could feel the tension mount in the small room. For a moment he could not bear to look at the table with its pile of envelopes and proxies and clicking adding machines. Instead he looked out of the window at downtown Dallas.

Suddenly the room behind him was quiet. The adding machines had stopped, so Schacter knew it was over. Slowly he turned back into the room. He did not have to go over to look at the totals to know who had won. One look at Horgan's face told him all he needed to know. The Texan was pallid beneath his deep tan.

Slowly the secretary of Caribtex read out the totals in a trembling voice. And well it might tremble, for his job was gone, as were those of most of the other men in the room. Under the cumulative voting laws of the corporation it was either one group or the other. There was no middle ground. For management: 1,100,021. For the opposition group: 1,600,422.

There was a silence in the room as Schacter walked around the table. The secretary made room for him. Schacter looked at him, then at the others. "Thank you, gentlemen."

The accountants began to gather up the records and put them away in boxes. Schacter glanced at them for a moment.

The best idea that Marcel had had was to have the court appoint a special company of accountants for counting the proxies. The company's accountants would never have given them a fair shake.

"There will be a special meeting of the new board of directors for the purpose of electing new officers tomorrow morning at nine o'clock."

He got up from the table and started toward the door. Marcel would be waiting for his call. Horgan's voice stopped him. "You tell yoh slimy little friend never to come down this way. 'Cause if'n he does somebody suah as hell will fill him full of lead."

Schacter nodded gravely and walked on out the door.

Marcel was drunk. He had been drinking steadily all afternoon while he waited for the call from Dallas. Now that it was all over the liquor seemed to roar through his body. He could feel himself swelling, his body growing taller until he could almost touch the ceiling. He walked over to the couch where the big-breasted blond sat watching him. He stood in front of her, weaving. "Do you know who I am?"

She sat there silently, looking up at him.

"You don't know." He reached for the drink he had left on the table and raised it to his lips. Some of it spilled on his jacket but he paid no attention. He drained the glass and threw it over his shoulder. It crashed against the wall.

"You don't know," he repeated, "nobody knows." His voice lowered and became confidential. "But soon they'll find out, because they can't stop me now. I'm the biggest man they ever saw."

"Man, are you stewed," she said.

Marcel paid no attention. He was tearing at his clothes, for suddenly they were choking him—too tight, too small. Finally they all lay in a pile on the floor. He climbed up on the couch naked and stood looking down at her. "Am I not the biggest man you ever saw?"

"Better come down from there before you kill yourself," she said, reaching up a hand to steady him.

Marcel slapped her hand away. "Answer my question."

Silently she nodded.

A suspicious look came into his face. "As big as Joe Karlo?"

The color drained from her face. "You—you know about Joe?"

He began to laugh wildly. "You stupid cunt!" he screamed. "I know everything about you. I know everything about everybody. I can even tell you what you both said in bed last night!"

"How—how do you know?"

"I know, that's all that matters." He laughed wildly. "And I know something else you don't know." He leaped from the couch and ran to a cabinet. He opened the doors and took out some photographs, waving them in her face. "You think he'll marry you, you think he's been saving all the money you gave him so the two of you can go away together? You stupid fool! You want to know where the money has been going all this time? Look!"

She stared at the photographs. A man stood smiling into the camera, one arm around a pleasant-looking young woman. His other arm was around three smiling children.

"You didn't know he was married, did you? You weren't aware the money you gave him last month went to buy them a station wagon?"

She suddenly felt sick. "I've got to go."

Marcel slapped her in the face, and she fell back onto the couch. "I didn't tell you you could go!"

He reached down with both hands and grabbed the front of her dress. The fabric came away with a rasping, tearing sound. He put his hand inside her brassiere and pulled her breasts up and out. She stared at him, a fear growing deep in her eyes as once more he stood over her. Slowly he lowered himself onto her breasts until he was sitting facing her.

He looked down at her and laughed. "Now, tell me. Examine it carefully. See, am I not the biggest man you ever saw?"

Despite his weight she managed to nod.

"I'm the biggest man in the world!" A glazed look came into his eyes. "Soon I'll own——" He tried to continue but suddenly he pitched forward, falling heavily across her.

She lay very still for a few moments, afraid to move. After a while she turned slightly, trying to wriggle out from under him. Slowly, almost gently, he slid to the floor and rolled over on his back. His mouth was open and as she watched in fascination he began to snore heavily.

She sat up on the couch. "You son of a bitch!" Then she noticed the photographs lying on the floor beside him and the tears came unexpectedly to her eyes. "All you sons of bitches!" she cried, wiping at her eyes with the back of her hand.

16

From the pool at the far end of the terraced lawn came the happy sound of children's laughter. The warm Côte d'Azur sun fell languidly upon the blue waters. It was not that long ago, Robert thought, that he and Caroline had shared that same pool with their friends and cousins. Not so long ago, before the war.

"You have a strange look on your face, Robert."

With an effort he brought his mind back to the present. He smiled at his English cousin. "I was thinking about when you and I were young."

Mavis made a face. "Don't remind me, I remember all too well. How you used to tease me because I was skin and bones. And now look at me."

Robert laughed. That at least was true. Mavis was skin and bones no longer, and neither was her sister. The two of them had settled into the comfortable figures of young British matrons. It was their five children and his son, Henri, who were making all the noise in the pool. "None of us has stayed exactly the same."

"Except Caroline," Enid said. "I don't know how she does it but she looks as young as ever. If anything her figure is even better than ever I remember."

"Are you talking about me?"

"Mavis would like to know the secret of your eternal youth," Robert said.

Caroline laughed. "It's no secret. I diet."

"I never could," Mavis said. "The children make me so nervous sometimes, all I can do is eat and eat."

Robert looked down the table toward his father. The baron looked slim and comfortable despite the weather. He was seventy-two years old but seemed much younger, especially his eyes. They never seemed to age. Right now they were alert and attentive as he listened to Sir Robert.

Sir Robert had put on weight but despite it his face had never quite lost the slightly rapacious look that he had never trusted. If anything the look was more pronounced than ever. Idly he wondered why he had never liked Sir Robert.

John, Mavis' husband, a tall, blond, athletic-looking Englishman, said, "Robert, it seems a grand day for a sail. How about coming out with us this afternoon?"

Robert looked down at the boat dock off which their English yacht was at anchor. "Not me, I haven't the energy of you English." He got to his feet slowly and stretched. "The only decent thing to do after a lunch like this is to take a nap."

He crossed the terrace and went into the house just as Denisonde came out. "Where are you going?"

Robert grinned. "I'm going upstairs to take a nap."

"Why don't you stretch out in the sun?" she asked. "You can sleep just as well there, and you'll get some color in your face. What's the sense of coming to the Riviera if not for that? You could just as well have stayed at the bank if you're going to spend all your time indoors."

Robert stood looking at her indulgently. "Finished?"

"Yes."

"What are you doing?"

"I'm bringing your father his medicine. If I don't remind him he'll never take it."

"*Bien.* When you've done that come upstairs and I will show you why it is always better to take a nap indoors."

It was after midnight and the big villa was silent when Robert made his way down to the library in search of something to read. He opened the door and as he went directly to the *bibliothèque*, his father's voice came from directly behind him. "You are awake?"

Robert turned. The baron was seated in one of the deep

easy chairs. "I could not sleep," Robert said. "I expect I slept too much this afternoon. But why are you awake?"

"I am old," his father replied. "When you are old you don't need as much sleep."

Robert smiled and took a book down from the shelf. Idly he glanced through it.

"Our cousin thinks it's time our banks merged," the baron said unexpectedly.

Robert looked up from the book. "What do you think?"

"Many years ago it was the ambition of my grandfather —one bank that would blanket all Europe." The baron looked up at Robert. "It was not such a bad idea then, perhaps it is an even better one now. The American banks grow larger every day, and even the Morgan bank is thinking of a merger. The American banks are our strongest competition. If our resources were pooled we could match them on any deal."

"I don't like it," Robert said suddenly.

The baron seemed curious. "Do you have a reason?"

"Not really. I just feel a merger would cost us our independence. We would not be able to act as freely as we do now."

"I am not at all convinced it would not be to our advantage. Certainly our cousin has been successful. His bank is twice the size of ours."

"That is no true measure," Robert replied quickly. "Not once have they had to suspend operations because of war or a change in government. How many have we had since the time of Napoleon? And each time we have had to rebuild from the ground up. Sir Robert was fortunate in having a continuous, stable government during all that time."

"Then a merger might be advantageous. Wars and governments would no longer affect us if our business was centered in London."

"If we're concerned only with safety, why not move our headquarters to New York? There we would be even safer."

The baron looked at him shrewdly. "You do not like our cousin, I gather."

Robert stared back at him for a moment. "No, I do not."

His father did not ask his reasons. "Even as a boy Sir Robert was always ambitious."

"If that were all I sensed in him I would not be worried."

The baron looked up. "You think he wants to control our bank, too?"

"Wouldn't he?" Robert asked. "You've admitted his is twice the size of ours. Is it not normal that the shark eats the sardines?"

"Perhaps. But aren't you forgetting one thing? I have a son, and Sir Robert has only daughters. The bylaws of both banks are similar in one respect. Only sons may inherit control. Our grandfather saw to that."

"But the sons of daughters may inherit," Robert said. "Already three of his five grandchildren are sons."

"Sons. That was the secret strength of the Rothschilds. They bred sons. We have not been so lucky—perhaps one to a generation. Sir Robert and I were the only ones in ours, you the only one in yours. And you have but one." He smiled suddenly at Robert. "What are you waiting for? You must apply yourself!"

Robert laughed. "I'm doing the best I can, *Papa*."

Robert looked down at the sheet of paper, then up at the accountant. "You've made no mistakes on this?"

The accountant shook his head. "Everything is verified, sir."

"Thank you."

Robert sat thoughtfully for a moment. For months someone had been buying up all the bank's paper and he had not until now been able to ascertain who. Now he knew. He should have realized before. He should have been aware that Sir Robert would not come to his father without a card up his sleeve; he was far too professional not to be prepared for a refusal. Suddenly it was all clear, even where Campion had got the money to meet his note.

He got up and with the sheet of paper in his hand went down to his father's office. He knocked and went in. "Did you know about this?" he asked, placing the paper in front of the baron.

The baron looked down at it. "I guessed as much," he admitted, "but I could not be sure."

"Then why didn't you stop him?" Robert asked. "He has almost enough of our paper to put us out of business."

The baron shrugged and leaned back in his chair. "I

569

couldn't see quite what difference it would make once we merged."

"You're not going to let him push us into a merger?"

"There is very little else I can do," the baron said. "I am old. I am tired. I have not the strength for another battle with our cousin."

Robert stared at his father angrily. "You may not, but I have! I will not let you trade away my children's future because yours has already passed. I will find a way to stop that greedy cousin of ours!" He stormed out of the office, slamming the door behind him.

The baron looked at the closed door for a moment, then slowly began to smile. He had waited a long time for this moment. When Robert would admit that he cared as much about the bank as he did. That Robert wanted it for his son as he had wanted it for Robert.

Now he could do what he wanted with a clear conscience. At last he could retire.

17

Slowly Robert turned the pages of the confidential ledger until he found what he sought. Then he sat there, studying the figures. This could be the answer. It all depended on how greedy Sir Robert really was.

Capital had always been the problem. It always was with a private bank. A publicly held bank had many ways of increasing its capital. It could merely issue stock to extend its capitalization if it should so desire. But De Coyne's was a private bank. There were no shareholders outside of the family. That was the way it had always been. They accounted to no one except themselves.

Many years ago his father had solved the problem of improving the bank's cash working position without borrowing money or diluting their ownership. He began to sell short-term notes at minimal discount. The reputation of the bank was such that the response was immediate. The public bought the notes without hesitation, in preference to other offerings promising greater gain, because they felt there was no risk. Never in the almost one hundred years of its existence had the De Coyne bank failed to meet an obligation. Before long such notes developed a reputation for being more stable than many of the currencies of Europe. Perhaps one of the reasons was that they were always payable in dollars, and in any country in the world.

Wisely the baron had anticipated the problem of the notes being hoarded and to counteract this he set up a repayment program. Ten percent of the notes outstanding were redeemable each year for new notes or for cash. To make certain of their redemption, interest was paid on the notes only until their due date; after that no interest was earned.

The plan had worked very well until almost five years ago when a small percentage of the notes due had not been presented either for exchange or for redemption. Automatically a transfer had been effected from working cash to reserve. It had grown with each succeeding year until now almost twenty million dollars lay idle in that reserve account.

Robert calculated swiftly. This money held in reserve alone meant a net reduction in possible earnings to the bank of close to three million dollars, the difference between what this sum could have earned and the interest they paid on the notes. But it meant something even more important. It limited the bank's ability to enter into new ventures and reduced their competitive position in the money market.

Robert stared down at the page in front of him. Right there lay the answer, if it worked. The Corteguayan investments, by far the most profitable the bank had. While it was true they had only a half-interest, since Sir Robert's bank in England held the other half, their share alone represented almost nineteen million dollars. Their profit from this was almost five million dollars a year.

Robert toyed idly with his pencil. It was a big profit to forego. Almost two-thirds of the total earnings of the bank after all operational expenses had been met. But it would be a bargain if it got their paper out of the grasp of the baron's English cousin. It would have to be handled delicately. Sir Robert must rise to the bait without ever becoming aware who was holding the other end of the line. Robert reached for the telephone.

"See if you can locate Monsieur Xenos for me." He listened to his secretary for a moment, then added, "Anywhere in the world. It is vital I speak with him."

Two young men were seated on either side of Sir Robert's desk when Dax was shown into the office. They both rose as Sir Robert extended his hand. "It's good of you to drop in, Dax. It's been a long time."

Dax took his hand, smiling. "Yes, sir, it has."

"You haven't met my sons-in-law, Victor Wadleigh and John Staunton."

"Mr. Wadleigh, Mr. Staunton."

"Please sit down," Sir Robert said, sinking back into his chair. "I suppose you're wondering why I asked to see you?"

"Not really," Dax replied. "I have a faint idea." He cast a questioning look at the two young men.

"You may speak frankly," Sir Robert said quickly. "They're both in the bank and quite privy to my affairs."

Dax nodded and smiled. "I imagine it's about the Corteguayan investments?"

"Exactly," Sir Robert said. He glanced at his sons-in-law, then back at Dax. "We've learned that you started negotiation with the baron's bank for the acquisition of their holdings in Corteguay."

"That's true," Dax admitted.

"I was not aware that you were still active in the affairs of your country."

"I'm not," Dax replied. "Actually, I am not acting for myself or for Corteguay. I represent a syndicate interested in the acquisition." He reached for a cigarette, and one of the young men sprang up to light it for him. "After what happened to me I have learned, though rather late in life, I must admit, that I have to look after myself."

Sir Robert nodded. This kind of language he had no difficulty in understanding. "I must say you have been treated rather shabbily after all you've done."

Dax did not answer.

"This group you represent—they're Americans, I imagine?"

Dax smiled. "That much I can admit."

"You wouldn't be at liberty to disclose to us just who they might be?"

Dax shook his head. "I could not disclose that even to you, Sir Robert."

"You are aware, of course, that we hold an equal investment in Corteguay and that our agreement would be necessary before the baron could sell your group his share?"

Dax nodded. "Robert mentioned that, but he said he expected no difficulty. He explained that he could always count on your cooperation."

Sir Robert was silent. The baron must be feeling the squeeze if he was considering such a sale. The Corteguayan investment was the most profitable the two banks had ever made. He also realized that he dared not withhold approval if the baron asked. If he did the baron would never consent to a merger.

In a way he felt himself between the devil and the deep blue sea. If he approved the deal, there was all that profit gone. If he withheld his approval, however, there would be open war between himself and the baron and no merger could be effectuated. Unless there was another way.

That was it, he thought suddenly, there was a third way. True, it would mean that the merger would have to be put off for a while. But even that was unimportant in the light of what would be gained for very little additional investment on his part.

He looked across the desk at Dax. In a way it would all depend on what Dax had meant when he said he had to look after himself. Sir Robert hesitated for a moment, remembering their conflict of many years ago. But only for a moment. Then his greed betrayed him into thinking that eventually all men came to be motivated by money. Rapidly he began to speak.

Robert could scarcely believe the triumph he felt, and in his elation he lapsed into an Americanism. "You mean he bit?"

Dax smiled. "Hook, line, and sinker."

The baron looked from one to the other, slightly puzzled. "Explain it to me."

Robert turned to his father. "When our honorable cousin learned that the Corteguayan investments might go else-

573

where, he decided to buy them for himself. First he bought Dax off by offering him twice as much as he thought the mythical syndicate was offering. Then he met what he thought was the syndicate's offer, twenty-five million dollars, the only provision being that instead of cash, twenty million would be in our own paper."

The baron smiled. "And what did you do?"

Robert smiled back at him. "What could I do? After all, blood is thicker than water, so I had to accept. His sons-in-law have just returned to London with the signed agreement."

The baron looked at Dax. "You have done well."

"Thank you," Dax replied, "though I really did nothing. I was merely the errand boy; it was all Robert's idea. I feel guilty about accepting your money."

"You shouldn't, you have earned it." The baron turned to his son. "You, too, have done well."

Robert smiled. Praise from his father was very rare. "I have something for you." He opened the briefcase which he had brought into his father's office and spread out the ornately printed forms upon his desk. "The paper—twenty million dollars' worth."

The baron looked down for a moment, then opened his desk drawer and took out a single sheet of paper. He wrote the date in his own hand across the top, then turned to Robert with a smile. "And I have something for you."

Robert looked down at the sheet of paper. Below the date were the typewritten words:

The De Coyne Bank announces today the retirement of the Baron Henri Raphael Sylvestre de Coyne from his office as President of the Bank, and the election of his son, Robert Raymonde Samuel de Coyne, as his successor. In so doing, the De Coyne Bank announces with pride, the office of President has now passed directly from father to son for the fourth generation.

There were tears in the old man's eyes as he looked at Robert. "It is my fondest wish," he said quietly, "that one day you will be able to do this for your son."

Robert leaned over his father's chair. He tasted the salt of the old man's tears as he pressed his lips first to one cheek, then the other. "Thank you, Father," he said humbly. "It is also my fondest wish."

18

Dee Dee came into the bedroom holding a newspaper. "Have you read this column of Irma Andersen's?"

Dax rolled over on his bed. "You know I don't read the columns."

That was something Dee Dee would never understand. As an actress she was constantly searching the papers for mention of herself. She subscribed to at least three different clipping services and would no more think of coming down to breakfast without the morning columns than she would of leaving the house without makeup.

The jet plane has given society a new freedom. Freedom from boredom. Bored? Get on a jet and tomorrow you're anywhere in the world you want to be. You could be in Paris attending the latest showing of the new Prince Nikovitch collection with Robert de Coyne, the new young head of the ancient De Coyne Bank, and his lovely wife, Denisonde, and charming sister, Caroline. You could be in London at Claridge's and lunching on the roast beef at the next table might be the Earl of Buckingham and Jeremy Hadley and perhaps even one or two visiting American congressmen. London is very 'in' politically this year. Or you could be on the Via Veneto in Rome rubbing elbows with Dee Dee Lester or any one of your favorite Hollwood movie stars flocking to what many think is rapidly becoming the new cinema capital of the world. Or you could be lying on the sand soaking up the sun on the Riviera, not even

575

knowing that the man with the beautiful tan lying next to you is the famous South American playboy Dax Xenos, and the beautiful girl in the brief bikini next to him Sue Ann Daley, probably the richest heiress in the world.

You, too, can join the fabulous jet set. You don't have to be a movie star, born into the four hundred, or a politician or a playboy. You don't even have to be rich. All you need is a ticket. The jets fly day and night.

Dee Dee put down the newspaper and looked at Dax. "What do you think of that?"

"If it's all that damn exciting, what the hell are we doing in New York?"

"That's not what I mean."

"The old dike must have a new client, the airlines."

"You're being deliberately stupid."

"Stupid? Let me see that newspaper." Dax took it from her hand and rapidly glanced at it. "I don't know what you're complaining about. She spelled your name right."

"Damn! You know perfectly well what I mean. Me in Rome, you on the Riviera!"

"Wrong on both counts as usual," Dax said, shaking his head. "We're in New York. Very bad reporting."

Dee Dee pulled the newspaper from his hand and hit him across the head with it. "With Sue Ann Daley, that's what I mean! The old bitch did that deliberately. She wanted to show we were apart."

"Well, we were."

"Then you admit you were on the Riviera with Sue Ann?"

"Of course. You didn't expect me to stay in all that accursed heat in Rome while you were making a picture, did you?"

"You came to New York with her; that's why I had to come here to find you."

Dax shrugged. "I was coming to New York anyway."

Dee Dee sat down suddenly. "I don't like it."

"Careful, you're beginning to act possessive."

Dee Dee looked at him with troubled eyes. "I think I'm beginning to fall in love with you."

"Don't! Love is not the 'in' thing this year, not even in the jet set."

Dax followed the maître d' into the bar. As usual, "21" was crowded. He nodded pleasantly to several people he knew on the way to his corner table.

"Sorry I'm late," he apologized as Jeremy Hadley rose to greet him.

"That's all right. I just got here myself."

They both sat down and Dax ordered a Bloody Mary. When the captain went away the two men looked at each other. "Well?"

Jeremy smiled. "I'm a little surprised that when I suggested lunch you chose '21' instead of the Colony."

Dax laughed. "I only take girls to the Colony."

"I bow to the leader."

"The leader?"

"Didn't you know? That's what they're calling you now."

Dax was honestly puzzled. "I can't see why."

"I suppose the newspapers started it. You've become the columnists' darling."

Dax grinned. "Oh, them. They're a bunch of old women. They have nothing else to write about."

"Not true," Jeremy replied quickly, "they have their pick of the field. They can write about any celebrity. But they write about you because you represent to them the new way of life. Somehow you always turn up at the right places, with the right people, at the right time. Do you know how many times a week your name is in the columns?"

"You mean I'm 'in'?"

"You're more than that." Jeremy smiled. "As far as the columns and their millions of readers go, Eisenhower could be in Topeka, Kansas, intead of the White House."

The waiter brought Dax's drink. He tasted it and nodded, and the waiter, who was hovering nearby, went away.

"As a matter of fact, that's why I suggested lunch."

"You mean you want to interview me?"

Jeremy laughed. "You think it's such a bad idea? Might be just the thing I need to hype up my readership."

"You're doing all right."

"I suppose so." Jeremy waited until Dax put down his drink. "This is off the record," he said, leaning forward, his voice lowering confidentially. "My friend the senator is thinking of getting married."

"I know, to that Back Bay girl. She's very nice."

577

Jeremy stared at him in amazement. "How did you know? It's all been kept very quiet. Not a word has appeared in the newspapers."

"Why should you be so surprised?" Dax asked. "If I'm as 'in' as you say, it's only normal that I hear things."

When he saw that Jeremy was still puzzled, he smiled. "It's really quite simple. When I was in Capri last month I went water-skiing with a girl who used to be what you Americans call his 'girlfriend.' I must say she was quite philosophical about it. Apparently she's been well taken care of."

"Oh, brother! I suppose you also know why we're lunching?"

"Not yet."

"If you know the girl he's going to marry you know the kind of a girl she is. Good family. Educated at the best schools, here and abroad. A very nice girl really, but a little distant, reserved, and cool. Slightly snobbish, the average American might think." He fell silent.

"I see," Dax said reflectively. "Not quite the image a man with ambitions to be President wants his wife to project."

"That's it in a way," Jeremy admitted.

"I still don't see what it has to do with me."

"I'm getting to that. There's a big flap going on about her clothes. She wants to go to Paris for her trousseau but he's against it. He's afraid there might be some political reaction. You know what I mean?"

Dax nodded. He had some idea of the complexities of American politics. In many ways the ILGWU commanded a great deal of respect.

"The senator asked me as a friend to help resolve the impasse," Jeremy continued, "and I came up with the idea of Prince Nikovitch. She'd purchased some things from him last year in Paris, so she approved of the idea. The senator was satisfied, too, since the prince is now American based."

"Sergei would be delighted."

"I'm sure, but the senator had one further reservation. He thought it might be more acceptable if the prince announced his intention of becoming an American citizen before any announcement was made. That way there should be very little criticism."

578

"That shouldn't present any problem. I'm sure he'd be agreeable."

"Would you speak to Sergei for us?" Jeremy asked. "I can't, my association with the senator is too well known."

"I'd be glad to. That's simple enough."

"There's another thing."

"Yes?"

"This may be trickier. My youngest brother, Kevin, is graduating from Harvard this year."

"The baby?"

Jeremy laughed. "The baby? You should see him, he's six foot two. Anyway, he and the senator's brother, who is in the same class, are going to Europe on their own this summer. And if I know those two, they won't be twenty minutes off the plane before the roof blows off."

"That sounds healthy."

"If it were just Kevin it wouldn't be so bad," Jeremy said, "but the senator's brother will attract the reporters."

"I see." Dax looked at Jeremy. "Your friend has many problems."

"We both know our younger brothers."

"What would you like me to do?"

"I was wondering if there is some way we could sort of keep an eye on them, see they don't get into trouble."

"That wouldn't be easy," Dax replied thoughtfully. "Young men move pretty quickly."

They sat silently for a moment, then Dax said, "If we could somehow control where they went and whom they met it would help."

Jeremy didn't answer.

"That might just be the way to do it." Dax looked at Jeremy. "I'll get in touch with an old friend of mine. She'll see to it that they are occupied from the moment they land."

"But how?"

Dax smiled. "You don't know Madame Blanchette. She's retired now but she will do it as a favor to me."

"They must never know that everything is set up for them. If they do, it will be the end."

"They'll never know what hit them." Dax laughed. "All I can say is that they may never want to come home. No matter where they go in Europe they'll be up to their elbows in cunt."

19

Dee Dee came into Dax's hotel suite in Rome while he was eating breakfast. "Where were you last night?"

He paused in the act of buttering a roll. "Out."

"With Sue Ann." She threw a newspaper down on the table in front of him. "Your picture is on the front page."

Dax looked down at it, then back at her. "Those *paparazzi* never really take good pictures, do they?"

"You didn't tell me Sue Ann was here."

Dax took another bite of the roll and a swallow of coffee. "I didn't think you cared about her that much."

"But we were supposed to have dinner last night," she all but wailed.

"That's right. I waited here for you until ten o'clock, then I called the studio. They said you'd be working until midnight finishing the picture so I figured you'd be too tired to do anything but go to sleep."

Dee Dee stared at him silently.

Calmly Dax buttered another roll. "Now be a good little girl and go back to your room and get some more sleep. You know I don't like arguments at breakfast."

"I'm getting sick and tired of having Sue Ann show up everywhere we go."

"I can't tell Sue Ann where to go. She pays her own way."

"You like having her follow you around."

Dax smiled. "It's not exactly bad for my ego."

"Oh, I hate you!"

"I have a theory," Dax replied. "She's really not following me, she's following you. I think she's in love with you."

580

Dee Dee was suddenly really angry. "You'll have to make up your mind. I won't have any more of it!"

"Don't push it," Dax said, his voice suddenly cold. "I don't like being pushed."

"I don't know what you see in her. She's like an animal."

"That's just it." His voice was still cool. "You go out with Sue Ann, you have a few laughs, you go to bed, that's all there is to it. No bullshit, no romance or lies about love—tomorrow is your own, no promises, no demands. Besides, she doesn't require applause every time she farts."

"And you think I do?"

"I didn't say that. You asked about Sue Ann, and I told you." Dax picked up another roll. "Now go away. I told you I don't like arguments at breakfast."

"You egotistical bastard!" Dee Dee exclaimed, her hand raised as if to swing at him.

Instinctively his arm shot up to ward off the blow, and by accident his half-closed fist caught her on the cheek. She stepped backward in surprise.

"You hit me!" she said in a shocked voice. She turned and ran to a mirror. "In the eye too." She studied herself. "It's turning black and blue!"

Dax got up curiously. He didn't think he had hit her that hard. Besides, he knew how prone she was to overdramatize anything. "Let me have a look at it."

Dee Dee turned to face him.

"It's nothing," he said, and began to laugh. "But it does look like you're getting a shiner. Let me get you something for it."

"Stay away from me, you beast! You're going to hit me again!"

"Come off it, Dee Dee. The picture was finished last night. Stop acting."

She turned and ran to the door. He caught her by the arm just as she opened it. She glared at him. "Make up your mind! It's me or her!"

Dax was still laughing as he tried to pull her back into the room. Angrily she pulled her arm free. "You'll never beat me up again!" she cried, and opened the door wide. She stepped out into the corridor just as the flashgun went off.

It made the newspapers all over the world.

There were even more photographs when she got off the plane the next day in New York wearing an eyepatch. For the first time in her life Dee Dee received all the publicity she had ever wanted. But it wasn't until a week later, when a reporter thrust a newspaper at her with a terse "Any comment, Miss Lester?" that she realized what she had done.

"No comment." Then she quickly turned her face away so that the reporter could not see the tears suddenly rushing to her eyes.

Dax and Sue Ann had been married that morning in Scotland.

"It's dark in here."

"I find it restful."

"And it stinks. You've been smoking those damn cigarettes again." *El Presidente* crossed the room and, pulling back the drapes, opened the windows. The warm sweet air came rushing in. He stood there for a moment breathing deeply, then turned to face her. "I don't understand what you get from them."

Amparo was sitting in a chair, half turned toward the window. Slowly she stubbed the cigarette out in an ash tray. "They relax me," she said quietly. "Sometimes things get to be too much for me. When I can't face myself or anyone else they bring me peace. They slow everything down so that I can see things more clearly and sort them out."

"They are a narcotic. They are worse even than whiskey."

"Not worse, not better," she said. "Different."

He came over to her chair and stood looking down at her. "I found out where the arms are coming from."

Amparo didn't look up. Her voice was without curiosity. "From where?"

"The American in Monte Carlo."

"But I thought they were Communist made."

"They are," *el Presidente* answered, "the American is the agent. It is he who ships them, he who sells them all over the world. The same guns have turned up in Cuba and also in Santo Domingo."

"Oh."

"He must be made to stop."

582

"How will you do that?" Amparo asked without any real concern. "There will only be others to take his place."

"We will have to deal with the others, too. Meanwhile we gain time to prepare."

"Prepare?" For the first time some expression came into Amparo's face. "Prepare for what—disaster?"

Her father didn't answer.

Amparo began to laugh quietly.

"What are you laughing at?"

"You," she answered, her voice reflective. "Cuba and Santo Domingo. Batista, Trujillo, and now you. You men with your cocks and guns and power. Can't you see that your time is drawing to a close? That you're already extinct, like the dinosaur?" Amparo closed her eyes wearily. "Why must you all try so hard to outlive your time? Why don't you all just go away quietly?"

"And who will take our places?"

Amparo didn't answer. Her eyes were still shut.

"The Communists. And what guarantees are there that things will be any better under them? None. Probably a lot worse."

Amparo opened her eyes but she did not look at him. "Perhaps the Communists must come before the people can think and do for themselves, as the night must grow darker before the day."

"If they come the night might never end."

Amparo's eyes seemed suddenly luminous. "Even at the two poles, where the nights seem to take forever, the day comes. The world has survived many things. It will survive the Communists exactly as it will survive you."

"I am thinking of sending Dax to negotiate with the American," her father said suddenly.

For the first time real curiosity came into her face. "How will you explain that to the people," she asked, "after what has already been told them?"

"The people?" *El Presidente* laughed. "It will be easy. The people believe what I tell them. I can be very magnanimous. For the many good services Dax has rendered our country, I shall order them to forgive him his one mistake."

"And you think Dax will be eager to do as you ask?"

"Dax is his father's son," her father said quietly, "and in a different way also mine. He has been my son ever since

I gave him over into Fat Cat's care and sent him to the mountains."

"And if he refuses?" Amparo's voice took on a peculiarly distant quality. "There is nothing you can do. He is now beyond your reach."

"He will not refuse," *el Presidente* answered steadily. "As his father did not refuse me even after my soldiers had killed his wife and daughter. It was for Corteguay that the father joined with me, and it will be for Corteguay that Dax will return."

"You are sure? Despite the fact that he may have made another life for himself in the two years he has been away?"

"You know he is married, then?"

"Yes," Amparo said, reaching for another cigarette. "I heard it on the American radio."

El Presidente stared at her for a moment, then nodded. "I am sure," he said. "Marriage will make no difference to Dax. He has been married before. One woman has never been more important to him than another."

"Why have you taken the trouble to tell me this?"

"You are my daughter," he said, smiling at her. "And having once been his wife, I thought you should be the first to know that he has been returned to my good graces."

When he looked back at her from the doorway Amparo was holding a match to a cigarette. Already its strange heavy aroma was again beginning to fill the room.

20

"Oh, Christ! Stop it! You're hurting me!" Sue Ann's voice was thin with pain, her hands suddenly beating on his back. She pushed him away and rolled over on her side, fighting for breath. The mattress lifted as Dax shifted his weight away from her.

584

Sue Ann heard the scratch of a match as he lit a cigarette. Gratefully she took it from his fingers and dragged deeply on it. The pain in her loins subsided as she heard Dax light another for himself. She turned her head to look at him.

He was seated on the edge of the bed, his lean, muscled, dark body scarcely moving, watching her with his inscrutable black eyes. "Better?"

"Much better, thank you." She lifted her head, resting her chin on one crooked elbow. "That never happened to me before. I've gone completely dry."

There was a flash of Dax's white teeth in the dimness of the room. "Maybe you've never been on a honeymoon before," he said, a faint note of humor in his voice.

"I've never spent four days in bed without ever leaving the room, if that's what you mean."

"Complaining already. The honeymoon is over."

Dax got up from the bed and went to the window and pulled back the drapes. The sunlight came tumbling into the room, and then he threw open the windows to let the cold Scottish sea air come rushing in. "It's a beautiful day outside."

Sue Ann dove under the covers. "Close the window before I freeze to death!"

Dax pulled the window shut and stood smiling down at her. Just her eyes and her white-blond hair were visible; the rest of her from the nose down was covered.

"What kind of man are you?"

He didn't answer.

"Has there ever been another like you?"

"There must have been," he replied, smiling slowly. "Adam began a long time ago."

"I don't believe it. I'm sorry, Dax," she said, apologizing suddenly.

"For what?"

"For pushing you away. I didn't want you to stop but I couldn't take it any more. The pain was too much."

"It's my fault. I wasn't thinking."

"I know," she answered in a low voice, "that's what's so wonderful about it. You don't, you just do."

Sue Ann watched as Dax left the window and crossed the room naked to the dresser. He picked up his wristwatch and looked at it silently.

"What time is it?"

A faint hint of laughter came into Dax's dark eyes. "I forgot to wind it. I wonder why?"

A soft look came into Sue Ann's face and she reached out and touched him gently. "Do you remember in Boston when I used to come to your room?"

Dax nodded.

"Did you ever think that someday we'd be married?" He shook his head. "Never."

"I did," she said, "once or twice. I wondered what it would be like being married to you."

"Now you know."

"Yes." Sue Ann pressed her lips lightly to his. "Now I know, and I wonder why I wasted all those years."

Dax put his hand down and stroked her hair gently. "We all waste years in one way or another."

Sue Ann turned her head slightly so that she could see his face. "Are you happy with me?"

"Yes, for the first time in my life I know exactly what's expected of me."

She half kissed, half bit him, then abruptly slid away. "Oh, yeah? Well, you can slow down, boy. I'm grabbing a hot shower."

He caught her in the shower stall just as the water came on. He lifted her up in his arms and held her against the wall. The bar of soap fell from her open hand. "Really?" he asked, his eyes laughing at her. "You're wet now, what excuse have you got?"

He let her slide gently down the wall onto him. "Oh, God! Be careful, you'll slip on the soap!" Then she felt him inside her and she closed her eyes, suddenly clinging to him frantically. "That's it! That's it. That's it!" she gasped in shuddering ecstasy.

Later, when they were lying on the bed again, quietly smoking, she turned to him. "I think I'll open the house in Palm Beach next month."

"O.K."

"It will be lovely there this time of the year. Winter in Europe never appealed to me."

Dax got out of bed and crossed the room.

"Where are you going?"

586

"I'm thirsty." He went into the other room and came back and stood drinking a glass of water.

Sue Ann watched him for a moment. "Besides, I bet my family is dying to see what you're like." She began to laugh. "My sweet Southernproper cousins will go out of their minds. Wait until they see how you fill out a pair of swimming shorts. They'll cream right in their cotton-pickin' pants."

The telephone began to ring as Dax put down the glass of water. "Who could that be?" Sue Ann asked. "Did you give anyone our number?"

"Only Fat Cat. I'll answer it." He picked up the receiver. "Hello?"

"It's Fat Cat," he whispered, covering the mouthpiece with his hand.

Sue Ann lit another cigarette and listened to his rapid Spanish without understanding a word. Idly she wondered how many languages he spoke. Mentally she ticked them off. Spanish, English, French, Italian, German. Suddenly she was very impressed. She had never been able to get past high-school French.

Dax put down the telephone and came over to the bed. "Our consulate in Paris has received an important letter for me from *el Presidente*."

"Will they send it on to you?"

Dax shook his head. "They are under instructions to deliver it to me personally. Would you mind very much if we went over there to get it?"

"Of course not. I was thinking about picking up some new clothes. After all, how would it look if I came home without a trousseau?"

"Pretty bad."

"When do you want to leave?"

"If we hurry we can make the late plane from Prestwick to London."

"The honeymoon *is* over."

Dax laughed.

She had a sudden idea. "Maybe it isn't. They say a drive through France is very romantic. We could pick up your Ferrari and the letter in Paris."

Dax shook his head. "I'm afraid not. Jeremy Hadley's kid brother Kevin and a friend just borrowed it to drive to Italy. They had a couple of girls with them."

587

Sue Ann had started to get out of bed but she stopped. "Girls?" she asked in a puzzled voice. "That's a big joke."

"What's so funny about that? Boys will do it, you know."

"I know, but not that kind of boy." Then Sue Ann noticed the peculiar look on his face. "Didn't you know?"

Dax shook his head silently.

"The kid's a swingin' fag."

Dax watched her go into the bathroom and close the door. A moment later he heard the shower running and he glanced at the telephone indecisively, then picked up a cigarette. It was too late to call Madame Blanchette. She must have thought him a stupid fool for not warning her.

Jeremy should have told him; no wonder he had been so concerned about publicity. Dax drew on his cigarette thoughtfully. Sue Ann had to be wrong, he thought suddenly. They had been in Europe all summer and Madame Blanchette hadn't said a word. Everything had to be all right or she would have found a way to let him know.

21

"I'm sorry, but I don't see what I can do."

Dax looked at the cherubic little man with blue eyes. He seemed more the small store merchant than the man who had taken over when Sir Peter Vorilov died. He looked at the two bodyguards lounging silently but alertly against the wall. Then he turned and looked out the window.

Barry Baxter had taken over everything. Vorilov's old house high on the hill looking down over Monaco, the city, the port, even the sea. He turned back to the American.

"I, too, am sorry, Mr. Baxter. Many men will continue to die needlessly."

"I'm not responsible for that. I'm a businessman. I operate on a cash-and-carry basis. What is done with my merchandise is not my concern."

"I will inform *el Presidente* of our discussions," Dax said and got to his feet.

Baxter also rose. "You understand my position? If I were to begin selecting my customers I'd be taking sides. I can't afford to do that."

Dax turned to leave, and Baxter came around the desk and walked him toward the door. "Please inform his excellency that we have a complete line of counter-insurgency armament highly suitable for use in guerrilla warfare. And all in first-class condition."

Dax nodded silently. As if by an invisible signal the door opened. Two additional bodyguards stood just outside. Dax turned to the American. "Good day, Mr. Baxter," he said formally. He did not offer his hand.

"Good day, Mr. Xenos. If there is any other way I can be of help to you, please don't hesitate to call on me."

The door closed behind him and Dax walked thoughtfully through the spacious entrance hall to the front door. They could obviously expect no cooperation from Baxter. He had thought that from the very beginning. The shipments of arms would have to be stopped in some other way, perhaps before they got into the country. And that was the problem. It could not be coming in by small boats. The quantity was too great. Somehow the *bandoleros* must have found another way.

Dax went out into the driveway and his chauffeur opened the car door respectfully. He looked up at the sky. It had suddenly clouded over with heavy dark clouds racing up the coast from Italy. He squinted at them critically. There would be heavy rain tonight. It was like that on the Riviera in late September.

"Back to the hotel, *monsieur?*" the chauffeur asked.

"*Oui,*" Dax answered absently.

The car stopped a moment for the gatekeeper to open the iron gate. Slowly the car rolled through. Dax glanced back idly over his shoulder at the white stone columns and suddenly he sat upright in his seat.

It was Vorilov's coat of arms still chiseled into the stone that reminded him of something. Once Sergei had mentioned that while he was secretary to Sir Peter he heard that Marcel was acting as the old man's agent in Macao, that that was how he earned the money to buy the Japanese freighters.

He twisted in his seat and looked back speculatively at the white house on the hill. Marcel was always complaining that his ships returned to Corteguay light. Had he found a way to increase his cargo? It would be almost no effort for Marcel to bring in weapons; he had practically the freedom of the port. After all, his was the only line authorized to come into Corteguay and *el Presidente* himself was its largest stockholder.

It was near midnight by the time they finished their dinner, and the rain was pelting against the windows of the dining room in the casino overlooking the sea.

"I feel lucky tonight," Sue Ann said.

Dax smiled. "They're waiting for you."

"Let me go to the little girls' room. Then I'll be ready to break the bank at Monte Carlo."

Dax half rose from his chair until Sue Ann had walked away, then sat down again. He gestured and the waiter refilled his coffee cup. He was just raising the cup to his lips when the maître d's voice came over his shoulder. "Monsieur Xenos?"

Dax looked up. *"Oui?"*

"There is a telephone call."

Dax followed him across the room and went into the small booth. The phone was lying on the table. He picked it up. "Hello?"

An American voice came over the wire, slightly thin and metallic. "Mr. Xenos, this is Barry Baxter."

"Yes, Mr. Baxter." Dax's voice was formal.

"You own a Ferrari with Paris plates?"

"Yes."

Baxter hesitated a moment. "There's been an accident on the Grand Corniche."

"A bad one?"

"Bad enough. Two people were killed."

Dax felt a chill settle over him. "Do you know who they were?"

"Not yet. I just picked it up over my police radio."

"Where? I'd better get out there right away."

"You'll never find it in this rain. I'll be down there in ten minutes to pick you up."

Slowly Dax put down the phone. Americans were strange.

Where business was concerned they wouldn't lift a finger to do you a favor, but the moment it was something personal it was quite another story. He went back to his table and quickly told Sue Ann.

"I'll come with you," she said.

"No, I want to attract as little attention as possible. You go on into the casino. I'll be back as soon as I can."

"Somehow I don't feel lucky any more."

"Do as I say. It will be better than waiting around in the suite wondering what happened."

As the big Rolls-Royce town car climbed the road to the Grand Corniche, Dax turned to Baxter. "Any later word?"

"No," Baxter said. "But there wouldn't be any. I told the *chef de police* we were on our way and he took the calls off the radio."

Dax looked at Baxter. One thing was sure. He was not stupid. Automatically he had done what he knew Dax would have wanted him to do. The big car continued climbing the mountain. At last it reached the corniche and turned toward Nice. About sixteen kilometers out from Monte Carlo it turned off on a small road leading down to the sea.

"This is a shortcut down to the Moyenne Corniche," Baxter said. "The accident occurred just around the next curve."

The headlights picked up the police cars as they took the curve, and the big car slowed and came to a stop. The *chef de police* was at their door almost before it opened. "Monsieur Baxter?" he asked respectfully.

Baxter gestured to Dax. "*C'est lui le patron de la Ferrari, Monsieur Xenos.*"

The police chief looked at Dax with somber eyes. "I am afraid your car is a complete wreck, *monsieur.*"

"I am not concerned about the car," Dax replied, getting out and starting off into the rain. The few policemen parted to let him through. The Ferrari lay on its side, its front completely telescoped against a tree. Slowly Dax walked around it. A body lay hanging down from behind the wheel, its arms outstretched along the seats.

A policeman's torch came on behind Dax. "*Il est mort.*"

Dax leaned over. It was Kevin, there could be no mistake about it. His face was completely unmarked, but the eyes were wide open and staring. The police chief came up to stand next to him.

"He doesn't seem to have a scratch," Dax said. "What killed him?"

"*Regardez.*" The police chief pointed.

The boy's groin beneath the steering wheel was a pool of already congealing blood. Dax turned back to the police chief. "But how? The steering wheel is intact."

"He bled to death." The police chief's voice was flat and emotionless. "Come with me."

Silently Dax followed him to a small clearing a little way from the front of the car. Another body was lying there on the grass, the rain already soaking through the torn coat and dress, the face covered by a handkerchief. The policeman knelt and lifted it. The face was a man's face, dark and congested.

"It is not a girl." The policeman's voice was still emotionless, "*C'est un transvestit de Juan-les-Pins.* They had to be out of their minds to try a thing like that on such a road in this rain."

Quietly Dax followed him back to Baxter's car. Baxter took one look at his face and turned quickly, reaching into the car. He came out with a bottle of whiskey and a glass. "You look like you could use a drink."

Gratefully Dax swallowed the whiskey. It burned its way down his throat. He took a deep breath. "Thank you. The accident is tragedy enough. I would appreciate it if none of the details got out."

Baxter looked at him shrewdly. "It's foolish to stand in the rain. Why don't we get into the car and talk?"

The police chief sat on the jump seat, looking back at them. "The photographs have already been taken," he said. "It is a requirement of the law."

"I understand," Baxter said, "but how unfortunate that no one realized the camera was broken."

"The journalists will ask questions," the policeman replied, "and my men do not make very much money."

"Of course," Dax answered, "we would not let them go unrewarded for their cooperation."

The policeman thought for a moment, then nodded his head. "*Bien*, we will do as you wish. It is true as you say that the tragedy is great enough without enlargement."

Suddenly Dax remembered about the senator's brother. "When they left Paris there was another boy and girl with them."

"There were only the two in the car, *monsieur*. My men have searched the area."

"I have to locate the other boy," Dax said. "They must have stopped somewhere while these two went on alone."

"We will find them for you, *monsieur*." The police chief got out of the car and walked over to his squad car. He spoke into his radio, and a few minutes later he came back to the limousine.

"The *gendarmerie* on Antibes reported seeing the car at Monsieur Hadley's villa. It left there at ten o'clock this evening. There were only two people in it."

Dax stared at him. For once he was grateful for the efficiency of the French police. Very little went on that they did not know about. He looked at Baxter.

Baxter nodded. "I'll be glad to drive you over there."

"Good."

Dax turned to the policeman. "*Merci*. I shall call you after I have spoken to the boy's family in the United States."

"Inform Monsieur Hadley of our extreme sympathy."

"I shall. Thank you."

The big car turned around and went back up the road slowly until they reached the Grand Corniche. Then it picked up speed as it turned toward Nice.

"I think the rain is beginning to stop."

"Yes," Dax replied, looking out of the car window. He would call Sue Ann as soon as he got to the villa. There was no point in her waiting up for him. He would put the senator's younger brother on the first plane out of the Nice airport in the morning.

"It's a terrible tragedy," Baxter said.

"Yes."

"I apologize for not walking over to the accident with you," Baxter said unexpectedly. "I'm sorry, I never could stand the sight of blood."

593

22

"I have a surprise for you," Sue Ann said as Dax came out onto the terrace for breakfast.

"Another?" he asked. "You'll have to stop. I have so much jewelry now I'm beginning to feel like a gigolo."

Sue Ann laughed, secretly pleased. She was always buying him presents. "Not jewelry this time, something you've always wanted."

Dax sat down and poured himself a cup of coffee. "O.K.," he said in mock resignation, "what is it this time?"

"I'm not going to tell you. Hurry up and finish your breakfast. We have to go into town for it."

Dax lifted the cover off the heavy silver serving dish and helped himself to a generous portion of ham and scrambled eggs. He spread butter liberally on several pieces of toast and began to eat.

The sound of a speedboat's motor came to him and he looked up. The boat was just pulling out from the dock with a girl behind it on water skis. "Who's that with all the energy this morning?"

Sue Ann smiled. "Cousin Mary Jane working off her frustrations."

"Frustrations?"

Sue Ann nodded. "She's got the hots for you."

"You think everyone has the hots for me," he said, taking another mouthful of scrambled eggs.

"Haven't they?" Sue Ann asked. "I know Mary Jane. Ever since she was a little girl she's always wanted what I had." She began to laugh. "I told you you'd drive them out of their minds."

"I hadn't noticed."

"I have. Even Simple Sam can't keep her eyes off you. You'd think she had enough going for her over at her own place."

Dax grinned. Simple Sam was a showgirl who had married the soft-drink scion who owned the estate next door. He walked around in a drunken fog most of the time, completely unaware that Simple Sam had stocked his estate with her boyfriends. They were in every available job from beach boy to butler. It was a very neat arrangement.

Dax gathered that Sue Ann and Harry had more or less grown up together and that in her own way she felt sorry for him. There wasn't any pretense of morality in Sue Ann's position, she was basically too honest about herself for that. She just didn't like the idea that Harry was being cheated so casually and deliberately.

"She's the only one who bugs me," Sue Ann said suddenly.

"What do you mean?"

"I can understand the others. They're simple little bitches and in a way if you banged them I couldn't get too angry. Look at the way they keep pushing their twats at you."

Dax grinned. "That's very generous of you."

"Not really. At least they want you for themselves. Simple Sam's another matter. She wants you just so she can say she's made as big a fool of me as she has of Harry."

Dax didn't answer. He reached for his coffee cup and drained it. "O.K., what's the big surprise?"

"I thought we were going into town," he said later as the car turned into the West Palm Beach airport.

"I have to stop here first. Come on."

Dax followed her to a small office just to the side of the terminal. "Did it get here yet?" she asked the man behind the counter.

"Yes, Mrs. Xenos. Right out back of the hanger. Follow me."

They went with the man around the building. He stopped and pointed. "There she is," he said, a note of satisfaction in his voice. "All fueled up and ready to go fourteen hundred miles. Isn't she a beauty?"

Dax stared at the sleek twin-engined plane gleaming like

595

polished silver in the bright sunlight; then he looked at Sue Ann.

"Surprised, darling?"

Dax turned back to the plane. He didn't have to act surprised. He was.

Dax lay outstretched, his face turned sideways and resting on his arms, his body burrowed into the warm sand. His brief white French swim trunks were scarcely a narrow band across his deeply tanned body. He lay motionless, without stirring in the hot sun.

"Are you awake?"

Dax's head moved slightly. "Yeah."

"I thought you might like a cold drink."

Dax turned his face up. Sue Ann's cousin Mary Jane was standing over him, a tall drink in each hand. He rolled over and sat up. "Thank you. That was very thoughtful of you."

Dax took the glass as she dropped onto the sand beside him. He turned over on his side to face her. "Cheers."

Then he noticed that she was staring, and he looked down at himself, following her eyes. Dax began to laugh. The heat from the sand had permeated his loins.

"I don't think it's funny," Mary Jane said testily. "You might as well be wearing nothing. I can see everything."

"Don't be hypocritical, cousin. You don't have to look, you know."

"Now you're being vulgar."

But Mary Jane still didn't raise her eyes. She squirmed slightly in the sand, and her hand moved as if drawn by a magnet. Dax leaned forward, placing a strong brown hand under her chin and drawing her face close to his. "Now, now, cousin," he teased. "You may look but you mustn't touch! I don't think Sue Ann would like that."

Angrily Mary Jane pulled her hand away and got to her feet. Her face was flushed. "Now I believe you're every bit the animal Sue Ann says you are!" she said haughtily and stalked away.

In a little while Sue Ann came over and sat down beside him. "What's Mary Jane so steamed up about? She claims you made a pass at her."

"Is that what she says?" Dax began to laugh. "She's

really angry because I had a hard on when she came over and I wouldn't let her touch it."

After a moment Sue Ann began to laugh. "I told you you'd drive them crazy. If you did have a hard on why didn't you call me? It seems a shame to waste it."

Dax rolled over on his back. "It really wasn't worth bothering you about," he said, smiling lazily. "It wasn't very much of a hard."

The sleek silver plane banked and swooped down onto the airstrip and rolled to a stop almost where the reporter was waiting. Dax climbed down from the cabin and walked over. "I'm Xenos," he said, his white teeth flashing in his tanned face.

"Stillwell, *Harper's Bazaar*," the reporter replied. They shook hands. "I didn't know whether your car would be at the airport. If it isn't we can call a taxi."

Dax smiled. "I called Sue Ann from the plane. The speedboat should be waiting for us at the dock at the end of the airport."

Sue Ann waved at them from the cockpit. "Have a good flight?" she called. "I thought I'd come over and pick you up myself."

"Pretty good." Dax jumped easily down into the cockpit and kissed her. "This is Mr. Stillwell."

"Hi. There are cold drinks on the bar."

Sue Ann climbed up and expertly snapped off the bowline. Carefully she began to coil it around the small stanchion. Then she walked around and did the same for the stern line. "Sit down," she said, going to the wheel, "we're ready to go." She pressed the ignition switch and the big motor started with a roar.

"Mr. Xenos," the reporter shouted over the noise, "don't you sometimes feel like a male Cinderella, being married to the richest girl in the world?"

Dax stared at him for a moment as if he could not believe his ears. Then his face darkened, and he walked over to him as the boat began slowly to move away from the dock. "Of all the stupid questions I've ever been asked," he said angrily, "that's the stupidest!" Then he picked up the reporter and, holding him out over the side of the boat, dropped him into the water.

The reporter thrashed about and yelled and finally began to swim back to the dock. He climbed up and stood there waving his arms at them.

"What on earth did you do that for?" Sue Ann asked.

"Did you hear the damn fool's question?" Dax yelled, repeating it.

Sue Ann stared into his angry face and suddenly began to laugh. "I was wondering when it would get around to you. They've asked that of every one of my husbands!"

"Is it O.K. if I use the plane to go up to Atlanta today?"

Dax rolled over and looked up. Sue Ann was standing next to the bed, already fully dressed. "Sure," he said sleepily, "want me to fly you up?"

"You don't have to. Why the hell should you have to hang around all day waiting for me? I'll get Bill Grady."

Bill Grady was the man they hired to take care of the plane and act as copilot. A former airlines pilot who had retired because of his age, he welcomed the job.

"O.K.," Dax said. He sat up in bed. "What do they want this time?"

"I don't know," Sue Ann answered vaguely. "I never know what they want. But they keep telling me that since I'm the principal stockholder I have to be there when certain decisions have to be made."

"Pretty rough being rich," Dax teased. "Some people think you have nothing to do but lie around and have a good time."

"Go back to sleep." Sue Ann stopped for a moment in the doorway. "I'll be back in time for dinner."

The door closed behind her and Dax reached for a cigarette. This was the fourth time in less than three weeks

Sue Ann had gone to Atlanta. He lit the cigarette and leaned back against the pillow.

Whichever lawyer her father had hired to establish the trust had been very clever. Written into it was the proviso that Sue Ann had to appear in person at the company's headquarters in Atlanta whenever summoned in order to maintain continuation of her equity. In that way her father had made sure of her presence in the country at least part of the time.

Dax ground out the cigarette and got out of bed. He went into the bathroom and looked at himself in the mirror. Thoughtfully he rubbed the stubble of his beard. No need to shave today; there wouldn't be anyone to see him. He reached for a pair of swim trunks.

Fat Cat was waiting on the terrace when he came up out of the water. "The two men *el Presidente* sent are here again."

"What for?" Dax asked. "I gave them my answer. What I did in Monte Carlo was done only as a favor."

Fat Cat shrugged. "They merely said it was important that they see you."

Dax hesitated. "All right. Tell them I'll see them as soon as I get dressed. Take them into the breakfast room."

The two men stood up and bowed formally when he came into the room a little later. "Señor Xenos."

"Señor Prieto. Señor Hoyos." Dax returned their bow, speaking in Spanish. "Please be seated. Would you like some coffee?"

"*Gracias.*"

They sat there silently while Fat Cat filled their cups and went away. Dax noticed the service door was slightly ajar and smiled to himself. Fat Cat was up to his old tricks. "To what do I owe the pleasure of your visit?" he asked politely.

The older man glanced at the other, then back at Dax. "*El Presidente* asked Señor Hoyos and myself to come here once more to try to prevail upon you to change your mind."

"I see. You explained my position to *el Presidente?*"

"We have done so," the younger man, Señor Hoyos, said quickly.

"Yes," Prieto continued, "but his excellency says that such personal reasons cannot be allowed to interfere at

599

a time like this. He asked us to explain again that Corteguay needs you. The *bandoleros* in the mountains are being welded together by Communists from the outside and unless steps are taken the country may soon be inundated by another bloody civil war. *El Presidente* is prepared to offer you the important post of ambassador at large, in addition to appointing you representative to the United Nations. He believes that only you can prevent the catastrophe that threatens our country."

Dax studied the two of them. Silently he lifted his coffee cup, then slowly returned it to the saucer. *"El Presidente* is the only man who can prevent that," he said quietly. "If he had given the people freedom to elect their own representatives, as he promised a long time ago, this might never have happened."

"El Presidente has authorized us to tell you that elections will be held as soon as stability has returned to the country."

"That is the same promise he made to my father almost thirty years ago."

"It would be foolish to hold elections today, *señor*. The Communists would only take over without a struggle." He glanced at his companion. "I agree with you, *señor*, that elections should have been held many years ago. But now they would only serve to retard the cause of freedom."

Dax looked down at his hands. "I'm sorry, gentlemen. In the time that has passed since *el Presidente* dismissed me from my country's services I have managed to make a new life for myself. I feel it only justice that my wife and I continue it."

"Your country is above all considerations, personal or otherwise," Prieto answered quickly.

"My love of Corteguay is unchanged. I repeat that my reasons are personal."

"In that case you leave us no alternative," Hoyos said. "It is with the greatest personal regrets we must give you this." He reached into his inside breast pocket.

Behind him Dax saw the serving door open. Fat Cat stared silently through it, a revolver in his hand. But at the same instant Hoyos' hand emerged from his pocket with a white envelope. Dax nodded imperceptibly as Hoyos held it.

The door closed silently behind Fat Cat. Dax took the envelope. "What is this?"

"Open it and see."

Dax ripped open the envelope and a number of contact photographs fell into his hand. There were about a dozen showing Sue Ann and another man in one frantic naked posture after another. He looked up.

"I am sorry, *señor*," Hoyos said. Neither of the two men would meet his eyes. "They were taken in Atlanta just last week with an infrared camera. Apparently your wife does not have the same high regard for your marriage that you do."

Dax looked down at the photographs again. For a moment he felt his anger rising, then it was gone as quickly as it came. He kept his face impassive as he spoke. "I am sorry, too, gentlemen. You have gone to all this trouble unnecessarily. My position remains unchanged."

Hoyos started to speak but the older man silenced him. "We will be at our hotel in Miami until the weekend," he said. "Should you change your mind, *señor*, call us there."

They bowed as Fat Cat came into the room and ushered them to the door. Dax stared after them for a moment, then went over to the small desk in the corner and threw the envelope into it. Silently he locked the drawer and put the key in his pocket. He was still standing there when Fat Cat came back into the room.

"Some breakfast?"

Dax shook his head. "No, thanks. I'm not hungry."

Dax was sitting on the terrace watching the sun go down when the telephone call came. The maid brought out the phone and plugged it into the jack. He picked it up.

"Hello, darling?"

"Yes."

"I'm terribly sorry, darling," Sue Ann said breathlessly, "but something just came up at the last minute and I'll have to stay over."

"I'll bet," he said dryly.

"What did you say?"

"Nothing."

"I'll be back tomorrow in time for dinner."

"O.K."

"Darling, what are you doing? You sound so distant."

"I'm just sitting on the terrace. Perhaps I'll go over to the club for dinner later."

"Do that," Sue Ann said, "it's better than sitting around in that big dump all by yourself. 'Bye now."

"Good-bye." Dax stared down at the telephone for a moment, then went inside to get changed.

———

24

———

Dax was standing alone at the bar when Harry Owens came over. As usual he was half-drunk. "Dax, ol' boy," he said happily, slapping him on the shoulder. "What're you doin' here?"

Dax smiled. He liked Harry. Harry was a gentle harmless sort of drunk. "Sue Ann's in Atlanta, so I thought I'd come over for dinner."

"Wonderful. Then you can join me and Sam. Our cook just up and quit. Sam'll be here in a minute. She stopped off you know where." Harry turned to the bar and picked up the martini the bartender had automatically set before him. "Haven't seen much of you lately, Dax."

"I've been sort of laying around."

"Laying around. That's very good!" Harry chortled, emptying his drink and reaching for another without even looking to see if another was there. It was and he picked it up. "Know just what you mean."

Simple Sam came up, her long red hair falling almost to her shoulders. "Dax." She smiled. "Where's Sue Ann?"

Harry answered before he could. "Dax is having dinner with us. Sue Ann's in Atlanta."

"Oh, lovely. I just ran into Mary Jane and asked her to join us. Ralph's in Washington again." Ralph was Mary Jane's husband, a tax lawyer who spent most of his time away from home.

Simple Sam turned as Mary Jane came up to them. "I've managed to get you the most divine dinner date, darling!"

Mary Jane looked at Dax. "This is a surprise," she said sarcastically. "Where's Sue Ann?"

"In Atlanta." Dax was getting tired of the question. It seemed to him that was all he had heard since he'd got to the club. "Shall we sit down? I'm hungry."

By dessert time Harry could hardly manage to keep erect. Dax had already danced once with Simple Sam; now he got up to dance with Mary Jane. As they walked onto the floor the orchestra went into a samba. Mary Jane was surprisingly light on her feet.

"You do the samba very well."

"Why shouldn't I?" Dax smiled. "Where I come from it's almost our native dance. You're very good too."

Mary Jane looked up at him. "It's rather a coincidence that you should come here the moment Sue Ann's away."

"What do you mean?"

"You know what I mean," she said snidely. "I saw the way you were looking at Simple Sam."

For no reason at all Dax felt himself growing annoyed. "There's a lot to look at," he said, knowing it would only infuriate Mary Jane more.

"You'd look at any woman who wore her dress cut down to her navel," Mary Jane replied coldly.

Dax looked down at the small breasts pushing against her dress, then up at her face. "I don't know. It would all depend."

He felt her grow stiff in his arms and miss a step. "I think you deliberately planned the whole thing. So will Sue Ann when I tell her."

"You do that. She'll believe it about as much as she did the last lie you told her."

Angrily Mary Jane pulled out of his arms and went back to the table. "It's getting late. I think I'll be going home."

"So soon?" Simple Sam said, her quick eyes noting Mary Jane's anger. "I thought we'd sit around and have a few drinks."

"No, thanks."

"I'll drive you home," Dax volunteered politely.

"Don't bother," she replied icily. "I have my own car."

"Now what's eating her?" Simple Sam asked, looking speculatively.

"She—"

"Don't tell me now," Sam said, placing a finger over his lips. "Tell me on the dance floor. You know how I love to rumba."

She pressed herself into his arms, her body moving sensuously against him. He had never danced a rumba so closely to anyone before. The warmth from her body came through the thin dress. He felt the thrust of her hips writhing against his and without thinking he responded.

She looked up at him with a half-smile. "I was beginning to think all those stories I'd heard about you weren't true."

Dax returned her smile, holding her now so that she could not move away from him even if she had wanted to. "And I'm beginning to believe that all those stories I heard about you are."

Sam looked up into his face. "Well, what are we going to do about it? Just talk?"

Dax glanced over his shoulder at their table. Harry was pouring himself another drink. "He'll pass out in another few minutes," she said callously.

"Then I'll drive you both home."

"No, I have a better idea. I'll meet you down at your boathouse in about half an hour."

"I'll be there."

Dax followed her back to the table and watched as she picked up her wrap and purse. "Come, Harry," she said, turning to her husband, "it's time for beddy-bye."

Once he thought he heard a sound outside and he walked out on the deck and around the boathouse but there was no one there. He went back inside and looked at his watch. Almost an hour had passed. Perhaps Sam wasn't coming. He went outside again and sat down on the bench looking out at the water. The yellow Florida moon danced on the waves. He lit a cigarette.

"Light one for me too." Sam's voice came from directly behind him.

Silently Dax gave her his cigarette and lit another for himself. "I was about to give you up."

604

She smiled in the glow of the cigarette. "I had to get laughing boy into bed. Sometimes that's not so easy."

Dax turned as she crossed in front of him to the doorway He heard the metallic slide of a zipper and by the time he looked up she was standing naked in the doorway. "Do all you Latin lovers talk so much?"

It was almost an hour later and they were lying on the huge couch smoking when the door opened. Dax sat up with a curse and Sam was grabbing for something to cover herself with when the light from the flashlight caught them.

Dax shielded his eyes with his arm, trying to see who was holding the light. He had just recognized Mary Jane when she spoke. "I suppose you still think I should believe that you met here by accident?"

"Don't be a damn fool, Mary Jane," he said harshly. "Put out that light before you wake the whole damn neighborhood."

She laughed. "It would serve you both right if I did." She stared at them. "See if Sue Ann won't believe this!"

"Put out that light," he repeated, walking toward her.

Mary Jane backed away slightly, lowering the light. "My my!" She laughed mockingly. "It doesn't look so big now, does it?" Then her voice faded as she kept backing away. She was still holding the light on him when her back came up against the wall and she could go no farther. Dax reached out and took the flashlight.

He threw it into a corner and pulled her away from the wall. "There's only one thing that will satisfy you, isn't there?" he asked angrily.

Mary Jane stared up into his face. Suddenly she began to twist in his grasp, her hands trying to beat at his face. "Let me go!"

Dax caught her hands and held them. With a sudden motion he ripped away her dress, exposing her small white breasts. He pushed her down on the floor and straddled her with both knees.

"Hold her hands!" he commanded Simple Sam harshly. "I know what she needs to keep her quiet!"

It was at breakfast two mornings later that the other photographs arrived. The envelope was addressed to Sue Ann. She opened it and the photographs spilled out onto the table. Sue Ann took one look at them and threw them angrily at Dax. "So this is what you do the moment my back is turned!"

He looked down at the photographs. There were all three of them. Simple Sam, Mary Jane, and himself. They were probably taken by the same camera. *El Presidente* hadn't missed a trick.

Dax looked at Sue Ann. "Before you get too angry," he said quietly, "perhaps you'd better take a look at these."

Sue Ann watched him cross to the little desk and, taking the key from his pocket, open the drawer. He came back to her with an envelope very much like the one that lay before her. He shook the photographs out on the table in front of her.

Sue Ann picked them up and looked at them silently. Then she looked over at him and the anger had gone out of her face. "*Touché*. When did you get these?"

"The day you went to Atlanta and didn't come home; the day before these were taken."

"Oh," she said. "I guess I'm not as controlled as I like to think I am. I wonder who took them?"

"I know who took them—*el Presidente*. He doesn't care what he does to my life or anyone else's so long as I come back to him."

"I see," she replied thoughtfully. "So when my pictures didn't work, he thought yours would."

"That's right."

Sue Ann was silent for a moment. "What are you going to do?"

He met her eyes. "I'm going back, of course."

"After all he's done to you?"

"Yes. Not for him or even because of him. For a lot of other reasons. For my country, my mother, my sister, my father. So they will not have died without reason."

Sue Ann looked at him steadily. "Do you want to get the divorce?"

"You do it. I won't have the time."

"My lawyer will make the usual settlement."

"I don't want anything. I don't need it."

"You'll keep the things I gave you? I'd like that."

"As you wish."

606

They stared at each other silently. "Well, I guess there's nothing else to be said."

"I guess not." Dax turned and started for the door. Her voice stopped him. He turned and looked back at her. "Yes, Sue Ann?"

She was holding two of the photographs in her hand. She looked from them up to him. "You know," she said, "I take a better picture than either of them!"

BOOK
6

POLITICS
and
VIOLENCE

"I don't like it," I said, as I turned the car into the narrow dirt road. "We should have heard the dogs by now."

"He keeps dogs?" the girl asked.

I glanced at her. Her young face was completely unaware. "Dogs, cats, goats, pigs, chickens, you name it. If he were on a highway in Florida he could put up a sign and call it an animal farm."

The house was still hidden behind the next hill. "Maybe he doesn't keep animals any more," she said. "It's been a long time since you were there."

I nodded. It had been a long time. Five or six years. "No, if there are no dogs then Martínez is dead. He's the one who gave me the only dog I ever had as a boy. A little yellow dung-colored mutt."

We crested the hill and the house lay in the shimmering heat of the small valley below. "Look," Fat Cat said, pointing.

I followed his fingers. High in the sky, circling lazily on the currents of air above the house, were two condors. As I watched, another awkwardly got up from the ground behind the house.

I didn't speak until the car stopped in front of the gate. Part of the wooden fence was down, and a few feet beyond it lay a dog, its skull broken and its brains spattered over the earth.

I turned off the motor and sat very still. The air smelled of death. That was the one thing that hadn't changed, that would never change. The peculiar smell and stillness of *la Violencia*.

I felt the hairs on the back of my neck stiffen. I glanced into the back at Fat Cat. He felt it too. Already his gun was in his hand. His face was damp with sweat.

I turned back to the girl. "Wait in the car until we go and see what happened."

Her face was white under the tan but she shook her head. "I will go with you," she said. "I will not stay here alone."

I glanced in the rear-view mirror. Fat Cat nodded imperceptibly. He got out of the car and held the door for the girl. I led the way up the path to the small house.

The door hung half open on broken hinges. There was no sound from inside the house. I gestured to Fat Cat, at the same time pushing the girl behind me against the wall. With a swift, sudden gesture Fat Cat kicked the door the rest of the way open and rushed inside. I was right behind him.

Almost as soon as I got inside the one-room shack I turned to keep the girl from entering. But I was too late. She stood there in the doorway, her face white and frozen with horror, staring at the headless body of Martínez, then at the grinning severed head in the center of the small wooden table facing the door.

I stepped in front of her quickly and pushed her back out of the doorway. She spun around weakly, and I caught her, thinking she was about to faint, but instead she leaned away from me and retched.

"Close your eyes and take deep breaths," I said, holding her by the shoulders. She had courage, this girl. It took a few minutes but she regained control of herself.

Fat Cat came out into the yard, holding a piece of paper in his hand. "The stove is still warm. They were here this morning before we got up."

I took the paper and read the penciled scrawl:

THIS IS THE FATE OF ALL WHO WOULD SERVE THE BETRAYERS OF OUR PEOPLE.

EL CONDOR

I folded the paper and stuck it in my pocket. I remembered the boy who had run away the night his father had been killed. Now the name was his and all the violence and death that went with it. And something more, something his father never had. Help from outside. He had been trained in political and guerrilla tactics.

But the weapons were the same as they had always been. Violence, terror, and death. I had seen many changes since my return to Corteguay, but this, it seemed, never changed. *La Violencia* was always with us.

I looked at the girl. "Are you better now?"

She nodded, wordlessly.

"Go back and sit in the car and wait for us."

She went back to the car and got into the front seat. I turned to Fat Cat. "I wonder why they did not come for us? We were less than ten miles away."

Fat Cat looked at me impassively. "Perhaps they did not know we were there."

"They knew," I said. "They left this note for us. They knew we would come looking for Martínez if he did not appear."

Fat Cat shrugged. "Perhaps they suspected a trap."

I nodded. That would be more like it. This was the first time I had come to my *hacienda* without the escort of soldiers *el Presidente* insisted accompany me every time I left the city. "Let's see if we can find a shovel," I said. "The least we can do for the old man is bury him so the buzzards and the jackals won't get to him."

Behind the house the goats, sheep, pigs, and chickens had all been slaughtered in their pens. Even the old gray mule that Martínez rode lay dead in its stall. I shook my head. There was the difference. Years ago all these animals would have been taken away by the *bandoleros*. But not now. This was pure destruction.

We found shovels and began to dig. The sun was beginning to go down by the time we finished. I threw the last shovel of dirt on the grave and stamped it down, then looked up at the sky. Ten or twelve of the big birds were hovering in the air over our heads.

"We'd better get out of here," I said. "I don't want to be caught on the road at night."

Fat Cat nodded. He threw his shovel on the ground. "I am ready." He glanced at the house. "Shall we burn it?"

I shook my head. "No, they would see the smoke. They would know we are here and they would come to investigate." I dropped my shovel. "Poor old man." I looked at Fat Cat. "Nothing ever really changes, does it?"

He grimaced. "Only the world outside."

I nodded. I knew what he meant. For others war and peace were subjects for discussion. The agony of death never

613

intruded into the council chambers, not its smell, its horror. Just the clean aseptic words that were recorded on tapes and written on paper.

Fat Cat followed me to the car and climbed into the back. I got in beside the girl. She looked at me, her eyes wide. I felt her shivering beside me in the sudden chill of dusk.

I switched on the ignition and looked at the fuel gauge. It registered less than a quarter full. I turned to Fat Cat. "Have we got gas enough to get back to the city?"

He nodded. "There are two ten-gallon containers in the trunk."

"Better fill the tank now," I said, "I don't want to stop on the road at night."

It was over three hundred miles to Curatu. I gave Fat Cat the trunk keys, and he walked around to the back of the car. I turned to the girl. She was still shivering. I put my jacket around her shoulders.

"Thanks."

I didn't answer.

"We're not going back to your *hacienda?*"

I shook my head. "Not with the *bandoleros* nearby."

She was silent for a moment. "I never realized it was like this."

I lit a *cigarrillo*. "No one ever does."

"My father said—"

I interrupted. "Your father!" I said angrily. "What does he know? He did not come from these mountains, he lived in the shelter of the university. Everything to him was abstract theory. What does he know about the stink of death?"

She pulled my jacket closer around her. "The guns," she said, almost to herself. "They were not intended for this."

"Guns are for killing," I replied brutally. "What did he think they were for—wall ornaments?"

"He does not understand about things like this," she insisted stubbornly. "They promised him—"

"They?" I interrupted again. "Who? The *bandoleros?* The *comunistas?* Those honorable men whose words have been trusted for generations? Your father is a fool, a dupe."

"It is the fault of *el Presidente!*" she answered angrily. "He was the first to break his word!"

"Your father was involved in a plot to assassinate *el Presi-*

dente. It failed, and he fled for his life. Now that he has safely reached another country he is sending guns to do what he could not do. It does not matter to him how many innocents like Martínez die in the process."

"Democracy," she said, "my father believes in democracy."

"So does everyone else. That word is responsible for as many crimes as love. Somehow it always comes down to one thing. Democracy is on as many sides as God."

"Then you think *el Presidente* is right, that the corruption of his government can be overlooked?"

I took the *cigarrillo* from my mouth. "No, it cannot be. But you are too young to remember what it was like before him. He represents simply one step forward. There is much more to be done. But not this way."

She turned and looked at the silent house. "You believe that, don't you?"

"Yes," I answered simply.

"You think that if the guns are stopped this will stop?"

"If the guns are stopped it will be a beginning."

I saw her shoulders straighten under the jacket as she turned to me. Her eyes searched mine. "Can I trust you?"

I didn't speak. Whatever answer she sought she would have to find it herself.

"You will not betray my father? Or me?"

This I could answer. "No."

She was silent for a moment, then took a deep breath. "Tomorrow morning, at the port of Curatu. There is a ship coming in on the morning tide. . . ."

This was the break I had been searching for all the month I had been home. Now there might be a way out of the maze of lies and deception that had been woven around me by everyone whom I had spoken to, from *el Presidente* on down.

Perhaps now I could find the truth that had eluded my father.

615

2

Beatriz Elisabeth Guayanos. That was her name. But I had not known that the first time I saw her in the Miami airport. I was waiting to board the plane to come home, and she was standing in front of the ticket counter.

It was the way she held her head high that first caught my eye. She was tall for a Latin American, with raven-black hair bound high in a chignon. Slim, yet faintly voluptuous, with a suggestion of exciting flesh beneath her summer black chiffon dress. Perhaps there was a little too much bust, a little too much roundness of the belly above the swelling curve of her hips for the American taste, but her kind of beauty had been classic among us for generations. In the end, though, it was her eyes that held me. Framed by the sweeping dark curves of her brows and lashes, they were the greenest eyes I had ever seen.

She became aware of my stare and turned away slightly with that air of disdain that only years of having a *dueña* can give. I smiled to myself. It had been a long time since I had seen that particular gesture.

She said something to the man at the ticket counter, and he turned involuntarily to look at me. I caught a glint of recognition in his eyes as he turned and spoke quickly to her. Now it was her turn to stare. I half held my smile. I knew that look. I could almost tell what they were thinking: what makes him such a cock? He's not that tall, not that good looking. Still, all those women, all the things they say about him. I wonder?

I saw her eyes turn frankly speculative. This time I did not contain my smile. I could feel the pulses quicken in me. This was the fever that had come with the first woman I had ever known, the challenge I could never resist. The look that seemed to ask: are you man enough?

You saw a woman. You wanted her. Nothing in the world mattered until you possessed her. You could not eat, you could not sleep. The agony of the damned was yours until you slaked it in the even greater agony of the flesh.

I began to walk toward her, and I saw the expression in her eyes change. For a moment I thought it was something like fear, then I felt a hand on my arm and turned.

Hoyos and Prieto were at my elbow. *"Buenos días, señores,"* I said politely.

"How fortunate, *señor,"* Hoyos said. "I am returning to Corteguay aboard the same plane."

"How fortunate indeed," I replied, but the sarcasm was lost on him. There was no need for *el Presidente* to have gone to all this trouble. I had given my word that I would return. Besides, I was impatient to go over to the girl.

This time it was Prieto, the younger of the two, who spoke. "And I am going to New York to prepare the consulate for your arrival. I am sure they will be most pleased to see you after you have finished consulting with *el Presidente."*

"Gracias," I said.

Just then a photographer and a reporter came up, and a flashbulb went off in my eyes. "Señor Xenos," the reporter asked, "what are your plans now that Miss Daley has filed for divorce?"

"I am returning home for a short vacation."

"And after that?"

"After that?" I smiled ruefully. "I haven't really thought much about it. I imagine I shall have to go back to work."

The reporter grinned. "It's a rough life."

I laughed. "It doesn't get any easier, that's for sure."

"Will you return to Miami?"

"I hope so," I said. "Miami is a lovely city."

"Thank you, Señor Xenos."

The reporter walked away, the photographer followed him. I turned and looked for the girl but she was gone.

Prieto touched my arm again. "You must excuse me, *señor,"* he said hastily. "I have urgent business to complete in Miami."

I nodded.

"Vaya con Dios," he said, already on his way to the exit.

"Adios," I called after him.

The loudspeaker overhead announced our flight. I ges-

617

tured to Fat Cat, who had been leaning against a post watching, and we started toward the boarding area. I saw her again as I started down the staircase. She was standing in the tourist-class queue.

She glanced up, saw me, and turned her head away haughtily. I smiled to myself as I came down the steps. This, too, was expected.

"Here we must part for the moment, *señor*," Hoyos said.

"But I thought we were returning on the same flight?"

"We are, *excelencia*." He smiled. "But an unimportant person like me travels *turista*."

"We will meet in Corteguay then."

"With God's help."

Fat Cat and I walked over to the first-class section. I flashed the boarding passes to the attendant and he waved us through. As I joined the others waiting to board, I looked over the railing into the tourist area. The girl had her face buried in a magazine but I was sure that she was aware of my eyes.

I looked at the man behind her. It was Hoyos. I felt a sudden impulse to exchange tickets with him, and almost before I realized, I was gesturing to him.

There was a puzzled look on his face as he came over to the railing that separated us. "Would you be kind enough to exchange seats with me, *señor*?" I asked.

"But why, *excelencia*? *Turista* is not half as comfortable as first."

I smiled at him and looked at the girl. He followed my eyes, then gave me a knowing look. "Of course, *excelencia*," he said quickly. "I am at your service."

We exchanged tickets and he went back through the gate. I didn't bother. I merely stepped over the section of railing between us.

"You can't do that, sir," an attendant called. "This is tourist."

"There's been a mistake." I smiled and waved Hoyos' ticket at him.

He studied my ticket and motioned me on.

I walked over and got into the line behind the girl. She looked back curiously.

"Are you going to Curatu?" I asked.

She did not answer.

"Vous parlez français?"

She shook her head. "No."

"Capite italiano?"

"No."

"Sprechen Sie deutsch?"

Again she shook her head, but this time there was a faint hint of a smile on her lips.

"Well," I finally said in Spanish, mock despair in my voice, "if you don't speak Spanish I'm probably waiting for the wrong plane."

She began to laugh. "You're waiting for the right plane, Mr. Xenos." Her English was accent free. "It's just that you're out of your class. You don't belong here with the common people."

I smiled at her. "That was most unfair of you. You know my name, and I don't know yours."

A curious look came into her eyes. "Guayanos," she said. "Beatriz Elisabeth Guayanos."

I looked at her. She seemed to be waiting for something. "Am I supposed to know you?" I asked. "Have we met?"

She shook her head. Her eyes looked into mine. "You knew my father, Dr. José Guayanos."

"Oh."

I knew her father, all right. He had been minister of education and later special assistant to *el Presidente*. He had also been involved in a plot to kill *el Presidente* which had backfired. He was the sole member of the group of would-be assailants who had escaped; all the others had gone before a firing squad. There were rumors that Guayanos was hiding somewhere in New York, still involved in a plot to overthrow the Corteguayan government.

"Yes, I knew your father," I said, meeting her eyes. "He seemed a very nice man."

"Perhaps now you would prefer to go back to first class?"

I smiled. "What for?"

She answered by gesturing across the railing. "The Old Fox."

"The Old Fox?" I questioned. I looked up and saw Hoyos reading his newspaper. "You mean Hoyos?"

"That's what we call him," she said. "He is chief of the secret police. *El Presidente* will hear about this."

"I couldn't care less," I said. "Internal politics are no

concern of mine, and if they were, it would not matter. I would still be here with you."

The color of her eyes went dark like the virgin emeralds found in our mines. "Why?"

"I had to find out if you smelled as beautiful as you look," I said, "and you do."

3

The police were everywhere when we landed, for *el Presidente* himself had come to meet me. The stewardess opened the door between the tourist and first class and walked over to me. "Señor Xenos, would you be good enough to leave the plane through the first-class exit?"

I nodded and turned to Beatriz. "Will you come with me?"

She shook her head. "It would be embarrassing for everyone."

"I will see you again? Where can I call you?"

"I will call you."

"When?"

"A day or two," she said. "You will be busy."

"Not later than tomorrow," I answered. "I won't be that busy."

"Tomorrow then." She held out her hand. *"Vaya con Dios."*

I kissed her hand. *"Hasta mañana."*

I followed the stewardess through to the first-class cabin. Fat Cat and Hoyos were waiting for me. "Was it a smooth flight?" Hoyos asked with a smile.

"Very smooth, thank you." I walked to the open cabin door. The bright sunlight made me blink for a moment. Then I saw *el Presidente*'s black limousine roll to a stop near the debarking stairs. A soldier ran around and opened the door.

El Presidente himself got out as I came down the steps. He walked toward me with open arms. "My son," he said emotionally, embracing me, "I knew you would not fail me."

"Excelencia."

I returned his embrace while all around us the photographers were shooting away from every angle. I was suddenly surprised at the slim frailty of the man inside the uniform. I looked down into his face; there were tears in his eyes. I noticed lines in that face I had never seen before, and his eyebrows, that were once jet black, now were almost silver white. Something inside me went suddenly very sad. It seemed only yesterday that I had left Corteguay, and he had seemed so young then, so strong. Now he was an old man.

"Come into the car," he said, taking my arm, "the sun is hot."

I followed him into the cool air-conditioned limousine. He sank back into the seat wearily, breathing heavily, and I sat silently, waiting for him to speak. He gestured to the driver, and the car began to move. I looked back through the window. The other passengers, who had been held up until I was down the steps, were beginning to disembark. I could not see the girl.

"Do not worry," *el Presidente* said, misinterpreting, "your luggage will be taken to the hotel. I have reserved the best suite for you."

"Thank you."

"But first there is much we must talk about. I thought we might have an early dinner alone at the palace where we will not be interrupted."

"I am at your disposal."

He smiled suddenly and placed a hand on my arm. "Come, you need not be so formal with me. You were not the last time."

I smiled back. "If memory serves, neither of us was."

He laughed. "It is done and forgotten. We are together again, that is all that matters."

I glanced out the window as we passed through the airport gates onto the highway. Police were lined up about every thirty yards as far as I could see. Each held a submachine gun at the ready.

"We are well protected."

"It is necessary," he replied. "The *bandoleros* are becoming increasingly bolder. Three times in the last month they have tried to get at me. Fortunately they failed."

I looked at him silently. There had to be something radically wrong if the *bandoleros* were bold enough to come this close to the city. Usually they stayed in the mountains.

He sensed what I was thinking. "These are not the *bandoleros* we once knew," he said, "these are something quite else. They are now a trained army led by Communist-schooled *guerrilleros* like el Condor."

"*El Condor?* But he is—"

"Yes, the old one is dead," el Presidente answered quickly, "but this is the son. He has taken his father's name."

"You mean the boy—"

El Presidente nodded. "He is a boy no longer. He has been trained in special schools in eastern Europe. Once we had him in prison but he was released during the amnesty at the time of your marriage to Amparo. Since then he has set up a guerrilla army, welding almost all the *bandoleros* into one loose federation."

"Wasn't that what you once did?" I asked.

"In a way, but this one has organized even better. He has aid from the outside, which we never had. Money and guns."

"The guns have not been stopped?"

"No. Of the many things that must be done, this, perhaps, is the most important. Once the guns are stopped his federation will fall apart by itself."

"The guns are coming in by sea," I said.

"My own cousin is in charge of customs at the port. He swears that could not be."

I didn't answer. As usual the truth was in no one's mouth. I glanced out the window. We were on the outskirts of the city. It was market day and the farmers were walking along behind their wagons at the side of the road. They trudged slowly and silently homeward. I stared at them.

Something was very wrong. Usually after market the *campesinos* were happy. They would be singing and laughing and jingling the coins in their pockets, proudly feeling how clever they had been in beating the city dwellers out of their cash. As I looked, one of them spat silently after the car.

I turned back to *el Presidente*. He had seen it too. His face

622

was white and drawn. "The poison has even begun to infect the common people."

"There must be something that can be done about that."

"What?" he asked. "I cannot put them all in jail. Everyone blames me for all his ills. God knows I have done the best I could for my people."

I stared at him. He really believed it. There was nothing I could say. Perhaps when the guns were stopped things would calm down and the people would listen to reason. In time, I thought, even *el Presidente* might listen.

Surely the bones in that old body must be weary from the burden of power they had borne so long.

"So you came back?" Amparo's voice was sarcastic in the dimly lit room.

"Yes," I replied, "I came back."

"Just as he said you would," she said scornfully, "like a puppy crawling back to its master."

I didn't answer. Instead I walked deeper into the room. I stopped in front of her chair and looked down at her. Her eyes were dark and luminous. Her pale, thin face looked as if she had not been out in the sun in years. There was a bitter twist to her mouth as she asked, "Why do you stare?"

"I want to look at you," I said. "It has been a long time."

Amparo turned her face away. "You do not have to look at me like that. I do not like it."

"All right." I sat down in a chair near her. "I was told that you had been ill."

"What else did they tell you?"

"Nothing."

"Nothing?" Her voice was skeptical.

"Nothing."

She was silent for a moment. "I have not been ill," she said. "That is merely the story he gives out. He does not approve of my actions so he forbids my appearing in public."

I didn't speak.

"I didn't think he would let you come to see me."

"Why?" I asked.

She glanced at me again, then turned her face away. An emptiness came into her voice. "I was wrong, he is smarter than that. He knew the best thing was to let you come. When you saw how I looked there could be nothing more between us."

"There is nothing wrong with the way you look, but what was between us was over a long time ago. It went wrong when we tried to recapture something that had disappeared with our childhood."

Amparo reached for a cigarette. I held a light for her. The faintly pungent odor of the tobacco filled the room. She let the smoke out slowly through her parted lips as she looked at me. "Poor Dax, you have not been lucky with your wives, have you?"

I didn't answer.

"It was because you let others choose you. Next time, you do the choosing."

I still didn't speak.

"But not the Guayanos girl," she said unexpectedly, "she will get you killed!"

I stared. "How do you know about her?"

Amparo laughed. "Everyone knows everything you do. There are no secrets in this city. Everybody's life is subject to el Presidente's scrutiny."

"But how do you know?" I persisted.

"I have friends in the secret police." She began to laugh. "Do you like your suite in the hotel?"

"Yes," I said, "it's the most luxurious suite there."

"It should be. It was designed expressly for el Presidente's important guests."

"If you are trying to tell me something," I said, annoyed, "tell me. Stop hinting like a child."

"You're the child." She got out of her chair and walked over to a cabinet and opened a drawer. "Come, I have something to show you."

I went over and looked down. A tape recorder was mounted in the drawer. "Listen," she said, pressing a button.

Presently from the speaker came the sound of a telephone ringing. Then there was a click and man's voice. "Hello."

It was a fraction of a second before I realized it was my own voice. Everyone thinks they sound completely different from the way they do.

Then I heard a girl's voice. "Señor Xenos?"

"Yes."

"Beatriz Guayanos. I promised I would call."

624

"I have been waiting all morning—"

Amparo hit the switch and the tape stopped. She looked at me. "You do not have to hear the rest. You already know what was said."

She went back to her chair and sat down. "It's not only the telephones. If there were a way to record your thoughts he would have a copy of those, too."

"But the tape? How did you get it?"

"Simple." She laughed. "He gave it to me. To prove to me something I had already realized a long time ago. But he was taking no chances."

I looked at her thoughtfully. "Why do you tell me all this?"

Amparo ground out her cigarette angrily in the tray. "Because I feel sorry for you. Because he will use you exactly the way he uses everyone and then when he is through he will cast you aside!"

"I know that."

"You knew that and still you came back?"

"Yes. I've always known it, even before my father died. My father realized it, too, but it did not matter. The important thing to my father was the good he could do. There are many men like your father, he is not the only one. They have their uses and in time they will disappear, the evil with them. All that will remain will be the positive things they have accomplished."

"You really believe that, don't you?"

"Yes. Just as I believe that someday Corteguay will be free, truly free."

Amparo laughed but there was no humor in it, only an empty, hollow mockery. "You are as big a fool as the others. Why can't you see that that is the secret of his strength— the unspoken promise that will never be kept."

I didn't answer, and Amparo came over and looked up into my face. There was a wildness in her eyes I had never seen there before.

"Corteguay will never be free so long as he is alive. He has played God too long to stop now."

I still did not speak.

Amparo turned away and picked up another cigarette. She looked into my eyes as I held the light for her. "If freedom is what you really want for Corteguay, the only way to get it is to kill him!"

I stared at her for a moment. There was not a flicker of expression on her face. I shook my head. "No," I said, "that is not the way of freedom. That is the way it always has been with us, and the people still are not free. This time the desire for freedom must come from them."

"The people," Amparo replied scornfully. "They think the way they are told to think."

"Not always. I have seen enough of the world to know that. Someday it will change here too."

"When it does we shall all be dead," she said, walking away from me. She stopped at the cabinet and closed the drawer, then looked back at me. "Except my father. He will live forever!"

I didn't answer.

Amparo took a deep drag on the cigarette, then let the smoke out slowly. "*El Presidente* was right. He is always right," she said almost in a whisper. "You are too much like your father!"

4

"This is Lieutenant Giraldo," *el Presidente* said. "I am making him personally responsible for your safety while you are here."

The young soldier saluted smartly. "*A su servicio, excelencia.*"

"Thank you, Lieutenant." I turned to *el Presidente*. "I feel rather foolish. Is this really necessary?"

El Presidente nodded. "Especially if you persist in going to your *hacienda* in the mountains. The *bandoleros* are very active in that region."

"I must go there. It has been too long since I visited the graves of my parents."

"Then Giraldo and his men will accompany you." There was a finality in that voice that brooked no argument. He turned to the soldier. "You will have your men at the ready, Lieutenant."

The soldier saluted smartly and left.

"You saw Amparo?"

"Yes."

A strange expression came into his face. I could not make out what it was. "What did you think?"

"Amparo has changed," I said cautiously.

He nodded. "Amparo is very ill."

"I could not tell. She seemed all right to me."

"Not physically," he said in a low voice, "up here." He tapped his brow with a finger.

I did not speak.

"I suppose she suggested you kill me?" His voice was casual.

My voice was as casual as his. "She did say something like that."

"Isn't that evidence of a sick mind?" There was a hint of anger beneath his controlled voice. "The desire to kill her own father?"

"Yes." There was no other answer I could give. "Have you thought of sending her to a doctor?"

"What could a doctor do?" he asked bitterly. "She is consumed by her hatred of me."

"There are doctors abroad who have worked with such cases."

"No," he said, "she must remain here. There is no telling what might happen if she were not here with me. There are those who would take advantage of her sickness." He changed the subject abruptly. "Have you spoken to the American consul?"

"No, I have an appointment with him this afternoon."

"Good," he said. "Let me know his reactions after the meeting."

"Twenty million dollars," he said, leaning back in his chair.

"Don't sound so shocked, George. It is nothing compared

to what you've given others. And it's merely a loan, not a grant. You've pissed away that much and more on Trujillo and Batista, not to mention others."

"I know, I know. But we knew exactly where we stood with them."

"I know," I replied sarcastically. "Maybe if you worried less about how you stood with them you'd be hated less by their people."

George Baldwin looked at me. "I don't want to get into a policy argument with you."

"I'm not arguing. A borrower does not have arguments with his banker."

"Oh, buddy. You're not mincing any words."

"The situation is too serious to fuck around," I said. "I'm not saying everything the old man has done is right. But he has done more for his country than the others. And don't forget he has accomplished it without the official help of the American government. Now the problem is no longer solely our own, it's one that involves all Latin America and yourselves. Like it or not, the Communists are in Latin America to stay. And it will be only your ignorance that will allow them to obtain control."

Baldwin's face grew serious. "What are you telling me?" He reached for a cigarette. "Are you beginning to fall for that Commie-under-every-bed bit, too?"

"No," I said, "but they're clever. They've allied themselves with many groups. In time you may even find yourself supporting one of them. When you do you'll have turned over a country to them."

"I can't believe that. We know who the Communists are."

"Do you?" I asked. "Maybe. But what if they are well concealed? Will you be able to discover them when they're hidden beneath the surface?"

He was silent.

"That is one way they'll take over," I said. "But there is another and that will be even easier for them. American support has come to mean stability for any Latin American government. Withdraw or withhold that support, and that government will fall. The first time you do so you'll be conceding that country to them."

George Baldwin smiled a bitter smile. "What you're saying is that we're damned if we do and damned if we don't."

"In a way, yes."

"That we must continue to support these two-bit dictators whether we like it or not?"

"Not entirely," I said, "there are valuable concessions that can be obtained in return for your aid. Like the ones we're willing to give."

"We've had samples of *el Presidente*'s concessions," Baldwin answered bluntly. "He's not especially noted for keeping his word."

"This time he must. He is approaching the end and he wishes to be remembered with respect."

George looked thoughtful. "He may already be too far gone to help."

"It is not for him that I am asking," I said. "It is for Corteguay."

George was silent, studying me.

"Each day that goes by," I added, "more guns are entering this country. Not just rifles, but big guns, mortars, and light cannon. It is only a question of time before they will be used. And the guns do not come from your factories but from behind the Iron Curtain. If a revolution succeeds, whom will the people be grateful to? You or those who helped them?"

George took a deep breath. "I will pass the word along. But I can't promise anything, you know that."

"I know." I got to my feet. "Thanks for listening to me."

He held out his hand. "If you find yourself free one evening give me a call. Perhaps you can join us for dinner."

"I'll try," I said.

But when I left the cool air-conditioned office and got out into the baking-hot street in front of the embassy, I knew I wouldn't. Just as I knew that the Americans would always follow their classic pattern. For whatever their reasons, they would keep hands off. And their money in their pockets.

I looked at my watch. It was a few minutes past four. Just after siesta. The streets were beginning to fill with people again. It was too early to go back to the palace. *El Presidente* would not be back in his office before five.

I strolled idly down the hill to the port, past the market where the peddlers were just beginning to uncover their afternoon wares. I smelled the aroma of tropical fruits and listened to the chattering of the women calling their invitations from the windows of the cheap cribs. I watched the children at play, barefoot and ragged, weaving their way in and out of the stalls in the secret games that I had long ago forgotten.

I bought a mango ice from a peddler and sat down on the same stone steps looking out over the harbor where I had sat savoring the same sticky sort of mess many years ago as a boy. I looked out over the water. There were only two ships in port and in the distance on the far side of the harbor I could see the rusting offshore oil derricks that had been abandoned not too long ago.

The shadows lengthened as the sun moved deeper into the west, and the smells of frying fish came to my nostrils as the fishermen began to cook and eat what they had been unable to sell. Curatu. At one time I had thought it the biggest city in the world.

I looked at my watch again. It was almost five. I got to my feet and as I began to walk back toward the city, a lottery peddler crossed my path trailing his string of tickets idly from his hand. A strip of them fluttered to the ground at my feet, and he walked on without so much as a backward glance.

I smiled. Nothing had changed. The tricks they used to hawk their tickets were still the ones they had used when I was a boy. If you called attention to the tickets they had dropped they would insist that Lady Luck had sent you an omen, that these were obviously the winning tickets you had always sought. It did not matter whether you wanted them or not; they would trail you for blocks insisting that you were missing the opportunity of a lifetime.

The ticket vendor went on a few paces, then, unable to resist the temptation, stopped and looked back at me. I grinned as I stepped over the tickets. His face darkened and he glowered at me as I came up to him. He reached out and grabbed my arm, silently pointing to the ground.

"So what?" I shrugged. "They're yours."

"Pick them up!" he hissed. "They contain a message for you!"

I glanced at him again, then I went back and picked up

the tickets. The message was scrawled in pencil across the back of one of them.

I spun around but the man was already gone. He had disappeared into the crowd walking around the market. I crumpled the tickets angrily and shoved them into my pocket. Suddenly the feeling of danger was very real as I stood there studying the crowds. Almost any one of them might be an agent of the *bandolero*.

I took a deep breath and resolved never to go out alone again without Fat Cat to protect my back. It had not taken them long to find out I had returned.

A lone taxi came cruising through the marketplace. I hailed it and got in with a feeling of relief. Now I realized why *el Presidente* took the precautions he took. Now I knew why he felt as he did. It would be a relief to go home, to go back into the mountains. At least up there you never had to worry about who might be standing behind you.

5

I looked out the car window in the direction that Fat Cat pointed. There was a faint wisp of smoke drifting lazily up from the chimney.

"Is anyone living in the house?" Lieutenant Giraldo asked.

I shook my head. "No, it's been closed ever since I first left Corteguay."

"Stop the car for a moment."

Giraldo got out and walked back to the jeep that had been following us. In the rear-view mirror I could see him talking to the soldiers. I saw them take up their rifles, and in a moment he came back to the car and got in beside me. "We can go now, but let them enter the courtyard first."

"It is probably nothing," I said.

"Probably. But there is no point to taking chances."

The jeep pulled in front of us before we entered the yard. I followed it and came to a stop in front of the *galería*. We sat there silently looking at the closed front door.

After a moment I got out of the car. "This is silly. If there were *bandoleros* in there they would have opened fire on us by now."

I started up the steps and just as I reached the top the front door began to open. I felt a sudden tightening in my gut. I heard the quick scramble of the soldiers behind me, then the rush of footsteps on the stairs. Without looking back I sensed that Fat Cat was right behind me.

"*Bienvenida a su casa,* Señor Xenos."

The voice that came from the shadowed doorway was a familiar one but it was a moment before I recognized the man who spoke.

"Martínez!"

The old man came out and we embraced. "Ah, *señor,*" he sighed. "It is good to see you again!"

"Martínez!" I smiled down at him. The old man who lived on the edge of our land perhaps ten miles from the *hacienda*. The old man who kept stray animals, who ate only vegetables because he could not bear to kill his chickens, the *campesino* who gave me the little puppy I had had as a boy.

"When I heard you had returned I knew it would not be long before you came home," he said. "I did not want you to return to a cold, empty house. So I started a fire and brought a few things for you to eat."

I could feel the tears coming to my eyes. "Thank you, Martínez."

I looked back at the soldiers. They were getting back into the jeep. I waved to the lieutenant. "Martínez is an old friend."

"I have straightened up and cleaned as much as I could, *señor,*" the old man continued as we walked into the house. "You should have given me more time. I would have found a woman to put it all in order."

"You have done fine, old friend. I am more than grateful."

"It is little enough to repay all your father has done for me."

Years ago my father had allowed Martínez to move into an old shack at the edge of the cane fields. It was his as long as he wanted it, my father had said, and in return for this he used to come down to the house once a week with a few chickens and occasionally a suckling pig. The animals were always alive though. La Perla would have to butcher them because the old man didn't have the heart.

"How has it gone with you, my friend?"

"It goes well."

"There has been no trouble?" I asked. "I have heard talk of *bandoleros.*"

"What would they want of me?" Martínez asked, opening his hands. "I have nothing. They do not bother me."

"Have you seen anything of them?"

"I see nothing," he replied, "just my companions, the animals who live with me. We are all happy together."

I looked at Lieutenant Giraldo. His face was impassive. He knew as well as I that even if the old man had seen the *bandoleros* only ten minutes ago he would not say anything.

"I have your permission to allow my men to erect their tent in the yard, *señor?*" Giraldo asked politely.

"Of course, Lieutenant."

"I will have them put up my tent as well."

"No, Lieutenant," I said, "I will not hear of it. You will stay in the house with me."

"You are most kind."

"I will bring in the food," Fat Cat said, and Martínez hurried after him.

I watched them go out the door. "What do you think, *excelencia?*" Giraldo asked. "Has the old man seen them?"

I turned to look at him. "Of course he has seen them, Lieutenant. But how do you think he has managed to live this long, alone and defenseless? He has learned to close his lips against his eyes."

I awoke to the familiar sound of birds calling to each other in the tree outside my window. For a moment I lay there half awake, half dreaming, and I was a boy again.

I looked up at the ceiling. It was yellowed and cracked now, but I remembered when it had been glistening white and I used to lie in bed and lose myself looking up at it. On very hot nights I would imagine it was the snow glistening on the mountaintops and I would feel cool and fall asleep.

As I lay there I could hear the sounds of the house as it used to be. The whisper of the barefooted servants walking past the door, the shrill voice of La Perla coming up from the kitchen, the creak of the wagons and the neighing of the horses, with my little dog barking and yapping at their heels.

I could hear my sister again, the sound of water splashing into her washbasin as she filled it from the pitcher, then the low music of her voice as she hummed to herself as she washed. And the soft footsteps of my mother as she hurried past my door, then the heavier tread of my father. Almost at any moment I expected to hear her ask La Perla, as she always did when she entered the kitchen, "Has Dax come down yet?"

And I remembered the faint exasperation that would come into her voice when she learned I had not. "That boy!" she would say to my father. "Someday when he is married and has children of his own he will discover how important it is to start the day early."

And then the amused low chuckle of my father as he soothed her. "He is still little more than a baby and already you have him married and with children!"

I half-smiled to myself, warm in the imagery of memory. Married and with children. How shocked my mother would have been had she known how it had really turned out with me. I wondered what she would have said. Nothing, probably. In the end it was always she who made the excuses for me. Nothing was ever my fault. Now I knew better. There was a weakness in me that had never existed in my father. My father had had a genuine capacity for love. All people felt it, though only my mother possessed it. For him there was never another woman.

Not so with me. I was too much the victim of my own loins. The sight of a woman, the smell of her, the taste of her, was enough to displace the one before. And the promise of the next served only to accentuate my greed. Somehow I had never experienced the tender, gentle love my

634

father had had for my mother. Perhaps I simply lacked the capacity.

My kind of love was another kind. It was physical, it was compulsive, demanding. I could be with a woman and satisfy both her and myself, saturating our senses to the point of complete exhaustion, and yet after it was over, I would again be alone. And so would she. Somehow it was as if we each knew in our secret souls that there was nothing more I had to give her.

Perhaps this was the something more that Caroline had sought in me and never found. Or the child that Giselle had always wanted and I would not give her. And even with the two who were most like me, professing to the same physical drives and nothing more—Amparo and Sue Ann—there was something missing. Or was it because we were too much alike, demanding only that which we had to give to each other?

We were like strangers on a brief voyage, exchanging a polite pleasantry, giving each other a small comfort because soon the voyage would be over. When we would look into each other's faces afterward there would be no signs of recognition. The night had passed and we were again alone. Each with the knowledge that we would pass through the harsh white light of day seeking still another stranger with whom we could pass the coming night, so we would not have to see ourselves in the clarity the next morning would reveal.

A sudden silence came to my ears. I listened but the song of the birds had vanished from the tree. I got out of bed and looked out the window. On the far side of the yard a soldier stood urinating against a post, another knelt in front of the tent making a fire.

There was a knock at the door behind me. It was faint at first and I scarcely heard it, for I was still lost in my thoughts. But the second time it was louder.

"¿Quién es?"

"Me."

I opened the door and Fat Cat stood in the opening, grumbling. "I have ham and *tortillas* and beans on the stove. I knocked before but you didn't hear me."

I smiled at him. "I was thinking of the house as it used to be."

635

Fat Cat stared at me for a moment, his eyes wise and penetrating. "It is good sometimes for a man to listen to the ghosts of his family."

I looked at him curiously. "What is it?"

"I, too, have been listening to your ghosts," he replied seriously.

"And what have they told you?" I asked with half a smile.

Fat Cat looked at me oddly. "They have lived too long here in this empty place. They are waiting for you to bring home a woman so they can leave in peace."

Then Fat Cat turned abruptly and walked on down the hall. I watched him descend the staircase and when I closed the door I could still hear the sound of his heavy footsteps. I went back to the bed and sat down, reaching for my shoes.

Perhaps that was it. I had never brought a woman home, except Amparo that one time. But then I had never met one who would love the place in the way I did. Then a thought came to me and I cursed myself for not thinking of it before. One. There might be one.

Beatriz. Almost from the moment I first saw her I had felt as if we belonged in the same world, the same place, the same time. I had not felt like that with any of the others.

Perhaps it could be as my mother hoped after all.

6

"I am giving a small dinner party," *el Presidente* had said. "You may bring someone if you like."

"I'll ask Amparo," I answered dutifully.

"No, Amparo is not to come."

I knew better than to ask why. If he did not want her, she would not be there.

"Bring the Guayanos girl if you like," he said unexpectedly.

"I thought—"

But *el Presidente* interrupted. "I do not fight children. It is her father with whom I quarreled."

I didn't speak. It was all very strange. I had the feeling he wanted Beatriz there.

"I've heard you have been seeing a great deal of her. It is true, is it not?"

"Yes," I answered.

"Then bring her." There was a finality in his voice that made it an order.

"How do I look?" Beatriz asked nervously as Fat Cat turned the car into the palace grounds.

I smiled. "You will be the most beautiful woman there."

As the car stopped a soldier opened the door. I got out first and helped Beatriz. The long dark gown set off her lush figure to perfection.

I smiled reassuringly as the butler announced us but I felt her hand tighten anxiously as we walked into the drawing room. A silence fell and the people there turned to look at us. They seemed as curious as I about the reception *el Presidente* would give the daughter of his foremost enemy.

El Presidente was dressed in a simple blue uniform without medals. Only his eyes and his step were young as ever as he crossed the room to us. He took Beatriz' hand and pressed it to his lips as she curtsied. "You are an even lovelier woman than you were a child," he said, smiling.

"Thank you, *excelencia*."

In the corner of the room a small orchestra began to play. "You are just in time," *el Presidente* continued, and with an old-fashioned kind of courtesy he bowed to me. "May I have just this one dance with her?"

I bowed and he led Beatriz to the edge of the dance floor. I watched them move away in a sedate waltz, then turned and walked over to the bar. "A whiskey and soda, please."

"What's up, Dax?" I turned and saw George Baldwin standing next to me. "I don't think I quite believe what I see. The old man dancing with the daughter of his most outspoken enemy?"

I looked at him and shrugged. "His quarrel is with her father, not her."

"That sounds to me like a quote," George replied shrewdly.

I lifted my drink. "It is."

"What's behind it?"

"I don't know," I answered frankly. "Perhaps he wants to indicate that he is not the monster you think him."

George smiled. "That's not it. It has to be something more than that. When did he ever give a damn about what people thought about him?"

There was a burst of laughter from the grand staircase and everyone's eyes turned. Amparo in a white gown stood at the top, swaying slightly and staring down at us. A young soldier, a captain by his uniform, tried to take her arm but angrily she shook him off. The music came to a stop.

"Go on, go on, don't stop," she called as she began to descend the staircase uncertainly. "I decided to come to the party after all."

I looked over at the dance floor and noticed *el Presidente* glaring up at her with implacable anger. I saw Beatriz, pale and somehow frightened, next to him, and I wanted to go to her. But instead I walked over to the staircase.

"Amparo," I said, taking her hand to steady her. I bowed and kissed it. "How good to see you again."

"Dax," Amparo replied uncertainly. Her eyes were dark, the pupils wide and distended. "Dax."

The music started up again and I led her onto the dance floor. I held her close so that she would not stumble. Her movements were stiff, awkward, and yet somehow loose and disjointed. She placed her head wearily against my chest and closed her eyes. "Dax," she whispered, shivering suddenly. "I'm afraid."

"Don't be," I said reassuringly. "You're safe now."

"No," she whispered, "I should not have come. He told me not to."

"But you are here now and it will be all right. You will see." The music stopped and I led her off the floor. "Come, let me get you a drink."

Amparo gripped my arm. "No," she said, a note of hysteria in her voice, "don't leave me."

I followed her eyes. *El Presidente* was approaching us, Beatriz on his arm, his face impassive.

"*Papá.*" There was something of the child seeking approval in Amparo's voice.

El Presidente didn't speak as he bent forward and kissed Amparo's cheek.

"I wanted to come, *Papá*," she said, still in that little girl's voice.

Her father looked at her for a long moment, then nodded slowly. He glanced at Beatriz, then at me. "You will excuse us?"

Beatriz nodded and I bowed.

"Come, Amparo," he said imperiously and, turning his back, began to walk away.

Almost as if she were mesmerized, Amparo started to follow her father. Then, unexpectedly, *el Presidente* turned back to Beatriz. "I almost forgot to thank you for the pleasure of the dance, *señorita*."

Beatriz curtsied.

El Presidente turned away and this time he took Amparo's arm and led her to a corner of the room. Consciously the guests moved away so that they might speak in privacy. Beatriz looked up at me, her face still pale. "The girl is sick," she said, a curious sympathy in her voice.

"Yes," I replied, watching them. But it was more than just being sick. I recognized that particular kind of sickness. I had seen it too often in the eyes of others who wished to escape reality. Amparo was a heroin addict.

Now I understood the dim lighting in her room. It was so that I would not see the needle marks in her arm.

After a quiet talk with Amparo she seemed to calm down, and when *el Presidente* led us into dinner she was on his arm. He placed her in the hostess' chair at the foot of the table. The nervousness had left her and after a while Amparo seemed almost her normal self. Her long blond hair and white dress with the sleeves reaching almost to her fingertips only served to accentuate the savage wildness of her beauty.

While we were having our coffee *el Presidente* got to his feet and cleared his throat. A silence passed down the table and all eyes turned toward him. He smiled benignly down at us.

"I suppose you are all wondering why I have given this dinner when for so long a time I have not entertained." Then, without waiting for an answer, he continued. "It is to honor a trusted and old friend, the son of an equally close friend and patriot. It gives me pleasure to announce the appointment, effective immediately, of his excellency Señor Diogenes Alejandro Xenos, as foreign minister and representative to the United Nations."

I felt Beatriz' hand pressing warmly against my arm as the guests began to applaud. All eyes turned toward me but I remained seated as *el Presidente* held up his hand.

"That I choose to fill these two most important positions with the same man is an indication of the esteem in which I personally hold him. It is also evidence of the regard in which I hold the United Nations."

Again there was applause and again *el Presidente* held up his hand.

"In these troubled times, for Corteguay and for the world, there is no greater need than for us to evidence our sincere desire for peace and unity within our own borders. And to further implement the strength of his position I make this offer now to all who dispute our policy. Complete and total political amnesty, free of all restraints. I invite such opponents to come and participate in a free election to be held within the near future. And to further assure all who doubt this, I hereby divorce myself from the position of Supreme Judge of the Court of Political Action and give such powers over into the hands of his excellency Señor Xenos."

Again there was applause. I noticed George Baldwin looking down the table at me skeptically from his seat near *el Presidente,* and I was aware what he was thinking. That I had known about this all along.

El Presidente began again as the applause faded. "I repeat my invitation." And this time he looked down the long table at me, though somehow I realized the words were intended for Beatriz' ears alone. "To all who seek to divide our country by speech or with guns, both here or abroad, come forward into the open. Entrust yourselves not to me but to Señor Xenos. Let us all work together as true patriots for a more glorious future for our beloved country."

He then sat down, and the applause this time was truly deafening. Little by little everyone turned toward me. *El Presidente* was smiling benignly. He gestured and I got to my feet as an attentive silence spread around the table. I looked down at their faces and somehow I knew that tomorrow whatever I said would be read or heard all over the world.

I began to speak slowly, choosing my words carefully. "There is very little I can say other than that I am humbled by this honor so unexpectedly and generously given." There was faint applause but it faded quickly. "There is one thing, however, that I wish to add. You have all been witness to the promise given."

I paused and looked at everyone at the table. There was a respectful silence as my eyes stopped on *el Presidente*'s face. It was a mask but his eyes glittered and there was a faint hint of irony in the curve of his lips. I stared at him for a moment before I spoke again.

"I will do everything in my power to see that promise kept."

I sat down and everyone seemed too surprised to applaud until *el Presidente* led them. The music began abruptly again in the other room and *el Presidente* got to his feet. The others rose and we followed him into the drawing room.

George Baldwin caught me at the end of the line of people who had come to congratulate me. We were soon alone and he looked at me with that quizzical look of his. "Does the old man really mean it?"

"You heard him," I answered noncommittally.

"I heard *you*," he said. "*You* meant what you said."

I didn't answer.

"If he didn't mean it, I wouldn't give two cents for your life now."

I just looked at him. I still didn't speak.

"The old son of a bitch," George said, a grudging admiration coming into his voice, "he did it again. Until tonight I wouldn't have given two cents for Corteguay's chances of getting an American loan. But now, I'm certain that Washington will feel differently about the whole thing."

We were silent in the back seat as Fat Cat drove through the dark streets to Beatriz' home. I lit a thin *cigarro* and looked out the window. The houses near the university, where her father had once been a professor, were more prosperous. She still lived in the one where she had been born. It was no mansion but it was set well back from the street and screened by a wooden fence covered with flowers.

When the car stopped I got out. I took Beatriz' hand. "I'll see you to the door."

Beatriz didn't speak but hurried past me through the gate. I followed her up the steps to the small porch and she turned to face me. I took her hand and bent to kiss her.

She averted her face. "No."

I looked at her.

Her eyes were an even darker green in the dim light coming through the window behind her. "I cannot see you again," she said. "It is all turning out as they said it would. You are a trap, for me and my father."

"They said?" I asked. "Who?"

Beatriz didn't look at me. "Friends."

"Friends? Or those who would have you and your father serve their ends?"

"It does not matter," she said, "I will not discuss politics with you."

"Good." I took her by the upper arm and roughly pulled her to me. I could feel her stiffen but she offered no resistance. "I was not attracted to you because of political discussions."

"Let me go," she said, her lips scarcely moving.

I kissed her, and for a moment I thought I could feel the warmth rising inside her, but then she spoke again, whispering against my lips. "Let me go, I am not one of your whores."

I released her. Her eyes were wide and staring. "Your friends have done their job well," I said bitterly. "They not only dictate your politics, but also your love."

"My friends have only my best interests at heart," she replied uncertainly. "Everyone knows about you. They do not wish me to be hurt."

"*Excelencia!* Look out!" Fat Cat's warning shout came from the car behind me.

I whirled, sensing a movement in the bushes at the side of the house, and at the same time flung out my arm, knocking Beatriz violently to the ground beside me. I heard the cough of a silenced gun, then the sound of disappearing footsteps as Fat Cat came running through the gate.

I scrambled to my feet and followed Fat Cat into the bushes. He stopped short and turned to me. "It's no use, we'll never find them in the dark."

I looked out across the field behind the house.

"Lucky for you I happened to warn you."

I turned. "Yes, thanks. You probably saved my life."

"It is too bad," Fat Cat said solemnly, though with the hint of a smile. "They came just when it was beginning to get interesting."

I stared at him and, turning, went back to Beatriz. She was just beginning to sit up, so I helped her to her feet. Her fine dark gown was a mess. "Are you all right?"

Beatriz nodded. "I—I think so." She looked at me. "Who were they?"

"Who else could they be?" I asked sarcastically. "Your friends, who, having your best interests at heart, came to kill me. Of course, if by accident you, too, had been hurt, no doubt they would have been terribly sorry."

Beatriz' eyes began to fill with tears. "I don't know what to think."

The door behind us opened and a woman in a wrapper, no doubt a servant, looked out. "What is it? What has happened?"

"Nothing. I will come in a moment. Go back to bed."

The door closed and Beatriz turned back to me. "Dax," she said, her hand reaching for mine.

Suddenly I was angry, and I ignored her hand. "Sorry,

I made a mistake. In my world only children do not know what to think. They have to be told. But men and women think for themselves."

I turned and walked back to the car. Fat Cat was already behind the wheel. "Move over," I said gruffly, and angrily threw the car into gear. As we turned the corner I heard him chuckling. "What's so funny, you idiot?"

"I've never seen you like this."

I didn't speak. Instead I horsed the car into the next turn with an angry screeching of brakes.

"You're like a child who has had his candy taken away."

"Shut up!" I shouted.

Fat Cat was silent for a moment, then he spoke more softly, almost to himself. "Yes, but you see she is the one."

I glanced at Fat Cat out of the corner of my eyes. "What?"

He looked at me, his eyes suddenly serious. "She is the one you will take home to free your *hacienda* from the ghosts of your family."

The telephone began ringing at seven the next morning. The calls were coming in from all over the world. The newspapers and wire services had not been sleeping. The first one I took was from Jeremy Hadley in New York.

"Dax, do I congratulate you or sympathize with you? What does it mean?"

"Nothing more than what you heard."

"There's a rumor going around that *el Presidente* is preparing to step down and turn the reins over to you."

"That is not true," I answered, "nothing has been said about that and nothing will be. *El Presidente* has merely announced that an election will be held in the near future. He said nothing about his succession."

"There is also a rumor that Dr. Guayanos is already in Corteguay."

"I have heard nothing concerning his whereabouts. So far as I know, he is still in exile."

"There is also talk that you have been seeing a great deal of his daughter and that you were instrumental in arranging a truce between Guayanos and *el Presidente*."

I stopped. Rumors. There were times when it seemed as if the world were made up of only two things. People. And rumors. I didn't know which there were more of.

"I have been seeing his daughter," I said, "but there have been no political discussions between us."

"Come on, Dax," Jeremy said, "you don't expect me to believe that? How could you avoid politics with the daughter of the leading opponent of your government's regime?"

"Simple, Jeremy," I said, "and you of all people should know that. Since when have I needed a reason other than that she is a beautiful woman?"

I could hear him chuckle. "I'm beginning to feel better already, you old dog. I was afraid you were beginning to go straight. Good luck."

I put down the telephone, and it began to ring again almost instantly. It was the assistant manager of the hotel. There was an anxious note in his voice. "The lobby is crowded with newspapermen and photographers, excellency. What shall I tell them?"

I thought for a moment. "Take them all into the dining room and serve them breakfast. Put it on my account. Then tell them I will be down as soon as I have shaved and dressed."

I put down the phone again but it rang before I could take my hand off it. "Yes?"

"This is Marcel," a familiar voice said in my ear. "Congratulations."

"Thank you."

"I know your father would be very proud at this moment." Marcel's voice was smooth.

"Yes, thank you," I said, wondering why Marcel had called. He was not the type to waste time on the courtesies.

"When do you expect to be in New York? There are many important matters we must clarify."

"I don't know. *El Presidente* has not given me a schedule yet." I was curious what he meant. "Is there something urgent, something that needs immediate attention?"

"No," Marcel said, his voice hesitating. Then it cleared. "You know that television thing I have here? Do you think it is needed down there?"

Then I realized what he was telling me, that he was aware the lines were tapped. "No," I answered, "I don't think so. I'm sure they have something very similar here."

"I thought so. Well, let me know when you are coming to New York. I will keep myself available for you."

"I will."

"And please congratulate *el Presidente* for me. Assure him of my respect and support."

I put down the phone and it began to ring again. I got out of the bed, ignoring it, and started for the bathroom just as Fat Cat came in the door.

"Tell them I'll accept no more calls for the present. Have them take messages."

Fat Cat nodded and started for the phone. I was almost through the bathroom door when he called to me. *"El Presidente."*

I took the phone from his outstretched hand. "Yes, excellency?"

The old man's voice was bright and cheerful. "Did you have a good night's rest?"

"Yes, sir."

"What are you doing?"

"I'm about to take a shower," I said, "then meet the newspapermen downstairs. I guess I have to see them?"

"Yes, that is one of the hazards of public life. They never leave you alone." He laughed easily. "When you are finished would you come over to the palace? There is someone here I would very much like to have you meet."

"I shall be there as soon as I can, excellency." Then my curiosity got the better of me. "Who is it? Anyone important?"

"That depends on one's point of view. If I were you, I should think him very important. But I am not you. And we think differently about many things. It will be interesting to see how you react when you meet him."

"Him?"

His easy chuckle came over the wire. "Yes, the man who tried to kill you last night. We captured him this morning."

646

8

It was the man I had first seen at the ticket counter with Beatriz at the airport in Miami. But he was no longer so neat and dapper as he stumbled into the room between the two soldiers. Both his eyes were blackened and there was blood crusted on his cheek and around his mouth.

"Do you know him?" *El Presidente* glanced at me shrewdly. "Have you ever seen him before?"

The man raised his head and looked at me, a frightened expression in his eyes.

"No," I said, "I never saw him before." There was no point in my involving Beatriz in this.

"Let me tell you who he is," *el Presidente* said. "He is the girl's uncle, Guayanos' brother."

Suddenly the stupidity of the whole thing got to me. I strode over to him. "You fool!" I said. "Why?"

He did not answer.

"Even if you had killed me, what good would it have done?" I shouted. "Didn't you realize that either of those two bullets might have killed Beatriz?"

An almost invisible change came into his eyes. "I did think of it," he answered in a low tired voice, "and that's why you are alive today. At the last minute I pulled the gun off target."

I stared at him.

El Presidente laughed. "Do you believe that?"

I didn't answer.

"The girl was probably in it with him. That's why he tells you that story."

"No! Beatriz knew nothing about it! She did not even know I was back in Corteguay!"

"Shut up!" *el Presidente* roared. He crossed in front of

me and slapped Beatriz' uncle hard across the face. His head snapped back and he almost fell. *El Presidente* hit him again.

"The guns?" he demanded. "Where are they being landed?"

"I know nothing about guns."

"You lie!" This time *el Presidente* kneed him savagely in the groin.

He doubled over, falling almost to his knees, and gasped with pain. "I know nothing," he said. "If I did, don't you think your police would have found it out before this?"

El Presidente looked down at him. A look of contempt came into his face. He turned to me. "It is worms like these who think they have the strength to govern."

I didn't answer.

El Presidente went back to his desk. He pressed a button on his intercom. "Ask Hoyos and Prieto to come in."

He looked over at me. "If it were not for the two of them, this miserable scum would have escaped us completely. They were following him from the moment he came ashore."

The two came into the room and stood in front of *el Presidente's* desk, their faces impassive.

"What else have you found out?"

Hoyos answered. "Nothing, excellency. There were no guns in the small boat. He came in alone."

"Did he contact the girl?"

"No, excellency. She was not at home when he first went there. He hid himself in the bushes and waited for her return."

"Why didn't you capture him then?" I asked.

"We waited because we thought he would deliver a message to her about the guns. We did not expect him to try to kill you."

I looked at Beatriz' uncle again. His face was pale and lined with pain. "Why did you try to kill me?"

His eyes met mine. "My niece is a good girl. I realized what you hoped to do to her."

"It was not a political plot then?"

He shook his head. "No, it had only to do with her. She is my brother's only child. I warned her of your reputation but apparently she had not heeded my advice."

"This is all nonsense!" *el Presidente* roared. "For the last time—where are the guns being landed?"

"I told you I do not know."

648

"Liar!" *el Presidente*'s voice was hoarse with anger. "Why did you return if not for the guns?"

Beatriz' uncle stared at him. "Where else do I have to go? Corteguay is my home."

El Presidente glared at him for a moment, then turned to Hoyos. "Take him to Escobar. You know what to do with him."

"*Sí, excelencia.*" Hoyos turned and started to lead the prisoner from the office.

"No!"

I knew what Escobar meant. It was the prison for those condemned to death. They all turned and stared at me curiously, *el Presidente* the most curious of all.

"Let him go!"

"Let him go?" *El Presidente*'s voice was shocked. "This man tried to kill you."

"Let him go," I repeated.

"You are a fool!" *el Presidente* shouted. "He will only try again. I know his kind."

I didn't answer.

"You have been too long in the outside world, you have forgotten what it is like here."

I stared at *el Presidente*, remembering his words once long ago when I was merely a boy and had sprung for the throat of another murderer. "There is no need to kill, my son," he had said. "You are no longer in the jungle."

"Have we returned to the jungle so soon?" I asked. *El Presidente* stared at me but I could see that he did not remember. "Last night you appointed me to the Court of Political Action. You surrendered to me all its powers."

He nodded slowly.

"Then the responsibility is mine. I have something more important for the prisoner to do than die." I looked at him. "I give you this message for your brother."

The prisoner looked at me suspiciously.

"In today's newspapers you will read that a complete amnesty has been granted to all political prisoners and refugees. You will also discover that I am now in charge of the Court. I have asked all who disagree with us to come and settle their differences before the people in a free election. Tell your brother it applies to him as well as to all Corteguayans."

Beatriz' uncle sneered. "It is but another trick. We know what happened after other amnesties."

"Then it is a good trick. Because it will allow you to walk from this room alive and a free man."

He stood there nervously. He glanced from one to the other of us as if he did not know what to believe.

El Presidente spoke finally in a disgusted voice. "Throw the worm out. Let us pray he is grateful for such justice."

There was a note of shock in Hoyos' voice. "You mean let him go? Just like that?"

"You heard his excellency," *el Presidente* said, "the prisoner is free."

Hoyos turned silently and left the room, pushing Beatriz' uncle before him. Prieto followed. A silence came into the room. *El President* and I stared at each other for a long time, then finally he began to smile. In a moment he began to roar with laughter.

I was bewildered. "What are you laughing at?"

"Until now," he gasped, "I was sure you had had her. Now I know that you have been no more successful than the others."

I didn't speak.

His laughter subsided to a chuckle. "Beautiful."

"What is beautiful?"

"Your plan." He smiled. "I take my hat off to you. It is so subtle, so clever that I myself would have been proud to have thought of it."

"Yes?" I wished to know how brilliant I had been.

"By freeing the uncle you gain her confidence, and by gaining her confidence you gain her person. Once you're inside her she will deliver her father into our hands." He looked at me shrewdly. "Have you ever known a woman able to keep her mouth shut while she was being fucked?"

650

9

Two weeks went by and still I had not heard from Beatriz.
Several times I found myself reaching for the telephone but
each time I stopped my hand. When she was ready it must be
on her terms.

Yet these were not quiet weeks. All the days and many of
the nights were spent in the office in the palace which *el
Presidente* had assigned to me. Across my desk flowed the
entire economic picture of the country, each chart and
analysis, as soon as it had been completed by the respective
departments. After a while it began to take shape.

One night as I was sitting in my office studying the final
summary, *el Presidente* came in. He walked up to my desk
and looked over my shoulder. "What do you think?"

I looked up. "If these figures the economists have reported
are accurate, we have a chance."

"We have a chance if we get financing. Have you heard
from our friend yet?"

I knew he meant George Baldwin. "No."

"I wonder why they are waiting."

"I don't know."

"Perhaps you should leave for New York without waiting
for their invitation."

"The Americans are a peculiar people," I said. "They
don't like people coming and asking for money unless they're
invited."

"You're not going to Washington," he answered, "you
would be going to New York. You have a right to be there;
after all, you are the head of our delegation to the United
Nations. And while you are there perhaps you can work
on the other."

"That might be a good idea." I looked at the old man
with respect. Not a day passed in which somehow he did not

651

earn a little more of my grudging admiration. He was old but far from stupid.

"It is better than sitting around here doing nothing. When will you leave?"

"Tuesday or Wednesday perhaps," I replied. "There are some personal matters I would like to attend to over the weekend."

He smiled. "You haven't heard from the girl yet?"

I shook my head.

El Presidente shrugged philosophically. "And nothing from her father either?"

"Nothing."

"Not one of them will accept," he said contemptuously. "They're all worms, afraid of the daylight."

I didn't answer. There was no use in pointing out that his last two amnesties had resulted in the death of all who surrendered. Why should they think this one would be any different?

El Presidente put his hand on my shoulder and patted it gently. "You'll learn. You should have killed the uncle when you had the chance. That's the one thing they understand."

He started for the door, then turned. "Good luck with the girl."

I nodded as he closed the door behind him. There was no sense in telling him that Beatriz didn't figure in my plans at all. This weekend there was much I had to do, and I wanted to do it alone.

I wanted to spend some time at my *hacienda* with the memory of my family. It would take at least two days' work with my own hands to straighten up the little cemetery. At last it would be neat and clean and planted with flowers again, the way I knew my mother would have wanted it.

I heard the motor of the car before it came around the curve at the crest of the hill. I put down the shovel with which I had been working and straightened up. I crossed to the old iron fence and picked up the rifle leaning against it. I pulled back the lever, throwing a cartridge into the chamber, and waited. I could see much better from here than from the front of the house, and whoever was coming couldn't see me.

Martínez had left for his shack almost an hour ago, and I

didn't expect Fat Cat until tomorrow. We had come up together on Friday but I sent him right back to the city to cover for me. If there was no answer in our suite I would soon be missed, and it would not take anyone long to figure out where I had gone. Then the soldiers would come, for Lieutenant Giraldo wasn't about to risk his commission by neglecting his duties.

I watched the car come to a stop at the top of the hill, then give the two honks of the horn that Fat Cat and I had agreed upon as a signal. When it started down again I ejected the shell from the chamber into my hand and fed it back into the magazine of the rifle. Then, holding the gun loosely in the crook of my arm, I started slowly back toward the house. My muscles ached with every step. It had been a long time since I had worked like this. But it felt good, and the tiny cemetery was beginning to look as I remembered it.

I stood on the front steps and watched curiously as the car approached. It had to be something important to bring Fat Cat back a day early. As the car turned into the yard I could see that there was another person in the front seat beside him.

The car stopped in front of me and Beatriz got out. For a moment she stood there staring up at me. I suppose I was a horrible sight—half naked to the waist, covered with dirt, and with a rifle in my arms. But she spoke quickly before I could say anything. "Don't be angry," she said, "I made Fat Cat bring me here."

I was too surprised to answer.

"I read in the papers that you were leaving for New York on Tuesday. I didn't want you to go away without my seeing you. I called the hotel twice on Friday but there was no answer. Then this morning I got through to Fat Cat. He didn't want to bring me but when I told him I would come anyway he reluctantly agreed."

I didn't move from the steps.

"You could have waited," I said. "I would have been back in Curatu on Monday."

Her eyes were as green as the leaves of the forest as she looked up at me. "I know," she answered, her voice suddenly trembling, "but I couldn't wait any longer. I almost waited too long as it was."

I came down the steps. In the narrow-cut, clinging slacks,

she was slimmer than I remembered. The open-collared, rolled-sleeved man's shirt made her seem like a little girl dressed in her brother's clothes. Except that the beautiful curve of her breasts would never allow a mistake like that. I stopped in front of her. "What were you waiting for?"

She returned my gaze almost defiantly. "For you to call me," she said, "and then when you did not I remembered what you said. Only children need to be told what to think. Men and women think for themselves."

"And what do you think?"

I could see the faint hint of color creeping up into her face from below the collar of her shirt. "I think—" She hesitated a moment. Her eyes fell, then came up to mine. "I think I've fallen in love with you."

Then she was in my arms.

I held the match to my *cigarro* and watched her leaning over the railing of the *galería* looking up at the night sky. I shook the match out as she came back to me. "Now I know why you love this place. It's so beautiful, you feel as if you were the only person in the whole world."

I smiled at her. "It's more than just that," I said quietly. "This is my home. I was born in that room at the head of the stairs. My mother and father and sister sleep in the soft earth behind the house. My roots are here."

She sat down opposite me and took my hand. "My father knew your father. He said he was a truly great man."

I looked away out into the night. I could hear the soft breeze singing in the field grass. "My father," I said, and stopped. How do you put goodness and warmth and love into words? I brought my eyes back to hers. "My father was a man, a real man. He found an excuse for everyone in this world except himself."

"You're like that too."

I stared at Beatriz for a moment, then got to my feet. "Time for bed. We farmers have to be up at sunrise."

Beatriz rose hesitantly. I saw her nervousness and smiled. She was still more of a child than she realized. "I've given you my sister's room," I said. "Fat Cat has prepared it for you."

I lay stretched out on my bed in the dark listening to the

654

hum of her voice and the splash of water from the pitcher in her room. This time the sound was real, not a dream. I listened carefully. Fat Cat had been right. There was not another sound in the house. The ghosts had all been freed.

I smiled to myself and turned over on my side and closed my eyes. After a while the humming stopped and I fell asleep. Suddenly I was wide awake again, for someone was in my room. I turned over in bed and my hand touched the full firmness of her breast. I felt the erect, bursting nipple through the thin nightgown.

Her voice was low. "They warned me about you. Didn't anyone ever warn you about girls like me? I didn't come here to be alone."

The fire from her ran down my arm, inflaming my body. I felt the muscles tighten and harden. I pulled her over to me and kissed her so hard she almost cried out. It was the first time for her and in a way almost the first for me. Better than it had ever been, better than I had ever dreamed it could be.

It was the only time any woman had ever cried out to me in the midst of her initial pain and agony and delight: "Give me your child, my lover. Fill me with your children!"

10

I awoke as the first golden streamer of sunlight came in the window. I turned slowly, holding my breath so that I would not disturb Beatriz. She lay partly on her side, partly on her back, the thin light sheet caught around her legs. Her lustrous, long black hair was spread out on the white pillow beneath her head. Her eyes were closed, her mouth slightly curved in a secret smile as she slept.

I looked down at her full strong breasts and I could see the faint blue tracings of her milk veins, leading to her nipples set in their plumlike frame. I let my eyes trace the lovely curve of her narrow waist over her hip and down the tiny moist forest of her mountain to the straight strong swelling of her thigh.

"Am I beautiful?" she asked softly.

I looked at her in surprise. Her dark green eyes were smiling at me. "I didn't know you were awake."

"Am I beautiful?"

I nodded. "Very beautiful."

She closed her eyes slowly. "Was I—was I all right?"

"You were wonderful," I answered quietly. And she was.

"I was afraid at first," she whispered. "Not for myself, but for you. So many things could go wrong. I heard such stories. You know. How painful it could be, how a girl could spoil everything for her husband. I wanted to be perfect for you. I wanted everything to be right."

"It was."

Beatriz opened her eyes and looked at me. "Did you mean it? What you said last night?" Then she stopped for a moment and added quickly, "No, you don't have to answer. It's not fair of me. I don't want you to feel you must lie to me."

"I usually don't answer such personal questions." I smiled at her. "But I'd like to answer that one."

She looked at me, her eyes wide.

"I meant what I said last night. I love you."

Beatriz smiled slowly and closed her eyes again. "I love you," she said, reaching out and touching me with her hand. With her eyes still closed, she bent down and kissed me.

Then she opened her eyes and looked up at me, her lips still against me. "It's so beautiful," she whispered, "so hard and strong. I never dreamed it would always be like this."

I began to laugh. But I was ready to kill myself rather than disillusion her.

"That's it," I said, putting the last flower into place and tamping the earth down around it. I straightened up and looked at Beatriz.

She stood there leaning against the fence, then came over and kissed me. "The next time I will help. This time I understood. You had to do it by yourself."

"I should have done it a long time ago."

"You could not help it, you were not home." She went

over and knelt beside my sister's grave. "So young," she said softly, "only thirteen. How did she die?"

I stared at her. "The *bandoleros* came down from the mountains," I said tightly. "They killed her, and my mother, and La Perla, our cook."

"Your father wasn't here?"

I shook my head. "There used to be a village a dozen miles from here. He was there."

"And you?"

"I was hiding in the cellar in back of a box my sister had pushed me behind."

"Then you saw—"

"Everything. And there was nothing I could do. When they finally discovered me I ran out into the road. Luckily my father was coming toward the *hacienda* with the general and his soldiers."

"The general?"

I nodded. "*El Presidente.* But that was a long time before he took over."

Beatriz got to her feet, and I saw the tears in her eyes. "Poor Dax," she whispered, "what a poor frightened baby you must have been."

"In a way it wasn't so bad," I said. "I was too young to understand really what had happened. But not my father, and he was never quite the same after that. Oh, he kept on living. Working. And taking care of me. But something had gone out of his life."

Beatriz came close and pressed her lips gently to mine. I could taste the salt of her tears. "Someday," she whispered, "this house will be alive again with the sounds of children. Your children. And then the memory will not be so bitter."

The sound of approaching footsteps came from behind me. I turned to see Fat Cat.

"It is past one o'clock," he said, "and Martínez is not yet here."

"Something must have held him up. Do we have food for lunch?"

"Yes, if you don't mind eating what you had for breakfast this morning."

Beatriz smiled and I laughed. "We don't mind. We like *tortillas* and beans."

He turned back toward the house and I gathered up the

657

tools—the shovel, the hoe and the rake—and slung them over my shoulder. "Can you carry the rifle?"

"Yes," she said, picking it up, the muzzle toward her.

"Not that way." I straightened the rifle in her hand. "Always keep the muzzle pointing away and down from you."

"I don't like guns. I never liked them." Beatriz looked at me. "I don't see why you feel you need one here. There isn't anyone for miles."

"See that tall grass?" I asked, pointing.

Beatriz nodded.

"A hundred men could be out there and you would never see them until they were upon you."

"And if there were," she said, "what could they hope to gain by attacking us?"

"What did they gain by attacking my mother and my sister?" I asked coldly.

Beatriz didn't answer.

"The only excuse they need is the guns. The guns give them a feeling of power, and they are getting more of them every day."

"Some of them must have guns to defend themselves."

"Against what? Whom?"

"Against the terrorist soldiers of the government," she replied defiantly.

I looked at her. "You don't know soldiers like I do," I said dryly. "I don't know one of them who really likes to fight. They are perfectly happy to hang around their warm barracks and never go out into the field where they might be hurt."

We were at the house now and I put down the tools and took the gun from her. "No, the only reason men want guns is to make war. If we could stop the guns perhaps we could prevent the bloodshed that is bound to follow. That is if we're not already too late."

We walked silently around to the front of the house. Fat Cat was waiting for us on the *galería*. He was silent until Beatriz had gone in to wash up, then he gestured to me.

"Look," he said, handing me a pair of field glasses. He pointed in the direction of Martínez' hut.

I put the glasses to my eyes and swept the horizon. "I don't see anything."

"In the sky, just above where the house is."

I looked again and then I saw them. Three condors floating lazily on the air currents. I put down the glasses. "So what?" I asked. "There is probably a dead animal in the field. You're getting to be an old woman."

"I don't like it," Fat Cat said stubbornly.

I stared at him. I'd known him long enough to trust his intuitions. In many ways he was like an animal of the forest. He could smell trouble before it arrived.

"All right," I said finally, "we'll go over there after lunch. O.K.?"

He looked at me with the quizzical expression he used whenever I dropped an English word into my Spanish. Finally he nodded. *"D'accord."*

"I don't want to leave here," Beatriz had whispered as we watched Fat Cat load our things into the car. "It's so calm and quiet and beautiful." She turned suddenly and pressed her head against my chest. "Promise me we'll come back here one day, Dax!"

"We'll come back."

But that had been before we got to Martínez' house and found what we did. Now she sat shivering in the seat beside me as we hurtled through the night toward the city. I wondered if she thought of returning to the *hacienda* now.

I glanced over at her for a moment. She sat wrapped in the car blanket to protect her from the chill of the night, her eyes staring straight ahead. I wondered what she was thinking, what she felt. And more than anything else I wondered if she regretted coming to me. But she didn't speak and I didn't press her. Beatriz had been through enough that day.

It was almost four in the morning when I finally stopped the car in front of her house. I got out and walked with her to the front door.

She turned. "You'll be careful, won't you?"

I nodded. I knew that she wanted to ask something more but had changed her mind. "Don't worry," I said, "I love you too much not to be."

Suddenly she flung her arms around me and started crying. "Dax, Dax!" she sobbed huskily. "Nothing makes sense any more. I don't know what to think."

"You did right. The guns must be stopped. And no one need ever know."

Beatriz looked up into my eyes for a long time. Gradually her tears stopped. "I believe you. Perhaps it's because I'm a woman, because I'm in love with you. But I believe you."

I kissed her. "Go in to sleep," I said gently, "you're exhausted."

She nodded. "Dax, I forgot to thank you."

"For what?"

"For my uncle. He told me what you did."

"Your uncle is a fool," I said harshly. "He might have killed you. And he should have realized he'd be caught."

"You don't understand. He worships my father and since my father is not here he thinks it is up to him to protect me." Beatriz laughed a little and I was relieved to hear the sound. "Actually more than half the time I have to protect him."

"Well, don't let him get into any more trouble."

She put her hand on my arm. "The amnesty? It's not just a trick this time?"

"It's not a trick."

Beatriz looked up into my eyes for a moment, then reached up swiftly and kissed me. "Good night."

11

The hold of the ship was dark and full of the heavy stench of the fuel oil in its tanks. "Is there a light in here?"

The captain nodded and gestured with his flashlight. A sailor turned on a switch, and two bulbs emitted a sick yellow glow. The tiny hold was filled with heavy wooden cases. I turned to Lieutenant Giraldo. "This looks like it."

"Open a case," Giraldo ordered.

Two of the soldiers pulled one down and began to pry it open with their machetes. I watched the captain. His face was impassive amidst the ripping sound of the wood.

"Guns!" The soldier's voice was harsh and echoed in the steel hold.

The captain's expression did not change. I turned and looked at the opened case. The automatic rifles gleamed black and shiny under their light protective film of oil. I picked one up and examined it. The markings were tiny but clearly etched. No attempt had been made to disguise them. KUPPEN FARBEN GESELLSCHAFT e.g. I knew what the small initials meant. East Germany. The old armament factory in the Russian Zone. They had kept the name because it still commanded respect in certain parts of the world. Who was to know that this company was under a completely different management than the one in the west which had been put out of the armament business?

I threw the rifle back at the soldier. "Open the other cases."

I turned back to the captain. "You have bills of lading for these?"

"Of course. They are part of a consignment for our next port of call."

"I see. May I see them?"

For the first time the captain's expression changed slightly. He glanced out of the corner of his eyes at the customs inspector who was standing silently next to him. "I do not have them."

"Then who does, Captain?"

He did not answer.

"Come, Captain," I said, "someone must have them."

He seemed to answer with difficulty. "I think they may have been included with other bills by mistake."

"You mean that customs has the bills?"

He nodded reluctantly.

I turned to the customs inspector. "Have you seen them?"

The man's eyes were frightened. "No, excellency," he stammered. "We are not permitted to see such bills. They are processed by the chief inspector himself."

I turned to Giraldo. "Leave half your men here. Bring the rest and come with me."

"*Si, excelencia!*" For the first time I noted a growing respect in the young lieutenant's eyes. It had not been there at six this morning when I strode into his barracks. He had protested that he had no authority to embark on such a raid, and that his only duty was to protect me.

"Then your duty is clear," I said, "you must accompany me for my own protection."

He had stared at me for a moment. "I will have to take it up with my superiors."

"Lieutenant, you will clear it with no one!" I had allowed my voice to grow sarcastic. "Your instructions are very explicit. How will it look if I tell *el Presidente* that you have already breached them? That I have just returned from two days in the mountains while ·you were lolling around your barracks?"

Giraldo had thought for a moment, but it did not take him long to decide which was the lesser of two evils. Even if his decision was wrong in accompanying me, at least it would not cost him his commission. If they ever found out I had been alone in the mountains he'd be lucky if all *el Presidente* did was strip him of his commission.

He had turned his men out and they piled into two jeeps and followed my car to the port. The ship was already secured to the pier. I stood there in the gray light of the morning and looked up at the foremast, where the ruby and green insignia of the Campion Lines flew. It would have to be one of his ships, I thought, as we began to climb the gangplank.

Now that we had found the guns, I could tell by his manner that Giraldo felt differently. All hesitancy was gone as he issued his orders. I turned to the captain and the customs inspector. "Will you both please come to the chief inspector's office with me?"

Without waiting for an answer, I climbed up the steel ladder to the open deck. After the stench of the hold the warm sweet sea air smelled good. I took a deep breath.

Fat Cat came hurrying down the deck. "*El Presidente* has just arrived!"

I stared at him. "Here?"

"*Sí.* On the docks. He is waiting for you."

I didn't speak. I didn't have to. Fat Cat knew what I was thinking. I could not make a move anywhere in the city that *el Presidente* didn't know about.

I followed Fat Cat to the edge of the gangplank and looked down. *El Presidente* was standing beside his big black limousine surrounded by soldiers. He looked up and saw me and waved. I returned the greeting and came down the gangplank. The soldiers parted to let me through.

"What did you find?"

I stared at el Presidente for a moment before I answered. "What I expected to find. Guns. Communist guns. The same kind you captured from the bandoleros in the mountains."

El Presidente looked at me for a moment, then turned away. "Hoyos!"

The policeman came quickly from behind the car. It was the first time I had ever seen him in uniform. The gold crescent of a colonel of the army shone on his shoulders. "Sí, excelencia!"

"Put a squad of men aboard the ship to take possession of the guns, Colonel."

"That won't be necessary, sir," I said quickly, "Lieutenant Giraldo's men are already guarding them."

"You have Giraldo with you? Good."

"I am on my way to the chief inspector's office. I have been told the bills of lading are there."

"I will go with you," el Presidente said grimly. "My cousin, it seems, has a great deal to explain."

The ship's captain and the customs inspector moved on ahead as we walked down the dock to the building that housed customs. El Presidente's voice was low as he took my arm confidentially. "How did you learn about the guns? From the girl?"

"No, from Martínez, the old farmer who lives near my hacienda. The bandoleros tortured him and left him for dead because he was my friend. He heard them talking." The lie was an apt one. They would have to dig him up to disprove it and they wouldn't bother.

"Martínez? You mean the animal man?"

I stared at el Presidente. Sometimes there was no end to the surprises he furnished me. It was at least thirty years since he had seen Martínez and yet he recalled him immediately. "Yes."

"I had no idea he was still alive," el Presidente said thoughtfully. "We used to get chickens from him. He must be a very old man by now."

We were at the door of the customs shed and Hoyos sprang forward to open it, then stepped aside to allow el Presidente and myself to enter. The two clerks seated at their desks looked up, startled.

"Is my cousin in?"

663

"I—I don't know," one of them answered nervously, half rising. "I will see, excellency."

"I will see for myself!"

The clerk sank back into his seat as *el Presidente* pushed past him into the private office. Through the open door I could see the chief inspector jump up from behind his desk and stand at attention.

"There are guns on that ship out there!" *el Presidente* roared.

The chief inspector's face was suddenly white. "Excellency, I did not know, believe me."

"Liar! Traitor! The bills of lading are here in your office, get them for me!" *El Presidente* strode toward the desk, his hand outstretched imperiously.

I walked into the office, with Hoyos at my shoulder, just as the chief inspector frantically pulled open a desk drawer. It stuck for a moment, then came open, and he reached in with his hand. There was a glint of metal, and a gun went off almost in my ear. The force of the bullet propelled the chief inspector back against the wall. He hung there for a moment, the surprise in his eyes abruptly fading to nothingness as he crumpled awkwardly to the floor.

I turned to Hoyos. He was standing there, the gun still smoking in his hand, his thin lips drawn back slightly. "I saw a gun!"

I didn't answer. Instead I went behind the desk, stepped over the dead man, and reached into the drawer. I took out the papers, which were held together by a large metal clamp. "That is your gun," I said quietly.

I saw the look that flashed between Hoyos and *el Presidente,* and I realized it wouldn't have mattered what the man had done. He was dead before we ever came into the office. I looked down at the papers, flipping through them rapidly, but the bills of lading, if there ever had been any, were gone.

There was more to the story of the guns than they were willing to have me discover.

12

"My cousin," *el Presidente* said. "My own flesh and blood."

I looked across his desk at him. Despite the black mourning band on his sleeve he did not sound any sorrier than he had yesterday in the customs office. I didn't speak.

"You were right," he continued, "the guns were coming in on the ships. I never would have believed it. I had put my own cousin in charge of the port. If I couldn't trust him, whom could I trust?"

Again I had no answer, but this much I knew: there was no one he really trusted, except himself.

"I have placed the port under Hoyos' jurisdiction," he continued. "The army will control it now."

"What happened to the customs people?" I asked.

"They are in jail. They were all in it with him."

"You found evidence?"

"I found guns," he replied. "What more evidence do I need? For those guns to get off that ship, everyone had to know about it."

"And the captain? What about him?"

"We let him go. What else could we do? Have him call the American Embassy and create a big stink when you are trying to borrow twenty million dollars?"

There was a peculiar logic to his statement. This was one time we couldn't afford any trouble. I got to my feet and walked over to the window.

The ship was still in the harbor. It was due to leave on the evening tide. If only it hadn't been a Campion ship flying our flag we could close the port to the whole fleet. But how could you seal the port to vessels flying your own flag? The guns would still come in. If they were to be stopped another way had to be found.

El Presidente came over to the window and stood beside me. "It is never simple."

I turned to look at him.

"When I was a young man I thought I knew all the answers. Then I came to the *palacia* and found there is no quick and easy answer for anything. The smallest matters have a way of growing into insurmountable problems. And all the time there are people pushing you. Do this. Do that. First one way, then another, until there are times you wish you could take back the words you once said out of ignorance. No man ever knows anything until he is in the lonely and precarious seat of power and realizes how little he actually knows."

"I will speak to Campion when I get to New York. Perhaps he will know a way to keep the guns from getting onto his ships."

"Do that," the old man said, "but it will not help. How can Campion personally approve every freight order his ships pick up? He would have to look into every hold, every crate. And if he did that how long do you think he would remain in business?"

"I shall speak to him anyway."

"I am beginning to think there is only one way to settle this. It is for me to lead an army into the mountains and clean out the cursed *bandoleros* once and for always. Kill every one of them."

"That is not the answer," I said. "You would have to kill the women and children, too, and you couldn't do that. Even if it were the only way, the world would turn away from us in horror."

"I know. The Americans would denounce us as a dictatorship and the Soviets would claim we were an extension of American imperialism."

El Presidente took a deep breath. "It's not easy. I sit here with my hands tied while every day a few more are murdered or subverted. And the only thing I can do is defend, never attack. It is a war without answer."

"The amnesty—"

He stared at me. "The amnesty is a failure! Has one single *bandolero* or revolutionary come forward? No, and they never will. You might as well accept it."

"It has been in effect only two weeks," I said. "They are still deliberating."

El Presidente walked away from me back to his desk. His voice was dry. "If you wish to continue to delude yourself, you can. I prefer to be realistic." He sat down heavily in his chair. "Take that little worm you allowed to escape with his life. Have you heard one word from him since? Or from his brother, that cowardly traitor? Or for that matter from the girl?"

I didn't answer. I couldn't tell *el Presidente* that I wouldn't even have known about the guns if it had not been for Beatriz. To me that was proof that the amnesty would at least be discussed and evaluated. I stopped in front of his desk. "You are not withdrawing your offer?"

"I don't have to," *el Presidente* replied contemptuously. "There is no need to withdraw a public offer that privately you know will never be accepted. At least this way the failure will be on their heads."

Then he changed the subject abruptly. "The girl? What are you planning to do about her?"

"I don't know. I hadn't thought about it."

"Better think about it, then. I have a feeling that somehow you've changed since you met her."

"What do you mean?"

"You have been in Corteguay for almost a month," he said, the hint of a smile at the corners of his mouth, "and there hasn't been the slightest hint of scandal. Not one father or husband has come forth with a complaint!"

As usual the drapes were drawn when I entered the room. "Amparo, I'm leaving tomorrow. I've come to say good-bye."

She looked up from the desk. Her voice sounded eerie, as if it were coming from a great distance. "That's very kind of you. You really didn't have to bother."

"I wanted to," I said, walking over to her. "I was wondering if there is anything I can do for you."

"For me?" There was an echo of surprise in her voice. "Why should you want to do anything for me?"

"For many reasons, most of which you know. But mainly because I don't like to see you like this."

Amparo looked straight into my eyes. Her own were calm

667

and distant, as if we were speaking about some other person. "You mean the drugs?"

"Yes. There are places where you could be helped, you know. Cured."

"What would you cure me of, Dax? Of the only peace I've ever known?"

"But it's not real peace, Amparo, even you know that. It's only an illusion."

Again Amparo looked at me with that strange calmness. "Would you have me go back to what I was before? Torturing myself, living in terror, half crazy all the time with wanting things I knew I could never have? No, thank you. I don't care if it is only an illusion. Let me keep it, Dax."

"But you're only half alive."

"Half alive is better than dead." She looked down at the desk in front of her and picked up a letter. "Look at this, Dax. Do you know what I have been doing?"

I shook my head.

"I've been trying to write a letter of condolence. For two days I've been trying to write the family of my cousin to explain to them how sorry I am that he had to die because of my father's ambitions."

Amparo's voice was beginning to take on a slight edge of hysteria. "Do you know how many times I have had to write to families of men my father has killed? I can't even count them any more, there are so many."

"It was an accident," I said, "your father was not to blame."

"It was no accident. The only accident was that somehow you found out something you were not meant to know. From that moment on my cousin was doomed. Last night I went to his house. Already his widow is in black, and his children are wide-eyed, not really understanding that their father has left them forever. I could not walk into that house knowing what I knew. So I came home, and ever since then I've been trying to write this letter."

Angrily Amparo crumpled the paper and threw it into the wastebasket. She reached for a cigarette and lit it with trembling fingers. After a few moments the trembling stopped, and she looked at me again. When she spoke, her voice was icily detached.

"How can you be so stupid, Dax? All the answers you

seek are in your own hands. Kill him, Dax, and all this will stop. I am beginning to think that even he is waiting for you to do it. He would welcome it."

That evening I stood in the doorway of Beatriz' house as her servant told me that she and her uncle had gone away. No, she did not know where they had gone.

It was not until the next morning, when I went to *el Presidente*'s office to say good-bye, that he informed me that the two of them had left on yesterday's Miami plane.

13

"This visit is strictly unofficial," Jeremy warned as we got out of the car. "If anyone asks, the senator will deny he ever spoke to you."

"I understand," I said. "I'm grateful that someone is at least willing to talk to me." And I meant it. Despite what George Baldwin had thought, there had been no official response from Washington.

I'd taken it for three weeks. Then the pressure began to build up inside me. The news from home hadn't been good. A village in the mountains had been completely taken over by the *bandoleros*. It had taken almost half an army division to drive them out, and when they did go they left nothing behind them. Every one of the inhabitants was dead. Fifty-seven persons—men, women, and children.

It was too big for even *el Presidente* to withhold from the newspapers, and they were filled with it. And no matter how objective they tried to make the story, it came out sounding as if the government were responsible and the *bandoleros* were some romantic figures out of America's highly distorted western past. The Communist and many European papers were far more blunt. They blatantly accused *el Presidente* of wiping out the village as an act of reprisal against a popular revolt. Several members of the Communist bloc even threatened to bring up the matter before the United Nations.

They didn't, of course, but all the talk and the threats did us no good. It became fashionable in America to regard *el Presidente* as another Perón, Batista, or Trujillo, and the American politician, ever sensitive to the moods of his constituents, was perfectly willing to sit on his hands as far as we were concerned.

It wasn't until I received a coded dispatch from *el Presidente* that I decided to see if I could force the issue. The *bandoleros*, actually, had held the army at bay for almost three days with mortar and cannon fire, and our losses were heavier than reported. Now it seemed likely that the enemy would simply move into another village and the same thing would happen all over again. If it did, it was not at all certain our army could dislodge them.

For once I was willing to accept what the old man said without question. I had seen the wanton destruction at Martínez' farm. I picked up the telephone and called Jeremy in Washington and read him *el Presidente*'s letter.

There was a silence on the wire after I had finished. After a moment he asked, "Have you shown this to anyone in our government?"

"Who is there to show it to?" I asked. "We stand already condemned in their eyes. Baldwin must have sent in a report, and yet I have heard from no one."

When Jeremy spoke his voice was casual. "Do you remember the old house up on the Cape?"

"Of course." It was the first summer I had been in the United States and I had spent a weekend there. "I didn't know you still had it."

"It's still in the family. I go up there every now and then when I can get away. I was planning to go this weekend. If you think you could stand the quiet, would you like to join me?"

"Very much." Jeremy had something on his mind or he wouldn't have asked me.

"Good. I'll pick you up at your office. Maybe we'll drive up."

"We'll do better than that, we'll fly up."

"I didn't know you had a plane."

"You haven't been reading your own newspapers," I said dryly. "Sue Ann has been very generous in her settlement."

Jeremy hadn't told me we were going to meet the senator until we got there. The Cape was usually fairly deserted at this time of the year, and the senator himself opened the door. He was dressed casually in a sweater, slacks, and sneakers. He seemed even younger than his thirty-five years.

"Hello," he said, holding out his hand, "I've been wanting to meet you for a long time. I never had the chance to thank you for what you did for my brother."

I glanced at Jeremy and saw the lines in his face tighten slightly. In some strange way he still blamed himself for the death of his brother. He felt it was somehow his fault, that he should have taken more precautions than he had. I didn't see where or how.

"I did what I could," I said.

We followed the senator into a small study. The house was silent. There didn't seem to be anyone else around.

"Care for a drink?"

"Not for me, thanks," I said.

He mixed a Scotch and water for Jeremy and himself and sat down opposite me. "Jeremy has already told you that this visit is entirely off the record. I don't know what I can do to help you, probably nothing. But I would like to hear you out just as a friend."

Again I glanced at Jeremy. "Tell him everything," he said.

I did just that. From the very beginning. I left nothing out. I began with a brief history of Corteguay and told him what it had been like before *el Presidente* came down from the mountains and took over. Then I told him what had happened in Corteguay since then. He listened quietly, intently, interrupting only to ask a clarifying question, and when the story was over almost two hours had passed.

"I'm afraid I've been rather long-winded."

"Not at all," the senator said. "I've been most interested."

"I'll take that drink now."

He got up and mixed drinks for us all. Then he turned back to me. "You say there have always been *bandoleros* but that now they are being supported by the Communists. You're sure of that, are you? Everyone who comes to us for help says that."

671

"I saw the guns myself," I said. "I held them in my hand. They were made in the old Von Kuppen factory in East Germany."

The senator nodded slowly. "I've heard some talk about that. Supposedly they're making only agricultural machinery." He reached for a cigarette, then discarded it for a cigar. He put it into his mouth without lighting it. "Your president is far from perfect, you know. He was pretty much of a bandit himself."

"What president is perfect?" I asked. "As sincere and honest as your own is, you must admit that the best that can be said for him is that he was a good general."

A faint hint of a smile crinkled the senator's eyes. I could see that he liked what I had said even if he didn't comment. He held a match to his cigar.

"This much I can say," I added. "At least when *el Presidente* came down from the mountains he represented only the people of Corteguay. He had no foreign support, not even America's. You had been too involved with the previous government to give him any comfort. What he did he did himself, with the aid of only Corteguayans."

"Do you think he represents the will of the majority of your people today?" the senator asked suddenly.

I looked at him for a moment before I answered. "I don't know. And I seriously doubt that any of my countrymen can tell you. He has promised an election so the people can decide, but an election with only one candidate would be a farce. And up to now no other candidate has presented himself."

"Have you ever heard of a man named Guayanos?" the senator asked shrewdly.

"I know about Dr. Guayanos, though I don't know him personally." Out of the corner of my eyes, I saw Jeremy glance at me, and I smiled. "I do know his daughter, however."

"I haven't met Dr. Guayanos or his daughter," the senator said seriously, "but there are several of my fellow congressmen who seem to believe what he told them. That the offer of an amnesty and an election is merely a trick to entice him back into the country where he would promptly be arrested or murdered."

For the first time I almost lost my temper. "Fifty-seven

men, women, and children died in a small village in my country less than two weeks ago. Perhaps the *bandoleros* killed them, perhaps the soldiers, which largely depends on what newspaper you read. But to me it doesn't matter who killed them. What is important is that they are dead, and the men responsible for their deaths are those who support the *bandoleros* with guns and money. The soldiers were not sent to attack a village of women and children. They were sent to free them from the *bandoleros*. For far too long my country has been governed by men who seized power through bloodshed. If Dr. Guayanos is as concerned as he professes, let him come forward and run for the presidency. The world will soon discover whether it is a trick or not. But I am afraid that in his own way Guayanos is no better than the others. It is much safer to seize power than to risk refusal by the electorate."

"Or his life," the senator said.

I stared at him. "Especially his life. Is his any more precious than any other?"

The senator looked at me thoughtfully for a moment. When he spoke his voice was gentle. "The world is filled with cowards who ask that heroes die for them."

A few minutes passed and I got to my feet. "I apologize for taking more of your time than I intended. Thank you for letting me."

"No, it is I who should thank you," the senator said, getting up out of his chair. "I have learned a great deal. But as I said, I don't know what I can do."

"You've listened, and that means a great deal. It's more than anyone else in your government has been willing to do."

We began to walk to the door. "I would like to see you again," the senator said. "Socially, so that we may become friends."

"I would like that."

"Would you accept a dinner invitation from my sister if you should get one?"

"It would be a pleasure."

"Good." The senator grinned and for a moment he looked like a triumphant little boy. "She would have killed me had you refused. She's been dying to meet you."

673

14

It was the Monday night after I returned from the Cape. Jeremy had gone back to Washington, where his news bureau had headquartered him, and I had spent a long frustrating day attending minor UN committee meetings. It was after eleven when I looked up from my desk in the consulate. I felt restless and knew I would not sleep. Suddenly I realized that I had not eaten dinner.

John Perona himself lifted the velvet rope at El Morocco to let me through the crowd. He groaned when he saw me.

I smiled at him. "You don't seem happy."

"Who could be happy in a place like this?" He looked out over the crowded rooms. "Problems, nothing but problems. I just finished telling my son that I hoped you wouldn't show up tonight, and here you are."

I grinned at him. "Why me especially?"

A reluctant smile came to his lips. "Every one of your ex-wives is here, plus three or four of your old girl friends."

I laughed. "Would you rather I told them to go somewhere else?"

He stared at me for a moment, not knowing if I were joking. Then he shook his head. "No, only tonight. It seems as if everyone in New York is here. Maybe in the whole world."

I followed him as he threaded his way through the tables to an empty banquette against the wall. He wasn't entirely wrong. Aly Khan and a party were at one table. Amos Abidijan, Marcel's former father-in-law, was at another. Aristotle and Tina Onassis were at their usual spot with Rubi and his new young French wife. The motion-picture colony was represented by Sam Spiegel and Darryl Zanuck, at separate tables, and at another the prominent international attorney Paul Gitlin held forth on his two favorite subjects, his weight and such important literary matters as royalty rates and motion-picture sales. His patient wife, Zelda, listened and waited her chance to get a word in sidewise.

I sat down and before I had a chance to order anything the wine steward set down a bottle of champagne, opened it and filled my glass. I looked up at Perona questioningly.

"You'll drink champagne tonight," he said. "We're too busy to serve anything else."

"Very uncivilized. Besides, I'm hungry."

"I'll have a captain take your order." Perona clapped his hands sharply and hurried away.

A captain materialized. *"Oui, monsieur?"*

I ordered a tossed green salad with oil, vinegar, and grosgrain Beluga caviar in the dressing, and a thick steak, medium rare, with french-fried potatoes. I leaned back, lit a cigar, and looked out over the room.

For a moment I felt like calling Perona back and informing him that though he hadn't been entirely wrong, neither had he been completely accurate. I had located Caroline and Sue Ann but I hadn't believed Amparo would be there and she wasn't. Then the waiter brought my salad, and I began to eat.

I had just finished when a voice came from in front of my table. "I can't believe my eyes. Things have certainly changed. *You* eating alone?"

I'd have known that gravelly voice anywhere. I got to my feet. "Irma Andersen."

"Dax, dear boy," she said, holding out her hand.

I kissed it, wondering if those pudgy little fingers had ever been young. "I've been working late and came out for a bit of supper. Would you care to join me, perhaps a glass of champagne?"

"No wine—my diet, you know. But I will sit with you for just a moment."

The waiter hurried over to hold her chair.

"Tell me," Irma said, settling herself, "what have you been doing with yourself? I thought I'd see more of you once you got back to New York."

"There have been problems."

"I know. It's terrible the things that are happening down there. People say there will soon be a revolution."

675

"People love to talk," I said. "There will be no revolution."

"Too bad. If there weren't all this talk there might be an opportunity to revive the tourist trade. People are looking for a new place to go. They're getting bored with the same old thing."

I looked at Irma speculatively. She was a shrewd old bitch and if she was talking it wasn't merely to listen to herself. "If you are saying that there will be no revolution and that things will soon quiet down, what you need is a new public-relations program."

Now I knew what Irma was getting at. I nodded in agreement. "You're absolutely right. But who outside of yourself could handle such a campaign effectively? No one. And you're far too busy."

She looked at me quizzically, then lowered her voice. "Frankly," she said, "I've been looking for something new. Now that Sergei is so well established I'm beginning to have more free time."

"Wonderful! Suppose I give you a call tomorrow? We can make a date to talk about it."

"Do that, dear boy," Irma said, getting to her feet. "Oh, by the way, did you know that Caroline de Coyne and Sue Ann Daley are here tonight?"

"I know, I saw them."

"And Mady Schneider and Dee Dee Lester and—" Irma would have continued but I held up my hand.

"You don't have to go on. I saw them all."

"And still you're eating alone?"

"Don't feel sorry for me." I laughed. "I like to eat alone sometimes."

But as it turned out I wasn't alone for long. Dania Farkas came in after her performance, and I invited her to join me. And perhaps because I was no longer alone the others came over. First Sue Ann, because she was curious to see if something was developing between Dania and myself. Next came Dee Dee, who never could resist making the scene when Sue Ann was present. And later Caroline, followed by Mady Schneider, who could never bear to be left out of anything.

Suddenly I became aware that an awkward silence had fallen over the table. They looked at each other and began to wonder why the hell they had come over. John Perona came hurrying over with two waiters, each carrying a bottle of champagne. He leaned over, a worried look in his eyes. "I hope there won't be any trouble," he said in a stage whisper.

Suddenly I laughed aloud. This was great, for a moment I was truly the Sultan of Morocco. "Don't worry, there won't be any trouble," I said reassuringly. "The ladies merely decided to hold an impromptu class reunion."

In the wave of laughter that followed, the tension left the table, and while we all talked and laughed, the others in the restaurant went back to their normal occupation, which was talking and minding everybody else's business.

It was two in the morning by the time I left the restaurant with Dania. "That was fun," she said, smiling. "Each of us looking at the others and wondering what each was thinking."

"It was amusing but I wouldn't like to do it every day. It's too wearing."

She laughed. "Come to my place for a nightcap. It will help settle you down."

"All right, but I can stay only a few minutes. I have a very full day tomorrow."

It was after five when I left her apartment, and I stared at myself in the mirrored elevator. I looked a wreck. There were two long scratches on the side of my neck and my ears were still ringing from her moans and squeals of pleasure. I looked at myself ruefully. It had turned out more than I bargained for.

The doorman looked at me silently as he let me out into the street. There was not a taxi in sight, so I started to walk west toward Park Avenue. There were always taxis there. I didn't notice the car that had pulled up alongside me until I heard her voice.

"Dax."

"Beatriz!"

I turned, staring.

She sat next to the driver, a curiously hurt look in her dark-green eyes. "We've been following you all night," she said, "hoping to find a moment when you'd be alone!"

15

One of the wonderful things about New York is that no
matter what time of day or night, there is always someplace to
go. At five in the morning, if you're on the east side of
Manhattan, the place to go is Reuben's, a delicatessen kind
of spot where you can get anything from a cup of coffee to a
full-course meal.

It was almost empty when Beatriz and I came in. There
were a few stragglers left from the night, and the morning
people hadn't yet stirred from their beds. The bored waiter
didn't even raise an eyebrow at my dinner jacket. He was
used to it; it was perfectly normal at that hour.

"What'll it be?"

"Coffee," I said, "lots of it. Strong and black."

I looked at Beatriz.

"I'll have coffee too."

The waiter nodded and went away. I reached for her hand
but she kept it on her side of the table. "I was worried when
I found you'd gone away," I said. "I thought about you every
day."

Beatriz looked at me, her eyes still full of hurt. "Your neck
is scratched, and there's blood on your collar."

"I'll speak to my barber," I answered lightly, "he'll have
to be more careful."

Beatriz didn't smile. "I don't think that's funny."

"Why didn't you tell me you were going away?"

She didn't answer until after the waiter brought our coffee. "You weren't that worried."

I took a deep sip of coffee. It was hot and its warmth
raced down to my stomach. I began to feel better. "I don't
want to bicker. Besides, that's not why you finally decided to
see me."

Beatriz looked down at her cup. Perhaps it wasn't fair of
me to throw it up to her but it was true. She raised her eyes

again. "My father did not believe what I told him. He says it's all a trick."

"Your father!" I exploded. "I suppose he thinks the fifty-seven dead *campesinos* of Matanza are a trick too?"

She didn't answer.

I thought of what the senator had said yesterday about the world being filled with cowards who asked that heroes die for them.

"What did you say?"

I hadn't realized I was speaking aloud. I repeated it, adding a few words of my own. "Your father is like a general sitting safely miles from the battlefront, comfortable in the realization that the blood he orders spilled will never soil his own hands. If your father truly believes he represents the will of the people, let him come forward and run against *el Presidente*. Or is he afraid he might lose and be exposed as a charlatan?"

Beatriz' lips tightened. "He would if he believed that *el Presidente* would keep his word about the amnesty!" she retorted angrily.

"*El Presidente will* keep his word!" I was equally heated; nothing was going right. "He has to, he has made the announcement to the world. Do you think he could go back on his word now?"

Beatriz stared at me. "You really believe that, don't you?"

"Yes." I subsided into an angry silence.

After a few minutes Beatriz said, "Would you be willing to meet my father and talk with him?"

"Yes, at any time."

"There would be no strings attached, and you would come alone?"

"Yes."

"I will speak to him." She got to her feet, and I started to get up also, but she gestured for me to remain seated. "Do not follow me."

"Beatriz," I said, reaching for her hand.

Again she kept away from me. "No. I made one mistake. I thought we lived in the same world, but about that one thing they were right. I can see that now."

"Beatriz. I can explain—"

"Don't!" she replied, her voice trembling. Then she turned quickly and hurried out of the restaurant.

I watched her go and something inside me ached. I got to my feet and through the huge windows I saw her get into the car as it moved away.

The waiter came over. "Will that be all, sir?"

"Yes."

It wasn't until I was outside again in the gray light of the morning that I remembered I hadn't asked her when we would meet again.

Marcel's voice was confidential on the telephone. "I have the information you asked me for."

"Good."

"Yes," he interrupted quickly. He did not trust telephones. "When can you come up and discuss it?"

I looked down at the clock calendar on my desk. "I have a dinner date this evening. Can I come up after that?"

"Fine. About what time?"

"Midnight too late?"

"No. I'll tell my man you're expected."

I put down the telephone thoughtfully. In a way I had never really expected Marcel to give me the information I sought. Not about the guns, or where the money came from that paid for them.

There was a knock at the door.

"Come in," I called.

Prieto came into the office, a newspaper in his hand. "Have you seen this?"

I looked down, following his finger. It was a small item buried on one of the inside pages of the *Herald Tribune*.

CORTEGUAYAN TO SPEAK

Dr. José Guayanos, former president of the University of Corteguay and once the vice president of that country, and presently living in exile in this country will speak tonight at Columbia University. His subject will be: The Need for Democratic Government in Corteguay.

I looked at Prieto. It had been more than a week since I had met Beatriz. This was the first word I had even indirectly had about her.

"What shall we do?" Prieto asked.

"Nothing."

"Nothing?" Prieto's voice was shocked. "You will allow him to spout his lies in this public place?"

I leaned back in my chair. "This is not Corteguay. Here everyone has the right to speak as he pleases."

"*El Presidente* will not like it. For more than two years now we have been searching for this man. Now he dares to come into the open with his false accusations."

"I do not give a damn what *el Presidente* likes or doesn't like!" Surely even Prieto could see that this was the first tentative step in testing the sincerity of the amnesty. The first faint glimmer of respect for Guayanos began to awaken in me. Even to speak out here must have taken a great deal of courage.

"But—" Prieto protested.

"This is my responsibility," I said sharply. "You will keep away from him! You will do nothing to interfere with him!"

Prieto stared at me for a moment. "*Sí, excelencia.*" Sullenly he started to leave the room.

"Prieto!" I said, calling him back. My voice was cold. "Remember what I say. If I find out that you or any of your men have been anywhere near him, I'll see to it that you are sent home in disgrace!"

Prieto's lips tightened grimly but he said nothing.

"Is that understood?"

"*Sí, excelencia.*"

I waited until he left the room, then picked up the telephone and called my apartment upstairs. I told Fat Cat to come down. As much as I would like to, I could not attend Guayanos' lecture. What went for Prieto also went for me. Even my appearance might be considered an intervention.

But there was nothing to prevent Fat Cat's going. I had the strange feeling that Guayanos expected me to send someone and that whom I chose might be very important. And Fat Cat seemed the best choice for several reasons.

He could by no means be considered political, and it was well known that his only relationship to me was a personal one. And I could trust Fat Cat to report accurately, without bias or distortion, exactly what Guayanos said, which was probably exactly what Guayanos wanted. And lastly, and not the least important, Fat Cat would be able to tell me if Prieto had kept his word.

16

The senator's sister met me at the door. "I'm Edie Smith," she said, smiling, "I'm so glad you could come. This is my husband, Jack."

The tall heavyset man behind her smiled. "Delighted to meet you, Mr. Xenos," he said, a faint midwestern twang in his voice.

"My pleasure, Mr. Smith."

"Come on into the living room," his wife said, taking my arm, "we're all having a drink in there."

There were six or seven people standing around, all of whom I knew except the senator's wife, a dark pretty girl seated in an armchair. Obviously she was pregnant.

"I believe the only ones you don't know are my brother and his wife. Let's fix that and the party can begin." Mrs. Smith was beautifully oriented politically. She knew exactly what she had to do.

I shook hands with the senator as if it were the first time, and bowed to his wife. Then I turned to the others.

Giselle looked at me reproachfully as I walked over to her. "Aren't you ashamed," she said in French, "that the only times we meet is in someone else's house? You've turned down our invitations to dinner so often I've stopped asking you."

I kissed her hand and glanced at Sergei. He had put on weight but he looked very well. "Don't stop asking," I replied. "The way things are going, God knows when I may need a good meal."

The smile left Sergei's face. "The news in the papers has not been good."

I nodded. "It is serious, my friend. Very serious."

Concern came into Giselle's voice. "You're not in any danger, are you?"

"How could I be?" I smiled at her. "I am here."

"But if they call you home—"

Sergei interrupted. "There's no need to worry, my dear, Dax knows how to take care of himself." He turned to me. "We think about you often. We are both deeply concerned."

"I know." I believed Sergei because there was enough time behind all of us to know who were our friends. I saw Giselle slip her hand into Sergei's and his reassuring squeeze. For a moment I envied them. "You both look very well. And how is Anastasia?"

"You should see her!" It was Giselle who answered, before Sergei had a chance to speak. There was a mother's pride in her voice. Then she laughed. "Or maybe you shouldn't. She's turning out to be a very beautiful girl."

Jeremy came over. "You three are grinning like Cheshire cats. Let me in on it."

But the senator's sister appeared and took Jeremy and me by the arm. "One of the prerogatives of being the hostess," she announced gaily, "is that one can preempt the only two bachelors in the room as dinner partners."

Everyone laughed, and we went in to dinner. Several times I caught myself watching Giselle and Sergei and each time I had to force myself to look away before it became too obvious. They were close. Warm. And each time I looked at them I could see myself with Beatriz. We could be like that. I felt it. If ever we got the chance.

After dinner the senator caught me in a corner of the room. "I haven't forgotten our little talk. I've been making a few quiet inquiries on my own."

"Thank you," I said. "Knowing that you are interested is a help."

"I hope to do more than that," he said, "and I may have some news for you next week. Will you be in New York?"

"I expect to be."

"I'll be in touch."

Then we moved out of the corner and over to his wife. She was once again back in the chair. The senator stopped in front of her and looked down. "How about it, little girl? Feeling tired?"

"A little."

"Let's go, then." He smiled. "We'll leave these young folk to their little orgy."

After the senator had left the party began to break up. I left with Giselle and Sergei. His car and chauffeur were just outside the door, and they suggested I come home with them for a drink. But I shook my head. "No, thanks. I've got a date."

Sergei grinned. "You dog. You haven't changed a bit."

I laughed. "I wish I could preserve your illusions. But it's business; I have to see Marcel."

"They say he never leaves his house," Giselle said.

"It's true," Sergei replied before I could answer. "I went there to see him once. The house is as closely guarded as a bank."

"You went to see him?" I asked. Sergei and Marcel never seemed to have had much in common.

"It was a few years back, when I first came over here," Sergei said. "You know the bastard. He wanted to sell me a piece of some company he had."

"Did you buy it?"

"Of course." Sergei smiled. "I don't like Marcel but the one thing he does know how to do is make money. I didn't even know what the company did but he made me president and every three months like clockwork I get twenty-five hundred dollars in dividends."

Giselle looked at me. "I remember that time in Texas—" Then she looked at Sergei and stopped.

I glanced at my watch. "I'd better get going."

I kissed Giselle on the cheek. Sergei took my hand. "You look tired and drawn," he said. "Try to slow down."

"I will once this mess is over."

"And come up your first free evening," Giselle said.

"I'll try."

I watched them get into the big Rolls-Royce with the gold crest on the door. They waved as the car pulled away, and I began to walk west. It was only a few blocks over to Park, where Marcel lived, and I got there a minute or two early.

When I rounded the corner a man was just leaving. He jumped into a taxi as I turned up the steps and rang the bell. I looked after the disappearing cab. There had been something familiar about the figure, but it was dark and I hadn't seen his face.

A light flashed on overhead and I was aware that the butler was studying me on the closed-circuit television. Then the light went off and the door slowly opened.

"Come in, Mr. Xenos," the butler said, "Mr. Campion is expecting you."

I followed him into the house. He took me up to the private elevator to Marcel's apartment and held the door. "Press the top button, please."

The door closed and the elevator started up. I got out on Marcel's floor. Marcel was just coming out of the guest room as I walked into his living room.

"Dax!" he exclaimed. "How good to see you again. A drink?"

I nodded and we walked over to the bar. Marcel took down a bottle of Scotch and poured some over the rocks. I took the glass. "How about you?"

Marcel shook his head. "Doctor's orders—it's bad for my ulcer."

"Cheers," I said. I took a swallow. "Hope he didn't take you off anything else."

Marcel laughed. "No, just liquor." He pressed the button under the bar. "Take a look at that."

I looked at the television screen. This time there was only one girl in the guest room. She was lying on the bed, completely nude, a bottle of champagne on the night table. She turned, reaching for a cigarette, and Marcel hit the off button. "Not bad, eh?"

I nodded.

"She's new. I just took her on the other day. You get bored with all of them after a while. They're all after the same thing—money."

I didn't say anything. What did he expect—romance?

"The cunts!" Marcel shouted, suddenly angry. "I think I'll have a drink after all. The damn doctors don't know everything."

I waited until he had poured a drink. "I don't want to keep you."

Marcel looked at me. "Have you heard anything from *el Presidente?*"

"No. Everything seems to be temporarily quiet."

685

"Do you think he can keep things under control?"

"I think so," I said. "Especially if we can discover the source of the guns and stop them."

Marcel took the hint. "I have the papers you wanted." He came out from behind the bar and went over to a desk. He took some papers out of the drawer and brought them to me.

I looked down at them. The shipping invoice was obviously in the name of a fictitious company and would probably be of no help, but the check in payment for the freight was legitimate. I turned the credit invoice over. The check number, the name of the account, and the bank were written across the back.

The account name was not familiar but the bank was. C.Z.I. I took a deep breath. This was more of a break than I had hoped for. It was one of the De Coyne banks.

"Does it mean anything to you?" Marcel asked curiously.

"Not much," I answered noncommittally, slipping the papers into my pocket, "but I'll look into it in the morning. Maybe I'll come up with something."

"I hope you have better luck than I did," Marcel said, "I found out nothing. You know how those damn Swiss banks are."

"I'll let you know. I hope all your captains are checking their cargoes. I wouldn't like it if *el Presidente* discovered any more guns coming in on your ships."

"They're all alerted," Marcel answered quickly, "and I think they'll be careful. But you can never tell. They like an extra buck now and then."

"For your sake I hope they restrain themselves. One more shipment and I'm afraid the old man will cancel your franchise."

"I'm doing the best I can."

I looked at Marcel curiously. He didn't seem at all disturbed over the threat, though the loss of the franchise would take his ships out from under the Corteguayan flag and quite probably put him out of business. Then I decided that he must have everything under control and thus didn't have to worry.

"Well, I'll be going," I said. "If I keep you too long your friend might fall asleep."

I put my glass down on the table and suddenly I knew who the man was I had seen leaving. Prieto. One of my cigars

686

lay half smoked in the ash tray. I remembered giving Prieto several a few days ago when he had said he liked their bouquet. I told Marcel good night and went down and got into a taxi.

I leaned back in the seat. Prieto. I wondered what his connection was with Marcel. I couldn't figure it out. But I had learned one thing at least. Prieto had not gone to the Guayanos meeting.

Fat Cat was waiting up for me.

"Well, how did it go?" I asked.

Fat Cat handed me a set of printed pages. "It's all there," he said. "He had it all ready for the press."

I didn't look at the papers. "Who else was there?"

"I didn't see Prieto."

I was silent.

"Oh," he added, as if it were an afterthought, "I saw the girl."

"Did she see you?"

He nodded.

"Did she say anything to you?"

"She did," he answered, a mocking smile around his eyes, "but I didn't understand it. It was something about meeting her at Reuben's tomorrow at midnight. I don't know anyone by that name, do you?"

17

"Dax, this is my father."

The thin-faced, pale man in the faded gray cardigan got up from behind the old wooden table. He held out his hand. His touch was thin and papery but somehow firm.

"Dr. Guayanos."

"Señor Xenos."

His lips moved stiffly, as if he were under some kind of strain. He glanced at the other men in the room, who were

687

watching us silently. "You have already met my brother," he said. "The other gentleman is a good friend who enjoys my every confidence."

I nodded. I could understand the reason for not naming him. But nothing was lost, since I recognized him instantly. Alberto Mendoza, a former army officer whom I had once met at a reception. I wondered if he knew that I had identified him.

We remained standing awkwardly for a moment, then Guayanos turned to the others. "Would you excuse us? I would like to speak with Señor Xenos alone."

Mendoza looked hesitantly at us.

"It is all right," Guayanos said quickly. "I am sure that Señor Xenos intends me no harm."

"Perhaps not," Mendoza said in a somewhat surly voice, "but the car might have been followed. I do not trust Prieto—"

Guayanos' brother spoke up. "The car was not followed. I am sure of that."

"How would you know?" Mendoza asked. "You were driving."

I did not speak. There was no point. I had let myself be blindfolded at Beatriz' request. I did not even know where we were.

"We weren't followed," Beatriz said flatly. "I watched from the rear window all the way."

Mendoza shot another sullen look at me, then silently walked from the room. Presently Beatriz and her uncle followed him. Once the door had closed behind them, Dr. Guayanos turned to me. "Won't you sit down?"

"Thank you." I sat down in a chair opposite him.

"I knew your father," he said. "A great man and a true patriot."

"Thank you."

He sank back into his own chair. "Like your father I was at first entranced by *el Presidente*. Then I became disillusioned." He glanced down at his thin white hands. "I could never understand why your father did not come out in opposition to *el Presidente*."

I looked straight into his eyes. "Because he believed that enough blood had already been shed in Corteguay. He did not want it to begin again. He was convinced that first the

688

country must be rebuilt. It was to that end he devoted himself."

"So did we all," Guayanos replied quickly. "But after a while it became apparent to even the most stupid of us that all we were doing was perpetuating *el Presidente* in his power. He took credit for everything that was accomplished."

"I see nothing wrong in that," I said. "From what I have observed of heads of state all over the world, they do exactly the same. And tell me this, Doctor. How much of it would ever have been accomplished had *el Presidente* not been there?"

Guayanos did not answer.

"Today all our children attend school until they are fourteen. Before *el Presidente* came to power only the rich could afford such schooling. Today forty percent of our population is literate, prior to that something like three percent—"

Guayanos held up his hand. "I know the statistics," he said wearily. "But they do not justify the corruption and the personal wealth *el Presidente* accumulated at the expense of the people."

"I agree. But it was still a great improvement over the past, when nothing at all filtered down."

I started to reach into my pocket for a cigarette and saw him start. "May I smoke?"

He relaxed. "Of course."

I took out a cigarette and lit it. "But all this discussion of the past proves nothing. It is the future with which we must concern ourselves. I think even *el Presidente* has come to that conclusion."

"Why suddenly now and not before?" Guayanos asked. "Nothing in the past seemed to concern him except the preservation of his own power."

"I can't answer that. To do so I would have to be able to enter his mind and know what he was thinking. My own feeling is that he is beginning to recognize his own mortality. He would like to be remembered as the great benefactor."

Guayanos was silent for a moment. "I don't believe that," he said flatly. "I think he is frightened. Frightened by the temper of the people, by their attraction to the *guerrilleros,* by the fact that open revolution has begun to threaten."

"If you really believe that, Dr. Guayanos, you are making a mistake. *El Presidente* is one of the few men I know who

689

does not know the meaning of fear. Moreover, he is clever and intelligent and he does think. He recognizes that these men you call *guerrilleros* are the same men who for years were called *bandoleros*, and whose very existence was devoted to loot, rapine, and murder. He also understands the political use made of them by the Communists. But the situation is volatile and many may die unnecessarily to gain what could be achieved by peaceful means."

Guayanos studied me for a moment. "You speak very much like your father."

I smiled. "I would not be his son if I did not."

"Then you think *el Presidente* is sincere in his offer of an election and amnesty?"

"I do. Why should he wish to see more bloodshed? He knows that unrest is holding back the progress of the country. If it were not for the *bandoleros*, the tourist trade alone could add fifty million dollars a year to our national income."

"Has a date been set for the election?"

I shook my head. "What for? No one has come forward to offer himself in opposition. An election with only one candidate would be a farce."

"What guarantees would be made for the safety of his opposition?"

"What guarantees would you require?"

He stared at me. "The freedom to move about the country as I wish, access to the newspapers and radio without restraint, the right to protect myself with men of my own choosing, even though some of them might be foreigners, and the election to be supervised by an impartial observer such as the United Nations or the Organization of American States."

"That seems reasonable to me," I said. "I will relay your suggestions to *el Presidente*. Now in turn may I ask something of you?"

He nodded, warily.

"Are you in a position to guarantee that illegal opposition to the government will cease?"

"I could make no such guarantee and you know it. My contacts with other groups are loose and tenuous at best. But I will say this. There would be no further opposition from my group, and I would use my influence on the others, too."

"Thank you. That was what I wanted to hear."

690

"I have no desire, either, to see further bloodshed."

I rose. "For the sake of our country let us hope there will be none."

Guayanos came around the table and walked to the door. Before he opened it he looked back at me. "I did not thank you for what you did for my brother. He has a quick temper; sometimes he does foolish things."

"Beatriz already explained that to me," I said, "but I did only what I thought was right."

For a moment it seemed as if Guayanos wanted to say something more but instead he opened the door. "Come in," he called "Señor Xenos and I have finished."

He turned and said almost regretfully, "I hope you will not mind if we ask you to submit again to the blindfold?"

I shook my head.

Beatriz came toward me, the black cloth in her hand. I leaned forward to make it easier for her. As I did I caught a glimpse of Mendoza's face over her shoulder, and suddenly I knew why he had acted toward me as he had. The reasons weren't solely political. He was also in love with Beatriz.

When the blindfold came off we were back in front of Reuben's. I blinked my eyes as I looked at Beatriz. "Would you like to come in for a cup of coffee?"

She stared into my eyes for a moment, then shook her head. "I think I had better go back."

I reached for her hand. She let me hold it but did not return the pressure. "I must see you," I said. "Alone. Not like this."

She didn't answer.

"Beatriz, I meant what I said that night. I wasn't playing games."

She looked at me, the tears seeming to blur the green of her eyes. "I—I don't understand you at all." She took back her hand and turned away. "You'd better go."

Silently I started to get out of the car.

"Dax, my father will be safe?" she asked. "You meant what you said?"

"Yes, Beatriz, I meant what I said."

"If—if something were to happen to him," she said huskily, "I would never stop blaming myself."

"Nothing will happen to him."

A moment later I watched as the car turned south on

691

Madison Avenue. For the first time I felt depressed and discouraged. A vague sense of impending doom seemed to settle around my shoulders. I shook my head angrily. Why should I feel like this?

I went into the restaurant and ordered a drink. The whiskey burned its way down and I could feel myself lift. But it was a false kind of lift. It would not be too far in the future that I would remember my words and wonder how I could ever have been such a fool as to make the one promise I could not keep.

18

El Presidente listened silently while I told him over the phone about my meeting with Dr. Guayanos. I listed the conditions he had asked for, and as I read the last, about impartial observers, there was a moment's silence. Then *el Presidente's* voice came roaring over the wire. "The son of a bitch! He's asking for everything except my vote."

I had to laugh. "I have a feeling he'd ask for that, too, if he thought he'd get it."

"What do you think? If I agree will he come back?"

"I think so."

"I don't like it. If we agree to impartial observers it will be the same as admitting we were wrong."

"What difference does that make?" I asked. "You do not expect him to win, do you? Your victory should make it sufficiently clear that you are wanted by the majority of the people."

"That's true. All right, I'll agree to his conditions with one of my own added. And this one has nothing to do with him, only with you."

"What is it?"

692

"That you join with me as my nominee for vice president. It has been on my mind for a long time now. I will not live forever. I want to be sure that the government continues in good hands."

This was something I had not counted on. Grudgingly I realized that the old man had me boxed in. If I really believed in what I said, I would have to go along with him. And if I did, it would effectively eliminate me as a future opposition candidate by placing me squarely in his corner.

"Why do you hesitate?" he asked sharply.

"I was surprised, and I am overwhelmed by the honor. But do you think you're doing the right thing? I could be a handicap to you. There are many at home who do not approve of me."

I did not go into the reasons. He knew them as well as I. The church, for one. There was not a Sunday that passed but from one pulpit or another I was castigated as a profligate and playboy.

"If I am not concerned," el Presidente asked, "why should you be?"

"Your excellency, I am both delighted and honored to accept your generous offer."

"Good." His voice lightened. "Then you may inform the traitor that his terms are accepted. And that the date set for election is Easter Sunday."

"Thank you, your excellency. I will so inform him."

"Do that. I will await word that you have spoken with him and then give the announcement to the press." He chuckled in a pleased tone. "You have done well, but then I never doubted for a moment that the girl would be putty in your hands."

There was a bitter taste in my mouth as I put down the telephone. Everyone had it figured out. Latin Lover Number One. I pushed the annoyance from my mind and reached for the telephone to call Guayanos. And then I realized that I had no way of reaching him until he was ready to contact me. I looked down at my desk calendar.

It was the eighth of January. He had better get in touch soon or the election would be over before he even was aware that he was a candidate.

It was four o'clock when I returned to my desk in the con-

693

sulate from one of those interminable meetings at the United Nations. Finally I had been able to stand it no longer and had slipped out in the middle. There was a message on my desk to call the senator. I picked up the telephone.

His secretary put me right through. "I think I have some good news for you," he said. "How soon can you get down here?"

I glanced at the clock. "I could make a six-o'clock plane. Is that too late for you?"

"No," he answered, "that will be fine. You should be able to make it by eight. Come right out to my house for dinner."

There were three others there besides the senator and myself. His wife did not join us, except for a drink, and then went up to lie down. I looked around the table as we sat down. Whatever the senator had to tell me had to be important, otherwise these men would not have been there. On my right was the Undersecretary of State for Latin American Affairs, and opposite us, side by side, sat the respective heads of the foreign-affairs committees of both the House and the Senate.

"We can wait until after dinner or begin with the soup," the senator said. "I don't mind talking shop at mealtimes."

"I defer to you, gentlemen," I said.

"Then let's begin now," the senator opposite me said.

"I have had a number of discussions with the gentlemen present about the situation in Corteguay," the senator began. "I told them in great detail about our discussion. They were as impressed as I. But we are agreed that there are certain questions we feel we must ask to clarify our thinking."

"Please feel free to ask whatever you wish."

For the next twenty minutes I went through a barrage of questions. Much to my surprise I found that these men were far better informed than I had thought. Very little of what had happened in Corteguay during the past twenty-five years had escaped their attention.

At the end we all sat back in a rare sort of mutual respect that doesn't happen very often in meetings of this kind. They had been brutally frank in their questions, and I had been painfully direct in my replies. The senator looked at me for a moment, then glanced around the table. He seemed to be seeking their permission to continue. One by one they nodded and he turned back to me.

694

"As you know," he said, "your application for a loan of twenty million dollars has been kicking around for some time."

I nodded.

"In a way this was because we did not know exactly what to do about it. We realized the Communist threat to your country and we would have liked to help combat it. On the other hand we were aware that the present government in the past has not been above corruption and political terrorism. In many quarters of the government, speaking frankly, your government is regarded as a classic example of fascism, and your president as no better than another dictator."

I didn't speak.

"With such conflict in our minds, you can realize the difficulties of our choice. But with the full agreement of the others at this table I venture to make this proposal."

I looked at him. His eyes were clear and serious.

"We are willing to sponsor a loan to Corteguay if the following condition could be met. If your president were willing to step aside in the interests of your country, in favor of you, there would be no difficulty in counting on the support of the United States."

I was silent. Slowly I let my eyes move around the table. They all watched me curiously. Finally I found the words I wanted.

"Speaking for myself, gentlemen, I thank you for your trust and confidence. But speaking for my country I deeply resent that you feel your money gives you the right to interfere in our internal affairs. And lastly, speaking for my president, I cannot answer for what he would do, but I can tell you what he has done just this morning."

They were interested now. Their instincts, sharpened by experience, warned them that they had almost walked into a trap.

"This morning I acceded to a request by my president that I join him as his candidate for vice president in an election to be held on Easter Sunday. Opposing *el Presidente* will be Dr. Guayanos. Dr. Guayanos and our president have agreed on certain aspects of the election, the principal one being that it will be conducted under the impartial auspices of the United Nations or the Organization of American States."

The senator looked at me ruefully. "You didn't tell me that over the phone."

"You didn't give me a chance."

His face went serious. "Do you think Guayanos has a chance?"

I shook my head. "You have a saying 'About as much chance as a snowball in hell.'"

"Nothing is ever certain in politics," the congressman across the table said.

"If Guayanos won I'm not sure I'd like it," the undersecretary said in his precise voice. "He plays it a little too close to the Communists to suit me. Mendoza, for instance, seems to have a personal passkey to the Kremlin."

I hid my surprise. That was something I had not known. But at least now I could establish the link between Guayanos and *el Condor*. Until now I had been unable to connect them.

"The entire thing is academic," I said. "*El Presidente* will win."

"And you will be vice president?"

"That's right."

The senator looked around the table again. "What do you think, gentlemen?"

I got to my feet. "I'll leave the room if you gentlemen would prefer to talk privately."

The senator waved me back to my seat. "We've been talking openly," he said, "and I don't see that we have anything to hide at this point."

The undersecretary said, "I for one would be willing to go along on the basis Señor Xenos has outlined."

The others raised their voices in assent.

"All right then, we are agreed," the senator said. He turned to me. "You can count on our support in favor of the loan as soon as the announcement of the election is officially confirmed."

I took a deep breath. For the first time in days I felt that I was making progress. But it all blew to hell the next morning. The dream exploded when I picked up the telephone on my desk and heard Beatriz' soft voice.

I could hardly keep the excitement out of my voice. "I'm glad you called," I said, the words tumbling from my lips.

"Tell your father that I have spoken with *el Presidente* and that he has agreed to all your father's conditions."

She didn't answer.

"Beatriz, didn't you understand?"

Again the strange silence.

"Beatriz."

But this time her voice cut me off. It was curiously strained. "Didn't you read the newspapers or listen to the radio this morning?"

"No, I was in Washington until late last night, and I slept all the way back on the train. I just got to my desk this minute. I haven't even had time to change my shirt."

For a moment her voice trembled, then it grew calm and cold. "You mean to say you know nothing even now?"

"About what?" I asked angrily. "Stop talking in riddles like a child."

There was still that icy calm in her voice. "At about two o'clock this morning my father went down for a breath of fresh air. As usual Mendoza was with him. A car drove by, a black car. Shots came from it. Mendoza got a bullet in his arm. My father died less than an hour later in an ambulance on the way to the hospital."

Suddenly her voice broke and the icy calm vanished. "Dax, you promised! You swore that nothing would happen to him, that he would be safe!"

"Beatriz, I didn't know. Please believe me! I didn't know!" More than anything I had ever wanted in this world I wanted her to believe me. "Where are you? I must see you."

"What for, Dax?" she asked in a suddenly exhausted voice. "To tell me more lies? To make other promises that you do not intend to keep? I can't go through that again."

"Beatriz." But the telephone had gone dead in my hand. I stared at it for a moment, then slammed it down. I got out of my chair and walked to the door.

"Tell Prieto to come in here!" I called angrily, and slammed the door shut. I had just about got back to my desk when my phone buzzed. I picked it up. "Yes?"

My secretary's voice sounded frightened. "I thought you knew, sir. Señor Prieto left for Corteguay this morning on the nine-o'clock plane."

Slowly I sank back into the chair. I felt my temples begin to throb. My head felt as if it were being squeezed in a vise.

Gone. Everything was gone. All the work, all the hopes, for nothing. I leaned forward on the desk, resting my aching temples in my hands, trying to think despite the terrible pain. Think. I had to think.

Somehow Prieto had managed to find out where Guayanos was. And the only way he could have done so was through me. I didn't see how but I had no doubt of his ability to do so without being detected. I remembered what he and Hoyos had done to me in Florida. I should have realized that he would find a way and sent him back before he could create such havoc.

But no. I was the clever one. I was so sure that everything would go exactly the way I wanted it. Prieto wouldn't dare go against me. Well, I wasn't smart. I was stupid. *El Presidente* was the one. He had sent Prieto to do what he knew I would not.

I felt a sudden nausea and just made it to the bathroom. I stood there retching until there was nothing left in my guts. Then I rinsed my face and came back to my desk. I sank into my chair and took a deep breath.

In my plethora of self-castigation and pity I had almost forgotten that the most important thing still remained undone.

The guns had to be stopped.

19

"The senator is steaming." Jeremy's voice crackled over the telephone. "He feels you used him and made a fool of him. He doesn't like it."

I listened wearily. By now I was tired of explanations. No one listened to them anyway. Or if they did, they didn't believe me. All judgments were preconceived. For a moment I wished there was no such thing as diplomatic immunity. Then they would have openly to prove what they thought.

But this way there was really nothing they could do to me. I didn't ever have to answer questions if I chose not to. So they were free to think as they liked and the shield of diplomatic immunity was as easy an out for them as for me.

"You told him what I told you yesterday?"

"Yes."

That was it. The same as the others.

"Perhaps if you hadn't been in the senator's house when it happened it might not have been so bad," Jeremy continued. "But since you were he feels you used him to establish an alibi."

I didn't answer. There was no point to it.

"You realize there's no chance for the loan now," Jeremy continued.

"I know."

My secretary came in and placed my attaché case on the desk. "The car is waiting outside to take you to the airport," she whispered.

"What are your plans now?" Jeremy asked.

Suddenly I was tired of confiding in other people. None of my plans seemed to materialize anyway, and in a way I couldn't blame people if they thought me a liar. "Right now I'm catching a plane for Paris."

"Paris?" Jeremy asked in surprise. "Have you gone out of your mind? You know what everyone will think."

"I don't give a damn what anyone thinks."

"You're acting like a fool. You sound as if you didn't even care any more."

"I don't," I replied bluntly.

Jeremy was silent for a moment. "I can't believe that, I know you. Why are you going to Paris?"

"To get laid!" I said savagely. "What in hell other reasons are there for going to Paris?"

I slammed down the receiver angrily. But in a moment I was sorry. I had no right to blow up at Jeremy like that. He was on my side. At least he still spoke to me.

I thought about picking up the phone and calling him back to apologize, but just then my secretary stuck her head in the door. "The driver says you'll just have time to make your plane if you hurry."

I picked up the attaché case and started out the door. There'd be time enough to call Jeremy when I got back.

It seemed strange to see Robert in his father's office, sitting behind that ornate desk in the baron's chair. But after a moment it did not seem strange at all; it was as if he had always sat there. He was after all born to it.

"You know the law," he said, "and the Swiss government is very strict. We could lose our license if we give you such information."

"I know the law," I said, staring at him, "that's why I came to you."

Robert was silent, a troubled look on his face. I didn't push it. He knew how close we had been to each other.

"How are Denisonde and the children?"

Robert flashed a smile. "Don't get me started. I'm a typical father."

I returned his smile. "I take it, then, they are well?"

He nodded. "You'll never know what it's all about until you have children of your own."

First Sergei, now Robert. There was something about them, a sense of belonging, of roots and of growth. That's what it was. I was like a tree whose top had been cut off, stunting its growth. "I envy you," I said sincerely.

Robert gave me a startled look. "That sounds odd coming from you."

"I know, I lead such a gay life. The playboy of the jet set."

"I didn't mean to offend you, Dax."

"I know," I said. "It's my fault, I'm edgy." I reached for a cigarette. "It seems everywhere I turn I run into a dead end."

Robert watched as I lit up. "What do you think will happen now?"

"I don't know. But if the guns are not stopped a lot of innocents are going to die."

Robert looked down at his desk. "You understand that I'm not trying to protect any interest of ours?"

I nodded. He didn't have to tell me that. I was there when he had unloaded his investments in Corteguay on his British cousins.

"It's just that I have a responsibility now," he went on. "There are many people depending on me."

I got to my feet. "I understand. I feel the same way, but in my case it's their lives, not their livelihood."

He didn't answer.

"Thanks anyway," I said. "I won't take up more of your time."

"What are you going to do?"

This time I was not being flippant when I answered, "I've got nothing better to do so I guess I'll look up a girl."

Marlene Von Kuppen. Just the other day I had read in Irma Andersen's column—or I had heard someone mention —that she was living in Paris. It was a long shot but it was better than nothing. It was just possible that she still was friendly enough with the people who could get me the information I wanted from East Germany. After all, she had been a Von Kuppen.

A friend of mine on one of the newspapers gave me her telephone number. I called almost all afternoon without getting any answer, but finally at five I got her. Her voice was husky, as if she had just awakened. "Hello."

"Marlene?"

"Yes. Who is this?"

"Diogenes Xenos."

"Who?"

"Dax."

"Dax," she repeated, and a faintly sarcastic note came into her voice. "Not *the* Dax?"

"Yes."

"To what do I owe the honor of this call?"

"I heard you were in Paris," I said. "I thought I'd find out if you were free this evening for dinner."

"I have a date." Then she became curious. "Isn't it rather late for you to call?"

It was now my turn to play it cute. "I've been ringing you all afternoon. When there was no answer I figured you were out."

"You've known me for a long time," she said. "Why now, all of a sudden?"

Ask an honest question, get a dishonest answer. "You *were* going around with a friend of mine."

"From what I heard, that never stopped you before."

"Jeremy happens to be a very close friend. But from the very first time I saw you that night at the beach house on Saint Tropez I said to myself—someday."

I heard a pleased note come into Marlene's voice, and I

701

knew I had her. "As I said, I do have an engagement to-night. How about tomorrow?"

"Someday is today and I've waited long enough," I said. "Why not break your date? I don't know where I'll be to-morrow."

Marlene hesitated a moment. "I don't know . . ." Then her voice was suddenly meek and compliant. "All right."

I put down the telephone and leaned back in my chair.

20

It was after three in the morning when the taxi stopped in front of her apartment on the Avenue Kléber. We sat there for a moment, then she flashed a curious look at me. "Would you like to come up?"

"Yes, thank you," I said, almost formally. "I would."

I paid the driver and we got out. Silently we crossed the tree-lined promenade over the small side roadway jammed with cars parked for the night. The streets were darkly wet and shining from the late-January rain that had stopped only a short while before, and the first of the falling autumn leaves felt soggy under our feet.

We stopped in front of her door, and she fished in her small purse for the key. Silently she handed it to me. I opened the door and we went in. The elevator took us to the third floor and with the same key I opened the door into her apartment.

As we walked into the living room she turned to me. "Would you like a drink?"

I nodded, and she indicated a small portable bar. "You'll find everything there. I'll be back in a moment."

She went into another room, and I poured myself a brandy. I took a sip and sat down on the couch. Something had gone wrong. I had blown it. Almost angrily I wondered what the hell was the matter with me.

Marlene came back into the room. She had changed from her evening gown into black velvet hostess pajamas with a short bolero jacket that almost met the top of the flowing harem trousers. When she moved there was just the slightest hint of the fair soft flesh beneath. The black looked very well with her blond hair and blue Nordic eyes.

"*Très jolie.*"

Marlene didn't answer. Instead she turned and poured a brandy for herself and sat down opposite me. She held up her glass. "Cheers."

"Cheers." We both sipped at our brandy. Marlene lowered her glass, and her eyes met mine steadily. "I'm not angry," she said quietly, "but why did you call me?"

I looked at her without answering. I was beginning to wonder about that myself. It had been nothing but a stupid idea from the very beginning.

"It wasn't what you said over the phone," she said. "I'm not a child. I know when a man is interested."

That was it. I don't know what I expected. Perhaps in some naïve way I thought I would find the same frightened girl who had come to my house at Saint Tropez seven years ago. But this was not the same girl. She was a woman now, grown up, self-possessed, in many ways a completely different person than I had expected. She knew at least as much if not more than I did.

"I'm sorry," I said lamely. "I've got problems and I guess I haven't been able to get them out of my mind."

"I know," Marlene replied, "I read the papers." She sipped again at her brandy. "But it wasn't only that, was it? You've got all the symptoms of a man, as the Americans would put it, carrying a torch."

"That too."

"I thought so. I know the signs, I've walked that street myself. And you thought the best cure was another woman and since you happened to be in Paris you thought of me." There was a strange sympathy in her eyes. "But it doesn't work that way, does it?"

"No, it doesn't."

"I know. I felt like that after Jeremy left. I didn't know what to do with myself. I really was in love with him, you know. I should have realized it was impossible from the beginning. First it was his politics, then his family. But all the time it was really me. I'm German, and for some people the war will never be over."

She continued to speak in the same half-introspective way. "I was a child, not even eighteen when I married. Fritz, to me, was the hero I had always dreamed of—tall and handsome and rich. But I didn't realize what he was really like. I didn't know about his 'boys,' and the sickness in him that demanded he inflict pain before he could achieve even the mildest orgasm. So when Jeremy came along it was no wonder that I fell in love with him. To me Jeremy was simple, direct, and uncomplicated. There was only one thing on his mind. I became aware for the first time of my power as a woman and also of my own needs."

Marlene looked at me. "Does that sound strange? Truly I didn't know until then. I had always blamed myself for my failure with Fritz. It had to be my fault, I thought; he told me so often enough."

A kind of stillness settled down upon us and in the silence Marlene got up and refilled our brandy glasses. Outside I heard the faint sound of the traffic on the circle around the nearby Arc de Triomphe.

"Was it like that with you too?"

"No," I replied, "only the end result was the same." Marlene's eyes were searching. "Does she love you?"

"I think so."

"Then she's a fool!" Marlene said vehemently. "What reason on earth could she have for not coming to you?"

"You read the papers," I said. "Her father's name is Guayanos."

"Oh, so that's it."

"Yes, and in a way that's why I called you. The guns that are being smuggled into my country are coming from the former Von Kuppen factories in East Germany. If this influx is not stopped there will be a war and many innocent people will die. I'm trying to find a way to put an end to it. But I can't until I learn who is paying for the guns. If I discover that, perhaps I can stop it. I was hoping you might know someone who could furnish me with that information."

"I don't know." Marlene hesitated. "It has been a long time."

"I'd be grateful for any bit of information you could give me," I said. "I've seen enough of war for my lifetime."

"So have I," she answered in a low voice. "I was a little girl in Berlin when the bombers came."

I didn't speak.

Marelene's eyes grew somber and thoughtful. "There was a man, a Swiss named Braunschweiger. He lived in Zurich, and I remember meeting him several times with Fritz. Officially we had nothing to do with the factories in East Germany, of course. But he knew what was going on there and furnished Fritz with regular reports."

An edge of excitement began to form inside me. "Do you think he might talk to me?"

"I don't know," she said. "I don't even know that he's still alive."

"It's worth trying. What's his address?"

"I don't remember, Dax. It was all very hush-hush. I'm sure his name is not even listed in any of the city directories. But I do remember the house. It had odd-shaped gables over the windows. I think I might be able to find it."

"I have no right to ask you this after this evening, but would you come to Zurich with me and try to find it?"

"You have every right," Marlene said, looking directly at me. "If it weren't for you I might never have gotten free of Fritz."

"Thank you," I replied gratefully as I got to my feet. "I'll call you tomorrow after I've made plane reservations."

Marlene got up out of her chair and came over to me. She looked into my face. "Today is already tomorrow, though tomorrow is a long way off. We are both here now, without illusions, empty and alone."

Perhaps it was the way Marlene said it but suddenly I saw in her what I had seen so many times in myself. The loneliness, the aching to touch, to share, the momentary need for another human being, the fear of the dark night. Or perhaps it was the female scent of her, the warmth emanating from her body, the glow of her flesh that not even velvet could hide. I put down my brandy glass and took her into my arms.

She was strong, stronger than I had ever thought. But I used her strength and she used mine, until we lay together in each other's arms completely spent. We were as secure in each other's warmth as two animals sleeping in the night.

21

It took us three days to find the house. Three days of driving up and down streets, along wide avenues, and exploring side streets. Like every city in the world, Zurich had changed. Old landmarks were gone, new buildings stood in their place. In the end we found the house by accident.

It was toward evening and already the chill of the night had come on. Marlene's face looked tired from the strain. I leaned forward and tapped on the glass that separated us from the chauffeur. "Take us back to the hotel as quickly as possible."

I leaned back and lit a cigarette. It was like searching for the pin in a bale of hay. I closed my eyes to rest them for a few minutes when suddenly I felt her hand on my arm.

"There!" Marlene said excitedly. "That street—I'm sure it's the one!"

I leaned forward and tapped on the glass. The driver pulled over to the curb. I turned to her. "Are you positive?"

Marlene was looking out of the rear window. "I don't know," she said hesitantly, "I thought it was."

My tiredness had suddenly disappeared. "Let's make sure," I replied opening the door, "let's have a look."

The chauffeur got out and came around the car. "Wait here," I said to him, taking Marlene's arm.

We walked back to the corner and stood looking down the street. It was a section that had once seen better days but seemed now to be devoted mostly to tourists' pensions. "What do you think?"

An excitement came into Marlene's face. "I'm almost afraid to say, but it could be. I seem to remember that the house was set back farther from the sidewalk than the others. And look, there in the middle of the block, you can't see one house because it is hidden by the others."

Marlene began to walk rapidly down the street. I followed her to the front of the house and together we stood staring at it. It was the house, all right. Gray stone and with odd gables shaped almost like a tricornered hat.

"Let's go."

I took her arm and we walked up to the front entrance. I pressed the bell and in a moment the door opened on an old woman dressed in a faded maid's uniform. *"Ja?"*

"Herr Braunschweiger?"

She looked at us suspiciously. "Who is calling?"

Unconsciously Marlene's voice took on that authority that only the German upper class use with their servants. "Frau Marlene von Kuppen," she answered icily.

It was the Von Kuppen name that did it. The old woman all but collapsed, prostrating herself. She ushered us into a small waiting room, apologizing all the time for making us wait, and ran to fetch her master.

I stepped back into the darkest corner when I heard heavy footsteps in the hall outside. The door opened and Braunschweiger came in, a big heavyset man in his late fifties. "Frau Von Kuppen," he said, clicking his heels smartly and bowing to kiss her hand. "It is a pleasure to see you again. I am honored that you should remember."

"Herr Braunschweiger."

The slightly fatuous smile faded as I stepped out from the corner. "Herr Braunschweiger, may I present his excellency Herr Xenos, Corteguayan Ambassador to the United Nations?"

"Your excellency," he said stiffly, clicking and bowing. "Herr Braunschweiger."

He looked at Marlene. "I do not understand," he said. "What is the purpose of this visit?"

"Ambassador Xenos can explain it far better than I," Marlene said. I noticed her stressing of the title. She knew what she was doing, for this obviously was a man impressed by titles.

"Herr Braunschweiger," I said, "I have certain important matters to discuss with you. Are we to talk standing in this uncomfortable little room?"

707

The arrogant tone worked. "Of course not, your excellency. Please. Come upstairs to my office."

We followed Braunschweiger up the stairs. It was a large, old-fashioned sort of room decorated in massive wood furniture of the old Teutonic school, and there was a fire going in the small grate set into the wall. He showed us to chairs, then went behind his desk and sat down. His voice was almost servile as he said, "Now, what can I do for you?"

I stared at him. "I want to know who is paying for the guns that the Von Kuppen factory in East Germany is shipping to my country."

Braunschweiger looked at me, then at Marlene, and finally back at me again. "There must be some mistake," he said. "It is my understanding that the factory is manufacturing only agricultural equipment. Besides, I would know nothing about their operations. It has been years since I was associated with the Von Kuppen Fabrik."

I stared back at him. "How many years, Herr Braunschweiger?"

He didn't answer.

"Before the war? After?"

"I don't see why that is any of your concern, sir," he answered stiffly, and got to his feet. "I see no purpose in continuing this discussion."

I remained in my chair, making my voice sound as threatening as possible. "We in the United Nations have access to a great deal of information which is not always given out to the public at large, or even to some of the governments concerned, Herr Braunschweiger. We know all about your former association with the Von Kuppen Fabrik. We also know much about your present affiliations."

I reached for a cigarette and slowly lit it to give him time to mull over what I had said. I casually let the smoke out as I continued to stare into his eyes. "We are not at this late date interested in raking over past history or bringing embarrassment to those who were involved in Von Kuppen. Particularly those who cooperate with us."

Fortunately Braunschweiger took the bait. "As a former manager of the plant, you must understand, I was in no way responsible for company policies. I was responsible only for production."

"But you were a member of the Nazi party," I said quietly.

708

It was a fairly safe assumption, since jobs such as his were not held by people who were not. "A very important member, actually, and as such in a position to know the purposes for which your product was intended."

Braunschweiger's face paled. He knew as well as I that toward the end of the war it was his factory that had supplied ninety percent of the poison gas used at Dachau and Auschwitz. "I knew nothing," he said stiffly. "I was merely an employee obeying orders."

"That sounds reasonable but of course you must realize that it is the exact defense offered by every defendant at the Nuremberg war trials."

"I am a Swiss citizen," Braunschweiger replied sharply. "I am protected by the Swiss constitution."

I stared at him. "How long do you think your government would protect you if they learned you had sold out to the Nazis?"

"They have done nothing to those who helped the Allies!"

"I know," I replied patiently, "but you made one grave error. You picked the wrong side, the side that lost."

Braunschweiger looked at me. He took off his glasses, then put them back on again. "It is impossible. Even if I wanted to give you such information I have no way of obtaining it."

"Too bad, Herr Braunschweiger," I said, getting up. "You realize, of course, that we can force you to testify?" I returned to Marlene. "Come, Frau Von Kuppen," I said formally, "it is useless to remain longer."

"Just a moment, your excellency!"

I turned back to Herr Braunschweiger.

"If I could manage to get you such information, this other business, it would be . . ." His words trailed off.

"It will be forgotten," I said. "No one need ever know." Which wasn't exactly accurate. I'd be willing to bet that no one could ever prove what I had managed to intuit.

Herr Braunschweiger took off his glasses again and polished them vigorously with his handkerchief. "It will not be easy. It will take me a few days."

"This is Tuesday," I replied. "My staff already has instructions to release our dossier on you Friday morning—unless they hear from me to the contrary."

"You will have the information you desire by Thursday night at the latest."

709

"I am staying at the Grande Hotel," I said, and looked over at Marlene. "Come, Frau Von Kuppen."

Herr Braunschweiger was still standing stiffly at attention as we went out the door.

Thursday morning Marlene stood looking over my shoulder as I read the report Herr Braunschweiger had sent by special messenger. She looked at me with a puzzled expression. "What does it mean?"

"It means we go back to Paris," I said grimly. If it meant what I thought it did, even Robert would not dare withhold the information he had denied me.

22

The press descended on us like a pack of wolves as we got off the plane at Orly. The French newspapers, with their nose for scandal, were out in force. The flashbulbs popped in our faces. One of the reporters waved a newspaper headline. It was *France-Soir* and the bold black type sprawled all over the top half of the front page. Typically French, it could be read a block away.

PLAYBOY-DIPLOMAT ON SWISS IDYLL
WITH FORMER VON KUPPEN HEIRESS!

I took Marlene's arm and bulled my way through. I was more angry with myself than at them. I should have known what to expect. Things were difficult enough as it was, and this sort of publicity wasn't going to make it any easier.

Finally, when we were almost at the car, one persistent reporter planted himself firmly in front of us. "Are you and Mrs. Von Kuppen planning to marry?"

I stared at him balefully without answering.

"Then why did you go to Switzerland?"

710

"To get my watch fixed, you idiot!" I said, roughly pushing him aside.

Marlene got into the car and I followed. We pulled away from the curb and Fat Cat looked back at me from his seat beside the driver. "I have a cable for you."

I took the blue envelope from his hand and opened it. I had no trouble reading it. *El Presidente* hadn't even bothered to put it into our simple code.

WHAT ARE YOU DOING IN EUROPE STOP GET BACK TO NEW YORK STOP THIS IS NO TIME FOR UNA PARRANDA STOP.

Una parranda. It had a peculiar meaning in our country. A wild party, an orgy. Angrily I crumpled the cablegram.

Marlene looked at me with wide eyes. "Bad news?"

"No," I answered tersely, "It's just that *el Presidente* is as bad as everybody else. He thinks I've been having a ball."

A faint hint of humor came into her eyes. "Well, I hope it hasn't exactly been dull."

I looked at her and I had to smile. "No, much of it wasn't bad at all."

"I thought so myself." Marlene laughed. "I doubt that I'll be able to walk for a week."

Robert sounded surprised at my voice on the telephone. "I thought you were in Switzerland."

He read the newspapers, too, it seemed. "I was," I replied. "I'd like to see you as soon as possible."

Robert hesitated a moment. "I'm very tied up today."

"It's important." I had to see him today. It was Friday, and tomorrow the Swiss banks would be closed.

He was silent for a moment. "I'm meeting my father for lunch at the Crillon. Would you like to join us? I know he would be delighted to see you."

"I'll be there."

"You're looking very well, sir."

The baron looked at me shrewdly, the old realist. "It's kind of you to say so, but the truth is I'm getting old."

A peculiar look passed between him and his son. I glanced at Robert. He seemed disturbed, peculiarly upset. "Father's been having a few aches and pains," he said. "I've been trying to convince him it's only the normal hazards of age."

The baron laughed. "How would you know? I'm the one with the years."

The waiter brought coffee, and the baron lifted his cup delicately. "I've just had a letter from Caroline. She mentioned seeing you a few weeks ago in New York."

"We had a drink together in El Morocco."

"Ah, El Morocco." The baron smiled. "It is like a club, you meet everyone there. But if you two have business to discuss go right ahead. Though I'm no longer active I'm still most interested."

"Thank you."

I meant it. Lunch was almost over and it seemed that Robert was never going to give me a chance. He didn't look particularly happy as he said, "If it's about the same subject I'm afraid my answer will still have to be no. You must be aware of our position."

"I didn't push it before, Robert," I replied, "and I won't now. But can't you reconsider your position?"

Robert was silent, a stubborn look on his face.

The baron studied us curiously. He took out a thin cigar and slowly lit it as the tension built between us. "I have no knowledge of this problem between you."

It certainly wasn't my place to tell him.

Robert looked at his father. "Dax has asked access to certain confidential and restricted information concerning our Swiss bank. I have refused it."

The baron nodded slowly. He looked down at his cigar. "Robert is quite correct," he said in a quiet voice. "Not only are the laws specific but also there is the matter of ethics."

"I understand, sir. But this is information vital to me."

"Important enough to ask a friend to breach his trust?"

"Not only that," I answered, "important enough to breach the friendship as well if necessary."

The baron was silent for a moment, then he turned to Robert. "How long have you known Dax?"

Robert looked at his father with surprise. "You know as well as I how long."

"Has Dax ever come to you before with such a request?"

Robert shook his head.

"Any request?"

"No."

712

"Have you ever gone to him for help?"

The baron's voice was mild but Robert was beginning to look uncomfortable. "You know that I have."

"I remember many things. How during the war Dax came to the aid of both you and your sister without even being asked. And I also recall how he came to our aid when we were in difficulties with our cousin. He didn't hesitate then either."

"That was different," Robert replied stubbornly. "We didn't ask him to betray a trust."

"We didn't?" The baron's voice was ironic. "If I remember correctly we asked him to lie for us. And whenever one man lies to another, no matter the provocation, I consider that betraying a trust. Don't you?"

"No!" Robert answered vehemently. "That was in a business deal. Under the circumstances we acted normally."

"Normally, perhaps, but morally?"

"Morality has nothing to do with it!" Robert replied, looking at his father angrily. "And you're a fine one to be preaching about morals."

The baron smiled. "I'm not; I'd be the first to admit that not everything I've ever done was moral. Also perhaps the first to admit that I might do so again. But at least I acted with a full realization of what I was doing. I did not try to delude myself as you are doing."

Robert was silent, staring at his father.

The baron turned to me. "I'm sorry, Dax, that I cannot be of assistance to you. I think you know me well enough to believe me when I say that if I still had the authority I would give you whatever information you desired."

"I believe you would, sir."

The baron got to his feet. "And now I must go. No, don't get up. Good-bye, Dax."

"Good-bye, sir."

The baron turned and looked at Robert, "My son," he said in a low voice, "the one thing worse than an old fool is a young fool who believes that there is nothing more to learn. You must learn to listen."

"I've listened," Robert replied tersely, "and my answer remains the same!"

"Then you haven't heard everything to which you listened. I distinctly heard Dax say that he wouldn't push if you re-

713

considered. And knowing Dax as well as I do I can only assume that this means he has the means to force this information out of you whether or not you wish to give it."

Robert glanced quickly at me and then, his face reddening, looked up at his father.

The baron placed a hand gently on his shoulder. "My son, in view of what you—we—owe Dax, wouldn't it have been easier to bend your so-called ethics a little? By giving a friend what he needed you would not have forced Dax to become an adversary."

In silence the two of us watched the baron thread his way through the tables to the door, then we looked at one another.

"Since his retirement my father has grown soft and sentimental," Robert said with a forced laugh. "It's an occupational disease of the aged."

Suddenly I was angry, and what Robert said about his father triggered it. How could a man know so much and yet have learned so little? "You're going to age a little in the next few minutes," I said grimly.

"Come off it, Dax!" He laughed. "You may fool my father with that act, but not me. I know better."

"You do?" I asked savagely. "Do you also know everything about a company called De Coyne Freight Forwarding?"

"Of course; it was formed for the purpose of expediting shipments to Corteguay. It was part of our original investment agreement, but you know that as well as I. Your own father signed the papers on behalf of Corteguay."

"The bank still owns the company?"

"No."

"Who does?"

A tight smile came back to Robert's lips. "I can't tell you that. When we had no further use for the company, after it had been inactive for a number of years, we sold it, agreeing to act as nominees and trustees of record for the new owners. It is perfectly legal under Swiss law, and is done all the time."

"Then so far as the public is concerned you're still the owners, responsible for the company's activities?"

"Yes." But a worried crease had appeared in Robert's face. "That's standard practice too; everyone knows it's just a subterfuge."

714

I looked at Robert, and let the worry deepen. After a few moments I said, "I assume you also know the present nature of the company's activities?"

"I have some idea," Robert answered warily.

I took the papers that Braunschweiger had furnished me and dropped them onto the table between us. I was about as subtle as a kick in the balls. "Then I take it the De Coyne Bank has no objections to acting as shipping agent for arms and weapons manufactured by the former Von Kuppen Fabrik in East Germany?"

The color abruptly drained out of Robert's face. "What—what do you mean?"

"Read the papers."

Robert picked up the summary of the contract between the East German government and the De Coyne Freight Forwarding Company, a Swiss corporation. When he looked up beads of sweat were standing out on his forehead. His mouth was slightly open, and he looked positively sick.

I didn't feel in the least sorry for him. Robert deserved this one, if only for his stupidity. The baron had been right, it would have been better if we had been able to achieve this as friends. Such a revelation could break the De Coyne Bank where nothing else had been able to. We were both aware that no one would believe the bank's protestations of innocence.

"You weren't as smart as you thought, Robert," I said quietly, "you've been had."

By that evening the records had been flown down from Switzerland, and Robert and I spent half the night in his office going over them. When I finally left, my attaché case stuffed with papers, I had the whole rotten story, and it wasn't pretty. For Marcel lay at the center of it like an octopus, his obscene tentacles reaching out in every direction.

In the morning I called Marlene to say good-bye.

"You're leaving?"

"I'm at the airport now."

"I'm sorry about the newspaper stories, Dax. I hope she doesn't believe them."

"It doesn't matter," I said, and I meant it. Too much had already gone wrong between Beatriz and me. "Anyway, it wasn't your fault, Marlene."

"Dax, it was good, wasn't it?" she asked hesitantly. "Between us, I mean."

"Yes, Marlene."

She was silent for a moment and when she spoke again her voice was so low I could scarcely hear. "*Auf wiedersehen*, Dax. Take care of yourself."

"Good-bye, Marlene."

23

As I walked through the outer office of the consulate I came upon Lieutenant Giraldo. I stopped, and he jumped to his feet, standing at attention. "Your excellency!"

"Lieutenant Giraldo." I held out my hand. "It is a surprise to see you in New York."

He took my hand and shook it formally. "To me too," he said. "During the Korean War I was given pilot training by the American Air Force. Now suddenly I find myself sent here for a refresher course."

"Refresher course?" I smiled. "But we have no airplanes."

"I know," Giraldo replied. "That's why they sent me back here."

"Come into my office." Giraldo followed me in, and I closed the door. "So you're a pilot."

"Yes, but only on single-engine prop aircraft. I am here to receive jet training."

"Jets?" *El Presidente* had great expectations. How he was going to fulfill them I didn't know. I sat down behind my desk. "How are things at home?"

"The same." Giraldo looked at me hesitantly. "Not good; the *bandoleros* grow bolder. There have been several more villages attacked, though this has not been reported in the newspapers. I think that is why I have been sent here. There is talk that we are somehow to get jets to use against them."

"And the guns?"

"I don't know. Hoyos is in charge of the port, so we hear

716

nothing. There has been no further report of shipments being intercepted."

I was silent. If my hunch was correct the guns were still coming in, and it would take more than a Hoyos to stop them.

"Curatu has become like an armed camp," Giraldo added. "There are soldiers everywhere. The populace is silent and tense, as if they are waiting for something to happen. After eight each night no one appears on the streets. It is like a city of ghosts."

"Perhaps soon things will improve," I said.

"I hope so," Giraldo replied earnestly, "it is terrible to exist like that. We are beginning to feel as if we are living in one tremendous prison."

Sergei's face was flushed and angry. "I'll kill the son of a bitch!"

I looked out the windows of his office. The late-afternoon sun was dazzling against the white towering buildings. My eyes smarted and felt heavy. The need for sleep was catching up with me. Somehow you never really rested on those long night flights.

"I should have known better!" Sergei was still reproaching himself. "Any time that bastard offers you something for nothing, watch out. I should have realized there'd be a catch in it."

I turned back to the room wearily. "You were greedy, Sergei. He had you before he even approached you."

"What's so wrong about trying to make a few dollars you can keep?" Sergei asked defensively. "The taxes here eat you alive. So you divert a little to Switzerland; everybody does it."

I let my eyes wander around his opulent office. I thought about his duplex apartment on Fifth Avenue and his magnificent home in Connecticut. I remembered the black and gold Rolls-Royce with his crest on the door. "When you had nothing you had no taxes to pay."

Sergei must have realized what I was thinking, for his eyes narrowed.

"You're a fool," I added. "To risk so much for so little, to put yourself in the hands of a thief for a few lousy dollars."

717

I was not telling Sergei anything he did not already know, but he was still defensive. "At least I wasn't the only one."

If Sergei wanted to console himself with that it was his privilege. Unfortunately he was right. Robert's greed had led him into the same trap, and only God and Marcel knew how many others.

After a few moments Sergei asked, "What do I do now?"

"You do nothing. I do it."

Sergei was only too glad to cooperate.

I went over the whole thing again in my mind. Marcel bought the company from Robert in Sergei's name, explaining that it was to be used for the shipment of Sergei's products from France to the United States. And Robert, knowing of Sergei's success and envisioning the tremendous volume of material to be moved, went for the deal without hesitation.

Then Marcel turned around and told Sergei that there was a small piece of the De Coyne Freight Forwarding Company available, and sold him five percent for practically nothing. The name De Coyne was synonymous with security in Sergei's mind, and when Marcel told him that he had spoken to Robert, who agreed that Sergei should become president, he was flattered. Nothing could have kept him out. The dividends that Sergei received and the commissions that the De Coyne Bank earned kept both satisfied and restrained their curiosity.

Actually, I blamed only myself for not discovering sooner what was going on. A suspicion had been lurking in the back of my mind ever since I first heard about the guns. Perhaps subconsciously I remembered the stories I had heard about Marcel buying his first few ships by selling arms in the Orient. He would not be unfamiliar with the inordinately high profits involved in gun-running. But in my own way I had been as stupid as the others.

I looked across the desk at Sergei. "As president of the company you signed papers?"

"Yes."

"Do you have them?"

Sergei shook his head. "No, Marcel kept all the records. He claimed it would be safer."

"What do you have then?"

"Only my stock certificates."

"Get them."

Sergei picked up the telephone on his desk. "Would you bring in the small red folder in my personal file, please?"

A moment later his secretary came in. "Is this what you wanted, your highness?"

I glanced up to see if she was serious. She was.

"Yes, thank you."

She turned and left the office. I couldn't help smiling. "Oh, brother," I said. "You finally made it, your royal-assed highness."

Sergei had the decency to blush. "It's been good business." He found the certificates and pushed them toward me. "Here."

I studied them carefully. They were the usual printed forms, green with golden-orange curlicues. The name of the company was printed at the top, and the number of shares each certificate represented was typed in. Down on the bottom, one in each corner, were the two authorized signatures. One, of course, was Sergei's, as president of the company. I looked at the other, expecting to find Marcel's, but I should have known better. With his instinct for self-preservation he wouldn't put his name to anything.

But the name I did find was even more illuminating, for it tied the guns, the *bandoleros*, and Dr. Guayanos' group into one neat little package. The other signature was that of Alberto Mendoza, as secretary of the company.

The ringing of the telephone seemed to come from a long way off. Sluggishly I fought my way out of sleep and picked up the phone. "Yes?"

It was one of the clerks in the consulate downstairs. "I have the information your excellency requested."

I sat on the edge of the bed in a fog, trying to remember what I had asked for. The clerk must have sensed the way I felt for in a moment he added, "About Alberto Mendoza, your excellency."

"Oh, yes," I said, awake now. "Would you bring it up to my apartment, please?"

I put down the telephone and looked at the clock. It was nearly midnight. I remembered coming back to the consulate after I had left Sergei and asking the clerk to get me a file on Mendoza. Then I had gone upstairs to take a shower.

But I had decided to stretch out on the bed for a few minutes first. And that was all I remembered until the telephone had rung.

My mouth felt as if it were stuffed with straw; my clothing was rumpled and stuck to me. I got up and stretched. When a soft knock came at the door I walked toward it, unbuttoning my shirt on the way.

Fat Cat's voice came through the closed door. "Señor Pérez is here."

"Send him in."

The door opened and a little gray-haired clerk entered timidly. "Come in, Pérez," I said. "It was very good of you to give up your evening."

"It was a pleasure, your excellency." The clerk handed me a typewritten sheet of paper. "Here is the information, sir."

"Thank you, Pérez."

"Will there be anything else, your excellency?"

"No, thank you. You have done more than enough. Good night."

"Good night, your excellency."

I put the sheet of paper on my dresser and read it as I undressed.

Alberto Mendoza: age 34, born 28 July, 1921, Curatu.
Parents: Pedro Mendoza, merchant; Dolores, née García.
Education: Jesuit School, Curatu. Grad. Honors 1939,
University of Mexico. Majored Economics and
Political Science; Honors, 1943, Colombia University, Bogotá. Master in Political Science,
1944.

Career: Appointed lieutenant to army, 1944, in July.
Courtmartial 10 Nov., 1945; charge: distributing Communist literature and attempting to
organize Communist cadres among the troops.
Verdict: guilty. Sentenced to ten years' hard
labor; pardoned in general political amnesty,
1950.

Other: Left Corteguay for Europe, 1950. Actions and
movements unaccounted for until September,
1954, when became associated with Guayanos.
Of his personal life nothing is known.

I sat down on the edge of the bed and took off my shoes. That seemed to clinch it. *El Presidente* had been right. He had said all along that Guayanos was Communist-sponsored. I thought of Beatriz, and I felt sick. With so much against us we had never had a chance. No wonder she had thought I had something to do with the death of her father.

I cursed aloud and suddenly I was wide awake. I couldn't go back to sleep now. I glanced at the clock again. Marcel would still be awake; he never went to bed before three in the morning. It still wasn't too late to do what I had to do.

24

Marcel was already half drunk when he opened the door. He stood in the foyer of his apartment, weaving slightly and smiling. He half fell against me, his hands clutching at my lapels. "Dax, you dog. I've been reading about you in the newspapers."

I gripped his elbow to keep him from falling. "I've been doing some reading, too."

The sarcasm was lost on Marcel. "You know," he said, peering into my face owlishly, "for a while I'd about given you up. I thought you'd turned square. Now I know better."

"Sure," I said soothingly.

"You came just in time. I was having a little party but it was getting dull. Come."

Grabbing me by the arm, he half pulled me into the living room. The room was in semidarkness. The overhead lights were off, and only the side lamps glowed dimly in the corners. Two women were seated on the couch, their faces half hidden in the shadows.

There was a curiously vicious edge to Marcel's voice as he said, "I think you know the girls. Beth, say hello to Dax."

The nearest girl looked up. "Hello."

I recognized the big-breasted blond. I had met her there before. "Hello, Beth."

"Don't just sit there like a stupid idiot," Marcel said sharply, "fix Dax a drink."

Silently Beth got up and walked over to the bar. The other girl sat without moving, her face partly averted.

"You know Dax," Marcel said to her sarcastically. "Is that the kind of greeting you usually give an old friend?"

The woman looked up at me, her long dark hair falling away from her face.

"Dania!"

"Yes, Dania," Marcel mimicked nastily. "You never expected to find her here, did you?"

I didn't answer.

"Not Dania Farkas," Marcel continued, slurring his words slightly, "she's too independent and important."

I still remained silent.

"Bullshit!" Marcel suddenly exploded. "She's as big a cunt as the others!"

Beth came back from the bar with a drink in each hand. Marcel took one and handed me the other. Beth went back to the bar and returned with drinks for Dania and herself. "Come on, Marcel," she said, "the party's getting to be a drag. Put on some music. Let's ball a little."

"No, I don't feel like it!" Marcel swallowed half his drink and sprawled onto the couch beside Dania. "Don't be so formal," he said, "you're among friends." He fumbled at the top of her dress and silently she pushed his hand away.

Beth hit the button on the record player and music swelled through the room. She leaned over Marcel, her breasts half pushing their way out of her dress. "Come on, let's ball."

Even I could see that she felt sorry for Dania.

Viciously Marcel knocked the drink from her hand. It flew across the room, shattering against the wall. "Turn off that goddam machine," he shouted. "I told you I didn't feel like it!"

For a moment hatred flashed from Beth's eyes. She would have killed him if she'd dared. But a moment later the music stopped.

"You're not on a stage in front of an audience now," Marcel said in a cold voice, turning back to Dania. "You don't have to playact. Not for me, or for Dax either. We both know

722

what you're like, we've both slept with you. You didn't think I knew?" He began to laugh. "I know everything. That night at El Morocco when he took you home. He didn't leave your apartment until five in the morning."

Without speaking Dania got to her feet. "Dax, would you please take me home?"

"Dax, would you please take me home?" Marcel mimicked.

"Do that!" he suddenly shouted. "They say you've got a great cock. Maybe she wants you to fuck her again. But it's a waste of time, Dax, you might as well be sticking your prick into a marble statue. She does nothing but lie there!"

Marcel looked at her, then at me. "She's a whore just like the others. You know why she came up here?" He didn't wait for an answer. "Because she still thinks she can get me to marry her. She's getting old and her voice is going and she's afraid she'll have nothing once that's gone!"

Marcel began to laugh, turning back to her, his voice sly and baiting. "But I'm not that much of a fool, am I? Why should I, when I've got my pick of all the cunt in the world? Dania will always be around as long as I have any money."

Dania's face was pale. "Dax, please—"

I'd had enough myself. "Come on, Dania."

"Go ahead," Marcel shouted. "Do you think I don't know what you were doing in Switzerland? A big man with the ladies, the world's number-one lover! Bah!" He spit on the floor at my feet. "The only brains you ever had were in your prick!"

My temper burst. I grabbed Marcel by the armpits and hauled him up from the couch. "You slimy little bastard, I ought to kill you!"

Marcel stared into my eyes balefully. "You haven't got the guts!"

I began to shake him as I would an animal, then I felt Dania's hand on my arm. "Dax! Dax! Please, stop!"

Angrily I threw Marcel back on the couch. He lay there slumped against the back. "See, I was right! You're still only a ladies' man. You haven't got the balls to do what you want!" Marcel caught his breath; his voice was quieter now. "Years ago I thought you had it, Dax. But whatever you had is gone now. You've lost it."

I glared at him, my contempt showing plainly.

Marcel laughed. "Don't give me that look. I've seen it before. It means you're feeling quite righteous and holy. Well, don't be; you always took the easy way out. You followed your cock and pretended that what you did not want to see never existed. All your life you've been playing at things but never really doing any of them. You've been kept, Dax—by *el Presidente,* by your wives, even by me. It's about time you really saw yourself for what you are. You're nothing but a stupid parasite, Dax, a well-dressed gigolo."

Marcel took a deep breath. "You think you found out something in Switzerland? Well, what are you going to do about it? Nothing. Because there's nothing you can do without destroying yourself and all your friends."

I looked at Marcel. For the first time I felt a chill of fear run through me. The man was deranged, mad.

Marcel picked up his drink, and suddenly his voice was calmer. "You think you could stop the guns, Dax? Do you know who else owns a piece of the company? *El Presidente.* Do you think I could have succeeded without his help? He wanted the money and he was not afraid of a little disturbance. It would help unite the country, he said, only now it's gotten a little bigger than he bargained for. Well, I'm not worrying, Dax. I'm in, no matter which side wins!"

I felt sick because I knew he was speaking the truth. I turned to Dania. "Let's go."

"Wait," Marcel called, "I'm not through with you yet." He fished in his pocket and came out with a key. "Come back after you're through fucking her." He threw the key at me. "We still have things to settle."

I caught the key and put it in my pocket.

"You leave, too!" Marcel suddenly screamed at Beth. "I'm getting sick and tired of you, too!"

Marcel followed us, drink in hand, to the elevator. The last words he said were, "You come back, Dax, and if I'm asleep wait until I wake up!"

Then the elevator came. As the butler let us out into the street I said, "I'll be back." And I meant it. The only way you could look at a man like Marcel was the way a surgeon considered a cancer. Left alone it would destroy everything around it; the only way was to cut it out. My mind was made up. Marcel had to die.

There was no other way.

724

25

"I won't need a taxi," Beth said as we came out onto the street. "I only live across the way. Marcel likes to have me close by. Well, good night."

We watched Beth run across the street into the lobby of an apartment house on the other side. A taxi pulled up and I opened the door. Dania got in. She leaned against me, and I could feel the trembling of her body through the mink coat. She began to cry silently. There was no sound at all, only weird racking sobs.

"Take it easy," I said, "you don't ever have to go back."

Dania looked at me. I could not make out the expression in her eyes; it was too dark. "If that were only true."

I stared at her. "Not you too?"

She nodded.

"But what could he do to you?"

"Everything," she said. "The only really big thing I have is my recording contract. Now he owns the record company."

"When did you find that out?"

"Tonight; that's why I was there. Marcel called me just before I went on and told me that he wanted me to come up there and talk about it. He flew into a rage when I said I was too tired. He told me that if I didn't show up right after the performance I'd never cut another record as long as he held my contract."

"How long does it have to run?"

"Long enough," she said. "Seven years."

"But he'd still have to pay you."

"Only the minimum. Most of my money comes from earnings in excess of guarantees. Besides, Marcel could virtually keep me out of every opera house in the world. Even if they wanted to use me they couldn't."

"What has a recording contract to do with your working?"

"A great deal," she said. "Most opera companies help make up their deficits by recording complete opera performances. The sale of such records and the broadcast rights run into a great deal of money. The recording companies who hold our contracts generally agree to it, even when they don't happen to be the company involved. It makes good sense for everyone. But Marcel could withhold such approval, and then what opera company would hire me?"

"Seven years isn't that long a time," I said.

Dania looked at me. "It is for me. I'm not a child any more, I'm over thirty. My voice will be gone by then. And even if it isn't, who would give me a job? There will be younger, newer singers. No one will even remember Dania Farkas."

When the taxi stopped in front of her house she was still shivering. "Would you come up with me, please? I can't bear to be alone."

I looked at her silently for a moment, then paid the driver. At the door to her apartment she turned to me. Her eyes were still red rimmed. "Would you like a cup of coffee?"

I nodded.

I walked into the living room, and she went on into the kitchen to make the coffee. Her record player was open and I looked down at the record on the turntable. It was her latest. I read the label: DANIA FARKAS SINGS CARMEN!

I pushed the button and a moment later that glorious rich voice filled the room. For a moment I closed my eyes. If ever an opera was written for a Latin American this one was, and if ever a singer had been born to sing Carmen she was that singer. For those brief moments of song Dania was Carmen.

She came back into the room carrying a tray. "I hope you won't mind; it's instant coffee."

I shrugged. "So long as it's hot."

"It's hot." Dania put the tray down on a small table. "Help yourself, I'll be right back."

I was on my second cup and the other side of the LP by the time Dania came back. She had changed into a long hostess gown. Silently she poured coffee for herself. She took a long sip and some color seemed to come back into her face.

"Marcel said it had taken him a long time to get control of the company."

726

I didn't answer.

"Once I cared about Marcel, I really cared. But he doesn't love anybody, only himself. To him we only exist to serve him."

The record came to a finish. I sat there for a moment, the music still echoing in my ears, then got to my feet. "I must go."

"Are you going back to his house?"

I nodded.

Dania got up and came over to me, resting her head against my chest. "Poor Dax," she whispered, "he has you just as he has all of us."

"He has nothing," I answered harshly, "nothing! No one! He'll find that out soon enough."

Dania's eyes searched mine for a moment. I think she intuitively knew what I was planning. "Don't do it, Dax," she said in a low voice, "he's not worth it!"

I didn't answer. I started for the door. As I opened it, Dania stopped me. "I'm not like that, Dax, am I? Like he said, a stick of wood?"

The bastard really knew how to stick it in where it hurt. Unerringly he had discovered Dania's area of greatest doubts. I shook my head and bent to kiss her cheek.

"No, you're not like that at all," I said. "Besides, what would a man like that know about women? If he didn't have all that money he'd be going steady with his fist!"

Fat Cat came into my room as I was loading the small revolver. He blinked his eyes rapidly and the sleep disappeared. "What are you planning to do?"

I snapped the barrel into place and spun the chamber. It clicked softly and rhythmically in my ears. "I'm going to do something I should have done a long time ago."

"Campion?"

I nodded.

Fat Cat hesitated a moment, then came toward me. "Better let me do it. I have had more experience."

"No," I said, slipping the gun into my jacket pocket.

"It will not look good, for you or for Corteguay. There is enough talk already about Guayanos."

"So there will be more talk," I said. "Besides, I have a better chance of convincing the police it was an accident than you.

Who is there who will doubt it when I say we were examining the gun and it went off?"

Fat Cat looked at me skeptically.

"After all," I said, "I am an ambassador, am I not?"

After a moment, Fat Cat shrugged his shoulders. "*Sí, excelencia.*" A faintly mocking glint came into his eyes but I could tell he was satisfied with me. "But, excellency, are you sure you remember how to work that thing?"

"I remember," I said.

"Be careful, then." He opened the door for me. "Don't shoot yourself."

Almost three hours after I had left Marcel's, the taciturn Oriental butler let me in again. It was a few minutes after four in the morning, but he looked as if he never slept.

"I have the key to the elevator," I said.

The butler nodded. "Mr. Campion told me. Don't forget to turn the key again when you get off."

I nodded. The door to Marcel's living room was open. I turned and locked the elevator door behind me and walked in. The lights were still on but the room was empty.

The door to Marcel's bedroom was ajar, so I walked over and looked in, restraining an impulse to shout at him. It made no sense to be polite to a man you had already made up your mind to kill. The room was dark. I switched on the lights. The bed was empty. It had not been slept in. I walked through to the dressing room, and then into the bathroom. Each was empty.

I came back into the living room and tried the door of the guest room. It was locked from the inside. Marcel had either called up another girl and gone in there with her or was asleep and with his usual paranoia had locked the door behind him. Either way, I wasn't about to wait to find out. I knocked loudly on the door and shouted. "Marcel!"

I waited a moment, then repeated my call. There was still no answer. I walked slowly back to the bar and poured myself a drink. At least I was sure he was alone. If anyone had been with him there would have been an answer. Probably he had gone in there and passed out.

I took a sip of my drink and glanced up at the paneling behind the bar. Then I remembered the closed-circuit television. I walked around behind the bar, found the button, and pressed it.

Silently the panel rolled back. It took a moment for the set to warm up. The first place I looked was on the bed. It was empty. Then I saw Marcel. Slowly I let the breath escape from my mouth. Someone had beat me to it; Marcel was already dead.

He was lying on his stomach on the floor beside the bed. His head was arched peculiarly, his eyes protruding from their sockets, his thick swollen tongue sticking out from his mouth. He was in his shirt sleeves, his collar open, and a black silken cord had been wound around his neck, then back to the hands tied behind his back, and from there to his ankles. It was pulled so tightly behind him that it made of his body a taut bow.

I stared at him for a moment, my drink forgotten. It was as viciously simple and neatly executed as anything I had ever seen. Whoever had done it had been a true professional, and there was no doubt in my mind that Marcel had been alive when the murderer left the room. But only for a few moments. Then he had killed himself by struggling to free himself, which only tightened the black silk cord around his miserable neck.

I took another sip of the drink, then reached for the telephone on the bar. I pressed the button marked BUTLER.

"Yes, Mr. Campion?" The Oriental voice had a peculiar sibilance over the telephone.

"This isn't Mr. Campion, it's Mr. Xenos. Did anyone come to see Mr. Campion while I was away?"

There was a slight hesitation. "No, sir, not to my knowledge. I didn't let anyone in the front door since you left with the ladies."

I looked at the television screen. "Then I suggest you call the police. Mr. Campion appears to be dead."

Slowly I put down the telephone and lit a cigarette. I sat there smoking and sipping my drink as I waited for the police to arrive. I remember the words of a bank robber I had once met named Willie Sutton. He had written a book about himself and for a while he was sort of a party pet.

"There isn't a safe, a vault, a bank or a prison made by man that another man could not find a way to break into or out of, if he wanted to badly enough."

I wondered grimly what Marcel would have said had he heard those words. Probably nothing. He thought he was the only one who had everything figured out. I smiled grimly to myself.

I wondered how much good all his money and his schemes were doing him now.

26

The murder of Marcel had all the classic elements the newspapers love, and they made the most of it. The well-guarded house, the impenetrable apartment, the locked room, and one of the richest, most hated men in the world as the victim. Added too were hints of international financial intrigue, and hundreds of photographs of beautiful women and expensive call girls. It was like Christmas for them every day. They had everything they needed except one thing. The murderer.

A captain of homicide put it very well late one afternoon about a week later in my office. By this time we had begun to feel as if we knew each other quite well. There had not been one day since the murder we had not seen each other. "Mr. Xenos," he said, knocking out his pipe in the ash tray on my desk, "it will take years to complete this investigation. And when we're finished we'll be no closer to who the murderer is than we are right now. It's not because we lack suspects. I could name at least fifty people who had good reason to kill him."

I smiled to myself. This cop was not stupid, just too polite to say that I was included.

"Each time we come back to his apartment. We're checked it thoroughly, over and over, backward and forward. And there is no possible way a murderer could get into the house without being noticed, much less upstairs."

"But one did," I said.

730

The policeman nodded. "Yes, one did. And it wasn't the servants either. The old joke about the butler won't work this time. They all have airtight alibis."

The captain got to his feet. "Well, I've taken as much of your time as I intend to." He held out his hand, a faint smile on his lips. "I'll be retiring at the end of the year, Mr. Xenos. Here's hoping I won't be seeing you again."

I took his hand, looking at him quizzically.

"I mean at least not under circumstances like these. Twice we've met in the last two months and each time a man had been killed."

Then I remembered. Of course. He had questioned me after the Guayanos killing. I shook his hand and laughed. "Wait a minute, Captain. You're making it sound as if it were dangerous for me to know anyone."

"I didn't mean that," he added hastily. "Oh, you know what I mean."

"Don't explain, Captain," I said, "I understand. By the way, would you do me a favor?"

"If I can."

"I would like to get in touch with the Guayanos girl. Would you know where I could reach her?"

A look of surprise came over his face. "Don't you know?" I shook my head.

"The day after we released the body she and her uncle took it home for burial."

"To Corteguay?"

The captain nodded. "Yes, that was why I thought you knew. Your embassy cleared the papers."

That explained it; I had been in Europe. "Did a man named Mendoza go with them?"

"I think so. At least he got on the plane with them, but there was one stop in Miami and he may have gotten off there. I can check it if you like."

I shook my head. "No, thanks, Captain. It's not that important."

The captain left the office and I sat brooding about it. Strange that I had heard nothing. There should have been word from Corteguay. Mendoza was not the sort of man Hoyos was likely to overlook. I called for our copies of the daily arrival and departure lists at the Curatu airport for that week.

Beatriz' name was recorded and so was her uncle's, but there was no name resembling Mendoza. I folded the sheets slowly. On the list or not, I was certain Mendoza was in Corteguay. A sense of foreboding came over me. For a moment I thought of sending a cable. But then I decided against it. I was not the secret police. Let Hoyos and Prieto do their own dirty work.

The revolution did not come until almost two months later. The first I heard about the uprising was on Easter Sunday morning, that same day originally planned for the election. I was in Dania's apartment. We were sitting up in bed having breakfast when she picked up the remote-control gadget that operated the television set at the foot of the bed. "Do you mind if I turn on the twelve-o'clock news?"

"Do I have to get dressed for it?" I asked.

Dania laughed, and pressed the button. A moment later the picture came on. As usual it was a soap commercial. Then one of those good-looking nothing types standard to television came on. "And now, ladies and gentlemen, from the CBS newsroom in New York—the news!"

The scene dissolved to the face of a serious man seated behind a desk. His somewhat pudgy face, rather prominent nose, bushy mustache, and slightly protruding eyes induced an immediate sense of confidence. This man knew what he was talking about, even if you were aware that he was reading what others had written for him.

I bit into a piece of toast and watched.

"Good morning, ladies and gentlemen." The big smooth voice flowed out into the room. "This is Walter Johnson, CBS News. Now for the first item.

"We have another bulletin on the fighting in Corteguay."

I just had time to glance at Dania before he continued. There was a wide, startled look in her eyes.

"Battles in the mountains between the government troops and the *guerrilleros* continued throughout the night. The rebels have captured two more villages and say that they have inflicted heavy casualties upon the government forces. According to their statements, picked up from their own radio station broadcasting in the field, they appear to be but sixty miles from the capital city of Curatu. They are in complete control of all the country to the north.

"Meanwhile to the south other rebel forces have been swelled by the mass defection of regular army troops joining them in their march north to link forces with the strong rebel concentration of troops on the other side of Curatu.

"In Curatu itself a military curfew has been established. The streets are empty but occasional bursts of gunfire are heard, especially in the port area, where soldiers are stationed to protect the sea approaches to the city. Almost anything seen moving is fired upon.

"Meanwhile, several times this morning, President de Cordoba took to the radio to make an impassioned plea to the populace to stay calm in the midst of this crisis. He implored responsible officials and the army to remain loyal to the government and steadfast and determined in what—and I quote—he called their 'opposition to the seductions and promises of the Communists to the south and the lawlessness and violence of the *bandoleros* to the north.' President de Cordoba termed the growing war not a revolution but the first overt invasion of Latin America by the Communists. He claimed—and again I quote—that it was 'planned, conceived, led, and supplied by men and forces from outside the country.' He further stated that he personally intends to take charge of the army tomorrow after he has made certain provisions for the orderly continuation of government. He promises—and again a quote—not to rest until he has 'driven the bandits over the borders and into the seas over which they came.' "

The camera switched to another angle, and the commentator picked up a sheet of paper. "The State Department in Washington has announced plans for the immediate safety and evacuation of any Americans in Corteguay should this become necessary."

He put that sheet down and picked up another. "Pan American Airlines has announced the temporary suspension of flights to Curatu until the situation has clarified. The daily flight schedules which have read New York, Miami, Curatu, Bogota, will now read New York, Miami, Bogota."

The camera angle again switched and this time the news analyst spoke without notes. "Attempts to reach the Corteguayan ambassador at the embassy here in New York have been without success. The doors of the Corteguayan consulate have been barred to the press since the early hours of

733

the morning. It is not known whether Señor Xenos, who has been in the news himself lately, is in the city or not.

"And now to other news. Here in New York, the Easter parade is—"

There was a click and the picture faded from the screen. I was out of the bed and half dressed when Dania turned to look at me.

"What does it all mean?" she asked.

I paused in the midst of buttoning my shirt and stared at her. What did it mean? A thousand thoughts flashed through my mind. Marcel could have been right. What right had I to spend nights away from the consulate when deep inside I had always known that at any moment the explosion might come? I didn't have to ask myself where my brains were; Marcel had told me very explicitly.

I felt a strange guilt, a personal sense of tragedy and loss that I had not known since the death of my father. I felt the sudden pressure and warmth of tears pressing against my eyes.

"What does it mean?" Dania repeated.

"It means," I replied dully, "that in everything I have ever done—everything I have tried—I have failed."

27

By the time I reached the consulate there was no time for self-reproach. I pushed my way through the throng of reporters with a curt "No comment," and managed finally to get inside. Fat Cat and one of the clerks had to lean against the door again until it was securely locked.

"Call the police," I ordered. "Ask their assistance in keeping the entrance clear." I turned to Fat Cat. "Come with me."

My secretary looked up from her desk, an expression of relief on her face. "There are many telephone calls," she said.

"El Presidente has been trying to reach you. So has the State Department in Washington——"

"Bring the list into my office," I said tersely. I shut my office door behind Fat Cat and myself, and turned. "Is it as bad as the television says?"

Fat Cat shrugged, his face impassive. *"Quién sabe?* No one is telling the truth at a time like this. But it is not good, that is for sure."

I nodded. "Is Giraldo still around?"

"Yes, he's upstairs monitoring the radio."

"Get him down here."

Fat Cat left the room without a word and I took the list of calls from my secretary. "Get *el Presidente,*" I said before I even looked at the list.

"Yes, excellency."

I sat down and studied the messages. It looked like for the first time the world was suddenly aware of Corteguay. There were calls from everyone——from the UN, from consulates of various countries, and from the newspapers. Not only had the State Department called but there had also been calls from the senator and the two other congressmen who had been at the dinner in Washington.

The telephone buzzed and I picked it up.

El Presidente's voice was harsh and angry. "Where in hell were you?" he demanded. "I have been trying to get you all night!"

I had no excuse to offer. I remained silent.

"If you were here I'd have had you shot!" he shouted.

I'd had enough. This kind of talk was leading nowhere. "Shoot me next week," I said grimly. "If we're still in business, that is. Meanwhile, exactly what is the situation?"

El Presidente was silent for a moment, then what I had said got through to him. His voice became calmer. "It is rough but I think we can hold out if the rest of the army remains loyal."

"Will they?"

"I don't know," he said, and for the first time I heard the weariness in his voice. "Some of those I thought would be with me to the death——Vasquez, Pardo, Mosquera——have already taken their regiments over to the rebels. Others, who I had thought would be the first to go, like Zuluaga and

735

Tulia, are still with me. It all depends now on how long I can keep them convinced that we will win."

"Will we?" I asked.

"If we get help, and if we can hold out long enough. I have a feeling the rebels decided to attack now because they knew the guns had been stopped. If they had waited longer their supplies would have dwindled away. For them it was now or never."

How exquisite an irony, I thought. The very thing I had hoped to accomplish on Marcel's death had resulted in the exact opposite of what I had planned. "What kind of help do you need?"

"Any kind I can get. Ask everyone—the United Nations, the United States, anyone who will listen. We need men, arms, money, anything they will give. They should realize by now that if they don't uphold us the Communists will take over."

"They might want to know who the Communists are," I said. "They are suspicious of name-calling."

"There will be a list on your telex within the hour. *El Condor*, Mendoza—"

"Mendoza got through?"

"Yes, he shaved off his mustache and walked past our police as if he were invisible. They were too busy staring at your girl."

"The girl is all right?"

"She is safe," he replied tersely. "What is the reaction up there? Do you think we can count on any support?"

"I don't know. It's too early to tell. I've had more telephone calls than I could answer."

"Then get on with it!"

"The newspapers are yelling for a statement," I said.

"Have they printed my speeches?"

"Yes. I have also heard excerpts on television."

"Then that's all they need know at the moment," *el Presidente* said, a pleased note in his voice. "I'll let you know when other statements are to be made."

I put down the telephone, and a moment later Fat Cat and Giraldo entered my office.

"How goes it?" Fat Cat asked.

"Under control, so far."

"*Bueno.*"

"You wanted to see me, *excelencia?*" Giraldo asked.

"Yes. You said you were checked out in small aircraft. Can you fly a twin-engine Beechcraft?"

"Yes, sir."

"Good," I said. I looked at Fat Cat. "Take him out to the airport and have him checked out in my plane. If he can fly it I want you both to take it to Florida."

"I can fly it, sir."

"O.K. I want you to take it into Broward Airport in Fort Lauderdale, just outside Miami. If you went into Miami you'd attract too much attention. When you get there call me. I may want to get to Corteguay in a hurry. Pan American has shut down its flight."

"Yes, sir," Giraldo said. He turned and left the office.

"You're a fool if you go now," Fat Cat said bluntly. "There's nothing you can do."

"I'm not planning to go now. I merely want the plane there in case I have to go."

"Then you'd be even more of a fool. The best thing you can do is stay here. You'll only get yourself killed."

Probably he was right. But there was nothing else I could do. For too long I had held myself aloof from things. "My father would have gone," I said.

Fat Cat looked at me silently for a moment. There were times when I could never be sure what he was thinking, and this was one of them. Finally he shrugged, his face still impassive. "If it is what you wish."

I watched the door close behind Fat Cat and looked down at the list of telephone messages on my desk. I picked up the phone and told my secretary to begin returning the calls. Everyone I spoke to sympathized with the situation but no one was willing to offer any concrete help. They were all watching and waiting.

The Secretary of the UN was most polite but also quite definite; it was not a matter for the Security Council. As far as the UN was concerned it was an internal matter and they had no right to interfere in the internal affairs of any country. But he thought it might be possible for me to address the General Assembly if the necessary waivers could be secured from members whose speeches were already scheduled for tomorrow's meeting. However, that was all he could do; he could promise nothing more.

The State Department merely wanted to talk about what provisions had been made for the safety of Americans in Corteguay. They had a destroyer standing off the coast ready to take out such Americans if necessary, and I assured them that all possible precautions were being taken, and that they would be advised if any further action was necessary.

The Latin American countries were all sympathetic but had similar problems. And Europe was only curious to the extent that they would be in any power play; they regarded it simply as a struggle between Western and Eastern spheres of influence. While I sensed they favored us, I felt they were willing to go along with the rebels should it become necessary. The only thing that was certain was that they did not want to become involved in any conflict. And to the emerging nations of Africa and Asia ours was a familiar story, and reminiscent of the very same problems they themselves were facing.

I finally got down the list to the senator, who came right to the point. "I'd like to see you tomorrow. Can you come down here?"

"I'm sorry. I'm expecting to address the General Assembly at the UN tomorrow afternoon."

The senator hesitated a moment. "Have you spoken to either of the congressmen?"

"No. I haven't had time to return all the calls."

"You don't need to," he said, "we'll come up there tomorrow. Do you think you could slip over to my sister's apartment without being observed?"

"I can try."

"What time?"

"Make it as early in the morning as you can," I said. "There's less chance of the reporters being wide awake."

"How about breakfast at six?"

"Good. I'll be there."

And I put down the telephone and thought for a moment. I wondered what the senator had on his mind. What more could he do when his government had turned me down cold? There seemed to be no immediate answers so I picked up the telephone again.

Fat Cat came in while I was waiting for the next call. "Why do I have to go with Giraldo? You know I know nothing about planes."

738

"But you could keep an eye on it."

Fat Cat was silent for a moment. "Don't you trust him?"

"I don't know," I said. "I'm taking no chances. That plane is the only way we have of getting home if we have to. So I don't want anything to happen to it."

"What do I do if he decides to sabotage it while we're in the air?"

I eyed him grimly. "Start praying," I said as the telephone began to ring. "*Vaya con Dios.*"

28

I made it without being observed by going out the basement door of the consulate and through the alleyway to the apartment next door. From there it was only a few minutes to the apartment of the senator's sister, so I walked over to Madison Avenue and hailed a taxi.

I had spoken twice during the night to *el Presidente*. The news had not been promising. The *bandoleros* in the north had pushed to within forty miles of Curatu and captured the gateway city to the road south. *El Presidente* had sent reserves to Santa Clara with orders to make a stand there or die. And Santa Clara was only eighteen miles from Curatu, just beyond the airport.

The only news that was good was by virtue of its not being bad. The defecting regiments in the south were stalled, apparently more by confusion than by any opposition they faced. Already several colonels were squabbling among themselves, yet despite this no great successes had been achieved by loyal troops. But at least this served to keep the rebels from going around Curatu and joining up with their comrades to the north. Once they achieved this Curatu would be cut off and the war would be as good as over.

The senator's sister let me in. Her face was serious. Like her brother she wasted no time on the amenities. "They're waiting in the dining room."

The senator was seated at the head of the table, the others grouped around him. There was one among them I had not expected. George Baldwin, from the American consulate in Curatu. I wondered how he came to be there.

The question was answered soon enough. He had been in Washington for the past week furnishing them his latest information. "We've been expecting something like this for a long time," he said, "but none of us knew exactly when."

"May I?" I asked, reaching for the percolator. The senator nodded and I filled my cup. I took a big swallow. "Gentlemen, you wanted to see me. Here I am."

"All of us here," the senator began without hesitation, "feel that we have done you a grave injustice. And because of it have perhaps made a very disastrous mistake."

I looked at him. "What brought you to that conclusion?"

The senator glanced at Baldwin, then back at me. "We had all assumed that you were involved in the death of Dr. Guayanos. When Baldwin got here last week he set us straight."

"That's right," Baldwin said. "We had it on pretty good authority that Mendoza had killed him."

"Mendoza?"

"Yes. Apparently Mendoza realized that if Guayanos took advantage of your president's offer, his own power and influence would soon disappear. It might even lead to his own exposure as the Communist in back of the gun-running. So Mendoza made arrangements to have Guayanos gunned down, aware that everyone would assume that either you or *el Presidente* had ordered it. The only reason he got hit was that after he threw himself to the ground a ricocheting bullet caught him in the arm."

"Who told you?" I asked.

"We have our sources of information. And in New York ours are better than yours."

I didn't argue that. It was ironic that all the time Beatriz had been blaming me for her father's death she was helping his real murderer escape. I turned back to the senator.

"This is to the good. I am most grateful to know of your change of attitude."

740

But they were aware that what I did not say was more important than what I had said. The important thing was what were they prepared to do. The senator took it upon himself to answer that. "All of us, including George, are willing to urge immediate consideration of a Corteguayan loan."

I looked at him steadily. "Thank you. I'm in no position to refuse but my own feelings are that as usual your government is too late to be of any significant help."

The senator looked at me. "What *could* we do that might help?"

I met his eyes. "You could ask your government to send in troops to restore order. Not to ensure *el Presidente*'s continuation but to give the people a chance to elect their own government in an objective election."

The senator's voice was shocked. "You know we couldn't do that! The whole world would censure us for interference."

I finished my coffee in silence. "Ask yourselves this one question, gentlemen. What have you been doing all these years if not interfering? By doing nothing, by not recognizing our government until it was virtually impossible to ignore it, and by offering a loan only if I usurped power. Don't you consider that interference, or is it merely good politics?"

I didn't wait for them to answer. I got to my feet. "My own feeling, gentlemen, is that the great powers of this world—and this includes you as well as Russia and China—are constantly interfering in the affairs of their smaller neighbors. Despite the nobility of your motives, which I am quite willing to concede, it is nothing more than that. Interference."

They were silent for a moment. Then George looked up. "What's the situation this morning?"

"Not good," I replied. "Government troops are taking up a stand at Santa Clara, just beyond the airport. Eighteen miles to the south lies Curatu. Thank you, gentlemen, for your consideration."

The senator walked me to the door. "I'm sorry, Dax. But what you are asking is impossible, and you know it. We wouldn't dare send troops into your country, even if requested to do so by your government. The whole world would damn us for an imperialistic action."

"Someday you will," I said, looking at him directly. "You'll have to face up to the fact that you really are responsible for what happens in your sphere of influence. You won't do it this time, perhaps not even the next time. But let one country fall to the Communists and you'll have to."

"I hope not," the senator replied seriously. "I wouldn't like to have to make a decision like that."

"One of the responsibilities of power is the obligation to make decisions."

An embarrassed look came into his eyes. "I personally made a mistake, Dax. I'm sorry for it."

"My father said to me once that mistakes were the beginnings of experience, and that experience was the beginning of wisdom."

We shook hands silently and I went back to the turmoil of the consulate. When I got there I found a message on my desk. The plane had arrived safely in Florida.

There was a faint polite smattering of applause after my speech but it seemed to be coming from the public galleries overhead rather than from the delegates gathered on the floor. Slowly I came down from the podium and walked down the long aisle to my desk. Behind me I heard the crisp rap of the gavel announcing the close of the assembly.

I looked neither to the right nor to the left as I took my seat. I had no desire to embarrass any of the delegates by seeming to seek their approval. Already many of them were on their way out of the great chamber. There was a strange silence in place of the normal chatter that usually attended their departure. Occasionally one or another of them would stop at my desk for a moment and murmur a kind word. But most went by silently, avoiding my eyes. I sank wearily into my chair. It was no good, nothing was. I had failed again.

What could I have told these men who already knew so much that would have altered the opinions they already had formed? I was not a speechmaker, a man of glib phrases and flaming oratory. Half the time I spoke words that were not even convincing to my own ears. Slowly I began to gather my papers together and put them into my attaché case.

The news that afternoon before I came to the assembly had not been good. That is, what news I could get, which was mostly from radio or television bulletins. I had not been able to get through to *el Presidente* all day. And just before I had left the consulate, the networks had reported that heavy fighting was taking place around Santa Clara, and that the government forces were falling back.

"It was a good speech," a voice said.

I looked up. It was Jeremy Hadley. There was an expression of sympathy in his eyes.

"You heard it?"

Jeremy nodded. "Every word. I was in the gallery. It was very good."

"But not good enough." I gestured toward the departing delegates. "They didn't seem to think it was much."

"They sensed it," he said. "It was the first time I ever saw them leave so quietly. There isn't one of them who doesn't feel in his secret heart a sense of shame because of it."

I laughed bitterly. "Fat lot of good that will do. By tomorrow they will have forgotten all about it. It will be nothing but a few thousand words buried among the millions already stored in the archives."

"You're wrong," Jeremy said quietly. "Years from now men will remember what you said here today."

"But not today, and for Corteguay today is what counts. There may be no tomorrow."

I finished putting the last of my papers in the attaché case and closed it with a snap of finality. I got to my feet. Together we began to walk up the aisle.

"What are your plans now?"

I stopped and looked at him. "Go home."

"To Corteguay?"

"Yes, I have done everything I could here. Now there is no place else for me to go."

"It will be dangerous."

I didn't answer.

"What good can you do there?" he asked in a concerned voice. "It's almost over."

"I don't know. But there is one thing I do know. I cannot remain here, or anywhere else, for that matter. I cannot live with the realization that this time, this one time, I may not have done all I could."

There was a strange respect in his eyes. "The better I think I know you, the less I do know you."

743

I didn't answer for a moment. Instead I turned and looked around the great empty chamber. So many hopes of men had been born here. And so many, like mine, would die.

Something of what I thought must have been in Jeremy's mind too, because when I turned back to him his face was sad. He held out his hand and I took it.

"In your own words, Dax," he said earnestly, *"vaya con Dios."*

<hr />

29

It was about four in the morning and still dark when we swung in over the shores of Corteguay. We were a little over four hours out of Panama City. I looked down, straining my eyes to pierce the darkness, but I could see nothing. Whatever lights there usually were were not on tonight.

I glanced down at the fuel gauge. It registered slightly more than half full, and the reserve tank had not been touched. I nodded in satisfaction. At least we had enough gas to get back if we had to.

"Turn on the radio," I said to Giraldo. "Let's see if we can pick up anything."

He nodded, his face an odd green from the cockpit lighting. He reached over and flipped the toggle switch. Samba music flooded the cabin.

"You've got Brazil."

Giraldo began to turn the dial. He stopped it at 120 megacycles. "That's Curatu," he said. "They're not on the air."

I waited a moment. Usually Curatu was on all night. But there was nothing. "Try the military and police bands."

Quickly Giraldo whirled the dial. First one, then the other. Still nothing.

"If I had some light," I said, "I'd try for a landing in a field. But I can't see."

"We could circle a little," Giraldo said. "It will not be long until dawn."

"No, we can't spare the fuel. We have to reserve enough to get back on."

"What are you going to do then?" Fat Cat asked from behind me.

I thought for a moment. "Try for the airport."

"And if Santa Clara has fallen? The airport is probably in their hands."

"We don't know that," I said. "Maybe we'll be able to tell when we come down. I won't cut the engines and if anything looks suspicious we'll cut out."

"Sweet Mother of God!" Fat Cat murmured.

I swung north over the sea. We wouldn't come inland until the last possible moment. "Turn to the air band."

Giraldo leaned forward and spun the dial. "All set."

Three minutes later I turned west toward land. The voice coming over the radio seemed suddenly to roar through the cabin. Whoever it was was speaking English but he seemed very nervous. His accent was so pronounced as to be almost unintelligible.

"Let me answer," I said quickly. My English was good enough to convince the average Corteguayan that I was foreign. At least over the telephone or radio.

I pressed down the button on the microphone. "This is private aircraft United States license number C310395 requesting permission to land at Curatu Airport. Please give us landing instructions. Over."

The voice was still nervous. "Would you identify yourself again, please?"

I repeated my request, speaking more slowly this time.

There was a second's silence, then a question: "How many on board your aircraft? Please state the purpose of your visit."

"Three aboard. Pilot, co-pilot, and one passenger. Aircraft chartered by American news service."

This time there was almost a full minute's wait. "You are on our radar screen about five miles west and three miles south of airport, heading north. You will continue until we give you the signal to turn south and take up your landing pattern. Acknowledge and repeat. Over."

I acknowledged and repeated.

"What do you think?" Fat Cat asked.

"Sounds O.K.," I said, "unless the army has gone over to the rebels." I adjusted my airspeed just as the radio came back on. "Anyway, we'll know in a few minutes."

They gave us the minimum lights necessary to land. As soon as our wheels touched the ground, they went off, and we taxied by our own landing lights toward the dimly lit terminal.

"Do you see anything?" Fat Cat asked.

"Not yet," Giraldo answered.

A moment later we reached the loading apron. Slowly I turned the plane around, keeping the motor running so we could get out the way we had come in if we had to.

Suddenly soldiers came running from all sides, surrounding the plane. There seemed to be at least forty of them, all with rifles.

"Are they ours or theirs?" Fat Cat's voice was puzzled.

I peered down at our landing beams. A short man marched pompously forward, dressed in a captain's uniform. I laughed suddenly and cut the engines. "Ours!"

"How do you know?"

"Look!" I said, pointing.

There was no mistaking the man. Prieto. All dressed up in an officer's uniform. I smiled to myself. Never in my life had I ever thought I would be glad to see Prieto again.

"How is it going?" I asked after we got into the terminal.

The single light on Prieto's desk glowed weakly as he poured coffee for us. "There is still fighting at Santa Clara."

I picked up the cup and sipped the coffee gratefully. "We had heard that Santa Clara had fallen."

"No, the rebels are a mile or so outside the town. They are dug in, waiting for the forces from the south to join them."

There was noise outside, then the sound of a shot and a man shouting. Silence. I looked at Prieto questioningly.

"The men here are nervous," he said with a slight smile. "They shoot at anything that moves, even shadows. Afterward they shout."

"Have any of the rebels tried to get through to here?"

"A few," Prieto said. "They are all dead." He reached for a cigarette, and I noticed the faint trembling of his fingers.

"We picked you up on our radar about fifty miles out. We thought it might be you but couldn't be sure until you had identified yourself."

"You expected me?"

"We had word from New York that you were on your way. It was *el Presidente* who figured that you might be coming in your own plane. He's had a car waiting for you since late this afternoon."

I finished the coffee and put down the cup. "Good," I said. "I am ready."

Prieto got to his feet slowly. "You thought I killed Guayanos, didn't you?"

I looked at him and nodded silently.

"You should have known better. If I had, I'd have made sure we got Mendoza, too. He was far more important."

I told Giraldo to stay with the plane until he had further orders from me, then Fat Cat and I got into the army jeep and went barreling off to the city. It was a six-place job and Fat Cat and I occupied the middle seats, with the driver and another soldier in front. Two more soldiers were on the seat behind us and all of them, except the driver, held their rifles at the alert.

We drove without headlights until we were within a mile of the city. There were times when I wondered how the driver could see but apparently he knew the road. By the time we did turn on the lights we really didn't need them. A faint hint of dawn was breaking in the east.

Twice, just outside the city and once at the entrance to the city itself, we were stopped by roadblocks. Each time the soldiers merely glanced in our car and waved us on. They had apparently been alerted to my arrival. It was daylight by the time the car turned into the courtyard of the *Palacio del Presidente*. We piled out and went inside.

An army captain was waiting at the door. "Señor Xenos," he said, waving us past the guards. "*El Presidente* has asked that you be brought to him immediately."

I followed him down the corridor to the presidential office. The captain knocked on the door politely, then without waiting for an answer opened it and stood aside.

El Presidente was standing in the center of a group of officers gathered around his desk. A sudden smile came to

747

his face as he looked up. He came quickly around the desk, throwing his arms wide to embrace me.

"Dax, my boy," he called warmly, "I'm so glad you got here in time for the finish!"

I stood there frozen in numbed surprise as I felt his lips kiss me on either cheek. I had not expected to find him like this. Cheerful, almost gay.

It was no way for a man to act at his own funeral.

30

I stood next to *el Presidente* looking down at the map spread out on the desk. It was covered with crosses and checkmarks, each in a different color. It made no sense to me until he explained it.

"The only chance they had was to win quickly. Speed. Three days, four days at the most, then, poof!" *El Presidente* snapped his fingers. "It would be gone like that."

A murmur of agreement came up from the officers around us.

"I realized that right away," he continued, a satisfied note in his voice. "They had just so many guns, so much ammunition. That was fine if they were merely to continue their raids, but it was nowhere near enough for a war. I made my decision immediately. Fall back from the mountains. Let them stretch their supply lines and use up their ammunition. Let them think they were winning so they would outrun their ability to supply themselves. And they did. They moved two hundred and forty miles from the mountains, leaving nothing behind them to maintain their supply lines. No trucks, only a few automobiles, and horses and donkeys." *El Presidente* laughed. "Think of it. Horses and donkeys in this age!"

Almost like a chorus, the officers behind us laughed, and were silent as soon as he began to speak again.

"We could hold at Santa Clara, and it was close enough to the city to make them feel they had a chance. They would pause there and call for reinforcements from the traitors in the south to help them push on to Curatu.

"But there was only one way for the traitors from the south to come to their aid. The way north was blocked by our loyal troops, so they had to move west, around us via the peninsula. Yesterday morning they began their move. By nightfall all three divisions, along with some of the rebels, were on the peninsula. Then we made our counter-move. Two armored divisions and three infantry sealed them off. There was no way for them to escape. There was only one direction in which they could go, and that was into the sea!"

El Presidente looked at me triumphantly. "The traitor colonels realized immediately that they were in a trap from which there was no hope of escape. Already, early this morning, I have had reports from the field that they are asking for conditions. And now that it is morning, long past the time for reinforcements to have arrived, the *bandoleros* at Santa Clara are beginning to realize they have extended themselves. Intelligence reports that already some of them are beginning to turn back. But they, too, are in for a surprise. Two armored divisions, brought in from the west, are now between them and the mountains. They will be cut to pieces!"

My head was spinning and my eyes felt heavy and leaden. "But the news," I said, "was so uniformly bad. They were winning."

"They were," *el Presidente* replied with a smile, "at first. And when I put my plan into effect I refused to allow any counterclaims to be made. One word about our possible victory and they might have pulled back in time to avoid the trap. I had made up my mind. This time they would not escape. Once and for all they had to learn that I am the government, that I am Corteguay!"

El Presidente looked at me silently for a moment, then turned to the others. "That will be all for the moment, gentlemen."

He did not speak until they had closed the door behind

749

them, then silently he made a spitting gesture at the floor.

"They are pigs and cowards! They think I do not know that they were waiting to see which side had the better chance of winning before they committed themselves!"

I looked at the old man. The years had seemingly fallen away from him. He seemed as strong and as full of vitality as he had ever been. It was the time of waiting that had drained his energies.

El Presidente placed his hand on my arm and looked into my eyes. "You were the only one I did not doubt," he said. "I knew you would come to stand beside me no matter what happened. I did not have to be told that you were on your way. I knew it."

I didn't answer.

He went to his chair and sat down. "You must be worn out from your trip. Go to my apartment and bathe and rest. There will be a fresh uniform for you when you awake."

"A uniform?"

"Yes, you are still a colonel in the army, aren't you? Besides, I have a mission for you. I am too busy here to get away. I have decided that you will go as my representative to arrange the surrender of the traitors in the south."

"The south?" I repeated.

"Yes. For the *bandoleros* in the north there will be no surrender. I shall kill them all!"

It was ten o'clock the following morning and the rain was beating heavily against the earth outside the farmer's cottage in which I awaited the rebel officers. Looking through the window, I could see several sheep and one goat grazing in the fields, oblivious to the water pouring down upon them.

Colonel Tulia came back from the open door. "They are coming."

I got to my feet and faced the door as he came around the table to stand slightly beside me. I heard the clank of rifles as the guards presented arms, then the door opened and they came in. Their uniforms were wet and dirty from the mud of the fields, and their faces drawn and exhausted. They stood just inside the door looking at us.

I already knew these men. Colonel Tulia had probably known them for years, by their Christian names; no doubt he had even socialized with their families. Yet we all stood there silently. The formalities had to be observed.

A young captain, one of Tulia's staff, made the introductions. "Colonel Vasquez, Colonel Pardo." He paused for a moment. "Colonel Xenos, Colonel Tulia."

The two officers stepped forward and saluted. We returned their salutes. The young captain closed the door.

"Won't you sit down, gentlemen?" I indicated the chairs at the table. I gestured to Fat Cat, who was standing in a corner behind us. "Will you have coffee brought in?"

Fat Cat nodded and turned, then, remembering, did an about-face and saluted awkwardly, almost bursting the seams of his too tight army blouse. I hid my smile as I returned his salute, and turned back to the others.

"There are only two of you, gentlemen," I said. "I had been led to understand there would be a third. A Colonel Mosquera, I believe?"

The two colonels shot a brief look at one another. "Colonel Mosquera was accidentally killed this morning while cleaning his revolver," Vasquez announced formally.

I glanced at Tulia. We both knew what that meant. It had been no accident; this was merely army language for suicide.

Fat Cat came back into the room with four steaming mugs of thick black Corteguayan coffee. I watched the two colonels pick up their mugs and sip at the coffee. A little color came back into their faces.

"Shall we proceed to the business at hand, gentlemen?" I asked.

They nodded.

I opened my attaché case and took out the typewritten forms and placed them on the table between us. "I assume that you gentlemen have already read the draft of this document which was handed you last night, and that you understand it and accept all its conditions?"

"There is but one condition that I would like your excellency's permission to discuss," Vasquez said.

"Proceed."

"It is clause six, pertaining to the punishment of individual personnel according to their rank, responsibility, and guilt as determined by court-martial."

"Yes, Colonel. Your question?"

"It is not a question," he answered. "Colonel Pardo and

I are quite willing to accept our punishment. But it is our feeling that it should be ours alone. The officers and men under us were merely doing their duty. They are good soldiers and have been taught to obey their superiors without question. Surely they share none of the responsibility for what happened."

"That is true," the other colonel interjected. "You cannot punish three whole regiments because they were misled."

"That is not our intention, gentlemen," I said. "Your men have been guilty of insurrection and rebellion against the government. I am sure they were aware at whom they were shooting, yet they aimed at their fellow soldiers."

The two officers did not answer.

"I have constructed clause six most carefully and explicitly," I continued. "Undue hardship and injustice can and will be avoided as much as is humanly possible. I call your attention to the words 'individual personnel.' This means there will be no mass trials where a man could be punished for the sins of his associates. Each man will be judged on his own."

"I ask amnesty for my men——" Vasquez' voice broke.

I looked at him sympathetically. "I'm sorry, Colonel. I have not the authority to change these conditions. They were read and approved by *el Presidente*."

Pardo hesitated a moment, then picked up the pen. "I will sign."

A moment later Vasquez also signed, then Tulia and I. We all got to our feet. "You will place yourselves and your men in the custody of Colonel Tulia," I said. "At the proper time he will issue further instructions."

"*Sí, Coronel.*" They both saluted.

I returned their salute and as they turned Colonel Vasquez stopped before me. "I apologize for my tears, excellency."

I looked at his sad, weary face. "Your tears do you honor, sir."

Vasquez turned again and continued out the door. The war in the south was over.

31

But the war in the north was not yet over. The *bandoleros* were not soldiers; they did not fight according to the rules of warfare. To them war was not a game like chess, when if the situation was hopeless one resigned. To them war was to the death. They would continue to kill until they themselves were killed.

And they died. By the hundreds. But in dying they also killed, not only soldiers but anyone and anything that lay in their path. They moved through the land like a plague, and like a plague their savagery was contagious. Our soldiers grew callous and careless. In a matter of days they became no better than their enemy. They, too, began to destroy everything that got in their way merely to get to the enemy.

The roads became clogged with *campesinos*, women and children fleeing first one way, then another. They were unsure who was their enemy or in which direction safety lay. The stories that came back to Curatu, carried by refugees, were almost too incredible to believe.

Murder and rape had become commonplace, death and torture a way of life. And the lawlessness was common to both the soldiers and the *bandoleros*. Between the two, entire villages were wiped out in the name of war. The *bandoleros* acted out of a fear that the villagers might lead the army to their hideouts, and the army reacted because they were afraid the *campesinos* might give comfort to the *bandoleros*. The helpless *campesinos*, caught in the middle, had no choice but to die, for if the soldiers did not kill them the *bandoleros* would.

And for every *bandolero* that the soldiers killed, at least one got through their lines. Relentlessly the army pushed after them. Each day the war became more vicious, more improbable. Because it was no longer even a battle. It was total extermination.

On the fifth morning after my return from the south, *el Presidente* asked if I would fly him over the battlefields. He wanted to see for himself the progress of the war. We flew in bright shining sunlight over the bleakest terrain man has ever seen. The earth had been truly scorched. In many places the winter harvest still smoldered in the fields, and animals lay dead and decaying. Entire villages had been fired, and the buildings which still remained were silent in their lonely emptiness. Nowhere was a sign of life visible.

Occasionally on the roads below us an army vehicle moved or a platoon of soldiers trudged toward the north. But outside of that the only people we saw were occasional straggles of refugees, bent under their packs and heading toward the safety of Curatu. It was not until we had almost reached the mountains, not far from my *hacienda*, that we witnessed actual war.

There we saw an entire regiment besieging a small village. They had surrounded it with cannon and mortar and were mercilessly lobbing shell after shell into the tiny hamlet. I did not see how anyone could remain alive after such a holocaust. I glanced over to see how *el Presidente* was reacting to it.

He was looking down, his face impassive. I sent the plane into a wide slow circle. Almost at the same instant two men broke from one of the houses below us, carrying rifles. Behind them came a woman, pulling a small child. She turned and ran between one of the houses. The men were obviously trying to cover her escape. The four of them made it almost to the back perimeter of the village before the two men were cut down in a murderous crossfire. The woman got to the last building and sank down, the child at her back.

I banked the plane again, looking over the side. The soldiers were moving in. Slowly and cautiously. There was no returning fire. Now a group of them was gathered around the woman and the child, who knelt there beside the building, staring up at them.

One of the soldiers gestured at her. Slowly she got to her feet and with an odd gesture dusted off her skirt. The soldier gestured again and she took the child's hand. He prodded her with the muzzle of his rifle and she stumbled to the door of the small cottage. He motioned for her to go inside. She hesitated. He raised his rifle threateningly. With a last backward glance she pushed the child before her and went in through the door. A moment later the soldier and several of his companions went in after her.

I glanced at *el Presidente* again. His lips were drawn back tightly over his teeth, his eyes shining. He looked up and noticed that I was watching him. For a long moment our eyes met, then his face became expressionless again.

"It will teach them a lesson," he said harshly, "the *bandoleros* and the *campesinos* who help them. It will be a long time before any of them will want to make war again."

"If that child lives," I said, "it will hate the government for all its life. If it is a boy, as soon as he is old enough, he too will go back into the mountains."

El Presidente knew what I was talking about. It had always been that way. The children who somehow survived *la Violencia* were scarred, something inside them became warped and they, too, carried the seeds of violence.

"It is war," *el Presidente* said emotionlessly, "and there is nothing that can be done about it."

"But they are soldiers, they are not animals! Where are the officers who are supposed to control them? Do you wish them to become the same as the *bandoleros?*"

El Presidente looked at me for a moment. "Yes, they are soldiers but they are also men. Men swollen with victory, or the fear of death, and faced with a sudden realization of the nothingness of their lives."

I didn't answer. I had no answer.

"We can go back now."

I nodded and began to bank left, then on a hunch decided to fly over my *hacienda*. We were scarcely ten minutes away. I came down to about a thousand feet. There was nothing left except a few charred and burned timbers and the stones of the foundations. Even the barns were gone.

Only the cemetery remained, its small white headstones standing like tiny beacons in the scorched fields around them. I glanced over at *el Presidente*. He was looking out the window but I doubt that he realized where we were. His face was expressionless.

I altered course to take us directly back to Curatu. There

was a strange tightness in my breast. Suddenly, for the first time in the last few hectic days, for perhaps the first time since I had arrived home, I thought of Beatriz.

Something inside me lightened. I was glad now that I had taken her there before it was too late. And I was glad that she had freed the ghosts of my family so they would not have to see their home burned down.

I stopped the plane and cut the engines right next to *el Presidente*'s big black limousine, which was parked on the field awaiting us. He turned to me before getting out. "Make sure your plane is in order. Tomorrow you are flying back to New York."

I nodded.

"I wish to talk to you tonight. Alone. We have many things to discuss. I think the Americans will give us that loan now. You will come to my apartment at eleven. I shall leave word to admit you. If I am not there you will wait for me."

"Yes, excellency."

El Presidente pushed open the cabin door, then looked back at me. "And by the way," he said, almost as if it were an afterthought, "this time you are not going merely as our ambassador. This time you are going as vice president of Corteguay. The news was announced over the radio at noon, about the time we were flying over your *hacienda*."

I was too stunned to speak.

El Presidente smiled briefly, then with a wave of his hand he was gone. I watched his car pull away and go roaring out the gates before I cut the engines in again and started to taxi to the hangar.

New York, I thought. It would be good to be back in New York again. There was nothing to keep me here now. Except one thing. Beatriz. I would not go back alone. This time she would go back with me. As my wife.

756

32

The change in my status was evident the moment I got down from the plane in the hangar. Giraldo, who had become accustomed to being with me and had grown rather careless about his uniform and his manners, now stood stiffly at attention, his uniform neatly brushed. The two mechanics behind him also stood at attention. Even Fat Cat, in his own sloppy way, seemed to stand straighter, though I could see from the look in his eyes that it was more for their benefit than for mine.

"Lieutenant—"

"*Si, excelencia!*" Giraldo had spoken before I'd a chance to finish.

I would have to remember now to speak more quickly or I should be giving all my orders in two installments. "Please have the plane serviced and thoroughly checked out."

"*Si, excelencia!*"

I looked at him. "I hadn't finished yet," I said mildly.

"*Perdone, excelencia!*"

I had to smile, I couldn't help it. "Fill the tanks and stand by. We are soon to return to New York."

"*Si, excelencia!*" Giraldo saluted sharply, then looked at me hesitantly. "May I offer your excellency my congratulations and best wishes in your new position, and assure you of my total loyalty?"

"Thank you, Giraldo."

Again he saluted, and this time I returned it. I went out of the hangar ringing with his orders to the mechanics. Already Giraldo saw himself as attached to the vice presidential staff.

Out of the corner of my eye I could see Fat Cat walking slightly behind me. He was still in that strange posture

757

which seemed so wrong and awkward for him. "You'd better relax," I said to him out of the corner of my mouth, "you'll break in two."

Almost immediately everything dropped. His chest deflated, and his stomach reappeared again. "Thank God!" he murmured gratefully. "I was beginning to think I would have to remain like this forever!"

The two soldiers who drove me were at attention beside the jeep. Everybody saluted. I saluted, then they saluted again, and finally to put an end to it I got into the car. We roared off toward town.

"How was it out there?" Fat Cat whispered under cover of the roar of the wind in our faces.

"Not pretty," I said. "It will be years before we recover from this." I was silent for a moment. "The *hacienda* is gone. There is nothing left but the cinders."

"You can build again."

I shook my head. "No. Another house, yes. But not that one." The feeling of the loss was beginning to register. It was as if a part of my life had vanished.

Fat Cat knew how I felt and changed the subject. "I was in the control tower when the news came over the radio. Everyone wanted to know what it meant."

I didn't answer.

"There were some who thought that at last the old man was getting ready to step down and turn it over to you. At least that's what they kept telling me."

"What did you tell them?"

"What could I tell them?" Fat Cat asked expressively. "Let them think I was a fool and didn't know? That it was as much a surprise to me as to them?"

I detected the faint note of reproach in his voice. "It was a complete surprise to me," I said.

Fat Cat looked at me for a moment, then decided I was telling the truth. The reproach faded from his eyes.

I soon discovered there were some advantages to my new position. We raced past the checkpoints without once being stopped, and when I got to the *Palacio del Presidente* I found I had been moved from the small office in which I had been installed on the day I arrived. I now had a large suite of offices next to *el Presidente*'s own.

758

By the time I reached them I had run a gauntlet of good wishes and protestations of undying loyalty. It was with a feeling of relief that I finally closed the door to my private office behind me. I walked around the desk and sat down in the chair. I leaned back, swinging, trying it out for comfort.

"You look as if you'd sat there all your life," Fat Cat said.

I looked over at him. "Don't you begin."

Fat Cat didn't answer.

"Go up to our *apartamiento* and bring down my suit. I want to get out of this uniform." Suddenly I didn't feel right in it any more.

Fat Cat nodded and left. A moment later I had my first official visitor. It was *Coronel* Tulia. "I'm sorry to disturb your excellency, but I have important papers that require your signature."

There was something about this tall reserved soldier that I liked. I felt none of the usual Latin American effusiveness in him, the false compliments or scraping to superiors. He had not even mentioned my new position.

"My signature?"

"Yes, as vice president."

"What are they?"

He took them from his briefcase and handed them to me. "Execution orders," he said briefly. "For Pardo and Vasquez."

I looked at him in surprise. "I wasn't advised of their court-martial."

"There has been no court-martial, excellency." Tulia's face was expressionless. "They were condemned by order of *el Presidente.*"

I stared at him. Tulia knew as well as I that this was contrary to clause six of the surrender agreement. Under its provisions no man could be judged without trial. "Then why didn't *el Presidente* sign the order of execution?"

"Under our constitution," he answered, "it is the vice president who has the power to set the final penalty in cases of treason. The president is considered to be the government and therefore in prejudice. Only if there is no vice president is the president empowered to act." Tulia paused for a moment, then added significantly, "You are now the vice president."

Tulia did not have to point out that. It had already begun to dawn on me. I looked down at the papers. Were *el Presi-*

dente to sign them an outcry would go up around the world; these men had been denied their rights under the surrender agreement. But not if I were to sign them. I would assume the responsibility.

I looked at Tulia. "If these men had come before a court-martial what do you think the verdict would have been?"

"I cannot guess the decisions of others."

"If you were to sit in judgment would you have found them guilty?"

Tulia hesitated a moment. "No."

"Despite the fact that they led their troops against their own government?"

"Yes." Tulia's answer came without hesitation. "You see, I know the facts of that decision."

"The truth?"

Tulia nodded.

"I would like to hear it."

For the first time I noticed the tension under which Tulia was laboring. Faint beads of perspiration dampened his forehead. Suddenly I realized the courage it took for him to come even this far with me. One word and he might stand beside the others in the dock.

"Sit down, Colonel," I said gently. "You are among friends."

Gratefully Tulia sank into the chair. To give him time to compose himself I took out a thin black cigar from my case and offered it to him. He shook his head so I lit it. Then I leaned back and waited.

"There were seven regiments in the field when the fighting began. Seven regiments, seven colonels, including Mosquera, who is now dead." Tulia leaned forward. "In many ways the rebel attack was what has become almost the classic opening in modern warfare. Like the German blitzkrieg of Poland and the Japanese attack on Pearl Harbor, it came without notice, without warning. And we were caught completely unaware.

"It was on a Saturday morning that the attacks began in the north. Nothing much was said about it at first because everyone assumed it was just another *bandolero* raid. By the time we realized that it was more than that the fighting had begun in the south. The news came while all seven of us were having dinner together at my headquarters. You cannot imagine the confusion and rumors. At one point during the night we even had a report that *el Presidente* had been assassinated, and that the rebels were in complete control of the government."

Tulia reached into his pocket and took out a cigarette. "It was at that moment that we got an invitation from the Communist, Mendoza, to join the revolution. He promised that we would be welcomed in the south as brothers in arms.

"The seven of us stood around the table looking down at the message. The lines to Curatu were down, we could not even reach the capital by radio. The outside news networks were spreading conflicting reports. Both Brazil and Colombia reported that the government had already fallen, and there was not one word from *el Presidente*. We did not know what to do.

"To continue the struggle if the government had already gone under could only result in unnecessary deaths. To join with the rebels if the government had not fallen could only assure them victory. It was Vasquez who finally came up with the solution to our dilemma. Vasquez, the gentle one with the wisdom of Solomon. Right there we formed a junta. We agreed that the three weakest regiments would go over to the rebels. They would delay and procrastinate until the situation clarified."

Tulia ground out his cigarette. "The three weakest regiments belonged to Pardo, Mosquera, and Vasquez. They deliberately led their regiments onto the peninsula, where they knew they would be trapped. Mendoza ranted and raved at their stupidity, but there was nothing he could do. It was already too late."

A curious speculation came into Tulia's voice. "I wonder if Mendoza suspected that we tricked him."

"Mendoza was captured?"

"Yes, but just last night he escaped."

That kind always got away; they were like rodents carrying the plague. I looked down at the papers.

"These are only the first you will be asked to sign," Colonel Tulia said suddenly. "Every officer in each of those regiments down to the rank of lieutenant has also been condemned. The typists are working overtime to prepare the execution orders."

"Every officer?" I asked incredulously.

761

"Yes, almost a hundred."

I stared down at the papers again. These were the kinds of men *el Presidente* wanted to kill while a man like Mendoza was running free to spread his poison? I got to my feet slowly.

"Leave the papers with me, Colonel. I think in view of what you've told me *el Presidente* should review the matter."

33

I got out of the jeep in front of Beatriz' house. The shutters were drawn, the house seemed empty. "Go around to the back," I ordered the two soldiers.

"*Si, excelencia.*" They went off at a trot.

"Come with me," I said to Fat Cat, and walked up to the front door. I pounded the heavy brass knocker. The sound echoed through the house. I waited a moment, then lifted it again.

There was no answer. I had a hunch. If Mendoza went anywhere, it would be here.

Fat Cat moved back and squinted up quizzically. "There's no one in there," he said. "Even the shutters are shut tight."

There was certainly no sign of any movement within the house. Slowly we began to walk around it, checking all the windows. They were all tightly shuttered except one, a small window on the second floor. I guessed it to be a bathroom window.

We passed the soldiers. "See anything?"

They shook their heads. Fat Cat and I continued on around. The small window was the only one we could find unshuttered. I stood there looking up at it. I couldn't be this wrong.

Fat Cat followed my eyes. "I could climb up that tree and get in the window."

I looked at Fat Cat and had to smile. "You couldn't get through that window if you were fifty pounds lighter."

"We could send one of the soldiers."

"No." If Beatriz was in the house I didn't want to take the chance of anything happening to her. "I'll go up myself."

I reached the lowest branch easily, and pulled myself up. Slowly I climbed but it wasn't as easy as it had been when I was a boy. I was blowing pretty hard by the time I finally got up there.

I reached over and pushed. The window seemed to be stuck. I could see no sign of a lock, so I hit the frame smartly with the edge of my fist. The sash quivered and moved slightly. I pushed it the rest of the way up and began to climb through.

"Be careful!" Fat Cat called.

I nodded and climbed through. I had been right; it was a bathroom. Cautiously I crossed to the door. I stood there quietly, listening.

There wasn't a sound in the house.

"Beatriz!" I called. My voice echoed through the rooms.

Slowly I moved out into the hallway. There were four doors opening onto it. Three of them must be bedrooms. The only one I didn't have to guess about was the door opposite the staircase. The small shield on it identified it as the linen closet.

I checked the far bedroom first. The faint residue of perfume told me that this was Beatriz' room. I went through it quickly. Her clothing was still in the closets; the dresser drawers had not even been disturbed. Wherever she had gone, it could not have been for long. Everything seemed in order. Even her suitcases were still in the closet.

The second room apparently was her uncle's. That, too, seemed undisturbed. The third was the smallest of the three, probably the maid's room. It was the only one in disorder. The bed was rumpled and unmade, as if it had just been slept in. But the closet was empty, as were the bureau drawers.

I walked back into the hallway deep in thought. It didn't make sense. Why should the maid's room look as if she had gone away? And yet her bed be the only one to have been slept in?

I started down the staircase, then changed my mind. Still puzzling over the disorder in the maid's room, I pulled open the door to the linen closet. My hunch was right but it almost cost me my life.

Mendoza came out of the closet like a projectile. I clutched at him and we went tumbling backward, over and over, down the staircase. We landed on the floor below, with him on top and my head bursting and my lungs gasping for breath. I saw a knife flash and desperately I grabbed for it. I could feel the strain in my arms as I battled my assailant to keep him from using it.

"Fat Cat!" I shouted. "Fat Cat!"

Violently he clamped a hand over my mouth to keep me from shouting again. The slight easing of pressure enabled me to twist the arm out and away from me. I heaved with my body and rolled him off me onto the floor.

We both came to our feet at almost the same instant. He lunged toward me, the knife still in his hand. I ducked away from the slashing blade. From behind me came a heavy pounding on the door. He cast a quick glance sideways, then back again before I could take advantage of it.

"I don't care about you, Mendoza," I gasped. "Where is Beatriz?"

"As if you didn't know!" he answered, and lunged at me.

I jumped aside again. "Beatriz, where is she?"

Now Mendoza actually seemed to be laughing. He had to be mad. He began to swing wildly at me, mumbling incoherently all the while, "You can't win! Someday we'll get you, all of you! You can't win!"

I was so busy keeping away from his knife that I didn't anticipate his sudden leap. He crashed into me, his weight carrying us to the floor. But this time I was faster. I rolled away from him and then back, catching his knife hand at his side just as it was coming up.

It was an old *bandolero* trick. I clamped one knee and a hand down on his knife arm, pinning it to the floor, then with a crooked elbow jammed into his throat just below his Adam's apple, I pushed with all my weight.

His free hand clawed wildly at my eyes but I twisted my head away. And all the while I put more and more weight on my elbow. I could almost hear the crunch as his windpipe crushed. Relentlessly I kept on applying pressure until at last

764

his hands stopped moving and his protruding eyes and tongue told me that he was dead.

Only then did I roll off and lie gasping on my back beside him. The pounding on the heavy door had ceased. In a few moments I heard the sound of a key turning and I began to sit up.

Fat Cat was the first in. He leaped over Mendoza's body and pulled me to my feet. "Are you all right?"

I nodded, turning.

Hoyos stood there, the key that had opened the door in his hand. Beatriz was beside him, her eyes wide and frightened.

No one had to tell me where Beatriz had been, for I could see the handcuffs still on her wrists. *El Presidente* had assured me she was safe, and he hadn't been altogether wrong. She had been very safe. In jail.

Beatriz sat over in one corner of the couch. She was still crying. I looked up and saw Hoyos watching us from the hallway. Mendoza's body already had been removed. I got out of my chair and closed the door. I came back to Beatriz and stood looking down at her.

"That's enough!" I said harshly.

She was surprised at the sharpness in my voice and looked up, her dark-green eyes still brimming with tears.

"You have cried enough, you're merely feeling sorry for yourself. It is time to stop."

"You killed him! Now that my uncle is dead in the fighting there is no one left. I am alone."

"You were alone before I killed him," I said patiently. "I tell you he was the one who had your father killed."

"I don't believe you!" Beatriz' eyes began to fill again with tears.

This time I lost my patience. Angrily I slapped her across the face. "Stop it!"

The shock dried her eyes, and she came up off the couch clawing at me. "I hate you! I hate you!"

I caught her arms and pinned them by holding her tight in an embrace. I felt the warmth of her firm young body through the thin soft dress. I looked down into her angry eyes and laughed. There was an almost instant surge of response in me to the touch of her, and I knew that she knew it.

Now she was very still, her eyes still angry. But it was another kind of anger, directed at herself, as if she had just proved something she had always known. "You animal. Now I suppose you're going to rape me."

"I should," I said, "it's probably what you need more than anything else."

She broke out of my embrace and stood there glaring at me, her magnificent breasts heaving. "I want to go away," she said, trying to control her voice, "I want to leave Corteguay. It's a sick land. Everything and everyone in it is sick." She turned away and went over to the window, her back to me. "It has taken too much out of me. I have nothing more to give. My father died because of it, my uncle—"

"I told you your uncle was a fool," I interrupted. "Who told him to join the rebels? Mendoza?"

Beatriz turned and stared at me. "You're very proud of yourself, aren't you? The little people have all been taught their lesson and put back in their proper places. Now you can go back to your soft willing women who make no demands upon you. You don't have to concern yourself over us any more. *El Presidente* will take care of everything, *el Presidente* will provide." Her voice was heavily sarcastic. "He'll provide—with prisons, or by extermination."

"No more," I said, suddenly weary.

"No more? You can stand there and say that with the blood of an innocent man on your hands? A man who wanted nothing but freedom for his people?"

"No, not that kind of man. A man who lied; to you, to your father, to everyone. A man who spread poison wherever he could. A man who was responsible not only for the death of your father but also probably for thousands of others these past few weeks. That's the kind of man you are talking about. I'm glad I killed him!"

"You're gloating over it," Beatriz replied, a note of contempt in her voice. "You make me sick."

We stood staring at each other, then her expression suddenly changed. "My God, I'm going to be sick!"

She ran past me into the kitchen and out the back door. I heard the rasping sounds of her retching, and when I got there she was leaning her head weakly against the cool clapboards of the house.

"Beatriz," I said, trying to take her into my arms.

"No, Dax," she replied huskily, "leave me alone."

For the first time I noticed how pale and drawn she had become. There were shadows under her eyes I had never seen there before. She turned to look at me, still speaking in that husky voice. "Just let me go away. Help me leave Corteguay, that's all I want from you."

I was silent for a moment but even then I couldn't keep all the anger out of my voice. "Pack a bag if that's what you want. I'll see to it that you're put on the first plane or boat out."

Then I walked back into the house. Halfway through the living room my anger disappeared and I began to smile. I wondered what Beatriz would say when she found out that the first plane out would be mine.

34

Colonel Tulia was waiting in my antechamber when I got back to the *Palacio del Presidente*. "Your excellency, I took the liberty of awaiting your return."

"I have not yet had time to discuss the matter with *el Presidente*."

"I know, I have already heard the news. Mendoza is dead. *El Presidente* announced it about an hour and a half ago."

I nodded. Hoyos was right on the job. I wondered if he also told *el Presidente* that I had ordered the release of Beatriz.

"The typists have completed their work," Tulia said. "I thought you might like to look at the rest of the execution orders before you spoke to him."

I sat down, and Tulia opened his briefcase. The papers made a neat stack on my desk. I picked off the top one and studied it. The name meant nothing to me, I had never even heard it before. But it was a young man, a lieutenant, only twenty-three years old.

I put the order down and lit a cigarette. I could not take my eyes from the stack of papers. It was the first time I had ever realized that death could be arranged so simply, so impersonally. All it would take was my signature and every one of these pieces of paper would turn into a dead man.

My signature. I inhaled deeply, letting the acrid smoke burn its way down into my lungs. I wondered how many more ways *el Presidente* had in the back of his mind to use me. I began to feel sick inside. How many more had to die to maintain his power?

I remembered the grim satisfaction in his voice that morning as I had banked the plane away from the little village. "It will teach them a lesson," he had said. "It will be a long time before any of them will want to make war again."

Suddenly the answer came from inside myself. As if it had always been there but I had refused to accept it. The lesson was as old as time. An Englishman had put it into neat and economical language: "Power tends to corrupt; absolute power corrupts absolutely."

El Presidente knew more than I had given him credit for. This was the ultimate temptation, and he knew it. The power of life or death. What greater power could be given to any man? He knew better than anyone that once I had signed those orders, no matter how noble my motive, I was committed to power. And once I was, my corruption was inevitable.

For what my father could not or would not see was that there is no middle ground; there are no grays, only black and white. And no matter how much might be gained for the moment, in the end more would be lost. I looked up. Colonel Tulia was watching me intently.

I took a deep breath. Suddenly for the first time in my life I felt free. I was my own man. I belonged to myself, not to the memory of my father, not to *el Presidente*, but only to myself. For the first time I knew my own mind.

"Colonel Tulia, how many executive officers are there besides yourself?"

"Five colonels," he replied, "including Hoyos, of the secret police, and Pardo and Vasquez, the prisoners. Only Zuluaga and myself, really; the others are in the field."

"Could a court-martial be convened?"

"If we included Hoyos." A light was beginning to show in his eyes. He realized what I was getting at. "Actually, only three officers are needed."

"And the prisoners?" I asked. "Are they also in Curatu?"

He nodded, then hesitated. "There is one difficulty. We need one more officer to preside as judge of the court."

I got to my feet. "That should present no problem, Colonel. I am still wearing the uniform of the army."

I looked down at my watch. "It is seven o'clock. Do you think you could have everyone here in an hour?"

I went upstairs to my room and shaved and took a shower. When I came down a few minutes before eight they were all there. Only Hoyos among them seemed uncomfortable.

I went around behind my desk and sat down. "We all know why we are here, gentlemen, let's get down to business."

Tulia turned to me. "It is the first order of the court to elect a presiding officer from among ourselves."

I nodded. A moment later I was elected.

"The next step is to present the court with the charges against the accused." Tulia stepped forward and laid a sheet of paper on my desk.

He had been very thorough. Somehow he had found the time to write out exactly what I should say. "*Coronel* Vasquez, this courtmartial is being held in accordance with army regulations and clause six of the document of surrender signed by you. . . ."

The two trials were over in a matter of minutes. Both officers were acquitted of all charges, by a vote of two to one. Hoyos, of course, was the one who voted the other way. As presiding officer I dismissed the charges and restored both Pardo and Vasquez to their full rank and pay without penalty.

Quickly Tulia wrote out a brief summary of the trial and we all signed it. I signed twice, once as presiding officer and again as vice president.

Vasquez reached across the desk to shake my hand. His grip was firm. "Thank you."

Hoyos slowly got to his feet. "Now that it is over, gentlemen, I'll be getting back to my duties."

"No!" I said sharply.

769

Hoyos turned to look at me questioningly, and a sudden silence fell over the room. He looked at the others, then back at me. "I have important matters waiting," he said, almost mildly.

"They will keep."

I didn't want Hoyos informing *el Presidente* of what had happened before I got to him. This was something I had to do for myself. "You will return to your seat and wait here with your fellow officers until I have informed *el Presidente* of the decisions of this court."

"You have no authority to detain me," he protested. "I am accountable only to *el Presidente*."

"As an officer of the army you are also accountable to the vice president."

Hoyos stared at me for a moment, then shrugged and returned to his chair. "Yes, excellency."

Something about the sound of his voice aroused my suspicion, and it took me only a few minutes to ascertain that the office was bugged. I picked up one of the tiny microphones and looked at him.

His face was pale but he didn't speak.

"Why didn't you tell me the office was wired?" I said. "We could have saved the time spent in writing a report if we had known that everything that was said was being taped."

35

It was perhaps an hour later when I presented myself at *el Presidente*'s *apartamiento*. But what I had to do might require that extra hour.

A servant let me in. "*El Presidente* is expecting you, excellency, but at eleven o'clock."

"It is an emergency," I said in my most authoritative voice. "I must see him immediately."

"He is with *la princesa*. *El Presidente* never allows us to disturb him when he is in her apartment."

"I shall return in an hour, then."

I turned from the door and went down the stairs and across the courtyard from *la residencia* to the little palace which Amparo now occupied. The soldiers on guard snapped to attention. "*El Presidente* has summoned me."

"*Sí, excelencia!*" Both saluted and one of them hastened to hold open the door.

I stepped inside. The little palace hadn't been changed since I had been there last. I had been only a boy then, the day the bomb had severed my father's arm. It was just as well that Amparo would be present at our meeting, for what I had to say would affect her, too. I knocked softly on the sitting-room door.

There was no answer.

I knocked again, this time a little louder.

Still no answer.

I turned the knob and walked in. Only one dim lamp lit the corner. I reached out and switched on the lights, and it was then I heard sounds coming from the bedroom. I crossed the room. The sounds were louder now, and I recognized them. I had been married to Amparo long enough.

The servant must have been mistaken. That or he had lied deliberately. *El Presidente* was not here. I had just turned to leave when a scream of pain shattered the room. Then there was another. It contained so much agony and terror that involuntarily I threw myself against the door and burst into the bedroom.

I was almost in the center before I could stop myself. I stood there staring, a nausea churning my stomach. They were naked on the bed, Amparo's legs wide, *el Presidente* on his knees between them, a huge black dildo strapped around his waist. In his hand he held a riding crop.

He turned to stare at me over his shoulder. "Dax, you've come just in time to help me punish her!"

The sound of his voice helped break my paralysis. I moved over to the bed and pulled him away from her. "Are you crazy?" I shouted. "Do you want to kill her?"

He got off the bed and stood glaring at me, the dildo

hanging down obscenely. I turned and bent over the bed. Amparo raised her head. "Dax," she whispered softly, "why did you do that? Now he'll be angry with you, too."

Then I noticed her eyes. They were wide and dilated and hazy with heroin. Slowly I pulled the sheet up to cover her. When I turned back, *el Presidente* had already unstrapped the dildo. It was lying on the floor. He picked up his trousers. "Dax," he said in a normal voice, as if nothing had happened, "have you signed the orders?"

"No, there are no orders to sign. A court-martial has acquitted them."

"A court-martial?" *El Presidente* turned, his trousers still dangling in front of him.

"Yes," I answered. "There will be no more executions, no more extermination of people. An hour ago I sent word to the field ordering a cease-fire. The army will only fight now if attacked."

He stared at me with unbelieving eyes. "Traitor!" he screamed suddenly, dropping the trousers. He held a revolver, which must have been in one of the pockets. "Traitor!" he screamed again, and pulled the trigger.

I froze, expecting a bullet, but the firing pin struck an empty chamber. I was on him before he could try a second time, and knocked the revolver from his hand. He leaped at me, screaming obscenities, his skinny arms flailing, his fingers gouging at my face and eyes. I tried to hold him but he pushed me and I stumbled over a chair. He dove after the revolver, and we thrashed around on the floor.

Suddenly I was aware of Amparo, dancing nakedly around us. "Kill him, Dax," she screamed excitedly, "kill him!"

El Presidente's fingers reached for the gun, and on his face was an expression I remembered from my childhood. It was the same look of concentration that had been on his face as he had held the machine gun for me. But I had been a child then and had not understoood about killing. I thought I was bringing my mother and sister back to life.

Angrily, and for the first time, I struck out at that leering face. *El Presidente* fell away from me, his head striking the floor. I got to my feet slowly, and picked up the revolver from the floor.

"Kill him, Dax!" Amparo whispered in my ear. "Now! This is your chance, kill him!"

I looked at *el Presidente,* lying motionless on the floor, then at the revolver in my hand. There were so many dead because of him. It would be only justice.

"Now, Dax! Now! Now! Now!"

Amparo's voice was an obscene chant in my ears. I raised the gun slowly, aiming it at him. He opened his eyes, and for a long moment we stared at each other.

Amparo began to giggle hysterically. "Kill! Kill! Kill!"

I felt my finger tensing on the trigger.

"No, Dax," he said quietly, his eyes without fear, "if you do you will be no different from me."

Abruptly I lowered the gun. The temptation was gone. I felt Amparo pummeling my shoulder angrily. I pushed her away wearily. "Get back into bed, Amparo."

She was suddenly silent as she crept back.

I looked at *el Presidente,* who was beginning to struggle to his feet. Suddenly I saw him for what he had become—a skinny, trembling old man. He seemed to age before my eyes as he stood there in his bony nakedness. Instinctively I put out a hand to steady him.

He glanced at me, then sank gratefully into a chair. "It's over?" It was more statement than question.

"Yes."

He was silent for a moment. "I've taught you well. What will happen now?"

I glanced toward Amparo. She was sitting up in bed, her hands clasped around her knees, watching. Her eyes seemed clearer now. The heroin was probably wearing off.

I turned to *el Presidente.* "Exile."

He nodded thoughtfully. "You were like a son. When my own sons died I gave you their place in my heart."

I didn't answer.

He looked over at Amparo. "When do we go?"

"Now," I said, "as soon as you're dressed."

"Where?" Amparo asked from the bed.

"First to Panama. After that, anywhere in Europe you choose. But first you must sign these papers."

"What papers?"

"Your resignation as president and an agreement to remain in voluntary exile for life."

"Give me a pen." He signed without even looking at them.

"I'll wait outside while you get dressed," I said.

I went into the sitting room and picked up a telephone and dialed my office. Tulia answered. "Send the car around to the little palace," I said wearily. "They're ready to go."

I put down the telephone, and then remembered the promise I had made Beatriz earlier in the day. I picked up the receiver and dialed her number.

"Do you still want to leave Corteguay?"

"Yes."

"Then be ready in a half an hour. I'll come around to pick you up."

Amparo came out of the bedroom, clutching a robe. "My father would like a fresh uniform. You know how he is. The one he is wearing is soiled."

I gestured at the phone.

She picked it up and dialed his apartment and asked a servant to bring over a clean uniform. Then she put the phone down and started back toward the bedroom.

"Amparo?"

She turned and looked at me.

"Why did you let him do that to you?"

"Because he was *el Presidente*," she said gently, "and because he was an old man and my father. There was no one else who would let him keep the illusion."

She turned and went back into the bedroom.

From outside I heard the sound of a car.

I took Beatriz' bag as she came out the door and locked it behind her. We walked slowly to the jeep. The others had already left for the airport.

"I promised you the first plane out," I said after we got in, "and I have kept my word. But I wish you'd think it over. In the next few days the commercial planes will be flying again."

"No," she answered, without looking at me, "I've already made up my mind."

"You're a stubborn broad."

She looked at me without speaking, and we rode most of the rest of the way in silence. It was only as we approached the airport that she spoke again. "Dax, you don't understand," she said suddenly, "I'm—"

"Don't understand what?"

"Nothing. It's just that I can't stay here. There are too many memories."

"All right," I answered, "you don't have to explain. Just promise me one thing."

"What?"

"That if you go to the States you'll let my friend Jeremy Hadley take you over to the State Department. They'll at least tell you the truth about what happened to your father."

She was silent for a moment. When she spoke again her voice was very low and there was something suspiciously like tears in it. "I will."

There was one last-minute addition to the passenger list. Hoyos. He came over to me while the others were boarding. "I have spoken with *el Presidente*. He is willing for me to accompany him if there is room in the plane."

I looked at him questioningly.

"I am much too old to develop new allegiances," he said. "There is no place for me here."

"You may go."

"Thank you, excellency." He hurried aboard.

El Presidente and Amparo were the first to board. They spoke to no one. I couldn't see his face—the collar of his greatcoat was pulled up around it—but at the last moment he turned and looked out. He seemed to be searching for something, but after a moment he disappeared inside.

Hoyos was next aboard. He scampered upward without a backward look. Beatriz was next. She turned and came over to me. She raised herself and kissed me quickly on the cheek. "Thank you, Dax." Then she turned and hurried up the stairs.

I stood there looking after her. Suddenly I began to feel better. Somehow I knew that in a few days, when I followed her to New York, things would work out between us.

The cabin door shut, and a moment later Giraldo began to turn the engines over. I listened critically. They were running as smooth as silk. He stuck his head out the window and gave me a thumbs-up. I gestured back at him.

"Remember to come back after you put down in Panama!" I shouted over the roar of the engines.

He nodded, grinning, then, cranking up the window, began to taxi out onto the apron. I watched the plane turn into position, and at a signal from the control tower go racing down the strip and off into the sky. I followed it until its blinking red and green lights vanished among the stars. Then I turned and looked at the others.

It was Vasquez who put it best:

"Once, perhaps, in every fifty or a hundred years a man like *el Presidente* comes along. A man whose capacity for good or for evil is so vast that it is almost beyond the comprehension of ordinary men. Such a man was he, and we shall not forget him. For the good things he has done, and for the bad. But the tragedy is that with so little effort on his part it might have all been good. I pray to God that we may never see his likes again."

It was after four in the morning, and we were still in my office. So much had already been done. The cease-fire order had been confirmed and the language of a blanket amnesty had been agreed upon. It would be issued in the morning.

"Gentlemen," I said, "it now becomes the duty of this junta to elect a provisional president to govern in its name until an election can be held. As agreed, I shall vote only in case of a tie. There are four votes among you."

Tulia got to his feet. "I have taken the liberty of getting in touch with the commanders in the field. They all agree that you are the logical person to carry on the government until an election can be held."

"I am honored, gentlemen, but my answer is the same as it was earlier this evening. No. The honor you do me is great but the temptation is even greater. For too long in our country this has been the classical means of seizing power. Just this once let it not be said that all of us acted out of personal motives, but only for the ultimate good of our country. Actually I no longer belong here. I have been away too long and know too little about the needs of our people. What is needed

776

is a man who knows and loves the people of Corteguay—all the people, the *campesino* and city dweller alike. There are good men among you. Select one and I will deem it an honor to serve under him."

Tulia looked at the others and then back at me. "In anticipation of your refusal we have made a second choice."

Vasquez got to his feet. "Colonel Tulia," he said in a hurt voice, "you forgot to consult me."

The others began to smile. Tulia, too, began to smile. "Would you accept my apologies, *Señor Presidente?*"

We walked down the hallway to *el Presidente*'s office. Now it was no longer his. I supposed in time we would get used to that, too. I opened the door and stood back. "Tomorrow morning this will be your office, *Señor Presidente.*"

Vasquez started forward, then stopped. He stood there for a moment looking in, then turned to me. "Tomorrow morning it will be mine," he said quietly, "but tonight—tonight it is yours. Without you there might not have been a tomorrow."

He pushed me gently through the door. "I will come back in the morning," he said. "Good night, *Señor Presidente.*"

One by one they bid me good night, and then walked down the corridor. I watched them until they had passed the guard at the far end, then turned to Fat Cat, who was standing silently against the wall.

"Shall we go in?"

"No," he said, shaking his head. "I have a premonition."

"You and your premonitions!" I laughed, and strode into the office.

I walked around the desk and sat down in the chair. It was just the kind of chair to make a man feel big and strong and powerful. I leaned back in it, putting my hands in my pockets. I felt *el Presidente*'s revolver in one of them, and I took it out and threw it to Fat Cat.

He caught it deftly. "Where did you get this?"

"*El Presidente* tried to kill me but it misfired."

A shadow flashed across Fat Cat's face. "That's twice today you escaped. The third is the unlucky time. Come, let us go from here."

I laughed. "I'll go after I've had one cup of coffee. There's a kitchen back there; go make us a pot."

777

Fat Cat looked at me hesitantly. "I don't like to leave you alone."

"What can happen to me in the time it takes to brew a pot of coffee?" I asked. "See, it's already daylight."

Fat Cat still didn't move.

I got to my feet and took a machete down from the wall where *el Presidente* had hung it. I placed it on the desk in front of me. "Besides, I have this."

Fat Cat shook his head and turned, still silent, and started back to the kitchen. I heard the faint rattle of pots and then the sound of water running. I got out of the chair and walked slowly around the office. It was still filled with memories of *el Presidente*. There were pictures of him everywhere I turned—medals, medallions, scrolls, cups, each engraved with his name.

The gray morning light began to fill the room. I walked over to the window and looked out at the city. The street lights were beginning to go out near the port and soon the first rays of the sun would be creeping in from behind the mountains to the east. I opened the wide French doors and went out into the garden to breathe the morning air.

It was sweet and fresh as I strolled across the garden to the wall to look east to the mountains and catch the first glimpse of the morning sun. Then I heard a faint sound behind me. I started to turn but suddenly I was caught in a grip of steel. An arm crooked around my neck from behind, and I was jerked backward almost off my feet as a harsh voice whispered in my ear. "Not a sound or you're a dead man!"

I tried to turn but the arm held me as if I were a baby. Again that voice in my ear. *"El Presidente*—where is he?"

The pressure relaxed slightly so that I could speak. "He is gone. Exiled."

The arm tightened again. "You lie!"

Another voice came from behind me. "It does not matter. This one is as good."

I stared as the man behind me came around to face me. He was one of the ugliest individuals I had ever seen. His mouth was twisted in a perpetual grin over blackened steel false teeth. His right hand was crushed, the fingers twisted, and a sawed-off double-barreled shotgun rested negligently in the crook of his other arm.

"Do you recognize me?"

I shook my head.

"Remember the boy whose father you talked into coming down from the mountains to be murdered?"

He began to laugh as he saw my eyes widen. "That's right, *el Condor*. I never forgot your face, how could you forget mine?"

I didn't answer. I couldn't have even if I had wanted to; the arm around my throat allowed me scarcely enough air to breathe.

"Let him go."

Abruptly the arm was taken from my neck, and I was hurled back against the wall. I stumbled and almost fell but managed to turn and face them. The other man was older, square and stockily built. There were two guns stuck into his belt.

"How does it feel to be trapped the way my father was trapped?" *el Condor* asked.

I didn't answer.

"I swore that I would not go back to the mountains this time without the blood of at least one of my father's assassins!"

I still didn't speak. I was tightening my muscles for an attempt to escape. Carefully I tried to gauge the distance between us. He was at least eight feet away.

"Assassin!" *el Condor* suddenly screamed. "You die!"

I sprang toward him at the same moment I saw the muzzle of the gun flash. At first I thought he had missed, then I was on the ground before him, staring up at him, and I knew he hadn't. But the strangest thing was that there was no pain. I had always thought there would be pain.

Everything seemed to slow down. Even *el Condor's* smile as he slowly raised the shotgun to fire again. Then a crazy thing happened. There was a flashing light and the arm that held the gun seemed to fly off from his shoulder and float lazily through the air. I saw *el Condor's* mouth open and heard his scream as the blood came gushing up. Then the light spun at him again and the scream was cut off.

I heard the shots, and I could count them as I turned my head. Three, four, five, six. There was a horrible look on Fat Cat's face as he walked steadily toward *el Condor*, the bloody machete held high in his two hands like a woodsman's ax.

Desperately the other *bandolero* clawed at the gun left in

779

his belt, but it would not obey his frightened fingers. He turned screaming and began to run. He had gone but four paces when Fat Cat threw the machete after him. Abruptly he seemed to break open from the back of his head to his spine. He plunged forward over some small bushes out of sight.

I twisted my head toward Fat Cat. He was walking toward me, then he seemed to stumble and fall. He lay stretched out on the ground only a few feet away.

"Fat Cat!" I called, but my voice was very weak.

At first I thought he did not hear me, then he raised his head and looked over at me. He began agonizingly to crawl slowly toward me, rolling, using his elbows, clawing his way. The blood was streaming from his mouth and the hole in the side of his neck.

I stared at him in shocked surprise. Fat Cat was dying. I couldn't believe it. Not Fat Cat. He could never die, he was indestructible. "Fat Cat, I'm sorry," I wanted to say, but I couldn't get the words out.

Now our faces were almost touching and we hung there together on the spinning earth staring into each other's eyes.

I felt the icy polar cold creeping upward through me. "Fat Cat, I'm cold," I whispered. Even as a child I had hated the cold. I loved the sun.

But the sun coming over the mountains now gave me no warmth. Only a bright dazzling light that hurt my eyes and made it difficult for me to see. I felt the cold getting colder and creeping ever higher.

"Fat Cat, I'm afraid," I whispered. I squinted my eyes against the sun so that I could see his face.

Fat Cat raised his head and into his eyes came a look I had never seen there before. It was all the looks of love in one expression. Of a friend, of a father, of a son. Then he pushed his hand out over mine and covered it. I gripped his fingers tightly.

His voice was hoarse but soft. "Hold my hand, child," he said, "and I will take you safely through the mountains."

Postscript

Hildebrandt, his chauffeur, was waiting as he came through the swinging doors from customs. "The car is just outside," he said, taking the valise. "Did you have a good flight, sir?"

Jeremy nodded. "It was a good flight."

They got into the big limousine and it sped rapidly off into the night. There was very little traffic at this hour and almost before he knew it, the car was racing past the multicolored lights of the World's Fair and onto the approaches of the Triborough Bridge.

"I called Mrs. Hadley when I heard your plane would be late."

"Thank you, Artie."

They came off the bridge onto the almost empty East River Drive and, racing downtown, turned off at the Sixty-third Street exit. A few blocks more and the car pulled to a stop on a quiet tree-lined street just east of Central Park.

She was waiting at the door as he crossed the sidewalk to the steps of the gray town house. He stepped inside and shut the door and took her into his arms. They clung together silently for a tiny quiet moment.

She felt the weariness and the ache of travel in him. And something more than that. A strange stillness of spirit that was somehow foreign to his nature. She kissed him gently, comfortingly. Then she took his hand and led him into the living room.

"It's the staff's day off," she said. "I've made sandwiches and coffee; they're in the kitchen."

"It's all right," Jeremy said. "I'm not really hungry."

She looked up into his face. "How was it?"

"Pretty awful." There were grim lines there she had never seen before. "I never knew there could be anything like that."

She nodded. "Was there anyone else there?"

Jeremy shook his head. "I was the only one."

She was silent, watching him.

"It wouldn't have been so bad if someone else had been there. But I was the only one. And there had always been so many people——"

"No more talk about it now," she said quickly, touching her finger to his lips. "You go wash up. You'll feel better after you eat something."

Jeremy went upstairs and into the bathroom. A few minutes later he peeked into the children's rooms. The girls first. Their room was the nearest.

They were fast asleep, their eyes tightly shut against the night. His golden girls. He smiled to himself. They were three and five years old and there was nothing that could wake them. Not even an earthquake.

But the boy was different. He slept lightly, and the slightest sound would waken him. Even now, as he came into the room, the boy stirred, then sat up in the bed. "Dad?" he asked in his nine-year-old voice.

"Yes, Dax."

"What kind of a plane did you come home on this time?"

"A 707," he answered, coming over to the side of the bed. He bent down and kissed the boy's forehead. "Now, go back to sleep."

"Yes, Dad," the boy said, lying down again. "Good night."

"Good night, son," Jeremy said gently, leaving the room.

She was waiting at the foot of the staircase when he came down. Silently he followed her into the breakfast nook just off the kitchen. The table was already set with sandwiches, coffee, and cake.

Unexpectedly he was hungry. He sat down and began to eat. She sat down opposite him and filled his coffee cup. He finished the sandwich and reached for his cup. "I was hungry," he said.

She smiled.

He took a sip of the hot coffee. His eyes were somber again. "No one came."

"Very few do," she said, "even under the best of circumstances. Ten years is a long time to be remembering."

"I wonder if we'll ever really know the story of that last day," he mused.

"Never," she said. "Within a few months they were all dead. Except Vasquez."

"Do you think he killed them?"

"Yes." Her voice was positive. "With Dax gone he knew the junta would fall apart. Who was there to be its conscience? Vasquez turned out to be no better than *el Presidente*."

"There is talk of revolution."

"Jeremy, I don't care." A faint edging of nerves came into her voice. "I told you, I don't care. I left it a long time ago because it was sick and all they ever thought about was death and destruction. I don't even want to hear about it any more."

"All right, all right," he said soothingly. "But I still remember sitting in the gallery at the UN when he made that last speech. The way he looked at them as he spoke. As if he was reminding the whole world of its conscience. 'Let there be no man among you to help another make war against his brother.'"

She looked at him without speaking.

Jeremy put his hand into his pocket and took out a ring. "They gave me this," he said, holding it out to her. "That is, I thought they had until I found out I was expected to buy it."

She took it from his hand and looked down at it. "I always wondered about the inscription."

"It's a class ring. He was in Jim's class at Harvard. We gave it to him when he had to leave before graduation."

She studied it.

"Upstairs, when I was in the boy's room, Beatriz, I was thinking. He's so much like his father. He should know."

"The boy knows one father. That's enough."

"He would be very proud of him."

"He's very proud of you," she replied.

"He's growing up," he persisted. "What if he should find out?"

"I'll take that chance," she insisted stubbornly.

"In fairness to his father?"

"No!" she said sharply. "His father is dead and fairness doesn't matter to him any more." Abruptly she got up and walked into the kitchen. From the table he saw her pull open the incinerator chute and drop the ring into it. He heard it tinkling on its way down.

"Why did you do that?" he asked when she came back to the table.

"Now he is gone," she said tightly, "and there is nothing left of him but a dream we all had when we were young."

Jeremy started to speak but then he saw the tears standing in her emerald eyes. Instead he too got up, taking her into his arms and holding her closely to him. He felt the trembling in her and the salt of her tears against his lips.

She was wrong. And he knew that she knew it.

There was always the boy upstairs.